THE METAPHYSICS OF SEX

ALSO BY VALERIE TOWNSEND BAYER

City of Childhood

THE
METAPHYSICS
OF
SEX

Valerie Townsend Bayer

—◆◆◆—

ST. MARTIN'S PRESS
NEW YORK

THE METAPHYSICS OF SEX. Copyright © 1992 by Valerie Townsend Bayer. All rights reserved. Printed in the United States of America. No part of this book may be used or reproduced in any manner whatsoever without written permission except in the case of brief quotations embodied in critical articles or reviews. For information, address St. Martin's Press, 175 Fifth Avenue, New York, N.Y. 10010.

Library of Congress Cataloging-in-Publication Data

Bayer, Valerie Townsend.
   The metaphysics of sex / Valerie Townsend Bayer.
      p.   cm.—(The Marlborough Gardens quartet)
   ISBN 0-312-08263-0 (hardcover)
   I. Title. II. Series.
PS3552.A 85878M48 1992
813'.54—dc20   92-24039
                                               CIP

First Edition: October 1992
1 3 5 7 9 10 8 6 4 2

To my beloved sons, Christopher and Shawn, who are the joy of my life, and to my editor, Maureen Baron, whose remarkably intuitive understanding of my work in progress was of invaluable assistance in molding it into its final form.

Descendants of Josephus Isaac Forster (Faustus)

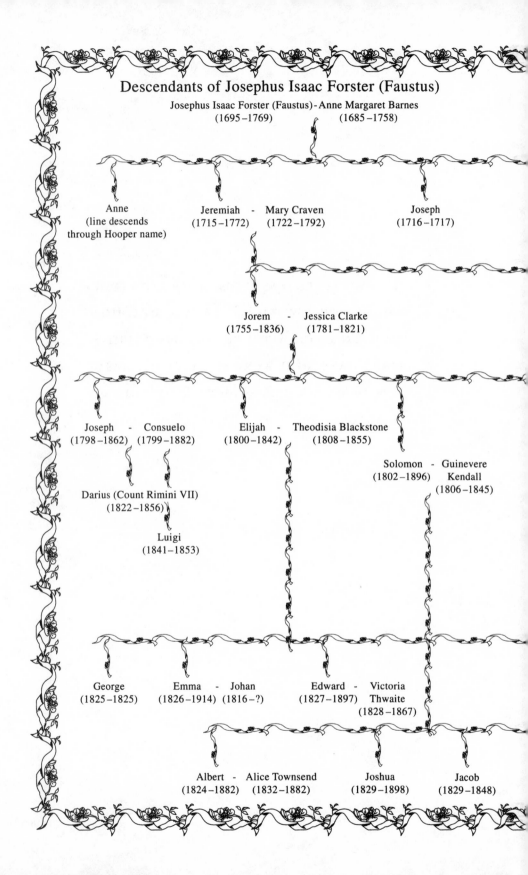

Josephus Isaac Forster (Faustus) - Anne Margaret Barnes
(1695–1769)   (1685–1758)

Anne
(line descends
through Hooper name)

Jeremiah - Mary Craven
(1715–1772) (1722–1792)

Joseph
(1716–1717)

Jorem - Jessica Clarke
(1755–1836) (1781–1821)

Joseph - Consuelo
(1798–1862) (1799–1882)

Elijah - Theodisia Blackstone
(1800–1842) (1808–1855)

Solomon - Guinevere
(1802–1896) Kendall
(1806–1845)

Darius (Count Rimini VII)
(1822–1856)

Luigi
(1841–1853)

George
(1825–1825)

Emma - Johan
(1826–1914) (1816–?)

Edward - Victoria
(1827–1897) Thwaite
(1828–1867)

Albert - Alice Townsend
(1824–1882) (1832–1882)

Joshua
(1829–1898)

Jacob
(1829–1848)

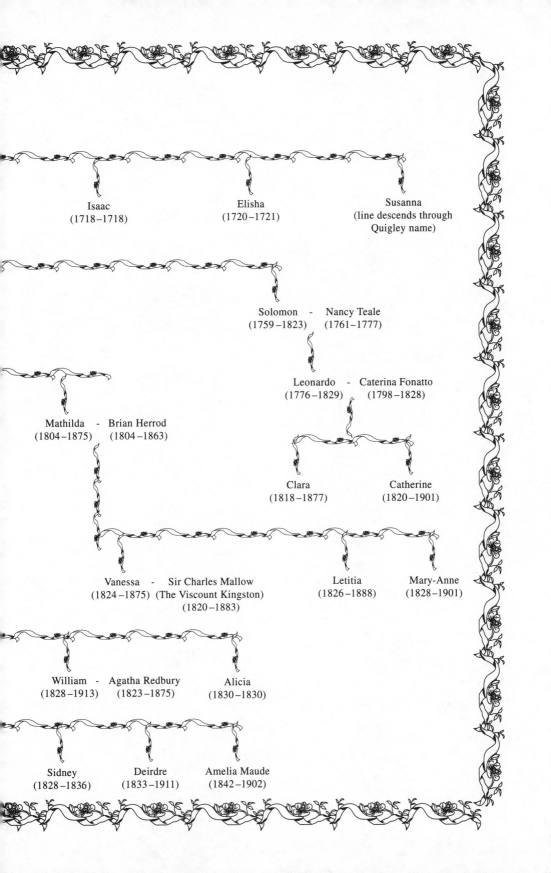

Isaac
(1718–1718)

Elisha
(1720–1721)

Susanna
(line descends through
Quigley name)

Solomon - Nancy Teale
(1759–1823)   (1761–1777)

Leonardo - Caterina Fonatto
(1776–1829)   (1798–1828)

Mathilda - Brian Herrod
(1804–1875)   (1804–1863)

Clara
(1818–1877)

Catherine
(1820–1901)

Vanessa - Sir Charles Mallow
(1824–1875) (The Viscount Kingston)
(1820–1883)

Letitia
(1826–1888)

Mary-Anne
(1828–1901)

William - Agatha Redbury
(1828–1913)   (1823–1875)

Alicia
(1830–1830)

Sidney
(1828–1836)

Deirdre
(1833–1911)

Amelia Maude
(1842–1902)

Next to the love of life, [sex] shows itself . . . as the strongest and most active of all motives, and incessantly lays claim to half the powers and thoughts of mankind.

—Schopenhauer
The World as Will and Representation

THE METAPHYSICS OF SEX

PRELIMINARY
COMMUNICATIONS

MARLBOROUGH GARDENS
23 APRIL 1937

*We enter the Gardens through the Great South Gate—the wind sharp
and cold from the northeast, in the west a thundercloud glowering.
Hand in hand we walk, past the oaks, the ashes, past the old quince
that sags against the broken panes of the winter garden . . .*

*As is our custom we tend the grave and chant the hymns in the temple and walk the established routes. All that is left to do now is to pay
homage to the goddess who stands alone behind the Temple of the
Virgin, secluded in her grove of poplar trees.*

*You reach the grove by the narrowest of paths—insignificant, trivial,
a frayed, tattered, pale brown ribbon of earth, barely visible—that begins in front of the temple and winds around halfway, where it suddenly veers off at a sharp angle and pierces the dark perimeter of the
small wood behind it.*

And there she stands—the goddess Nemesis,[1] *Dispenser of Vengeance and Justice—in the center of the clearing. Young, beautiful, the
corners of her lips uplifted in their sixth-century smile, her stone hair
twisted into stone antlers, her stone fingers holding stone apple
boughs.*

*In windy March, wine-colored catkins adorn the poplars, and on
those days when the wind has been particularly high, the bare earth at*

---

1. Nemesis was the last statue Kevin Francini, the Gardens' landscape architect, bought
from his friend James Titmouse, a sculptor, and placed in the Gardens before he disappeared in 1820.

sunset is stained with purple streaks . . . as if blood had been spilled.

It was to Nemesis that Emma brought her offerings, and witnessed the crackling of the boughs, the barley in flames. It was to her she paid homage, and stood with bowed head in front of her reciting the ancient prayers of justice. As we do now . . . as Nicholas once did. . . .

Returning home we pass Jorem's[2] house, which stands just outside of the Great East Gate. A pink glowing ruin in the setting sun, its soft red brick and dove-gray stone are overlaid with moss and lichen, creating a tapestry of yearning and regret; the pink glow transforming ruptured sashes, broken lintels, boarded windows into something picturesque. Even the copper tub half entangled in the weeds beguiles.

I make the tea this afternoon from the dried leaves of the mullein weed. At one time it was thought to be a remedy for leprosy. "A mild narcotic," so wrote Mrs. Farnley[3] opposite its name. In a subdued mood (the day has been strenuous) we drink the somewhat bitter tea out of cups painted by Vanessa as we search through the Forster archives to track down Nicholas Renton, Lord of the Underworld, who lived in Jorem's house after Jorem died.

Except for our two assistants (I shall speak about them later) we no longer see anyone anymore. We are no longer interested in "the world at large." Here in Marlborough Gardens we have everything we need. We have each other and we have "them."

On Sunday we walked to the East Meadow in Marlborough Marshes, where the wild cyclamen and hellbores grow. According to Emma, Nicholas Renton was first sighted by Clara, Emma's governess, in the Gardens in the spring of 1838. But we know for a fact that it was on May 21, 1837,[4] to be exact, that Nicholas first entered the Gardens with Kevin Francini, his chief lieutenant, to pay homage to the goddess Nemesis and to survey the realm that he hoped one day to claim for himself alone. Part of our story is about his quest and the evil that resulted from it.

During that interval Nicholas and his "cohorts" lived in the labyrinthine cellars of Jessie Malkin's brothel biding their time, watching for straws in the wind to show them when the time would be ripe for their undertakings, while at night they spied on the Forster men who came to the brothel on a regular basis.

---

2. Jorem Forster (1755–1836), creator of Marlborough Gardens.
3. Georgiana Farnley (1798–1896), Elijah and Theodisia Forster's housekeeper par excellence.
4. Date found in Kevin Francini's memoir *The Life and Times of Nicholas Renton.* Privately published.—*R. Lowe*

Some words about the text:

The Metaphysics of Sex *is the second book of a tetralogy about a Victorian banking family, the Forsters.*

The author, Emma Adelaide Louisa Forster, began the novel when she was twenty-eight years old in Florence, Italy, while visiting her cousin Count Darius Rimini VII, and completed it in Marlborough Gardens, London, England, thirty-four years later.

It is dedicated to her cousin, the world-renowned poet Amelia Maude Renton-Forster, Guinivere Forster's last child.

Emma's original novel was a protracted, rambling undertaking of 932 pages. Conceivably the author did not fully gather up the skeins of the narrative that she had set in motion because it was never intended for publication. Passages are left to drift inconclusively, characters are introduced never to be seen or heard of again. At other times extraneous information congeals the narrative flow.

We have tried to remove these impediments, as well as eliminate Emma's lengthy discourses on Clara Lustig's teaching methods and Clara's long essay on Faust.[5] We have also added to the text by interpolating material from the Forster archives into the text itself in the form of diaries, journals, letters, account books, etc., as well as other material we thought crucial to the psychological comprehension of the text.[6] Furthermore we have included "intimate" matters concerning the Forsters' personal lives that some people might consider "bad taste" but that we believe enhance the vitality and effectiveness of our psychohistory. *In all of this we have scrupulously adhered to Emma's real purpose in writing* The Metaphysics of Sex, *which was a serious, analytic, ongoing, and detailed sexual account of her family.*

Emma Forster was not only a novelist, she was also a critic and an early adherent of Sigmund Freud, and one of the first readers and admirers of Freud and Breur's Studies in Hysteria. *Her last literary endeavor was, in fact, an excellent translation of Freud's brilliant and ingenious essay "Three Contributions to Sexuality."* The Metaphysics of Sex *reflects that interest in sundry ways on all levels.*

5. However, we have not discarded the material. This fall we are publishing the aforesaid material in two separate volumes titled *On Teaching Classics,* by C. F. Lustig, and *The Inner German: Faust,* by C. F. Lustig. They are part of our proposed series on education designed to meet the needs of nonspecialist readers.

6. For instance, in *The Metaphysics of Sex* the children play the role the adults played in *City of Childhood:* that is, for the most part they are *unseen,* yet they are an ultimate part of the reality of Marlborough Gardens. Lowe has composed a series of vignettes culled from the Forster archives that she has named "Notes from Warrenton." We have interspersed a selection into the book.

In our reconstruction *we have clung fast to the adage To Cite Obscenity Is Not to Be Obscene. We assume our readers can assess the material for themselves without the intervention of censorship by us, the editors.*

Emma disapproved of writing that draws attention to itself—"Work that smells of oil" (Trollope). She cultivated a style that was unpretentious and unaffected. In accord with that principle we have in our *reconstruction used certain vulgarisms that we are certain she would have employed were she writing her novel in these modern times.*

—❧⟶⊷◈⊶⟵❧—

My name is Harriet Van Buren. I am an American, an Episcopalian, born in Cleveland, Ohio, in 1898. Rachel Lowe, my companion, is an English Jew, born in Paddington, London, in 1900. Since 1929 we have been the caretakers of Marlborough Gardens and the keepers of the Forster archives.

In the winter of 1936 we bought a hand press and established the Mantikos Press. The primary motive was to publish selected works from the Forster archives, so that the general public might have access to them. We began by printing a hundred copies of Albert Forster's quaint but fetching Reminiscences of Marlborough Gardens, *illustrated by Vanessa Forster Herrod.*

The business of operating and cleaning the machinery, besides the binding and the pasting, proved to be too much for us. We inserted an advertisement for two assistants in the London Times *with excellent results. We wish to express our gratitude and thanks to Dorothea Rutledge and Irene Debenham (recent graduates of Newnham College) for their invaluable assistance. We are indebted to them not only for their physical labor but for their expert advice on certain sexual and psychological problems concerning the Forsters, both women having read for the moral/science tripos.*

Our publications may be purchased at our bookstore, the Phoenix, at 43 Marlborough Gardens. Our hours are flexible. You need only ring the bell.

THE METAPHYSICS OF SEX

PART I: 1837–1839

EMMA FORSTER

Edited by H. Van Buren and R. Lowe

I

NICHOLAS RENTON:
THE OUTSIDER

Of stocky build, he had a beautiful profile, and binding eyes. Maligned, misunderstood, defamed, he once told me that he believed he was the illegitimate son of my grandfather, Jorem, and hence Marlborough Gardens was as much his as it was ours.

—Emma Forster, *The Weimar Journal*

Some people say that he is the bastard son of a French count, others the whoreson of an English duke. I say his father is the Devil, and he was spawned in Hell.

—Clara Forster Lustig's
Boxwood Letters

Simply put: Nicholas Renton was an outsider, trying to get inside.

—William M. Forster's Stud Book
(1851)

O N a dewy Sunday morning in late May, two men in beaver hats stood in front of the Great North Gate of Marlborough Gardens. When the shorter of the two, Nicholas Renton, nodded, Kevin Francini unbuttoned his black redingote and withdrew from his vest pocket the silver key given to him by Jorem Forster almost two decades earlier. Sliding the key into the lock, an unobtrusive detail in the bronze rim of the five-layered shield of Achilles depicting, among other things, the city of war and the city of peace, he turned it. The great iron gate swung on its oiled hinges and the two men slipped inside. Kevin closed the gate behind them.

They walked quickly in silence down the wide clean avenue of earth that cut through Blenheim Wood towards Blenheim Cliffs, where Darius once led his cousins into battle. The *tap tap tap* of their boots sent birds flying upward, and a turtle dove, disturbed, flew from its nest, the white fan of its tail gleaming in the twilight of the wood.

There was no need to talk. The two men understood one another. Besides, the walk through the Gardens had been planned in every detail months before. Today was the beginning of an adventure whose idea had been formed many years ago in Nicholas's mind, in Newgate Prison, the man-made hell where he had been born and forced to live until Jasper T. Hemsley, Esquire,[7] a London barrister, had come with orders to release him.

There was no need to talk because Kevin, whose whole life was now involved in obeying and pleasing the man he called "Commander," had read the expression on his master's face: There will be silence. Kevin, artist, architect, and former opium addict, had the face of a dreamer— an open unguarded face, benign yet indifferent, his light blue eyes turned toward inner visions.

Not so Nicholas. His face, forged in the desperate struggle to survive, resembled a hawk's face: the deep-set vivid green eyes ever watchful, ever observant of the movement of others, the barest flicker of motion capturing his complete attention.

But today, deep in thought, Nicholas barely heard the passionate song of the nightingales, or noted the dark air shimmering with their wings.

No one ever asked Nicholas outright where he had come from— sprung from, hatched, been spawned. He gave the impression of not being altogether human, as if he had not gone through the normal birthing process. And he had never volunteered. Closemouthed generally, though he could exhort his troops eloquently when need be, he was as silent as the tomb about his early life.

Alone in his chambers at the end of the day before undressing (he had no valet and didn't want one), Nicholas would sometimes stroke his clothes, run his hands over the woolen or cotton sleeves of his jacket, caress the cloth of his trousers, or hold the jeweled stickpin he had chosen to wear that day, turning it over and over—the ruby, the diamond, or the pearl—in his broad strong fingers. Sometimes he would

7. Jasper T. Hemsley was the executor of Jorem Forster's estate. Called to the bar in 1823, he resided in Inns of Court 1828–1853, published in collaboration with Sir Ravenscourt "A Commentary on Cicero."—*R. Lowe*

place his Spanish leather boots in front of the hearth and stare at them, turning them this way and that way, moving them about in the firelight. Or he might pick up one of the boots, examine it slowly under the lamplight, bring it to his nose, inhale the scent of the leather, and wonder at the workmanship. At other times he might recite to himself the names of the different kinds of wood in the house: "Walnut, mahogany, satinwood, oak, beech, elm, ash, cherry, applewood . . ." imagining as he recited the words the various pieces of furniture he owned that were constructed from those woods: the writing tables, chests and double chests, bureaus, china cabinets, chairs, beds, sofas, and settees. Removing his cravat he would inspect its stitchery. Still holding the expensive silk to his cheek, he might make a close study of his mahogany table with its side board pedestals inlaid with satinwood and mounted with ormolu. Or walking over to his cabinet, he might take out and study a miraculous Venetian goblet he had bought recently—incredibly beautiful—its stem base merging from Parma violet to amethyst to tawny orange to its golden yellow rim.

Things! The luxury and splendour of *things*! Rich costly extravagant *things*. The voluptuousness, the sensibility of *things*. *Things* made for him, bought by him, sometimes stolen for him.

Oh, it was a lie that things meant nothing to the soul. To Nicholas's soul they meant everything! The real crime was not having things! And those who sermonized, preached against things—philosophers, ministers, pedagogues—were unmitigated liars.

The value of things: Wasn't the real truth, if there was such a thing as truth at all, that things, just things, in themselves were wonderful? Why have eyes if not to see the wondrous things mankind made for itself: paintings, statues, cities . . . the list was endless. Why have hands if not to stroke and touch satin, lace, leather . . . oh, the list was indeed endless. Only when he was made calm and secure by things, his things, for a brief time sated, only then did he allow himself to think about his childhood.

He remembered only too well the place where there were *no* things. That stinking, dark, and dismal place.

Meat. Gobbets of meat. That was his first clear memory. Perhaps he had been six years old . . . a turnkey had thrown a sack filled with putrid meat into the middle of the ward, crying out "There's meat for you!" and a fight had ensued. And Dame Lou, his prison mother. "Get some for yourself, Nick, and some for me!" she had said, and he had dived into the bodies wrestling and fighting with one another, grabbing the meat and chewing it while fighting off the others. Frightened, the sweat pouring off him, he had clawed his way out, stuffing the meat in his shirt to bring to Dame Lou.

And the stench of the stone ward! Until the end of his life he remembered that stink, so that whenever he passed an open cesspool he would say to himself: Newgate!

Yes, only those people who had *things,* or who were paid to say that things were unimportant, proclaimed that things, material things, could never be the source of true contentment or happiness.

Who was his mother? Who was his father?

"A young lass, she were, your mammie," Dame Lou had told him. "She died soon enough, mebbe a month or two after ye were born, coughin' and wheezin' her way to death. Paper lungs, toy lungs, lungs that a doll might have. Not like us, Nicholas. You have to be strong to breathe this air. Strong and willing. Like you are, Nicholas. Aye, a young lass she were, no more than seventeen, I reckon. A child. T'was she that named you Nicholas, but t'was I who gave you your last name. Same as mine. Nicholas Renton, a Newgate lad."

But sometimes she told him other stories. When she was drunk she would tantalize him with allusions and insinuations. She had found him wrapped in an old torn blanket in the corner of the stone yard; he had been brought to Newgate by a man who had left him there . . . "you're the bastard son of a real mucky-muck, a financial wizard" . . . "if you knew who your real father was you'd be proud, but I promised I'd never tell." And she never did tell him no matter how hard he tried to get her to. But no matter, he had found out, hadn't he?

Had he loved Dame Lou? He had wept when she died. He was ten then. He had known no other mother. She had saved him, protected him; without her, he would have died.

The two men stood at the cliffs now all golden with coltsfoot, overlooking the marshes and beyond the marshes and its canal out to the shimmering lake. Here, thought Nicholas, was a place to dream in. Detached from time.

The air was already heavy with the scent of flowers and the droning hum of bees. Milton's immortal words flowed effortlessly into his consciousness:

> *A happy set of various view*
> *Groves whose rich trees wept balm*
> *Betwixt them lawns or level downs*
> *Or palmy hillock. Flowers of all hue*
> *And without Thorn, the Rose . . .*

Kevin leading the way, the men walked down the cliff to the marshes alive with daisies and cuckooflowers. They followed the canal, rich in shrubs and old roses, to the lake, where the black swans with their coral beaks lived. Swimming in twos towards them (nature's faithful lovers), the swans glided away once they understood that the two gentlemen in beaver hats had not come to feed them.

—◆⊙◇⊙◆—

One day a new prisoner unlike anyone Nicholas had evern known arrived in Newgate. A gentleman by the name of Charles Mallet. A bold man, an audacious man, a man who had his meals sent in and his linen sent out to be laundered. A man who made fun of the prisoners Nicholas was frightened of, a man who seemed to view everything differently, who made jokes, who continually amused, a man who was cocksure of himself. He seemed to have an endless supply of coins. "Patrons, patrons," he would say. "All from patrons. My name is Charles Mallet. Mark it well. I am an English poet, an English astrologer, and above all an English gentleman!"

One day Lou, ambitious for Nicholas, went up to the strange, outlandish man and placing a hand on him asked if he would teach her "son" to read.

"Remove your paws, you flea-ridden harpy, or I shall have you whipped and then quartered!" was his first response. And then, pointing to Nicholas: "That thing! That lump, blob! Pray tell me, is it human? Can it speak? In a world full of lunatics, Madam, you are the queen of lunatics! Teach that thing? Never! And take your loathsome and repellent visage far away from mine!"

But she persisted, ignoring his waspish manner, his narrow self-absorption, for she understood human nature. And she knew that although a pretty girl might say no at first to the ugly brute pursuing her, human vanity, being what it is, would transform what at first appeared annoying to the girl into a compliment to her beauty. So Dame Lou trailed after Mallet, ever pressing her demand.

And one day after she had asked him yet again, he suddenly apologized for insulting her and her "son."

"The idea, Madam, has taken hold," he told her. "It might help pass the time in this stinking hellhole. When my friend Titmouse comes to visit me again I shall ask him to bring some books with him." But then a crafty look came on his face. She had not expected this. "If I do agree to teach Nicholas, your so-called son, to read, you must do something for me in return. My motto, Madam, is quid pro quo . . . something for something. You were a whoremonger, weren't you? Now don't deny it. You sold fake virgins, children under twelve . . . ah, the boy, he didn't know, did he? Thrown in for stealing a bit of bread, you told him? Well, now he does. I know a bawd when I see one, Madam. So I shall teach your precious Nicholas, but in return you shall provide me with fresh girls—not diseased, mind you, and apple-breasted, mind you. And that, madam, will be my quid pro quo. Come here boy! Is he deaf?"

"No, he ain't deaf. He's scairt of you."

"Well *that's* a good beginning. Tell him I shall beat him hard and *now* if he doesn't come immediately!"

"Go ahead, Nicholas." She pushed him towards his tutor. "He wants to do you some good. He do. Ye need not be afraid of him. His bark's worse than his bite, ain't it?" she said, looking at Mallet.

The poet snarled: "Madam! From now on you will hold your tongue. Either he is my pupil or he is not. He will come of his own free will, or our short-lived relationship is over! Come over, boy. You're a bit short for your age, aren't you? And quite ugly. But perhaps there's a brain underneath your lice-infected hair. Yes, a brain waiting to be jostled into action. Who knows? Recite after me, boy . . . let me hear your voice. Listen closely. I shall only say it once: 'Milton! thou shouldst be living at this hour!' "

Nicholas repeated it as well as he could.

" 'Thou'! 'Thou,' you numbskull! Not 'dow'! 'Thou.' Watch my tongue."

Nicholas tried again.

"Good. 'England hath need of thee . . .' "

And so at the age of eight Nicholas began to learn the Wordsworth sonnet.

———◆◇◆◇◆———

South to north, north to east, east to west the two men went. Up flights of steps, down flights of steps, up sloped paths, down sloped paths strewn with sharp-edged gravel, past walls with wild roses run up to great heights, on to terraces filled with sweet-smelling shrubs, through a field of apple trees whose rosy boughs leaned down to cowslips and daffodils.

Nicholas felt the enchantment, the richness, the palpable gift of being well taken care of. Prepared as he had been for "unparalleled beauty," the reality of the Gardens had surpassed his expectations. Kevin had described the Gardens and its creation to him many times; how once upon a time a London banker by the name of Jorem Forster had hired him, Kevin Francini, a starving artist and Homeric scholar, to create a paradise for his grandchildren; how it had taken three years and ten thousand pounds to build, and how finally before its completion he, Kevin, had run away. "This *is* paradise," Nicholas murmured to himself. "Paradise."

They walked down a grassy lane that wound its way under arches heavy with blue and white delphinium, beyond which a small pond reflected a blue sky. For there was water everywhere: trickling streams, murmuring brooks, tinkling fountains, rills, pools, lakes, canals . . .

For the first time Nicholas spoke: "The grove. Are we headed back toward the grove?"

"We are almost there," said Kevin, pointing to the top of a small hill. "There, up there on the rise is the temple. It is behind that."

Nicholas looked in the direction that Kevin was pointing and saw the temple, its Doric columns awash in the rosy-colored air, a sharp contrast to the dark apertures between.

You reach the grove by the narrowest of footpaths—insignificant, trivial, a frayed, tattered, pale brown ribbon of earth, barely visible . . .

Kevin, holding the branches apart, let Nicholas enter first. Head bent down, Nicholas watched his boots crush the loathsome toothwart that makes its home in dead vegetation, its pink fleshy waxy stems sticking to the soles of his boots.

And then they were there. In the clearing where the goddess stood, daughter of Chaos and Darkness, the Goddess of Chastisement and Vengeance, the Goddess of Righteous Indignation.

A miracle of balance, her stone draperies lifted and twisted behind her as if an eternal wind was blowing, her right leg bent toward, her toes barely grazing the pedestal on which she stood, a sixth-century smile curling about her exquisite lips, untamed locks tumbling down her shoulders onto her exposed breasts.

They fell to their knees, Nicholas in his bottle-green coat with its bronze satin lining and stone-colored trousers, his curious toadstone pin gleaming in the folds of his striped silk cravat; beside him, Kevin in his redingote and brown trousers.

"Restore to me, Goddess," said Nicholas, his voice hoarse with anxiety, "that which is mine! Punish those who have transgressed and grant me the courage for the undertaking ahead . . ."

———

Charles Mallet began his tutoring by teaching Nicholas what he called his Newgate alphabet.

"Every letter shall stand for something connected to prison life . . . G for gaol, T for turnkey, C for crime, and so forth. We shall begin with the letter A. Pay close attention, boy. A is for Aban-doned, which is what we are, and A-bused, which is what we also are because we are Ab-errant, A-lien, Anom-alous, and so they insist that we be

Ab-ject and Ab-jure our past life, A-tone for our past Au-dacities, and bow forever more to their Au-thority. *That* is the letter *A*, Nicholas. Do you Ap-prehend, As-similate, Ab-sorb?"

At first Nicholas understood nothing. But after a year of struggle, during which he thought he would kill either himself or his tutor, he began to learn to read. And when Mallet saw that Nicholas could read he began to study Milton with him, "for," he said, "I am, among many other things, Nicholas, a Miltonian scholar, in particular *Paradise Lost.*" It was an inspired choice.

"It is the story of loss," said Mallet, "the loss of Utopia . . . Heaven . . . Eden. You are to learn the first six lines of Book One. The measure is English heroic verse without rhyme, as that of Homer in Greek and of Virgil in Latin."

As he struggled to learn Milton's great poem, a slow conversion took place in Nicholas's mind. Newgate became Hell, the region of sorrow, the black fire and the horror where Satan lived, where he, Nicholas lived . . .

> *A dungeon horrible on all sides around,*
> *As one great furnace flamed, yet from those flames*
> *No light, but rather darkness visible.*

and Eden the place he had come from—and to whence he must return.

And so his young mind, which had almost been destroyed by despair, gradually began to take hope and comfort in the power and grandeur of Milton's Satan, in the opulence and dignity of the fallen angels; for Nicholas read and understood the poem to be in praise of Satan. Perhaps to amuse himself, Mallet did nothing to correct Nicholas's perception.

❖

Rising now, the two men brushed the dirt off their trouser knees and left the Gardens. Together they slowly walked around the outside of the Gardens, Kevin pointing out to Nicholas the houses in which Jorem's children lived, giving a clear and concise description of each of their households.

"But I've written all this down for your perusal. It is already in your files. Jorem, as you know, had four children: three sons, Joseph, Elijah, and Solomon, and one daughter, Mathilda. They married, respectively, Consuelo, Theodisia, Guinivere, and Brian Herrod. In all they had fourteen children, some of whom have died—"

"Yes, I know all that. Jorem's house . . . who lives there now?" Nicholas asked as they passed the red brick structure. A servant girl was scrubbing the steps.

"A widower, Sir Timothy Eveshem. Fifty-six years old. Has a B.A. from Trinity College, Cambridge. Former resident and superintendent of Benares—"

"Yes, yes, I shall read your report of him later."

Soon the Forsters (those who were in London) would convene at Elijah's house for their traditional Sunday afternoon dinner, secure in their wealth, smug and complacent, unaware that Nicholas Renton even existed. That was in 1837. It would be one year before they knew of his existence, and then they would know him as Isaac Coverly, a retired tea merchant and former resident of Macao.

Mallet had remained in Newgate for three years until finally one of his "patrons" took pity and paid his debts. Before he left he gave Nicholas "two last words of advice from your old tutor, my dear boy. This first is not to follow in my footsteps. You see before you, simply put, an artist manqué—unfulfilled and unsuccessful.

"Art is hard work, my boy—*ars longa, vita brevis,* as they say—and I have cared too much for women and too little for my craft. If you are to be a criminal, and I predict you shall be, the stars have said so, be the *king* of criminals. Pay attention to your craft, whatever it is, whether it be philosophy or theft.

"Secondly—come closer to me. Regard this watch. Notice the exquisite workmanship, regard my linen, examine the leather of my shoes, and remember, Nicholas, that even the most imbecilic prince—and there have been many of them—know more than you merely by the virtue of having lived with *things.* You have no things. You have nothing. Things are the beginning of culture, my boy . . . civilization. Remember that when you leave Newgate—and you will, my boy, my charts have predicted it—*acquire things!*"

A year later, the lawyer Jasper T. Hemsley came with the proper papers for Nicholas's release. He was twelve years old. He left with the only thing he owned—his dog-eared copy of *Paradise Lost.*

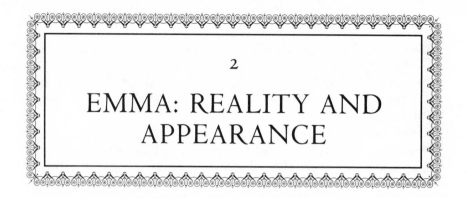

2

EMMA: REALITY AND APPEARANCE

I met Emma when she was ten years old and I was fourteen. I fell in love with her then. I have never stopped loving her.

—Count Darius Rimini to Albert
Forster, 1846

No, I did not love her. My sister was not lovable. She was too opinionated, too ambitious. She had a predatory, calculating look about her, as if she was measuring you for the pot.

—W. M. Forster's Australian Papers

Thin, bony, clever . . . obsessive, passionate, vulnerable. . . . She has a strong sexual drive. She should be easy to seduce.

—C. F. Lustig's Boxwood Letters

I first noticed Nicholas Renton when my governess, Clara Lustig, pointed him out to me. He was strolling down the path to the lake in front of us. I was twelve years old at the time. Nicholas told me later that he had been watching me for some time. And not only me but my brothers Edward and William and all my cousins too.

Clara had a clever tongue, and she dubbed him then and there the Troll of Marlborough Gardens. In a way she was right; that is, he was shorter than the average man, though remarkably handsome. Still, there was something fabled and legendary about his looks, as if he might have stepped out of a Norse fairy tale. He must have heard us walking behind him, perhaps he had heard Clara's unkind remark, because he turned around and faced us. Smiling, he removed his hat and bowed.

Before I went to sleep that night I thought about Clara and what she had said—everything Clara said was important to me; she was the center of my life. I was deeply in love with her. I wondered why Clara had not told me that she knew him, for I was quite certain that she did. I knew Clara. I was a Clara watcher. Nothing she did or said escaped my attention. They, the Troll and she, had met before. I was certain of that. So then why hadn't she told me?

Soon after that my father, Elijah, invited Nicholas—or Isaac Coverly, as he then called himself—to our house. That year, as I recall, was the year of the outsider. It was the year Clara and Nicholas came to Marlborough Gardens and did what they came to do. But enough about them. This is my story. They shall tell their own story. In their own time. . . .

———◆◇◆———

My adolescence was marked by personal eccentricities, sporadic but intense masturbation, sustained eavesdropping, and out-and-out theft.

I shall begin with an incident that occurred the day before my father, Elijah Forster, returned from the Continent. He had been there on business for almost six months. The year was 1837.

A chimney sweep got stuck in the flue of my mother's sitting room, a flue that ran from that room to my parent's bedroom on the floor above, and from there to my room on the third floor. The nameless sweep, however, was lucky. His master dismantled the chimney by loosening the bricks one by one so that the boy could squeeze himself down to safety without injuring himself.

After this dramatic rescue, Mrs. Farnley, our housekeeper, gave the boy and his master sweets and several glasses of wine. My mother, Theodisia, gave the boy a sixpence so that when they left with the tools of their trade—scrapers, brushes, wipes, brooms, and whisks—they were cheerfully singing some verses from "The Legend of the Toby Jug." An altogether happy ending.

However, at the time no one realized that the master sweep had not only rescued his apprentice but also created an air passage that would enable me to hear (as if I were in the same room with them) my parents' private conversations in their bedroom below.

When I first heard the disembodied voices I did not connect them to my parents. I thought it was the mice whose twitterings and scamperings I heard every night before I went to sleep. Gradually, however, I began to realize that this was quite a different aggregate of sounds.

I also began to notice that if I stood close by the hearth the sounds were more audible.

One day on impulse I stuck my head inside the hearth and realized with a shock of dread that the sounds were my parents' voices; that they originated from the room below, my parents' bedroom; and that henceforth, if I so desired (and I did), I was privy to their most intimate conversations. Though I had no idea at the time how this singular phenomenon had come about, I felt a sudden elation at the same time that I felt dizzy with fear. But for the most part I was delighted, as one is with an unexpected and unusual gift. As the days and months went by my interest in their private lives increased, and I went to my room each night after dinner as eagerly as an opium addict scurries to his den.

At the time I was the only child living at home; my brothers, Edward and William, were away at Warrenton, the public school they and all my male cousins attended.

After the eavesdropping began, I took to watching my parents at dinner with an intensity that had they only noticed might have led to my being apprehended. But though I was my father's favorite I was not expected to participate in their conversations. It was enough of a privilege for me to be there rather than eating upstairs with my nurse, Nanny Grindal, a woman I disliked. My father loved me, but he would not abide what he called "juvenile jabber."

Each night I ate the wonderful meals prepared for us by Mrs. Lovesley, our cook—mutton roasts, boiled leg of lamb, rumps of veal, roast pigs (during the hunting season there would arrive each week from Saddler's Grove, our country estate, large hampers filled with game), partridges, pigeons, ducks, geese, rabbits—all prepared with savory sauces cooked in wine or cream and served with capers and sweet mustard. Oh, the food I enjoyed at that table! So very different from the Spartan nursery fare I was used to.

I watched them, scanning my father's face as he said grace, glancing at my mother from time to time, listening to them converse with one another in cold, contemptuous tones on impersonal and banal themes, wondering as I chewed a piece of pork or mutton at the vast difference between their public and their private discourse with one another.

Of course I would be in bed hours before them. I remember waiting, forcing myself to stay awake, awaiting for the sound of their bedroom door opening and then shutting—the soft thud of the door acting as the muffled prelude to the sound of their voices. And I would already be there, seated on a stool near the hearth waiting for the sound of my father's voice: rich, deep, variable, a growl of a sound, an alloy of arrogance and power, a conductor of sexual pleasure—I had only to hear his voice and my spine would begin to tingle—and the other sound, my mother's voice: uneven, low, indistinct, whining, defensive, devious . . .

—◆◇◇◆—

My father, Elijah Joseph Forster, was a handsome, virile type, shrewd and successful in business. "A jewel of a man," as they say, with a sexual preference for working women (cooks, laundresses, ladies' maids, and prostitutes), entrapped in a loveless union imposed by parental will.

When he was twenty-two his father, Jorem, had forced him to marry Theodisia Blackstone, a yeoman's daughter, a woman Elijah neither loved nor desired, threatening disinheritance if he did not. The marriage was the fulfillment of a guarantee that Jorem had made to Theodisia's father, Seth Blackstone, that one of his sons would marry one of Blackstone's daughters—a corporal reiumbursement, so to speak, to the man for befriending Jorem when he was young and friendless.

During the courtship Theodisia fell in love with Elijah, though he was cold to her and did not in any way encourage her spontaneous displays of affection towards him. After they were married she continued to show him her desire to please him, but by the time I was born my mother had been made to understand the hopelessness of her love.

A month before I was born, she discovered that her husband had taken a mistress, Lucinda Dillard (her ladies' maid). Inexperienced and lacking counsel, Theodisia foolishly confronted her husband and accused him of "betraying their love." He told her then that not only did he not love her but that he never had and never would. Though she was only eighteen her youthful bloom began to wither, and by the age of twenty-five she had the desiccated look of a much older woman.

She kept herself busy nevertheless with charity work, the running of the household, social functions, crafts (she had a penchant for wool carving[8]), and numerous pregnancies, for though her husband might not love her, she learned to her increasing bitterness that he still wanted sex with her from time to time. She had five children: the firstborn, George, who died immediately; myself, Emma Adelaide Louisa Forster; my brother Edward (my father's heir); William, my younger brother, whom she adored; and her last child, a stillborn girl named Alicia, born in 1830.

---

8. A variation of Berlin work (a form of hand-worked textile). This technique was called "raised work," "reed stitch," or "wool carving." It was used for cushions and fire screens.—*R. Lowe*

I was my father's favorite, and though I knew my mother disliked me it did not really affect me until my brothers and my cousins were sent away to school and my father for business reasons had to spend the better part of six months on the Continent.

With him away, I began to feel abandoned. Entirely forsaken. Left for no apparent reason to live in my own society, to form my own reality. "More and more the world became a dream and the dream became the world."

My father returned from Germany in late November of 1837, and it was then that my life as a serious eavesdropper began.

On the night my father returned, we assembled—I; my mother; Nanny Grindal; Mrs. Farnley, our housekeeper; Mrs. Lovesley, our cook; and two of our maids, Daisy and Tags—in the great hall to wait for Poppa, Elijah Forster, our master.

We stood there shivering though log fires burned and blazed in the two great hearths on either side of the entrance door.

Our house and its interior had been designed by James Titmouse, a sculptor and friend of the artist Kevin Francini, who had created, together with my grandfather, Jorem, the phantasmagorical world of Marlborough Gardens. The house faced the Great South Gate of the Gardens. My grandfather Jorem's house and the houses lived in by his sons Solomon and Joseph faced the Gardens from the east, west, and north, in that order, like cardinal points of the compass. My Aunt Mathilda's house stood between Solomon's and Joseph's houses.

Mr. Titmouse, like Mr. Francini, had been a great admirer of Homer's *Iliad* and Mr. Walpole's Strawberry Hill, and so, though the facade of our house was conventional, the interior was not. He did in the interior what Francini had done in the Gardens, that is, transmuted his fantasies into his work, using rich wood panelings, baroque ornamentation, odd-shaped rooms, marble extravanganzas, and star-spangled ceilings.

Our entrance hall was a large octagonal space whose walls were papered with a trompe l'oeil panorama of the ancient city of Troy by moonlight. Arm in arm, gorgeous, sensual, their bodies luminous in the silvery light, wandered three sets of lovers: Zeus and Ganeymede, Aphrodite and Mars, Apollo and Daphne, while in the middle distance beyond the ramparts, in the marshes facing the sea, huntsmen rode on their steeds.

From the center of the hall's star-spangled domed ceiling hung a huge gold-and-crystal chandelier, which, when its thousand candles were lit, glittered like a golden star. On either side of the entrance door two mammoth fireplaces towered over us; with huge andirons in the shape of flames, and hanging on the wall in individual niches were pokers and shovels whose metal shafts were carved with demon faces.

Some days before, our coachman, Norris, who slept in the coach house a few blocks away, had gone to fetch Poppa at Albion, a country estate outside of Exeter owned by my grandfather's friend, Miles Ryder. My father had stopped there for a few days after his arrival at Dover, on his way home to us.

"According to my calculations," my father wrote to my mother, "barring accidents such as overflowing rivers, fog or snow, or coupling reins not crossed, pole-chains gone, or Norris too much in whiskey to use his whip well, expect your lord and master home on November 17, an hour before midnight."

My heart ached for the sight of him. My eleventh birthday had occurred during his absence, and though I had received some letters from him, none had acknowledged that most important event. I could only think that my father had stopped loving me, that I had done something to offend him. And since it was only his love that sustained me, though I would not have phrased it that way then, I wondered what would happen to me now.

The two mantel clocks on either side of the entrance door began to chime the hour: eleven o'clock. "Dear Jesus, sweet Jesus," I prayed, "let Poppa come home on time!" Moments after the last chime rang we heard the thunderous clatter of hooves on the cobblestones outside and the landau groaning and shrieking to a stop, its wheels scraping the stones. My prayers had been answered!

Hurriedly, Mrs. Farnley undid the cumbersome iron bolts and pushed the doors wide open. I could see snow on the ground and fog and steam rising from the four chestnuts. The carriage lamps were lit.

The footmen, having jumped off their perch, were already removing the luggage from the boot while Norris, his cape flying in the wind, leaped down from his box, let down the double folding steps, and opened the carriage door. And there he was! Poppa! Stepping down to the walk . . . framed in the yellow light of the carriage lamps, superlatively handsome in his greatcoat with its fur collar and fur cuffs, telling Norris, as he came towards us down the short walk, that next time they made such a journey "you'd better put the mare next to the wheel!"

"Good evening, sir," Mrs. Farnley cried out to him.

"Good evening, Mrs. Farnley," he said, as he walked up the short flight of steps and crossed over the threshold into the hall, bringing the cold air in with him.

He had blond hair. Blond like the Vikings and the Norse gods of old. His hair was the color of burnished gold. The tips of his mustache and whiskers curled like gold filaments. Majestic. His top hat, tilted, pressed down on a blond mane of thick, long, lustrous hair. Yellow leather gloves clutched a stout cane whose knob was made of ivory and gold. A lion of a man, he stood there, the master of all he surveyed. Behind my father, Norris and Daisy and Tags and the footmen carried in his luggage: handbags, portmanteaus, cases, all sizes and shapes, stacked around him like dwarfs or gnomes of some strange country of which he was king. Then at a discreet signal from Mrs. Farnley the bags were magically whisked away by Daisy and Tags to wherever they were supposed to go.

"Your journey, I trust, was satisfactory," my mother said in the neutral voice she always used when addressing him in public.

Her face was as bland as her voice. And yet she had been quite lively in his absence, I realized. The transformation to this dull, spiritless creature standing there tonight had begun, I realized, on the day she had received his letter with its exact and meticulous instructions about preparations for his return. The change had been subtly wrought but accumulative, apparently, for by the time of his arrival she was totally lacking in distinctive character.

"It was tolerable," he answered. His cold glance rested on her briefly as Mrs. Farnley removed his coat, cane, and gloves and disappeared into the cloakroom with them. He walked over to one of the fireplaces and stood in front of it, his back to us, warming his hands, and then, suddenly, he turned around, his face warm, friendly, lit with smiles, and opening up his arms he called me to him.

"Emmy, Emmy, pretty penny come . . . come here to me. I have brought you many gifts, for I understand that I must be forgiven for not being present at your birthday celebration. That was very bad of me. But before I give you them—and truly they are wonderful—you must assure me that you have forgiven me for not being there. Do you forgive me? Can you forgive me? Tell me that you do!"

Did I forgive him! "Oh, yes, yes, yes, yes!" I assured him. I did forgive him. I should always forgive him no matter what he did. And though I did not mean to, indeed I tried not to, my tears overflowed and I wept with joy. Poppa had returned! I was once more his "Emmy, Emmy, pretty penny," for that is what he called me, and his "blue-eyed darling." Enfolding me in his arms, he told Mrs. Farnley to lay out a small supper for him. "Some hot soups, cold meat, a little wine, fruit and cheese."

It was almost midnight. He had traveled from Frankfurt to Paris and then to Calais. Yes, the crossing to Dover had been rough. And then to Albion and from Albion to us. Now he was tired, he said. Gently he let go of me, and when Mrs. Farnley returned to tell him that his meal was ready I went upstairs to bed.

———◦✦◦✦◦———

I was tired when I went to bed that night and so I fell asleep immediately. It was the following night that their voices awakened me, and the night after that, being awakened again, I began to listen.

"Come here!" said my father.

"But you said that you were tired."

"I am, so you will oblige me, Theodisia, by not giving me any trouble."

"I detest you."

"I don't believe you. I think you are as eager as I am. Take off your clothes or I shall rip them off you. Now lie down there."

"On the floor!"

"Yes. On the rug in front of the fireplace. Right there. Good. Now spread your legs . . . wider, damn you! Wider!"

Silence, then grunts and groans as if furniture was being lifted and moved. I heard him say, "Tell me you like it! Say it!" I heard her muffled screams, "Yes, yes, I like it." I heard him cry out "Bitch!" and then moments later I heard him say in his ordinary tone of voice, "See to it, Theodisia, that the Strooksburys dine with us next week. I have a business proposition that might interest him. . . ."

I was not sexually naive. My cousin Darius[9] had explained certain sexual things to me. I knew what a penis was. Darius had shown me his and then he had suggested that I undress and when I did he explained and identified to me my own genitalia. After that anatomy lesson, when we were dressed again, he explained to me the nuts and bolts of human

9. Darius Marcus Georgione Forster, Count Rimini VII, b. 1822, was the only son of Joseph and Consuelo Forster. An extraordinarily creative, if decadent, person, he was expelled from Warrenton (the public school the Forster males attended) in 1836 for an act of sodomy with another boy. Bored and restless in Marlborough Gardens, he became the children's mentor during eight crucial months of their lives. As their mentor he taught them among other things the "art" of war. In the spring of 1837 he led one faction of cousins against another on Marlborough Marshes in a battle the children referred to as the Marlborough Wars. Involved in a love/hate relationship with his mother, Consuelo (a famous composer and musician), he attempted suicide when he discovered shortly after his military victory that Consuelo had run away to Florence (her native city) with his father's valet, Ricci. Darius's suicide was aborted by Emma's father, Elijah. Darius's relationship to Emma was quite different. She had "suffered" as he had. But she was not only an object of his compassion, she was also an object of his love and devotion. His attitude towards her was similar to what a medieval knight must have felt for his lady love. As children they exchanged vows. Complex, charismatic, Darius affected the children's lives profoundly. See *City of Childhood,* Book I of Marlborough Gardens.—*R. Lowe*

sexual intercourse, and though it made no sense to me at the time (I was ten years old) I never doubted that what he had told me was true. But it had been basically an abstract and technical explanation rather than a blood and flesh one.

Darius had not told me that a woman might object to the procedure, but I certainly understood that what my father was doing to my mother was being done against her will. Not that I cared. I adored my father. Passionately. His treatment of my mother, for whom I did not care, his coldness to her, his apparent violence to her, did not lessen my love for him.

On the contrary, I became more enamored of him. My father's sexual advances towards my mother stimulated my own sexual desires, and though I did not absolutely comprehend my parents' physical actions, gradually, over the weeks and months that I eavesdropped as they had "sex," I would find myself sexually aroused, and I would begin to masturbate as my father forced himself on my mother. When he uttered "Bitch!" I would climax.

I began stealing small things that belong to my father, items I thought he might not miss—a garter, an old hat, a worn cravat—and as they had sex I would press the stolen item to my chest as I gratified myself. But he did miss them, and there were rows and servants threatened with dismissal over these stolen articles of clothing. I kept them all under a floorboard that I had loosened beneath my bed. For all I know they may still be there.

As for my mother . . . had my father cut her up into small pieces and had Mrs. Lovesley like Atreus served them up to us in a stew, I would have joined my father gladly in this diabolical meal. I was savage and primitive in my hatred of her. How dare she refuse my father anything!

Gradually over a period of time I began to realize as I listened to them that not only did they have a fixed and limited number of topics on which they spoke—money, society, mutual friends, household matters, current events—but that certain categories, such as money, aroused my father's sexual desires, or should I say lust.

For instance, my father might be lecturing my mother on certain economic principles (my father was a Ricardian and a Benthamite) during which she was made to understand that "profit" was a positive good and "loss" a positive evil when his voice would change. The customary fundamentally demeaning tone in which he addressed my mother would contain a few plaintive notes. I could hear in that voice reverberations of the voice he used when he talked to me during the visits he made to me just before my bedtime.

Seemingly out of the blue he would say to my mother, "You look quite lovely tonight, my dear." At first somewhat amorous and loving in his declarations, he would become increasingly aggressive and hostile towards my mother as she parried, fenced, and tried to repulse him, at which point he would drag her (I presumed drag, for what else could make that sound but heels scraping across a wooden floor) to bed, where he quickly mounted and raped her.

How did I know he mounted and raped her? At the time I didn't. It is only over the years that I have been able to interpret her woeful cries, her little bleats of pain; his shout of triumph when he first overcame her, and his strange-sounding muffled cry when the tumescent organ released its seed into her, followed by the epithet "Bitch!" And so it went, the forces between them pulling them towards each other and away from each other. Again and again.

Truthfully it was only years later, actually, when I came back from visiting my cousin Darius in Florence in 1856 that I began to sympathize with my mother (somewhat) and see the world more from her point of view. For by then much had happened to me . . . enough to make me understand my character and the limitations of my nature. The best and worst had befallen me.

It was, by the way, through my pernicious habit of eavesdropping that I first heard about Clara. . . .

How is it, and why is it, that love dies, or is even born, or changes? I am, of course, thinking of Clara as I write this . . . not that Clara ever loved me. Oh, no, she made that clear to me from the beginning. She was my friend, she said. She felt affection towards me. It was *I* who fell in love.

It is a dreary truism that eavesdroppers seldom hear kind things said about themselves—I did not—but is it their fault or is it a comment on human nature? Before I continue any further I wish to say a last word about another aspect of my parents' liaison. It is this: though my father was undoubtedly at the helm—it was he who commanded, judged, castigated, decreed, and was obeyed—there were times an ambiguous shift took place when Theodisia, if not capable of wielding absolute power, could prevail somewhat. And that was when he lusted after her and she had not as yet satisfied him. During that period (of grace, shall we say?) the lines of force shifted and moved from the male to the female. During that brief interim she said things she would not have dared to otherwise. It was during one of those times that I first heard them speak of Clara. When exactly I've forgotten, but I do know that Christmas and New Year's had come and gone. And that it was so cold that I even thought of forgoing my nightly eavesdropping.

<hr>

"There really isn't any point in asking me to do something I cannot do, is there, Elijah? I am as kind to Emma as I can be. She seems senseless to me."

"It's because you are cold and unfeeling to her. Cold and distant. Alone with me, Emma is sensible. And amusing besides. She chatters away like a bright little monkey. . . . You have three children, Theodisia, not just one. If you could but spare her just a morsel of some of the love you lavish on William it would satisfy me. It would do your soul good to try to love her—"

"Oh, do spare me one of your duller homilies. I wonder if you realize how frightened I was after she was born that I might give birth to another child with just such a mark as she has. [I have not mentioned my birthmark since it was truly nothing, and only a woman with a cold heart and little intelligence would have made anything of it. It was, and still is, on my left temple. Hardly noticeable . . . round, the size of a guinea.] Who will marry her? Don't glare at me. You know I am speaking the truth. Furthermore, why does she have it? There is no one on my side of the family that does."

"A rhetorical question, I presume. You are as unnatural a mother as you are a wife, my dear. A veritable freak of nature, but it's not about you that I wish to speak. It is about Emma. She is almost twelve years old now. She is all alone. Her brothers and all her cousins have gone off to school. You pay no attention to her. Grindal, who was supposed to keep watch over her, has been sent to Saddler's Grove because of that ridiculous business with Joseph's groom.

"Emma must be educated, civilized, prepared to take her place in society. She does nothing. She has nothing to do. In her case, an education will prove important. At any rate, I have employed a governess."

"A governess? Whatever for? Mrs. Bottome [our minister's wife] teaches her embroidery, some grammar—"

"If it were you I was raising I would leave you in Bottome's hands, a suitable match, but Emma is my daughter, and she is to have something considerably better. Indeed, she shall have the very best."

"Then why not send her to the academy her cousin Vanessa and her sisters attend?"

"To be mocked and jeered at by her peers for something she cannot help, a birthmark? Something no larger than the nail on my thumb?

No, I know how cruel your sex is. My daughter shall be educated at home."

A few nights later I heard the following:

"How many times have I told you not to sit Mrs. Strooksbury on my right? She's an opinionated bore. Uninteresting and contentious besides. It does seem to me a fairly small favor to ask of someone to whom so much is granted—fine clothes, fine food, a luxurious home— with little to do. See to it, Theodisia, that it does not happen again. Oh, by the way, I have received an answer from Clara, Mrs. Clara Lustig. She will be arriving in London in a fortnight."

"Mrs. Clara Lustig? Who is she?"

"She is the woman I have hired to educate Emma."

"But you have never mentioned her before to me."

"I have now. I told you just the other day I was going to hire a governess. Have you forgotten already? Incidentally, she is my second cousin. Surely you have no objections to that."

"Of course not . . . though I don't quite know what you mean. I mean, I don't object to having a second cousin. Why would I? But who is she really? Where did you meet her? You've told me nothing."

"There's nothing to tell. Emma needs a governess. I have hired one. Were it left to you Emma would rot. You've made it clear to me, clear to her, clear to everyone, that you don't care for her. She must be protected from you . . . and since Mrs. Lustig is a relation she shall sup with us. You are to be polite to her. You are not to treat her as a servant."

There was silence for a minute or two.

"Where did you meet her? Or have you known about her all this time?"

"Women! You cannot control your curiosity, can you? You must know everything. Well, I shall take pity and tell you. . . . I met her in Germany, in Frankfurt at the house of Frederick Lustig, a banker with whom we do business. Meinheer Lustig was kind enough to invite me to his house for dinner. Clara, his daughter-in-law, is a widow. She was married to his older son Franz, who died recently. I met her there."

"Oh . . . but how did you find out that you were related to one another?"

"I suppose I shall have to tell you or you shall annoy me until I do. After dinner she and her brother-in-law, Johan, played a piano duet. Haydn, and well done it was. I complimented her, and when she thanked me in English I complimented her on her English accent, whereupon she told me that she was English and that she had been born in the Cotswalds in a village called Ashville. [Both my mother, her parents, and my father's father had been born in Ashville.] And that, to make a long story short, is how I subsequently discovered that my father and her grandfather were brothers. Now you know all."

"I suppose she is pretty—"

"No. Actually she is quite plain."

"Oh?"

"Yes. She has none of the usual physical snares to catch men that women generally have. Her bosom is small. Her skin is sallow—her mother was of Italian descent—her eyes are too large, her nose too long. She is underweight—"

"But someone married her, you said. . . ."

"Yes, and a handsome fellow, too, I was made to understand. Exactly like his brother Johan, one of those pink and blond German types with deep blue eyes. Oh, I imagine her Franz could have had his pick, as they say."

"But he chose her."

There was another long pause.

"Mrs. Lustig is exceptionally bright. Well educated. But even more important to me than that, Theodisia, is her soothing manner. I hope this will have an effect on Emma."

"Did you tell Mrs. Lustig about . . . oh, you know what I mean!"

"Yes, I know what you mean. I explained the problem to her and she was quite knowledgeable about it. Almost as if she were a doctor. She wanted to know whether the birthmark was pigmented or nonpigmented, whether the nevus was superficially flat, I think she said, or whether it was raised. And was it port-wine in color or blue-black?"

"How did she know to ask such questions?"

"She told me that her father, my cousin, had been a doctor. For a short time when she was young he used her as an assistant."

"But when did she tell you this? Surely not at the dinner party?"

"No, I saw her several times after that. I decided almost instantly upon meeting her that she might be the governess I was seeking, but I did not ask her until I knew her better. By the time I left Frankfurt she had promised to consider my offer."

"You saw her several times—"

"Oh, for God's sake, Theodisia, spare me your fits of jealousy. I assure you that you shall never know or meet the woman who is my mistress of the moment. I prefer my women with more flesh on their bones, prettier faces, and less grey matter than Clara."

"What have you told her about me?"

"I told her that my daughter has a mother who is a shallow, selfish woman who does not love her."

"I will not have her here!"

"It is not for you to decide that matter. Whether you like it or not she will arrive here in a fortnight. I intend to have her educate Emma. And I intend that you shall be cooperative. These are my intentions. Do you understand me?"

I knew my father's wishes would have to be obeyed. He ruled the household. As I said, I loved him passionately. I did not think him unkind. Indeed, I worshiped him, but I was beginning to understand that his behavior towards my mother could be construed as unkind. I began to wonder why he disliked her so much. And why she disliked me.

As for the unknown woman, Clara, I was terrified to meet her, and was incensed that my father had told Theodisia about her before he had told me. After listening to their conversation that night I was sick to my stomach. A nevus! So that was its official name!

I did not want to meet her, the woman who already knew so much about me. If and when I was summoned to the library to meet her I would refuse to go. Refuse! In a fortnight she would be waiting for me to meet her there, a thin plain woman with sallow skin and eyes too large for her. I would not do it. I would refuse! Blue-black . . . port-wine. I stared at myself in the mirror over the bureau; it was too dark to see. I moved over to the window. I wondered would I die if I pitched myself headlong out of the window at this height or would I just end up a battered heap of broken bones? I prayed to be taken with a fatal illness. Opening my arms wide I asked to be "afflicted."

The following day after supper my father told me he wished to speak to me privately. I was to go to the library and wait for him there.

When he came in I noticed with pleasure how very handsome he was. How beautiful his thick blond hair was, oiled, scented and curled, and distributed in a beard of moderate size, side whiskers, and a mustache. A striking figure in resplendent clothes.

That evening he was dressed in a swallow-blue coat, a buff waistcoat, and white corduroy trousers. In his blue satin cravat nested a gold stickpin molded in the form of Pegasus. His gold watch chain looped through a left buttonhole and curved across his broad chest. How utterly attractive he was. I adored him.

I loved the library. It was his room. The furniture was comfortable and masculine, deep red and brown leather. A fire hissed and crackled on the white marble hearth. Rows of books lined the shelves.

"I have engaged a governess for you, Emma. She will arrive some-times in early March."

"But I don't want a governess! I don't need one!"

"I believe I am the best judge of that, Emma."

"I don't want one. I . . . I shall run away!"

"You shall not. It may be that you do not want a governess, but she is coming nevertheless. I intend to see that you are well educated."

"But I don't want to be educated."

"Education is one of those things that no one wants but one always appreciates afterwards. You will be a good student. You have the makings of a good mind."

"How do you know that, Poppa?"

"I know about such things. I also know, Emma, that you are reluctant to meet a stranger, and I can understand that, but I have told her about you. In . . . every particular."

"Oh. And what did she say?"

"She said she knew about such things, and that beauty is but skin deep and that it is the soul that God judges, not our physicality."

"Is that what she said, Poppa? She said nothing more?"

"Nothing more, Emma."

———◈⬩◯◈⬩———

Two weeks later on a Thursday in the late afternoon Daisy came to my room and announced that I was wanted downstairs in the library to meet my new governess.

She was wearing a grey silk dress and she looked almost like a Quaker except for the green ribbon on her dark silk bonnet.

My father was right about one thing, I could see that immediately. Clara Lustig was not pretty. Indeed, she was quite plain. Her lips were thin, pale, her complexion uniformly sallow. But all of this was immediately forgotten when one took in her eyes: enormous, hooded, set in deep sockets, alive with mysterious shadows. I did not shrink from looking at her, examining her. For a moment it seemed to me as if I was once more looking into my beloved Darius's eyes. They were amazingly like his; they held enormous comprehension like his, and something else . . . something that I could not define but somehow felt. A penetrating look, I decided, but not cruel. (Not like Nanny Grindal.) I glanced down at her slippers. They were surprisingly elegant: slim brown sandals, cut high and fastened with an ankle strap. Dainty, as dainty as her hands; her fingers, long, tapered, and beautifully shaped, clasped each other. A golden wedding band and above it a small garnet ring glimmered on the pale flesh of her fingers.

My father introduced us, declaring immediately afterwards that he would withdraw so that we could become acquainted, but as he made to leave the room she rose from her chair and walked towards him hurriedly. She stood between him and the door. I heard her whisper, "Then it is understood, Sir, that I am to have complete control?"

"Yes, Madam. Now if you will excuse me, I shall take leave of both of you." With that my father left the room, closing the door softly behind him.

She said nothing. Nor did she look at me. Instead she returned to her chair, sat down, and stared into space.

For some reason it did not disturb me—she was so still and quiet— I only wondered what she could be thinking of or looking at. At any rate I felt relieved that she was not staring at me, and then I realized that she had not really looked at me at all since I had come into the room. I was seated on a chair about six feet away from her. Suddenly she turned towards me and gave me the full weight of her concentration. I colored, I know. I could feel the heat as my blood crept up my neck and slowly flooded my face. I would have run away but I simply could not move.

"Come here, Emma." Her voice was low, but it held the definitive note of authority.

I moved towards her.

"Closer."

I stood in front of her. I was tall for my age. She was small for hers. It gave me some measure of comfort.

"My name is Clara Forster Lustig," she began. "I am related to you, but I shall give a complete genealogy of our family and our specific connection with one another some other time. For now it is enough for you to know that I am twenty-two years old; that I have been widowed recently. My husband's name was Franz Karl Lustig. He died young, he was only twenty-nine, of a sudden heart attack. He seemed in perfect health but apparently he wasn't. My father, your father's cousin, was a doctor. He died some years ago. I have one sister, Catherine, who is married to a clerk, a decent man. They have children. I shall tell you about them some other time." She paused. "I was born in Ashville, a small village in the Cotswalds, the same place your grandfather Jorem was born.

"I met your father at my in-laws' house in Frankfurt in Germany. When your father asked me if I would consider being a governess—I had been governess to Franz's nephews[10] before we married—I thought about it seriously. I had been thinking of the possibility of returning to England—it is, after all, my home—but I had no financial means with which to do so. Your father's generous offer gave me the oppor-

---

10. Clara Lustig was eighteen when she was hired through an acquaintance by Lisette Falkenstein, Franz's older sister, as governess for her two sons.—*R. Lowe*

tunity. Besides, the thought of teaching pleased me. I think at heart I am a teacher. That is enough for you to know about me for the time being . . . now, you must tell me about yourself."

I had not wanted to meet her, I had dreaded it, I had even thought of killing myself rather than meeting her. I had conjured up all kinds of scenes in my head about the first meeting, not knowing what to expect, but what was happening now was something I never could have conceived.

No adult had ever spoken to me that way before. Not even my father, whom I knew loved me and I believe understood me. No adult had ever shown me such respect, a consideration that implied I had worth, that I was to be taken seriously. For the sharing of her life with me just now and the promise of more to come . . . what else could it mean but that?

I could say nothing. I was too overwhelmed with emotion.

When my silence continued she said, "I shall wait until you have collected your thoughts."

Instead of answering I began to cry. Sobs like jagged bits of flesh welled up in my throat and broke loose. I stood there, my head bowed, in front of her, crying as I had never cried before. Crying tears I had not known up until that time I possessed. All the loneliness, terror, and humiliation of not understanding anything, of not knowing who I was, all the feelings I had bottled up in me this past year, ever since Darius had been sent away, came pouring out. I felt her take my hands in hers . . . she turned them over and held them firmly.

"You have fine hands, Emma, capable of doing all sorts of work. Emotion is a fine thing, of course, but we must not let ourselves be carried away by grief . . . or by love . . . or by joy. Control is always better. Duty, discipline, control, work, these are the things that will carry us through.

"I imagine you have no Latin, no Greek . . ." My head shook no at each subject she mentioned. I did not mean to lie, but I did. Darius had taught me Greek along with other things. But for some reason I did not want her to know that.

"Well, then perhaps a little piano or drawing . . ." I shook my head again. "Hmmm . . . not even that. A veritable tabula rasa. Good! A clean slate. I like that. Now, take my handkerchief and dry your eyes, and after you have done so I shall be obliged to you if you will please show me to my room."

We ascended the staircase to the third floor. Leading the way, I showed her to a small room, somewhat larger than mine, and more comfortably furnished, the former day nursery where my brothers and Tansy, Grindal's former assistant, had slept.

As Clara stood there in the center of the room, a small thin figure dressed in grey silk, I suddenly recalled the Creature of Light, a character in my grandfather Jorem's "Tale of the Black Swan." The last words of my grandfather's story flooded back into my mind: "And if you are wondering who or what the Creature of Light really was, why I shall tell you. The Creature of Light who lodged herself and remained forever in Maartel's heart is what we mortals, for want of a better word, call Hope. . . ."

Yes, I thought, staring at her, yes, that is who she is, that is who she must be—the Creature of Light called Hope.

A Note of Explanation: Clara's Letters

According to Emma's diary, Emma found Clara's letters in a box-wood box hidden in Johan Lustig's home in Frankfurt, Germany.

The letters had been torn in two and three parts and more. We do not know if Clara was the one who tore them up, but presumably it was Emma who pasted them together. We know she carried "the traitors" (Emma's name for the letters) back with her to England on one of her numerous trips back to Marlborough Gardens in the eighties, for she mentions this specifically in her Weimar journal.

We have taken the liberty of interpolating them into the text of The Metaphysics of Sex *when and where we thought it was suitable.*
—R. Lowe and H. Van Buren

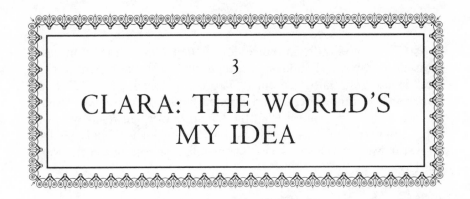

3

CLARA: THE WORLD'S MY IDEA

. . . as I watched Clara move about the room I felt a stab of pain around the region of my heart. Such was the quality of my fevered imagination at the time. I watched as she put away her clothes and set her brushes on the bureau. An excitement seized me. Suddenly I wished to know everything, everything she could teach me! My father had been right as always.

—Emma Forster, *The Metaphysics of Sex*

43 MARLBOROUGH GARDENS
23 APRIL 1838

Mᴀ dear Johan,

Forgive me for not writing sooner.

I arrived on English soil from Calais, March 12, weary and wet after a most uncomfortable crossing, the sea covered with perpetual foam, violent and rolling, as were my organs, which did not settle until I saw the Cliffs and we were finally at anchorage at Dover.

Disembarking, I wandered on the sands, whereupon my luggage was snatched by two murderous-looking porters and carried to a post chaise whose horses looked as if they might fall down dead at any moment, where it was tossed into the hind boot.

And myself, forthwith, lifted and tossed by the same murderous-looking porters into the dank and dark interior of the chaise. My fellow passengers, six on the inside, three on the outside, spent the ten-hour ride to London drinking whiskey except for one other woman who like myself wished she had.

England. My native land. London . . . the sound of my own language. Oh, it was good to be back.

I stayed at a coaching inn called the King's Head where I had been instructed to await my employer's coach. And so I had the pleasure of dining at the inn. I need only tell you the menu to have your instant commiseration. A piece of pork without flavoring or seasoning of any kind with a dish of beans followed by a floury pudding. Thank God, the next evening as was prearranged I was called for by the Forsters' sullen coachman, Norris, and whisked off to Marlborough Gardens in a most comfortable landau with plated door handles and painted vermillion moldings, and two footmen in livery trimmed with lace.

An hour's journey, through a light snow, the wind blowing, stars shining, a cold night but with windows that fit tight, with my seat comfortably padded, a fur robe wrapped around my lap, my feet resting on a Wilton carpet, my back resting on a quilted cushion, I was comfortable enough. Ah to have money! What pleasure it brings.

As you know I have reason to dislike the Forsters, so you can imagine the intensity, the range of my emotions when I finally entered their home late that night. How many times I have dreamed of that moment. And now I was there inside ensconced in their establishment. Invited in, begged to come! Paid well to do so.

So here I am. And we shall see, shan't we. I shall describe them, the tribe, in my next letter.

> *auf Wiedersehen, mein Kamerad,*
> Clara

3 May 1838, Marlborough Gardens

My dear Johan,

Why is that from the very first moment we met we understood each other so well? I have little or no use of your family, as you know. Except, of course, for my beloved Franz, my late husband, the soul of integrity. For me there shall never be another. He had my heart, what there was of it, and my small portion of sexual feeling . . . but that is not what we have between us, is it? What did you call it once? "Einmal freundlich," was it not? Yes, I agree you are my friend; I shall always be yours.

I had my first "interrogation" by my employer, my cousin Elijah, this very evening in his study-cum-library. À propos, the house is remarkable, if that is the right word. Perhaps "disturbing" is a more appropriate word. There is a dearth of rectangular rooms at 43 Marlborough Gardens! We live, breathe, and suffer in octagons, pentagons, triangles, squares, and rounds! A maddening state of affairs. Oh, for the comfort, the peace, and serenity of a mundane rectangular room.

Elijah: He is most irritating. But you have met him so you know what I mean. Everything he does—the tone of his voice, his choice of vocabulary, the look on his face, in short, everything—exemplifies his contempt for the female sex—he does not treat me so, of course—but the habit is so pernicious he cannot help but speak to me at times in a demeaning tone. However, he is also an epitome of masculine virility, which in itself is sexually arousing. I remember we spoke about this in Frankfurt but what we did not speak about because it was not present at the time is my budding sexual desire for him. I hope this admission does not disturb you. But we made a pact, didn't we, to tell each other *everything*.

As you know I held out for an unheard-of salary and did not yield until I won it, as well as the understanding that my position would not interfere with my other goal in London, that of establishing myself as a critic for either the *Westminster Review*, *Blackwoods*, or the *Edinburgh Review*. Frankly, I do not know why he hired me unless he felt that because I was "family" I might prove more "trustworthy." Or perhaps, who knows, it was a tacit attempt on his part to right a wrong. As you know, London is filled with women, mostly vicars' daughters, far more agreeable than me (but then who isn't) who would have been as suitable for the position. However, he chose me. He would not take no for an answer.

He interrogates me as to his daughter's progress on a regular basis on Tuesday evenings in his study after dinner. I am invited to join him in a glass of Madeira, which I drink greedily as he proceeds to question me. He is meticulous and knowledgeable. He understands Emma quite well, her impulsive, ardent nature, her unique intelligence that seems so intimately connected to her emotional process. "Emma feels things," he told me. "It is through her feelings that she arrives at intellectual decisions. Unlike me. I come to mine having either forgotten my emotions or never having had them in the first place."

I found being locked up with Elijah in that small space—sealed as it were, from the rest of the household—sexually stimulating. He is seductive. Last night he was wearing brown breeches, a rose-colored waistcoat, a yellow figured silk neck-cloth, a faint scent. He looked as rakish as a horse dealer, I thought. When he bent towards me to hand me my glass of wine, I believe there was a distinct pause in which he registered the fact that I was not only a governess but a "woman."

About Emma: She is unusually bright *and* unusually vulnerable. So I am convinced that all shall go the way we have planned.

> *auf Wiedersehen, mein Kamerad,*
> Clara

8 May 1838, 43 Marlborough Gardens

Dear Johan,

At the risk of sounding foolish or like the mindless heroine of the latest Gothic novel, I "sense" something has happened here that is—what?—unusual. Sui generis. For despite the beauty (Marlborough Gardens is truly magnificent) and the luxury of the Forster way of life, "a shadow hangs over" the whole family. I know—shades of Mrs. Radcliffe and Clara Reeve & Co.[11] Still, those ladies with their *intuitions* were on to something. Environments do exude atmosphere. Places do have power. I shall find out what it is, of course, but until then I dismiss it. After all I have brought my own serious mischief with me, as you know. Still, it makes me uneasy. So forgive me if I am not my usual steadfast sardonic self.

From the very beginning I was invited to eat my meals with them. I am not adverse to dining with a Forster, but the

---

11. Clara is referring to a group of female novelists—Mrs. Radcliffe, Clara Reeve, Sophie Lee, Charlotte Smith, Charlotte Dacre—known as Gothic novelists, female specialists of "tales of terror."—*R. Lowe*

tension at the dinner table between Elijah and wife, Theodisia, may prove too unbearable even for me. This is an armed
camp.

He behaves towards his wife as if she were his enemy. Fully
armored and not the "wee timorous beastie" she actually is.
I do not know why as yet except that I have noticed that like
most despots it is the victim's cowardice that seems to stimulate the sadism.

She is blond, too, like him. But while he is radiant and
glows with good health and is vigorous and virile she is faded,
wasted. She responds to his brutality in whispers. She seems
dull-witted, hardly a worthy opponent to draw so much fire.
Marriage! A strange institution, *nicht wahr*?

On Sundays the entire family convenes here for dinner.
Elijah's brother Solomon and his wife, Guinivere; their sister,
Mathilda, with her husband, Brian Herrod; and Joseph, the
oldest brother, sans wife, his wife having decamped with her
husband's valet two years ago! The servants cannot wait to
tell one the bad tidings about their masters and mistresses.
I had barely unpacked when Daisy, one of the upstairs maids,
told me this bit of interesting gossip. However, the most
interesting thing about it is that the runaway wife is none
other than the Contessa Consuelo Rimini, the well-known
composer and pianist we had the pleasure of hearing play in
Weimar a year ago! Oh, how I wish I could turn back the
clock. . . .

Their collective progeny[12], except for Deirdre (Guinivere's
youngest child) and Emma, are away at various schools, including the Contessa's son, Darius Rimini, who according
to Daisy attempted suicide when the Contessa "abandoned"
him. I shall say more about him later, but from the little I
know Darius seems to be the most intriguing of them all.
Putting aside my "premonitions" and my prejudices, I must
admit that all in all the Forsters are a decidedly handsome
lot: energetic, large-boned, blond, heroic types. Solomon
and Joseph, like Elijah, are over six feet tall; they resemble

12. "Perhaps you should have the following précis: the male Forsters attend Warrenton,
a public school in Leicester; Edward and William, Emma's brothers, are there now, as
are Guinivere's sons, Albert and the twins Joshua and Jacob. Darius, the Contessa's
son, attended Warrenton but was expelled (rest assured I shall find out why) and is now
attending a Catholic academy, Somerset, in Wiltshire. As for Mathilda's brood—
Vanessa, Letitia, and Mary-Anne—they are frittering their time away in some silly
female academy." From C. Lustig's additional note at the end of her letter.—*R. Lowe*

one another most markedly in the eyes, which are an unusual dark and vivid blue, and in the shape of their faces, squarish. Solomon, Jorem's youngest son, is a bit plumper than his brothers, but his nose is as finely chiseled as theirs. Grouped together they resemble a pride of lions.

And though their sister, Mathilda, is by no means a beauty, she is as the French say *jolie laide,* a tall, handsome, matronly looking woman with a confident air about her which is most attractive. She too has blond hair, if not as golden as her brothers', just as thick, which she wears in loose curls over her ears. Dressed in a mustard-colored silk gown with high puffed sleeves, her ample bosom adorned with jewels, Mathilda looked as wealthy and sleek and self-satisfied as her brothers. I sensed that she took an instant liking to me. I was, she implied by her actions (in the way she addressed me), after all, a member of the family, *a Forster*, albeit not as well-to-do, but nonetheless the genuine genealogical article, a *true* Forster and not like the other two, i.e., Theodisia and Guinivere.

Her husband, Brian, who never left her side, and who seemed half her size, a slender brunette, graceful and lively, is looked down on by the Forster men, for he too is after all *not* a Forster. Not that it seems to bother him, for he chatters away and expresses his views freely on all subjects.

À propos, I was told yesterday by Mrs. Farnley, Elijah's formidable housekeeper, that Mathilda's oldest daughter, Vanessa, is considered the family beauty. "She is expected to marry into aristocracy," she said.

It is amusing to look into Deirdre's face—she is a well-behaved, rosy, blond creature—and see her father's deep-set dark blue eyes and long upper lip set in a shape that resembles her mother's. Compared to Deirdre, Emma, my charge, looks positively scraggly. Underweight, far too intense . . . but I will write you about her in a special letter. Emma deserves a letter all to herself.

The dinner conversations were the usual explosive ravings about the Corn Laws and the Anti-Corn Law League that had just been formed in Manchester. You tell me you know something about English politics, hence my reportage. I should tell you, I suppose, that Elijah is a Whig and Solomon a Tory. It seemed to me their fulminations were subtly encouraged by Brian. As for Joseph, he ignored the ruckus entirely. Instead, as his two brothers ranted he quietly kept helping himself to more and more wine, and when Mrs. Farnley removed the bottle from the table and put it on the sideboard, Joseph made a point of getting up and bringing the bottle back and placing it next to his serving plate.

As expected, the women said nothing—except for Mathilda, who admonished her brothers to cool their tempers.

As for myself, I cared about nothing else but the food, I confess. The soup was heavenly, a light vegetable broth full of pearl barley, carrots, and shredded cabbage, followed by braised goose in a sweet Madeira-flavored sauce and garnished with roast potatoes and apricot patties served on Derby china and accompanied by three different kinds of wines: a pale rosé, a more robust claret, and a sweet Rhennish wine. I would not have cared had they come to blows. No, the poor relation ate her full and wondered, as always, why those who had so much were not more grateful.

By the end of the meal I think I understood quite well how they related to one another, who was the most powerful, who the least. But family life is the same everywhere, isn't it? Each member jockeying for position in the family constellation—even unto death. The women as well as the men. But since I consider it boring in novels to be introduced to a plethora of characters, no matter how skillful or original the author is, I will send another letter[13] describing in greater detail my first impressions of the lay of the land, so to speak.

However, there is one person I shall speak about more fully and that is Guinivere, Solomon's wife. In the mythology of family life there is always the evil one (Elijah, I believe, in this case) and the good one. Guinivere is obviously the "good" one.

I cannot tell you how irritating this concept is to me. I mean a "good" woman. What in the world does that mean? It brings to mind Medea's statement: I know the good but I do the bad (Euripides' answer to Socrates).

What does it mean? Does it mean that she knows her place? Has never offered an opinion? Has never worked for a living? Has never had an original thought or a creative impulse? Has never been witty or uproarious or rambunctious or rude or seductive (Heaven forbid!) or experienced anything vital, a spark of life!

But besides being "good" she is "bereaved." One of her

13. So far we have been unable to locate this letter.—R. Lowe

children, a boy named Sidney, died two years ago at the age of eight. So Guinivere, besides being "good," is now "sacrosanct." He was buried in the Rose Garden here at Marlborough Gardens, and not in the family plot at Saddler's Grove. A strange place to bury a child, don't you think? Anyway, she irritates me as much as Elijah does, though for different reasons. I suspect that she would be the first to condemn me were she to find out my true nature. She has a heart-shaped face, her facial physiognomy so in keeping with her character (a true wedding of form and content) it nauseates me.

Even as I write this, I know your letter in reply shall quiz me mercilessly in respect to my maunderings about her. And on first meeting! And so I have looked into myself in preparation and have asked myself the same question: why is it that I spontaneously detest a woman I hardly know?

But I am, as you know (have I not confessed it to you countless times), an envious—even spiteful—type, and Oh my dear Johan! what a relief it was to tell you that and not have you turn away from me. So I confess there is something about her that ignites my envy, genuinely chafes my soul. Far more than Mathilda, who is—what? loud? senseless? boring?

And I think I know what you will tell me . . . you have told it to me before. You will tell me I envy her because she is capable of love. Yes, and that I (by my own admission) am no longer. Well, you are right, not even you, Johan, evoke that emotion in me. So be warned.

Auf Wiedersehen, mein guter Kamerad,
Clara

(No Date)

Dear Johan,
It is difficult when you are poor, when you are lonely, when you have no power whatsoever over your life, to be pleasant, or honest, or forthright . . . and even though I have trusted you more than I have trusted others, even Franz, I have not been altogether candid with you. There are certain things in my past that I have withheld from you. Unfortunately I no longer can. I must tell you now. Not out of a desire to confess, believe me, but out of necessity. Someone out of my past has "caught up" with me, a man called Nicholas Renton.

I shall not make excuses for myself. I detest people who

do. I shall write down the facts. If you decide to break with me after reading this letter, I shall understand.

Before I came to Germany to work for your sister's family I was employed as a governess to Lord and Lady Headly's three young daughters on an estate in West Riding. When Lord and Lady Headly left to sojourn in Italy, I remained behind with their daughters. At that time, I was contacted by a man and asked if I would be willing to assist his "company" (his word) in their plans for stealing Lady Headly's considerable fortune in jewels. I would be paid handsomely, he said, for my cooperation.

He was a neat, polite, soft-spoken, older man, a Mr. Kevin Francini. He impressed with his good manners, his . . . compassion (I can call it nothing less) for my circumstances. He seemed to know everything about me.

To make a long story short: I "assisted" them. I assisted them by doing precisely nothing; that is, I raised no hue or cry when they entered the household, or when they very calmly and deliberately went about their business of stealing my mistress's jewels. À propos, I am certain that they were assisted by others on the staff as well, and on as agreeable terms as mine. The jewels were stolen, paste put in their place. They seemed to have complete knowledge as to where they were as well as exactly what they were. Even then I admired the thieves' operation. And had the jewels not been sent to be cleaned—the Headlys were invited to Windsor to celebrate the Queen's [14] birthday—I doubt if the theft would have been as yet discovered. By that time of course I was in Germany.

What does this have to do with present circumstances?

Yesterday I received a note from the same Kevin Francini asking me to meet him and a Mr. Nicholas Renton at his house on Wicklow Street. Mr. Renton, he wrote, "wishes to use your services again."

I shall keep you informed. That is, if you still wish to correspond with me. Now I shall speak of more pleasant things: Elijah. Elijah and myself.

I think I have written to you about my sexual desire for him. Well, it grows stronger every day. Powerful, mysterious, uncanny, this sexual instinct, this desire to mate, to become one with someone—for how long? Five minutes? Not much

14. Queen Adelaide, wife of King William IV.—*R. Lowe*

longer, but for that five minutes of pleasure what will we not do? What will *I* not do? And he too is interested. I know it, and knowing all the while that my knowing it, and feeling it, and transmitting it, encourages his sexual interest in me.

Strange, isn't it, how Greek art paid homage (again and again) to the male body while we (since the Renaissance) focus on the woman? When I am with him I understand only too well the Greek passion for the male form. He is an English Apollo Belvedere. And here I am. Ugly. Yes, please do not protest, or tell me what I can see with my own two eyes is not true. Do not belittle my own observation of myself. How can I attract him? He is not like your brother, Franz, the soul of honor. Elijah is interested more in the flesh than in the spirit. My avowed purpose in coming to this household as the poor relative was to reenact Cousin Bette. To prey on their weaknesses, to spoil their triumphs in every way I could. And now I think only of how I can attract him to me. I perceive my mounting sexual desire for him as a sickness. Enough . . .

Emma has confessed to me about her first love, the Contessa's son, her cousin Darius. They saw one another naked, Emma told me, but from what I understand there was no actual sexual act, only arousal. She also told me that Darius was expelled from Warrenton, the public school the Forsters attend, because he had "befriended" an Indian boy named Dee Jee, the son of a Rajah. I need not spell it out to you, I know, but the Contessa's son is apparently a catamite.

I sense there are other secrets as well. They will come— all her confessions—one by one. In time Emma will turn her life and will over to me. She longs to; she wants to. She is a lonely child, because as I mentioned, except for Deirdre, all her cousins and her brothers are away at school. Unloved, except by her father . . .

I am here. My intelligence sensitive to hers. With the greatest caution I turn the tumblers of her emotions and when I hear the click I know that I have passed one more barrier, and continue to the next. Soon all will be tumbled, soon I will be in possession of her heart, and so shall you—as we planned some time ago.

I must remember what I told you a few letters ago: *mit Geduld kommet alles* (with patience comes everything).

Alles Beste, mein einziger freund,
Clara

P.S. Did I mention that though Darius writes Emma regularly she never receives the letters? Mrs. Farnley has orders to bring any letter that Darius writes to Emma to Elijah personally. (Daisy, the perennial gossip, told me.) Emma complains to me how heartbroken she is that though she writes Darius, he has as yet "never once written me!" I am tempted to tell her, but of course I won't. The time is not ripe for you to start writing her, but soon it will be.

NOTE

There is a great deal of internal evidence in the Forster archives of Clara's hatred of the London branch of the Forsters, but there is only a single reference (albeit suspect) as to why.

What we do know comes from one of Emma's journals, written in the 1860s, and the information, scant as it is, is sandwiched between what were apparently far more pressing matters at the time. According to Johan, Emma writes, Clara's dislike of the London Forsters stemmed from their insolent treatment of her mother (Caterina Fonatto), who went to them for monetary help after the death of her husband, Clara's father, Leonardo Joseph Forster, and was denied it. When they refused her summarily, Caterina returned to Ashville in a daze that never dissolved. "All her fantasies were shattered. Unable to live in the real world, she died shortly afterwards. Clara and her sister (Catherine) were taken to the local orphanage."

Well and good, except for the fact that Leonardo, Clara's father, died one year after his wife. It is this kind of misinformation that makes the text so ambiguous. Is it forgetfulness? If it is, on whose part? Joseph's? Emma's? Clara's? Or is it a deliberate effort to miscommunicate. If so, why? We do not know the answer and we may never solve this puzzle but we do know that by the time Emma wrote this, she was no longer interested in Clara. She was obsessed with Johan.

—R. Lowe and H. Van Buren

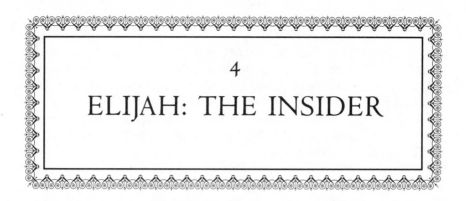

4
ELIJAH: THE INSIDER

Despite his scandalous behavior he was well liked and respected in the city for his financial acumen.

—Edward A. Forster: *Bankers Magazine*, Vol. 32, "Commerce and History"

Committed to excess, a bestial man, he was doglike in his pursuit of the scent of sex, and the scent of money.

—William M. Forster's Australian Papers

My father was a curious amalgam of cold prudential calculation and romantic sentiment.

—Emma Forster, *The Hours Between*

FROM the beginning Elijah Forster had health, good looks, and ability. A man of superabundant energy, he thrived on hard work and all its details. A self-confident, even a courageous man, he had been taught to shun emotion, to be calculating, arrogant, and snobbish. Unusually attractive to both men and women, he had a strong appetite for food, drink, gambling, and sex. He knew where to go to satisfy each of these pleasures and he did so frequently.

Confining himself mostly to women, he surprised himself occasionally by being possessed with an urgent desire for a man.

One afternoon in early May while taking the shortcut through the Burlington Arcade to Picadilly (he was on his way to the club), he spotted a young man just after he had passed the two beadles in charge of the preservation of morality in the arcade. What he considered his "type" was a youth with faunlike slanting eyes, ivory skin, and dark chestnut hair hanging in long waving curls.

The faun lingered provocatively in front of a shop filled with paintings of harlots and portraits of mortal angels in low-cut dresses, beside views of Venice and Constantinople.

Elijah joined him there, brushing up against him. The boy, slim, dark, saucy, malevolent-looking, greedy—all sexually stimulating qualities to Elijah—moved away, but not before a quick glance at Elijah's fine frock coat, the diamond in his cravat.

With a delicate shake of his rotund hips, the boy disappeared into the dark doorway next to the shop.

Elijah, his heart pounding, followed him up the steps to the apartment above the shop, where for the pleasure of playing the active role, Elijah paid the boy the sum of one guinea.

After it was over Elijah washed his genitalia and hands in hot water and the boy handed him a towel. Elijah buttoned his dark olive frock coat—he had not undressed, just dropped his trousers—adjusted his black silk bow, put on his hat, and left.

Elijah preferred his sexual outlets to be working-class like the young boy he had just had. Like his mistress, Moly, Mrs. Farnley's niece. At least Mrs. Farnley said she was her niece. Did he believe her? Perhaps, though he knew Mrs. Farnley was both a liar and a cheat. . . .

—◆◇◆—

Servants' quarters were never visited by the Forsters. Theodisia never entered the kitchen or Mrs. Farnley's suite of rooms over the kitchen, a snug little harbor that Mrs. Farnley had furnished with odds and ends from Saddler's Grove, the Forsters' country estate, where she had worked until she came to Marlborough Gardens years earlier.

Elijah had never ventured beyond the baize doors either, and never would have except that one night Emma was taken ill, and in desperation (Grindal was nowhere to be found) he had come looking for Mrs. Farnley just as she and her niece Mary (Moly's real name) were having a bite to eat.

One glance and he wanted the girl, though he left the room quickly enough after he explained his reason for seeking out Mrs. Farnley.

And thank God he had, for Emma had high fever and was about to convulse. Had it not been for Mrs. Farnley and Tansy, Grindal's assistant, Emma might have died. But they plunged her in cold water and then, rubbing her dry with huge towels, they had wrapped her in cold dry sheets until her fever had broken and she was out of danger.

The next day Mary told Mrs. Farnley that a gentleman (she didn't realize it was Elijah) had stopped her outside the house as she was returning from an errand and had pressed into her hand a bouquet of flowers with a note inside it. Would her aunt read it to her? Mrs. Farnley did: "Tell Mrs. Farnley I want to meet you."

There'd be no stopping him, Mrs. Farnley knew. If she tried to she might even be dismissed. And she didn't want that. Elijah was a good master, according to Mrs. Farnley. That meant he was manageable; he left her alone; he gave her complete authority in household matters. Mrs. Farnley could do as she pleased—and she did.

She was virtually in control of every operation in the household. Nothing was done without her consent. It was Mrs. Farnley who gave orders to the greengrocer and the butcher, collecting part of their percentage. It was Mrs. Farnley who sold the household drippings to dealers who retailed it to those unable to buy butter for their bread. It was Mrs. Farnley who was in charge of engaging and dismissing servants. And her ledgers, which in ordinary households were examined by the mistress of the house, in this case were inspected by the master, who had never once questioned her figures. No, it was a job that suited her very well.

She recalled how Elijah had hounded another girl. A parlormaid she had hired some years earlier. Not that the girl had been that pretty, but she had been big-breasted . . . yes . . . unusually so. Unwisely the girl held Elijah at arm's length and he had cornered the poor fool one day in Theodisia's sitting room when Theodisia was out. The maid had screamed but no one had dared come to her rescue and he had raped her. Nor had that been the end of it. Oh no. For her "disobedience" (Elijah's word) she had been thrown out on the street. Yes, Elijah thwarted was a dangerous animal. But after all, weren't most men? She herself had never known a man who wasn't. Elijah was not the exception, he was the rule.

From that time on, it had been her policy to occasionally hire a servant she thought Elijah might want sexually and whom she felt would be compliant. In most cases she had been right. They had been bedded and then got rid of discreetly. But her niece . . . well now, that was family, wasn't it?

Three years ago Mrs. Farnley's brother Caleb's wife had come to her and begged her to take their daughter, Mary, into service.

"T'will be the best deed you ever done, Mrs. Farnley, if you take Mary, for I swear I canno' longer protec' her. They be threatenen' me, tellin' me they be killin' me if I stand in their way." She was referring to Mrs. Farnley's brother, Caleb, and his son, Noah, Mary's brother. "T'is their right to 'ave her, they be sayin'. They be mad. She be drivin' them mad."

Mrs. Farnley looked at the young girl sitting so quietly beside her mother, the girl who had driven her father and her brother mad. No more than fourteen, if that. Not really beautiful . . . yet there was a sexuality about her, wasn't there? A promise of something—what? Pleasure . . . supreme pleasure . . . and it shone through the plain ugly dress she had on. A combination of features and expression, an impression of rosy health that would attract old men, young men . . . all men.

Why, wondered Mrs. Farnley, as she looked at the girl, why had God created that? A walking, living temptation. Not that the girl knew it, poor thing. Her own father lusting after her! Yes, best have her here. But keep her hidden from Elijah.

Without telling anyone that the new girl was a relative—the less they knew the better—she had put the girl to work in the kitchen as a scullion. But when Mrs. Lovesley had become too nosy, she had given the girl the job of taking care of the slops, a disagreeable job, but absolutely safe. Only the back stairs were used. Elijah would never see her. And he wouldn't have, except for Emma being sick.

Well, now that the cat was out of the bag they might as well make the best of it, Mrs. Farnley decided. She did not like what she was going to propose to her niece, but between two evil alternatives you still had to choose the best, didn't you? The one that brought in a little profit at least.

So she told Mary the following morning who her suitor really was and exactly what he wanted from her, explaining at the same time that the longer Elijah waited for what she would have to give him anyway, the more irate he would become (gentlemen being what they are), but if Mary would leave the matter in her hands she thought she would be able to come to a "suitable arrangement."

Working together they had managed to maneuver Elijah into making Moly his mistress, setting her up in a small house in St. John's Wood, and providing her with a good allowance for clothes and a maid (one that Mrs. Farnley hired) and even a pension plan of sorts.

For Mrs. Farnley was only too aware of Jessie Malkin's brothel on the corner of Wickfield and Collards Lane—hadn't a few of her maids wound up working for Jessie? Well, no relative of hers would wind up working in a whorehouse if she could help it. Moly had been only too willing to cooperate. So they had done well together. And Theodisia none the wiser.

The streets were thronged. It was an unusually warm day for May. Elijah observed the torrent of vehicles . . . gigs, wagons, hackney coaches—great lumbering squares pulled by horses with droopy heads and scanty manes and tails—the sort that weren't allowed to stand in Marlborough Gardens.

Thwarted ambitions gnawed at him. The Marlebone Cricket Club . . .

He remembered the day his father, Jorem, had taken him there, after he had entered Oxford, writing his name down on the candidate list. "Elijah Forster, Esquire, of Marlborough Gardens, London, and Saddler's Grove, and St. John's College, Oxford; proposed by Jorem Forster, Esquire, and Baron Ravenscroft." It had been one of the few happy moments he had shared with his father.

Why had his father been denied a title, he wondered. Jorem had wanted a peerage but he had not been granted one. Why? Peerages had been granted for successful exploitation of mines; even brewers had been knighted! It rankled.

Elijah owned factories, mills, warehouses, joint stock companies, was the head of the Forster Midland Bank, and was rich, very rich. But not an aristocrat. Engaged as he was in the "despised" trade of making money instead of receiving it like a gentleman in the form of tithes and rents, he was lumped together with clerks, menial shopkeepers, and tradesfolk. *That* was not just.

Justice! Even in his youth he had sided with Thrasymachus. He recalled Dr. Pond's exegis of the Republic, his dislike of Thrasymachus. "A man of meretricious value," he had told the class. But Dr. Pond was wrong. What was justice but the interest of the stronger? What else could it be? He looked about him. Here on the streets of London . . . wasn't it true here on the streets of London? Might makes right. Absolutely. That is why he, Elijah, was not the cross sweeper, or a chimney sweep, or a . . . woman.

A man in order to succeed must "stand in" and "stand well" with the stronger party, help his friends, injure his enemies, and even commit injustice, if needs be, but not suffer it. He had a horror of passivity. He thought of his brother Joseph: passive, weak, a slave to Consuelo. Look what had happened to him. He drank more and more now. Once he had even shown up at the bank drunk. Well, Joseph had been "just." "Just" to Consuelo, "just" to the boy Darius. And what had happened to him . . . the honor men bestow on tyrants reveals their real convictions. "The shepherd fattens sheep not for their good but to eat them." Thrasymachus was right.

He had come to the tip of the Strand, which led to Temple's Lincoln Inn.

He thought of his sons William and Edward. He didn't like William. A mother's darling—and Edward, his heir? A cold unimaginative type, suitable, though, for what he was destined. The law? Yes, now that was a possibility . . . the legal profession had long been a route to wealth and nobility. All sorts of work in that profession: the management of vast estate conveyancy work, private bills in Parliament, turnpike trusts, besides wills, leases, marriage settlements . . .

And William. The army. Theodisia wouldn't like that. Perhaps the baron (Ravenscroft) could procure him a commission, even a governorship of a garrison town. India. . . .

Waukenphast's Boots. Elijah always smiled when he came to that shop. A sign in the window read: "The celebrated tour Boots at 28 s. are the perfection of walking boots combining durability and lightness." He had never gone in.

Money. He wanted money. As much money as could get. Money, the elixir of life. Strooksbury had mentioned a new acquaintance of his, a retired tea merchant . . . what was his name? Coverly? Yes, Isaac Coverly. "A very wealthy man," Strooksbury had told him. Retired. Looking to invest. He would introduce them. Elijah would ask Strooksbury to bring him to dinner one evening next week.

When he had visited Miles Ryder at Albion some months ago, Ryder had told Elijah something about Jorem's affairs that had whetted his appetite. Fancy finding out after so many years that his father had been Miles's partner in the opium trade. The old man had been secretive about that, hadn't he? The books had shown tea investments. Miles Ryder, called the Prince of Macao, had wealth the equivalent of kings. Albion, his estate in Essex, was beyond belief.

Elijah passed Ambrecht Nelson and Co., homeopathic specialists and analytical chemists. Ever since he was a child and had accompanied his father to his club on St. James Street, he had been fascinated with the medicine chest displayed in the window. He read the small handwritten labels pasted on the vials. "Arnica Montana: fetid breath, the spitting of blood"; "Chamilla: convulsions and dentition"; "Podophullum: inaction of the liver" . . . twenty-four vials of pilules or tinctures, and his favorite: "Ignatia: hysterics, grief, or disappointment," a pale lavender liquid.

Elijah needed money. He loved money. He wanted money. More than he had, though he had a great deal. His passion for gambling, which he kept under control, still cost him a pretty penny, as did his passion for women. And as he grew older these appetites instead of decreasing seemed to be getting more insistent. Coverly. "Naive . . . eager to invest," Strooksbury had described him. But why was Strooksbury passing the man on to him? Why not keep Coverly to himself?

In front of the club he noticed a portly looking coachman sitting on a very high coach box, wearing white gloves, a nosegay in his buttonhole, holding the reins of four horses perfectly matched. That meant Sir Ravencroft's son, Lord Cecil, was inside.

The stone letters carved above the lintel read: *"Carpe diem quam minimum credula postero"* (Seize the day, putting as little trust as may be in the morrow). With a glance at the familiar motto, Elijah quickly ran up the wide shallow steps and entered the club.

—◆◇◆—

Elijah, wearing his damask dressing gown with the lace cuffs and Levantine Moroccan leather slippers, sat in a chair drawn up to a partially open window in Moly's bedroom.

Almost entirely relaxed, almost entirely satisfied. He had just had sex with Moly, who now was being bathed by her maidservant. Yes, Moly soothed. His body felt temporarily at peace. Yes, Moly calmed. He had poked and probed her where and when he wanted to, for as long as he wanted to, the way he wanted to. It had been quite good. God, he disliked women who were coquettish! Who thought they had to seduce. How ridiculous they looked when they cold-bloodedly decided to entice. Cobras, wolves, that's what they looked like . . . if they only knew. No, he did not fancy being a woman's dupe. If the world was divided between victims and predators, and sometimes he thought it was as simple as that, he chose to be a predator.

Two facets of his character had remained unaltered as long as he could remember: his love of sex and his love of money . . . oh yes, there was a third: his love of clothes. Not that he was a dandy. As a matter of fact, he disliked fops. Had contempt for them. But he felt neither shame nor guilt dressing up, rather a sense of release and excitement. The feel of silk and satin, velvet, good linen, and fine leather on his hands and feet gave him enormous pleasure.

He looked down at the lace cuffs of his sleeves—exquisite—three tiers, which had to be removed and sewn back on again every time the robe was cleaned. He moved his wrists, felt the lace graze the backs of his hands. He expanded his naked chest inside his robe, felt the black satin lining of the robe brush against him . . . a "shimmering stroke."

He had designed the room. Chosen the bed, the chairs, the carpeting, the drapes, the bed linen. The bed fit his body, the width and length of it. Everything in the room was the way he wanted it. Including Moly. In particular Moly's behavior.

Moly came into the room with her brown curly hair still damp wearing a dressing gown of peach-colored satin with an ivory design of fans sprinkled throughout.

She was smiling, happy, content. Dora Finley (Moly's maid) had cleaned her private parts gently, and her rectum, for Elijah had taken her twice from behind. Sometimes he used an unguent, but today he hadn't. So it had hurt a little.

He liked mounting her from behind and clasping her breasts tight as he came. Sometimes he lashed her with a riding crop, but very gently. She remained dressed for that. He would order her to kneel and put her head on a chair, and then he would lift her skirts over her head and flick her buttocks with the crop "until they were rosy" and then mount her right there.

Moly knew him well. When he asked her to come over to him now she knew what he wanted before he said anything. But she waited passively. She also knew he did not like her to initiate anything. She thought of her aunt, Mrs. Farnley. Tomorrow was Wednesday, her day off. She would come over as usual and together they would go to the dressmakers', the same dressmaker Theodisia used. Did Elijah know, she wondered? She heard him cough slightly and looked up. Well, he was ready now, wasn't he?

He took her hand and placed it under his robe. She held his organ not tightly but as he had taught her to, and rubbed the tip of it exactly as he had taught her to. It grew larger as she held it.

He seemed insatiable at times. This afternoon was one of those times. "Kneel." She did, and he placed it in her mouth. "Suck." She did, and he thrust it into her mouth deeper . . . deeper . . .

Then suddenly he stood up. Was it over then? No. Wordlessly he motioned her to the bed. And when she went there he told her to lay face down and again took her from behind. "Ahhhhhhhh!" she said as he had taught her to. "I like that. Oh, I like that! Oh, again. . . . Don't stop ever. . . ."

Elijah got off her immediately after coming and went into the bathroom. He stared at himself in the looking glass. God, he was handsome! Grimacing, he checked his teeth. Perfect. He smiled to himself. He was pleased, too, with the fact that he had the newfangled bathtub in and the newfangled commode installed. He opened the door of the small room where the commode stood alone and urinated, watching with satisfaction the stream of urine flow into the water. He flushed. Everything was better than at home. Newer, more convenient. Up-to-date. He went back into the bedroom; Moly, lying under the covers, smiled at him.

As usual she reminded him of someone he once knew. Sometimes he almost remembered but not quite. Not always, of course . . . only when her head was at a certain angle, when her eyes and the curve of her cheek were just so . . . she reminded him of someone.

As he came towards her she lifted her face up and then of course he knew. Millie . . . his father's housekeeper's assistant. Sweet, silly, foolish Millie. Such a long time ago (Elijah was generally very careful to not remember his childhood). She had fed him, he remembered, and when he didn't want to eat she had told him stories, coaxed him into opening his mouth, danced for him to make him laugh. Oh, he had loved her. . . .

And then one day she was gone . . . without explanation. That had *not* been *just.* . . .

He never saw her again. Never. Millie. Brown curly hair, the curve of her cheeks, the color of her skin. Moly looked like her, didn't she? Moly, the nectar of the gods, the draught of Nepenthe, forgetfulness, the losing of all earthly cares. Moly . . . well, well, well. Suddenly he thought of Jorem, his dead father. An irrational hatred swept over him. If his father were alive now standing next to him he would strangle him.

He smiled at his young mistress. "We're going out tonight. Have Dora dress you, my dear." His voice was tender. His sarcasm, his biting remarks, his savage verbal cruelty were all reserved for Theodisia and thoughts of his dead father. He hated both of them.

"What shall I wear?"

"Something that becomes a lady, my dear. Tonight we are going to visit Malkin's brothel. We have been invited to meet Jessie's new partner, a gentleman by the name of Nicholas Renton."

"They need cleaning, but they're the best quality. Remarkable luster and the size, without measuring, I'd say at least seven to eight millimeters," said the man in a prim, educated voice to Kevin. The speaker was seated next to Kevin Francini in one of the rooms in the vast basement of Jessie's brothel. The long rope of pearls glowed pink against the palm of Kevin's hand. He ran the rope through his fingers. "Beautiful, quite beautiful. Lady Yarmouth's pearls, you say . . . anything else?" Kevin asked, as he laid the pearls aside.

The man seated next to him pulled out a brooch. He watched Kevin's face and saw with satisfaction Kevin draw in his breath.

Kevin said: "T'was worth all the work, wasn't it?" Taking the brooch, which was shaped like a flower with blue sapphire petals perched on a gold stem, with green emerald leaves, and with a brilliant diamond at the center of the flower, Kevin studied it. "Without weighing it I'd say sixteen or seventeen carats . . . that is for the center diamond."

The man smiled: "I've weighed it, Sir. It's exactly sixteen point fifty-nine carats."

Thomas, Jessie's oldest son, came into the room. All five of her sons worked in the brothel in various capacities.

"Nicholas says you're to come right away. Now! Elijah Forster's just come in with his slut, Moly."

Kevin rose instantly and followed the boy out of the room and up the stairs to the second-floor landing where Nicholas Renton and Samuel Stokes were waiting. Samuel Stokes, one of Nicholas's three lieutenants, a failed priest and an alcoholic, was to play the part of Nicholas Renton for the crowd downstairs. A tall, handsome man with a white mustache, dressed in evening clothes and the picture of respectability, Stokes exuded an aura of goodwill. The three men looked down at Elijah and Moly as they stood in the hall below.

—◆◇◇◆—

Fitzroy, Jessie's youngest son, the image of his dead father, Lord Henry Fitzcrawford, took Elijah's frock coat, cane, and hat. James, his older brother, a weedy-looking lad, escorted Elijah and Moly into the lounge, a large room filled with chaises and couches and divans. In the back of the room, a long table had been spread with all sorts of cold meat, champagne, and bottles of wine.

There were a number of people present already: some stockbrokers, a sprinkling of Lords, two M.P.s . . . and women with white shoulders and swelling breasts, most of them young but all well dressed with impudent faces.

Jessica, spotting Elijah coming into the drawing room with Moly, detached herself from the group of men she was with. Pressing down the bodice of her gown so that her breasts stuck out, she called to him, "Elijah! You've arrived just in time. Come here to us." She turned to the elderly man beside her whom Elijah knew and didn't like, full of boring anecdotes about the good old days of George III and the Regent. "There, do tell him what you have told me."

The man smiled, revealing missing teeth and began again: "It happened last spring to me. I was riding in Rotten Row and this pretty woman on a bay passes me. She smiles, I follow—"

Someone new came into the room. All heads turned to see if it was Nicholas Renton. But it was only Langly, a bootmaker, who would later on in the evening put on women's clothes and pirouette about with makeup and a wig. A regular, he came once a month.

Everyone was waiting for the new owner to arrive. They had all been invited to meet him. Nicholas Renton . . . a master crook, the head of London's underworld. Elijah remembered what Redfield said about him: ". . . a totally evil man that everyone wants to know. He has the Midas touch, they say. And for that they are prepared to put up with the Devil himself."

Restless as always, Elijah moved away, noticing a new girl, a young beauty, dressed in pink tulle. Cat-faced, with a small circle of admirers around her.

Jessica, who had followed him, noticed his interest. "Swiss from Lausanne. She arrived last night. Madelaine. But best of all she has a twin sister who arrives tomorrow."

Ignoring Jessica, Elijah moved on. He wondered who in the room would have her first. Lord Rosedale? Redfield? Strooksbury, whom he noticed talking to Cora, an older woman, heavily roughed, wearing too much jewelry?

How soon women lose their beauty. He remembered when he first met Cora . . . as they grew older they began to look like men, unattractive men . . . their features coarsening, their hair falling out, their teeth loosening . . . disgusting . . . their jowls thickening . . . revolting. Well, he was in a jolly mood, wasn't he? What was wrong with him? But it was true. Men aged slower and better, ripened like wine . . . he was sure.

Elijah bowed perfunctorily to Strooksbury—tomorrow he would speak to him about Coverly. Elijah made his way to the table in the back. As the waiter filled his glass, Elijah looked around. Moly was seated on a couch listening to a redheaded girl who had put on too much weight. He remembered her as talking too much. He hated women who talked too much. Paula. Yes, that was her name.

Still there was something decidedly agreeable about the room. An ideal male's world, in a sense. The idea that he could have any woman here, whenever and for however long he wanted her, made him feel safe. These women were not his enemies. They did as they were paid to do. That and nothing more. There were no surprises, no unexpected outbursts. He thought of Theodisia. . . .

Yes, of course that was it! There were no rivals here. No, here everything was shared. All the women . . .

A man joined them. Coutledge. Elijah knew him from Warrenton. He cried all the time—a momma's boy, he remembered. A judge now, wasn't he? A magistrate. Known for his harsh sentences, his indifference to the poor.

"I'll have a little of everything," the momma's boy told the waiter behind the table who proceeded to fill a plate with all the smoked meats and fish and delicacies on the table. "And hock; I don't like champagne. French piss," he said to Elijah. He took the plate, the napkin and fork, and began to eat. "I understand there'll be a show after he arrives, Mr. Nicholas Renton . . ."

"I suppose so," Elijah said. "There's a rumor he was born in Newgate. I wonder if it's true."

"Yes. Made something of himself, didn't he? Can't say that for most criminals. Most are caught and hung. That is, if I have anything to say about it—"

"Gentlemen! Ladies!" Jessica was clapping her hands, standing in the middle of the room next to an unusually tall man. The man wore a double-breasted tail coat with gilt buttons. His gloves were of white kid. Taking his arm, she said, "Our new Master of Revels! Mr. Nicholas Renton himself!"

There was applause. The man bowed. He smiled quietly, said a few words into Jessie's ear, and she left the room.

The crowd waited. They expected him to speak. The room was silent. The men had all heard of Renton. That he was brilliant, unusual, strange. They were willing to commit to him, but Renton just stood there with a bemused look on his face.

Suddenly young Fitzroy, flashing an impudent smile, went up to the beauty in pink tulle and lifted one of her breasts out of her bodice and lay his head on it. Someone laughed, and the crowd broke up into small groups again.

Well, thought Elijah, Nicholas Renton was not what anyone expected. Certainly not what he had expected. A respectable elderly-looking gentleman. Elijah had expected to meet a man who, though crude and uncouth, exuded power. An irresistible force. Out of the corner of his eye he saw a troupe of naked women enter the room. The show was about to begin.

Suddenly Elijah was bored. Suddenly he detested everyone in the room. Everyone and everything around him seemed ridiculous. Those absurd naked women! Why had he come? There was not a single person he cared about in this room. Not even Moly. But what should he do? Should he go to Crockford's? He hadn't been there for a while. But the last time he had played there he had lost . . . disastrously. But what then? He must leave. He would not stay. Why was everything so bleak suddenly? What was wrong with him? And then he had an absurd thought. If only he could fall in love. . . .

Emma. He would go home and see Emma. She was the only person who mattered to him. He loved her . . . against reason. What other way was there to love? He would go home. If he stayed here he would do something ridiculous . . . he would smash something . . . or strike someone.

Emma would be asleep, of course. He wouldn't wake her. He would watch her as she slept, her guardian angel. As for Moly . . . she was still listening to the redhead. Well, he needn't say good-bye. He'd tell Norris to pick her up later and drive her home. God, he could not stay here another moment! Not another moment!

5

EMMA: FURTHER ELABORATIONS

That the relationship between Clara and myself ended badly, that it caused me more pain than any other, is true, but let me say here and now that it also had caused me the greatest joy, the greatest happiness.

—Emma Forster, *The Metaphysics of Sex*

10 APRIL 1853, HOTEL DE BRIENNE, CHAMPS-ELYSEES, PARIS

I have decided to stay longer in Paris than I intended to. I give myself all sorts of reasons: the Opera Comique is giving a performance this Tuesday of *The Damnation of Faust,* the following Friday they will perform, at the L'Opera, Mendelssohn's oratorio "Elijah." How can I miss that, I ask myself? But I know none of that is true. I am staying here because somewhere in my being there is a small voice that whispers to me: You will find her in the streets of Paris. You will turn a corner and there she will be, or pass a bookstall and she will be standing there, her nose in a book, browsing. Yes, you will find her in a small side street seated in a cheap café having her dinner. She will look up, she will see you, and then you will be in each other's arms crying and laughing.

Of course I am talking about Clara. Who else would I stay in Paris for? Didn't she tell me once that if she ever disappeared I would find her in Paris, on the Left Bank browsing, or having a glass of wine in a café. It was her dream city.

I walked most of the day in those sections of Paris that I think she would be in, if she were here at all. I leave the hotel early and come home late, exhausted but still eager to search for her. If she is here I will find her. I would know if she were dead. . . .

—◆◦◇◦◆—

Within a week of Clara's arrival that spring of 1838, we began to work.

"As much as I know," she said, "I shall impart." And indeed it was a great deal.

Her first subject was the Greek language. I had not told her (as a matter of fact, I never did) that Darius had begun teaching me and my cousins Greek, that I was not a "tabula rasa" as she thought. I lied out of a desire to be hers completely from the very beginning. I wished to be nothing, to be only whatever she wanted me to be. "Of myself I am nothing, it is he that doeth the work"—I remember actually saying that to myself when I was with her.

As was her custom she first gave a brief introductory lecture.

"Because the Greek language is inflected—do not fidget, Emma, patience is the cornerstone of learning—Greek syntax, that is, the arrangement of words in sentences, s-y-n-t-a-x, is more varied than ours. For example, Emma, in the English sentence 'It ravages one's nerves to be amiable every day to the same human being' [as you can see, she had a dry wit[15]] the syntax—arrangement of words—is set in the familiar, to our ears that is, nominative predicate sequence. The Greeks, however, could say and did say: 'Ravages one's nerves it to the same human being to be every day amiable,' or 'Day every ravages one's to be nerves amiable it to the human same being,' or 'Ravages day every amiable it to be one's nerves to human being the same.' Emma! Pray do not daydream when I am lecturing to you—"

She was wrong of course. I never daydreamed when she spoke to me. Though I understood that her interest in me might not be out of personal liking, but was due to the fact that my father had hired her to instruct me, it did not deter me from giving her what she wanted from the very beginning: hard work, complete attention, complete obedience. As with Darius, I was only too eager to give her exactly what she wanted.

If I concealed from her certain things that she had a right to know

15. Indeed she did. But this particular time Clara was quoting Benjamin Disraeli. —R. Lowe

as my teacher, why should I complain that she concealed so much from me?

We lied to one another. I lied because I wanted to be hers, completely. She lied because she wanted to remain herself.

She ended her first lecture with the dry observation that "the study of grammar and grammatical forms can seem tedious, but this is only an attitude, albeit a prevalent one." And she gave me my first Greek aphorism to learn by heart: *Skaion to ploutein kalo meden eidenai* ("It is a boorish thing to be wealthy, and to know nothing else").

Poppa was right on both counts: I enjoyed learning, and Clara was an excellent teacher—a bit too didactic perhaps for some tastes, not for mine. Her primary value lay in her seductive powers, her ability to enthrall, to lead me despite my resistance through the dark complexity of problems where, fatigued and lost, I might have thrown up my hands in despair. But there she would be, farther up the path, her siren voice beckoning me onwards. She was as imaginative as my cousin Darius had been, and as just, though she lacked an essential quality that Darius possessed.

Though we were together every day she still remained strangely aloof. Generous in her praise of me when she thought I deserved it, she never offered the deep emotional intimacy that I longed for and once had with Darius. Despite the fact that she continued to tell me from time to time anecdotes about her past life, her way of relating them was odd. For instance, one day she described to me the exact moment her beloved Franz confessed his love for her.

"Did I tell you he was extraordinarily handsome? He was. The epitome of masculinity, combined with the sensitivity of an intelligent female. He knelt in front of me, on one knee—a mating ritual unique to our society—and told me that he loved me and wanted me to be his wife and fervently hoped that I felt the same way. And then he slipped this ring"—she pointed to the small garnet ring on her finger that had been an object of my speculations for some time—"the *verlobungsring* [engagement ring] on my finger."

What had meant *everything* to her was the fact that he had "chosen" her. I was certain of that. I felt it intuitively. Yet she told it to me as if she were merely explicating one more rule of grammar. That is, though her explanation was detailed and even vivid, she spoke about it as if it had not happened to *her* . . . as if it were not personal.

About a month after her arrival, I discovered, much to my dismay, that Clara's way of handling what she "disapproved" of was quite as chilling, if not worse, than that of my nurse, Grindal, who had beaten me whenever she found fault with my behavior.

I assumed and still do that Clara had knocked—she was not impolite, nor was she intrusive—but I was as usual so intent on listening to "them" I did not hear her. My parents were discussing her.

"Well, you've had your way," my mother was saying, "in this matter. I hope you are satisfied but I do not like her looks. She looks sly, as if she might steal the silver—"

"Oh, at least that. You are an unmitigated fool, Theodisia."

"Ugly women are not necessarily honest—"

"That has the ring of an aphorism. May I quote you?"

I have no idea how long Clara had been standing there, but when I realized that she was, I have never felt, before or since, such an urgency to magically disappear. Every muscle in my body wanted to flee, every nerve was sending me urgent signals. I urinated where I stood; I could feel it trickling down my inner thighs. I turned scarlet. I felt hot and cold, both at the same time. And still their voices went on! I think I must have gone temporarily mad because when my mother next spoke it seemed to me as if the words were coming out of my mouth. And what words! The worst possible.

"And she has a slightly disagreeable odor about her that is distinctly unpleasant."

Faint! I told myself. Faint! I screamed to myself. But I could not even do that. I could only stand there, my body bolt upright, rigid with fear.

"I knocked, Emma," Clara said. "Several times. Apparently you did not hear me . . . you were so engrossed in your work. By all means do continue. What I have to say to you can wait until morning. Good night."

Throughout this quiet explanation of her presence there was not the slightest change in her expression. She left acknowledging nothing.

I was alone. What if I tell her, my thoughts raced wildly as the door shut, that it was the very first time it had happened? That it was a fluke? A chance event? A freak accident? Would she believe me?

Should I run to her room, now, immediately, and throw myself at her feet and tell her that? Or would she think me a liar to boot? But the way she behaved! It was as if she had heard nothing. Was that possible? Of course not! Oh, the shame of it! The humiliation! And worse: Would she tell them? But at this point I stopped thinking. Instead an overwhelming desire to vomit seized me, and I grabbed my chamber pot from underneath my bed and threw up in it. Somehow I fell asleep, hours later, wondering how I could ever face her again.

The following day, dreading it, I met her as usual in the schoolroom, which was the old day nursery where I had once slept side by side with Nanny Grindal. Our beds were still there, and William's chair, but it now also contained two school desks and a large blackboard and several bookcases and two straight-backed chairs.

Clara was seated at her desk, her face composed as ever, her head bent over a book she was reading. When I came in she looked up, and I searched her face as she began to outline the topics we were to cover in the next quarter of the school year. There was no change. She looked exactly the same. Behaved exactly the same. Her voice was still low-pitched, quiet but authoritative . . . but I did not believe it.

I was quite sophisticated in that respect, having learned from my eavesdropping that though adults may behave in public as if nothing disturbed them, they could and did act swiftly in a way that made no mistake about how they really felt in private. I wondered what she would do. I found out soon enough.

After lunch she informed me that today we would commence the practice of a daily constitutional in the park for one hour. When I remonstrated—the day was miserable, the weather raw and wet—she paid me no mind and put on her coat while she waited for me to do likewise.

The wind was fierce. Spring was late that year, and even though it was already May the trees were still not in leaf. We walked through the length of the Gardens, bleak and deserted, side by side, in silence.

That night after supper, I went to my room. Her assignments were always onerous, but the ones she had given that day seemed worse than ever. The complete conjugation of three Greek verbs, ten lines of translation, and the maxim *Nipseon anomema me monan opsein* ("Wash your sins, not only your face") to memorize.

Though I always resisted the work initially, I would soon become absorbed, for though I protested I really did find the study of Greek fascinating. Hence it was not until I had completed my studies that I realized how silent it was. I was used to the chronic bickering and occasional full-scale flareups of my parents' unfortunate style of relating to one another. They had not gone out for the evening, so I knew they were there below me in their room.

I inspected the hearth. As I suspected, it had been plastered up. Who had done it? Which of the maids or the footmen? And had they been told anything? Was my humiliation and shame to include them too? I did not dare ask her. She had had it done and that was that.

As our subsequent relationship proved, that was the way Clara handled most disciplinary actions. Without discussion of any sort—very much like my father, actually—if she thought she was right, she did it, without consulting anyone.

After the inspection, a horrible thought came to me: what might she have done had she discovered me masturbating? A fleeting thought too awful to contemplate. But forewarned is forearmed. In future, I remember thinking to myself, I would have to be doubly careful. I could see Clara was a blessing, but a mixed one, decidedly.

As I grew older and reflected on my experience with Clara, one of the conclusions I came to (there were many) was that the development of my intellect had been achieved in part by a sacrifice of my bodily appetites, for after that unexpected intrusion and action on her part, I never really enjoyed masturbating as much, though I continued nevertheless.

I wanted her love. I worked very hard so that she would love me. I was obedient, cheerful, neat. I knew her approval was conditional, but I was willing to meet her conditions. All of them. No matter what they were.

I was in love with her and had no idea I was. Did she? I believe she did. But I also believe it made no difference to her as far as judging or assessing my work. Just as I believe she might have been ruthless enough to use that love as a means to make me study all the harder.

Love was not something that seemed to be important to her. It did not seem to be part of her nature. While I, on the other hand, craved it. She was passionate, yes, but about causes, not about people; about intellectual puzzles, not about human beings.

Clara became part of the household, a familiar figure. Someone whom Grindal disliked (she returned only too soon from Saddler's Grove). Someone whom Theodisia ignored, and with whom my father occasionally had a glass of port while he interrogated her as to the state of my intellectual progress.

When my brothers, Edward and William, came home from Warrenton on holidays, she would take us to various sights and events about town. Once she took us to the British Museum to see Lord Elgin's marbles (the Parthenon frieze, except for the west face and the last slab of the north frieze).

My brothers liked her, particularly Edward, with whom she discussed music. She treated them with the same respect she had shown me. She was just, considerate, reasonable. But—and that "but" made all the difference—she was cold. Sometimes unbearably so.

There were times I wanted to be held, to feel someone else's physical warmth, to be enclosed in someone's arms. And when I felt that way, that I wanted to touch her and be touched by her, she became colder still, more remote. Untouchable. When that happened, I found myself longing perversely for Nanny Grindal. For though Grindal had been unjust, a petty tyrant, a physical abuser, nevertheless it seemed to me when I lay alone in my bed at night longing to be touched that being beaten by Grindal was better than being taught by Clara.

What I wanted was love; what I got was justice.

6

FURTHER INFORMATION ABOUT THE TIMES AND LIFE OF NICHOLAS RENTON

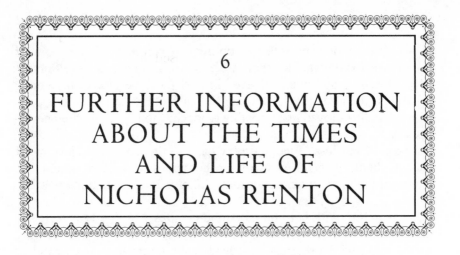

Though few knew of him, Renton was a force to be reckoned with in London. A cunning and crafty man, his exploits outdid any criminal in the past. In truth he was lord of the underworld.

—*Newgate Notorieties,* Parsons
Ackerman, Keeper of
Newgate

There has been much specious cogitation by the hoi polloi concerning a man named Nicholas Renton and his purported "empire of crime." There is no proof, no documentation, nor shall there ever be, for no such person ever existed.

—*Reports,* No. 743, The London
Society for the Suppression
of Mendacity

NICHOLAS and his three lieutenants—Samuel Stokes, Kevin Francini, and Anthony Kerr—were in the cavernous basement of Jessie's brothel, in Nicholas's office, the former kitchen of Malkin's house.

The basement had been gutted recently by Kevin and a crew of workers who had installed hot water pipes and water closets, workrooms of various kinds, and several ingenious methods of escape through varying trapdoors that led to passages beneath the basement to the alleys of Wickfield and Collard's Lane.

At the back of the house Kevin had exposed the foundation and built a wide ditch. Tearing out the original windows, he had replaced them with tall wide windows so that the grey light of London could pour into the workrooms.

Though Nicholas's office was large, it was sparsely furnished, monastic in feeling, containing only a high-topped clerk's desk, a few wooden chairs, a table, and an oak stand, all of which were huddled together in the rear. Over near the windows stood what looked like an unfinished dollhouse.

The sun had almost set and the room was darkening, but from the back of the room a continuous flickering stream of light came forth. A large crystal ball set in a shallow green glass and placed in the center of the oak stand released the bright points of light. Next to it, in a reed basket on the narrow table, lay a pair of diamond earrings and a tiara (formerly possessed by the Bonaparte family), glittering in the crepuscular gloom. At a signal given by Kevin, Stokes lit one of the lamps.

"Fitzroy is a catamite," Nicholas said. "Tell his mother that in case she doesn't know—which is unlikely. Tell her also that I don't want him poaching. There are houses that cater to his taste. Tell him to go to Windmill Street, from there to Covent Garden he can have his pick of 'she shirts' . . . as if he didn't know. He is not to solicit our customers."As always, Nicholas's voice was low. Low but resonant. A baritone, he spoke slowly and the prolongation of his vowels would sometimes tremble in the air like a dying chord. But though his range was low his voice had a brilliant timbre and great expressive power.

Kevin remembered the first time he had heard Nicholas speak. He had landed in one of Nicholas's shelters "down and out," at the end of his rope. (Nicholas had constructed shelters for the poor in every major slum in London. It was from these shelters that he drew most of his gang recruits.) Kevin was in the first stages of opium withdrawal when he first heard Nicholas's voice—when he came to, so to speak. He never forgot that moment. For though he did not recall what Nicholas had said he remembered forever how the sound of his voice had moved him—thrilled him, really—how it had reached something within him that had not lived or stirred for years.

Sometimes when Nicholas spoke at length, Kevin would envision Nicholas's voice in the shape of a wide wave moving out from the abdomen, forcing the diaphragm to push air out from the lungs and upwards to the vocal cords to produce the desired effect: sonorous, plangent . . . hypnotic. As he began to know Nicholas better, Kevin understood that nothing, certainly not his voice and its effect, had been left to chance. No, Nicholas was like a trained singer. Like Desmothenes, he had practiced.

Nicholas continued speaking, his face a quiet, expressionless mask. There was no democracy in his organization. His empire was not a community of equals. It was rather a hierarchy of ordered parts; to be part of his system was to be a subordinate. No one dared to ever interrupt Nicholas except Kevin and the hunchback Toby Cole.[16]

Anthony Kerr, whose sobriquet was Angel, and indeed he looked like one, stood next to Stokes listening attentively. He was a beauty of a man in a black suit with gold cuff links, immaculate white cuffs, and cravat à la Beau Brummel. The former rake who had aristocratic connections had been going to "rack and ruin" until he met up with Nicholas in a gambling club and was recruited to take charge of the women in the group. It proved to be a brilliant decision.

"Tell Malkin," Nicholas advised Angel, "she is to leave immediately for Hull tonight. A shipment of German whores is supposed to arrive tomorrow. Tell her also she is not to bid for the girl who might have a craving for flagellation. Old Fitzcrawford catered to that perversion. Tell her I do not. I shall not have it. Tell her that."

Fitzcrawford, Jessie's lover, had recently died of a seizure at Epsom Downs when his horse, on which he had placed an unusually large bet, came in first. Though he had fathered five children on her, he had left Jessie and them with no provision. His brother, and heir, a hunting-shooting aristocrat, was about to chuck "the trollop and her whelps" out on the street and sell the property to St. Giles Church, which had immediately put in an offer of purchase when his lawyer wrote him that a Nicholas Renton wished to purchase the said property and "was willing to pay ten thousand guineas for it! Will you consider it?"

With commendable brevity the heir replied in one word: "Assuredly!" and so the house and the land on which it stood were sold to Nicholas Renton.

The new Honorable, on receipt of the guineas, ordered a new hunting jacket with long swallow tails from a shop in Picadilly, and bought a pack of hounds from his neighbor, Lord Omerstead, and on October first was ready to ride to hounds astride his new hunter, which out of gratitude he christened Nick.

While he spoke, Nicholas kept fingering (a habit of his) the curious toadstone he always wore on his neck on a thin gold chain. He had bought it from an old Jew, the owner of a rag shop on Aldgate Street, who swore to him that he himself had cut it out of the marrow of the brain of an earth toad, and that when the moon was waning, he had placed the stone in a fine linen cloth for forty days to guarantee its power. Engraved on the face of it was the figure of Hecate.

---

16. Toby Cole was Dame Lou's "baby girl," the child she had with the turnkey Emmet Cole. A seamstress, she lived with Nicholas, who had adopted her as his "sister."

Nicholas stood silent in thought. The men waited for him to speak again. There was no banter among them as there is among equals. Finally after some minutes of silence Nicholas began speaking again, slowly, as if out of a body of analytic thought. His was a quiet manner but it conveyed absolute conviction.

Stroking the toadstone, Nicholas asked Kevin: "Now that you've ferreted out Jessie's real accounts, tell me, how much was the whore holding back?"

"Twelve percent, Commander. A hundred and nineteen pounds per week . . . more or less."

Kevin, who was forty years old, looked double that. Though he had stopped smoking opium more than ten years earlier, it had left him knife-thin and cadaverous, with sunken cheeks and heavily wrinkled skin. Every trace of the golden lad Jorem had once known had disappeared.

Nicholas glanced at Anthony, who was smiling now, revealing his short white even teeth.

"Well, well, Anthony, have one of your chats with Jessie. Explain to the old dear, in detail, as only you can, exactly what will happen to her"—here he paused momentarily, and then spat out the next word— "pudendum . . . which, though it may be decrepit and decayed, I daresay she still values. Explain to her what will happen to it were she to contemplate doing such a thing to our organization. And tell her she must pay back double what she has withheld. I am too coarse, too ungentlemanly for such a delicate task. And . . . keep her far away from me! The sooner we leave here the better."

"About the matter of leaving, Nicholas," said Kevin. "I have good news. For you, though not for poor Sir Timothy Evershem. He is very ill. His housekeeper told one of the Malkin brood that she fears the poor gentleman will soon 'pass over.' So presumably the house shall be vacant soon . . . and hence for rent . . . Jorem's house . . ."

"Jorem's house . . ." An unfathomable emotion crossed Nicholas's face and disappeared.

"Yes, Commander. Do you wish me to 'facilitate' his death? It can be easily arranged. Mrs. Skipton, the gentleman's housekeeper, is amenable to any arrangement, as long as it puts money in her pocket."

"No, Kevin. We shall leave Sir Timothy's death to chance. I am not ready yet. I need to cultivate the ground first. Now to current business— Kevin, you placed a thousand pounds into the greedy paws of Mrs. Strooksbury as a donation for her forthcoming ball to aid and assist abandoned children? Yes or No."

"Yes," replied Kevin.

"And I am to dine once more tomorrow night with Mr. and Mrs. Strooksbury, at their home. In Portland Place. Yes or No."

"Yes," replied Kevin.

"The Strooksburys! What a pair. He is a greedy lecher, she a greedy termagant. Well, tell me, gentlemen, truthfully how do I look? Elijah's tailor, shirtmaker, and bootmaker have done well by me, haven't they?"

Nicholas was wearing tight white corduroy trousers, a double-breasted waistcoat of figured silk with a long pointed waistline, and high boots with curving tops reaching just below the knee known as Hessian boots. His black curly hair was brushed forward towards the front of his wide brow on either side of his head. He was clean-shaven except for short side whiskers.

There was a general murmur of assent. And indeed he looked very attractive. He was short but very handsome and he could, when he wished to, exude an energy that was captivating. Nicholas was exactly five feet and three inches tall. He was neither a midget nor a dwarf. Still, he identified with both and collected all sorts of information, historical and medical, about them.

After discovering that Kevin had once been a pupil of Fuseli, he had commissioned him to paint a portrait of the midget Jeffry Hudson, the court jester and loyal soldier to Charles the First of England. It hung in his bedroom facing his bed, next to Kevin's copy of Velasquez's portrait of Antonio Ingles, the Spanish court dwarf.

"The hour grows late. I am expecting someone this evening. We shall have to wait until tomorrow to go over the Yarmouth robbery and the spoils. You said, Sam, that the sapphire ring is quite extraordinary . . ."

"Yes, Commander, one of the most beautiful I have ever had the privilege to see," Stokes replied.

"Show it to me tomorrow then. Perhaps I will add it to my collection."

The men knew he was referring to his private jewel collection, which contained the finest and most select pieces that came into his hands via the criminal exploits of his organization.

The sapphire together with some other pieces had been stolen by the gang a month ago in a daring daylight robbery, an event that had caused a public outcry and an insistence on doubling the police force, building more prisons, and passing stricter laws concerning felonies.

"There is a tradition," said Nicholas, "that says Moses was given the law on tablets of sapphire. This is a star sapphire you say? How many carats?"

"Roughly speaking, Sir, I would say a hundred and forty-seven carats. A beautiful rich blue color and three perfect cross lines to produce the star," Stokes said.

"After contemplating their beauty, what do you intend to do with these treasures?" Kevin asked suddenly.

Nicholas smiled—Kevin was given far more latitude than either Stokes or Kerr.

"What do I intend to do with them?" repeated Nicholas. "Why, Kevin, I shall lay them at the feet of the woman with whom I fall in love. Good night, gentlemen."

Dismissed, they left the room. Nicholas walked over to the reed basket in which the earrings and tiara lay. Smiling, he held up the jewels. He had not told anyone, not even Kevin, but he was quite sure he had already met that woman—last night seated across from him at the Strooksbury dinner table. She was the beautiful golden-haired Guinivere, Solomon Forster's wife. He slipped the jewels into his pocket.

Nicholas walked over to the dollhouse and, kneeling down in front of it, looked through its windows. He wondered if she would be there tomorrow night, the peerless, the exquisite, Guinivere—whom he thought of as an orchid on a dung heap.

———◆◦◯◦◆———

Nicholas knew all about evil, the evil originated by human beings, and the evil originated by angels.

In Newgate he had seen with his own eyes the most base, the most destructive and repellent acts. By the time he became Charles Mallet's pupil he had seen everything: he had seen men and women manipulate and mutilate each other in diverse ways, out of spite, out of passion, out of boredom . . . once he had seen a prisoner tear a baby out of its mother's arms and smash its skull against a stone wall for crying just a bit too long, a bit too loud.

He himself had been brought to the prison (so Dame Lou had told him) as a babe in his mother's arms before the turn of the nineteenth century. She had been lowered with her babe into a subterranean pit that had an open sewer running through the center of it, overcrowded with wretches who fought with rats for the meager pittance of food thrown to them through a trapdoor, who slept on bundles of lice-ridden straw, who shit and pissed in the same place where they slept and fucked.

Evil was very real to Nicholas. It was corporeal, material, palpable. It had its own smell. Mephitic . . . the smell of fear, hopelessness, despair. A foul and noisome smell, the smell of sweat, piss, shit, blood, vomit, the rancid fetid stink of bodies that were never washed, the stench of flesh rotting in the airless dark of Newgate. *That* was the reek of evil. . . .

Nothing in the prison was sweet-scented, sweet-sounding, sweet-tempered. And the thirst! He remembered the awful thirst, for in Newgate water was controlled by jailers who brought it or didn't bring it as they wished. He had seen for himself the callous indifference of the turnkeys who ruled the prison. He had seen what happens to men, women, and children living at the "mercy" of other men, their jailers.

"And these denizens of Newgate," Charles Mallet would say to Nicholas, his voice sleek with insinuation, "which is situated, by the way, on God's green earth, these denizens, they tell me, are created, like me and thee, Nicholas, in the image of God—*imago dei*. Now truthfully, Nicholas, can you believe that for even a minute?"

Mallet had then posed the age-old question to him: "If God is all-powerful, he must be able to prevent evil. Then how is it that evil exists?"

Of course Nicholas couldn't answer. For a long time he didn't even comprehend the question. First of all he had no time for the question, he was too busy surviving. But Mallet's query sank deep into his mind, and as time went on it collected a curious body of thought around it. Gradually it seemed to Nicholas to be part of a mystery that he did not, and might never, understand.

Because even before he had met Mallet and started reading Milton with him, Nicholas had intimations, hints, and suggestions unsullied by the corroding touch of consciousness of what this "good" that Mallet spoke about in such mocking tones might be. For though he had been reared in the soil of evil, he had received signs from his innermost depths that something besides the world of Newgate existed somewhere. And nothing he had seen or done in Newgate or had had done to him had expunged that feeling. That too was part of the mystery.

But when he began reading *Paradise Lost* and followed in his imagination Satan's leap over the wall into Eden to perch in the branches of the Tree of Life, to view the lush panorama of groves of trees, open fields, glittering streams running over golden sands, *all* the beautiful things with which the world abounded

> . . . *flowers of all hue,*
> *And without thorn the rose* . . .

everything suddenly connected deep within Nicholas's soul. That first radiant image burned into his brain and formed the core of his faith and his belief.

Years later, when as an old man he thought back on his strange and eventful life, it seemed to him that he had also found particles of that radiance in certain people, even in Mallet himself, though he knew the poet would have laughed at him and denied it.

There was yet another mystery. A great mystery and a great paradox. He had wanted to speak to Mallet about that too. But though he had looked for Mallet off and on in London for years he never found him. The mystery was this: despite the evil and the horror he experienced there, Nicholas Renton had been happy in Newgate. Yes, happy. He remembered "good" times.

He had been a "Newgate lad," someone special, spoiled by the inmates and one of the turnkeys, a man called Alfred Duggins who out of his own pocket had bought him toys. He had been trusted by the old lags, and cuddled up against Dame Lou at night he had been content, content and happy.

It was as if he had two minds, one that remembered only the horror and denied the good, and the other that somehow forgot the evil and remembered only the good.

He was nourished by everything. A crumb was sufficient for a loaf. And when he left Newgate, Nicholas was eager to test himself in action in what he called "the battlefield of life." When he did leave (he was twelve years old), he exchanged the evils of Newgate for the evils of London. But he had expected to. He had looked forward to it.

For years he had heard about the infamous "Holy Land," the center of the worst slum in London, from inmates who had come from there, and when he was released he made straight for it.

But if he was eager, he was also terrified. He had never been outside before. He remembered the fear that possessed him when he passed through the great spiked gate of the prison to the outside, glancing in wonder at the huge stone statues of Ceres and Flores standing in their niches outside the prison.

The first night he slept on Saffron Hill, in one of the booths of Covent Garden, among the rotting garbage of the stalls, frightened out of his wits. But the following day he followed an evil-looking beggar (he would ask no one the way) and entered the Holy Land.

Years later, he stood on the highest point in Holy Land so that he could see the whole rookery sprawled out beneath him: the maze of courts, the labyrinth of twisted streets and alleys, the network of yards and lanes, the winding ditches filled with sewage. And he remembered with pride how he had learned the paths of escape through secret apertures, concealed passages, skylights, manholes, trapdoors, tunnels, and hidden exits and entrances to cellars connected to cellars, so that one could pass under a series of houses into another part of the slum, safe from one's pursuers.

Soon he joined a gang of boys and girls exactly like himself, ready and willing to do anything to survive. Children who had stolen from the time they could walk; children who had run away from workhouses, who had been in prisons or reformatories; runaways from industrial schools; children who knew about White Street, the twice-weekly mart underneath the railway viaduct where you could sell yourself for the night or the week to some man or woman.

The leader of the gang was a boy of seventeen called Jack. On Nicholas's thirteenth birthday Jack gave him a girl, a thin silent girl three years older than himself. After raping her he settled down with her, more or less, and thirty others like himself in a four-room tenement next to a slaughterhouse and studied crime.

When he began making money Nicholas bought himself a blue velveteen coat, and heavily braided "calf clingers" that were tight at the knees, and black leather ankle boots with an elaborate stitched pattern of hearts and roses.

He went to "flash" houses where he gambled and drank "blue ruin" and then came home and beat up the tall thin older girl whose name was Alice. And he was happy. Looking back he could not deny that. He had loved the excitement of it. He had loved stealing; he had loved the chase. He had loved belonging to a gang that had accepted him. He knew only too well what "they," the ones he stole from, thought of his kind—thieves, murderers, whores. Despised by them, rated worthless, a nothing in their eyes, he "belonged" in the Holy Land, "belonged" in Jack's gang. Soon he forgot Mallet, forgot Milton, forgot his mysterious feelings.

Had he not fallen and sprained his ankle during the execution of a crime—a group of them on a cold snowy night in January had enticed a drunken fool into an alley, and after beating him senseless were stripping him when some of his companions came looking for him and began chasing them—he might have just become another Jack and never met David Kitto.

When he twisted his ankle and fell, he was left by his peers to be caught. Instead, he crawled on his hands and knees into the doorway of a secondhand shop off Oxford Street on Chauncy Lane, and crouched down as his pursuers thundered past.

It snowed most of the night and, knowing he would freeze to death if he slept, he tried to stay awake by staring though the side of the window at things in it—pieces of lace, shoe buckles, old boots, umbrellas, canes, riding whips, a child's coffin—and putting them in alphabetical order.

Early next morning—he was just about to drift off towards death— the owner of the shop opened the door and saw him huddled in the doorway.

"What be ye?" roared the tall ferocious man with red inflamed eyes, like burning coals, and wild black whiskers. He bent down to examine Nicholas. "Be ye a manikin of a boy, a true homunculus . . . or be ye a vanishin' point, I be thinkin'."

Nicholas had never been as frightened in his life as when David Kitto bent over him smelling of smoke. The boy almost fainted. He was positive it was Satan himself!

When Nicholas said nothing, David continued in a somewhat more kindly tone. "Well, ye look near to dyin' so ye be welcome to come in . . ." At that point Nicholas sneezed and began coughing. "Speak up, lad, did ye say somethin'?" When the boy continued to sneeze, Kitto's voice rose sharply. "Aye, ye're welcome to come in but be ye rowdy, or a mischief maker, *out ye go!* Back on the streets of this barbaric city, and God go with ye, lad, for you'll need Him for sure."

Saying that, he scooped up the boy in his large arms and carried him inside to the back of the store, where he placed him in front of a hearth filled with the largest blazing fire Nicholas had ever seen.

Poor Nicholas thought he was in Hell. Satan had found him out at last and had carried him to Hell! He was sure he smelled the brimstone and the ever-burning sulfur and then he heard the monster screaming for what sounded to Nicholas like "kettles." Oh, God, thought Nicholas, save me! Save me! He was to be cooked—and then eaten!

Nicholas fainted.

Moments later when he came to, he almost fainted again. He was surrounded by giants. Might they not be, Nicholas thought in panic, Beelzebub himself and his awful companions, Moloch and Belial?

"Ah! Look now, he's awake. Well, boy," said Kitto, "be ye ready to introduce yourself? Or are we never to know who ye are? Come now, little lad, I've had enough of your coyness."

Saying this he reached down and shook Nicholas's hand. "I be David Kitto, and these—" he pointed to the grimy giants—"these be the Toddlers . . . Brucie, Jamie, and Ken—"

"Ach! You're daft, mon!" Out from the shadows came the hulking figure of a woman. "What do ye know about anythin'? You've scared him half to death. Tell the lad he's safe here with us and that we'll not turn him in. Then ye'll see some sense returnin' to him, ye bloody daft fire monster!"

The two monsters stood over him now. Would they begin fighting with one another, wondered Nicholas. And the fire! He had never been so hot before. If only they would move him just a bit away from the flames that seemed to be reaching out their red-hot tongues to scald him.

"That be Kate, my wife," said David sweetly, "Mistress of the Kettle, the bane of my life. Ye'll sleep with the Toddlers tonight. An' dinna let them crowd ye, for they'll try. . . ."

It was all too much for Nicholas. The last thing he remembered before passing out again were the smiles on the Toddlers' faces.

Nicholas was to stay with the Kittos for four years, until he was eighteen. From then, he learned all about the silver trade, for David had once been a silversmith, trained in Glasgow, where he had owned his own shop until his partner, a thin harried man, ran away with most of the stock.

Kitto had come to London with Kate and the Toddlers to open up a secondhand shop and in order to survive had become a fence, putting stolen silver objects "back into legitimate circulation, my dear boy," said David, "by transforming them."

Nicholas began working for them. His first task was sweeping the store and running errands, which were always "urgent," all over London. Jamie taught him to polish silver. Brucie made him understand the beauty of silver.

"You see this old piece," Brucie said, fishing out a small platter from one of the large bins that were placed all over the shop, "the softness of the texture, Nicholas, the color. . . . That is what they call patina." Brucie said the word clearly and slowly. "Pa-tin-a. It's a beauty that only time can make, that and the cleanin' and usin' of it. Now hold it up in the light, Nicholas." Nicholas held the platter up in the pale yellow shaft of daylight that had managed to eke its way through the dirty pane of glass on the side of the store that faced the alley. "You see its soft bluish color. Only old silver, Nicholas, good old silver, has it. Beautiful, ain't it?"

Nicholas remembered the first year they celebrated Christmas. Kitto took down the great Monteith bowl that was stored on top of the shelf in his room—"A kinsman of mine, Monteith, on my mother's side, a great silversmith, the inventor of a bowl with a removable rim"—and Kate filled it with spirits, water, lemon juice, sugar, and spices. There were many toasts to get through, beginning with themselves and the Toddlers, that were done first singly, then as a couple, then as a family group, and then to Nicholas and countless people he had never heard of, and lastly to Kitto's former partner, Joseph McKenna, for after all it was the Christian thing to do, wasn't it, to forgive one's enemies, Kitto said.

And then there was much gaiety and laughter as the Toddlers moved the bins and counters and made room to dance and the Kettle taught Nicholas the old country dance called the Roger Coverly.

That first Christmas Kitto had given him a watch. He still had the silver watch, a proceed from a robbery. The owner's name had been carefully removed and replaced by Nicholas Renton's name and the year 1814. That was the Christmas Nicholas felt he had been adopted, so to speak, by the Kittos. Loved and accepted by them.

Then three years later, only a week before Christmas, the police came and arrested Kitto and the Toddlers and they were sent to Newgate in a coach, handcuffed to one another. When Kate rented an attic room near the prison, she made Nicholas the temporary caretaker of the shop and her kettle. Nicholas was alone again.

—◆◈◇◈◆—

For a time Nicholas joined the thieves he had met through the Kittos and became a successful cracksman. He was useful to his friends because not only was he bright and agile but he was also small, so he could get into places that were difficult for others to get into. And he might have become, like David Kitto, a fence except that a sudden, great, and unexpected thing happened: he inherited a thousand pounds! A veritable fortune!

Alfred Duggins, the turnkey who had befriended Nicholas in Newgate, died leaving Nicholas as his sole beneficiary in his will. It was mostly money but also gems like rings and brooches that had been given to Duggins by grateful prisoners for services rendered. The total value was just a bit over a thousand pounds. A young lawyer's clerk named Daniel Griffiths found Nicholas at the shop where Kate had said they would find him.

When he signed the proper papers and collected his money, Nicholas immediately went to Newgate and gave Kitto and the Toddlers half of his inheritance. Then he took some rooms for himself in Cheapside (Milton's birthplace), telling the elderly widow he rented from that his name was Alfred Duggins and that he was a law clerk recuperating from an illness, to insure that she would leave him alone. He wanted to be left alone. Entirely alone. He wanted to think about what to do with the rest of his life.

He was nineteen years old. He spent the next year reading, thinking, planning. He had seen in Newgate how the weak and humble had been ground down, how the meek had gone to the wall, how the strong and merciless had flourished. Power and might, that is what life was about. *That* was justice. He thought about evil and good and the "good" people he had met in his life—Dame Lou, Mallet, David Kitto, the Toddlers, and Kate. He wanted more out of life than they had gotten. Much much more . . .

He remembered what Mallet had told him about Alexander the Great:

"When Alexander pressed east to Gordian to revenge himself on the Persians he was told about the Gordian knot—how a Phrigian king more than a hundred years ago had tied his chariot reins so tightly and so intricately that no one had been able to untie them. And that an oracle had pronounced that whoever loosed the knot would become master of Asia. So there stood Alexander in front of the Gordian knot. What do you think he did, Nicholas?

"But before I tell you I will tell you this: what he did is the difference between those who *become* masters and those who *serve* masters. He lifted his sword, Nicholas, and he *cut* the knot. A sudden bold stroke where others had tried and failed by more subtle and ingenious methods; he cut the knot. A month later he defeated Darius at Issua. He was nineteen years old, Nicholas, nineteen. . . ."

Nicholas stayed in Cheapside for ten months, and when he left he had begun to work out in his mind the basic structure of his criminal empire.

—◆◇◆—

There was a knock on the door. A moment later Dame Lou's "baby girl," Toby Cole, sashayed in, an impudent look on her face.

"Well, the she-jackal is here," Toby announced.

Nicholas laughed. "Naturally. You didn't think for a moment, did you, that she wouldn't come?" He took out his watch. "And five minutes early, to boot. Well, put Miss Lustig in the room with a peephole. I want to see how she takes waiting—"

"For the sword to drop—"

"Exactly. You were polite?"

"Yes."

"But you don't like her."

"No."

"Come here first." He knelt down in front of the dollhouse. "Yesterday Daisy told me that the still room is right there, behind the kitchen . . . .

7
CLARA'S LETTERS: OBJECT FINDING

1 JUNE 1838

My dear Johan,

An incident!

I have not described my charge, Emma, in much detail. I shall do so now. Imagine a thin, tall, serious-looking girl with flaxen hair whose clothes hang on her no matter what we do. Naked, her bones stick out. Delicate bones, quite beautiful in their articulation, long fingers and long elegant toes, quite refined, her features small and regular. And though she is wealthy and even healthy, she has hollow cheeks as if she were a beggar girl.

Intense, uncomfortable in her skin, her eyes always solemn, always staring, she only smiles when her father pays attention to her, and then her face "glows." Emma is shamelessly, passionately in love with him. And I suspect him to be afflicted with the same madness. She has a bright, quick, lively intelligence but is decidedly odd. And what makes her even odder is the fact that on her left temple there is a birthmark, small, no larger than my thumbnail, which she tries to hide by standing in such a way as to keep it out of your sight. She has proven a good pupil though. Now to the incident!

I came into her room some weeks ago without knocking—after all, I am not a servant, am I?—and found her standing of all places right at the hearth, practically in the hearth! There was a reason, as you shall shortly hear.

Let me explain first that her parents' bedroom lies directly below and she could hear their conversations. She was listening to them as I came in. I heard something unintelligible. I realized at once what she was doing there. I have never seen anyone so frightened. I thought that she would faint, but she did not. First pale, then scarlet, first limp, then rigid, she hung on to consciousness. I said nothing but informed Mrs. Farnley the following day, and she made arrangements with the chimney sweep to reset the bricks. Mrs. Farnley swore to me she would not tell a soul.

Before doing so I was careful not to inform Emma as to my intentions and took her for a walk in the Gardens. When we returned it was *fait accompli*. So ended the matter, but I believe I have a firmer hold over my pupil than ever before, which of course, as you and I have discussed, suits our purposes. Remember: *Mit gedult kommet alles.*

> *auf Wiedersehen, mein Kamerad,*
> *deine Schwägerin,*
> Clara

2 July 1838

My dear Johan,
England is not Germany. What I mean is that Respectability and Sin are cheek-by-jowl in this country. One can literally move in a matter of seconds from the sacred to the profane sphere, unlike Frankfurt, where city planning, as you know, is arranged differently, *n'est-ce pas,* clear divisions being made, boundaries being set.

I refer specifically to Jessie Malkin's brothel, which Forster men attend "religiously" and which is on the northeast corner of Wickfield and Collard lanes directly opposite St. Giles, the church they attend on Sunday mornings. They say Jessie's lover, Lord Fitzcrawford, bequeathed it to her. She and her five loathsome sons run it.

Nicholas Renton has made his headquarters in her establishment, in the cellar. The cellar has been greatly enlarged by his lieutenant, Kevin Francini (have I mentioned him to you? we detest one another). Nicholas also keeps a ferocious-looking dog named Tartarus chained in his vestibule.

Improbable, even childish, I grant you, except that the establishment is so particular, so concrete, and Mr. Renton so obviously serious in his intentions, that one accepts unreservedly the vehemence of his desires (though one is not sure actually what they might be). And his perception of himself (though one is not sure what that might be either). Still, one is made to feel that in this subterranean fire-lit world—there are innumerable torcheres, candelabras, tapers, sconces—his will "prevailith" absolutely.

As I wrote, I was disturbed to find out that he was in the vicinity of the Gardens. I had hoped never to see him or have anything more to do with him again. And when he let me know through one of his minions that he wished to speak to me, I wondered what he wanted from me this time.

About a month ago I was "summoned" to his royal presence and informed of his desires. He did not equivocate with me but came straight to the point, because he obviously felt he did not have to be charming, or circumspect, or prudent, or politic with me—I was in his pocket, so to speak.

I believe him to be totally deranged. However, cynic that I am, that has not led me to doubt that he will succeed in whatever mad designs he has—history teaches us that the world has been run by lunatics for surprising lengths of time. And even successfully. Renton's strength lies in his ability to totally ignore reality whenever it opposes his dreams.

And so he told me what he wanted from me.

"I want information," he said, "about your employers: what they do, what they talk about; in short, all the particulars of their lives. No detail is unimportant. Remember, it is not for you to judge what is important and what is not. You are also to provide me with lists of things they own— all their possessions. Begin with their silver: their sugar bowls, their creamers, their chocolate pots, their service plates, their salts—include the hallmarks, and the tone . . . old silver has a soft bluish tone to it—their porringers, candlesticks, epergnes, chafing dishes; in short, everything."

Now you understand why I thought I was visiting a madman. He also ordered me to begin a sort of notebook, a daily account of what I see and an account of Elijah's Sunday afternoon dinners.

I am paid for this, quite handsomely. As Wednesday afternoon is the only afternoon I am free, I go to his house then, once a month. I am secretly picked up by his coachman where no one can observe me.

I have been to visit Nicholas once and he has listened to my report with the utmost interest and absorption.

You write that there are anti-Jewish disturbances in Germany. But why do you insist on involving yourself? I know that you are related to the Rothschilds through your mother's family, the Schnappers, but you were not circumcised, or at least I assume not, since my husband was not. I hope this does not offend you.

Your package of books arrived yesterday. Thank you for including Heine's *Letters from Paris*. I solemnly promise to read them all and discuss them with you as long and as thoroughly as you wish.

> *Until we meet again, mein liebster,*
> Clara

28 August 1838

My dear Johan,

Congratulations on your victory! You have humbled the beautiful baroness. Your description of her—her mounting anxiety at the ball when you flirted with her younger sister, her face draining of color when you persisted—was masterful. I could see it happening as I read. You should write novels, Johan.

I too have had success in my way. It concerns Elijah. But first Nicholas . . .

In making the lists for Nicholas, my eyes were opened to the material grandeur of the Forster possessions—their enormous temporal wealth. As you know, I have never cared for material things. I have never thought that *things* comprise the highest good, or the highest value in life. What I craved (and still do) was recognition for my intellectual gifts, respect for my work. But something strange has happened to me, for in describing such objects to him—he insists on the most minute details—"There is no such thing as a trivial detail," he told me, "and pray do not invent; you are not the only informant I have in the household"—I have in some inexplicable way felt myself becoming seduced by the richness and wonder of *things*.

I am beginning to understand Nicholas's near-demonic devotion to the objects of this world. Is it possible to "spiritually" awaken to materialism?

When I describe their possessions he insists that I convey to him the exact form, the size, the depth, the height, the color, all its "dependent" qualities, for, unlike Aristotle,

Nicholas is convinced that matter alone determines what a thing is.

And once I have described the object to his satisfaction, he then stares into space as if he were reconstructing it in some concrete way, making it his own, so to speak. Only after the mental operation is completed does he ask me to continue.

He pays me many guineas for this information, and he is generous. It will soon amount to enough money, which I shall send you, so that you can visit me. But not yet. The ground is not yet prepared sufficiently for you so that you may reap what I have sown for you.

Now, Elijah. I want him to see me as a woman he desires. And yet I dislike him so. So much of my energy is spent in his presence trying to preserve my female pride, for though he is not as sarcastic with me as with his wife, still when I leave him I feel as if I have been pricked all over.

I am insane. I who never believed I could be shaken by lust for a man have now capsized. Something will happen. He will want me sexually. My wanting him as much as I do will stimulate him to want me. To "take" me. Perhaps the "poor relative," the outcast, will have a good time in life yet. Do I shock you? I shock myself. How can I want him? He is so damnably egotistical. And yet my body does. It hopes, it prays, it longs, it thirsts for sex with him. It is obsessed.

In the Symposium, Aristophanes talks about love, describing love, and the agonies of love as a separation from the loved one, insisting that we are only half of what we really are, that we have from birth been severed from the other half and that until we are joined, united—reunited—we shall not feel whole. That passionate love is really the yearning for the divided half of ourselves. "Let everyone find his own favorite (man or woman) and so revert to his primal estate." Enough! I am obsessed.

Clara

10 October 1838

Dear Johan,

I know what it is to stand outside the pleasant world clasping my empty bowl, my face creased into what I sincerely hope is a pleasant and attractive smile, while at the same time I long with all my heart to tear down their world, destroy it, annihilate those who ignore me, who do not know or wish to see my worth. I can only hope to injure them in some frightful psychological way, for I have no physical force, no actual power, only a clever and manipulative mind. I have no money, no connections, nor do I possess the kind of physical beauty that can make use of men. As you know I am not one to shrink from looking ugly facts in their ugly faces. Had I not met your brother, Franz, I might never have known what happiness was.

Well now I am here, inside their world, a part of them, certainly a part of Emma. I dine with them, partake in their conversations, partake of their feelings. I am no longer the beggar with the bowl. Or perhaps I feel that because there is someone in the household who is worse off than I am. I mean Theodisia.

I am beginning to have some sympathy for her, foolish and silly though she seems to be. He is so savage with her, so brutal. It is uncomfortable to witness it. And he now torments her in a new way.

She loves no one but her son William, a petulant selfish boy—I have met him—he is the sole object of her love. She is passionately fond of him, much like Elijah is of Emma. Perhaps too much so . . . it is through William that he torments her. In this household the parents look not to one another but to their children for emotional fulfillment. They have another son, a boy named Edward, Elijah's heir, tall and as good-looking as his father. But neither she or Elijah seem to care for him, though he is treated by them and by the servants with the kind of deference one expects an heir to be treated. I have met him, of course. And though he is reserved, I sense quiet suffering.

But to get back to William and Theodisia: Elijah has forbidden her to correspond with William. And she may not send him cakes or cookies or money. It will make him a weakling, he told her. It will interfere with his studies. Finally yesterday he forbade her to visit him. She tried to control herself but couldn't. She became hysterical and had to leave the table. I was told by him to follow her and "calm her if that is at all possible." As I said, I dislike the man. It is my body, with a life of its own, that does not.

We are all star-crossed lovers in this household. At least the women are: Theodisia for William; I for Elijah . . . and Emma for me. Because of course I know she is in love with me. Passionately, as passionately as only a young girl can be when she falls in love with an older woman who means everything to her. She watches my every move, savors my every word. If only her father would. In the meantime I am preparing the ground for your entry into this little establishment. In four more years our Emma will be sixteen, and you, knowing her inside and out, will be able to maneuver her as skillfully as a captain pilots his craft. It will be "fair sailing." She shall fall in love with you. I am sure of it. I am priming her for you. But you must promise me one thing: do not fall in love with her. But of course you shan't—love is not an emotion you are too familiar with, *nicht wahr?*

Clara

8

THEODISIA:
QUID PRO QUO

Darius claims to have discovered a new play—*Iocasta Regula*—
written by Sophocles. It is about how Iocasta lusted after Oed-
ipus, her son, even though she knew he was her son. We are to
perform it at the Palazzo. Darius will play Iocasta, of course . . .

—Emma Forster, the *Florentine Journals,* 1856

Most of us carry in our hearts the Jocasta who begs Oed-
ipus, for God's sake, not to enquire further.

—Schopenhauer, in a letter to Goethe

THEODISIA was in hysterics. She ran screaming around the room,
beating herself with her hands. Then she began to batter her head
against the wall, sobbing, crying, moaning. Mrs. Farnley, hearing her
shrieks, ran upstairs to her room, opened the door, rushed in, and tried
to catch her.

In her right hand Theodisia held a letter.

"Please God!" Theodisia screamed. "Please God, let it not happen!
I will kill myself if it does! I will, I will! Oh, the monster, I will kill
him! I will kill him! I can't stand it! I can't stand it anymore! Oh, my
William! My little William!"

Mrs. Farnley caught her finally and, being considerably stronger than
Theodisia, was able to hold her still. She held her firmly in her large
strong arms.

"There, there, little one. Tell me what's wrong. Is William sick? What
is it? Now tell me . . . dry your tears and tell me."

Theodisia, her head resting on Mrs. Farnley's bosom, murmured something unintelligible. Drooling saliva on Mrs. Farnley's crisp white collar, which she had just put on that morning, Theodisia began sobbing again and let out a new pack of cries.

"Here, let me see the letter," said Mrs. Farnley, trying to pry it gently out of Theodisia's clenched fingers.

"No! You may not have it! It is mine! Mine!" And then she sagged in the housekeeper's arms and lost consciousness for a moment, which allowed Mrs. Farnley to remove the letter from Theodisia's limp hand. Picking her up in her arms, she carried Theodisia to the bed, where she lay her down gently. Theodisia curled up on the bed, weeping softly while Mrs. Farnley read the letter. It was from William.

13 November 1838

Dear Momma,

Since for reasons unknown to me you have stopped writing me letters, or sending me biscuits, cakes, jams and jellies, or any monies, I have decided to do away with myself.

I do hope when you receive this letter that you will suffer and understand a bit therefore how I have suffered at Warrenton and am still doing so. This past month I have waited every day for your letters and your packages. I have received nothing. In your last letter (a whole month ago!) you told me Poppa does not want you to write me as often as you have and that since I receive letters and packages from Poppa I should be satisfied. But I do not feel the same way towards him as I do towards you.

Until I went away to school I did not realize how much you meant to me.

When you are standing at my open grave (I would like to be buried next to Sidney), just before they lower my coffin, I hope you will remember how Sidney's Momma, Aunt Guinivere, had to be led away, for she was crying so hard the funeral could not proceed. Perhaps then you will realize the horror of what you have done.

In the event that I might change my mind about killing myself, I wish you to know that there is one thing that I shall *never* change my mind about: I shall *never* forgive you.

Your younger son,
William Marcus Forster, Esquire
Muckrake Hall, Warrenton
Little Claybrook,
Leicestershire, England

Mrs. Farnley folded the letter neatly in two and put it back into the limp fingers of her mistress. Theodisia was now quiet, her eyes open, staring blankly in front of her.

"Ah, Madam, you know William. He didn't do it, believe me, Madam. Nor will he. The lad is angry, but then he doesn't understand." Mrs. Farnley bent down and stroked Theodisia's damp forehead—was she ill, too? "He did nothing harmful to himself. Believe me, he shall come home for Christmas. William will not kill himself before getting his presents. Of that you can be sure, Madam. Had anything happened, we would have heard by now." Poor silly thing, thought Mrs. Farnley. So frightened and so powerless. The master had indeed been cruel. "You must not let the Master see this letter. Do you understand? He will retaliate by punishing William. Come now, pull yourself together. Try to be sensible . . ."

"What shall I do?" A new freshet of tears poured out of Theodisia's eyes. "You must help me, Mrs. Farnley. You must. You must go down there—"

"But how can I, Madam? On what pretext?"

"I shall give you anything, anything you want, if you will only do it. Go there, please! Tell me, what piece of jewelry of mine have you long admired? Tell me. It is yours!"

"Well now, since you've asked, Madam, I have always thought the little diamond ring in the shape of a flower the prettiest thing I have ever seen."

"It is yours! Only go. This instant. I shall contrive some excuse. A sick aunt who has no one in the world except you, an aunt with a bit of money. He would understand that, wouldn't he? Your keeping an interest in a possible inheritance. Yes, your master would understand that."

If Mrs. Farnley was surprised at how quickly Theodisia had thought of a lie she did not show it. Her face was blank as she watched the suddenly energized Theodisia move swiftly off the bed and to her bureau and in a twinkling of an eye pull out from the back of one of the drawers a small purse from which she took out some gold sovereigns. Then she opened her jewel box on top of the bureau, took the ring out, and pressed it into Mrs. Farnley's open hand.

"Here, take it! It is yours. And take the money too. It is not much, but give it to William. Tell him it is from me. Tell him I love him. That he has all my love." Theodisia closed her eyes and holding her arms she swayed slightly back and forth. "Go! Do not stop until you've seen he's all right. That he is alive! And then come straight back and tell me!"

"I will go now. I shall come back as soon as possible. Norris will find someone to take me. And he will keep his mouth shut. I'll see to that. But in the meantime you must stop crying. Have you forgotten that Mrs. Strooksbury is coming to tea? She sees everything and is delighted to spread a bit of scandal whenever she can. Bathe your eyes in some cold water so as not to look as if you've been crying. And remember, not a word of this to Master." For a moment Mrs. Farnley hesitated . . . should she or should she not say what she really felt? Looking at her mistress, so silly, so helpless, Mrs. Farnley boldly overstepped her place. "Remember, Madam, Mr. Forster is a vindictive man, especially when he feels deep inside his heart that he is wrong."

"You are right, Mrs. Farnley. How wise you are. And he has done wrong, hasn't he? He is a cruel man, isn't he?"

"Perhaps, but you must not be a silly woman. I shall lay out your lilac wool. . . ."

Theodisia was pouring a cup of tea for Mrs. Strooksbury (". . . three lumps, please, and a dash of milk"), when Clara and Emma came into the room. A look of dislike passed over Theodisia's childlike vapid features.

She was seated behind an enormous and elaborate Georgian tea service, which rested on a long narrow table covered by a spotless white cloth. An assortment of mouth-watering tarts, cakes, biscuits, buns, and tissue-thin crustless sandwiches were displayed on silver trays.

Theodisia's look was not lost on Mrs. Strooksbury, who collected these outward signs of inner feelings and brought them home with her, as one might a pastry, to mull over them at leisure. Theodisia was a fool, Mrs. Strooksbury decided for the hundredth time. *She* would have withered Mrs. Lustig with a look of cold disdain. It was the only way to treat servants, particularly governesses, who were sometimes imbued with the odd notion that they actually might be equal to their mistresses because of their so-called education, a smattering of Latin and Greek. But it was all a matter of breeding, wasn't it?

"No, Theodisia," Mrs. Strooksbury said, "do not bother to pour for Millicent . . ." She was referring to her daughter, a drab thing, except for her startling red hair, who sat next to her. "Millicent never drinks tea, or imbibes wine. Both make her bilious."

Mrs. Strooksbury was stout and ugly. Nevertheless she was always dressed in the height of fashion, as if to say, "Yes, I am stout and I am ugly and I shall make the most of it!"

Her enormous bosom was draped today in a dress of magenta wool and blue corduroy trim, adorned by buttons made of mother-of-pearl whose motif swept downwards to the broad hem of her skirt. Her hat, brown velvet, an "extravaganza," was girdled with magenta ribbons and surmounted by black plumes. Set diagonally on her oak-colored curls, the hat waved and dipped as she spoke. Her hair was arranged in rigid rows of curls on either side of a face brazenly repellent with its fleshy lips, its broad-tipped snout, its small brown eyes.

"As I was saying," continued Mrs. Strooksbury, "Lady Alysbury has unfortunately been taken ill, so that the burden of arranging this great charitable event—the aid and assistance of orphan children abandoned so heartlessly in the streets of London—shall fall entirely on my shoulders, Theodisia. Therefore I shall need your help. There shall be a musicale first, then a supper, and after that a ball. It is a great pity your sister-in-law, Consuelo, still remains in Italy. She could have played for us. But perhaps it is for the best, for it has been rumored, Theodisia, that she claims to be a serious musician. That is a mistake a lady should never make."

Theodisia shook her head, and her silken clusters of blond curls bobbed up and down in agreement.

Underweight, small in bone and stature, Theodisia had the appearance of a child dressed up in her mother's clothes. A colorless blonde with thin bloodless lips. A yeoman's daughter. A fact that played havoc with her social nerves. She was quite sure that everyone in her social set—factory owners, heads of trading houses and brokerage firms, controllers of joint stock companies, the husbands and their wives—looked down their noses—small, large, crooked, bumpy, curved, hooked, aquiline . . . all sorts of noses, yes, but all of them far better than her own—at her.

Theodisia had asked her beloved Gwinnie (Solomon's wife) to be present this afternoon, to give her support, while she entertained the "star" of their social set, Mrs. Strooksbury, a corn merchant's daughter, married to one of the heads of a trading and brokerage house with whom Elijah did business. The combination of Mrs. Strooksbury's antecedents coupled with her social position disabled Theo completely. Everyone intimidated Theo, but Mrs. Strooksbury—strident, commanding, aggressive, formidable, the self-elected arbiter of their set's morals and behavior—just a bit more. Where was Gwinnie?

"I will not take no for an answer, Theodisia. It is an honor to be asked to assist Lady Alysbury—"

The door opened again and Guinivere came in, rosy-cheeked, a little flustered, speaking, as she hurriedly advanced to her sister-in-law behind the tea table.

"Dear Theo, I am sorry I am late. But poor Deirdre was feverish and weepy besides . . . she must be coming down with something. And

Jakes the nanny as well. So there was nothing else to do but bed them both! With the housekeeper's help, of course. Ah, Mrs. Strooksbury, it is always a pleasure to see you. And what a perfectly splendid hat! So becoming . . . and Millicent, my dear . . ." She went over to the girl, who was smiling at her, and gave her a small kiss on the cheek. "Such beautiful hair," Guinivere said as she caressed one of the girl's ringlets. "And Emma . . ." She hurried over to her niece and putting her arms around her gave her a kiss too. "Mrs. Lustig . . ." Turning, to Theodisia she said, "I shall have tea . . . plain with a wedge of lemon, if I may. . . ."

Theodisia poured and handed Guinivere her cup and saucer, on which she put a small silver spoon. Oh, Gwinnie was wonderful, wasn't she? She made everything look so simple. But of course it really was, wasn't it? She was the only one who found even entering a room difficult. Dear Gwinnie. Theo began to relax a little. Nothing too awful or terrible could happen now that Gwinnie was here.

"May I have a strawberry tart?" Emma asked.

"You know you are not to speak until spoken to, Emma," Clara said.

"Come side beside me, Emma," Gwinnie said, "and bring me two strawberry tarts, one for you and one for me." The child always looked so frightened and disturbed. She thought of her own plump, happy, darling Deirdre.

Emma hesitated. Could she? Would Momma object? Then she saw her aunt smile at her mother, and saw her mother nod at her. She still hesitated.

"For heaven's sake, Emma," her mother said, "do as you're told. Your Aunt Guinivere is waiting."

Chewing nervously on her bottom lip, Emma walked over to the table. Choosing the two largest strawberry tarts, she put one each on separate plates and took them over to her aunt. Handing Guinivere one of the plates, she sat down on the chair next to her.

"But you've forgotten the napkins and the forks," her mother said in an irritable voice.

Emma went over to the table again to get two white linen napkins and two silver forks. Her face grave and unsmiling, she returned to her aunt and gave her one of each. She sat down again on the chair next to her aunt and picking up her fork cut into the tart slowly and carefully. When her aunt reached out to stroke her head, she moved away.

Guinivere put her hand down. Really, something should be done about Emma. She was strange. Different. Jakes had told her about the beatings Grindal had given Emma when she was younger. But Grindal was no longer in charge, thank God, though the governess Elijah had hired didn't seem much better. Cousin or no cousin there was something about Mrs. Lustig that Guinivere didn't like. What Emma needed was love. Mrs. Lustig did not seem capable of that. She sighed. After all, Theo did not love Emma, her own daughter. She loved only William. Guinivere lifted her fork filled with Mrs. Lovesley's strawberry tart to her mouth . . . delicious . . . she smiled warmly at her sister-in-law.

"My dear Guinivere," Mrs. Strooksbury said, "as always you have chosen the exactly right moment to arrive. I was just about to embark on Lady Alysbury's background and connections. It is always worthwhile, I am sure you will agree, to discuss such impeccable pedigrees. Now, when the Right Honorable Augustus Randall, Viscount and Baron Wenthworth, died without issue, and the barony henceforth became extinct in eighteen twenty-three, it was revived in eighteen thirty-two in the person of Lady Randall Alysbury, the daughter of Sir Randolph Randall Talbot-Randall, who was related to—"

Mrs. Strooksbury's flow of genealogical wonders was interrupted by the door opening once more. She glared at Daisy, but the glare was transformed into a brilliant smile when she saw that Daisy was followed by Elijah. The Master had come home.

"Poppa!" Emma cried as she ran to him.

"You are home earlier than usual," Theodisia observed with alarm.

"An accurate observation, my dear. You are to be commended for it. Is that not so, ladies? Where is Mrs. Farnley?" Elijah asked while stroking Emma's flaxen hair.

How does he do it, thought Guinivere? Include us all into an instant conspiracy against his wife, so that her remark, uttered out of surprise and panic, now protrudes in a telling way against her?

"She received a message this morning that her aunt was dying and was asking for her. She will be back this evening."

"Really. Mrs. Farnley has an aunt?" Elijah smiled at Guinivere and Mrs. Strooksbury. "The lady must have some 'shekels' then, otherwise Mrs. Farnley would be here as always. Well, let us hope it is not a large inheritance. We could not do without Mrs. Farnley, could we, Theodisia? But I am pleased my 'early' homecoming has insured my meeting the redoubtable, resplendent Mrs. Strooksbury and her lovely daughter, Millicent, and . . . my charming sister-in-law, Guinivere, who seems to grow more beautiful every day."

Popping a small tart into his mouth, he swallowed it whole and cried out: "Good heavens, what have I consumed? It has the texture of gooseberries. I'm quite sure of that, but the flavor, very odd, very strange indeed. Alas! I fear I have been poisoned. Emma!" He pretended to stagger.

"Poppa!"

It was pure slapstick, but he knew his daughter would enjoy the bogus drama. It was an old nursery game that he impulsively decided to play with her in front of an audience.

He turned to his wife. "Really, Theodisia, you had better instruct Mrs. Lovesley that if she insists on serving whatever it was I just 'et' she must provide a list of ingredients. Isn't that so, Emma?"

"Yes, Momma. You really must."

Theodisia did not reply. She looked frightened.

"Well, Sir," said Mrs. Strooksbury, smiling broadly at Elijah, "before you succumb . . ." What a fool Theodisia was! Certainly she was not the proper wife for him. And by the looks of her not an ounce of passion in her . . . but then all families had problems, didn't they . . . and secrets. "There are some things I must discuss with you, Elijah."

"I am at your service, Ma'am," said Elijah. "Come sit beside me, Emma, and we shall hear what Mrs. Strooksbury has in store for me."

"Church business, Elijah. Do not frown. The point is, if there is to be a new vestry, as Reverend Bottome spoke about in the last church meeting, I say let part of the cost be defrayed by a grant from the Church Building Society, of which I happen to be head, and part by the vicar himself! His living, after all, my husband tells me, is valued at two hundred sixty-five pounds per annum. A handsome sum, you will admit, Sir."

"I respectfully bow to your wishes, Madam."

Such a handsome man, thought Mrs. Strooksbury. A pity that his wife did not know how to manage him.

Guinivere rose.

"But you are not leaving now that I have arrived, are you?" Elijah asked.

He had sensed for some time now that Guinivere disapproved of him. He wondered what Solomon had told her. Had he told her about his mistress? Possibly. Or was it the way he treated Theodisia? Some women enjoyed watching another woman be insulted by a man. But he suspected that Guinivere was not one of those. Well, he did not need her approval. Still, it rankled. He was a vain man; he wanted to be liked regardless.

"No, of course not, Elijah. But your early arrival did remind me that I must be home to attend to my own family. Deirdre and Jakes are both ill. So you must excuse me, Elijah, Mrs. Strooksbury, Millicent, dear Theodisia . . . Emma . . ."

The fact that she had excluded Clara in her good-byes was noticed by no one, except Clara, of course.

Much later that evening, after supper, when her husband had gone out again—"Church business," he had told her—Theodisia, in the safety of her boudoir, pulled out of her jewel casket the creased, tear-stained letter from her son William, the letter she had already read countless times, to read it once more. Finishing, she sighed and then slipped the letter back into the casket, underneath the letters Edward had written her.

William. She had wanted to run all the way to Warrenton, to Muckrake Hall, to gather him up in her arms and take him home.

She saw his sweet face before her, so like her brother William, his eyes brilliant with tears . . . longing for her. Oh, it was impossible! Impossible! She could not go on this way any longer. Without him! Forbidden to write her own son! Forbidden to send him food—and now forbidden to visit him at all!

Elijah! How she hated him! Dead, she wished him dead! Her sweet William, silken and soft, an angel from Heaven, banished to Warrenton! Oh yes, yes, she knew it had to be done. Sons separated from their mothers . . . torn, yes, torn from their arms! She knew that, but she also knew, *knew* Elijah had exulted in it! Delighted in it. Delighted in tearing William away from her. She had seen it in Elijah's eyes when she had cried, that terrible morning when her William had climbed into the coach with Edward and his cousins Albert, Joshua, and Jacob, and they had ridden off together to Warrenton. A year and a half ago. That terrible, terrible morning! She lived and relived that moment in her mind . . . again and again as if it had happened only yesterday.

That morning she had almost fainted. At first Elijah had laughed and then just as William had been lifted into the coach by Norris, Elijah had told her—in front of William!—that she was "harmful" to William. "Warrenton shall make a man of him." She had wanted to spit in his face then and there. "A man! Like you! Without a morsel of tenderness, without compassion!" she had wanted to scream. Was that a man? Oh, the darling, the poor darling. Cold and hungry. They never fed them enough at school, she knew that.

She recalled how Guinivere had tried to comfort her in those first few months, pointing out gently to Theodisia that her sons had departed too. Neither of them had mentioned Sidney, who had departed forever. If that were to happen to her she did not think she could survive.

But she was not Guinivere. She did not have Guinivere's strength . . . besides, Guinivere had Solomon. Solomon was a kind man, if a little boring. Theodisia had been left with Elijah. . . .

Several hours later when Elijah returned he found Theodisia asleep, huddled on her side of the bed. Shall he, he wondered. Yes. He pulled her to him so that she faced him, and despite her muttered protests he thrust his penis into her vagina, and moving it in and out angrily had an orgasm, released her, and fell back on his side of the bed into a dreamless sleep.

Awake now and unable to sleep, Theodisia began to think. She might be just a yeoman's daughter, that much she conceded to him, but her family—her mother, her father, her sisters, her brothers—never, never behaved like the Forsters, heartless and brutal. They were a kind, hard-working people. She thought with shame how Elijah had behaved towards her parents when they had come up to London to visit her. How cutting, how sarcastic he had been to them. He had discouraged their visits. She hardly saw them anymore, for they had understood immediately. They had obeyed his wishes. Later they had written her telling her that though they loved her dearly, they did not want to be the cause of trouble between her and her husband. Perhaps, they wrote, it would be best therefore to stay away. For it had been, they said, such an incredible piece of luck that she had the opportunity to marry into such a fine family as the Forsters in the first place.

Like most victims Theodisia had a malicious streak in her. Underneath the vapid prettiness, the childish ways, was pure vengeance. It was what kept her alive. Dreams of revenge . . . of terrible things happening to each and every Forster. Sometimes she envisioned Mathilda's beautiful daughter Vanessa riding a horse and being thrown, disfigured and crippled forever. And Mathilda dying of a wasting disease, in agony, suffering. Joseph drunk, falling down the stairs and breaking his neck.

Elijah! One day she would pay back Elijah for what he had done to her. She would strike him down when he was at his weakest. The moment would come. She was sure of it. That was why she clung to life.

How vulnerable Elijah was where Emma was concerned. He was not invincible, as she thought he was when she first married him. One day he would be laid low by her hands.

9

GUINIVERE

. . . a (mother's) love for its offspring, has like the sexual impulse, a strength far surpassing that of the efforts which are directed merely towards itself as individual.

—Schopenhauer, *The World as Will and Representation*

A little more than two years had passed since Guinivere's son Sidney had died.[17] The intense pain had subsided, the pain that gnawed at her as if it were a sharp-toothed animal, scratching and biting her, wild with grief, never resting. That had left her, but . . . not entirely. Sometimes it would be awakened, prodded into action, by a mere sliver of thought, a random remark made by someone. . . . She would know then that her grief had not died as yet, but was lying there inside her like some reservoir, ready to be used when necessary. Why it should be necessary, she didn't know.

The visit to his grave in the Gardens, which she still made once a week, had taken on a ritual aspect, creating a pattern that in some way substituted for the actual feelings of grief, acting as a talisman against further pain.

If she came once a week and repeated the words she had fashioned for herself to express the unbearable loss, the pain seemed satisfied, the ritual became its food. Gradually in time the fact of his death became what might be termed "bearable." That is, if his name for some reason

17. Sidney Augustus Forster died at 6:12 A.M. on December 18, 1836, of complications brought on by measles. He was buried in the Rose Garden in Marlborough Gardens close by the East Gate.—*R. Lowe*

or other was uttered in conversation the tears did not immediately flow, or if they did, the flow had shrunk, as it were, to a trickle. And if she thought of him when she was alone by chance she no longer felt stricken. No, she was no longer overwhelmed by grief. She was despondent (a fact she kept to herself), but, thank God, she was no longer tormented.

In all this welter of emotions she had been alone. Except for Albert, her eldest son, who had accompanied her frequently to Sidney's grave. But now that he was at Warrenton there was no one.

Yes, the grief was "manageable" now; she could be Solomon's wife again, Deirdre's and her sons' mother; she could attend to other needs besides her own. Her grief was now "acceptable" to Solomon. He had been annoyed, impatient with what he termed her "morbid" behavior. He had told her that he understood her grief, but that she must accept two things, the first being Sidney's death (which was God's will), the second that life goes on. "I have suffered, too, my dear. I loved Sidney as much as you did, but moderation in *all* things. 'Everybody who understands his business avoids alike excess and deficiency; he seeks and chooses the mean.' Aristotle, *Nichomachean Ethics,* volume two, Guinivere."

She had said: "I believe you, Solomon. You loved Sidney. He was your son, too. I do not blame you in any way."

She did not say what she really thought: "You loved Sidney but you did not carry him in your body, he was not flesh of your flesh, your blood did not feed him, your milk did not nourish him." She did not say: "Sidney died not knowing or believing that I truly loved him. That I loved him as much as he had wanted me to love him."

But had she? That guilt, too, thank God, had lessened. All had lessened, but not much had lightened. She still lived in a dull grey world, though she kept herself busy. Sometimes it seemed immaterial to her whether she lived or died. Sometimes she thought death might be preferable. Death and reunion with Sidney. Was that evil, she wondered.

Sometimes she dreamed of Sidney. He would call to her, and she would rise out of her bed and go to him. Together they would wander through fields of flowers, his small hand in hers, warm, soft, and she would kiss the hand from time to time. When they came to the top of the hill they would lie down together in the warm sun-filled air. She would tell him stories and he would play with her hair, and then they would lie down together, he cuddled up against her. Alone in the other world with Sidney. Just Sidney and herself, a son and his mother.

Today she carried fresh sprigs of holly to the grave. She was dressed warmly (she no longer wore black). Her green cape was lined with squirrel fur, as were her long green gloves. Underneath her full-skirted cashmere dress she wore two flannel petticoats. A black bonnet trimmed with green satin ribbons almost hid her hair, except for two long blond curls on either side of her sweet face. On a chain around her neck she wore a locket filled with Sidney's hair. She had had a jeweler make up similar lockets for each of her children, and had elicited from each of them a solemn promise that they would always wear them in remembrance. They must never forget Sidney.

Still, even she agreed with Solomon's "life must go on" attitude. Was it cynical or realistic? And why say "must" when it did whether it must or must not? Wasn't that its nature? Its unrelenting continuity. Never ceasing, never stopping to console—or to forgive. Just on and on . . . Senseless. Meaningless.

She knelt down by the grave on the small verge of dried grass. She prayed for forgiveness for herself, she prayed for her children, her husband; momentarily Emma's face—pinched, unhappy, lonely—was suspended in front of her. She went on to bless her and her brothers . . . all those she knew and cared for, loved. What more could she do? What more could anyone? Enough. She would go home now and write her letters, discuss Deirdre with Jakes (they had quarreled, Jakes's feelings were hurt), talk to Deirdre, talk to Cook about dinner tonight. . . .

Joseph was coming to dinner. She must warn Mrs. Bridgewater not to keep filling Joseph's glass though he might ask her to.

"He drinks too much," Solomon said. "Far too much for his own good, Guinivere. What he does in his house I can say nothing about. There I have no jurisdiction. But I do in mine. He has practically stopped coming to the bank. He does not pull his weight there. A glass of wine perhaps, even two, but no more than that! Tell the servants that."

Joseph. Consuelo and Ricci! Ricci! Joseph's valet! Unthinkable that. What was it like for them now, the two lovers, a year later? And Darius, Consuelo's son! Did Consuelo miss him? Oh, she must! No matter what Elijah and Solomon said about her . . . What did men know anyway about mothers and their sons?

She started walking towards the Winter Garden. She wanted to see the new plant the head gardener had told her about, a form of cactus that flowered, a braclea, he had called it. "And in its spikey center, Madam, where you would think nothing would or could grow, there grows a strange flower, strange but beautiful." There was still time.

Crossing Nannies Plain, she hurried down the path to the iron-ribbed structure, painted white, that in this brilliant cold bluish light of winter looked almost like a huge diamond, the rays of sun reflecting and refracting in and out of its multiple panes of glass like so many facets.

Inside, the greenhouse was moist and hot—several large tile stoves were kept burning night and day throughout the winter months. A green moist world . . . one could almost hear the "purr-r-r" of growth: vigorous, healthy, splashed with gorgeous vibrant color.

The gardener had told her where the plant was to be found. She was walking down the center lane underneath the long rectangular glass roof when she saw a man standing at the end of the path, in the middle of it. She was startled. What in the world was he doing here? And then she remembered: of course, it was Thursday! Every Tuesday and Thursday the Gardens were open to the public, including the Winter Garden. The pitiless light revealed to her both the man's strangeness and his charm. He was beautifully dressed. A light blue frock coat with a black velvet collar with a cord edging, white trousers, a spotless cravat—and then she suddenly realized that she *had* met him. At Mrs. Strooksbury's house. A charity ball. . . .

Momentarily, she wished she had come to see the plant at some other time. Guinivere was shy by nature, especially when it came to strangers, and this man, odd, different—yet attractive, even handsome, in fact— was after all still a relative stranger. Even though she had met him before, she had barely said a word to him. Or he to her. She smiled at him now because she felt helpless. He did not return her smile. He only stared at her. She continued to smile. What strange eyes he had— green eyes, hawk's eyes—wary, tense, unwavering. Should she continue down the path, she wondered. Or should she turn around? But she couldn't do that, could she? He was Mrs. Strooksbury's friend. She continued down the path, her mind forming innocuous sentences such as "How pleasant to see you again, Mr.—" But she didn't recall his name. "Winter blooms are so extraordinary . . ." One part of her mind continued while at the same time another part of her mind wondered anxiously: Would he let her pass? But of course he would. Why wouldn't he? The path between the tables was narrow, edged with plants. He wasn't moving. Would he let her pass . . . he looked as if he actually might not.

All of these thoughts went through her head in seconds. And then she saw him move backwards, still facing her, still looking at her, and suddenly when he reached the end of the path, he turned the corner and disappeared from view. She listened to the *tap tap* of his heels as he walked farther and farther away, until she heard the north door of the Winter Garden open and close.

He was gone. She felt an instant relief.

Continuing on to the place where the gardener said the plant would be, she saw it was there. Quite a strange-looking plant, the blossom, in the shape of a jagged spear, had striated leaves . . . such an odd-looking man. His eyes, she could still see them staring at her. Had he found her odd, too? But of course, she thought, I shall probably never see him again.

But she was wrong. She saw Isaac Coverly the following week . . . on Christmas day at Elijah's house.

R. Lowe's Note from Warrenton: Albert

1838

When Albert went back to school that year, there was a new boy there who reminded him of his dead brother, Sidney. A frail, blond boy with the same serious expression on his face, the same bluish hollows under his high cheekbones, the same narrow chin with its sharp indentation.

Even the twins commented on the resemblance. "I thought it was Sidney," Jacob said, "even though I knew it couldn't be. Sidney's dead."

Each of Guinivere's children wore the locket that held a strand of their dead brother's hair. "Wear this forever," their mother had told them. "Do not forget him. Never forget your brother."

The boy's name was Thomas Malfitte. His father was an architect. When the older boys started teasing him Albert immediately intervened and became his protector.

Albert and Thomas became friends and then added a third boy, Ramkree, the son of a Maharajah, the brother of the boy, Dee Jee, who had known Darius.

Sometimes when the three of them would roam the countryside on an afternoon something Thomas would say or do would remind Albert suddenly of his brother. Whatever it was it was so fleeting Albert couldn't pin it down, so that when it happened again he would be taken once more by surprise.

Thomas's gaze whenever Albert looked at him seemed to be fastened on him, Albert. But that too reminded Albert of Sidney. They were so very much alike. Except that the living boy's eyes were a lighter blue, almost a pale violet, as if they were the eyes of someone who had come back from the dead—as if they had been rinsed or as if the death experience had been an immersion into water. For whatever reason, Thomas's eyes glistened with a watery quality.

One of the school's traditions was for each form to choose a play and, during the week before they went home for Christmas holidays, to perform it for the "edification and enjoyment" of the other forms. Without consulting anyone Ramkree took it upon himself to choose the play for their form. "I shall be Hecuba," he said. "I like the play. She reminds me of my grandmother, and Agamemnon of my father. I also have an uncle as evil as Polymestor. I shall play Hecuba. You, Albert, shall play Agamemnon."

But Albert had a cold so that he couldn't rehearse. Ramkree then told Edward that he must play Agamemnon. However, on the night of the performance Albert was well enough to attend and he did so.

Everyone was there, all the forms, the masters . . . even the house-mothers. Albert sat in the front row, between his twin brothers, Joshua and Jacob.

The curtains opened and the stage was bare. Then from the back of it as if from a hidden depth arose the slight childlike figure of Polydo-rus (Hecuba's child), wraithlike, played by Thomas. He wafted to-wards the flickering candles of the rim of the proscenium, his arms wide, and in a high and silvery voice he said: "Here I am . . . the child of Priam and Hecuba. . . ."

Albert almost swooned. He knew now without a doubt that Sidney had come back from the dead in the body of Thomas. Half-conscious, he listened to the stage-child, the child-ghost (Sidney) explain how he had been murdered by Polymestor. Though why Sidney had returned, Albert didn't know. Up till now, Albert had thought that Sidney was quite satisfied to just accompany him throughout life as a ghost. Albert returned to full consciousness by the time Thomas had finished his long speech. He glanced sideways at each of his cousins. They had noticed nothing. He sighed in relief.

Albert had great sympathy for his mother's grief, and when he went home on holidays or at half term he would always accompany her to Sidney's graveside. He was aware that his father behaved in an impa-tient manner towards Guinivere where it concerned Sidney, that he was quite angry with her "prolonged" mourning. Albert did not hate his father, but he did not love him either. It was Guinivere, his mother, whom he loved, it was she who claimed his entire heart. When he saw his father sometimes behave impatiently with her, he tried to be even more gentle himself. But why did she grieve so, he wondered.

After Sidney decided to inhabit Thomas's body, Albert wondered if it might not cheer her up a bit if he told her the good news. Perhaps if she knew about Thomas she might not grieve so. But when he arrived home at Christmas he forgot all about it, for once he saw his cousin Vanessa at Elijah's house on Christmas Day, he fell instantly and pas-sionately in love.

10

CHRISTMAS IN MARLBOROUGH GARDENS

. . . we really possess only half a consciousness. With this we grope about in the labyrinth of our life and in the obscurity of our investigations; bright moments illuminate our path like flashes of lightning.

—Schopenhauer, The *World as Will and Representation,* trans. C. Lustig

. . . we live in ignorance of the desires that offend morality, the desires that nature has forced upon us and after their unveiling we may well prefer to avert our gaze from the scenes of childhood.

—Freud, *Interpretation of Dreams,* underlined in Emma's copy

Fᴏʀ Emma the Christmas of 1838 was the last perfect Christmas of her youth. A memory marked with magical signs, an immortal place where she had once felt loved and protected in the comfortable and wealthy bosom of her family. A talisman to which she could and did escape when the external present was either too terrifying or too sordid. A cluster of bright memories connected by luminous threads. A past treasure out of which she could draw courage, sustenance, and the desire to go on.

The fact that another part of her mind might mock and ridicule this sentimentality did not impinge on its magical effect.

Deeply embedded in that particular chain of memory was a moment of supreme passion that she no longer recalled consciously, an incandescent moment that though it blazed, sank instantly into the depths of her unconscious, where it lay a hidden but sensational remembrance. That instant in time, powerful and thrilling, when on Christmas Day she mysteriously *felt* that she had been "chosen" by her father, Elijah, even as Clara had been "chosen" by Franz.

The concatenation of these submerged impressions always began with the image of snow. Pure white snow falling out of an opaque sky . . . each flake perfectly formed.

All through Christmas Eve it snowed, white flakes pouring out of low-lying clouds. Snow on snow, for it had snowed the day before. In Marlborough Gardens the snow lay thick on all the paths, shimmered on the frozen lake, weighted the branches, bending them towards the ground. And amidst it all the statues shrouded in white took on mysterious forms.

Outside on Elijah's sloped roof chunks of snow fell from time to time from the eaves with a soft thud to the ground below while inside Elijah, Theodisia, and the children slept.

Edward and William had come home the night before from Warrenton by coach and helped decorate the huge fir tree that had been cut down in Blenheim Wood two days earlier. Carried by a troop of gardeners into Elijah's house, the tree was placed in an enormous tub in their drawing room. Green baize and sand surrounded it. Tomorrow they would light its candles (time was measured out in traditions during this season).

During the early hours of the morning William dreamt of the "Weihnachtsmann," who carried not toys but switches in his sack, a small ugly wooden figure that had once belonged to their great-great-grandfather, Josephus Faustus. Josephus (Elijah always gave his ancestor his German name) had brought it with him, Elijah told the children, when he had come to England from Rechtdorp, a small town in Germany, in 1710, over a hundred years earlier. Edward had placed the carved figure (another tradition) carefully and solemnly in the exact center of the mantel.

While William was still dreaming, Mrs. Lovesley, who had never been married but had three children, two boys and a girl, and God knows where they were now, was standing in the center of the kitchen at a wooden table stuffing a goose with a roast duck (another Forster tradition) while keeping a fierce eye on her kitchen help.

Mrs. Lovesley was not drunk yet, though she would be before Christmas dinner was over. "The bread!" she screamed at Jupie, the small girl who was pounding the almonds at the table beside her. The girl rushed to the brick oven and, burning her fingers, pulled out the loaves. Mrs. Lovesley glared. Yes, they were done the way the Master liked them: crisp and dark.

Only she spoke, shouted, screamed in the kitchen. There was absolute silence except for her, queen of her realm, moving with drunken dignity among her pots, her pans, her scales. . . .

She went over the dinner in her mind: Jerusalem soup to start with— the bacon had come from the pigs of Saddler's Grove. Just before the holidays the hampers had arrived and been stored in the larder; hares with their long ears dangling, geese, ducks, hams, and tongue. Cook gazed with satisfaction at her sideboard, now crammed with steak-and-kidney pies, ham-and-turkey pies, a roast leg of mutton, oysters and jellied eels, and a large roast goose with her special Madeira sauce.

The guests would start coming at around noon, she reckoned, straight from church as usual, but dinner wouldn't be served until three. As was the custom, the Forsters would go to church without breakfasting to hear Reverend Bottome deliver his Christmas sermon. How many hours did that give her? She picked up her tankard of ale, finished it, and growled menacingly at the child who was blowing on her burned fingers. "More ale! Now!" The child hurried to get it.

Mrs. Farnley came into the kitchen, composed as always. Well, thought Mrs. Farnley, she was well on her way, wasn't she? Two sheets to the wind already, not swearing yet, but almost. Last year Lovesley had tossed her skirts over her head and waltzed into the stewing stove where three steam kettles had fallen on her.

"It's Christmas," said Mrs. Farnley, "I wish you would remember that, Mrs. Lovesley."

"Aye! It's Christmas, which means I 'as to work twice as 'ard, don't I, Mrs. Farnley? Not like some people I know."

Ignoring the cook's comments, Mrs. Farnley began labeling the cards that would be attached to the fifteen small plum puddings wrapped in oiled paper sitting on the top shelf of the huge doorless cupboard in the rear of the kitchen. They would be taken to the bank after Boxing Day and distributed to the employees. Beneath the puddings, on a shelf by itself, stood the family pudding, as large as a cannonball. On the shelf below in bowls and plates were the Lebkuchen (honey cakes) and Eir Kringels (egg biscuits) and loaves of gingerbread, all made from recipes handed down through generations of Forsters. Links with their German past.

For three weeks now Mrs. Farnley had supervised the maids, scolding, encouraging, and driving them until every carpet had been cleaned, every piece of silver plate polished, every mirror washed, the wainscoting cleaned with stale porter and the wallpaper cleaned with three-day-old bread. Garlands of English ivy and pine wreaths with their grey-green foliage graced every doorway in the house.

She was also in charge of the table, the setting, its decorations; and the sideboard with its flagons, its cups, its beakers; and the wines. Three dozen bottles of special Port from Macao had arrived yesterday afternoon, a gift from Mr. Ryder with a card sending his regrets. The Master had said to use them today. The Wassail Bowl too—Mrs. Farnley looked at her watch.

"The mistress," said Mrs. Farnley to a maid, "will be awake shortly. Go upstairs and wait for her. I have laid out her dress, everything that is needed . . ." Seeing the fear in the girl's pockmarked face, she added, "There'll be no need to dress her hair. She will be wearing a turban. Go now, quick!"

When the children came home from church they went to Mrs. Farnley's parlor, as was their custom, where she had laid out three small glasses of her homemade coltsfoot wine and a plate of biscuits. Beneath her own tree, which was so small she called it Elf Tree, she had placed the presents she had made during the year for the children: two long mufflers for the boys, and an exquisitely stitched purse for Emma.

Mrs. Farnley was not fond of children. She had little or no maternal feelings. She did not have a "loving nature," as Guinivere did, for instance. But she retained firm beliefs about Forster rituals even though they seemed to her to be a curious mixture of German and English rites. Though she did not know Latin she agreed completely with *Quando Romae sum, ieiuno Sabbato* ("When in Rome I fast on Saturday").

As the children chatted among themselves Mrs. Farnley studied them. Emma had grown this year, more intense than ever before. An intelligent child, she supposed, but disturbing. The housekeeper disliked Mrs. Lustig, still since she had come they were dressing Emma better, weren't they? Mrs. Farnley approved of what Emma was wearing today: a pink glacé silk with a crimson velvet sash. Actually she looked quite pretty. Her straight blond hair had been drawn back over her ears and tied in large bow of pink ribbon. In her ears she wore the small coral earrings that her Aunt Guinivere had given her the Christmas Sidney had died.

Both boys wore short blue jackets with gilt buttons. Their hair smelled of bergamot and lavender. Edward was wearing his first cravat. Mrs. Farnley passed her finger along its upper ridge in order to make it lay smooth.

"Master Edward," Mrs. Farnley said, "I believe it is time to prepare the Wassail Bowl."

The children rose and followed her down the stairs to the basement. Each child had a special task in preparing the punch for the bowl. Papa would be the first one to dip his cup in it and make the pronouncement: "As fine as the nectar of the gods. Well done, children!"

Daisy, who had been pressed into kitchen service, helped them put on large smocks that covered their entire figures. Emma began to cut the apples that Jupie set in front of her in quarters, her face grave and serious. Edward uncorked the dozen bottles of blackberry wine, the traditional wine used by the Forsters for their Wassail. William's job was to collect the glass jars of spices—ginger, nutmeg, cardamom, and cloves—and bring them to the table. Everything must be done perfectly so that Poppa could make his toast.

When that stage of preparation was complete Mrs. Farnley took the fruit, adding some dried apricots and cherries to it (another Forster tradition), and put it all in an enormous pan that was already on the stove. Then she added William's spices and several cups of sugar. Finally she poured the wine in and as the mixture simmered each of the children stood on a crate and took turns stirring it with a wooden spoon as the servants watched. Mrs. Lovesley, a little more drunk than she had been half an hour earlier, swayed gently to and fro in front of them.

When Jupie returned from the pantry with the roasted apples (Mrs. Lovesley had prepared them some hours before) Emma was stirring the mixture for the last time as the sugar had finally dissolved. Mrs. Farnley increased the heat for a moment or two and then brought the liquid back to a simmer for about ten minutes, after which the two women removed the pan and placed it on a wooden table, and covered it with a lid to let the mixture infuse. They were straining the wine into the large Wassail Bowl when a maid came back into the kitchen and told the children, "Your Aunt Guinivere and Uncle Solomon and Uncle Joseph have arrived—"

Tearing off their smocks, the children ran out screaming and up the stairs and through the green baize doors to the entrance hall, where Joseph, Solomon, and Guinivere (looking beautiful in a white velvet cloak) and their children were divesting themselves of their coats, cloaks, hats, gloves, sticks, bonnets, and boots, piling them all onto a waif called Nora who had come from the London League to "assist" the Forsters in their celebrations.

Solomon gave a woolen bag of parcels to Mrs. Farnley, who had followed the children up the stairs. The group entered the drawing room and breathed in the pungent fragrance of the Christmas tree whose tapers were now all lit.

"Beautiful, beautiful," Solomon pronounced.

"Yes, yes, as always," Joseph agreed.

Mrs. Farnley added Solomon's brightly wrapped beribboned parcels to the others underneath the boughs of the three—green, red, yellow parcels all done up in contrasting ribbons and bows with name tags on them.

Over ten feet tall, the tree sparkled and glittered. At the top of the tree four waxen angels held aloft a star made of spun glass. Following the German tradition, every branch was laden with good things to eat like Pfefferkuchen, and Marzipan made into the shapes of apples, oranges, and pears. Perched on the higher branches were fairies and elves, while on the lower branches, where the children could reach them, were gaily painted wooden dolls, drummer boys, fiddlers, and horn players.

Elijah, resplendent in a purple satin stock over a white vest and white shirt that ended in pleated cuffs à la Disraeli and stone-colored trousers, stood near the hearth in which the Yule log lay. At his side, Theodisia was dressed in green velvet, her blond hair covered by a turban. In the back of the room, on a straight-backed chair, barely visible, sat Clara Lustig dressed in her usual grey silk.

The children ran to the tree and read off the name tags: "To Emma from Aunt Gwinnie," "To Albert from Poppa," "To William from Uncle Solomon. . . ." What could be inside? Each present was picked up and examined and shaken, and as his or her name was read out the child would run up to the donor and beg and ask and plead, "What is it? Is it a soldier? Skates? Is it a doll? If it's not a doll, what is it?"

"Children" someone warned, "do be careful. Don't race around. Remember you are not to open your presents until after the Yule log has been lighted [another Forster tradition]. So calm yourselves."

But they couldn't, of course. They were almost in a frenzy. They couldn't keep still and calm and they moved and jerked around, and squealed and giggled and shouted and whispered conspiratorially with one another.

Each time the front door opened the children would run out squealing and return with the Redburys and their children, three sons and a daughter, or the Barings and their children. And the Wiltons, the Chesterfields . . . the Strooksburys arrived not only with their five children but with Mrs. Strooksbury's aged parents, Mr. and Mrs. Overton, the ancient father dressed in knee breeches and silk stockings. A bachelor whom the children didn't know arrived with his aged aunt and her companion. And then someone they had met the evening before, Mrs.

Strooksbury's friend, the retired tea merchant Mr. Isaac Coverly, appeared carrying two bags of gifts.

"I do wish Aunt Mathilda would get here," complained William to Theodisia. "She's always late, isn't she, Momma?" The children knew they would have to wait for that branch of the family to arrive before the Yule log could be lighted and they would be allowed to open their presents. Oh, it was maddening. Where were Aunt Mathilda and Uncle Brian?

Finally, as the clock struck two o'clock, Elijah, who was just as annoyed as the children—where were Mathilda and her brood?—was just about to give them permission to open their presents regardless when they arrived.

Vanessa came into the room last, her parents and her sisters entering first like heralds preceding royalty. And perhaps rightfully so. For a hush fell on the company as she stood there in the doorway of the room alone in her fourteen-year-old beauty.

Mathilda had dressed Vanessa in amethyst velvet trimmed with silver brocade. A small corsage of pink roses clung to her slender waist. Around her throat a diamond and amethyst necklace whose stone had been part of the King's Ransom[18] sparkled.

She stood there receiving homage—as she would for years to come—then, smiling, she went up to her Uncle Elijah, curtsied, rose gracefully, and moving into his open arms gave him a kiss. Albert, the twins, and Edward looked at her as if they were seeing her for the first time in their lives.

"Well, now that we are all here," said Elijah, looking pointedly at his sister, "we can light the Yule log. Are you ready, Deirdre?"

She nodded. As the youngest child in the family it was her duty to light the log, decorated with purple flowers, that was resting on its bed of hot ashes. Deirdre was the one who must pour the wine out of the large carafe onto the log. She was always fearful of dropping it. "Do everything slowly," Guinivere had told her, "and you shall do everything right."

Mrs. Farnley handed her the carafe. Deirdre tilted the bottle slowly until it was on its side. When the wine had been poured and the bottle was upside down Mrs. Farnley took it out of her hands, somewhat brusquely, and handed her a box of matches. This was the part that frightened Deirdre. Taking a match out of the box, she knelt down, struck the match, and then, reaching out her hand, lit the wine-soaked log. Instantaneously the log was wreathed in blue and yellow flames.

18. Vanessa's grandfather, Jorem Forster, bequeathed a ransom in jewels to his favorite granddaughter, Vanessa Herrod. See Chapter 8 in *City of Childhood.—R. Lowe*

Elijah lifted her up and then announced: "Children, you may open your presents now."

Soon the room was strewn with the flotsam and jetsam of scraps of glittering paper and ribbon. After a while the children's enthusiastic squeals subsided, their faces aglow, their curls in a tangle—even Vanessa's—and they settled in to admire their gifts.

Emma opened Poppa's present last. A small parcel wrapped in gold paper and tied with a silver string. Restraining herself, she unwrapped it carefully, folding the paper neatly and curling the string around her fingers into a circle, which she then placed on top of the paper. It was a small green leather box with an embossed golden *E* in its center. Before opening it she looked for Elijah—she was quite sure he was watching her. He was. He was standing, talking to Mrs. Strooksbury, but he was looking at her. She looked down and opened the box.

Inside it on dark blue velvet lay a ring, a garnet stone surrounded by a band of gold. She put it on her left forefinger and stretched her hand out before her, moving it back and forth, watching it catch the light. Suddenly, a wordless intuition seized her—and she understood that *she* had been "chosen." Like Franz had "chosen" Clara. She lifted up her glowing face. He was still watching her as she knew he would be. She smiled across the room at him, her face radiant with love. A moment in time that sank back into her unconscious to lie there glowing and winking in the depths of her mind, just as the garnet glowed and winked on her finger.

Guileless. Ingenuous, thought Elijah, looking at Emma, feeling a sudden foreboding, a surge of anxiety while pretending to listen to Mrs. Strooksbury's boring prattle. He wanted to go to Emma immediately, but he didn't. Instead he found himself generating suitable replies to the woman's irrelevant chatter.

He had been afraid the ring was too grown-up for Emma. Theodisia was against it. "It is inappropriate," she had said, and of course that decided the matter for him. He would give the ring to Emma.

Later in the evening it occurred to Elijah that no one had ever looked at him the way Emma had that afternoon.

The sound of the bell announcing dinner was heard. Mrs. Farnley stood in the doorway, her face stern but her eyes twinkling.

"Dinner is served," she said.

Elijah and Theodisia leading the way, the other Forsters and their friends following, they entered the dining room from whence delicious aromas had been drifting through the cracks of the doors for hours.

During the second course a raging quarrel broke out between Mr. Strooksbury and the eldest son of Mr. Baring about the Corn Laws, just as it had the year before. Solomon was just about to join the argument on Mr. Baring's side when Elijah rose and clinking his glass with a fork said firmly but good-humoredly, "Gentlemen, gentlemen, let us not forget that this is the season of peace and forgiveness . . . *and* remembrance. I propose a toast to absent friends; to loved ones who have departed; to my father, Jorem Forster . . . to my nephew . . . Sidney Forster." There was a hush and Clara, glancing at Guinivere, saw that her eyes were bright with tears. She also saw that Nicholas Renton, who for some reason was using the name Isaac Coverly, and who was sitting next to Guinivere, placed his hand on hers.

But in a few minutes Joseph, who was a bit drunk by this time, began a long and boring story about a man who was mad for snuff: "Possessed enough snuffboxes to enable him to use a different one every day of the year. Clothes, carriages, horses, and furniture all snuff-colored . . ." until his sister whispered to him, "Keep quiet!" After that everyone seemed to regain their good humor.

After dinner the cloth was removed and the dessert plates set. The room was darkened and Mrs. Farnley entered with Cook's masterpiece, the plum pudding, a wreath of fire blazing around the cake.

When they returned to the drawing room it had been tidied up and the hall table had been moved in set with the Wassail Bowl and its cups. Elijah dipped his cup in, sipped from it, and announced: "As fine as the nectar of the gods! Well done, children."

Then there were recitations by the children: Emma recited "To a Skylark" by Percy Bysshe Shelley. Each of her male cousins recited from Horace, first in Latin, and then in English for the benefit of the ladies. Several of the gentlemen pleaded with Vanessa to sing, and she finally consented to sing a few carols.

While the children were playing Snap Dragon the musicians arrived: two violinists, a cellist, and a pianist. The servants rolled up the rugs and shoved them into Theodisia's morning room.

At this point Joseph, taking his gold watch from his vest pocket, announced in loud tones that it was time for Jorem's Christmas story, and left the room. The children followed him as if he were the Pied Piper, out of the room and across the hall to the library, where chairs had been set up.

After everyone was seated Joseph cleared his throat.

The children knew the story, having heard it every Christmas of their lives, but every Christmas it was as if they heard it for the first time. Even Vanessa had come with them to hear it again.

"Now you do know," Joseph said, beginning the story,[19] "of course that the animals in Marlborough Gardens celebrated also Christmas—including the ferrets, nasty little creatures wearing their 'copes,' but Father Christmas had presents for them too—"

Joseph, his back to the door, heard someone enter the library. His back stiffened. It was probably Mathilda, who would tell him he was too drunk to tell the story. Well, he wasn't and he would. He turned around. But it was Mr. Coverly, Mrs. Strooksbury's friend. Joseph smiled. What did he want?

"Is it permitted?"

"To join the children? Yes, of course. Do come in and sit down. There." Joseph pointed to an empty chair between Emma and Edward. Odd, thought Joseph. Odd thing to do, but then Mr. Coverly was odd, wasn't he?

Nicholas's heart was beating rapidly. He had not wanted to "follow" Joseph—it was inappropriate—but it had proven irresistible. To hear Joseph tell Jorem's Christmas story in Elijah's house was a temptation he could not forgo. Momentarily envisioning himself as a child born not in Newgate but in Marlborough Gardens, Nicholas sat down between a brother and sister.

Joseph smiled at him again and continued the story.

—◆◦◦◦◆—

Sleepy, sated, gloriously full, the children went upstairs, where cots had been put up for them, for they would stay the night at Elijah's house; their maids would call for them in the morning. Moving up the stairs, the children heard the lighthearted laughter of the adults and the strains of the dance music.

Much later that night the Forsters and their friends went, as they did each Christmas, to ice skate on the lake. Wearing boots, cloaks, mantles, coats, muffled to the ears with hats and bonnets and with warm gloves and hands in muffs, they entered the Great South Gate and walked to the lake along a path that was lit with lanterns. The moon shone cold and bright.

The ice was lit with lanterns too. In a shed put up for the occasion, Mathilda's housekeeper, Mrs. Page, sat supervising urns of hot chocolate, though she had brandy for the gentlemen if they wished. Men

19. See *City of Childhood* for the Christmas story.—*R. Lowe*

and women both began removing their shoes and putting on their skates. They stepped onto the ice, warm with food and drink and good feeling. The musicians, who had followed them, stood on the bank playing waltzes.

Gliding along the ice in the moonlight, the Forsters and their friends resembled swans. Now and then, they encircled the statue of old Neptune, garlanded with a Christmas wreath, in the center of the lake.

When it grew colder and the moon moved closer to the horizon they wandered back to Elijah's house. Someone began to sing "Good King Wenceslas" and they all joined in, and so ended Christmas Day, 25 December 1838.

—◦◦◦◦—

1840

A whole year passed before Sir Timothy Eveshem finally died and, at last, vacated Jorem's house. During that year Nicholas, posing as Isaac Coverly, cultivated the Forsters. Solomon had pronounced him *gemütlich,* using a German term he had learned from his father, Jorem, whose English had been sprinkled with a few German expressions. Yes, Mr. Isaac Coverley was *gemütlich.*

Admittedly it was a short time for the Forsters to accept an outsider into their circle, but how could one dislike a man who, when invited to dinner, was always sure to send a basket of fruit or game or a bottle of wine—an expensive Moselle—to his hosts the day before? Or for the ladies a beautifully arranged corsage delivered by one of his exceptionally well-behaved servants? Mr. Coverly was captivating. Nothing less. They began to think of him with affection. And they prided themselves on admitting a relative stranger into their midst.

The Forster women took to him, too. Even before the men did. Strangely enough, Mr. Coverly seemed genuinely interested in their mundane lives: their problems with servants (he always had a word of advice on how to get the most work out of them) and their children. He made a point of remembering all the children's names and their respective ages. A woman could talk comfortably and as long as she wanted with him. And not only about children, but about other minor trepidations, fears that perhaps their own husbands might be impatient about, or even mock or ridicule.

The Forsters listened with sympathy when, some months after they met him, he related the terrible tragedy that had befallen his young wife and two sons in Switzerland many years ago. Buried in an avalanche in Simplon Pass! Unbelievable! And despite that catastrophe—how many people could have survived such a staggering blow?—he was always agreeable. Gracious even when a fierce political argument might break out among the gentlemen. Once the gentlemen had almost come to blows while dining at his house,[20] but Mr. Coverly's consummate tact (the "politesse" of a true gentleman, Brian had observed) soothed everyone's ruffled feathers.

Of course there was the matter of Kevin Francini. Working for Mr. Coverly! Where had he been all these years? Though none of the Forsters asked him this question directly, they had hinted at it, but to no avail. He pretended not to understand.

Mathilda in particular wondered. Seeing Kevin again brought back vivid memories of the time when as a young girl she had been in love with him, the beautiful young man her father had employed to help him create Marlborough Gardens. He had been the most handsome young man she had ever seen. Tall, broad-shouldered, with thick curly chestnut hair that hung in ringlets . . . rose-colored lips . . . their middle fullness drawn into a line that ended in a sort of secret and perpetual smile—that she had visualized kissing.

It began the day of the dedication ceremony—the day that the four Achilles' shields had been soldered to the four gates of the Garden. She recalled that there had been speeches, and that the Duke of Norwood, one of the many dignitaries present, had given a speech connecting natural beauty to classical antiquity and to God's will. Jorem's eyes had filled with tears but her eyes had been fastened on one face only: Kevin Francini's. *That* was the afternoon she had fallen totally and feverishly in love with Mr. Francini.

A month later, on a hot and humid night, she and Kevin were walking through the luminous mists to Blenheim Cliffs. "I want to show you something," he said, and taking her hand had led her to the new unfinished summerhouse, the belvedere.

"Your father does not know about it yet," he said as he pulled her inside it.

She gazed at the life-size statue of Apollo, naked except for sandals and a short cape flung over his outstretched right arm.

Suddenly Kevin drew her towards him. "Tell me you love me," he said. She was frightened, but when he kissed her something inside her opened up and she said, "Yes, I love you." He had fallen on his knees and proposed marriage to her. "Yes," she had said. "Yes."

---

20. Nicholas Renton had many houses available to him in London for whatever purposes he desired. During the time he was first posing as Isaac Coverly he reciprocated the Forsters' hospitality by inviting them to dine at a house located near their bank.

Who had told Jorem, she wondered. For when she came home that night—an hour before dawn—Jorem was waiting for her and he locked her in her room. The following day Jorem rushed her off to a boarding school in Essex, the same school Vanessa and her sisters went to now. She sat by his side while he told the headmistress that "Certain facts seem to indicate that my daughter is in need of being closely supervised." It was the most humiliating moment of her life. Six months later, when she returned, Kevin had vanished. What was he doing here now working for Mr. Coverly?

THE METAPHYSICS OF SEX

PART II: 1840–1841

Emma Forster

Edited by H. Van Buren and R. Lowe

PRELIMINARY COMMUNICATIONS

MARLBOROUGH GARDENS,
MIDSUMMER'S NIGHT, 1937

*There is a certain spot of ground in Blenheim Forest near Calypso's
Cave that is known as Piece of Moonlight. Here, on nights when the
moon is full, the glade is transformed into a silver paradise.*

*On those nights Lowe and I go there and pay our respects to an-
cient powers. Dancing under the pale moon, our heads held back, our
robes and long hair swirling in the languid air, we hum the ancient
melody.*

*Teasel with heads of silver-white grows here. And santolinas, dense
and mounding with soft stems and silver-felted threadlike leaves;
goat's beard with its tiny silver flowers; and feathery plumes of
meadow sweet, and silver-gray clematis. Peering out from the cloud-
gray rock, alpine buttercups and gentian—Kevin Francini's "gray garden," which he named Titania's Bower and some Forster (who, exactly, we do not know) renamed Piece of Moonlight.*

*Seated on a carpet of lamb's ears (Stachy lanata), a thick mat of
silver-gray leaves, Lowe unpacks our midnight repast: unleavened
bread, some figs and a honey ale that she made last month from one
of Mathilda's housekeeper Mrs. Page's recipes.*

*Moonlight sifts down through the canopy of juniper leaves. Drowsy
from wine, I nestle down on the soft velvety leaves of pale primulas,
my head resting on Lowe's lap, her dark hair black as printer's ink.*

*Except for the sound of Blenheim Brook babbling over its
pebbly bottom on its way to the cliff there is silence. Everything
sleeps. . . .*

We walk home along the banks of the brook, inhaling the scent of the lilies and the violets that grow there. The moon is reflected in the flowing curve of its waters, our way lighted by the fireflies, our skirts and slippers soaked with dew.

It is one of those nights when we decide to work throughout the night on various tasks related to the Forster archives.

I work on a study of Darius; his fundamental thinking on human nature and his belief in the necessity of war.[21] *A biographical sketch, which includes a brief account of Darius's absorption with Jessie Malkin's five sons, is followed by an analysis of his military theories.*

Lowe, influenced by Emma's interest in Freud, and using Freud's study of Leonardo da Vinci as her model, is writing a psycho-history of Nicholas's early life in order to determine why Nicholas, having made the decision to ruin Elijah and seduce Guinivere, hesitated. "What is it, then, that inhibits him in accomplishing the task?" (The Interpretation of Dreams, *Sigmund Freud*).

At dawn we gather in the library in the lodge, a beautiful room with tall windows between the bookcases looking on to the inner court that separates the main house from the lodge. Sinking into luxurious armchairs, I listen to Lowe read aloud from Emma's translation of Freud's Three Contributions to the Theory of Sex:

"Contribution II, Infantile sexuality: The Neglect of the Infantile. It is part of the folklore about the sexual instinct that it is not present in childhood; and that it makes its first appearance in the period of life called puberty . . ."

As the first rays of sunlight stream into the windows Lowe stops, ending with: "He who perceives the sated child sink back from the mother's breast, and fall asleep with reddened cheeks and blissful smile, must admit that this scene remains characteristic of the appearance of complete sexual fulfillment in later life."

---

21. In 1837, on May 26, the Forster children fought a battle on Marlborough Marshes. Darius led one army; Albert led the opposing. See *City of Childhood.—R. Lowe*

I I

NICHOLAS GIVES A BALL

The ultimate aim of all love affairs, whether played in the sock or in the buskin, is actually more important than all other aims in man's life; and therefore it is quite worthy of the profound seriousness with which everyone pursues it.

—Schopenhauer, *The World as Will and Representation*

ON the second of January 1840 at precisely 10:16 P.M., Sir Timothy Eveshem finally breathed his last. About an hour later Mrs. Skipton, his housekeeper, pocketed a nice piece of change for herself when she reported her employer's death to Kevin, with whom she had an "arrangement."

On the fourth of January, Nicholas sent a long, beautifully worded letter to Elijah requesting the privilege of renting Jorem's house, offering at the same time an enormous sum of money for that privilege. The offer was accepted on the tenth of that month and within a fortnight (January 23) Nicholas moved into Jorem's house.

Almost immediately he began making the necessary structural changes in the cellar and at the rear of the house. At the same time, guided by Kevin's remarkable visual memory, he restored the drawing rooms, the library, the study, and the ballroom on the second floor to their original splendor.

When all was completed, near the end of February, Nicholas decided to give a ball followed by a supper. "To repay in part," he told his new friends, their "generous hospitality," their "bountiful kindness."

The Forsters accepted with pleasure.

Kevin was given the task of arranging the ball.

"I want them to remember this ball forever," Nicholas said. "Do not spare the expense. Do what is necessary, and then—do what is outrageous."

———◦◦⊙◦◦———

As always Kevin was sensitive to Nicholas's unexpressed desires. He was certain that Nicholas was thinking about love . . . about falling in love. He, as well as Stokes and Angel, had noticed Nicholas's interest in Guinivere. Last month she and her husband (they were the only couple invited) had dined with Nicholas at his house on Holborn Street.

Nicholas had been unable to keep his eyes off her. His concentration on her had been so blatant it was a wonder that the husband had not noticed. But, Kevin thought, men like Solomon were born cuckolds. Uxurious but unimaginative. Considerate but self-involved. And Guinivere? She had said little throughout the evening, but Kevin knew that it was impossible even for a woman as "good" as Guinivere to withstand worship. Nicholas had gazed at her as if she were a goddess and he a lowly supplicant. Kevin recalled that Nicholas had said, when asked what he intended to do with his treasure in jewels: "I shall lay them at the feet of the woman with whom I fall in love." It was foolish of Nicholas to fall in love with Guinivere, a "good" woman *and* a Forster, but Kevin knew he could do nothing about it. Long ago he had realized that people commit their follies first, and then afterwards contrive their reasons, sometimes enormously elaborate reasons, for having done so. Sometimes Nicholas reminded Kevin of a hawk, at other times of a cheetah, but these past few months Nicholas brought to mind the figure of the childlike Eros, the youngest of the gods. Eros and Aphrodite. Nicholas and Guinivere.

The theme of the ball, Kevin decided, would be love . . . romantic love.

Watteau's painting . . . sunset . . . the stylish ladies . . . the gorgeous pastel trains of their dresses, trailing, soft and lambent . . . walking with their lovers at sunset to embark on the boat sailing to the island of Cythera. . . .

And another picture, the one Botticelli painted for Lorenzo de' Medici . . . Venus . . . driven by the west winds, gliding over the waves in a seashell . . . to the isle of Cythera.

First a blue-green carpet was laid in the large octagonal hall and run up the broad staircase. Next the walls were swathed in shimmering silken drapes of soft pink and pale gold, fastened with gilded arrows. Then in the niches of the great hall Kevin painted, in tempera, Aphrodite of Melos, Aphrodite of Cnidus, of Canova, of Capua . . . and at the head of the stairs he placed a life-size stone copy of the delicately formed Aphrodite, the work of the late Attic sculptor Cleomenes.

On the eve of the ball, the banister of the great staircase was festooned with white and pink roses. Set on every landing were huge silver tubs filled with fresh-cut flowers of delicate hues. Elongated flames from the two hearths that burned all night danced in time with the light of silver torcheres that hung on the walls.

As each carriage arrived, footmen dressed in shell pink livery and powdered wigs assisted the beautifully gowned women out of their carriages, and led them up the front stairs; their male escorts, chins set firmly over their well-starched cravats, followed. Chatting, jostling each other, the men and women moved slowly up the great stairs to the sound of an orchestra playing Handel's "Water Music."

At the top of the stairs Angel, acting as a butler, announced each new arrival. "Mr. and Mrs. Elijah Forster," "Mr. and Mrs. Brian Herrod . . ."

Mrs. Strooksbury arrived wearing black satin, lace, and diamonds. Guinivere wore pale pink velvet, her long blond hair done in a coronet, a wreath of small white roses woven into it. Theodisia, dressed in green silk, wore garnets; Mathilda, red taffeta and diamonds.

Inside the ballroom Nicholas, suited in black silk and velvet tartan waistcoat, greeted them. A black pearl glowed at the center of his white silk stock.

The ball opened with a traditional country dance—the ladies lined up on one side, the men on the other. After the dance the floor cleared, and servants came into the room bearing trays filled with refreshments and drinks.

More and more people arrived and the ballroom grew crowded. Everyone was dancing. As they swirled around the room the women's dresses—all the colors of the rainbow—were reflected in the wall of mirrors Nicholas had constructed. Jewels shone on their ears, their fingers, and shimmered on their breasts as they waltzed around on gentlemen's arms.

The Forster men were taller than the other men, their sleek blond heads glowing above the rest as they danced with their wives and their friends' wives. They felt perfectly at home in their father's house.

During a pause in the dancing, Theodisia went to speak to Guinivere, who was standing next to an open window fanning herself. She had danced with Elijah, Joseph, and her husband, Solomon.

"You look so beautiful this evening," said Theodisia. "You always look beautiful but tonight even more so."

Guinivere smiled. "Thank you. And you look wonderful. That color suits you. It complements your skin." Nicholas, who was dancing with Mrs. Redbury, whirled by and nodded. "Tell me Theo, what do you think of Mr. Coverly?"

"Oh, he must be enormously wealthy, Gwinnie. I know he is unusually generous. Just the other day he sent us a basket of fruit from one of his estates in Hampshire."

"Ah, he sent us one too. . . ."

At this point the "generous" man came over to them, bowed to Theodisia, and asked Guinivere to dance with him.

Guinivere blushed. Why did she, she wondered. She looked around for her husband, who was talking to Mr. Strooksbury and Joseph in a corner of the room. The musicians were into the second measure as Nicholas held out his arm to her, looking intently into her eyes.

Disconcerted, frowning slightly, she placed her small gloved hand on his arm as he led her onto the dance floor. As the notes of the violin sounded, he placed his arm around her waist and began to waltz her past a row of seated women chatting among themselves.

Up and down they went, turning, her pink velvet skirt flaring out. He held her by the waist lightly but firmly. Though he said nothing, it seemed to her as if he were speaking. His dark green eyes never left hers. It seemed to her as if they were asking her something. Beseeching. His green eyes had black shining centers, as black and as lustrous as the cloth of his evening jacket. She felt as if the whole room were watching them.

The musicians, seated on a broad dais decorated with myrtle, played on. Guinivere tore her gaze away from him. No one was watching them. It was all in her mind. Above her she heard the mellifluous cooing of the white doves in the cages that were hung from the ceiling. And then she saw the reflection in the wall of mirrors: Nicholas, diminutive but handsome, quite handsome, electrifying really, and herself looking unusually beautiful. Her heart began to beat faster as they danced 'round and 'round without speaking—not a word, not a single word—until the music finally ended, when he murmured into her ear, "Thank you," and led her gently back to the spot from which he had taken her.

The music started up again—a quadrille, the Lancers. He extended his arm again towards her. Without thinking Guinivere went with him, and they began moving quickly through the intricate figures of the dance. In the two-hand turn, he held her hand tightly as they both turned; in the ladies' chain, he caught her left hand and turned her into place beside himself. When the dance ended, he signaled the band to play on. He held her, refusing to let her go. A waltz this time. His arm around her waist began to feel like a cord of flame. She tried to speak, to say something, something neutral, innocuous . . . trivial. But every-

thing she thought of seemed exaggeratedly important and of great moment. She felt intoxicated. But because she had never felt that way
before—for though she loved Solomon she had never experienced passion—she could not understand what it was. She only knew that she
felt alive for the first time in her life. And it was frightening her. She
also sensed in some strange way that Isaac Coverly knew what was
happening to her. So she said nothing. But her cheeks were pink with
excitement and her eyes shone.

She was used to feeling almost childlike at Solomon's side. He was
very tall and serious. But Isaac was her height. It was as if he were her
twin. There was a spray of white roses in his lapel. How strange but
apropos, she thought, that he should be wearing white roses like herself.
The room . . . so very lovely . . . captivating, really. She felt as if she
were in some kind of spell. The music ended.

He returned her to Mrs. Strooksbury. This time, Guinivere told herself, when the music began again she would say no. She would say: I
am too tired. But when the music started up again, he asked Mrs.
Strooksbury to dance. Beaming, the other woman went off with him
to dance in three-quarter time.

Guinivere, settling down alone on a settee, watched Brian talk to
Elijah. She was sure they were discussing Joseph. They had put him in
one of the rooms downstairs, with the help of the butler, after he had
fallen on the dance floor. Solomon joined them.

Who would take him home, she wondered. Suddenly she understood:
Love! It was "love" that had done this to Joseph. Joseph had "loved"
Consuelo but she had left him. Involuntarily she shuddered, and then
she saw her husband looking at her, nodding. Automatically she smiled
at him.

Someone began playing a Mozart sonata, and when that was finished
supper was announced and the crowd began moving down the stairs to
the rooms set aside for the feast Mrs. Kitto (now Nicholas's housekeeper) had prepared for them.

After supper, Guinivere and Solomon said their good-nights and
walked home, their carriage following behind them.

—◆≈◇◇≈◆—

Later that night Guinivere listened to Solomon discuss Joseph as he
undressed in one of the alcoves of their bedroom, an enormous room,
actually two rooms made into one, furnished with an enormous bed
that they shared. She lay in bed waiting for him.

"He is a disaster!" he said. "He gets worse and worse. Something
will have to be done, but what? We've spoken to him. We've suggested

he go away for a while. But he won't, he said. He's too busy. Busy! With what? Certainly not with working—"

"Joseph . . . is brokenhearted." Her voice was solemn. The words had come out of her mouth unexpectedly.

Solomon came out of the alcove in his nightshirt, a look of surprise on his face. He went over to the bed and sat down on it. "Oh, Gwinnie," he said, reaching for her hands, "I do love you so. You are the kindest, the most wonderful woman in the world."

"It is true, you know. He loved Consuelo and she abandoned him."

"Yes, and for whom? A servant. Well, perhaps he is brokenhearted, but we still must do something about him." He got into bed and lay next to her. Since Sidney's death they rarely had intercourse. Unlike Elijah, Solomon was a considerate man. He sensed her reluctance and had respected it. Instead of imposing something on her against her will he had taken a mistress, Mrs. Cornwind, the greengrocer's widow. She resembled Guinivere somewhat and he had trained her subsequently to act more and more like Guinivere. Tonight he wondered whether Guinivere might not be ready to have sex with him. She had looked so unusually alive and beautiful at the hall. He put his hand on her thigh. In the past when he had done that, if she was "ready" she had indicated that she was by moving her thigh just a little, a fraction of an inch towards him. He always wondered whether or not she knew that. But tonight there was no response.

They said good-night to one another as they had every night of their married life.

"Good night, my darling Gwinnie, may you have pleasant dreams."

"Good night, my dearest Solomon, may you have them too."

Lying awake she heard Solomon snoring softly at her side. For the first time since Sidney's death Guinivere did not think of her son as her last thought of the day. She thought of Isaac Coverly. She felt his arm around her waist. And when she finally fell asleep, she dreamt that she was wandering through Marlborough Gardens searching for the place that the children called Piece of Moonlight.

12

PREDILECTIONS AND INTENTIONS

The madness of Eros seizes one's heart without choosing it, connecting 'her divine soul to her mortal libido' (Plato, Symp. 202E). For the energy that carries the soul to its highest pinnacle is the same energy present in the instinct that immortalizes the human race.

—Clara F. Lustig, "The Right to Lose One's Head," *Blackwood's Edinburgh Magazine,* Vol. 5, 1840

Though crippled and deformed, Toby, Nicholas's adopted sister, was filled with quicksilver energy. Moving like some incredible tumbler, her thin, twisted limbs in constant motion, her head like the head of a small bird, jerking forward and back, peering, listening . . . ready to fly, plunge, scuttle away, but chattering as she sewed—the rich gold velvet slipping through her small clever hands like a river of gold. Cutting and stitching away, the golden-colored thread melting into the material that quivered and lurched like a living thing as she moved this way and that.

"Oh! She'll look like a queen when I get through with it, Master, a fairy queen. . . ."

Around the small seamstress's feet flowed gillings of ribbon, gauze, lace, and the like. On the table next to her lay her surgical kit, as she called it: scissors of different lengths, razors, hooks, measuring sticks, boxes of pins, spools of different colored threads, and needles of all sizes. And wrapped in cotton, her tailor's chalk.

"Now a tiny gusset here," the small creature said, turning the material. "Gussets galore! Aye, and tucks and pleats! Aye, I like them all. So cunning and clever they are. And this, the finest velvet!" She began joining a side seam. "Perhaps an edging of lace, dear Master, inserted on the shoulder?" Her small head bent to one side as she looked up at Nicholas in a questioning way.

"It is you, Toby, who is the master in this predicament. Not I. I rely solely on your judgment what will be best . . . most elegant . . . most ladylike."

A small smile flashed on Toby's face as she dived down into the heaps of lace around her skirt. "Ah, that a darling piece," she crooned. "Now wouldn't you like to be sewn, you darling thing, just there on the lady's bodice," she said to the small strip of ecru lace she began to stick rapidly on the shoulder seam, "on to Milady Guinivere's ball gown."

They were in the bedroom Kevin had designed for Nicholas, a huge room created out of three rooms in the rear of the house. One end was occupied by a single narrow bed, a ladder-back chair, and a desk, all of which stood crowded together on the bare wooden floor while the rest of the room, sumptuously carpeted, was occupied by four very large dollhouses (each of them over four feet tall) that were exact replicas of Elijah's, Solomon's, Joseph's, and Mathilda's houses. They had been two years in the making—the first finished was Solomon's— and now, three months after Nicholas had moved into Jorem's house, they were finally installed.

The dollhouses were set on turntables so that by merely giving the structure a slight push one could turn the house any way one wanted. The backs were permanently open, but the facades could be removed too. Tacked on the wall above each house were carefully printed lists of numerous articles of furniture, cutlery, silver, dinnerware, clothing, books, etc. that the house contained. Each article that had been duplicated in miniature from the list had a red check beside it.

This morning Elijah's house was turned and its facade had been removed so that one could see in. Emma and Clara were in the schoolroom on the third floor. Emma, seated on a chair, poring over a book, was dressed in a blue blouse and pinafore with black boots and brown stockings. Behind her desk sat Clara, dressed in her grey silk and with a cap on her head. The dolls were approximately a foot tall, articulate, and easily recognizable.

Theodisia and Elijah had been placed in bed together, while the servant Daisy lurked in the open doorway. Mrs. Lovesley was in her kitchen with two servants, Jupie and Cora, preparing breakfast. A kipper rested on the kitchen table. And Mrs. Farnley stood in front of the sideboard in the dining room.

What was astonishing were the accurate likenesses. Theodisia looked unhappy, Elijah looked successful, Mrs. Farnley looked composed and competent, Mrs. Lovesley looked tipsy. And Emma gazed worshipfully into the glass eyes of her mentor, the cold, aloof Clara.

Toby left her sewing and went up to Solomon's house to remove its facade. Inside, each piece of furniture was an exact duplicate of the original in scale. She looked at Guinivere's bedroom, sitting room, and boudoir. The closet door was open and she could see the tiny dresses hanging there.

In the sitting room, on a rose-colored divan, sat Guinivere dressed in white muslin, a teal-blue sash around her waist, the only doll present in the house except for Mrs. Bridgewater, mending some clothes in her sitting room on the first floor behind the kitchen. Great care had been taken in creating Guinivere's face and figure. Her wig was made of human hair the exact color of Guinivere's, pale gold, and her doll's face was innocent and placid as she sat reading Bulwer-Lytton's *Pelham, or The Adventures of a Gentleman.*

Mathilda's and Joseph's houses were both shut.

Ever since Clara and others had begun to give Nicholas lists, meticulous in every detail, his workmen had been building the dollhouses and Toby had been making the dolls and their individual wardrobes.

Toby's childhood had had no dolls in it. Or any other kind of toy. After Dame Lou's baby girl was born, her father, Emmet Cole, the turnkey, had taken her away from Dame Lou and given her to a "baby farmer" named Mother Scarlet to raise. Miraculously surviving the woman's brutality, Toby grew up to first assist and then apprentice herself to a dressmaker. Five years older than Nicholas, she had visited Newgate on a regular basis bringing food and liquor with her for Dame Lou and Nicholas.

After two years at the dressmakers', she became an improver, then a second hand, and finally learned to design, cut, and arrange work. During the season (March till the middle of July) she had worked sixteen to eighteen hours a day for nine shillings a week. Once Nicholas was successful, he looked for and found her working in a large establishment and brought her home to live with him.

She held up the dress to the Guinivere doll. Taking a tape measure out of one of her many pockets, she measured the length of the figure and the dress she was making.

"Now, my Lady Guinivere, you shall be taken to the privacy of your boudoir, where I shall undress you and try on your new ball gown. Come now, don't fuss. It's all for your own good, you'll see . . ." And then, without looking at Nicholas, she continued. "Tell me, dear Master, is she really as passive and as lifeless as this doll looks? Has she no fire? She seems rather dull to me. What do you see in her?"

"Compared to you, Toby, she *is* dull, I confess."

"Ah . . ."

"But it is because her life has been dull. Except for the death of her son Sidney, nothing has ever happened to her that was unusual in any way. Of course Sidney's death was not that unusual either. Children often die. What was unusual was that she did not recover from his death. She found herself becoming more involved with the dead boy than with her living children."

"How do you know all of this? You have only met her a few times. And always with other people present. What a fool you are to fall in love the way you have. Because you have, haven't you? But that is not love, what you are feeling. That is sickness."

"Whatever it is, Toby, I have not chosen it. It was preordained. I have been chosen to experience it. Do not laugh, Toby. I believe it. And what is more I do so gladly. You see, I have lived my entire life, until I met her, without knowing what it was to fall in love. Now I know. And I shall be forever grateful to her for that. I love you and I love Kevin, but I am *in* love with Guinivere. Guinivere . . . I do not even expect or want or desire her to be in love with me. It is enough for me to love her. You call her dull and passive, but I am grateful for her passivity. I do not wish her to respond. I wish only to look, to contemplate, to think, to dream of her. At this moment she is perfect to me. There is not the slightest blemish on my love for her. I mean nothing to her now. She has met me, as you say, only a few times. Her eyes took me in without approval or revulsion, they merely saw me, as she would see a blade of grass, her servant, a passerby—"

"I do not believe that. Nor do I think that you do. But perhaps the lady is a somnambulist! Perhaps she is blind!"

"Perhaps you are right on both counts. . . . I shall not forsake you, Toby."

"You have already!"

"What do you mean?"

"Yes, you have forsaken me. You are a fool. Mooning over her, imagining her not as she is but as you wish her to be. I am jealous, of course. No one shall ever feel that way about me. As long as I live. It does not happen to the physically misshapen . . . and it shall not happen to you either, Nicholas! You love. But shall you be loved? I doubt it. Certainly not by her. But perhaps I should follow in your footsteps. Perhaps I should at least partake in love. Who shall I fall in love with though?" The door opened and Kevin walked in. "Shall I fall in love with Kevin after all these years? Why not? I shall begin by telling you, Kevin, that I have conceived an enormous sexual passion for you. I can no longer sleep at night, tossing and turning as I do, yearning for you. There, what do you say to that, Kevin?"

"At last the love I have for you is finally being returned. Dear Toby, I have loved you for years. Does this mean we are engaged?"

"Bah!" She bit her lips and growled. "Men! Impossible creatures! I am leaving and I am taking my surgical kit with me!" She sashayed over to the table, swept all her tools of the trade into a large bag, and limped past Kevin without looking at him, and past Nicholas without saying good-bye.

Nicholas went over to Solomon's house and turned Guinivere right side up, since Toby had left her standing on her head in the boudoir.

"I have the information you asked me to get for you," said Kevin.

"Good. I am longing to hear from your very own lips about the secret financial life of my neighbor and landlord, Elijah Forster. I was right, of course, to suspect he had one. Men like him generally do. Hidden and concealed from Solomon, the pillar of society, and Joseph, the weakling and drunkard. And since Elijah's province in the bank is foreign investments, I assume it has to do with that."

"Exactly. I see I need say no more. Well and good, I shall listen—"

"Forgive me for showing off, Kevin. Something Clara said to me one day tipped me off. Who lives in Essex? Why does he go there regularly? I see by the look on your face you know."

"I do. The man who lives in Essex—at a place called Albion, by the way—is none other than Miles Ryder, our old friend."

"Really. Miles Ryder, the opium trader. Isn't he the same gentleman for whom we arranged a burglary last year?"

"The very same, Sir. We arranged to burglarize his brother's estate in Scotland and steal not only the jewels but specific pieces of furniture desirable to him, for 'sentimental reasons,' he told us, which now grace his estate in Essex."

"A small world, as they say . . ."

"As you know, Commander, Ryder went out to India thirty years ago as an officer in the East India Company but eventually went into business for himself in Macao. The opium business. In ten years he was so successful he was dubbed the Prince of Macao. *But* did you know that it was Jorem Forster who staked him in the opium business? And that the Forster Midland Bank received annually a percentage of profit from Ryder's firm in the East, which the books carried as a tea account? Elijah found out about it. I don't know how, but ever since he has been interested in renewing and increasing the percentage in Ryder's trade. That is why he has cultivated Miles Ryder."

"So what's the difficulty, as if I didn't know?"

"Exactly. A matter of capital. Besides the necessity for maintaining secrecy about this part of the business from his brothers. He is eager, very eager, to invest personally in Ryder's firm but he cannot divert a sufficient amount of the bank's capital without making Solomon suspicious. So he is looking for capital. He is, as you would say, 'vulnerable' to approach from us. By the way, do you intend to ruin him?"

"Perhaps . . . I certainly intend to injure his pocketbook and his self-esteem. I intend to manipulate him. I intend to puncture his pride."

"Why?"

"Because it will satisfy me to do so. It will satisfy me to cheat and humiliate him. I also want him to know that I have done that."

"Why?"

Nicholas did not answer at once. He never let his feelings show, even though at times they were so intense that he thought only a bullet through the brain would relieve him. At times his brain felt swollen with venom, as if a poisonous snake lived inside the coils of his mind, a viper injecting the twisted brain matter with lethal toxins. And yet nothing of this extreme state of feeling ever showed in his face. There was no sign, no chill along one's spine when one met him, no onrush of intuition that foreshadowed danger. So controlled was he that not even Kevin, closer to him than any other human being besides Toby, suspected the depths of his murderous passions.

"I suggest that you do not pursue this further, Kevin."

But Kevin persisted nevertheless. "What profit can there be in ruining Elijah? Why does he mean so much to you? Perhaps if you told me I could help you ruin him. I'm not averse to it. My loyalty is to you, not Jorem's children."

Nicholas stared at Kevin. He trusted Kevin. Kevin was loyal. Should he tell Kevin that Elijah was his half brother and that Jorem was his father? But like a uxorious husband who suspects his wife of infidelity, he backed away from disclosing these inner thoughts to Kevin. He did not wish to see in Kevin's face the slightest doubt about this supposition, though to Nicholas's mind it was no longer a supposition or an interesting idea, but a fact. Still, he did not wish to state his case. He did not wish to argue or to frighten Kevin into agreement.

"I believe you are loyal to me. And that you will never betray me, will you, Kevin?"

"I never shall," Kevin said simply.

"Forgive my anger."

"Forgiven. By the way, I almost forgot, Mr. Strooksbury is waiting to speak to you in the library. . . ."

"Yes, of course. Go . . . I shall come down shortly. I wish to be alone for a few minutes."

When Kevin left, Nicholas went over to the Guinivere doll and picked her up. Holding the doll in his hand, he looked into the blue glass eyes and said, "One day you will tell me, 'I love you.' You will look into my eyes and tell me that." He put her down gently on the small rose-colored divan. He picked up the Elijah doll then, and after staring at it for a moment or two, tore off his head. Moving to the mirror, he composed his face into agreeable lines. Now he was ready to speak to Mr. Strooksbury. After all, Mr. Strooksbury was a useful connection.

13

ELIJAH

Elijah loved Joseph far more than he loved Solomon. But even though he had usurped Joseph's place as head of the family, a part of him still lived, intact, as the three-year-old child who had worshiped his older brother.

—R. Lowe, *On the Character and Diffusion of Forster Culture,* three black-and-white plates. Mantikos Press, London, 1938, one pound

ELIJAH seldom dreamed, or if he did he rarely remembered it. But when he did, he categorized his dreams the way he had been taught to do at Warrenton, where he learned from Homer's *Iliad* the fundamental distinction between significant and insignificant dreams; between the dreams that come from the "gate of ivory" that deceive, "bringing words that find no fulfillment," and the dreams that come from the "gate of polished horn" and "bring true issues to pass."

Elijah was basically a prudent man, even though he was inclined to be capricious in sexual matters, so when he awakened from this particular dream he took careful notice of it.

He had dreamt that his father, Jorem, standing at the end of his bed, had told him that he, Elijah, was not to come over . . . yet. That Joseph needed him. That though his time had almost run its course, it was not yet over. And then Jorem's ghost disappeared. Elijah awakened angry, anxious, and suspicious.

The issue was: had the dream come through the gate of ivory or the gate of horn? Was it meant to deceive? Or was it meant to be prophetic? As for Jorem, Elijah didn't trust him at all. Was his ghost, then, still wandering about Marlborough Gardens? Part of the message seemed quite clear: he was not to join Jorem in whatever world he was wandering in for the moment. But the ominous "almost run its course" disturbed him. It was true he had not been feeling all that well lately. A chronic fatigue, something he had never experienced before, plagued him. Perhaps he should see Dr. Harlowe, but he hated doctors. All doctors. He had nothing but contempt for Solomon, who, after Sidney's death, complained of heart pain and then put himself, without any reservations at all, into the hands of Dr. Blundell (or Dr. Blunder, as Elijah called him), a medical idiot who spouted a theory called the Open Pore. Because of him, Solomon wore those ridiculous clothes, jackets and pants that had vents sewn into them so that "God's blood could circulate freely," and wore open-heeled shoes so that "the feet, the very soul [pun intended] of the body, could breathe God's good air."

All these thoughts were going through Elijah's mind before he actually stepped out of bed, while he lay next to his wife, his body carefully not touching hers. He hated touching her body except for sex. He looked at the fraction of light coming through the drawn drapes making a single track that divided the room. What time was it? He read the face of the clock: five A.M. Usually he awakened at seven.

He rose and put on his heavy satin robe and slippers. Moving his shoulders up and down, he shivered momentarily as if to throw off the remembrance of the dream. Jorem was dead. Dead. He would not return here. He would never see Jorem alive again. But what was the purpose of the dream? Was it to inform him that after death they would meet again? A melancholy thought. He glanced at his wife. He hated the thought of dying. Hated it. And yet one did. You might live until you were a hundred, there were a few who did, but they died too. Before forty he had never given it a thought, but now that he was in his fortieth year it seemed to him that a day did not pass when at one point or another he did not think of death. The end of his heart beating, his mind thinking, his blood flowing . . . he found his hand on his penis. He looked at Theodisia lying there on her back, her mouth slightly open. Vulnerable. No, not her. He would rather masturbate. In his mind he mounted her and stabbed her with his penis again and again, lacerating her vagina. God, he hated her! To die and see Jorem again! He came and the semen, spouting like a small geyser, flowed over his finger and dripped onto his thighs. He wiped his hands, his penis, and his thighs perfunctorily with his robe, and went to his dressing room, where he poured himself a glass of wine. Somewhere deep inside him the worm of doubt was opposed; he dismissed the dream.

The evening before, Joseph had come to dinner at Elijah's, sober, for a change, and over a splendid round of veal had told him quietly that some days ago he had received a letter from Consuelo.

"Well, I can see by your face it was not a billet-doux. What does the bitch have to say for herself?" asked Elijah.

"She wants us to return her dowry," said Joseph bluntly.

Elijah looked at Clara and then at Emma. The governess rose instantly, and motioning to Emma, left the room with her.

"Really. Well, that's impossible right now. You'll have to tell her that. We can't afford it. Besides, if I remember correctly, at the time Poppa received the dowry, every last shilling of it was paid out again to cover her father's gambling debts, which, by the way, was the principal reason that sack of depravity and bankruptcy, Count Rimini, allowed his daughter to marry 'out of his class,' as he put it."

"She is pregnant," said Joseph.

Theodisia gasped. Elijah glared at her.

"Leave the room, Theodisia, and tell Mrs. Farnley to bring the port and cigars in here."

When his wife left, Elijah laughed and said: "Well, let Ricci support the new bambino."

"It is not Ricci's bambino."

"What? The slut! Not a penny, not a single penny of our hard-earned money will go to her. Do you understand, Joseph? Not a penny. I shall fight you hard on this. Hard. And be assured so shall Solomon."

"Slut or not, Elijah, we are not divorced; she is still my wife. The child will therefore be my legal responsibility. I must by law support it. If you do fight me on this issue, I shall be forced to sell my bank stock to whomever will pay my price. I am determined to send her the money one way or the other."

Elijah let out a yell of anger and began to pound the table with his fist. "Then you must divorce her!"

"Oh, I should like to. Very much. But, as you know, adultery is not grounds for divorce. Only an act of Parliament can do that, and at very great expense. It would be almost as expensive as the return of the dowry. I can get a decree—I have looked into the matter—Mr. Hemsley tells me. I spoke to him a few days ago. I can get something called *a mensa et thoro*, meaning 'from bed and board,' which would mean that I am no longer bound to support her, but I don't wish to do that."

"I see. *You* don't want to. So because you don't want to, *we* must support her. You have done nothing at the bank for almost the last three years. The few times you have actually come to work, you have been conspicuously inebriated, incapable of making sensible decisions. There isn't a clerk who doesn't have contempt for you. I myself have seen them laugh at you behind your back. Furthermore, I have been told lately by some of our colleagues that you have been responsible for our losing some new accounts. And you don't want to. No one respects you anymore, Joseph. You are, by the way, about to be black-balled from the Hebrides Club. And why? For what reason? That woman never loved you! It's been almost three years . . . other women run away from their husbands and their husbands celebrate! No, we have been patient and understanding too long. Enough is enough! It is bad enough she left you, but for you to lose all self-respect is far, far worse!"

Elijah had expressed his anger, but now he was frightened. Joseph looked so miserable. Elijah was afraid that he was actually going to cry. "Have you thought of taking her back?"

"She does not wish to come back! She makes that point explicit in her letter." Joseph pulled the letter out of his pocket and read it aloud: "I thank God on my knees every day that I am not in England! We two never should have married! Send me the money you rightfully owe me. Remember that I was forced to marry you. I never loved you. . . ." Joseph choked back his tears. "She is right, Elijah. The marriage was wrong from the start . . . a misalliance . . . you yourself called it that! And you were right. But the worst part—"

Elijah put his forefinger to his lips, commanding Joseph to be silent, as Mrs. Farnley came in with a bottle of port, wineglasses, and biscuits. She placed them on the table and left.

"No! I will not be silent any longer! Since her departure, since Darius's attempt at suicide, I have had to face certain things about myself. I have changed, Elijah. I am not the same man I was when I lived with her. Then I pretended that she loved me. I could not bear to face the fact that she did not. But now everything is clear, though it is hateful. But I no longer live in a dream. And sometimes I wonder at that monstrous passion I felt for her. Was that love? No, don't turn away, Elijah. For you everything was . . . *is* much easier than for me. I don't know why, but it is—"

"I don't think you should continue. You are overwrought."

"Overwrought . . . yes. But it has not muddled my thinking. On the contrary, like fine wine, it has stimulated it. Did I love Consuelo? I thought I did. It felt that way to me. You know, Elijah, her leaving me . . . at first I admit it was unbearable. But over the last year—Well, I will speak no more about it. You know nothing about my life . . . what I do with my time . . . how I occupy myself—"

"Well, you certainly don't occupy yourself with bank business!" interjected Elijah in a venomous tone.

"What I think about . . . what I do," Joseph continued. It was almost as if Elijah had not spoken. "And you need not worry, I shall not tell you. But I do have this final thing to say about the matter—her dowry must be returned. She has damaged me, her son, our family—all of this is true—but she has suffered too. I know that now."

"Oh, for God's sake! You are being a sentimental fool. I told you we cannot afford the loss of ten thousand pounds."

"I cannot afford not to give it to her. If you force me to, Elijah, I'll sell my shares of bank stock. It should be sufficient for her to live modestly in Florence—that is, if her father does not get hold of it. Furthermore, I shall provide for the child in my will. Darius must not hear of this— What I mean is, he will find out soon enough when he returns to Italy this summer— What I mean is, I do not wish to discuss it with him . . ."

"Perhaps the bitch will die in childbirth. How old is she?" Elijah asked bitterly.

"That is a possibility, isn't it?" said Joseph as he got up to leave. "Thank you for the dinner. My compliments to Mrs. Farnley and Mrs. Lovesley. You do well for yourself, don't you, Elijah?"

<hr/>

"He was always strange," Solomon said after Elijah told him the story. He watched Elijah toy with the cutlery. His eyes closed as if to wipe out the vision of Joseph.

The two brothers were dining at their club, the Hebrides. It was a relatively new club started by themselves and other bankers with merchants and ship owners. It was not like the Potters, to which they also belonged, which had magnificent drawing rooms, splendid paintings, a more subdued atmosphere, or Crockford's, where Elijah gambled and which was known for its excellent East India and West India Madeira and sherry and its superb service. But the Hebrides had among its members both Rothschilds, Nathan and Lionel, and all the Barings.

"Don't you recall," Solomon continued, "Poppa named him Stillwater? 'So tell us, Sir Stillwater, what are some of your deep thoughts today?' He used to tease him about how silent he was. But Poppa was wrong, he never should have allowed Joseph to marry that woman. That was a mistake. If Albert or the twins—or Deirdre, God forbid!—ever came to me with the proposal Joseph came to Poppa with, I would threaten disinheritance! But of course they won't. They are not like Joseph."

"If we don't give him the money, he has threatened to sell his share of the stock."

"Poppa had just bought Saddler's Grove and he wanted an aristocrat in the family—"

"Damn it, Solomon! All that took place years ago! We're living now. We shall have to give him the money."

"Must we?"

"Well, what's the alternative? A strange partner? No, we shall have to."

Solomon dipped his spoon into the mock turtle soup and brought it carefully up to his lips and swallowed the soup.

"Did I tell you," he said, "that Redbury is in trouble? He came to borrow money from us yesterday. I had the impression he had been asking all over town. His assets are negligible. Of course, I had to refuse . . . and he cried, Elijah, he actually cried! I told him that we had the deepest compassion for him, but it was better that he cried than we cried. Of course he understood that. As a matter of fact, my joke seemed to cheer him up. But times are hard, Elijah. It's not a good time for us to have to part with capital to give to that blasted woman!"

"I know. It's what I told Joseph. It's all this wild speculation going on. All that is needed to form a company nowadays is a map of England, a pair of compasses, a pencil and a ruler, and a Parliamentary agent. And then they come to us with their propositions." He raised his hand to summon a waiter. "I shall have Madeira and a roast haunch of mutton—"

"Dr. Blundell will not allow me to eat such things. No wine for me. Tell the waiter I shall have broiled fish with steamed vegetables."

"Tell him yourself."

———◆◇◆———

When Solomon left, Elijah went to the game room to find someone for a game of cards, but there was no one there he wanted to be with.

Ordering a bottle of brandy from one of the staff, he went to one of the drawing rooms and sat in front of the fireplace and stared at the small figure of Nelson, his medals shining, on the deck of the *Victory* in the oil painting that hung above the mantel. Damn Joseph! Damn Consuelo!

Pregnant! And who was the father anyway? He hadn't asked Joseph that. The woman should have been sterilized! Damn! Money. That's what it always came down to. Always. Filthy lucre. He thought about Miles Ryder and the last time he had seen him. He had had dinner with him and his black steward Pierre Mboza, a young boy of sixteen. Whoever heard of such a thing? One didn't dine with one's steward!

The most beautiful, the most magnificent dinner service he had ever seen. Better than the Duke of Norwood's. Rockingham with Famous Houses of England painted on the plates. Gold cutlery! The stemware! As well as glorious food and wine!

There had been four of them. A Mr. Gonzalef or Gorsalef, a German, a former minister, Miles had told him later, just arrived from Macao. The conversation had been all about the trade. The opium trade. Gorsalef or Gonzalef—what the devil was his name anyway?—had been telling them about a shipment of opium that had gone down in a typhoon off the China coast. They had lost the entire shipment, he had said, ninety thousand pounds' worth.

"But as you know, Miles, that is just a drop in the bucket, *nicht wahr?*"

A drop in the bucket! Elijah had said nothing, of course, but he remembered thinking, God, the profit that must be had in that trade! And Jorem had been part of it. Well, he wanted to be part of it too. More than he was now. He had given Miles as much money as he could without making Solomon or Brian suspicious. But with Joseph's demand there would be no extra money.

What Lionel Strooksbury had told him came to mind: "Isaac Coverly is a very wealthy man with no wife and children. He had assured me several times he is eager to invest in something, anything; he's not particular . . .

Coverly now lived in Jorem's house. Elijah had taken care of renting him the house, being careful not to tell either of his brothers about the extra five thousand pounds, which he had pocketed but lost in a few nights at Crockford's.

Isaac Coverly . . . he remembered the splendor of the ball. That must have cost him a pretty penny. Damn! He had forgotten to ask Miles about him. A retired tea merchant . . . Miles would know about him. Miles knew everyone. Coverly was such an amiable fellow, and so generous. Lately he had been dining with them on Sunday afternoons. Like a member of the family. Perhaps it was time to follow up on Strooksbury's suggestion.

Darius . . . poor Darius. He thought of the boy momentarily. He had been to him once at Somerset. That was more than Joseph, his own father, had done. Darius has seemed all right. Not that he had said much. He hadn't asked about anyone except Emma. Darius had given him a letter for her. It was still in his desk drawer in the library. There was no point in giving it to Emma. The less they had to do with one another the better.

Emma seemed happier now. So he had been right to hire Clara Lustig. Clara . . . he wondered would it be insane to seduce her. But that was the wrong word, wasn't it? If anything it was she who was seductive. No, she was certainly not beautiful; still, there is something very attractive about even a plain woman who makes her sexual needs known. For he was not unaware of her sexual hunger for him. In that sense she was almost irresistible.

Should he have her? He laughed quietly to himself. What harm could it do? No harm at all, if no one found out. Mrs. Farnley would find out. She found out about everything. A useful woman to keep on one's side. And there was Moly, her vested interest. How would she feel about that? But the woman herself, Clara *Lustig,* aptly named . . . once begun . . . the woman was a live volcano ready to erupt. For a moment he saw his household and everyone in it covered with lava. . . . He laughed out loud. But then he thought of Emma. No, he couldn't. Women! He desired them and detested them both at once . . . *odi et amo.* Whores? No, he was not in the mood for whores.

The following Saturday Elijah was in his library reading a newly published explorer's account of a trip down the Amazon when Emma came in without knocking and said that Momma had told her to remind him he was to accompany her to a concert at Lady Alysbury's house.

"Good God, Emma, you've almost made me drop my book. You're remarkably stealthy. Well, what have I said now? You look faint. Tell your Momma that the answer is no. I dislike fiddlers. And I particularly dislike German composers. Schubert, isn't it? Have you studied any of his pieces on the piano, Emma?"

"No, Poppa."

"Come back after you've told her. We shall go for a walk together, you and I. Perhaps to Calypso's Cave. . . .

When she returned he said to her, "Tell your governess to join us."

"She won't want to go. She doesn't enjoy walking."

"Ask her anyway."

The day was fairly warm but cloudy. The sun's rays pierced the clouds like scimitars. It felt almost like spring. The air smelled of fresh earth, the special smell of spring when everything is returning to life again. Emma, at first exuberant, ran ahead of the adults, exclaiming when she found the dog's-tooth violets just now coming into flower underneath the beech trees. At first Clara and her father were responsive to her, but then she noticed with some alarm that they were becoming far more interested in their conversation than they were in her discoveries.

"My wife knows nothing about music. She detests it," Elijah said, walking at a determinedly slow pace. "It's all cacophony to her. And yet she insists on attending concerts. The performance does not grip, exhaust, or refresh her, but she will take note, assiduously, for whose edification I don't know, of every dress and every hat that every woman is wearing."

"I saw the program. You wife showed it to me. A string quartet by Schubert, the one in D-minor. Poor Schubert. 'I am the most unfortunate, the most miserable being in the world.' He wrote that in a letter two years before he died. Did you know he died at the age of thirty-one?"

"Thank you for that bit of information. I see I chose my daughter's teacher wisely. You will, I am sure, be able to fill in the cracks of my education on innumerable topics. However, it only makes me feel most fortunate that God did not see fit to create me as an artist. Poverty, misunderstanding, ill health, and failure would not have suited me."

"No, it would not have. But then I'm sure it did not suit them either. For someone who is not an artist you seem to be quite familiar with their struggle."

"I am one of those people, Mrs. Lustig, who diligently investigates subjects that do not appeal to me."

Clara laughed. He smiled and she noticed how attractive his smile was.

"My brother's wife, the runaway—I'm quite sure you know all the details—the one they call the Contessa, inspired me to become interested in music and composers. I detested her sufficiently to investigate both art and music. I disliked the idea of a woman, particularly her, knowing more about something than I did. I disliked her arrogance. I disliked the fact that she was a brilliant composer—oh, yes, I know she is, Mrs. Lustig. But it seemed absurd to me that God had placed that kind of ability and talent into a woman's head. But you are an artist of sorts, aren't you? I remember our discussion in Frankfurt when I first met you. You told me then that you were hesitant about accepting the position I offered you because you hoped to earn your living by writing. Fiction, Mrs. Lustig?"

"I do not aspire to fiction, Mr. Forster. I have an analytic, critical mind. I am not a true artist, though I am not a handmaiden either."

"The inevitable question: have you been published? Will I one of these days inadvertently stumble across your name in some quarterly?"

She smiled. "Yes."

"Yes, and no more. I see I must coax you to reveal more."

She smiled again. "I have written a review and a newspaper published in Coventry by Mr. Hennel has seen fit to print it."

"Mr. Hennel, the well-known agnostic. You keep dangerous company, Mrs. Lustig."

"I do."

He laughed. "Don't you believe that all books are potentially dangerous? I do. Sometimes I think we should destroy all presses and most books."

"Oh, I agree. And authors too. Particularly poets. A great conflagration of artists would be best for society. Of course, we are merely paraphrasing what Plato said so many years ago."

They had reached the cave. Emma had attempted several times to interrupt their conversation, but her father made her understand in no uncertain terms that she was to leave them alone. The same jealousy that had once made her detest her cousin Albert—why had Darius been interested in him?—became active again. What did these two people, her father and her governess, see in one another? Because they *were* interested in one another, she could see that. And why were they excluding her? How could they? Her beloved Poppa. Her beloved Clara. It was if suddenly she did not exist for either of them.

"Look," whispered Elijah to Clara, "look there just underneath the trees—" He turned her body towards a copse where a fox, thoroughly startled by their presence, was holding a rabbit by its throat. Clara watched as the fox tore open the rabbit's throat, heard the animal's dying scream. Glaring at them fiercely, the fox turned away with his trophy, the blood dripping down his muzzle, and fled deep into the nearby thicket.

"Now there is nature, Mrs. Lustig, red in tooth and claw. The population of foxes has increased. We shall have to do something about it. The wood is full of vixen dens, the gardeners tell me. Perhaps a shooting party would be a good idea. Next Sunday after dinner . . . by the way, do you shoot? Mrs. Lustig?"

"No, I have never used a gun. Country sports have not been part of my life . . . the pleasures of the hunt. Mine has been the life of an impoverished scholar. Another kind of person that I should think that you would also thank God you are not."

"Yes. I enjoy the life I live for the most part. I enjoy money, intrigue, women, food, drink, and gambling. . . . I sometimes wonder what I would have done had I been born a woman. My daughter, for instance, so eager now, so full of enthusiasm . . . where will all that brightness, that eagerness go? If she marries it will be transmitted to her sons, perhaps; that is, if she does not turn sour before then. Still, I detest women who insist on 'leading their own life' like my sister-in-law Consuelo. What grief and anguish she has caused with her lawless libidinous nature. That is what happens to women who have freedom. Do you agree?"

"Yes, but—'What is life without the golden Aphrodite?' "[22]

Elijah laughed. "Lawless and libidinous . . . how appealing that assonance is." He looked at her. "I do not like intelligent women, Mrs. Lustig, but I find you singularly attractive. Or is 'challenging' a better word?"

Before Clara could answer Emma returned and complained about being cold and wanting to return home. She was angry with both of them.

"Well then," her father said, "return home by yourself with your tail between your cold little legs while we older people continue onwards to the cave and brave the elements."

Her father had never spoken to Emma like that before. The sneering words, the contemptuous tone . . . that was the way he spoke to Momma. Tears came to her eyes.

"Forgive me, Sir," said Clara. "I too am cold, so I will return with Emma, if you don't mind."

"Go, both of you!" he said, walking abruptly away from them.

"Oh, Clara! What shall we do? He is angry at both of us now."

"Nothing. He will get over his anger. Come, let us go home and I shall play a new piece for you, the 'Heidenroslein' by Schubert. Charming but simple." She began to hum it. "I learned to play it when I was your age."

But Emma was watching her father walk away.

"I can't see him anymore, Clara."

"Neither can I. Let us go."

"But what about Poppa?"

"It would not surprise me in the least, Emma, if your father was home by the time we arrived."

And as usual Clara was right.

---

22. Clara is quoting Mimnermus, the elegaic poet and musician. His *floruit* is given as 632–29 B.C. One could also translate the line as "What is life without sexual love?" —*R. Lowe*

14

KEVIN FRANCINI

I realize of course that I am a figure of fun to him, and that he laughs at me, and even mocks me occasionally, but I cannot help but like him more and more each day. Decidedly it is one of the pleasures of growing old that one is able to love the person that does not love you.

—Jorem Isaac Forster, Letter,
14 June 1813

KEVIN was dreaming about the flower: five feet high . . . its large leaves serrated, lobed, embracing the sea-green stem on which they were placed alternately. The flower itself white . . . moon-white, grey-white, terminal . . . a delicate violet tinging its base . . . two leaves composed the calyx, four petals the corolla . . . drooping shyly . . . the perfect dream flower to send one into dreams . . . the beautiful white poppy from which they gather opium. Ying-suh was what the Chinese called it. . . .

Like a number of addicts Kevin had made a special point of knowing everything there was to know about opium. The best opium: the best opium burned in powerful jets when you held it up to the spirit lamp—the odor resembling ignited naptha—swelled to twice its bulk, and was exhausted quickly, losing more than half its weight, leaving the greyish cokelike substance behind, ashes that broke up easily under the fingers.

The nearer opium approached a deep rich chestnut color the purer. The more it approached a consistency of cream cheese the more genuine. The taste should be bitter and enduring with a slight sweet tack; a very small portion would give sensations to the tongue.

And the pipe. Different in construction from common tobacco pipes. Formed from a straight round piece of bamboo or ivory that was perforated through its length till about two or three inches from the end, where there was a singular round bowl covered up with a very small hole in its top. Reclining then with a little box of opium, a lamp burning, and a needle four inches long terminating in a sharp point at one end and a spatula at the other end, his head supported on a pillow, he was ready. The attendant, a Chinese man, would place upon the spatula end of the needle a modicum of opium, the size of a pin's head, place the opium on the opening of the bowl of the pipe, fire it with the lamp, and then with the sharp end of the needle push it in. After that he would hand the pipe to Kevin, who would inhale, retaining the smoke as long as possible, letting it slowly disperse and escape finally through his nostrils, though sometimes he swallowed it. Between six and twelve pipes, depending on how much money he had.

The den itself was near the East India docks above a rag shop. Knock three times and the knock would be returned. Then he would whisper his name and hear the bolts slide, and the door would be opened a crack; he would be looked at, recognized, and allowed to come in.

The room was low-ceilinged, dirty, devoid of furniture except for wooden bunks one on top of the other and a few scattered chairs. A dozen men might be there already lying stretched out, their faces flushed, some of them muttering to themselves, others uttering obscenities, or comatose, dead to appearance, their faces idiotic in a deathlike stupor. It smelled of smoke, stale urine, feces, disinfectant, and naptha. Later on in the night the den assumed the appearance of a death house. Ghastly white faces, faces like grinning skulls, bodies bone-thin, skeletal.

And for what? For the inner glow of warmth, for the profound sense of well-being . . . guilt, fear, conflict, tension all melted away, and the imagination soaring . . . all the paintings he ever wanted to paint were all there completed in his mind, stunning . . . effortless . . . just by inhaling the magical smoke, raised above mundane problems, able to solve them without effort. The world as it should be, an abyss of divine enjoyment. That was in the beginning . . . though at the very first it produced nausea and vomiting.

By nature a loner, like De Quincy, he allowed himself the drug only when he was in unusually good spirits as a "luxury." But as time went on all that changed; as his need for the drug grew his world narrowed down to only himself and the drug. If he didn't have it for a day he would begin to twitch, then nausea, and then every muscle and every joint would ache—but worse than that, far worse, was the fear, the lawless terror that would invade, storm through his body, claim possession, and pour its poison into every cell, every organ, his mind insane with panic. The only thing in his life then was the need for the drug. . . .

Jorem loving him . . . that had frightened him. Why he didn't know, but he had not wanted that. He had wanted to be free to smoke and eat opium as much and as often as he wanted. He had wanted to give himself completely to the drug. And so he ran away, took a room near the docks where he knew the captains of the East India Company ate and drank and dealt drugs, they and their crews. He needed nothing except money to buy the drug with. After selling his paintings, his paints, his brushes, his few belongings, he sold his body to old men who lurked in the narrow streets in the East End. Finally he moved into the opium den and for sweeping and cleaning up was allowed to have the leavings.

Then one day, no different from any other, he changed his routine, the routine he had had for the last three years, day in and day out. He decided to go around the corner—just that—and have lunch in the shelter, a shelter that he had known about for the last two years. The shelter was run by a mysterious man named Nicholas Renton, a person he had heard about from time to time and whom he had occasionally seen, a short well-dressed gentleman. He had had no appetite for food for years, only for the drug, but that morning the thought popped into his head to go there and have lunch. Why he didn't know. He had not had a thought in his head about anything but opium for years.

It was a Tuesday, he remembered, eighteen years ago, a rainy cold November day. He was sensitive to the weather, particularly the cold, on a day like that he would not have put a toe outside the door. Nevertheless, he walked around the corner as if he were compelled and entered the shelter for the first time. Weighing six stone, in filthy rags, lousy, and smelling to high heaven, he sat down at the table with others like himself and ate a morsel of bread and a few swallows of soup. John Nash, the old man who ran the place, told him when he was about to leave that if he liked he could sleep there. And that if he wanted to he could clean himself up, but if he didn't that would be all right too. He was welcome to come back again.

The next day Kevin went back, though he didn't know why, and then one day a month later he told his Chinese friend that he was moving out, that he was moving around the corner.

—◆◌◇◌◆—

Ever since Kevin could remember, his constant companion had been fear—and something else . . . a mysterious desire to belong to something, to pass over into that universe where I and Thou were one. Sometimes when he had finished a painting depicting one of the dreams that lived inside his head, looking at the canvas later, it seemed to him as if he had painted a part of his soul, as if the act of painting had been an act of self-enlightenment . . . an act of illumination. For a few brief moments he experienced ecstasy. The first time he smoked opium the same thing had happened to him, as if he had connected to something within himself. He began to call that experience in his mind Root of All Roots, unaware that others had felt the way he did, and that this strange phrase had been used by early Kabbalists when they spoke about the living God, *deus absconditus,* the God who is hidden in his own self.

It was this sensation he had hunted for all his life and this sensation he had fled.

When he was coming out of the worst of his withdrawal Kevin met Nicholas. The first part of returning to the world remained clouded. It was not until years later that he recalled meeting John Nash, or remembered coming to the shelter, or remembered moving out of the Chinaman's den. What he remembered clearly, though—vividly—was Nicholas. Nicholas's voice, and how his heart had begun to beat rapidly when he heard it, and how at the same time he experienced momentarily the possibility of joy. Why, he didn't know, but it had happened.

One day Nicholas asked Kevin if he wanted to work with him. Not *for* him. Kevin said yes; it began like that. He felt nothing was vile in Nicholas's eyes, including himself, though he himself felt base and depraved. Gradually he became part of Nicholas's world, the world under the world in which the rich and privileged lived. In his heart he believed Nicholas had delivered him. And so the child of Newgate, the great sinner, the archthief, the master criminal, Nicholas Renton, became Kevin's saviour.

"They did very well in the panic of eighteen twenty-five," said Kevin. "In the mad boom of 'twenty-four Jorem stood aloof but when the panic started he began buying stock from the overloaded for profitable though reasonable prices. Seventy banks failed—three hundred were suspended—but Forster Midland did not. When a run began on his bank Jorem personally informed the crowd that one-pound notes would be paid first, five-pound notes the next day, and ten-pound notes the day after, and the panic was relieved. I think Nathan Rothschild advised him. They were fast friends by then. . . ."

Kevin was giving a quick history of Forster Midland Bank to Nicholas, who had received a note the day before from Elijah requesting a meeting with him. He was certain that it would be a request for money.

"—and they also did well in the crisis of 'thirty-five. They took a conservative position and issued no more notes, raised their discount rates, and refused to make advances even to good firms. They seem to know what they are doing. Really, were it not for Elijah's extravagant tastes and his gambling, he would be in an excellent financial position, even though they'll have to return the dowry. You know about the ten thousand pounds, of course. But Elijah hungers for money. If his family is not to be knighted only money will slake his thirst for fame, for power, for recognition. Besides, as we know he desperately wants money now in order to invest in Ryder and Company—"

"Ryder. Miles Ryder, the opium trader?"

"The same."

"And it was Jorem, you told me, who staked Mr. Ryder many years ago? And Jorem kept his hand in the drug business, carrying it in his books as the tea account."

"Yes."

"And now Elijah wants to open up the account again. Reawaken old interests, as it were."

"Yes."

"Thank you. Anything more?"

"Yes, before I forget, Commander, I have another piece of news for you. Quite intriguing—"

"What is it?"

"I went down to Curzon Street as usual to rescue and recruit and who do you think was there . . . buying."

"Who?"

"Evan Taylor, Mr. Strooksbury's manservant."

"What did he buy?"

"A twelve-year-old girl."

"Did he recognize you?"

"Yes, we recognized one another."

"It was for his master. I am sure of that. Perhaps we should keep a closer watch on Mr. Strooksbury. . . ."

———◆◆◆◆———

Kevin led Elijah into Nicholas's study.

"Make yourself comfortable, Sir. I shall inform Mr. Coverly that you have arrived."

"Thank you, Kevin."

Elijah stared at Kevin's back as he left the room. He still could not get used to it. Kevin working for Mr. Coverly. But as what? What did he actually do for him? Was he the man's secretary? His confidential clerk? His steward? (Coverly had spoken of estates.) And his behaviour. After the initial recognition and acknowledgment it was as if they had never known one another. Elijah looked around the room.

Bizarre! The room was exactly the way he remembered it when his father had lived here. He was quite sure the other tenant had used it as a gun room. Now everything was the way it used to be again: the same rug, the same desk, chairs, lamps . . . it was as if he had gone back in time. He had been punished in this room, he remembered. Humiliated. It was in this room that Jorem had informed him he was to marry Theodisia. . . . Kevin must have told Coverly how to decorate. But for what purpose? It gave Elijah a decidedly queasy feeling. He had half a mind to leave. He took out his watch—if the gentleman kept him waiting for longer than a quarter of an hour, he would do just that, take his leave. And what about the rest of the house? He thought back to the ball. The ballroom had been so wildly decorated he couldn't tell. Now he noticed the flowers in the vase on the desk in front of him. Jorem's favorite . . . from the Winter Garden, of course . . . Bengal roses. Was it a coincidence or was it deliberate? But of course he was acting like a fool. Coverly was not a gun man. He wanted a study. Still, so had Eveshem, he remembered, except it was a different room. The furniture? They had found it in the attic, the old desk, the globe, the chairs and tables, even the prints, where they had been stored after Jorem's death. No one in the family had wanted any of it. Kevin had found them probably, and had told Coverly, who decided to use them. Kevin, no doubt, had placed them in their original settings. Having reasoned all that out, Elijah began to feel better. But . . . it had given him a bit of a start.

A few minutes later Nicholas came into the room. Smiling. Effusive.

"Ah, Mr. Forster, my esteemed landlord. I hope the room brings back pleasant memories. Your father's former employee, Kevin Francini, assisted me in decorating this room. He found the furniture in the attic and thought it might be interesting to re-create the past. A droll idea, isn't it?"

"Oh, yes . . . very."

"You said in your note, Sir, that you wish to speak to me about a private matter. I hope I have not transgressed in some way, inadvertently committed a breach or an infraction of some kind. . . . I am aware of the rules that your family has set down concerning the Gardens; I hope I have not violated any of them in the last eight months."

"No, no, nothing like that, Mr. Coverly," said Elijah, laughing. "You are, believe me, Sir, the most desirable of tenants. We desire nothing less, my brothers and I, than that you continue to lease the house as long as you wish. No, Sir, what I have come to see you about is something entirely different. How shall I begin? I think it was Mr. Redbury, or was it Mr. Strooksbury . . . yes, it was Mr. Strooksbury who told me that you were very interested in these turbulent financial times in finding some lucrative market to invest a portion of your monies in . . ."

As Elijah spoke, Nicholas took in his graceful, elegant mien. He noticed that Elijah's shirt was a striped cotton imported from China. He knew where Elijah had them made, and for how much. A handsome man, stunning, really, Nicholas had to admit, admiring his long curled hair, his silken blond whiskers. He listened as Elijah, interpreting Nicholas's silence as encouragement and permission, held forth on the great financial opportunities there were in investments in South America. Tin mines in Peru, gold mines in Brazil, plantations in Argentina, sugar in Cuba. All were golden opportunities to turn comparatively small sums of money into fortunes, if not overnight, almost overnight. While Elijah spoke, Nicholas detached and reviewed in his mind all the facts that Kevin, Clara, Mrs. Farnley, Mrs. Capacity, Mr. Strooksbury, Daisy, and Moly had given him. The sum and substance of the man, Jorem's middle son, Elijah Forster. Hundreds of facts, the whole of Elijah in a sense, but no, not everything, not his innermost thoughts . . . not his soul. And it was his soul that Nicholas wanted. Wasn't it? And the only way he could obtain that was to get Elijah to sell it to him. And he would. If he were pushed far enough. Hard enough . . .

"So you feel the tin mines in Peru might be the best investment at this time, do you, Sir?" asked Nicholas, finally intervening in Elijah's lengthy panegyric about the wisdom and soundness of financial speculation guided by someone like himself whose thumb could be said to be firmly placed on the fiscal pulse as it were. Rolling out figures and percentages, creating a magic of plenty, an adventure that could not fail, risk capital that was not risk capital but a sure thing, Elijah threw out numbers whose luster glistened in the air.

"Yes, I do. Señor Juan Esposito is a great personal friend of mine. Besides, we have agents of our own down in Peru. I have seen the ore itself, Mr. Coverly, I personally can vouch for it. I myself have invested—"

"You need say no more, Sir. Well now, I trust you implicitly. Would you say one thousand pounds would be sufficient? To start with, of course," said Nicholas, his face a study in anticipation and hope.

One thousand pounds! Elijah had not expected that much. He studied the face before him. The man was much wealthier than Strooksbury realized. Such a small undistinguished man. And so wealthy. A tea

merchant . . . Elijah felt himself tremble. If he played his cards right—
it was the same sensation he had when he held a winning hand at
Crockford's—he could get huge sums of money from Mr. Coverly.
Because all the money Mr. Coverly would give him would go into his
own investments in Ryder's firm. The vision of Ryder's Albion and its
incredible riches came to mind. With an investment in Ryder's firm,
what couldn't he buy for himself? All this took but a second so that it
was as he was saying yes that all this passed through his mind. "Yes, it
will, Mr. Coverly."

"Well then, Kevin will draw up the proper contracts. You say that
according to your figures my thousand will triple in six months. That
they have started mining there already and it is believed to be the biggest
tin mine in history, Sir. Well, Mr. Forster, I am a lucky man to get in
at the beginning, so to speak. The quicker we move the better for me,
I presume. So why not make it five thousand pounds? I have the fullest
confidence in your financial wisdom. Kevin will draw up the contract
in a matter of days. Shall he bring it to your house or to the bank for
your perusal and signature?"

"My house, Sir, if you don't mind. I do not want anyone else to get
wind of this because if they do there will be a stampede. Give it into
the hands of Mrs. Farnley, my housekeeper. I shall alert her and I shall
return the documents to you the following day." Elijah took out his
watch, not that he wanted to leave the man, on the contrary, he felt
kindly towards him—it had been so easy, there had been no objections,
no questions, no frustrations at all—no, it was not the man but the
room. The memories the room brought back were too oppressive. "Forgive me, I must leave now. I have an appointment in the City. It was a
pleasure to do business with you."

As soon as Elijah left Kevin came into the room.

"Well?"

But Nicholas was not in the mood for camaraderie of any kind. He
was put out, Kevin noticed. By what, he wondered. "Did it go as you
planned it would?"

Nicholas did not answer Kevin directly, instead he gave him the details
of the proposal, telling him to draw up the proper papers to cover the
transaction. He gave Kevin all the information as briefly as possible.
When Kevin made a joke about the five thousand pounds, referring to
it as an act of charity, Nicholas did not respond.

"Yes, now if you would leave me . . . I feel a mood coming on. I
want to be left alone."

Kevin was familiar with Nicholas's "moods," which sometimes lasted
for days: he would seclude himself, seeing no one, nor would he speak
to anyone. During that time he ate his meals alone, and seldom if

ever left his room. Nor did he ever explain before or after what was wrong.

As soon as Kevin left, Nicholas moved over to the mirror and stared at himself. The image of Elijah towered over his handsome head. Damn Elijah! Damn him! The vision faded. He turned away from his reflection.

Why did he torture himself this way? Why did he involve himself in such nonsense—the spying, the reports, the lists . . . the scene with Clara flashed through his mind. He had tortured her. Why? *Cui bono?* as Kevin would say. Was he insane? Perhaps . . . Perhaps it wasn't true. Perhaps he wasn't Jorem's child. . . . Perhaps it was all a figment of his imagination. And then an emotion so twisted, so torturous, possessed him, leaving him momentarily breathless. Hatred and longing invaded him simultaneously, smouldered down the pathway of his nerves, spilled into his blood . . . an overpowering hatred for himself, a desperate yearning to be Elijah . . . he hated the man, and yet with all his heart he wanted to be the man he was determined to exterminate. He staggered, bent his head, for once he allowed his feelings to have their way . . . deadly images erupted in his mind . . .

He must stop himself. It was dangerous what he was doing. He must preserve his balance . . . he must remember that Jorem *was* his father. Everything was going as he had planned it long ago.

He had to be alone now. In the mood he was in people disgusted him. He felt like a pariah, a murderer. Evil. Guilty. Better to ride it out alone. Away from people. Never ask anyone for help. Never ask anyone to understand. Never ask for love when he needed it the most. He would rather die than do that. No, best to be alone then. It would pass, as it always did, and he would come forth again into the world he had created by himself, for himself, master of his universe. The head of an organization that lived on the underbelly of the greatest empire on earth in this century.

Nicholas never drank, except when he felt the way he did now. He rang the bell and when Mrs. Kitto came he sent her away to fetch Toby. Toby was the only person he could tolerate at such times. Toby was the past. Toby understood despair and terror. And Toby asked no questions. Toby would see to it that when he drank himself into oblivion he would not harm himself or others. And Toby would tell no one.

When Toby came into the room Nicholas had already started drinking. They went upstairs together.

At the end of the fifth day, Toby opened the door and let herself out, and said to Kevin, who had stationed himself outside the door, that Nicholas wanted to know had the contracts been completed. And if they had, had they been signed.

"Tell him they have, Toby."

"He says he'll try a bit of nourishment now, some gruel, some tea, and a dry biscuit."

The next day Anthony Kerr received instructions from Nicholas to go to Reade and Sterns, watchmakers, and have a watch made for him, an exact copy of Elijah's. Toby was already making a suit similar to Elijah's for Nicholas: brown checked trousers, a cotton pleated shirt, and a green double-breasted frock coat.

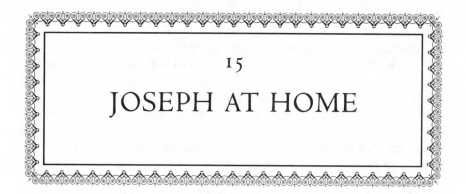

15

JOSEPH AT HOME

Yesterday Darius told me that years ago he and a school friend had come down from Cambridge for the day and that on their way to the Haymarket they had passed Joseph, who had looked straight at him without a sign of recognition.

—Emma Forster, *The Florentine Diary*

JOSEPH was hunched up in bed rocking back and forth and crying. Maria, the maid, the young wife Ricci had left behind when he ran off with Consuelo, was angry. It was early morning. Usually, she would awaken Joseph by climbing into bed with him, holding him for a few minutes in her arms like a child, and then if he wanted sex with her, she would comply.

After that, she would get out of bed, open the blinds, and go back to the bed, where she would hoist him up while telling him to open up his eyes "like a good boy." His eyes open, she would lead him to the commode, put him on it, and when he had finished his business she would wipe him and, after a cursory wash-up, coax him into his clothes.

Then she would go downstairs. Three quarters of an hour later, he would come into the dining room looking like the president of a bank. Breakfast was always the same: four rashers of bacon, a broiled kidney, a grilled tomato, and strong coffee. He would never eat anything, but he would sip the coffee.

The morning regimen had been established less than a week after Consuelo's flight to Florence with Ricci, Joseph's valet. But today Joseph was awake when she entered. She wondered what would he do if she ever returned to Italy, which she threatened to do quite often.

"She's left me! Forever and ever! She will never come back!"

She should have known he would begin to behave like this after the letter had come last month. But he seemed so calm at first. She had read it, of course. Her mistress was going to have a baby; Consuelo the slut would have the bambino of a man other than Ricci. Whore! Sometimes when he cried like this, Maria wondered if he realized that Consuelo had left over three years ago. His grief seemed so fresh. He cried as if it had happened the day before, shamelessly, unembarrassed by her presence.

"Never! She says so in her letter." Joseph waved Consuelo's letter, the tears falling on his cheeks. "Listen: 'I will never return. Never. I never loved you. I do not regret leaving England. Do not come after me.' " He broke into fresh sobs.

Maria now did what she had done the morning after the lovers' flight, after Elijah had cut Darius down: she went over to the bureau, took out the bottle of whiskey, and filled a glass, and handed it to him. He drank it down. And held out the glass to her. She poured him another one and he drank that one down too.

A few minutes later he seemed to have composed himself. "Why haven't you made the fire? It's freezing in here. Make it and put this in the flames," Joseph said, handing her the letter.

She took the letter and started making the fire. "You are a funny-acting Englishman," she said to him in Italian. In front of the other servants they spoke English. At this time Maria had only two young girls from the London League to assist her. Thin things without a spark of life in them. Maria feared they would die soon. She worked them hard. "Ah, your brothers, they should see you now. But they do not care about you at all. They care nothing for you! Your brother Solomon and your brother Elijah they never come here. Only your sister visits. She is a kind woman and I think she truly loves you. Your brothers don't. And Darius, he hates you. Ricci told me that."

What had happened to Maria in England—her young husband, Ricci, running off with the Contessa (she never thought of the woman as Mrs. Joseph Forster)—had upset her, but she accepted it as part of her life. She had, after all, been brought up in Tuscany, where her mistress, the Marchesa, the Contessa's aunt, had been accused of poisoning her husband and her two sons so that she and her lover, a riding master, could live in idyllic peace with one another. For centuries, the Riminis had been connected to one scandal or another.

"You are right," Joseph said. "They don't care about me. Elijah cares only about money. And Solomon only about his health and . . . oh, yes, and Aristotle. Some day I must read you his essay on Aristotle. I shall tie you to a chair, and even though you beg and plead

I shall not untie you until you have heard every word of it. He gave me a copy of it last week. In the brothel, no less."

"Why do you not take me to the brothel? Your brother Solomon takes Mrs. Cornwind, his new mistress, and Elijah takes Moly. Am I not as good as either of them?" She pulled down her blouse and exposed her full young breasts.

Joseph smiled and threw a kiss to her. "You are better and I really would like to, but there are some things an Englishman cannot do. I may take a friend to a brothel, my mistress to a brothel, I may even take my cat or dog, but I may not, no never, take my servant. Such is English custom. Though I may bugger you in the privacy of my bedroom."

"Tonight Grindal eats with us."

"Oh . . . Why? I don't like her."

"She says she has much to tell us. About your brother and Emma's governess, Miss Slyboots, and Mr. Coverly and Miss Slyboots."

"Grindal is too fat."

"Yes, but she eats because she longs for Ricci [before Ricci had run off he had been Grindal's lover] just as you drink because you long for the Contessa, that *strega*."

"I wish you would not call my wife that."

"I believe that Grindal loved Ricci even more than I loved Ricci."

Since the lovers had fled to Florence, leaving Maria and Grindal behind, the women had become friends of a sort. After all, they had both loved Ricci. And Ricci had loved both of them. It was Maria who had reached out the hand of friendship to her erstwhile enemy one day when she saw Grindal in the Gardens, overweight and shabby-looking, as if she no longer cared about living. Impetuously she had run to Grindal and embraced her, but Grindal had almost fainted, thinking that she was being ambushed once again by Maria. When she realized it was not an attack but an embrace she responded in kind. So from that time on Maria invited her to dine with them occasionally.

That night at dinner, Grindal, her face flushed from wine, her stomach amply filled with Maria's pasta and sausages, told them what she knew about Clara.

"I followed Miss Slyboots on her day off. And where do you think she went?"

"Where?" asked Maria.

"She stepped into a coach on Collards Lane."

"So—" said Maria.

"Oh, do be silent, you silly thing. It was Mr. Coverly's coach. I recognized the coachman."

"Ah, she is his mistress then?" asked Maria.

"Now, I don't know about that. She might be, but if she is then she has two men, for I know for a fact that a week ago she became my master's mistress! And it was him that came to her. I saw them—"

Joseph sat with the two servants, his face impassive, wondering about himself and his brothers. Why did they live the way they did? Why had Consuelo left him? Why did Elijah have to have every woman he met? Why was Solomon such a blathering idiot? Why was he sitting here with these women? Though he was fond of Maria, he detested Grindal. The child beater. Maria had told him how Grindal used to beat Emma mercilessly, and how Darius had intervened and stopped her. She must be well over ten stone now. Her once flawless white skin was now grimy and splotched. The fat had distorted her features, fleshed out her nose so that it looked like a snout, and her eyes had gotten smaller, or was it that the added flesh around them made them appear that way. He looked at her, feeling disgust. The child beater stuffing her face now with the small oily popovers Maria had made for dessert. He poured more whiskey into his glass and drank it. He drank a bit more than usual that night.

After Grindal left, Maria helped him up the stairs.

Upstairs he told her to leave him. "Leave me alone! Damn you! Don't come near me, do you hear me? I don't want your filthy peasant paws all over me!" he roared. "You stink. You stink of garlic and stupidity and vulgarity! Leave me alone. If you come near me I'll strangle you!"

"I'll leave you alone, you stupid Englishman! I hope you choke in your vomit!" said Maria, slamming the door on her way out.

Alone on his bed he stared at a chair across the room. He would dismiss her. He would send her back to Florence. He would ask Elijah to find him a good, kind, decent woman like Mrs. Farnley to take care of him . . . Darius! Elijah had told him—was it yesterday, or the day before, what difference did it make—Elijah had told him he had gone to see him again. Why? Who had asked him to? To Somerset. This spring. How had he dared to see Darius without asking for permission! Why had Elijah done that? What had Elijah told him? Oh yes, it was coming back to him . . . the boy was doing well, he said, he was sure to win a scholarship to Oxford or Cambridge . . . Darius looked well . . . he was grateful Elijah had come, he had thanked Elijah for . . . "your interest" is what he had said.

"I think he wants to see you," Elijah had said. "You should go to see him, Joseph."

"I don't wish to."

"You are his father, Joseph."

"Am I?"

"Of course you are. You have a responsibility to him."

"I shall never see him again, if I can arrange it. And there's no use speaking about it to me again. I'm very annoyed that you have interfered as much as you have. I don't wish you to see him again without asking me first for my permission."

Joseph slid off the bed and onto his knees. He began to pray. He prayed for himself and for Darius. He hated Darius; he would never forgive him. He had depended on Darius to keep Consuelo here with him. And Darius had failed. Darius had betrayed him. She had gone off anyway, leaving her precious Darius behind. He would never forgive him but still he prayed for him. He prayed because he could not stand the pain, and it seemed to him that after he prayed for his son, whom he did not love, whom he never wished to see again, he felt somewhat better.

He got back into bed. After an hour or so of trying to fall asleep and being unable to, he got out of bed and went downstairs to the studio, Consuelo's piano room.

Was Maria up? He listened for sounds. Should he go to her room and peer in? Should he go to the kitchen? No, what difference did it make? It was no business of Maria's anyway. He took the studio key out of his pocket and opened the door and closed it behind him, being careful to lock the door again.

There it was. As he had left it. The oil painting on the easel was a large canvas five feet by six feet of his sister-in-law Guinivere naked. A smile came across Joseph's face. He began to laugh. In his mind's eye he saw his family—Mathilda, Elijah, Solomon, Guinivere herself!— looking at the painting, their outrage, their horror . . . Oh, he could not stop laughing. Oh, it was too funny, too funny for words. Tears streamed down his cheeks. Oh, how he would like to show the painting to Elijah, the womanizer. Solomon the prude. And to Consuelo! That she-wolf! That vampire! What was it she had always said to him (and with such contempt) when he wanted to spend a little time with her, just half an hour, for God's sake! But she was always busy, busy: "Why don't you take up painting, Joseph, you seem to have a flair for it." Well, he *had* after she left. And yes, he did seem to have a "flair" for it, didn't he?

Before he had "taken up" painting, Joseph had first taken an ax to Consuelo's piano, and though Maria had tried to stop him he had destroyed it. He had taken the pieces out into the Gardens and burned them; then he had taken a hammer to the keys, and when that hadn't worked he had put them into bags filled with heavy stones and had thrown them into the lake.

It must have been six months later when the thought of painting had come to him. He painted her, of course, at first. Over and over again. Consuelo, the bitch goddess; Consuelo, the vampire. Standing there, wearing her robe day after day, painting her, it seemed to give him relief. And then, he didn't know when it had happened, he became interested in color, in painting itself. Sometimes months would go by and he would do nothing, he would not even think about painting, and then after he'd drunk himself into a stupor something inside him would tell him he was ready to paint. He would tell Maria not to disturb him and he would lock himself in the studio and stay up all night and paint.

He read books about painting now, and he experimented with different mediums. He went to museums. He knew about Turner, Constable, Crome, Girtman, Fuseli, Bonnington . . . but it was the Frenchman Delacroix whom he admired most of all. In particular his nudes, alive with sexual vitality. Sometimes he wondered what Consuelo would have made of all of this.

He had painted Guinivere lying on a divan, her golden flesh luminous against the dark amethyst velvets of the couch, the curves of her golden breasts repeated in the curves of her swelling hips, her body a welter of serpentine curves.

What in the world had possessed him to paint Gwinnie that way, he wondered. For though he liked Guinivere well enough (much better than Theodisia, for whom he had contempt), and even felt compassion for her grief, she was a bit too saintly for his tastes. For all his complaining he preferred the Consuelos and the Marias of the world. Women who had a bite to them. He definitely preferred female demons to female saints. So what had possessed him . . . he thought back. Had he been secretly attracted to Gwinnie sexually, and now that Consuelo was gone his real feelings for his sister-in-law had finally emerged, crawled out into the light of day? Hardly. No, he didn't think so. He had no sexual desire for Gwinnie. There was something decidedly a-sexual about her. . . .

Then why? Why had he painted her . . . as if she were in heat? A bitch in heat. He thought back to the last time he had seen her some weeks ago. Where? At Elijah's. He had felt good enough to attend Sunday dinner. She had been seated next to Coverly. He, Joseph, had sat across from both of them at the dinner table. And then Guinivere had blushed. He had wondered why. *That* was it. He remembered wondering at the time if Mr. Coverly had said something to her that would cause her to blush. She had lowered her head, lifting it a moment later—that beautiful head so gracefully placed on the beautiful stem of her neck—and looking straight at Coverly she had smiled. It had been the smile, of course. He had never seen Gwinnie smile in that way. There had been something so inviting that the phrase he had learned at Warrenton came back to him: "What is life, what is joy, without the golden Aphrodite?" Yes, Gwinnie had looked like that, the goddess Aphrodite. And at Elijah's dinner table. Had he been the only one to see that fleeting moment? He remembered he had glanced around the table. Everything seemed as always, that is Elijah was pontificating and Solomon was quoting Aristotle. He had been the only one looking at both of them—Guinivere and Isaac Coverly—the only one to see the blush expand and fade, the only one to see that radiant smile.

And then what Grindal had said hours ago came back to him. Elijah and Clara Lustig! And what was Coverly doing with Clara? Whatever it was, he was quite sure *that* wasn't sexual. But was Coverly pursuing Gwinnie? Should he tell Elijah what he suspected? Or Solomon? But what did he suspect anyway? That Coverly was planning to "ravish" Guinivere and Guinivere was planning to be "ravished"?

It was from that time on he had begun to think of Gwinnie naked. He had begun the canvas then. No one had noticed but him . . . Joseph the fool, Joseph the drunkard . . . Joseph the cuckold. He would keep his suspicions to himself. They had been vicious about the dowry. Solomon especially.

He stared at the life-size nude. The shading on the thigh needed some work. . . . He began to hum as he worked, mixing the colors white, carmine, a pinch of lemon yellow, unaware that he was humming one of his wife's musical compositions, one that she had written in this room when she had lived here with him.

Sometime later Maria knocked on the door. He didn't answer because he didn't hear her. She began to bang on the door. This time he heard her and didn't answer.

"Good night, you rotten Englishman," she said in a friendly voice. He could hear her walking away as he picked up the brush and began painting Guinivere's nipples.

16

A LETTER FROM WILLIAM

Dear Emma,
Do send me immediately some sealing wax and India rubber.
I am in urgent need of them. I have written Poppa about this
matter but he has chosen to ignore it.

Last night Albert's fag threw a package into my window
which turned out to be a quarter of a duck. I fail to understand why Albert and the twins receive these marvelous packages of edibles from home and we (Edward and I) do not.
I do not see how I am expected to construe and learn Latin
accidence on boiled milk and stale bread, which for the most
part is my daily diet.[23]

Yesterday I ate well enough. I was taken out to dinner by,
of all people (if I were home at your side I would make you
beg before I told you), our cousin Darius. Yes! He is in
Cambridge now. We shall go to Oxford, an inferior school,
he says, because our fathers went there. He said he shall stay
there until he is elected to the Apostles and then he shall
refuse and return to his palazzo in Florence. He came with
a sallow-faced, grubby-looking boy, whom he called Bumbles. Bumbles does everything for him. He helped him into
the carriage when we went to the Castle, which is the best
inn hereabouts, and helped him out! He carried his cloak
and at the table unfolded his napkin for him and even cut
up his meat for him! Veal cutlets! Heavenly most wonderful
veal cutlets! Lit his cigar for him. And for dessert Devonshire

---

23. There are diaries of famous men who in their eighties (Lord Curzon for one) still
wake up feeling starved, until they remember they are no longer at school.—*R. Lowe*

cream and raspberry tarts! When I grow up I want to have a Bumbles. I would dearly love it. Whatever Darius says—and of course Darius does say wonderful things, but not always—Bumbles always agrees with him.

Darius, by the way, is quite angry with you, Emma. He has written you countless times he told me, and you have never replied. But I told him that it was probably not your fault. That Poppa probably intercepted and did not pass his letters on to you. I told him frankly that Poppa did not like him, that though he saved his life when he cut him down (for after all Poppa is a Christian gentleman) Poppa did not approve of him or his mother and never would. He thanked me and said he understood. So you need not worry, Emma, I have taken care of the matter for you.

Now I must tell you something that must go no further. Albert and Edward fought with one another over Vanessa. This past Christmas they both fell in love with her. Edward, who promised never to fall in love, has. I sincerely hope that does not happen to me. Albert has written twelve poems to her and sent them to her! Edward is writing an epic poem in Latin about the Trojan War, which he has dedicated to her. He has written over one hundred lines already.

They fought behind the Eagle Yard, where we drink, though Mr. Keefe informs us that he will be closed on Sunday afternoons from now on by order of Her Majesty the Queen. However, he has a cellar where we can fight and play games and bet—that is, if we pay enough. And there will be liquor there and glasses and if we leave money we will be able to drink, and that is how we shall circumvent the decree.

They fought for over half an hour, both of them stripped to the waist like professional boxers, Emma. And they were both—and this you must *never* tell—drunk on brandy. Edward has no friends, so I had to be his second. As for Albert, he has so many friends there was almost another fight over who would be his second. Edward and Albert fought until neither of them could stand but merely clung to one another. Then Edward fell and Albert fell forward on him. Edward did not come to for hours and the senior Master told Albert that if Edward died Albert would have to stay home for "one half." Edward finally came to. However, they no longer speak to one another. I hardly speak to Edward either. He has become a misanthrope. I did not tell you this sooner because you were particularly obnoxious to me when I was home last.

Darius told me that I must forgive you when I complained to him about you. So I have.

At dinner Darius told me that the "Contessa," his mother, is expecting another child. He hopes it will die. He dislikes his mother as much as I dislike ours. When Mrs. Farnley came to rescue me from starvation, she told me that it was not Mater's fault that she did not write or visit because Poppa had forbidden her to. But I did not believe her. If Momma truly loved me as she says she does she would have found a way. I am quite certain I would have.

Next Christmas I shall be a remove higher and I shall have certain liberties. I cannot wait until I am in fifth form and can have a fag whom I shall flog unmercifully.

And now I have no more news to tell you.

Pray answer this epistle soon and tell me if, as I have instructed Grindal countless times, she has finally packed up my soldiers as she said she would and put them in the place where I told her to in the attic.

Ave atque vale (hail and fairwell).
Your frater, William

P.S. We are studying Suetonius' *De Vita Caesarium*. I find Gaius Caesar (Caligula) quite entertaining. Have you read him yet?

Emma read the letter quickly in her room after dinner. She was not too interested in William anymore. She no longer liked him. He had been insufferably rude to her the last time he was home. In everything he said to her was the implication that *he* was a boy; she a mere girl. That *he* would grow up to be a man! She a mere woman. He had been insufferable! So the startling information about Darius's letters did not immediately affect her. And then when it did she was sick with rage! Darius's letters withheld from her! But who could have done that? The answer came as soon as she thought it. Her father, of course! Who else but him? But how *could* he have done that? To *her*! And why? Darius! So then her beloved Darius had *not* abandoned her! Darius *had* written her! He had *not* forgotten her. He *still* loved her. Another violent rush of emotion seized her. Poppa! She must do something now! Immediately! Her body demanded action. She could not keep still she was in such a fury. She would *demand* an explanation from Poppa! It was after dinner; he would be in his library now.

Swiftly she ran out of her room and down the stairs. She would threaten! She would insist! She would demand! All sorts of wild thoughts went through her head. Tears flowed down her cheeks. Rage, sorrow, and confusion mingled with fear. Rage hurled her down the stairs. And then suddenly she was there, there before she knew it, outside her father's library door, her hand on the large carved wooden knob, and she was suddenly petrified. She stood there for a few seconds, shaking, her heart thudding . . . Oh, God, what should she do? She was in agony . . . and then from somewhere inside her head she heard Clara's voice sound in her mind: "Do nothing now. Go back upstairs to your room. Control yourself . . ." and an enormous feeling of relief poured through her. She need not do anything *now*. All this happened in a matter of seconds. The curved edge of the knob pressed hard into the sweaty palm of her hand—"control," that was almost the very first word Clara had spoken to her. A sigh escaped her—though there was still a part of her that wanted to rush in and attack her father physically, Emma let go of the knob. Clara was right. Having let go, she stood there for a few seconds and then she put her ear to the door. Hearing nothing from inside she turned around, walked back across the hall, and made her way slowly back up the stairs. Clara was always right, of course.

On her way back to her room she saw what could have been: she saw herself rushing in, confronting Poppa, hysterical, totally out of control, making a fool of herself and accomplishing nothing. Thank God that hadn't happened! She would go upstairs instead and . . . think. She would think about what to do. She would be clever like Clara. And she would tell no one—not even Clara—about William's letter. Not until many years later did it occur to Emma that she herself had conjured up Clara's voice inside her head so that she would not have to come face-to-face with Poppa.

As she walked up the stairs to her room she remembered Darius and the Order of Ramini,[24] and the vow she and her brothers and cousins had taken never to divulge anything about this secret organization. She had kept that secret. They *all* (her brothers and her cousins) had kept that secret. She had been ten years old then. Now she was thirteen and wiser. She would be silent. She would be cunning, even more cunning than she had been then. She would think and she would . . . plan. Seated at her desk, pen in hand, she asked herself this question: what would Darius do if he were faced with this situation?

The letters . . . she wondered, had Poppa kept them or destroyed

---

24. In November of 1836 Emma's cousin Darius (Count Rimini VII) proclaimed himself the Grand Duke of Marlborough Gardens and established the Great and Sacred Order of Rimini. She, her brothers, and all her male cousins took an oath to keep this "secret from everyone . . . our nannies and our parents . . . never to be revealed even under threat of physical torture." See *City of Childhood,* Chapter 9.—*R. Lowe*

them? Well, she would somehow find out about that too. But first things first. She would first write William—how dare he say she was obnoxious! If anyone was obnoxious it was him! Caligula entertaining!—and arrange with him to immediately tell Darius that (1) she had never received any letters from him, (2) that she was certain they had purposefully been withheld from her, and (3) that if Darius still wanted to write to her, and she fervently hoped he did, he should enclose his letters in William's letters. But then she wondered if perhaps she should make this arrangement with Edward—William would certainly demand something in return. On the other hand, William was certainly right about what he had said about Edward. Edward *had* changed. Edward was no longer the confident older brother he used to be, her defender . . . besides, the fewer people who knew about it the better. No, avaricious, greedy William would have to be the go-between.

That night she wrote William a letter calculated to appeal to both those defects of his character and enclosed a generous amount of sealing wax and India rubber.

Several days later she began thinking about the possible reasons Poppa might have had for doing what he had done. Poppa had once described Darius as "unsavoury." She remembered that she had looked up the word. There had been several meanings. She was quite sure Poppa did not think Darius was "insipid" or "disagreeable," but there was another meaning—"morally offensive"—and she suspected it was that meaning that her father intended when he used the word in relation to Darius. Now she wondered what exactly had been Darius's moral offence. Whatever it had been, if indeed it existed at all, it made no difference to her. To her Darius had been kindness itself. She loved Darius. She always would love Darius. It was uncomfortable to disobey Poppa, to lie and to connive behind his back, because she loved Poppa, but she would not give up Darius, not even for him.

Though the original savage anger began to fade from her consciousness, it surfaced, now and then, oddly enough, when she was not with Poppa, in his presence. She would be reading a book, or doing her lessons, or walking . . . and the thought of Poppa's intercepting Darius's letters to her would come to mind and she would experience a sudden spurt of fierce anger. That frightened her so badly that she felt compelled, when she said her customary prayers at night, to also pray for the desire to forgive Poppa.

17

CLARA

Men devise dogmatic codes; create philosophical systems like: morality is the intelligible doing of the state, or "world history is world action," and they are always expressed in high-sounding phrases for their *own* benefit.

—Emma Forster, *Conversation with Clara,* privately printed (1901)

CLARA was on her way to Nicholas. Walking quickly (it was a cold December day) towards Collards Lane, where Nicholas's coach was waiting for her, she looked like a well-groomed, glossy blackbird in her black caped mantle and black feathered bonnet—Mathilda's castoffs. A chronic diet of good food and money in her purse had filled out the empty pockets of her flesh and her soul. Good mutton, game pies, and sugary cream-filled desserts and puddings had plumped out her cheeks and added an inch or two to the pinched waist and erased the starved look she had had when she had come from Germany nearly two years before.

Yes, there had been some success, she thought. There was Emma, her pupil (she was very much aware of the importance she had in Emma's mind). And Elijah! (She must write to Johan about that! A discreet letter, but informative.) Within the complex hierarchy of the household she had contrived, successfully, to create a special niche for herself, wherein she was respected and appreciated.

She had no idea that Mrs. Farnley disliked her, or that Daisy considered her a fool. For all her intelligence Clara had no real understanding of people. She could and did write acidulous and even entertaining accounts of their foibles to Johan, assessing them accurately enough, but she had no means of penetrating an artful dissemblance. She was a bright, clever woman who, though she appreciated her own emotions, was incapable of experiencing others emotionally.

And then there was her "literary" success. Recently she had written an impassioned reply to somebody's prudish attack on Wollstonecraft's private life. She had dashed off the article in white anger, entitling it "The Divine Right to Lose One's Head," and had sent it off to *Blackwood's* magazine. It had been accepted. They were also considering an article she had written a year ago on Aphra Ben.

All these thoughts were going through her adroit mind, which was as always quickly sorting the incoming information about the world and the people in it into separate tidy compartments shut off from one another, so that she, Clara, could act out antithetical goals. No, she did not wish to be tied to one end, one final goal. She preferred five different personas, each carrying on with maximum energy. And if the ends were contrary, *tant pis,* she was quite sure she could control the results.

She was extraordinarily bright, but like Kant—and she was not as bright as he was; she could not have written the antimonies, the thirty-eight glorious pages of German metaphysics—she "knew" so much and simultaneously so little.

Her article on Wollstonecraft, maintaining the right to lose one's reason when the heart was involved, was *not* her credo. Reason was her mistress. "We rationalize so that we can attain our moral . . . or immoral . . . ends," she once told Emma. That is what she believed in, placed her faith in, not that unpredictable "the heart has its reasons" school. She had defended Wollstonecraft's *right* to lose her reason. A principle was involved. The dissolution of reason, well, that was another question.

She crossed the avenue. Down the next street she saw a carriage draw up to Guinivere's house. Mrs. Strooksbury's carriage. Mrs. Strooksbury was dropping Guinivere off. On Wednesdays the two women worked for the London League in the Bethnal Green slum. She had never been asked to join them or the London League. Had she, she would have refused. That was not a place she wanted to visit, nor did she wish to work there in that rubble of humanity. It was a lie, of course, but a lie that the women adhered to, that their work in the League in any way ameliorated the hideous conditions of the men and women in the slum. A lie to salvage their consciences, so that they could come home, as they were doing now, and enjoy without guilt the things they had and others didn't. Give up your riches and follow me! Hardly likely. They would fight to the last iota to keep what they had—"If not for ourselves, for our children."

She despised hypocrites, having no idea that she might be considered one.

Today Nicholas would pay her once again for telling him what he wanted to know about the Forsters. She knew, at least one part of her mind knew, that she did not have to "comply." That Nicholas could not really report her without revealing his own part in the thefts. Nevertheless, the fact that Nicholas existed at all made her uneasy. Nicholas brought to mind Hegel's repellent dialectic of master and servant in which the master seeks the destruction of the other because he perceives him as a rival existence. She had the feeling that Nicholas felt that way about her. But even if he didn't feel that way about her—she no longer concerned herself with why Nicholas wanted what he wanted, although it certainly was not to burgle—she knew in relation to him she had no power at all. Sometimes that fact just made her feel uneasy, at other times it terrified her. That was why she complied. In the last year, Nicholas, as Isaac Coverly, had become a "friend of the family." And recently on several Sunday afternoons he had been invited to dine *en famille* at Elijah's.

After having written to Johan about their "arrangement," Clara had dismissed it from her mind. The "arrangement" had been placed in her brain in the "Nicholas" file, while the several ten-pound notes Nicholas gave her each time she visited him had been placed in a locked drawer of her bureau. The bundle of ten-pound notes (over two hundred pounds!), as yet unused, gave off all by itself a mysterious sense of power. She had never had so much money before. That too was part of her success, besides Emma, Elijah, the servants, and her articles. The thought of all this success made her giddy. It gave her a feeling of power and pleasure to have secrets. To work secretly for Nicholas, to work for and against the Forsters.

Elijah. *That* was another file. There had been moments of passion with her husband, Franz—Franz and her father were the only men she had ever respected—but only moments. He was too gentle, too thoughtful to arouse naked passion. He had been a good man like her father. A rare quality in mankind.

She saw Guinivere ascend the steps of her house. Suddenly hatred engulfed her. The difference in their destinies, hers and Guinivere's. She saw herself transcendent, floating above the scene, looking down at the earth below, herself a figure trudging its way to Nicholas's coach and on the same map Guinivere entering the lavish interior of her house. The chronic fear of poverty . . . the luxury of the other woman's life . . . With ruthless discipline Clara cut off her feelings. Such musing would do her no good. The map faded. She had better things to do. She straightened her shoulders underneath the wool of her warm coat.

What had Mathilda said: "I have no use for this anymore. I thought you might want it." Mathilda was nicer to her than either Guinivere or Theodisia. She hurried on past Guinivere's house.

Ah, there was Nicholas's carriage at the usual place. The coachman was hostile as usual, though he opened the door for her and helped her in. They drove off through the narrow twisting lanes that lay behind Marlborough Gardens to Jorem's house. To the back door. No one must know of her visits.

Piles of garbage were everywhere in the back alleys. Groups of people, savage-looking men and women in dirty clothes, stood about blocking the road. She shuddered as the carriage made its way through them, the coachman screaming and yelling at them—"Make way!"—brandishing his whip and threatening to beat them to death if they didn't move. Forced to give way, their faces leered at her through the windows of the coach—the stuff of nightmares. She recoiled into the shadows of the interior. Why did he take this route through this sea of human excrement?

When they arrived at the back entrance of Jorem's house, the footman opened the door, helped her down the steps, and let her in the small red-painted door in the brick wall that protected the back of the house. To insure his privacy Nicholas had added several feet of wall to the existing wall and had had four-foot-high iron spikes drilled into the top.

Several brutal-looking dogs, mastiffs, tied to stakes by strong chains, lunged at her, baring their teeth. The first time, no one had warned her, she had almost fainted when they lunged. Now she knew the chains were strong and short. They could not reach her. Nicholas had told her they were loosed only at night.

The entire foundation of the house had been exposed. Windows up to fifteen feet high had been put in, and to further insure light a deep ditch had been built out from the foundation that you crossed over by way of a wooden bridge to get to the rear door, over which a name plate spelled out the word "Vallombrosa" . . . shady places. She knew the word, of course. It was from *Paradise Lost,* Book I: "Thick as autumnal leaves that strew the brooks of Vallombrosa . . ." But it made no sense since every tree on the grounds had been cut down to let in as much light as possible.

She knocked—there was no bell—and waited. No one came. She knocked again and finally the door was opened by that loathsome creature who always let her in, Toby.

Sometimes during the "visit" Toby would return with tea. For him. Not her. *One* teacup. Clara looked past the woman, wishing to disguise the surge of repugnance she felt on seeing Toby. Never a word of welcome. Always sullen. Today Toby said: "The master says today you are to wait in the mural room. Follow me."

The mural room. What in the world was that? Up till now Clara had met the "master" in a small room in the basement, down the hall from the workrooms. A squalid little room without drapes, without a carpet, only an old ugly desk and two wooden chairs.

She followed Toby down the dark corridor past a series of closed doors from behind which she heard sawing and what sounded like grinding. Then she passed one that was open. Quickly she looked in and saw Kevin Francini. He was talking to a man who looked like a beggar. But when Francini noticed her he stopped abruptly and, giving her a malevolent look, came to the door and closed it in her face.

Let me see, she thought, since all the Forster houses were similarly laid out—she must be going past what would have been, in Elijah's house, Theodisia's morning room. So that must have been what? The dining room? But the corridors twisted and turned and she was disoriented when Toby stopped to open a door to a staircase. She followed her up the stairs and down another corridor to a door on the left. Where was she? She was totally confused.

Opening up the door Toby motioned Clara in and said: "You're to wait in here, the master says." And then left her.

The room was large and the ceiling was vaulted, but how could that be? Then she realized on closer inspection that it was a trompe l'oeil. A brilliant and exceedingly clever one. "The mural room," Toby had said. And indeed there it was. She stared at the frescoed ceiling.

In the center was an empty sapphire throne. From it azure and gold curved ribs extended to the wainscoting. On either side of the ceiling, locked in combat, were two armies, two bands of angels. One side was obviously the worse for wear, their glorious wings clipped and torn, their naked breasts bleeding, their brazen chariots overturned, while on the other side stood the obvious victors, their shields shining, unsullied, some of whom were climbing upward towards the empty throne, their naked bodies becoming more luminous and radiant as they approached it. Below . . . the burning lake stretched. The opening scenes of Milton's poem ran through her mind. Vallombrosa, of course . . .

> *His legions, angel forms, who lay entranced*
> *Thick as autumnal leaves that strew the brooks of*
> *Vallombrosa . . .*

Paradise Lost, Book 1 . . . but so very different. For in this struggle it was Satan and his cohorts who were clearly winning. One could not mistake the fallen angel, Satan, larger and more radiant than all the other angels. His right hand almost touched the throne. In another moment the throne would be his.

Clara looked away. She was an avowed atheist, still it was disturbing to see Satan as victor. Shocking really . . . and then the next thought came: but of course that was exactly what Nicholas had intended. He had meant for her to be horrified. Shaken. That was why they were meeting here, in this room. He had meant to frighten her. To offend her. But why? She felt fear, repugnance, but deliberately cut herself off from the awareness. She would think about it later, in the relative security of Elijah's house.

Now she would examine the rest of the room. Calmly. . . . She walked closer to the wall. Paintings of dwarfs and midgets! All of them signed by Kevin Francini! Grotesque! The strange fresco, the freakish paintings, the hunchback Toby, the waiting, the change in routine, everything in the past quarter of an hour suddenly converged to unnerve her. She felt assaulted, brutalized. A wave of nausea threatened to overwhelm her.

Her mind was under attack by another mind. She understood that now. Resolutely she shut down all sensation and gradually the flood of disgust that momentarily had threatened to overcome her receded. Her nose had been shoved willy-nilly into the bloody center of another human being's heart. Nicholas's heart. Why, she didn't know, but it had been calculated. She was certain of that. Her mind cooled down. It became amused. Ironical. Curious. She would wait for him here. Detached. Composed. All this took place in less than a minute.

She sat down on the couch. Primly she clasped her hands in front of her. She must divert herself. Think of something quite different from this shoddy, melodramatic high jinks, this Grand Guignol milieu. Elijah. He had come to her at last . . . early one morning . . . in urgent need. Calmly as she sat there she forced herself to compose a letter to Johan as she waited for Nicholas to appear.

Dear Johan,

Elijah came to me one morning. Stealing in like a phantom lover . . . Arrogant. Clever. Lustful. . . . My door was open. It had been open for some time now, waiting for him. Softly he entered, swiftly he got into bed, placing his hand over my mouth gently, ever so gently but ready to clamp down if I screamed, while he drew me towards him, his strong arm around my waist. . . .

"Do you promise not to scream?" he asked me. I nodded yes and he removed his hand from my mouth to stroke my breast. "Put your hand on me. Put your hand on me, and stroke it, Clara. Do that. Ahhhh! Yes!" Then passion overwhelmed him, overwhelmed me. He lifted up my nightgown and spread my legs with his hands. "Ahhhh! Yes!" Then he

put the tip of his penis on the tip of my clitoris and moved it back and forth, in and out. Minutes later he came. All passion spent. He was about to leave when I said softly "Again" in a tone that made it swell and pulse once more. "Clara!" he whispered, and moaned when I took his organ into my hand and moved my hand up and down, gently but firmly. "Now, enter," I whispered, and he did and I murmured "Yes, yes, yes . . ." And then I came and he had to clamp down on my mouth to muffle my screams of joy, yes, and of pleasure. There we lay snugly together, my thin body enveloped in his fleshy one. We knew the time was short but we could not part. We lay there sated, blissful, I in his arms, he grateful and surprised perhaps, I deep in an animal satisfaction, my body fed. . . . Serene. And then I heard a noise. "Get under the bed," I whispered. "It's Emma, I know her step!" He hurled himself out of bed and lay on the cold barren floor beneath my bed. Seconds later the door opened and Emma said, "I've had a bad dream. May I come in?" she asked, and crawled into bed with me.

"Put your head upon my shoulder," I told her. "Go back to sleep, Emma." Five minutes later, though it seemed more like an hour, she was asleep. Without moving I lowered my hand over the side of the bed, motioning him to go. He did. Not looking at either of us, he fled. Half an hour later Emma awakened and I walked her to the door, my nightdress still wet with his semen. We walked past Grindal's door. She stared at us while we walked past. . . .

That was it. The end of the letter she would not send. She looked at the clock ticking away on the desk. She had been waiting ten minutes.

Behind her the door opened. She turned around to see Nicholas coming into the room. His handsome face bland as always. She rose.

This month Nicholas had wanted her to keep a record of what they ate each night. What in the world did he want with that?

He took the list from her and said, "Sit down, Mrs. Lustig. There is something I wish to discuss with you." He waited until she was seated again before continuing. "You are acquainted with Mrs. Solomon Forster, are you not?"

"I have met her. I would not say that we were 'acquainted.' "

He said nothing for a few moments. Instead he stared past her, and then, not looking at her, he said: "The best way to gather information about someone is to ask questions. Until I ask you, Mrs. Lustig, how you feel about me I shall not know. Now your answer may be a tissue of lies, or half-truths skillfully embroidered. On the other hand, you may be frank and truthful, but I shall know nothing in either case until I ask you. I may then tell you how I feel about you. How I have developed an uncontrollable sexual passion for you—Oh, do not be disturbed, Mrs. Lustig, I am merely illustrating what interrogation can develop into. As it sometimes does in police circles . . . into criminal convictions . . ."

She was as close to fainting as she had ever been in her life. His voice. Low. Venomous. Each word dripping with insinuation, each word stripping her of any feeling of self-worth. But what was he talking about anyway? Sexual passion . . . criminal convictions . . . What did he mean by that? She couldn't understand what he was talking about. But what difference did that make? That was not the point. The point was the obvious and blatant *contempt* he had for her. No matter how hard she tried, she could not shut that out. It shriveled her. She clutched her reticule to her chest as if it would save her.

"Are you ill, Mrs. Lustig?"

"No . . . Mr. Renton, a temporary migraine."

"Then I may continue . . ."

"Yes."

"So instead of list making—I have, after all, other ways and means of gathering the kind of information you have given me—"

Her mind revived somewhat. He was telling her, wasn't he, that others in the household, other servants—Mrs. Farnley? Grindal? Daisy? Norris? which of them?—were also in his employ in some way or other. She handed him the list of foods and menus.

"I want you to ask questions about Mrs. Solomon Forster. I want to know all about Mrs. Solomon Forster. I want to know about her personal life. See to it, Mrs. Lustig! Ask questions about her past. I am interested particularly in her childhood. You will do that, will you not, Mrs. Lustig?"

The last words were said in such a menacing tone that she had to counsel herself to remain calm and composed.

Nicholas glanced up at the mural. "Report back to me a month from now. The first week in January. Kevin will arrange it. Good day to you, Mrs. Lustig. Toby will show you out." He rose from his chair. "I owe you some money, I believe, Mrs. Lustig." And taking a ten-pound note from his pants pocket he walked over to her, opened up the hand clutching the reticule, and placed the note in it. He left her holding the note in her hand.

Toby took Clara back the way she had come, through the dark corridors, down the stairs, past the workrooms (all the doors were shut this time), to the back door of the house with the name plate Vallombrosa on it.

Clara crossed over the moat between the snarling dogs and opened the door in the wall. Just outside were the carriage and the coachman. She got inside and they went back through the same stinking sea of humanity to the same spot where he had picked her up. Her mind swarming with thoughts, she walked home slowly.

Just before she reached home—it was nearing five o'clock, she looked around her. It was cold but quite, quite beautiful. The sky was luminous. An absolutely pink cloud passed quickly behind the bare limbs of the oak in front of Elijah's house. In the distance the mauve horizon. A beautiful December twilight.

She hesitated before entering the house. Perhaps she should go away. Run away. But where to?

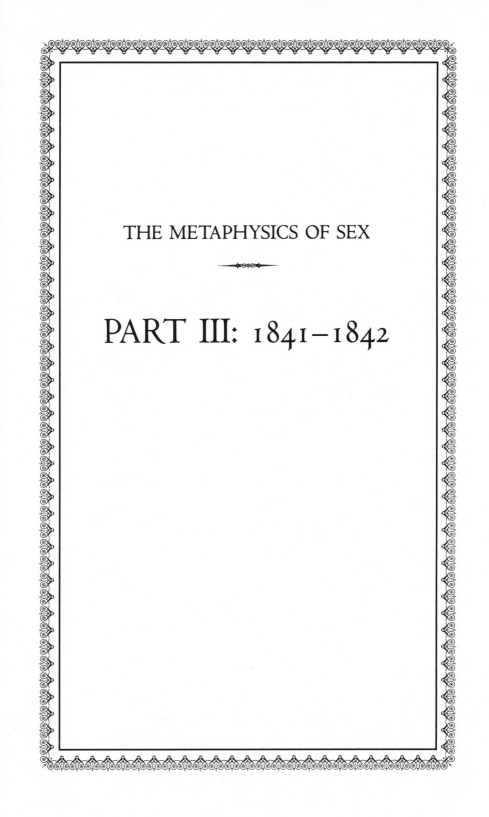

THE METAPHYSICS OF SEX

PART III: 1841–1842

PRELIMINARY
CONCLUSIONS

AUGUST 1937
MARLBOROUGH GARDENS

*Last night Harriet dreamed about Darius again. It is always the same
dream. The dream begins with the arrival of Darius to Marlborough
Gardens, to his house, No. 26 Marlborough Gardens. The "dream"
house looks exactly like Kevin Francini's aquatint, which depicted
the original Marlborough Gardens houses in their semirural grandeur . . . their leafy Gainsborough charm. The jalousies and railings
now gleam with fresh paint. Lavender and hydrangea bloom in the
garden and the red brick abounds with climbers. The panes sparkle
and through the gold-fringed drapes one can see the gilt harp that
Darius once played.*

*"And he looks," Harriet says, "exactly like his portrait in the Pitti
Palace."* [25] *Darius has returned, according to Harriet, has come back
to Marlborough Gardens, because he has fallen in love with Harriet.
He wants her to return with him to his time, a time in which the past
and future are irrelevant, for the time in his world is the eternal
now. . . . The dream ends just before the moment of departure, as
Darius assists Harriet up the steps into his landau.*

It is, of course, a wish-fulfillment dream. I have read Freud's Interpretation of Dreams *(as she has). The dream is perfectly straightfor-
ward. There is nothing complex about it. Somewhere in a footnote
Freud cites that children have far more complex and obscure dreams
than adults, whose dreams are simple and infantile in character. So*

25. See *City of Childhood*, Chapter 8.—*R. Lowe*

then what does it mean? Simply this: Harriet is in love with Darius so she dreams that Darius is in love with her.

I confess Harriet's obsession with Darius arouses jealousy in me. It is now over seven years since we went back to the estate agent, Mr. Chalmers of Chalmers Ltd.,[26] from whom Harriet bought the house, in an attempt to discover if there were any living Forster heirs still in possession of the remaining Forster houses. But neither Mr. Chalmers nor Chalmers Ltd. were to be found on Oxford Street. If in seven years, I tell myself, none have appeared, it is doubtful that any will. But I breathed a sigh of relief when we returned from the Gardens this afternoon to pass by Darius's house and saw that it is still boarded up and looks as depressing and shabby as ever. I am not fond of men of that type: irresponsible seducers who override with impunity the mores of society. I wonder, can one be jealous of a dead man?

We have spent the evening in Harriet's bedroom with our two assistants, Dorothea Rutledge and Irene Debenham, discussing and reading out loud Freud's Contributions to the Theory of Sex, *Contribution Two: Infantile Sexuality. Harriet is not feeling well. Dorothea and Irene are seated on a love seat while I am stretched out full-length next to Harriet, who holds court in lemon yellow crepe de chine pajamas.*

It was Dorothea's turn to read aloud:

"One of the surest premonitions," Dorothea reads, "of later eccentricity or nervousness is when an infant obstinately refuses to empty his bowel when placed on the chamber by the nurse, and controls this function at his own pleasure. It naturally does not concern him that he will soil his bed; all he cares for is not to lose the subsidiary pleasure in defecating. Educators have again shown the right inkling when they designate children who withhold these functions as naughty . . ."

Dorothea stopped here and put the book down, and then suddenly, apparently she felt compelled, told us that she had spent the year 1933 in Germany.

"I was studying at the University of Berlin—developing a treatise on the Meistersingers, and the legend of Tristan and Isolde. One evening I left the university—it was a warm May evening—and I saw hundred of students, much to my amazement, burning books at a square on Unter den Linden right opposite the university. They were using

26. See *City of Childhood*, Chapter 3.—*R. Lowe*

torches. I stopped to watch. I was fascinated in a strange sort of way. The boy next to me—I knew him slightly—tossed all of Freud's books into the flames . . . including this one."

Involuntarily I felt my body stiffen, and I looked at Harriet. She too looked startled, as if she had suffered a mild shock. I took the opportunity then and there to explain carefully to Dorothea how we— Harriet and I—had deliberately chosen a quiet life, withdrawn from the vulgarities of the world to pursue our "vocation"—the writing of the history of the Forster family—far, far from the horrors of modern history.

"Our lives may seem restricted to some persons but we have created for ourselves what few people ever succeed in doing—a private life in which we have achieved perfect contentment."

No more was said about the matter and we spent the rest of the evening editing the first part of Forbidden Objects, *Emma Forster's passionate account of her love affair with Johan Lustig.*

But later on that night when Harriet and I were alone, my mind kept going back to what Dorothea had said. Though I did not articulate my anxiety to Harriet, I wondered—how long would it be possible to keep the "world" out? And the wistful phrase "Can the ant ever leave the anthill?" reverberated in my mind. . . .

18

EMMA'S TRAVEL DIARY

4 APRIL 1853
HOTEL DE BRIENNE, PARIS

THERE is a man staying at the hotel who bears a strong resemblance to my father, not only physically but in how he relates to things, objects as well as people; how he presents himself in the world, how he secures space in it, the way his head moves on the column of his neck . . . graceful, elegant, and withal virile, a gorgeous masculine sexual force.

Like my father he is dressed in the height of fashion. My eyes are fastened on him. It is an effort not to look at him. I long to pore over his imperial face, look deep within those eyes, examine exactly how the golden russet-colored hair grows out from the smooth-pored skin.

He seems to be the same age as my father when he began his ineluctable decline, that is, in his prime, his early forties—but when are men like that not in their prime? Rudely I stare at him. Rudely I gape.

My father was my first sexual passion. The early chaste rapture that I experienced in my father's arms, that "bliss," has never yet been duplicated with others, neither men nor women, not even with Johan, for whom I would have given my life. That was the supreme, the complete and utter, pleasure.

I decided to ask one of the porters to tell me who the gentleman was. Count Wilenski. And he was aware of my interest in him. Though he did not cater to it, still, like any courtesan he was unusually sentient. It gave a modicum of calculation to all his movements. Like a spoiled child from time to time he would glance at me to see if I was still watching him.

Count Wilenski stirred deep deep chords within me. Memories of early betrayal and a sense of shame and sorrow . . .

I still recall how, one day, I happened to notice that my parents were smiling and laughing with one another, actually enjoying each other's company! I was appalled. How had this come about? Could it be true that these two enemies, forever sniping at one another, lacerating one another in so many ways, had "magically" reconciled and were about to "engage" in an amiable marriage? Like Aunt Guinivere and Uncle Solomon? And when had it happened? The idea totally demoralized me.

At dinner I noticed with rising nausea how they flirted with one another. My father was, in fact, deferential to my mother once or twice. And I saw that she was looking younger, yes, and plumper, not as thin and haggard as before. She seemed to glow. She had never "glowed" before.

His voice when he addressed her was actually warm and cordial. Gone was the mocking, biting tone, that special tone he used only with her. He even asked her one evening about her day with genuine concern if she had "enjoyed" herself!

When had it happened? It had happened, I told myself, while in order to please Clara and win her, I had thrown myself into my studies—I wished to be brilliant for her, learned, successful. It had happened when I was translating Horace and I let myself sink deep into the Symposium and dream of love. Clara was instilling an education into me that was a bit too ripe for my age, perhaps, for it is not true that classics or classicists are dry as dust. On the contrary, the richest, the most purple pages of prose were written by Plato. There were pages of Phaedrus that kept me awake at night with sexual desire. *That* was when it had happened. That was when they had drawn together. And if they were now one, suddenly joined together, where was I in relation to them? In relation to my father, in particular? I grew sick with fear. At the time it seemed to me as if my life depended on their remaining enemies.

No matter how hard I tried to win Clara, to please her, gratify her, submit to her, I knew on one level of consciousness that she really did not love me, that her feelings were for some reason placed elsewhere. She held me off. I could come close but no closer. So that all I had was Poppa, and now it looked to me as if that was no longer to be.

A tragic situation. Oh, it was not the kind of tragedy that Aristotle wrote about with his strict rules and regulations as to what constitutes tragedy: one must be highborn, prosperous, no vice or depravity should be the cause of his downfall, and so on. No. I was none of those things. I was powerless, vicious, eaten up with the sins of jealousy and envy, and in chronic terror. I was fourteen and going insane with fear and dread. And that is a tragedy.

I decided to ask Mrs. Farnley, who knew about everything that went on in the household. She would be able to tell me, that is, if she wanted to, because I had noticed how she too had begun to be protective towards my mother. It occurred to me that she might even prefer her to me, though I had always felt she had strong feelings of loyalty towards me.

While I was debating the wisdom of this action I remembered that three months earlier my mother had gone home to Ashville to see her father, who was dying. Her mother had died the year before. On her return, things had changed. But of course the next question was: Why? And the next: How could I find out?

I decided to revert to my old habits. I decided to eavesdrop again. I lurked in corners hoping to catch some clue as to what was going on. I scrutinized the mail. I peered through keyholes. . . .

I awakened in the middle of a dialogue between my mother and father. I had fallen asleep in the window embrasure of the library behind its thick curtains. In a moment of desperation, I had decided to secrete myself there in order to eavesdrop on their conversation.

It had become their habit, after dinner, to take a stroll in the Gardens and to return for a light dessert, which Mrs. Farnley served them in the library.

After dinner I had hidden myself behind the curtains. If I were caught I had prepared an appropriate lie: I had gone into the library (I had free entry to my father's library) to find a book, had started reading it, and had fallen asleep. Perhaps because I wanted to behave as authentically as possible, I had fallen asleep. My father was speaking:

". . . but to have left you the lion's share! And what a share! Not only the farm, but investments besides . . . and how cunning he was. What an astute investor! Oh, how I wish he would have come to me, not for advice, my dear, but to give it! Truly he was a financial genius. A truly remarkable man. I am sorry I did not know him better. You are to be commended, Theo, for having such a father. I am still agreeably surprised at your . . . or shall I say "our" good fortune."

"You may say *our* good fortune, Elijah."

I could not see their faces. Nor did I dare even to peep through the slit of the curtains, but their voices said enough. I knew (my heart sank) that despite his abuse of her for all these years, she had fallen in love with him once more. (I knew from Mrs. Farnley how much in love my mother had been with him when they were first married). Her voice was sugar sweet. Simpering.

He continued as if she had not spoken, as if in that short sentence of hers, she had not declared her love for him. I knew my father. I knew he was aware, sometimes preternaturally aware, of other people's feelings towards him. It was not that he hadn't heard her or registered it, oh no, her response had been weighed and assessed, and it had proved to him that she loved him still, despite the abuse, so it was not necessary for him to stop, to acknowledge her love, was it? After all, there was another point he wanted to make just then.

But at the same time my heart sank, my mind deduced another message: he didn't love her. He doesn't love her, I kept repeating to myself. It was not her he loved but her newly inherited money. For I understood immediately what they were discussing. Apparently her father had left her a great deal of money. I knew my father loved money, but it seemed to me that he loved me just a bit more than he loved money.

He was speaking again. I had been so deep in thought, so flooded with relief, I had missed the beginning of the sentence. When I began to listen I realized he was talking about me.

". . . money should go towards Emma's dowry. Let us say five thousand pounds."

"No, Elijah. She has a large enough dowry as it is. If there is to be a five-thousand-pound gift to the children it will be placed in William's account. He has nothing. He is neither the heir nor does he have a dowry."

"I have made provision for him, Theo. . . ." My father's voice was still cordial. "His education—Dr. Pond has written me that they are pleased with his progress in the classics—his family connections, all will contribute to his doing well in worldly terms. He will have hundreds of opportunities. He will be able to pick and choose. Perhaps an army career. And there is always the bank. But Emma . . . now there is a bit of a problem, isn't there?"

"I wish you would be more precise, Elijah."

"I have denied it, I agree. I could not admit it, but I do now. Emma is somewhat different from girls her own age. Painfully shy, awkward . . . I had hoped that Mrs. Lustig would make the difference, and she has to some extent but not quite enough. Our duckling has not become a swan as yet. Besides, there is the matter of the nevus. Nowadays men tend to look at women through the eyes of avarice, not through the eyes of love. Emma will need a bit more than other girls to balance the scales—"

"It is *my* inheritance, Elijah. You cannot force me to give it to you."

"My dear, I do wish you were agreeable to my wishes. I find your sudden flairs of independence somewhat annoying. There can only be one captain to a ship, one commander, not two, in the vessel, shall we say, of marriage. I have already discussed the matter with Mr. Redbury. He is willing to commit one of his sons provided the dowry is large enough . . . I have assured him this will be so, Theo."

They went on. Their voices were raised now. In my narrow enclosure I repeated my father's last speech to myself. "One of his sons!" "Painfully shy!" "Different from other girls!" How could my father speak of me this way? How could my father do this to me? One of Redbury's sons. I hated each and every one of them! Didn't he know that? To be given in marriage to one of them! It was unthinkable! The red planet of anger invaded the dark secrecy of my space. I remember nothing else after that. I must have fainted, overcome with emotion.

Hours later when I came to, the room was dark and cold. I pulled back the drapes and stepped out of my hiding place, replaced the book, and crept up the stairs to my room (no one had missed me, apparently) and collapsed on my bed.

The tears came slowly but they came. I wept. Wept because I still loved my father though at the moment I hated him. Wept because I had trusted that he loved me unconditionally and forever. Wept because he had betrayed me. And then I thought of Darius, and how I had not really understood his rage and sorrow when his beloved mother, Consuelo, had abandoned him for Ricci. And I wept once more because I had betrayed Darius.

The following day I wrote a secret letter to Darius, pouring out my soul to him. A week later, thanks to William, his letter to me took away all the pain.

⟡

Spring is late this year. There have been several snowfalls in the mountains, and the passes, the traveling bureau told me, are still closed. It might be another month. Darius has written to me saying that if I do not come to Florence by the end of the month he shall come to Paris to fetch me. I believe him. Darius can do anything he sets his mind to. Darius created a universe for us when we were children. From his recent letters I gather he has created another one equally as fascinating and as dangerous in Florence. He is still the archseducer, the archmagician. I cannot wait to see him.

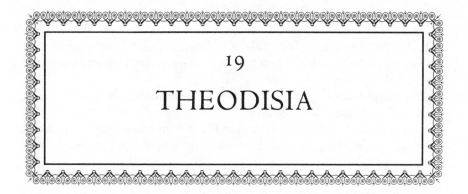

We have nothing new to say on the question of the origin of these . . . *hypnoid states*. They often, it would seem, grow out of the day-dreams which are so common even in healthy people, and to which needlework and similar occupations render women especially prone.

—Breuer and Freud, *Studies in Hysteria,* underlined in Emma's copy

T HEODISIA was frightened: having conceded to Elijah in the matter of Emma's dowry, she had found out soon enough that it was her inheritance and not herself that Elijah cared about. Looking at Elijah now, seated on the couch with William, his arm around him, she suddenly saw her hands detach themselves from her arms and float across the room and begin to choke Elijah. Magically strong, her fingers pressed hard into the sides of Elijah's neck, the two thumbs pressing into the jugular. Die, she screamed silently. Choke! Her hatred had deepened . . . had become almost uncontrollable.

When the boys had arrived home two days earlier, on one of the long weekends Warrenton provided for in its school calendar, William had ignored her. Nor had he spoken to her since . . . except once—a spasm of pain flickered through her head as she recalled the occasion—when Elijah had insisted!

"Now, old chap, mustn't be rude to Momma. She deserves better than that. Give her a kiss and tell her that you missed her. I know she missed you."

And so William had. Her William.

There was nothing she could do. Nothing. She looked down at her hands. Useless hands. Theodisia rose from her chair and walked over to her standing worktable and withdrew from it her embroidery frame and sat down next to the workbasket.

The night before Edward had recited a Horatian ode that had contained the phrase *Dulce et decorum est pro patria mori* ("It is sweet and proper to die for one's fatherland"). Elijah had suggested that she embroider the moral so that Edward could take it back to school with him.

Elijah had joined Edward in the recitation. He had learned the same ode at Warrenton. Asking William to join them, all together they recited the last sentence: *Raro antecedentem scelestum deseruit pede Poena claudo.* William had translated for her: "Rarely does Vengeance, albeit lame in one foot, fail to overtake the Sinner, Momma." And then Clara, who was sitting with Emma, began to recite another Horatian ode. Something to do with winter . . . She hated them—Clara, Edward, Elijah—reciting their Latin phrases and showing off—all of them, except William.

Theodisia looked at William now. He was seated next to Elijah, who had his arm around him. The boy's face shone. She knew that Elijah wrote to him. And that a month ago he had gone to visit him. The boy was basking in what he thought was his father's love for him. Die! screamed Theodisia silently across the room as she threaded the needle and began to embroider.

"Well, Theo, do you want to hear about your younger son's hunting adventure, or are you too busy with Edward's gift? Feckless woman. Once she loved you best, William. Ah well, *nihil est ab omni parte beatum*, eh, William? Quickly, Edward, name the poet and the ode."

"The sixteenth ode, Book Two, Horace, Sir."

"Right you are. Well done, lad. William, go to your mother and tell her what you told me. He's turning into quite an amusing chap, Theo. Go on . . . sit next to your mother."

William went over to her and sat down on a chair next to her. "I've learned to shoot rabbits, Momma. And I do it very well." He turned to his father. "I may go back to visit with Lord Andrew, mayn't I, Poppa? He's asked if I would. We had so much fun together last time—"

"Yes, of course. I know Lord Andrew's father, splendid chap, but we'll talk about it later. Tell Momma your adventures. She's very eager to hear about them. She's missed you."

"The secret of stalking, Momma, is standing still . . ." William went on to explain to her.

Theodisia plied her needle in and out of the linen. She would have to undo it, she realized, because she was doing it all wrong. There *must* be a way to defeat Elijah. To hurt him as he hurt her.

". . . but you may only break its hind legs, therefore it's better to empty the second barrel, otherwise they would die in misery. I bagged eight rabbits while I was there, Momma."

"It all sounds splendid, William. And did Lord Andrew's cook serve rabbit for supper?"

"Yes, Momma. Jugged hare."

"It is delicious, isn't it?"

"William," said Elijah, "come back here and tell me about Old Bogey. Has he caned you yet?"

"He has, Poppa."

"And you didn't cry, did you? That always whetted his appetite. Any sign of weakness. Marvelous teacher. Could talk on anything. Anything he chose to. We used to take walks with him just to listen to him expound on any subject that might cross his mind. A brilliant man—"

"He remembers you, Poppa," said Edward. "He told me to tell you that he thinks I am every bit as handsome as you were when you were a boy. Were you one of his favorites?"

"Yes, I and another boy named Barnett . . . pale as a white rose. We used to call him Albion. He died at Naverino. . . ."

The door opened and Clara and Emma came in. Emma looking quite pretty in a yellow muslin dress with green piping.

"Well, Emma," said Elijah, "tell us what you thought of United Service Museum.[27] How did you like the model of the field and battle of Waterloo? And the jaws of the shark in the tin box? Shall I continue to subscribe or should I cancel?" He said this in a light, flirtatious manner while smiling at her.

"I think you should become a member for life, Poppa. I quite enjoyed the model of the battle of Trafalgar, and the Grecian vases. Clara proclaimed it to be a remarkable collection."

Theodisia glanced at Clara in her new brown silk dress with lace cuffs and collar. For a plain-looking woman she looked quite pretty. She was silent most of the time at least, and seemingly unassuming. However, Theodisia did not trust her. Somehow she was certain that Mrs. Lustig was their enemy. She could not prove it, of course, but she sensed it. She looked over at her husband: talking authoritatively as always, this time about Greek art. Elijah's dark brown coat was open, revealing his white satin vest, a golden watch chain . . . she hated him, but he was a very handsome man nevertheless. Always so well dressed. Now he began discussing Warrenton. How successful his school career had been. How he had learned everything that was praiseworthy there: honor,

27. This institution near Whitehall Palace occupied a portion of Middle Scotland Yard. Founded in 1831, it contained a collection of arms, accoutrements, and models. Admission was free to soldiers, sailors, and the general public by a member's order. —R. Lowe

sportsmanship, fellowship . . . The needle pierced her finger. She made no outcry. She let the blood flow onto the linen.

"Dolly"—Elijah laughed—"Dolly is what they used to call me, Edward. Because of my pink-and-white complexion. 'Get me a candlestick, Dolly!' " Edward and William giggled somewhat self-consciously. " 'Dolly, do you want to get your ears boxed! You've let the fire go out and where's my tea? Do you call these shoes clean, Dolly?' I do hope you are all sticking together, you and your cousins, the five of you against your Masters. They can be tough brutes, you know. But it's all in your best interest, of course. Remember that."

"I'm one of three fags, Sir," said Edward, "for Marcus Simpson, who is the Marquis of Waterford. Really quite a nice chap. He won't let anyone beat us but himself. He's quite fair. He doesn't make us cut his hair at midnight or go to the Black Bull tavern and get him brandy or gin or anything like that. Poor Albert's having a terrible time with his prefect. No matter what he does he can't please him."

"Well, just remember you've got to be jolly in the face of all this abuse. They can smell a spoiled mother's darling right off, and if they do, that boy's in trouble."

"Albert's prefect pinches him. And when he takes a bath you can see his arms are full of black-and-blue marks," William told his father.

Theodisia was appalled as always. Her brothers had never gone to school. They had learned their letters from the village priest and a spinster woman in a Dames school. She was afraid to ask William who his "prefect" was. They all seemed to have one, though. She wasn't quite sure what a prefect was. She would ask Guinivere.

"And your prefect, William, what about him?" asked Elijah.

"Well, Sir, I and Lord Andrew fag for Edgar Abington. He's Andrew's cousin. He's over six feet tall and he's the best boater in the school. We cook sausages for him, for one thing. He's really a capital fellow. He lets us eat his leftovers."

Elijah turned to Emma. "Mrs. Lustig tells me that you too have learned a Horatian ode. Recite it for us now."

Emma stood up and moved to the center of the room, where she stood in front of her father, her face beaming, her head held high. "Ode Eleven, Poppa . . ." She ended some moments later, raising her voice slightly as she recited the famous last line: *"Carpe diem! quam minimum credula postero."*

"Excellent, Emma. And the pronunciation was absolutely correct. Far better than yours, Edward. You have a tendency to impede the iambic flow. And so your sister wins the palm, Edward. Better luck next time."

Annoyed, Edward challenged Emma. "Can you recite the beginning of the *Iliad*?" And before she could answer he began rattling off the first six lines.

When he had finished she gave him a cool look and said, "I can, Edward, and not only that I can recite the entire description of Achilles' shield, whose replicas hang on the Gardens' gates. I'm quite sure you can't do that."

"Children! Silence! Or I shall punish all of you," said their father.

All three children froze.

Pointing to Edward and Emma, he motioned them to sit. "I admire competition . . . it is, after all, the cornerstone of stamina. But not rowdiness. The best will out, never fear. I shall see to that. But since you are so eager to compete—"

Theodisia could contain herself no longer. "It is not *they* who are eager to compete. It is *you*, Elijah. *You* who are forcing them to compete with one another!"

Elijah turned to her in genuine surprise. "Why, Theo, I almost forgot that you were present. You have been so quiet. And so this is what you observe. You think I am cruel to the children. Because I want them to study hard, to be prepared for life when they become adults. To use their minds, their ability, to become acquainted with the best minds the world has to offer. To learn as much as they are capable of learning. And this is cruel. You take me to task for *this*, Theodisia?"

Theodisia said nothing.

"Come now, Theo, is it fair to criticize and then not reply when I defend my position? Surely you must have something to say to us about what I have just said."

The brothers looked straight ahead, at neither parent. Emma looked at Clara. What would happen now? Edward felt intensely uncomfortable, as he always did when his father behaved that way towards his mother. He didn't understand it, but he wanted to run away and hide when it happened. Emma, though she still disliked her mother, was beginning to dislike seeing her humiliated in public even more. She felt somehow threatened. William felt guilty. Had it been his fault? Why was Poppa so cruel to their mother, the children wondered.

"Nothing. No comment. Well, Theodisia, as usual you have spoiled our good time. Here is a Latin quotation you might want to learn by heart: *Orandum est ut sit mens sana in corpore sano.* 'Your prayer must be for a sound mind in a sound body.' Juvenal, boys, a man who in later life you will appreciate more and more."

Theodisia went back to her embroidery. The others turned their attention away from her. Elijah was now regaling them with stories about the Grand Tour he had taken when he was seventeen with their Uncle Joseph. Elijah had taken William away from her. She would take

Emma away from him. And if she couldn't do that, she would do something injurious to his "Emmy Emmy." She looked at her daughter, the only female Elijah loved, furtively. She looked at William. There must be a way . . . there must be.

Theodisia was staring at herself in the mirror of her vanity table in her boudoir. The next day was the anniversary of her marriage to *him* . . . in the small church outside Saddler's Grove, All Saints Church. Seventeen years before. An abyss . . . though she had not known it at the time. On the contrary, at the time it appeared to her as a pinnacle.

She recalled her life before the marriage. Herself as a young girl, the simple life of her family, farmers, descendants of wealthy yeomen, the warmth, the love . . . the family had been large, eight brothers, five sisters (she used the past tense when she thought of her family, as if all her siblings were dead like her parents) . . . her past life, all her remembrances, every image, was bathed in an amber glow, like a series of beautiful genre paintings: the first canvas was of the honey-colored stone manor house she was born in, hung with creepers and clematis, set among fields cropped close by the small herd of sheep. In the distance the flanks of limestone hills rose gently. The second canvas: herself as a small child standing in a doorway in a clean linen smock watching her father, a clay pipe in his mouth, standing on a knoll against a skyline, whistling to the old shepherd dog, Larry.

She remembered the large open fireplace, the glow of the pine floors—there was no Heppelwhite, no Sheraton, no Chippendale, no Adam here, no silver—instead, oak tables, pewter and brass and . . . jugged hare, a fresh rabbit that one of her brothers might have "potted," simmering for hours in an earthen stone pot with savory fresh vegetables and herbs. And there in the corner of the canvas she had painted for herself was her dear mother dressed in a cap and gown and an enormous apron taking a pie out of the oven.

Now everything in the past was set in the glow of time, like precious fragments of a life that while she had lived it she had not valued. She saw the last seventeen years of her life as a prison that she herself had helped to build.

Except for William. Everything had been Elijah's. The house, the children, her life . . . but when she had carried William, she knew from the very beginning that this baby was different. Why? She had thought about that often and had come to the conclusion that it was only because she had willed it. She had to have something in her life that was hers, otherwise she could not go on. She began to love the child even before he was born, as he was growing in her womb. He was beautiful even moments after birth, not like the others had been, ugly screaming red things. She had named him William (Elijah had allowed her that) after the brother she loved the most. The brother she no longer saw. A brother Elijah had forbidden to come to the house . . .

There was a tap on the door and Mrs. Farnley entered.

They went through day's menu and discussed the Sunday dinner arrangements. The Lustigs of Frankfurt were coming to visit London at Elijah's invitation. There had been some talk of a merger, though Solomon was not all in favor of it.

As Mrs. Farnley was about to leave, she turned at the door and said, "Madam, I wish to speak to you about something else . . . a personal matter, if you can spare the time."

"Yes . . . what is it?"

"It is Mrs. Lustig, Madam."

Theodisia looked at Mrs. Farnley. "What about her?"

Mrs. Farnley hesitated, wondering if she had made a mistake. If she had estimated the situation correctly, her information would be appreciated, but if she were mistaken . . . well, it was too late to turn back.

"Mrs. Lustig is sleeping with a man."

There was a moment of silence in which both women stared at one another.

"Come, Mrs. Farnley," said Theodisia, "let us move away from the door." And she led her housekeeper into the bedroom to one of the two large Chippendale chairs, newly reupholstered, close by the window overlooking the Gardens. "Sit down, Mrs. Farnley, and tell me about it. How do you know?"

"One of the servants, Madam, brought it to my attention."

She did not tell Theodisia that she knew everything that went on in the household, that she made it her business to know, that she had disliked Clara from the start, and that she had ordered Grindal to spy on her. Farnley had kept a dossier on Clara's activities ever since the governess had told her to have Emma's fireplace re-bricked. The less Theodisia, or anyone, knew about her machinations the better, as far as she was concerned.

Normally she would have said nothing. But this involved her niece Moly. She could control Moly. But not Clara. She liked to have control—not only over the house but its occupants as well. How else could a household run smoothly and efficiently? And she had wanted for some time to form a closer alliance with her mistress. For the past month Elijah had not looked well to her. If he fell ill . . . Anyway, she thought this was the time.

"Tell me what you know."

No, thought Mrs. Farnley, she had not made a mistake. She took a small notebook out of her pocket and recited certain dates. "It may have started sooner, Madam. The watcher only records when it began—that is, as far as the watcher knows."

Theodisia frowned. "There were no nocturnal visits during the month of February." That was the month Elijah had gone to Germany again.

Mrs. Farnley's face was expressionless when she answered. "None, Madam." She watched Theodisia closely. Would she come to the answer herself or would she have to be told? She waited. When she saw the flush of color creep up over Theodisia's face she knew her mistress had figured out who the man was. Theodisia's face remained calm, but Mrs. Farnley noticed that her hands were now tearing at the edges of the small lace handkerchief she had taken out of the pocket of her morning robe.

Theodisia could not bring herself to say thank you to the woman; instead she said: "You may go now, Mrs. Farnley."

⚜

Mrs. Farnley, in the privacy and comfort of her sitting room, was darning one of the master's socks. Had she done the right thing? She had, she decided.

In the beginning she had disliked Theodisia when she came to the house as a bride. Such a foolish young girl. So silly. So vulnerable. As a rule, Mrs. Farnley disliked vulnerable people, particularly women. Life was a serious business, fraught with pitfalls and problems. The first rule was to take care of yourself. People who didn't fell by the wayside. And that was their fault. If you couldn't take care of yourself, if life was too much for you, then you deserved what happened to you.

She admired Elijah. That was the way to conduct oneself in life. You took advantage of other people's weaknesses lest they take advantage of yours. Once upon a time she had been half in love with Elijah, but he had never availed himself of the opportunity . . . as he had with Clara Lustig!

Yes, it was the sealing of the fireplace that had decided it for her. Cold-blooded, even more cold-blooded than herself. Oh, she had known immediately what it had been all about when Clara had told her what to do about it. The child had been eavesdropping on her parents. On their private conversations. Emma had changed after Clara came . . . fallen in love with her. That's what had happened, and the parents blind to it. Everyone blind to it but her. No, she owed no allegiance to that bitch. Nor to Elijah, for that matter.

In the last few years, Theodisia had turned to her more and more for comfort and advice. And so it was to Theodisia that Mrs. Farnley had decided to be loyal. Better she heard about their carrying on from her than from some malicious servant. Or from Elijah. She would put nothing past Elijah.

Let her do what she wanted with the information. The housekeeper was not like Elijah. She did not underestimate Theodisia. Beneath the girlish tears and hysteria there was a strength that had not showed itself as yet. But it would one day. She was sure of that. All things in due time. . . .

She laid down her darning and examined it. Faultless. Perfect. The sock was as good as new.

⋯⋯⋯

Normally Theodisia's silence did not bother Elijah unduly. Actually, it was the way he liked her best. What was the Greek aphorism? Sophocles . . . ah, yes: "Silence is a woman's best adornment." Exactly. But tonight it bothered him for some reason.

It was not her usual sullen silence, or her "weary" silence, the silence that had a desperate quality about it. A silence that spelled out resignation. It certainly was not a comfortable silence. But then nothing was "comfortable" about her. Everything was a problem. No, this silence was different. . . .

Elijah was sensitive to people's moods and emotions. Not that he gave in to them, or empathized. Or identified with them. He had an almost female receptiveness, which he used to protect himself. It accounted for his success in business as well as in the boudoir. He found himself thinking: Could it be that somehow she had found out about Clara? But that was impossible. Even if the servants knew (and they must) he was sure they sympathized with him. They didn't like his wife, he was aware of that. They would not have told her. No, it wasn't that. But there was something. Well, he would wait. Sooner or later she would tell him.

"Did you do as I told you, Theo? Did you speak to Hollis, the gardener? It's absolutely essential that the trees be irrigated properly. And the soil sweetened. Did you remember what I told you to tell him?"

"Yes, I did. He said he would do exactly as you asked. He has already begun."

"And Mrs. Farnley . . . did you speak to her about the dinner?"

Elijah was referring to the special dinner party he was giving in honor of the Lustigs, whom he had finally persuaded to visit London. Johan, their son, who had been expected to accompany them, had decided that he could not interrupt his studies at the university after all. Elijah was interested in establishing closer financial ties with the Lustigs. If he could rely on the Lustigs of Frankfurt as the remarkable Rothschilds relied on one another, the two families, the Forsters and the Lustigs, could become one international financial force.

"Well, tell me, what did she decide? Which dinnerware and what is she serving?" He still did not trust Theodisia to do these things.

She told him and he nodded. "Good, very good . . ." But no, it was not good, not good at all. Theodisia was definitely holding something back from him. He felt her malice. Suddenly he had to know. It was this hint of defiance on her part that was making him angry. "Well, out with it, woman! There's something in your infinitesimal mind that is burning to be let out! So out with it! I'm tired of waiting."

"I don't know what you're talking about. And why must you raise your voice?"

"Oh, you don't, do you?" He walked over to her. She was lying on the bed, her head nestled in the pillows. A part of him was surprised by his actions, but his impulses overrode his good sense, and he grabbed her roughly. "Either you tell me now or I will shake it out of you. Do you think I don't know when you are holding something back from me, Theodisia? You are a very poor liar. You want to tell me something, something scandalous, something vicious, by the look on your face—" He pulled her off the pillows and held her arms in a punishing grasp. "Tell me now!"

"All right, all right, Elijah. Remove your hands. And stand over there." She pointed to the bureau. "I shall tell you. But you're insane . . . that's why I have difficulty telling you things—"

"What things?"

"Things, Elijah. Anything. Your manner is frightening. One doesn't know what you'll do. You're unpredictable. Especially when it concerns . . . Emma—"

"Emma! It has something to do with her?"

"Yes, it has something to do with your precious Emma."

"Tell me!"

"This afternoon, I remembered, after I had spoken to the gardener, what you had wanted me to tell him about the soil, so I went back to his shed. The door was open and I walked in. He wasn't there but Emma was. Emma and a boy. A dirty, wretched boy. They were both half undressed—"

"You're lying! You bitch!"

"I'm not lying! I'm not. I knew you would behave like this. I knew it! That's why I was afraid to tell you." Theodisia burst into tears.

He grabbed her and put his hands around her neck. "You're lying, aren't you, Theodisia? You're lying . . ." He began to press his fingers against her throat.

"I'm not," she gasped. "I'm not, Elijah."

Suddenly he threw her from him and went to his dressing room. Minutes later he emerged fully dressed, took one look at her, and left.

Lying in bed, still, Theodisia kept going over what Mrs. Farnley had told her. Clara Lustig . . . Elijah and Clara! In her house! With their daughter's governess! She remembered her first ladies' maid—Lucinda Dillard. The agony of that! She still hated her. She remembered every moment of the humiliation. And the servants . . . they had all known. Every single one of them. Wounded. In pain. That was how she had felt. And worse than that.

She had thought about it all afternoon while visiting Lady Alysbury and listening to her and Josephine Redbury discuss church business, the Woman's League, and Isaac Coverly; and all through dinner with her husband, Emma, and Clara: how to hurt Elijah, cause Elijah as much pain as he caused her.

She happened to be glancing at her husband when Mrs. Farnley brought in the dessert after dinner, Emma's favorite. She saw her husband's look of joy—yes, it had been joy—as he watched his daughter's pleasure eating it. She made up her mind then. It was a lie, of course. But she would have told him anything, anything, to get back at him. To make him suffer. Now he suffered as much as she did.

Someone was shaking her. "What is it? What are you doing?" she cried out, waking.

It was her husband; he had returned.

"Clara . . . Clara . . . where was she? How was it that Emma was alone? Damn you! Answer me!"

He had lit the bedside lamp. Behind him his shadow on the wall was enormous.

"Clara? Wait, I'll tell you. I'm still half asleep. You'll have to wait a second. Give me a second. Clara . . . yes, today is Wednesday, Elijah. Don't you remember, Wednesday afternoon is her time off. . . ."

"I don't believe for a second what you have told me. Not a word of it! You're an evil bitch! You're worse than I thought!" Throwing her down on the bed, he left once more.

He was right, thought Theodisia dully. I am evil, and I shall be punished for what I've done today. She began to weep.

———◆◇◆———

The following morning Mrs. Farnley told her that in the middle of the night the master had gone to Clara's room, yanked her out of bed, and had screamed and yelled at her. Finally, he had threatened to send her packing if she didn't take better care of Emma than she did. And then he had come to Mrs. Farnley's room and demanded to know if she had seen any strange boys hanging around the Gardens, and if there ever were any she was to come to him personally and report the fact. Then he demanded to know where Hollis was, and when she told him (the gardeners slept in rooms in the attic), he had gone off to find Hollis. When he returned he had ordered the housekeeper to bring a bottle of whiskey to the library; then he had drunk himself into a stupor.

20

CLARA

5 MARCH 1841

D
ear Johan,

Something extraordinary happened last Friday night at Mathilda Herrod's house. It has unsettled all of us in one way or
another, though we do not speak to one another about it. It
was so bizarre . . . so totally unexpected . . . so shocking,
really.

I have not written you before this because I have been too
dejected to write. So many things have gone wrong—everything has gone wrong—but this news cannot wait. I must
speak to someone about it.

I was invited along with Elijah and Theodisia to Mathilda's
for dinner since two of the guests were in my-laws, your
parents. I know you decided because of obligations you had
at school that it was best not to accompany them, and that
we both agreed it would be better that you should wait to
meet Emma, still, it was only when I saw them *without* you
that I realized how much I longed to see you, to speak to
you in person.

There were sixteen of us at dinner—besides all the Forsters, Mathilda had invited the Strooksburys, the Redburys,
Nicholas Renton, and two other insignificant couples whom
I shall not bother to identify except to say that they were
dutifully grateful to be dining with their "betters." The dinner was one of several in honor of your parents' visit to Merrie
England. Your mother, by the way, as usual managed to
ignore me as if I didn't exist. She has never forgiven me for
having married her beloved Franz. . . . As to what hap-

pened, you must bear with me. I must tell it in my own way.

Mathilda is a woman who presides over infinitesimals. (Yes, I know she is kind to me, but she has also been insufferably patronizing). Nothing is too mundane, or commonplace, or boring, not to warrant her full attention and absorb her entire intellect. She is a woman obsessed with insignificant details, regularly leaving out the heart of the matter. I say this so that you will understand the atmosphere in which the following bizarre accident occurred—or was it fate? I do not know what to call it.

It was understood that the guests were not to be bright or amusing (and they were not), that conversation was to be kept on a trivial plane (and it was). With such rules in operation there was no room (so we thought) or possibility for catastrophe, one that might ruin a good dinner, or worse, one's digestion.

The wines were glorious. The food, under the lash and ministrations of the cook, was divine. Nothing sparkled (except the wine) . . . there was not an iota of wit, not even an attempt, and had there been it would have been snuffed out immediately by one of Mathilda's damp glares. No new paths of insight to jar our concentration on the incomparable wines and delicious food coursing down our gullets. Not until the fowl was served were there any surprises.

One course after another—in these bourgeois households one must be prepared to work hard at the dinner trough (and I do). No sound except chewing and pulpification, the soothing and rhythmical clicking of the cutlery, an occasional sigh. But when the pièce de résistance was served—braised wild ducklings enrobed in Madeira sauce—we heard a strange and ominous noise.

Your father looked first to his left, then to his right. The noise increased. And such a strange noise. What was it? And where was it coming from? Nervously we looked around. Again the noise. This time it sounded more urgent. Mr. Strooksbury, who was seated on my left, stopped chewing and looked across at his wife, who was seated opposite him between Solomon and Elijah.

The noise—or was it a strangled cry?—was coming from his wife, Sybella Strooksbury. Her face, startlingly clear above the bright flames of the twin silver candlesticks situated in the center of the table, was an ugly red, her eyes were wide with fear, her large chest, made larger by her gaspings, expanded as she struggled to inhale life-giving air.

Throwing his cutlery down in an unprecedentedly decisive and energetic move, Strooksbury ran around the table, behind Mathilda, who was frowning with displeasure at his wife. But even before he got there Solomon and Elijah were both beating the poor woman repeatedly on her back.

Something unintelligible screeched forth from her mouth. Her head snapped back as if an all-consuming rage possessed her, as she tried clumsily with her arms to throw off once and for all her persecutors. Growling and slobbering like some fierce tormented animal, she finally tried to raise herself and almost did, but instead she fell forward just as her husband reached her, dead. All in what? Two minutes?

Mathilda summoned her startled footmen, who came and began to remove the dead Mrs. Strooksbury from the table, when the husband, quite berserk, screamed at them—"Stop! Unhand her!"—taking hold of their livery, tugging desperately at their scarlet jackets. Except for Elijah and Solomon, the rest of the table, including myself, just sat there, mute and paralyzed with terror. The two men released her and she slumped at the table like some large ungainly wounded bird, almost sliding off her chair except that Solomon caught her and held her fast.

So there it was. Death! Unbelievable. Unsuitable. A jagged clump of tragedy—the death of Mrs. Sybella Strooksbury, beloved wife, at Mathilda Herrod's dinner party in honor of your parents. Profane. Absurd. Ridiculous . . .

Did your father write to you about this? He seemed literally frightened out of his wits.

The unfortunate woman's death (I attended the funeral service yesterday) has somehow or other, however, given me the necessary energy to write you. It seems to have acted as a restorative in its way. Life, miserable as it is, seems more attractive than its alternative. At least it does to me. It is too late tonight to write you of all my woes but I shall tomorrow. . . .

The following evening:
I feel bitter, old and totally alone. Despairing, in fact.

There are things I have not told you. Things I have kept from you. . . .

I came to London, if you remember, to achieve history. Yes, I came to London in the same way, one might say, as an eager contestant might have traveled to the games, the Olympian or Pythian games. To win the footrace, or the chariot race . . . (Pindar has long been a favorite of mine).

And some months ago I thought I had "in the sweetness of my youth, swiftly fulfilled my hopes on wings of soaring valor. . . . And no less swiftly fell to ground again" (I quote from memory, forgive me, Johan).

My defeat . . . I cannot tell you how unbearable that feels! I shall not lie to you. I cannot tell myself that losing is all right. It is not. It never can be. There are no second, no third prizes! No silver, no bronze medals . . . only the "pale-skinned (olive) wreath." I do not have it in me to be Christian, meek and mild, to turn the other cheek. Only victory is glorious, worth living for. Pindar did not write his odes to those who lost. He knew that

> . . . *when they meet their mothers*
> *Have no sweet or joyful laughter around them,*
> *In back streets shunning hostile eyes*
> *They cower; Disaster has bitten them.*
>
> —*Pythian VIII*, 5

Those who are successful are envied, yet it is better to be envied than to be obscure, for those who do not count are "invisible."

Because my defeat is of my own making does not ease the pain. On the contrary. Oh, how quickly I became craven, asking nothing in return! I am speaking about Elijah, of course. And I told myself it was to be only a sexual exchange! That my body lusted, that my mind would somehow remain free, rise above the sordid brutality, for yes, he was brutal, and yes, it was sordid. There was no tenderness on his part towards me ever. Tenderness is what he feels for Emma, whom he loves. And where there is sex and no love there is only sordidness, dirt, muck . . . filth.

One morning—did I write you? (I know that I did not)—his daughter came into my bed. Thank God I heard her! Do you understand? The father underneath the bed, the daughter in it. Sordid. Vile. And yet I yearned for his flesh, as if his flesh had tentacles drawing me to him. I can no longer study, or write. I should have known better. For a woman like myself survival depends upon my mind controlling my body. I should have known better. I who had no feeling for years am now filled with them. Envy, jealousy, longing . . . oh, that is the worst! I long to be loved by him, long to be enveloped in the hairy torso of his body. Held. Crushed. Wanted by him.

I shall end up killing myself. But I have even wilder thoughts than that. What would my suicide be but a mere sordid detail in the Forsters' lives? Puzzling perhaps, annoying, but quickly forgotten. I have thought of going to Nicholas Renton and begging him to take me into his organization for any purpose whatsoever. I, who was so eager to come to London a mere two years ago. If only you would have come, Johan! I would have felt better. I know it. Just to see your dear face again, hear your voice . . .

Theodisia knows what happened between me and Elijah. I am sure of it. Mrs. Farnley must have told her. Farnley knows and controls everything. She might have been my ally, but I made a mistake there too. I did not realize her strength until it was too late. And it *is* too late.

He is finished with me. He told me so. It has something to do with Emma. He holds me responsible for something that is not my fault. I still do not understand his accusations; however, I do understand he is through with me.

But I must check my anger, swallow it, live with a fire raging in my blood, smile when I wish to bite, stroke when I wish to scratch, act humbly when I wish to kill. He has not spoken to me in private since that time, the middle of the night, when he came to me with his accusations about Emma.

Chapman has rejected my article on Faust. He claims my reading of it is eccentric. Perhaps he is right. I live out of joint in my own time. The friends I have made, except for Sophie Hussaye, a writer like myself, I know only superficially. Truth be told, they look on me not as a writer but as a governess, and an eccentric one at that. Those few who think I'm bright, think me a bit too bright for comfort—theirs, of course.

I see nothing ahead but servitude of the worst kind. "Better to reign in Hell than serve in Heaven . . ." Yes, but I cannot find a hell in which to reign. Nicholas now wants to use me as a procurer. The golden Guinivere shall be his. . . .

Your distraught sister,
Clara

P.S. Ignore this letter. These ravings. I shall collect myself in time, as I always have. I shall calm down. I shall begin to plan again. Nothing that has happened has changed our master plan. I shall not be dismissed. And nothing will be said to me directly. Theodisia would not dare, and if Elijah knows that Theodisia knows he will not care. Everything will go on as always. If he does mention it, it will only be to torture her, not me. He has forgotten about me. Besides, there are some new and promising possibilities which I have not mentioned to you as yet. Elijah is *not* the only male in the household. But enough said.

Clara

21

NICHOLAS AND GUINIVERE

It is a voluptuous delusion which leads a man to believe that he will find a greater pleasure in the arms of a woman whose beauty appeals to him than in those of any other.

—Schopenhauer, *The World as Will and Representation,* trans. Clara Lustig

GUINIVERE was beautiful. She did not have the kind of beauty Vanessa had, the kind of beauty that made men restless, stirring in them not only sexual desire but a craving for conquest. She did not have the wild grace of a Diana, or the fearful authority of an Athena, or even the imperial majesty of a Juno. Hers was a beauty that certain Italian painters, struggling to create a new form that would depict tenderness and compassion, an asexual spiritual beauty, had brought into existence: the unearthly beauty of the Madonna of the Renaissance, a "holy" mother, beautiful and good, suckling a babe on her breast.

Like her prototypes, Guinivere's perfect features were set in an oval frame that ticked out a timeless serenity, the kind of ideal beauty that a boy finds in his mother's face when she bends over him to kiss him good-night. Guinivere smiled, and, smiling, soothed, unlike Vanessa, who heated men's blood, or Emma, who might never be considered beautiful but whose smile was radiant. Guinivere's was the kind of beauty that men worshiped and women forgave. When Solomon first saw her at a hunt ball given by one of his friends in Shalford, a small village north of London, he knew immediately that he wanted

"Gwinnie" to be his, the mother of his children. As did so many other young men in the neighborhood. But she chose Solomon. Why? The question did not occur to her at the time. She married Solomon after a brief courtship when she was just seventeen, pleasing both her parents, and Jorem as well as Solomon. In an indirect and complex way she found out why she had chosen Solomon during the winter of 1840–1841.

That winter was hard, long and bitter. Continuous snow and sleet and hard rain. Many children and their mothers died in the streets of London. Beggars froze to death in doorways. The poor, the weak, the infirm, those without shelter, had been carried off. Died without complaint, without sound, quietly snuffed out, whispering deaths, sometimes with crosses in their hands. Sometimes in church doorways. The theatre season was, however, brilliant, and the prostitution traffic increased tenfold that year.

During that winter Guinivere and Sybella Strooksbury had worked hard, both women having been chosen to set up and establish the London League's[28] new Mission House in a building that had been a former brothel in Whitechapel, at the top of Goulson Street, a block past the Jews' New School. Its previous owner, Lord Longford, the fifth Earl of Tavistock, one of the League's trustees, had sold it to the LLGW for a considerable profit. The money needed to buy the building and refurbish it had somehow miraculously been given to them by an anonymous donor. Guinivere did not question it. She had accepted it simply as a gift from God and had felt enormous gratitude.

Some months after Sybella's death, however, while going through Sybella's desk, Guinivere found some letters from Isaac Coverly to Sybella and discovered that the anonymous donor had been none other than Isaac Coverly. That was impressive, but what was even more impressive were the letters in which he wrote knowledgeably about the problems of women who were abandoned and utterly impoverished. He seemed to really understand their plight . . . their despair. His donation had been the largest sum of money ever given to the League by an individual. Why hadn't Sybella told her, she wondered. Isaac Coverly's last letter was a reply to Sybella's request that he become a lieutenant in the organization, a rank that would entitle him to attend board meetings and to speak, though it would not entitle him to vote.

28. By the year 1841 the London League was the largest charity organization in England. Its full name was the London League of Gentlewomen for the Rehabilitation of Fallen Women and Their Progeny. From 1818, the year it was founded (Jorem Forster had been one of its founders), until 1901, the year of Queen Victoria's death (the queen herself was a trustee), Forster men and women were associated with it in one capacity or another.—*H. Van Buren*

It included an invitation to tea at his home to discuss the possibility. It was dated December 18. Almost four months before.

Guinivere had seen Coverly at Elijah's and Mathilda's houses several times since the ball he gave. At first, after the ball, she had been somewhat constrained in his presence, but when it seemed clear to her that he did not seek out her company as he had at the ball she began to relax. His intense interest in her, which had made her feel uncomfortable at his party—she had forgotten the strange feeling of pleasure and excitement it gave her—seemed to have vanished. He seemed, on the contrary, to now purposely avoid and ignore her. Had it been otherwise, she told herself, she would never have decided on her own to contact him on London League stationery to suggest that, if it were satisfactory to him, she, Mrs. Solomon Forster, as a representative of the LLGW, would like to continue discussions with him concerning his future activity with the League, "arrangements that had been initiated by her dear departed colleague and friend, Mrs. Lionel Strooksbury."

⟡

And so it was that in early March, Guinivere dressed in lilac wool trimmed with white braid, sat opposite Nicholas Renton in Jorem's study, the lilac streamers of her white silk bonnet mingling with the ash-gold of her curls.

The fact that she was there, that she sat there so beautiful and so composed in front of him, in his house, in his study, was a miracle to Nicholas. He examined her carefully, though covertly, repeating to himself every article of clothing she wore—the lilac gloves with their three mother-of-pearl buttons, the adorable small white lace reticule, the lace frill that decorated the puffed shoulders, the way the lines of the bodice curved gently inwards beneath her small breasts—remembering the while to keep his face devoid of any excitement. Each detail, everything, must be remembered so that he could relate it precisely to Toby.

Not wanting to frighten her—she must feel perfectly secure with him—with the intensity of his feelings, he kept the conversation as long as possible in the lifeless channels of etiquette. As far as Nicholas was concerned their relationship was beginning. He must do nothing to startle her, so that it would . . . it *must* . . . continue. He lowered his head when the delicate scent of her perfume reached his nostrils. She must not see its effect on him.

"Perhaps you have been wondering, Mrs. Forster, about my acute interest in the League."

"Yes, I confess curiosity, Mr. Coverly. But the reason I came was to personally thank you on behalf of our organization for your overwhelming generosity. I had no idea as to the extent of your donation until I examined Mrs. Strooksbury's accounts . . . also your deep understanding and compassion . . ." She smiled at him. "I read your correspondence. . . ."

He thought over what he knew about her. The Lustig woman had not failed. Guinivere Lucinda Kendall, the oldest daughter of John Kendall, a lieutenant-colonel in Her Majesty's army. Clara had even gone so far as to find out the details of Guinivere's wedding to Solomon . . . the details of her wedding dress . . . Now that she was here Nicholas did not want her to leave. But she must not for a moment suspect that. He would control his rapture, for what was it if not rapture, that she was here. If he extended his hand he could touch her. He controlled himself.

"My dear Mrs. Forster, the poor are always with us. That fact is a mystery in itself. However, I am interested in the poor. I myself have set up shelters, not only in London but in Manchester . . . now *there* is a place to study the poor. Your charity cares for women, mine concentrates exclusively on men. Perhaps you might like to accompany me one day . . . when I make my rounds."

He sensed the interest she had in him, an interest that she did not as yet perceive herself, but it was important—everything at this stage must be handled with the utmost tact—to proceed slowly. She must be drawn closer, she must not be allowed to pull away, but all the time she must be made to feel that it is—was—her choice. That she was free, absolutely free, while in fact the moment she had come into his house she had already become his.

"How long, Mrs. Forster, have you been engaged in volunteer work for the London League?"

The boring chatter about charity work went on. He was good at it. He understood organizations, he also understood how to disarm, and there was something here to disarm, for there had been in Guinivere's mind a slight hesitation about coming to see Mr. Coverly. Usually when the League's volunteers visited a donor they went in twos. But on impulse she had decided to come alone, a fact that she discussed with no one.

Mrs. Kitto brought in the tea service.

"T'is the last of the plum jam, Master," She said this as if she were announcing the last bottle of Napoleon brandy. She set the tray down on the table in front of Guinivere.

He leaned towards her. "The plums are from Jorem's plum tree, which was given to him by a gentleman by the name of Miles Ryder, many years ago. Do you know of him?"

"Yes, I do, Mr. Coverly. I have even met him once or twice in my brother-in-law Elijah's house. I know the Gardens contain several rare species of flowers from the East that were also a gift to my father-in-law from the same gentleman."

Mrs. Kitto presented Guinivere with a cup of tea and a plate on which a thin slice of bread spread with plum jam lay. She did the same for her master and then withdrew.

Nicholas watched as Guinivere opened her mouth and bit into the bread with her white teeth. He watched as she chewed the bread and swallowed it. "It's quite delicious," she said. "The taste is so delicate." In his mind he saw her for a brief moment unclothed, sitting there, lifting her cup to her mouth . . . He rose from his chair. She set down her cup and rose. She had to go, she said. She was late. She thanked him for everything. She stood there in front of him. He looked into her eyes. She dropped her gloves. He bent down and picked them up and handed them to her. Thanking him, she moved hurriedly away from him towards the door. When she was at the door he asked: "Mrs. Forster, would you consider coming with me one day to my shelters? I would appreciate your opinion of them."

Standing at the door, she replied, "Yes, Mr. Coverly, I would like that." And left.

Some moments later Kevin came into the room.

"You think I have lost my mind, don't you?" Nicholas said, smiling. "To fall in love with a married woman who is virtuous. What profit can there be in that?" Nicholas motioned to Kevin to sit down.

"What you must understand, Kevin, is that the fact that I can 'love' at all is a miracle in itself to me. I have always thought of love as a peculiar luxury reserved for human beings. Yes, some part of me still thinks of myself as an animal or subhuman. And that is what I was, until I fell in love. And I *am* in love. Totally. Rapturously. But you wonder, I can see it on your face, why Guinivere? Why her? Well, I shall tell you . . . because she is good. For it is goodness that attracts me, lures me, lays me low, seduces me. I know that there are other women far more stimulating, more seductive, even more beautiful. But were Guinivere seductive I would not love her. Were she "stimulating" I would not have the slightest interest in her. No. It is her . . . passiveness, coupled with her innocence, that I find that acts as an aphrodisiac for me. I can only love the good. I love rare commodities . . . the most precious, the most unobtainable things. And what is more rare than a "good person"? The quality of goodness for me is what evil is for most people, the great temptation. I have decided she is to be the mother of my child."

Kevin shook his head. "You speak as if that would be an easy thing to do. I don't think so. She may betray her husband mentally, even emotionally, but she will never break her marriage vows. Even if she disliked him, and she does not. It is you who will have your heart broken, Nicholas. But why speak of it? Nothing will happen. You will never be able to possess her sexually—"

"You are making me very angry, Kevin. You speak as if I were some kind of monster. As if I could not attract her physically—"

"On the contrary, you will become each other's biggest temptation. You are not only physically attractive to her—I have seen that with my own eyes, though she herself does not realize it—but she believes you to be a gentleman whose intentions towards his fellow men are fundamentally benevolent, a quality that is of the utmost importance to her . . . as you know . . . as you have counted on—"

"Enough. Tell me, Kevin, truthfully, what do you think of her?"

"What do I think of her? Well, first of all, I do not think she is all that good. Though I'm not all that sure what you mean by that term. It is a most ambiguous word that can and does lead to widely different conclusions. However, leaving that aside, Nicholas, she strikes me as too shallow to be considered "good." Her mind does not soar; she is not overly imaginative. The event of her life was the death of her son, and her subsequent grief. And in that matter I concur with her husband. In my opinion, there is a morbid quality attached to her. She suits her husband, Solomon, the average man personified; for you see, Nicholas, I think of her as an average woman. Neither good nor bad. She is not evil, I grant you that, but then she has not been tempted . . . physically, her body—"

"That will do, Kevin," Nicholas said, laughing.

"Her body," Kevin continued, "is too childlike for my taste. I prefer larger-breasted, more buxom women, the Mathildas of the world. Not that we ever had the pleasure of intercourse, nor shall we ever . . . the drug robbed me of that ability long ago. No, my bird"—Kevin patted his penis—"shall ne'er fly from its nest again. Falling in love . . . perhaps that is the most dangerous act performed in the world. Few survive it, barely a handful."

"We shall both survive. Were she available and were we encouraged by both our families to reproduce our glorious selves I would not be interested. But our love has a hopeless, doomed quality about it. We are fated to become romantic lovers—" Nicholas stopped.

Mrs. Kitto stood in the doorway, her huge frame filling the entire space.

"Mr. Lionel Strooksbury is waitin' in the parlor to speak to Mr. Isaac Coverly."

Kevin and Nicholas looked at one another.

"Well, show him in, Mrs. Kitto. Show him in here," said Nicholas.

Nicholas had laughed at Kevin's reaction, but he was annoyed with him. Kevin was wrong. He knew women, he understood them; Guinivere would be his.

———◆◇◆———

The fact that Guinivere succumbed to him sexually within just barely a month gave Nicholas not only intense pleasure but a feeling of triumph. He had taken an enormous risk and he had won. He could not help boasting of his conquest to Kevin, who had predicted: "Nothing will happen. You will never be able to posses her sexually—"

Kevin was greatly surprised, and he wondered why Guinivere had yielded so easily, but he said nothing about this to Nicholas.

22

GUINIVERE

If the woman finally submits to the sexual act, the clitoris becomes stimulated and its role is to conduct the excitement to the
adjacent genital parts; it acts here like a chip of pinewood, which
is utilized to set fire to the harder wood.

—Freud, *Three Contributions to the
Theory of Sex,* Contribution III,
The Transformations of Puberty

To Guinivere it seemed as if she had entered a magical realm when
she became acquainted with Nicholas Renton (he told her his real name
after they became lovers). A realm, however, that was not unfamiliar
to her in certain respects, for it reminded her in a way of the stories
that her mother had told her when she was a little girl.

Whenever Guinivere went to visit Nicholas, and Toby, the little hunchback, opened the door for her, she felt as she crossed the threshold as
if she were entering one of her mother's fairy tales. Tales about elves
and gnomes who lived in caves, and who were miners and gem experts,
friendly and helpful, but spiteful and vindictive when crossed. Nicholas,
she suspected, would be frightening too, if angered. They were also
supposed to have magical powers, even the power to make themselves
invisible. The longer she knew Nicholas the more she thought it might
be true of him as well.

On her third or fourth visit—she could not remember exactly—
Nicholas had taken her downstairs to the gem rooms, a series of rooms
whose wide windows stretched from floor to ceiling. Rooms in which
workmen sat at benches weighing, sawing, sanding, and lathing, and
whose walls were covered with a bewildering assortment of shears,

mallets, and hammers, the shelves crowded with mortars and pestles, vises, pitch bowls, engraving blocks, firing racks, and trivets. And there between the benches, standing quite casually, were coffers filled with cut stones. Aquamarines! Peridots! Turquoises from Turkey!

He had introduced her to one of his men, "a descendant of the famous Venetian jeweler Peruzzi . . ." Opals as large as hazelnuts, sea-green emeralds, tourmalines from Brazil. And rubies—dark male rubies and lighter female rubies. "Embedded in the flesh, the owner can pass unscathed through all perils," he told her. He showed her the male ruby that was embedded in his upper arm; an inextinguishable flame that burned in his flesh.

The diamonds and pearls he saved for the last. Hundreds of pearls of all sizes and luster and color. Among them a perfect strand of drop-shaped black pearls, his most highly prized possession. He put it around her neck. "It has been waiting for you," he told her.

He told her many things. Some of which she would think about when she was in bed with Solomon. Strange, interesting things. He told her about the toadstone; about the fact that light from an emerald, a diamond, and a ruby travels at different rates of speed; that the great Cardinal Mazerin invented the "rose cut" . . .

And he gave her jewels. Overwhelmed her with jewels. And though at first she resisted, she yielded finally. Wearing them naked in front of him . . . pendants of gold and enamel, rubies and pearls, girandolle earrings, tiaras, and two diamond bracelets that Nicholas told her had once belonged to the Bonapartes. But all that came later . . . after they had become lovers.

One day he showed her a crystal ball the size of a large melon with a gold ring encircling its middle.

"It once belonged," he told her, "to a knight crusader who brought it back with him from Jerusalem."

The ball was quartz in which the crystallization had been interrupted from time to time, so that between the successive transparent layers there was an occasional opaque layer. One could see the "phantom," the name for such opaque layers, quite clearly.

"The *Hollenzwang,* a sixteenth-century treatise," Nicholas told her, "by Dr. Faustus gives detailed directions for the consecration of crystal. Work should be done in the hour of Mars, on the first, eighth, fifteenth, or twenty-second hour of a Tuesday . . ." That and the following all happened on Guinivere's fifth visit to Nicholas.

Nicholas removed the crystal from its sheath, a yellow silk handkerchief, and placed the crystal in a green bowl that lay on a purple cloth, the crystal's convex surface multiplying the reflections into a dizzying tapestry of light points.

"Before I ever came to Marlborough Gardens," Nicholas said, "I stood one day in front of this crystal ball, and, after staring for a long time into it, I saw deep within its center an image of the Gardens, winking and shimmering like an immense emerald in a blaze of green lights . . . Blenheim Wood, the marshes stretching to the lake, the temple and behind it, in the grove, the statue of Nemesis, all golden in a golden light. I had never heard of Marlborough Gardens before. It was the year before I met Kevin Francini. But I knew then that it was a vision of my future . . . and that someday I would claim the Gardens as my own."

Then Nicholas asked Guinivere to gaze into the crystal. She didn't want to. For some reason it frightened her. But she wanted to please him; it was already difficult for her to refuse him anything. So despite her forebodings she did as he wished.

At first she saw nothing. She told him so but he insisted that she keep staring into the crystal. And then, after a few minutes of looking at the crystal's smooth and lustrous surface, she saw deep within its center the conception of a vague and shadowy form . . . she began to tremble . . . the form began to slowly coalesce, but even before it fused, took shape, she *knew* it would be Sidney. There he stood, a small figure of light, as if on a stage. . . . She heard him whisper to her: "I am here, I am waiting. . . ." She faltered. She trembled. Closing her eyes, she swooned. Nicholas caught her just before she fell.

Guinivere awakened in a room she had never seen before. She was lying on a wide divan, wearing a pale lilac-colored silk robe that was open . . . someone had removed her dress, her underclothes, her corset . . . he was there on his knees beside her. Naked. Perfectly formed. The body of a youth . . . a stripling. Somewhere in the depths of her mind an image flickered momentarily . . . familiar . . . but the moment passed. She felt no fear. She felt desire, the same excitement she had felt when she had danced with him at the ball he had given in Jorem's house.

She lay there, odalesque, mother of five, divested of her class, her station in life, a naked timeless nymph, her golden skin luminous against the dark, purple velvet of the divan. Her outward appearance, which had belied her sensuality, now lay open to his admiration and his passion. A torso dazzling in its curves, its small waist, its swelling hips, its large golden breasts. One of her hands grazed her golden fleece.

He opened the robe farther. "Your breasts . . . they are so much larger than I thought they would be. . . ."

She gazed into his eyes, which seemed to her like twin-orbed dark crystals. She heard herself say, "My love, my love . . ." and she stretched out her arms to him.

He moved towards her, his penis hard and upright, his small hands pushing her golden thighs apart . . . he thrust his penis into the golden fleece . . . and all the darkness of his life melted in that moment. He was one with his golden Aphrodite, healed and whole.

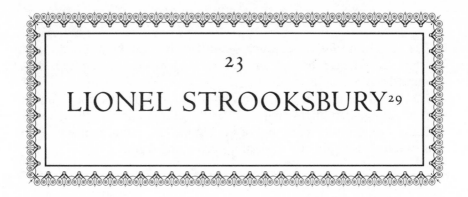

It is instructive to know that under the influence of seduction, the child may become polymorphous-perverse and may be misled into all sorts of transgressions.

> —Freud, *Three Contributions to the Theory of Sex, Contribution II*

Finally, it is evident that mental application, or concentration of attention on an intellectual accomplishment, will result, especially in youthful persons . . . in sexual excitement.

> —*Ibid.*

Aᴇᴛᴇʀ the peculiar and sudden death of Mrs. Strooksbury, the widower became a frequent dinner guest at our home. My father seemed fascinated by Mr. Strooksbury's grief.

"There is something admirable about a gentleman evincing such sorrow. Frankly, I had no idea he even loved her. Invite him often, Theodisia." And, encouraged by his reaction to Mr. Strooksbury's mourning for his wife, she did so.

Until then I had hardly noticed Mr. Strooksbury. I shall call him by his last name though on the first evening he dined with us he requested that we call him by his Christian name. "And you must too, Emma.

---

29. In Emma's original novel *The Metaphysics of Sex,* this chapter is numbered 28 and is entitled "Accountings." Except for tightening the action we have made very few revisions.—*R. Lowe*

My five children in the privacy of my home do so. My name is Lionel."

"My late wife had advanced pedagogic views," he continued while unfolding his napkin. "Her sister's husband, Herbert Quincy, a lecturer at Cambridge on education, held monthly seminars on modern parenting. We were privileged to be part of his circle. He has recently written a book called *The Rights of Children*. It is awaiting publication."

I could see that my father was about to say something uncommonly sardonic, but Mr. Strooksbury foiled him by beginning to cry. "Forgive me, it is the memory of those happy, happy evenings that caused me to break down. Pay no attention."

The rest of the dinner was eaten in relative silence.

Mr. Strooksbury sat on my left, opposite Clara, who sat on my father's right. It might have been the second or third time he came to dine, I don't recall exactly, that I mustered up enough courage to covertly glance at his profile—I was shy with strangers—and then I began to take notice of his smell. For though he wore a heavy cologne, as Poppa did, it mingled with but did not cover his pervasive and unique scent. An admixture of flowers, the carnation and the orchid, and of fruit, the apple and the pear, and, yes, like the mole and weasel too—a sweet savory smell. A musklike smell. But of course by this time I had my own share of musky smells. I had begun menstruating a year earlier, so it was not his smell that shocked me but the "intimacy" of it. For what was this odor if not his essence?

One was not immediately aware of it, but gradually as dinner progressed I would begin to smell him, and when I did I felt compelled to look at him, quickly, furtively, which though he never turned his head towards me, he seemed to sense and respond to in some indefinable way. Furthermore, in the same indefinable way I understood him to quite enjoy it.

His skin was pale. His full set of whiskers, sideburns, and mustache were crisp, curly, and ginger-colored. His features were not outstanding in any way; he was not handsome, but neither was he ugly. An average-size nose, undistinguished lips, medium-size eyes set in a squarish head. No, nothing stood out except for his odd smell.

He was always dressed in black with a wide mourning band on his right arm, the arm that faced me. His hushed manner, his grief-stricken air, his face set in mournful lines, all spoke and declared his recent bereavement. And yet, as mournful as he appeared, as lifeless as his conversation was, I sensed a liveliness about him. So much so that sometimes, after some particularly doleful speech about his late departed wife, I half expected him to suddenly and incongruously wink at me.

When I told that to Clara, for I told her everything, of course, she belittled my observations. Actually, she perceived the man as "inconsequential," beneath her analytic notice—so I stopped mentioning him to her.

His dinner conversation (and therefore ours) revolved exclusively around his dead wife, Mrs. Strooksbury, or Sybella, for he referred to her by her Christian name.

"Her real nature was that of a doe." For a moment, we had no idea who he was talking about. "A sweet and docile nature, ever ready to administer to the diseased, the sick in mind and body, the lost, the forsaken, the vile wretches who infect our city like a malignant growth, those females—I hope I offend no one—through the auspices of the London League. And perhaps—the thought has occurred to me from time to time—her death . . . might it not have been the result of her Sisyphean labors in the London League? I hope I offend no one by that observation."

My father would listen to these ruminations and pronouncements patiently but with an enigmatic smile on his handsome features. He was not without humor, and I believe that one of the reasons Mr. Strooksbury was invited so often was that it amused Poppa to hear his colleague Lionel speak about the dead Sybella in this way. As for my mother, her look was one of perpetual surprise: this was not the woman *she* remembered!

"Charitable to a fault . . ." Lionel was in the middle of one of his panegyrics when suddenly he lifted his right forefinger and held it upright above his soup plate. "Silence, silence everyone," he said. (Since as usual he had been the only one speaking, did he mean to silence himself, I wondered.) "I feel her presence . . . at this very moment . . . my dear Sybella . . . Yes! She is with us now! Here in this room. Do you feel it, Sir?" Mr. Strooksbury asked, looking straight at Poppa over his full plate of bone marrow soup.

"Perhaps, Lionel, we should set another plate!" My father was annoyed.

"You are right, Elijah. I speak too much of her. I must let Sybella go, reluctant though I am. I must live . . . on . . . without her." And a loud groan suddenly came forth from him that frightened all of us.

My father started up in his chair—not another death at the dinner table!—letting his napkin fall to the floor. "Sir, are you all right? Mrs. Farnley, more wine for Mr. Strooksbury."

"I am all right. But yes, a bit more wine, thank you. A bit of indigestion, that is all, Sir. Marrow soup does not always agree with me."

During the next course (crimped skate) he was relatively silent, except to lift his glass and say, "Incomparable one, I salute you wherever you are."

I watched as he chewed his fish, his mouth slightly open. After each swallow he would take a sip of wine, after which he would take his napkin and pat his lips carefully, first the upper, then the lower, then the corners. He repeated the process until the fish had completely disappeared from his plate.

One more habit and then I shall leave off. One that never failed to enthrall me. In his encomiums to his wife he would lift his eyes heavenward, staring at the carved ceiling with fervor and concentration, at which time his pupils would disappear from sight and only the semicircular rims of the whites remain. (Entranced, I would in my own room attempt to do the same thing, holding a mirror above my head.) He also did this when he praised Clara's piano playing for he would sometimes stay for the entire evening. "Fluid, limpid, perfectly phrased," he would murmur, and lift his head, his pupils vanishing from sight.

One day in the early fall of the year, Mr. Strooksbury came to call in the afternoon, to ask permission of my mother to take me with Clara out for a walk in the Gardens. My mother, who I knew detested Clara, consented happily, having jumped to the conclusion that now that he was a widower, Mr. Strooksbury might be interested in Clara as a replacement for Sybella.

We walked towards Swan Lake while Mr. Strooksbury discoursed knowledgeably about the flora and the fauna of the Gardens, as expertly as Clara did. At the lake, whose surface was afloat with massive beds of nymphea, he lectured on hermaphroditic organisms such as the nymphea as we gazed on the bronze-colored leaves bobbing in the wind.

The walks became a habit. My mother looked forward to getting rid of Clara permanently via Mr. Strooksbury.

One day we were on our way as usual to the lake when he stumbled and fell against Clara. "Pardon, pardon me, Mrs. Lustig, I am afraid I was dizzy for a second. I'd best sit down," he said, as he walked over to a nearby bench and sat down.

He did look pale, I thought. And then he plunged his head straight down between his bony knees and began to groan.

Clara said, "I shall go for help immediately. I shall leave Emma here, Mr. Strooksbury, in case you become incapacitated." To me she said, "I shall be back as soon as possible. Stay there with him on the bench. Be brave." And off she went.

When she was no longer in view, Mr. Strooksbury stopped groaning and, lifting his head from between his knees, he smiled up at me. I returned his smile, happy to see that he had quite recovered. Then quite suddenly he lifted his gloved hand and touched me on my breast, which was sheathed in the plum-colored material of my jacket. Being unable to make sense out of that action, and thinking it part of his strange condition, I did nothing; that is, I did not scream or move away. . . .   "Emma," he said. "Emma . . ."

"Yes, Mr. Strooksbury."

"Lionel, please, Emma. Lionel . . ."

"Yes, Lionel."

"You have beautiful breasts, Emma."

I sat there very still, not daring to move, hoping that Clara would return quickly, for obviously Mr. Strooksbury had gone mad. At the same time my terrible curiosity, which has never left me, wondered what Mr. Strooksbury would do next. But he did nothing; he behaved as if nothing had happened between us. And when Clara returned with two burly men to carry Mr. Strooksbury out of the Gardens to the hospital, he had already launched into a speech about toads and frogs with frequent allusions to Aristophanes.

Tipping the brutes handsomely, and thanking Clara effusively, Mr. Strooksbury assured us that there was no longer any cause for alarm. That he felt as fit as a fiddle. He even stood up and executed a few dancing steps for us.

The only moral conflict I experienced later that day was whether or not to tell Clara about what had happened in her absence. She was, after all, the repository of every thought, every feeling and action of my life. But somewhere deep inside me I made the decision not to. I remembered the fireplace incident. By not telling her, I once again had a private life. She had betrayed me then. I would betray her now.

Not telling Clara made an enormous difference. I lay in bed that night and repeated to myself countless times Mr. Strooksbury's strange words: "You have beautiful breasts."

I felt my breasts in the dark. Visualized them, my nipples' rosy aureoles, their small pink tips. I remembered Grindal's nipples. How horrified I had been when as a child I had watched her stroke them (when she was my nanny she had slept in the same room with me), as I stroked mine now. I repeated the phrase, "You have beautiful breasts, Emma."

From that day on I began to think of him. Would he dine with us tonight? Would he take us for a walk? And if he did, would he touch my breasts again? I was fifteen years old, vulnerable to all kinds of sensations, some of which Clara had explained to me. I had the strange sensation that my breasts seemed to be pleading with me, "Let him, let him . . ."

My father had ordered my mother to take more of an interest in my wardrobe, so I was taken to dressmakers and milliners, and I was beginning, I thought, to look quite pretty for once in my life. As for my mother, who seemed to have a genuine interest in me for once, I began to enjoy a sort of camaraderie with her. Something I had never experienced before. I remember giggling together with her for the first time, and enjoying it. I liked being "mothered," but when I commented on it to Clara she gave me a rather strange look and said in a dry tone that almost sounded bitter, "Cui buono?"

Despite myself, my body seemed to have desires of its own. I remembered how when I was younger I had wanted . . . *longed* . . . to be touched. That at times I had behaved badly so that Grindal *would* spank me, since that seemed to be the only way I could obtain physical closeness. Then Clara had come and I had longed for her to touch me. But she never had, except once or twice when I had a nightmare and I had crept into her bed. Clara, Grindal, my mother . . . the desire to be touched, fondled, handled, held, became an overwhelming obsession. I longed for the magical comfort of a bosom. Is it any wonder that I allowed Mr. Strooksbury "liberties"? What a strange word we have coined for such activities.

Thereafter, when we walked together in the Gardens, Mr. Strooksbury would contrive in endless ways to rid us of Clara, and as soon as she had left would take "liberties" with me. Plant kisses on my throat, run his hands up and down my bosom, embrace me, whisper to me, "Lionel wants you, Lionel needs you . . ."

His ardor seemed to increase as the weather grew colder. It was late autumn now. With an open mouth, his breath visible in small puffs of white air, he would nibble on my fingers, my ears, as he kept his eyes on the path. And then, seeing Clara return, he would momentarily fix on me a stern but conspiratorial look and his lips would mouth the word "Silence," and we would resume casual natural poses as she came back into view.

Throughout all of this activity on his part I did nothing, as if I were paralyzed. Nor did I make a sound, though I felt enormous physical pleasure and was in a constant fever of desire. He suddenly seemed handsome to me. Clever. Daring.

I knew, of course, that all that was happening between us was strictly forbidden. And that I should have reported it to Clara. To my father. And that they would have been outraged! Mr. Strooksbury was a forty-seven-year-old widower; I was a fifteen-year-old virgin, the respectable daughter of his closest friend. Yet I did nothing. I wanted it to continue. I realize that now. I accept that about myself.

This is not a social tract. I am not interested in judgment, accusations, or punishment. Perhaps some day society will evolve to a state in which there will be special places available to young girls who are starved for human touch, human affection, human embraces, and men (or women) who are starved for our embraces, and both will give to one another without private censure or public condemnation.

The conspiratorial aspects of my relationship with Mr. Strooksbury reminded me of my former life with Darius, our War Games, our preparations, our battle . . . our final victory. Here was another secret world. Inhabited by two people this time: me and Mr. Strooksbury. What "Lionel" offered my starving body was too utterly delicious to deny either myself or him.

Our threesomes continued. One day the weather was bitter cold, and he suggested that instead of a walk through the Gardens we go to a café instead. I had been there with Clara one or twice before.

We were shown to a red-velvet-covered booth in which a round table nestled, covered with a large, spotless tablecloth and napkins, glasses, and cutlery. Mr. Strooksbury arranged the seating. He would sit between us, he said. I on his right, Clara on his left.

The waiter, a handsome man, came over to us and took our order. "The lady will have lemon tea, the young lady will have hot chocolate," Lionel ordered. "I shall have a double brandy. And, oh yes, a plate of petit fours."

When the waiter left, Lionel said, "I do not like to see a waiter whose cuffs are soiled. In a public establishment cleanliness must be observed. It is the first rule of public dining. I shall report him to the proprietor, a friend of mine."

As he said this I felt his right hand upon my left thigh. At the same time I watched with fascination his left hand play with his knife and fork. I glanced at Clara, who was looking around the room as she answered him. "Yes, I agree, though I didn't notice that his cuffs were soiled."

There we sat, Mr. Strooksbury, Clara, and I in a well-lit restaurant, amid its cheerful bustle with its buzz of conversation, the waiters moving to and fro, patrons leaving and coming in, while beneath the dark circumference of the table Mr. Strooksbury began to move his hand gently up and down my left thigh.

The contrast, the separation between the visible and the invisible, between public and private, between open and secret, mundi and arcane mundi, between the upper part of my body, in full view, and the concealed lower part . . . this bifurcation . . . only increased my pleasure. I did not move away. Or remove his hand.

I listened as they conversed: knowledgeably, intellectually . . . competitively. I listened as they quoted Aristotle, Plato, spoke learnedly about revolutions, aristocracy, debacles, Robespierre, Rousseau . . .

He said: "Aristotle says that men are slaves by nature . . ." as he relentlessly pursued with his right hand his hidden sexual desires.

"Yes," said Clara, "but have you forgotten that a man who does not deserve to be in a condition of slavery is not a slave?"

"Would you agree," he asked her, "with Cicero when he says Syrians are people born for slavery . . ." while his right hand begged, coaxed, pleaded with me to open my young virginal thighs, so that he could slip his hand between them and move up towards my "seat of Satan," as Grindal called it.

She sipped her tea; he drank his brandy.

"Who was it," she asked, "That said Christian slaves should not wish to be set free at the public cost, lest they become slaves of lust?"

I felt my thighs open slightly while his hand groped eagerly upon my pantaloons towards my clitoris.

Their conversation, my fixed smile (Clara, Clara, how is it that you noticed nothing, suspected nothing?), the tearoom, the activity above my waist, and below it, their eerie philosophical observations, are embedded in my brain and have made strange connections.

I remember wondering if what was happening in this booth at this table was happening in other booths, at other tables. I was painfully aware how two things were happening at once, how the mind was carrying on a conversation on one level, while the body was carrying on a conversation on an entirely different level, and that both were connected, nevertheless, in some mysterious way, though one was visible and the other invisible.

Now his hand pushed farther up my thighs. Gently, almost playfully, he persisted. Unable to resist, I let him. Onward and upwards the hand traveled. The dread of discovery with what was happening out of sight, in front of my beloved Clara, only added to this delicious sensation. Barely listening to what they were saying, I gave myself up to what I was experiencing, counseling myself not to faint, so wonderful were the feelings I was going through. Then he made to move his hand away. I looked at him. He winked covertly and moved his hand back again.

At that moment Clara reminded me to drink my chocolate, which I had left untasted. In a delirium of sensation I drank it. It was the first time I had acknowledged in any way that I was experiencing sensations caused by him, and I could tell that he was pleased.

I came as he was discussing Rousseau and Kant's admiration for him. ". . . Kant adds that when one follows a law reason has dictated or made, then like Rousseau's citizens I am free, even though I, a sensuous being, am under a law."

Removing his hand from beneath the table, he used it to pop a petit four into his mouth and to pick another up and pop it into mine.

"Children should be cossetted, spoiled, and stroked, don't you think so, Mrs. Lustig?"

—◆◇◆—

The following Wednesday afternoon Clara went out, as usual, without telling anyone, also as usual, where she was going or what she would be doing. Though she did tell me once that she had made a friend, a Miss Sophie Hussaye, a writer like herself, and so I assumed that she went to visit her.

We had arranged, Mr. Strooksbury and I, that I should leave a side door open. It was relatively safe. Most of the servants had the same afternoon off, and my mother would be spending her afternoon as usual at the London League. It was the first of our assignations.

I have had many lovers. I am old now and what seemed at one time immoral and perverse no longer seems that way. Looking back, I realize that Lionel was an excellent lover. Among the best. He had several qualities that made him so. He was eager to please; he did not take offence at being directed; he picked up on the slightest cues. He had a robust and sensual nature, but was neither coercive or brutal in any way. On the contrary, he was both gentle and imaginative. True, he was eccentric, a mite peculiar, as they say, but for a young virgin, which is what I was, after all, he proved to be a true blessing.

He would enter my room and, giving me a cheerful smile, remove his hat and lay down his cane. I would be waiting, prim and girlish, seated with my legs decorously crossed on my narrow bed. Behind me hung a portrait of the Duke of Wellington, a former enthusiasm of mine. Lionel would sit beside me quietly for a few minutes. And when he saw desire in my face, and only then, he would begin to play with my breasts, as he had the first time, murmuring that magical phrase, "You have beautiful breasts, Emma." He would run his finger around the convolutions of my ear, never progressing further until he sensed my arousal, until he sensed I was eager for more. It is a source of perpetual wonder to me, considering the great risk involved, that he sat there calmly for those few minutes it took to arouse me.

So skillfully did he lead me on that I was only too willing and eager for him to lift up my skirts with one hand as he opened his fly with the other, and place his erect penis into the wetness that expected him (I had in anticipation of his visit removed my pantaloons), was only too eager for him.

As he began to slip his penis in and out of me, as his breathing grew more rapid, as his pale cheeks turned ruddy, he spoke to me about his deep desire for me. And perhaps it is that, more than anything else—

his declaration of deep desire for me—that brought me to climax. With the full weight of Lionel's body on my own (he never removed his jacket, though he did remove his frock coat), I listened in a sort of daze as I experienced the complete satisfaction that the close physical contact gave me, the satisfaction that I had longed for ever since I could remember. I felt worthy for the first time in my life. I was his primary object. My mind flashed with images of Grindal's bosom, Poppa's broad chest, Momma's lap, in which William used to lay his head, as Lionel droned on in marked contrast to the quick, sharp, pounding thrusts of his hidden penis. I felt intense joy as I climaxed.

I kept a secret and accurate record in a small notebook of our activities, which I named "Accounting," so I know for a fact that it was the fifth time that we were "accounting" when we were discovered by Mrs. Farnley.

So engrossed were we with one another that we never heard her enter, and it was only when I saw her sharp-featured squarish face, a mask of horror, over his left shoulder that I realized we had been found out.

"Get off her, you disgusting creature!" Mrs. Farnley screamed, accompanying her words with a physical attack on him, trying to draw him off me. He weighed considerably less than she, so that the two of them fell backwards onto the floor, whereupon, though startled out of his wits, he had enough presence of mind to draw his trousers back up again. Darting out of the room, he left behind him his coat, his cane, his beaver hat, his gloves, all of which he had so neatly placed on the school desk but a few minutes ago.

Mrs. Farnley, seated on the floor, looking stupefied, said nothing to me, but a moment later she began to cry. It was the first time I had ever seen her cry. It impressed me. I think that was the first time I took into account how others might view what had happened between Mr. Strooksbury and myself.

I rose. Pulling down my skirts, I stood in front of her, waiting for her to do something. But she only continued to weep. For five minutes the only sound that seemed to exist was the sound of her sobbing. Then, removing a handkerchief from her pocket, she wiped her face clean of tears, stood up, and left the room, all without saying a single word to me.

I got back on my bed again and lay down thinking of nothing.

Several hours later Daisy knocked on my door and came in. Poppa wished to speak to me in the library, she said. I remember scanning her face closely, trying to determine if she knew what had happened. But I could tell nothing.

Slowly, my feet dragging, I went down the stairs to my tribunal.

Guilty. I would be found guilty. I would be punished. Would I be hung or guillotined, I remember wondering. His library study was a room off the great hall, and I remember standing in that hall looking at the door before me. *All* of me, every cell of my body, urged me to run away, to disappear forever, and yet so ingrained was my obedience to my father that I found myself, albeit filled with fear, rebellion . . . intense reluctance, moments later opening the door of his study.

My father was seated behind his desk. He pointed to the chair in front of the desk. I sat down on it. We sat facing one another. Silence. I looked at him as a dog looks at its master, I even assumed a hangdog look. I was mortally frightened, but I was also thinking furiously: Certainly Mrs. Farnley had told him what she had seen. But what had she seen, actually? I also wondered, since it had been her afternoon off, why hadn't she taken it? And why had she come upstairs to my room? Something she rarely did, if ever. But these thoughts were overridden with terror. What would happen to me now? What would Poppa do? Would he kill Mr. Strooksbury, I wondered.

Mrs. Farnley had waited for Poppa in the vestibule until he came home. I was sure of that. "I must speak to you, Sir, immediately, upon an urgent matter." But what had she seen, actually? And had she exculpated me? Was there one villain in this affair or two? For as much as I felt guilty, I still hoped not to be punished, but to be spared on the grounds of innocence.

Finally my father spoke: "There is a matter that I must discuss with you, Emma, that I find quite difficult to do. I am certain, dear child, that you know to what I am referring—" He stopped speaking.

I noticed that like Mrs. Farnley, my father had been weeping. His eyes were red and somewhat swollen. Would he cry in front of me, I wondered.

"You must know," he began again, "to what I am referring—"

"Perhaps I do, Poppa," I said interrupting him. "The last time I saw Mrs. Farnley she seemed somewhat perturbed—"

"Emma!"

"Yes, Poppa."

His voice broke. "Do not think for a moment, dear child, for a moment, that I hold you responsible for what happened in any way. In any way! You are innocent. It is *I* who have failed you! It is *my* fault! I have failed as your protector, your guardian—" He could no longer continue. Tears coursed down his cheeks.

A hardness came over me. A feeling of spite. On the one hand, I was truly grief-stricken that I had caused my father such pain, but on the other hand, I did not wish to be the one to comfort him, to absolve *him* of blame. Were not his tears in some indefinable way asking for my forgiveness? I thought of Darius's letters, the ones he had deliberately withheld from me. How I had suffered, believing Darius no longer loved me. I mistrusted him now.

"I take it, Poppa, you are referring to your colleague, Mr. Strooksbury."

I heard him gasp and then I heard him say, "I understand from Mrs. Farnley that Mr. Strooksbury has taken certain . . . liberties . . . with you. He should not have done that, Emma. He is a monster!" As he said this he came around the desk and reached out to me, drawing me towards him. Holding me in his arms, he stroked my nevus and murmured in my ear. "My poor child, my poor, poor child . . ."

I recoiled at these words. Something of my fierce anger towards him must have penetrated his self-pity, because he released me.

Straightening, he said to me, "You need not worry, Emma. No one aside from Mrs. Farnley and me shall ever know. I shall attend to everything, every detail. We need never mention it again."

I never saw Mr. Strooksbury again alone after that, though I did see him on several social occasions, for my father, deathly afraid of even a breath of scandal, did not dare break off with him socially either . . . or financially.

That night I lay in my bed repeating my father's words: "My poor, poor child . . ." Lionel had not thought so. To him I had been the object of desire, albeit a forbidden object. Mrs. Farnley had removed Mr. Strooksbury's frock coat, his gloves, and his cane, but his beaver hat had rolled under the bed, where I had found it. I whispered to myself, "Lionel, my beloved monster, my seducer, my molester . . ." as I stroked his hat, and then placing the stiff rim between my thighs I pressed it hard up against my clitoris. Repeating over and over again "My beloved monster, my seducer, my molester," I finally fell into a deep sleep.

24

GUINIVERE

... the will to live is primarily an effort to maintain the individual; yet this is only a stage towards the effort to reproduce the species ... the sexual impulse is therefore the most complete manifestation of the will to live ...

—Schopenhauer, *The World as Will and Representation*, trans. Clara Lustig

In the most crucial decisions of our life ... we act not out of cool detached intellect but out of a deep inner impulse that comes from the core of our being ... an impulse that is present in our prophetic dreams that are forgotten when we awaken.

—*Ibid.*

GUINIVERE *knew* that she was pregnant even before she began to miss her menstrual periods. From the moment her sexual life had begun with Nicholas, her body (the sleeping beauty) had awakened and with it, its own preternatural awareness of itself. A person she did not know heretofore had emerged from somewhere deep within her to share a life with Nicholas. A hidden life. For that was the way she thought of it, if she thought of it at all. A hidden life, a sexual life that made her other life, the one she lived with Solomon, a living death to her. With Nicholas she felt as if she had developed a fever that, instead of debilitating her, had given her an extraordinary energy. She had never looked so well. When Albert came home from Warrenton, he commented on it. Even Solomon noticed it and concluded that at last his wife had relinquished her grief. And hoped if that were true perhaps she would allow him his conjugal rights again, though on reflection he decided the thought was not worthy of him. Still, it gave him hope.

When she was alone in her dressing room she would examine herself in the mirror . . . her body, her flesh that had become real to her, her flesh that had been kissed, stroked, caressed by Nicholas . . . her body that had given birth to her children and had nursed them. Feverish, yes, that is how she felt. On fire. She saw her body now through Nicholas's eyes: full-breasted, narrow-waisted, wide-hipped, slender thighs, legs, arms . . . seductive. Enticing. Her upper arms were perfectly shaped, rounded, her elbows invitingly dimpled. Gazing at herself she would hear his moan of passion, and his voice, thrilling, saying again and again, "Beautiful! So very beautiful!" Sometimes she tried to remember her virginal body, what she had looked like when she was sixteen, before she met Solomon. But there was no memory forthcoming. She had never looked at herself naked at sixteen. She regretted it now.

She remembered the first time they had made love. Though she had opened her arms to him—her body ached to be held—she had been overwhelmed by his passion, his lust for her, by the reality of his sex. Lying naked next to him in the glow of lamplight, she had seen the penis swell, become erect. He had placed her hand on it, kissed her hand, parted her thighs, and entered her almost at the same time. He moved on top of her, his eyes boring into hers, his green eyes flashing, looking frightened, and as if he were in pain, murmuring her name again and again: "Guinivere, Guinivere, Guinivere . . ." She felt him stiffen momentarily, as if death gripped him, and then he had cried out in ectasy and fear, and he had fallen at her side like someone slain. It was over. She had felt nothing. But that all had changed . . .

The wonder of it was that it had. That he had understood that she had felt nothing. And so step by step he had taught her how to feel something, and then how to feel more. And more . . .

For the first time in her life she began resorting to subterfuge, something she would have considered degrading, immoral, at one time. But now she would do anything to be with Nicholas. She found it amusing that she seemed to have sort of a natural skill for deception. It amazed her that she could carry on her daily tasks, her parish duties, her domestic chores, her charity work, while thinking of how to arrange a meeting with Nicholas. As the months passed an impulse that grew stronger took hold of her. She wanted them all to know—her two sisters-in-law, her two brothers-in-law, Solomon. Sometimes it was an effort *not* to tell them. Now when she met him at Mathilda's house, or Elijah's, or her own—for Nicholas had become an official "friend of the family"—she wanted to place her arms around him and announce to them *all,* This is my lover, my paramour, the object of my sexual passion, Nicholas. It seemed miraculous to her that she could move among them with him present as if he were not even there. As if he were not her lover. How was it, she wondered, that no one saw their deep passion for one another, their deep love for one another? But perhaps someone did. Joseph sometimes looked at her strangely. Solomon had begun commenting on the fact that she seemed "a bit too lively." Harping really. "A bit too buoyant, perhaps, Gwinnie. Are you well? Do you have a fever?" Yes, yes, yes, she wanted to tell him. Yes, I have a fever . . . the fever of love.

Nicholas told her about his criminal empire. He did not hide it from her. On the contrary, he offered it to her. She knew as much about it as Kevin Francini. And he told her all about Toby, and the Kittos, and the Toddlers. And Dame Lou and Charles Mallet. Once he took her to the Holy Land and stood with her at the highest point and told her about his past life there . . .

"When I was released from Newgate I went to see the lawyer, Jasper Hemsley. I wanted to know who had arranged for my release. But he wouldn't see me. I tried many times and finally he did only to tell me that he had promised someone he would never disclose the name of my benefactor. 'I shall not,' he told me. 'The matter is closed forever.' Later when I met Kevin, he told me that Jasper Hemsley was Jorem's lawyer, and I thought again what Dame Lou had told me about my parents. How my father was a well-known man in the city, very wealthy, and that he made his money from lending money. I realized then that Jorem Forster was my father, that I was his illegitimate son."

One day Nicholas asked her, "Do I resemble Jorem? You knew him. Do I?"

"Not in coloring, nor in bone structure," she had told him. "But your eyes . . . they are exactly alike . . . Though his eyes were blue, they were set the same way in the head. Deep and intense. Yes, the eyes are alike."

Toby cooked for them. Sometimes Guinivere was ravenously hungry after sex. She who never had an appetite now looked forward eagerly to eating; her awakened sexuality had awakened everything, including her appetite. Instead of the bourgeois fare the Forsters usually ate— roast pig, mutton roast, venison, boiled leg of lamb cooked with lard and mutton drippings—Toby's cuisine was more refined and more amusing. She might prepare veal sweetbreads with capers and sprinkle crushed pinenuts over them, or there might be fresh carp from the small muddy pond behind the Tower Farfrum[30] cooked in Malaga and gar-

30. The Tower Farfrum stood in Marlborough Marshes just inside the West Gate. It had

nished with slivers of ginger and roast grasshoppers, one of Kevin's Chinese recipes. Food to stimulate and satisfy the palate.

They met twice a week for four hours in the afternoon. Toby would help her undress. Nicholas would not be there yet. And while she waited, wrapped in an embroidered Chinese gown, she might nibble on one of Toby's dishes. Or lie down on the bed, her head nestled in the silk pillows, her loosed hair streaming like a shower of gold over the pillows, the silk sheets, her robe open, revealing the golden-tinged flesh of her body, and wait for him.

She would keep her eyes closed as he came to the bed and stretched out next to her, his warm body smelling of spice. "My love, my Guinivere," he would whisper, his hand stroking her nipples, and then as he sucked them she could feel them harden. Sometimes later in that very same day, when she was at home alone in her boudoir, she would stare at her nipples in the vanity mirror as Jakes undressed her. These were the nipples Nicholas sucked, she would say to herself, the same nipples that had fed her children, and her mind, drawn into the past, would once again experience the small mouth with the tongue curled around the nipple, sucking the milk out of her with such force, such eagerness. As much pleasure now as then but different . . . and yet not so different. Her body, which had been cold and unfeeling as she allowed Solomon to do what he wanted, was now flooded with feeling, sensation, emotion . . . all the cells of her body, her entire being, rocked with pleasure, and when she was penetrated, and he called out to her, she would experience bliss . . . complete contentment.

Every part of her body had been touched, kissed, and licked by Nicholas. It was as if they were children. The great solemn burden called "civilization" or "culture," with its duties and responsibilities, had been removed and they were children once again, in this miraculous room together made for bliss and pleasure. Afterwards there was a hip bath. Toby would carry it in and bring steaming-hot kettles of water and abundant towels, and they would bathe and soap one another, and splash one another, rub each other dry with towels until each of them was pink and rosy. On cold days there would be a fire and they would stretch out in front of it on the rug and lie there locked in each other's arms, naked, in front of the flames.

When Solomon had to travel to the Continent in Elijah's place—for Elijah had told him he would no longer do so because he was not feeling well, Guinivere and Nicholas spent even more time together. And she became even more daring. She would slip out at night to his house and

been conceived by Kevin as "a place where children can play as they wish . . . far from their nannies and their parents." From Jorem's letter, dated 4 May, 1818.—*R. Lowe* spend part of the night there, or he would come to her and he would slip out in the early dawn.

On warm nights they might go to Marlborough Gardens and swim in the silver water of the lake, liquid moonlight, their arms slipping in and out of the lisping water, or mired in the water lilies feel the minnows nibble on this strange new food. Barefoot with wet hair, clothed, they would walk to Piece of Moonlight and lie huddled in each other's arms in one long fiery embrace.

She was thirty-five years old, mother of five children, and for the first time in her life she felt fully alive. She felt as if she suddenly understood the wind, weather, trees, animals, nature . . . her own purpose in life: to experience pleasure fully, fearlessly, unsedated. She was grateful, grateful that she was beautiful, that he, her lover, her magician/lover, had fallen in love with her.

On the afternoon that she *knew* she was pregnant, she went to meet Nicholas as usual, bringing with her a present she knew he would want. She had written to her brother who still lived in the house she had grown up in, asking him to go up to the old nursery and forage around for one of her playthings, anything that was there that she had used as a child. This morning the package had come: a small collection of dolls. She chose one as her present to Nicholas. She knew and understood that he wanted her childhood, not only the stories she told him over and over again but something more tangible. She was bringing him Isabella, her favorite doll.

As usual she took a circuitous route through the Gardens and, slipping around to the side of his house, opened the door with her key, entered, walked down to the end of a corridor, and pushed open the door on her right. A small paradise, a suite of rooms: a dressing room, a bedroom, and a sitting room, awaited her. Each of the rooms faced the walled garden Kevin had designed.

Removing her gloves, hat, and veil, she unwrapped the package she had carried with her and placed the doll on the bed. She undressed, took the pins out of her heavy golden hair so that it tumbled down onto her rosy breasts, her coral nipples. She saw him in the mirror first. Holding her hands towards the mirror, she embraced his reflection. Dark apricot-colored skin shining, his penis semierect, he walked towards her with grace. Cupid, he was like Cupid, she thought, a perfect Cupid. Agile and adroit. As their fingers touched, the spark of desire once more shot up into a sudden flame, fiercer than ever before. For a second she lost consciousness. She shuddered, the feeling she had for him was so powerful, so intense, and did not lessen—on the contrary, each time she saw him it seemed stronger. She wondered if he felt the same way.

They murmured words of love to one another. Love and adoration. And gratitude. They laughed, they giggled, they played hide-and-seek in the confines of their small paradise: "I will find you," he growled, "I will find you and when I do I shall eat you up!" as blindfolded he would search for her.

He questioned her about her life before they met. Her wedding— he wanted to know every detail. Her brother Stephen, what did he look like? Her parents, her Nanny Rose, her governess Mademoiselle Elise. She in turn would listen to him speak about his "Empire of Crime."

Sometimes she might tell him about Albert, or the twins or Deirdre. He would rarely comment, he would just listen, his green eyes fastened on her, serious, burning. One day she told him that when she was young she had studied the piano. The next day there was a small piano in the sitting room, and she played for him. They were like two children in a fairy tale who had found one another in an enchanted wood. Only the passion was real. Only the love.

They made love that afternoon and afterwards they fell asleep. When she awakened, his head was on her breast, his moist mouth slightly open. She hadn't told him she was pregnant. Now that she had a secret life she would have secrets from him too. She smiled at that. The child growing in her would be her love child. She had heard the phrase and she had never connected to it. She had known, of course, what it meant. It meant a child born out of wedlock, something that was shameful, forbidden. Now she had a love child growing in her. The darling, darling thing, she said to herself. A child created fully and wholly out of the love they had for one another. Each cell of its small unformed body created out of their natural passion . . . their mutual joy. No, she would not tell him. He would find out in time, wouldn't he?

But—she *would* tell Solomon. He must believe the child was his. She marveled at her new guile, new cunning. Nothing must come between her and Nicholas. Nothing must prevent the birth of the child that was the outgrowth, the flowering, of their love. She began to make plans . . .

RESEARCH PAPER:
DESIGN AND CHANCE

Il est plus aise de connoitre l'homme en general, que de connoitre un homme en particular.

—La Rochefoucauld

My father Solomon Forster lived on and on and . . . on until he was almost the combined age of my two uncles, Elijah and Joseph, at their death, ninety-four years old, and that was good wasn't it, because he didn't really "flower" until he was well past fifty.

—Deirdre F. Bowles to Emma Forster
(8 August 1904)

Principal Sources: 1. A Little Learning—, Emma Forster, unfinished manuscript; 2. Solomon's diary: 1842

Introduction, research and editing: Rachel Lowe

Commentary and editing: Harriet Van Buren

INTRODUCTION

There is very little actual information about Solomon in the archives, except for occasional references and Emma's unfinished essay. One would have thought that Amelia Maude Forster, the esteemed and renowned poet, the child he adored, might have written a poem about him, or dedicated a poem to him, but even in that quarter there is silence.

Solomon was neither brilliant, wicked, nor saintly; he was, by his own admission, a "moderate man." No one ever quoted Solomon, no one claimed to have heard him say anything witty or clever. Yet by the end of his long life this rather dull man wedged in his narrow sphere of thought and action somehow bumbled his way into a joyful understanding of the meaning of love. How did he do it? Il y a un mystere dans l'espirit des gens qui n'en ont pas *("There is a mystery in the minds of men who have none").*

Since we, like Emma,[31] *are engaged in writing a history of the Forsters, we consider it important not only to relate the events of Solomon's life but also to attempt to establish his motives, his intentions. How did a silly man become a profoundly wise one? Certainly he is a prime example of the theory that a man's nature is not fixed once and for all.*

A LITTLE LEARNING—

Though my grandfather, Jorem Forster, did state somewhere in his journals that he thought his son Solomon was "a bit smug," he was nevertheless Jorem's favorite child. The reason seems obvious to me. Solomon never gave Jorem any trouble.[32]

He was not in the least like his biblical namesake. It was not in his character to call for the sword. Had he been given the matter of the

---

31. Emma, though a novelist, was primarily interested in history. Influenced by Clara, her interest lay both in Greek historians, particularly Plutarch, with his emphasis on the psychological aspects of his portraits, and German historians. It would be well to remember that a part of her life was lived in Germany. She was influenced by Dilthey and his sharp distinctions between Naturwissenschaften and his Geisteswissenschaften, as well as Ranke and Marx. Marx's startling idea that society's structure and its historical developments are determined by the "material conditions of life" aroused her. Paradoxically, she never relinquished her belief that from time to time there were "miraculous" interferences with natural laws. Like many of the Forsters, confronted with the unseen, she leaned towards the way of mysticism.—*H. Van Buren*

32. "Parents rarely admit the truth of how they feel about their children, to themselves or others. The real truth is that the parent prefers the tractable, malleable, easily controlled child. And why not? It seems sensible to me. Do we ever like anyone (adult, child, dog, or horse) who is not compliant, well-behaved, submissive, and obedient? It is the rare parent who loves the child who is different, the child who tiresomely insists on being herself or himself. And varying and ingenious forms of punishment (psychological and corporal) are meted out to children who rebel and struggle, for some perverted reason, to become themselves. 'Obey . . . or be beaten,' or worse than that, be 'reasoned with.' Surely, it is truly cruel to be consistently and relentlessly 'reasoned' out of what one desires. Be it a toy or a lover. One eventually loses all connection with one's *real* yearnings while being made to conform to the 'right' forms of behaviour. Hope withers." —*Emma Forster*

two harlots and the baby to adjudicate, he would have arranged for joint custody. He had no dramatic flair.

As for the Judaic commandment "Thou shalt honor thy father and thy mother" . . . well, that was not, according to Solomon's way of thinking, proper dialectical material. He did not have to be "commanded" to "honor" his father. He perceived it in Aristotelean terms: he, Solomon, was a son; Jorem was his father. Ipso facto, a son by definition "honors" his father. He cannot *not* honor his father. Since that cannot happen, it cannot be thought of. Q.E.D.

Solomon revered Aristotle. It was Solomon's bad fortune—or good fortune—to read Aristotle *sine Praejudicio* (without prejudice).

When he first read Aristotle at Warrenton, and later on at Oxford, it seemed to him that he himself could have written many of the texts (in particular, *Nichomachean Ethics*) so in tune was the thought and the underlying feeling with his own.

He had read the "other man's" work—*The Republic*—and had been horrified. Wives and children in common! Women given the same duties as men in the state!

Modeling himself after his ideal, he tried to be neither boastful nor self-depreciatory, neither a buffoon nor boorish, neither obsequious nor a flatterer, neither rash nor craven, neither a profligate nor stingy, but instead a pleasant, friendly, courageous, generous man, a human exemplar of the golden mean. His imagination remained, however, exclusively matter-of-fact.

Such a question as Elijah posed—Was it unfair of Jorem to leave Vanessa the King's Ransom?—did not enter his mind. He did not understand Elijah's anger towards Jorem, his tempestuous nature, his chronic restlessness; he did not comprehend Joseph's immoderate behaviour after Consuelo left him; he did not sympathize with Guinivere's grief.

However, as far as Joseph was concerned, Solomon had done what he could for his brother. He consulted Aristotle. And reading there that cabbage cured the ill effects of drinking, he had told Maria, Joseph's cook, to serve his brother cabbage frequently.

Joseph's non-Aristotelean, immoderate mode of behaviour upset Solomon. Had Guinivere left him . . . but the very thought was absurd! It was not proper dialectical material, since first, it could not happen, hence second, it could not be thought of. If cabbage did not work for Joseph, (if Maria did in fact serve him cabbage), it was not Aristotle's fault.

Solomon agreed, of course, with his mentor's theories of time, his theories of motion, his doctrine of chance, etc., but it was his practical advice to and about mankind that he concentrated on. For instance, according to Aristotle's theory of physiognomy, large protruding ears indicated both loquacity and stupidity. That described his sister, Mathilda. While high foreheads like Joseph's (who took after Momma) meant slower minds, rounder foreheads (like Elijah's) were hot-tempered. Exactly. And wide foreheads (like his own and Jorem's) indicated extraordinary faculties. Exactly.

As for wives and home economics . . . he himself had bought a translation of Aristotle's *Economics,* Book One, and had underlined certain passages for Guinivere, such as: "The well-ordered wife will consider the behaviour of her husband as a model for her own life."

He did have problems with *Historia Animalium,* even though he agreed with the passage that stated that women were more compassionate than men and had a greater propensity to tears. But the observation that females were naturally libidinous, and incited males to copulation and to cry out during the act of coition, puzzled him. Thank God this did not seem to apply to Guinivere.

However, ever since Sidney's death the plain fact of the matter was that Gwinnie did not want to copulate. Not that she had ever been enthusiastic, but now she refused. Taking his cue from *Nichomachean Ethics*—"He who avoids all pleasure, like a boor is an insensible sort of person"—he felt justified in taking a mistress, the recently widowed Mrs. Cornwind. Though he continued to love his wife, for love was more a question of friendship, said the master, than a matter of intercourse.

Unlike Elijah, who was a Whig, Solomon was a Tory. To be a Whig was to be associated with reform and the new industrial interests. It was the latter connectedness that determined Elijah's vote. There was no doubt in Solomon's mind what party Aristotle would have belonged to were he alive in these turbulent times of reform, the Chartist movement, the Free Trade movement. Had he not said in *Politics*: "A democracy considers only the poor, a democracy is a government in the hands of low birth, poverty, and vulgar employments . . ."?

However, despite the problems of the world ever since June 20, 1837, Solomon felt deep within him that everything would be all right. That was the day King William IV had died and the Archbishop of Canterbury and the Lord Chamberlain had hurried to Kensington to inform Alexandrina Victoria that she was now queen.

The accession of the girl-queen caused an almost instinctive conviction in Solomon that a new and better epoch had begun. Last February, when Victoria had married Prince Albert, son of the Duke of Saxe-Coburg-Gotha, Solomon had been there to see the royal procession wend its way through the streets of London to the Westminster Church for the coronation ceremony.

Some time after that he began a short treatise on Aristotle entitled "The Good Life."

COMMENTARY

How to explain the "flowering"? How did this ordinary man leave his mundane world of common sense and step into another universe where "flowers sang and notes of music shone"? The problem is charting his path to ecstasy. Nothing in his life seemed to point that way. We do know from his diary (circa 1842) that he did have a vision—a vision of an angel—and that it coincided with the birth of his wife's last child, Amelia Maude, in 1842.

Solomon's diary

28 August 1842
He was not a large angel. In fact he was quite small in stature. Still he was quite beautiful. Were it not for his wings I might have thought him to be a visitor to the house, so natural did he appear. What am I to think?

Not until a full year later was there another such occurrence.

I have seen Him again. He seems to hover about Amelia Maude. Can it be her Guardian Angel? Whoever or whatever it is I felt a sense of unusal peace after its visitation as I did the last time. The air seems sweeter, the light more brilliant, a feeling of deep gratitude but to whom and for what I cannot say . . .

Apparently there were only two visitations. At least there is no mention of other such incidents.

What are we to make of it? The falling sickness? Hysteria? A bilious attack? A pathological occurrence of a diseased mind? A hallucination, albeit a friendly one? Or was it an actualization of a deep spiritual feeling, a connection to another world, another plane of experience? Marlborough Gardens lends itself to such thoughts. There are things that have happened to us here that are unaccountable by way of so-called rational thought.

Socrates says in *Phaedrus:* "The greatest blessings come to us by way of madness" *(Ta megista twn agathown hmin gignetai dia manias).*

Near the end of his life, at the age of ninety, Solomon wrote an explanation of his life that we have published as *The Way of Solomon*. Since it reads like something Jorem would have written, as if the oracle (Jorem) and the muse (Solomon) were united, Lowe says that Jorem's ghost found sanctuary in Solomon and lived on through him. We are aware that neither of these explanations would satisfy a Marxist. Or a Dilthean. Or a Rankian. Though they would satisfy Plutarch.

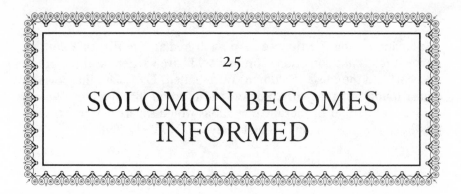

25

SOLOMON BECOMES INFORMED

All men by nature are motivated by the desire to know.

—Aristotle, *Metaphysics*

It is equally true that an object may exist even though knowledge of it does not exist.

—Aristotle, *Categories*

IN December Solomon received two pieces of information. The first in the beginning of the month, the second on Christmas Eve. Both items perplexed him, but one gave him pleasure and the other, if not pain, certainly discomfort. And both made him anxious.

The one that distressed him was provided by Elijah, who notified him at lunch one day at the Hebrides, without any apology or real explanation, that he would no longer be having the traditional Christmas celebration at his house. Elijah suggested that either ". . . you or Mathilda take charge of the affair." He no longer felt "convival."

Though he had been thrown into a state of instant confusion, Solomon had attempted then and there to find out what this radical *volte-face* was all about, but had given up in the face of Elijah's reticence. Unlike Elijah, who when he was young had looked up to Joseph as the elder brother, Solomon had always perceived both of his brothers through his father's eyes, that is, Elijah was unruly, hence unpredictable, hence unreliable; Joseph was possibly a fool. However, he loved Elijah, and ever since Elijah had insisted that he would no longer travel for the firm (two months before) Solomon had been concerned about him. Not consistently and not even too much (that was not his nature), still he had wondered about the decision—was Elijah secretly ill? Of course he had immediately acquiesced when Elijah had told him that he must take his place traveling. As a matter of fact, the trip to the Continent had been interesting . . . and enjoyable. He had taken Mrs. Cornwind with him, a fact that he had, of course, kept hidden from both brothers. Perhaps it had been imprudent of him, tempting Providence, as it were, but as Aristotle had said, "The irrational emotions seem to be as truly human as reason itself.' He was lonely. Ever since Sidney's death Gwinnie had not really been "available" for him.

The second piece of information was about Gwinnie. That had been given to him on Christmas Eve by Mrs. Farnley, who had come to the house to assist Mrs. Bridgewater.

Elijah had been unable to come. He was ill with a chest cold, said Theodisia, who had come with her children, accompanied by Mr. Coverly. Solomon had forgotten about Elijah, and he felt guilty. There was something wrong with Elijah. He must find out what it was. But the day was so happy and joyous and agreeable even without Elijah that it slipped his mind once more.

After dinner, just before the musicians arrived, Mrs. Farnley had called him aside and quietly congratulated him.

"On what, Mrs. Farnley?" he had asked.

"Excuse me, Sir, have I spoken out of turn?"

"No, No," he had assured her. "Pray tell me what am I to be congratulated about. I insist."

Then she had told him that she thought, but of course she had blundered, and would he please forgive her, and so on, that his Gwinnie was "expecting." This piece of news had completely confused him. Throughout the festivities he had hardly spoken, instead he had gone over and over again in his mind when exactly he and Gwinnie had last done "wooings" (his word for copulation), because of course they had, because Gwinnie was "expecting." Not for a second did Solomon question Mrs. Farnley's information. Mrs. Farnley was infallible. He wanted to speak to Elijah about it but he was not here.

He waited for Gwinnie to tell him. But Gwinnie didn't. And for some reason or other he found that he could not ask Gwinnie directly, though the unresolved situation—was she pregnant or wasn't she?—made him anxious.

One night two weeks later he came home and found Gwinnie waiting for him in the drawing room as usual. A room he had had a hand in decorating, for though Solomon might not have intuited people's inner feelings or understood or even caught those countless mute, soundless interactions between people—things that would be immediately apparent to someone like Nicholas, for instance—he did, like most of the Forsters, have an unusual sensitivity to form and color in the shape of objects.

So he noticed the moment he entered the room that Gwinnie was wearing a new dress. Unusually fine for an evening at home. A green watered silk with an elongated bodice and a low pointe waist. Short-sleeved and low-cut. Most attractive. She looks better than she has in a long time, he thought. As he greeted her and said the usual things, he remembered suddenly for some reason what he had thought when he had looked at her from across the room at a friend's house last year . . . Redbury's? . . . She's lost her girlish charm.

That's what had gone through his mind. Not that it meant anything to him. Gwinnie was his wife. He would love Gwinnie till his death. He had chosen her because he loved her, not for her beauty, rank, or wealth . . . none of these had been considerations. But now, tonight, she did look beautiful as she had when she was carrying Albert, their firstborn.

"Joseph told me that he has been asked to resign from the club. He also told me that he has been to see Darius at Somerset. Had he told me I might have gone with him. Perhaps we should invite Darius to stay with us this June . . ."

"We can, of course, if you wish," said Gwinnie. "But I am sure he will go to Florence as always."

"Yes, I know, but it will be a kind thing to do, don't you think?"

"Yes."

Solomon stared at Gwinnie. He couldn't help it. He stared at her figure. Could he detect a swelling underneath the skirt of her dress? He thought he could. Should he say something? And why didn't Gwinnie? He would tonight, he decided.

The door opened and Jakes and Deirdre came in. He felt relieved. The child ran to him. "Poppa! Poppa! I can recite a song now from *The Merchant of Venice,*" and without waiting did so.

> *Tell me where is fancie bred*
> *In the heart, or in the head:*
> *How begot, how nourished*
>
> *Reply . . . reply . . .*

When Deirdre lost her place Gwinnie coached her. At the end of the recital both Gwinnie and Solomon joined her in saying "Ding dong bell." Self-satisfied, plump little creature, thought Solomon. Filled with love for her, he picked her up and kissed her.

"You must have your bath now, Miss Deirdre," said Jakes.

"No! No! No!" screamed Deirdre. "I don't want a bath! I want to stay with Poppa!" The child was carried out screaming.

He began discussing the weather: "You know, my dear, the fogs this January are worse than ever, the afternoons are literally pitch-black. Torches appear on all the streets. Yesterday Clarence [their coachman] had to lead the horses by foot. River traffic had been suspended. Bottle-green, the fog, as green as your pretty dress—I don't think you've worn it before—have you? [He was nervous and that was a shame, to be nervous in his own house with his own wife.] Something will have to be done. It is the result of imperfect drainage being impregnated"— he looked straight at her, was she blushing?— "with smoke from hundreds of thousands of coal fires . . . By the way, are we dining at home tonight, Gwinnie?"

"Yes. Alone . . . together."

"Good. I like that best really. We haven't done that for a long time."

<hr/>

Guinivere undressed, assisted as usual by her maid, Sally, in her dressing room, an alcove off the bedroom. Solomon preferred to take care of himself in his own dressing room.

Solomon was not in the habit of watching Guinivere undress, not since their honeymoon in Rome, but tonight he had undressed himself quickly, putting on his nightshirt and cap, and had stepped into their large bed to purposely watch Gwinnie being disrobed.

By the time he had slipped into bed, the maid had already unbuttoned Guinivere's dress and was lifting it up over her arms. Then Sally took it to the wardrobe, where she shook it out gently and hung it up. So there was Gwinnie in her half-length linen chemise and stays and petticoats. Adorable. Her small waist . . . the way the whalebone of her stays lifted up her breasts, which shone in the lamplight like two half peaches nestled in a basket of lace. Caressable . . . Gwinnie bent down and began to remove her stockings. She held them up before she put them on a small table next to her. Twin thin flounders, he thought. The maid returned carrying Gwinnie's nightdress, ivory linen and eyelet with pink ribbons and piqué. He suddenly remembered how in the latter part of Gwinnie's pregnancies she had always had her bosom and her belly bound with white bandages. She had suckled all their children. She had refused to have a wet nurse. "Breasts must not be larger than two turtledove eggs." Ridiculous how certain phrases once heard were never forgotten. Strooksbury had told him that. He thought of his mistress, Mrs. Cornwind, and the varied bottles and boxes that cluttered her dressing table, all filled with various lotions and papers, black for the eyebrows, red for the face, white "prepared from real pearls," she claimed.

Gwinnie stepped out of her petticoats. She was wearing, he saw, those newfangled drawers, two unconnected tubes that tied to the waist by strings, the latest fashion from Paris. The maid began to undo the stay-laces . . . Gwinnie was wearing short stays! She was not wearing a pregnant stay! He remembered that had been made of dimity silk and had completely enveloped her body from her shoulders to below her hips, elaborately boned. Mrs. Farnley, "the infallible," was wrong. Gwinnie was not pregnant!

The maid took off Gwinnie's chemise, and naked, his wife lifted up her arms so that Sally could slip the nightgown with its beribboned collar and its frilled cuffs over her body. Beautiful. Quite beautiful, still, his Gwinnie, even after the birth of five children. He felt his penis harden.

Seated at the dressing table, Guinivere looked into the mirror as the maid brushed out her long thick golden hair and then placed a cap of French lace on her head. Dismissing the girl, Guinivere snuffed out her candle and crawled into bed. They lay side by side. Solomon was aware of her body for the first time in many months. A longing came over him that was almost desperation as they lay there in the dark. He began to hope . . . Oh, Gwinnie . . . He placed his hand on her thigh and waited for that almost infinitesimal movement, so subtle, so discreet . . . He was amazed when he felt Gwinnie move closer to him and—his Gwinnie!—put her hand on his penis. In a delirium of joy, he felt his penis instantly harden. Overcome with passion, he lifted up her nightdress and thrust it in.

—◆⋅⊶⊶⋅◆—

A month later, when Gwinnie told him that she was pregnant, he was overjoyed. And the following day when his family and their friends gathered for Sunday dinner at Elijah's house (at least Elijah had not terminated those social gatherings!), he could not help but announce *sotto voce* to certain individual people like Mathilda, Brian, Joseph, Mr. and Mrs. Redbury, even Mr. Coverly, that his beloved Guinivere was "expecting." He was disappointed in Joseph's reaction. He had given Solomon an odd look and said nothing except, dryly, "Congrat-ulations." Joseph was getting worse. In time (following his pattern of self-delusion) Solomon remembered the sequence of events in the following manner: Mrs. Farnley had told him at a Sunday dinner at Elijah's that she thought it would be a good thing for Guinivere to conceive again. That it might get her over Sidney's death.

"And do you know, Mrs. Farnley was right," said Solomon to all who would listen.

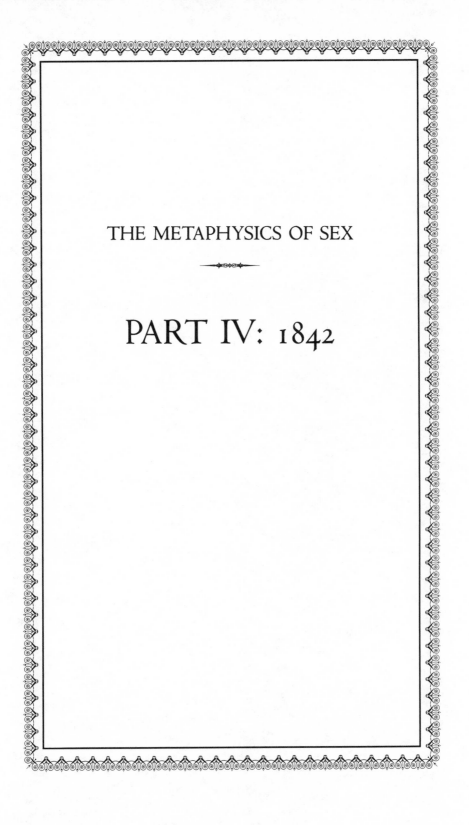

THE METAPHYSICS OF SEX

PART IV: 1842

PRELIMINARY
CONCLUSIONS

14 JULY 1937
MARLBOROUGH GARDENS

Lowe and I have just returned from our annual pilgrimage to Warren-
ton, which stands a few miles outside Little Claybrook, a typical colli-
ery village of the great northern coalfield: one long row of low-roofed
brick houses with shorter rows nearby behind which dug-out and
abandoned coal pits lay. A melancholy landscape. In Little Claybrook
in the graveyard of the old Norman church we found Farnley head-
stones. Though not Mrs. Farnley's, of course. She and Grindal were
buried behind the church yard of St. Swithins, just outside the remains
of Saddler's Grove. But the graves of her husband and her brother
and other family members were there. Our assumption, based on the
evidence, is that Mrs. Farnley was born here and met Jorem Forster
here. Perhaps she worked for the school in some capacity; at any rate,
she became his servant at a date that is as yet undetermined. The earli-
est record we have of Mrs. Farnley is a brief notation in Mrs. Capaci-
ty's Book of Accounts, circa 1822. It is the listing of the sum of
money paid to her in that year—four pounds and three shillings.

Places have power. Vicinities, localities, have a potency and energy
all their own. As we traversed the town, ate our dinner at the Castle,
revisited Warrenton, we felt the presence of the dead, and the passage
of time that separated us from them seemed annihilated. As we walked
in their steps, saw through their eyes, followed their movements, we
thought we understood only too well the underlying patterns of their
thoughts.

Warrenton, originally a twelfth-century monastery dedicated to St.

Augustine, stands in fields of pink sweet clover. Today it is no longer a school but a private dwelling owned by a wealthy American banker, a Virginian by the name of James Robertson, whose mother was a descendant of Dr. Pond. Robertson had visited the school when he was a young man, so when it came on the market in 1921 he bought it and began a careful plan of restoration. We introduced ourselves some years ago and have become friends to some extent.

The house covers a much larger space of ground than one would at first suppose, while the roofs of different heights and chimneys of different forms and sizes give it a picturesque appearance. One enters through an ivy-covered Norman gate with three arches that forms one side of a quadrangle. The center of the courtyard is smooth green grass. The first of the three other sides of the quadrangle is formed by a long low building, the acutal remains of the monastery, where Dr. Pond and his family resided. The second side was added in the fourteenth century by the Nevills, relatives of the Ponds. It is this wing of the edifice that the Ponds, who inherited the house in 1727, turned into a school. The wing has been converted back into its former medieval splendor and is now the present owner's residence. The entrance door is square and low with great bow windows in mullioned stone frames on either side. The rooms are large and well furnished. Gone are the bleak cubicles the male Forsters lived in when they attended Warrenton. Nor do the classrooms exist. Only the school's motto, etched in the ancient glass, remains: Per ardua ad astra *("Through difficulty to the stars"), a portrait of Dr. Pond: severe, staid, yet pensive, the eyes filled with serious thought. As for the school records: "Discarded . . . had to be . . . completely mildewed," Mr. Robertson told us on our first visit.*

As we wandered through the surrounding gardens, down the ancient grass walks, we felt the boys' presence: Albert's poignant apprehension; William's burgeoning conceit; Edward's increasing despair . . .

That night while riding home to Marlborough Gardens, we discussed in detail the difference between Edward's and William's response to Warrenton. Lowe said: "The Forsters moved like sleepwalkers throughout their lives. Perhaps we all do. But they knew nothing about what really motivated them. Take Edward, for instance. Edward fell in love with Darius, though he did not call it that, of course, after Darius was sent away . . . after Darius had left Marlborough Gardens. Not like Albert, who was almost immediately smitten. And after that every person that Edward fell in love with, except for a momentary and irregular desire for Vanessa—Clara, Victoria, Reverend Blackstone—resembled Darius in some way or another. A vital truth about his life that he never realized consciously."

Lowe is right. We know more about them than they knew about themselves. It gives one a strange feeling of omniscience. It is a risky business this traveling back and forth in time.

Arriving home in the early afternoon, we went for a walk in the Gardens and were struck once more with Francini's ingenious landscape effects. He designed the Gardens when he was a fairly well advanced opium addict. And though it is true that the Gardens do not have that logical unity that defines classicism, for instance—too many disparate ideas contend with one another—still there is so much that is imaginative, so much that is pleasurable, that it borders on genius. We walked from one delightful scene to another: from the darkenss of a dell made deeper by a carpet of blue-green myrtle to a sunny open space made brighter by the yellow-green ground cover of moneywort, to following a path that winds mysteriously out of sight past a stone fountain, to the meadow that Francini designed specifically so that at a certain time of day in summer the shadows that fleck the ground under the trees become in the late afternoon a breathtaking chiaroscuro. Even now, a hundred years later, the scintillation of light and dark gives the whole scene an incomparable sense of delicacy. A fitting prelude to the dark wood that lies behind it.

<hr />

1842. One could say that 1842 was the Forsters' "dark wood." The year in which the "underlying patterns of thought" overflowed into disastrous actions in their lives. The year in which submerged configurations and designs evolved and dispelled their poisons and set the stage for their futures.

In this section of the book we had to rely heavily on other sources besides Emma's novel The Metaphysics of Sex. *In her novel her attention is almost exclusively focused on herself, Clara, and Johan, ignoring for the most part important and actual circumstances and events. Little is said about the other members of the family, in particular Elijah, for whom the year 1842 was, to put it mildly, critical. The following is a partial list of sources we have used to flesh out her account.*

1. Mrs. Farnley's Day Book for the year 1842
2. "A Short Memoir of Nicholas Renton, *Entrepreneur Extraordinaire,*" by Kevin Francini. Privately printed, 1888
3. *A History of the Forster Midland Bank,* by Albert Forster, Edinburgh, Adam & Black
4. *Tales of a Ladies' Maid,* by Dora Finley[33]

33. Dora Finley, a former governess, was hired by Mrs. Farnley as a maid for her niece Moly, Elijah's mistress. See *City of Childhood* and *The Metaphysics of Sex.*—R. Lowe

NOTE FROM WARRENTON: EDWARD

I was never jealous of Edward, even though he was the heir. I knew Momma loved me best of all. Poor Edward. Emma was of course Poppa's "all in all." Everyone liked Edward and even deferred to him, but no one really loved him when he was a child. I realize that now.

—William M. Forster, *Australian Letters*

The first term at Warrenton was not nearly as bad for Edward as it was for his brother or his cousins. Ironically, the fact that neither Elijah nor Theodisia particularly cared for him, for he sensed they were not "fond" of him in the same way they were about his sister, Emma, and his brother, William, made Warrenton with its official detachment from any compassion, and with its emphasis on competition, not unlike what he had experienced in the bosom of his family. Though Mrs. Farnley, and Grindal on rare occasions, were affectionate (he was, after all, the heir) he had never really been involved in a physically tender intimate relationship with any adult. Had he been asked "Who are you?" he would have said "I am the heir." The harsh brutality that was part of daily life at Warrenton did not affect him as much as it did his brother or his cousins.

The fact that his parents did not act and feel towards him as they felt towards William and Emma (for he knew very well that they were receiving a mysterious something that he was not) connected in his mind to the other fact, that he, Edward Marcus Forster, was (after all) his father's heir. Being the heir was to be connected to future privilege and responsibility and apparently engendered such things as admiration and respect from other people. All of that would have been sufficiently satisfactory to make up for that mysterious missing substance had it not been for another fact: his cousin Albert, Albert too was an "heir." But it had not escaped Edward's notice that Albert, like Emma and William, was also the recipient of this clandestine substance. His Aunt Guinivere felt towards Albert the way his father felt towards Emma, the way his mother felt towards William. They were all the recipients of that mysterious thing called love.

Of course he rarely thought about it at all, though sometimes for no reason that he could understand the uncomfortable question would flash through his head: Why is it that Momma and Poppa do not love me? It was all too much for him though, a tremendous puzzle, be-

cause at the same time he sensed . . . he knew absolutely . . . that in a certain way he was also very important to both of them. These thoughts all went on in one part of his mind while in another part, a part that he did not yet have access to, a new idea was forming that had to do with a growing desire to exchange (if it were possible) all this privilege and responsibility that he had for the love his brother, his sister, and his cousins were receiving. But that idea, the idea of a sacrificial exchange, in effect, did not surface until much later in his life, though he acted out of this suppressed longing well before it ever became a conscious thought.

So the first term went fairly well. He adjusted to it far better than William and better than Albert, who was concerned about his mother and haunted by his dead brother. As a matter of fact, he bought a violin for himself, remembering what Darius had said about Elijah, who had refused to allow Edward to study any musical instrument: "Your father is incapable of creating beauty and is envious of those who do." Secretly Edward began to take lessons from a violin teacher named Dr. Fritz Hergzborg, a musical scholar he found in Hammer's Lane near the school.

It wasn't until the second year that he began to dislike school and long to be elsewhere. The dislike began when he was defeated ignominiously by Albert in a fight over Vanessa, but increased primarily because of William and Elijah's new attention to William's achievements in school.

William began at Warrenton as the smallest and the weakest member of the Forster faction. But soon after his arrival, despite the self-pitying letters that he had sent his mother, which almost drove her to suicide, he learned he could survive very well, thank you. He was protected physically by Albert, the twins, and Edward, but he also knew intuitively how to connive and manipulate circumstances to suit himself; skills he had unwittingly learned in his relationship with his mother. From the beginning his personality was geared to search out the lay of the land and, unlike Edward, he had seen instantly how to go about it at school. True, Warrenton was not home, and there was a part of him that particularly missed the love in his mother's eyes when she looked at him; certainly no one at Warrenton looked at him that way, at least not yet, but there were compensations. He was free! For after the first term the paramount feeling he experienced was a heady sense of freedom! A sense of adventure. Though he would not have said: I feel free now! It was what he felt. By the end of the term William saw quite clearly how he could carve a satisfactory niche for himself at his father's school. He had a knack for knowing what people might want from him, which included his tutors as well as his peers.

He also discovered that he was unusually bright, and a quick learner. Accidence and construing came naturally to him, as mathematics did to his cousin Jacob. He also had a prodigious memory, and so after his series of "lamentation" letters, he settled down to work.

He kept thinking to himself more and more: Soon I shall be a re-move higher and I shall have "liberties." He had stopped writing Theodisia out of genuine anger at what he perceived as a gross be-trayal on her part, and then when he perceived that this withdrawal from his mother was approved of by Elijah he was intrigued. For ever since he had gone off to his father's school he wanted to be his fa-ther's son, not his mother's child. He wanted what he perceived Ed-ward to have with Elijah. For from his vantage point it seemed to him that Elijah loved Edward far more than he loved him.

⸺⋆⊙⋆⸺

After a humiliating experience during Holy Week holidays, Edward began to actively dislike Warrenton. Edward had lost to William, by a significant margin, during one of those fiercely competitive games Eli-jah loved to devise for his sons when they came home on holidays or at half term. "Putting the ponies through their paces," he called it.

Elijah and his brothers, Solomon and Joseph, had been introduced to Aristotle, Plato, the Roman poets—Virgil, Ovid, and Catullus— there; parts of Thucydides, Hesiod, and Herodotus were the main fare at Warrenton. Elijah, brighter, more capable intellectually, than either of his brothers, had become fascinated as a young boy by Aristotle's Prior Analytics, *a text in which Aristotle proved each individual fact is what it is because of why it is, using a method of proof called the syllogism. In part, Elijah had won the most prestigious prize given by Dr. Pond for correctly identifying all of the "figures" listed in* Prior Analytics. *"A truly astonishing intellectual feat," as Dr. Pond had said when he gave Elijah the* corona triumphalis *(laurel crown). And it was.*

The competition between Edward and William, the one that shat-tered Edward's confidence in himself, had involved the "figures."

Elijah had stood behind the kidney-shaped desk in his study, one hand on his hip, the other in front of him holding a stopwatch, and shouted out the terms of the figures: "The Celerent, the Festino, the Barbara, the Darii, the Ferio!" Then, giving them the major and the minor premise of the syllogism, he expected the boys to shout out the conclusion and identify the form in a strictly designated time.

Elijah had been fair—according to his own dictum, at least. He had written an identical letter to each of his sons informing them of his intentions, so that they could prepare for the contest.

*But Edward had confused two figures in his mind and his father
had stopped him. When he returned to Warrenton after that defeat Edward began to withdraw emotionally from his brother and his cousins.
Not that anyone noticed. For he spent the days as usual. That is, he
rose at six and began translating his Ovid, or Horace, or Tacitus, until
eight, when he breakfasted on boiled milk and butterless bread. And
then as usual he memorized lines until eleven; from eleven until one
he played games, though if he could manage it, he wandered off by
himself. Dinner was at one o'clock, after which he read English and
did sums until supper at five forty-five. Then prayers and bed. And all
through the day you might get beaten or kicked by the headmaster or
his assistant because you had not construed properly.*

*Edward found himself thinking more and more often of Marlbor-
ough Gardens and . . . Darius. One day he began to play what he
called in his mind the Path game. He would first choose the season
and then choose the Marlborough gate and then wander in his mind
down the path. One of the points of the game, he had decided quite
early on, was to see everything clearly, as if he were actually there.
But sometimes when that happened it frightened him. Sometimes it
was so clear he felt as if he were actually in Marlborough Gardens
and not at Warrenton. Even though it frightened him, he nevertheless
continued to play the game.*

*He also began remembering the games he and his cousins had
played in Marlborough Gardens. He remembered the game Trafalgar[34]
and played it out in his mind, reciting to himself Nelson's last words:
"Kiss me, Hardy . . . I am a dead man." He remembered how he had
loved . . . worshipped . . . Albert. And now at Warrenton they hardly
spoke to one another. Albert spent all of his time with a boy named
Thomas and Ramkree, an Indian boy.*

*One time Edward spent the whole day thinking about his dead cousin,
Sidney. First he thought about how much he had disliked him. And then
of Sidney's death. And Sidney's funeral. How at that time he had felt
nothing when he looked down at Sidney in his coffin on that bitter-cold
morning in December in the ice-cold chapel of St. Giles Church. Then
one night six years after Sidney's death, Edward lay in his narrow bed
in his cubicle at Warrenton and cried because Sidney had died. He
wondered about that. He remembered he had felt nothing at the graveside.
Nothing. But now he suspected that beneath that nothing feeling he had
felt like screaming and screaming and screaming and running away,
instead of standing there next to his father and Emma watching the*

---

34. Trafalgar was the game his cousin Albert had devised and which he and his cousins
had played in Marlborough Gardens until Darius, their Italian cousin, came home from
Warrenton and taught them other games. See *City of Childhood.—R. Lowe*

gravediggers lower Sidney's coffin into the hard ground. So perhaps that was what that strange nothing feeling had been. Perhaps it was better to feel nothing than what he felt now: a terrible desire to scream and scream and scream.

Edward never saw Sidney's ghost as Albert and the twins did, but once or twice during the second year when the despair inside him had grown intolerable he thought he saw Darius, even though he knew very well that was of course impossible. Darius was in Somerset, a Catholic academy in Hampshire.

The last time he had been home, three or four months earlier, Edward had been a witness to a terrible quarrel between his Poppa and Uncle Joseph.

He had been showing his father his Latin translations as well as an epic he had started writing about Ulysses and Calypso—how it was that they had come to live in Marlborough Gardens in Blenheim Woods— when Mrs. Farnley had come in and told Poppa that Joseph was outside and insisted on seeing him immediately.

So Poppa had gone out to see Joseph, and a moment later they had come into the library. Poppa had been so agitated by what Joseph was telling him he had forgotten that Edward was there. The brothers were quarreling bitterly. Uncle Joseph was shouting that he hated Darius: "I hate him. I hate Consuelo! I hate you."

Joseph hated Elijah, he said, because he had saved Darius. "It would have been better to let Darius die!" And then Joseph tore up the letter that he was holding in his hand, which was from Darius, congratulating Joseph on being "a legal father again, if not an actual one!" The pieces of paper fell like confetti to the rug.

Joseph began to pull out the hair on his own head, holding his thick blond hair in his hands, pulling and tugging at it while Elijah tried to stop him. "You should have killed me that day!" Joseph shouted. "I should have killed myself! I should have had the courage that Darius had. At least he tried to do away with himself!" And when Elijah tried to comfort him, when he tried to put his arms around him, Joseph thrust him off and ran out. Elijah followed him, leaving Edward alone.

Since then Edward had thought more and more about Darius. He went over in his mind all the times he and his cousins had spent with Darius . . . the fall of 1836, the spring of 1837, Darius's War Lectures, the preparations for battle, the battle itself. He went over the scenes of battle, in particular Albert's defeat, his humiliation, his disgrace . . . He knew now why Darius had insisted that Albert walk around the tower three times, that was as many times as Hector had been dragged by Achilles' chariot—his heels lashed together—around the walls of Troy. Darius/Achilles, the victor of the Marlborough Wars . . .

Most of all he thought about Darius himself, how he had looked, what he had said, and how he, Edward, felt about it.

And so it was that during those lonely years at Warrenton Sidney and Darius became "alive" to Edward. They began, particularly Darius, to live in his imagination. As did Marlborough Gardens.

One day Edward tried to talk to William about Marlborough Gardens, about the battle, about Darius . . . but William was not interested. William could not understand what was wrong with Edward. Why didn't he get along? Why was he so serious? Why couldn't he laugh at himself? That's what the other boys wanted. Why couldn't he do that. Why? It was as if Edward had set himself against the school. He would never like Warrenton. Never adjust.

One night Edward had a dream about Darius. He remembered that just before Darius had left for Somerset he had told them (Edward and Emma) that their real name was Faustus and that they were descendants— they, the Forsters—of Dr. Faustus, the great German necromancer. That it was their great-great-grandfather, Josephus Faustus (1694–1769) who had changed his name from Faustus to Forster upon arriving in England. Then he told them that he, Darius, through his Persian[35] ancestors, was a descendant of the Minotaur of Crete.

Edward began to dream that he was living in Blenheim Wood, in Calypso's Cave in Marlborough Gardens, which was now the home of a minotaur named Dr. Faustus, who promised if he tarried awhile with him he would be given a gift that would change his life. As many times as he dreamt the dream he could never find out what the gift was because just before the minotaur was about to tell him he awoke.

The recurrent dream began just before he reached such a level of despair that he might have gone over the edge and into the abyss without anyone knowing or even caring.

Everyone he knew was far far too busy with their lives.

—R. Lowe

35. The name Darius means "holding firm the good" in old Persian. It was his family's custom (the Riminis') to christen the firstborn son Darius, in honor, they said, of their ancestor, a Persian noble who supposedly in 401 B.C. joined the Ten Thousand in their legendary march back to the Greek coast of the Euxine Sea. See *City of Childhood* —R. Lowe

Let us introduce two expressions, the sexual object, i.e., the person from whom the sexual attraction radiates, and the sexual aim, i.e., the aim towards which the instinct grapples.

—Sigmund Freud, *Three Contributions to the Theory of Sex*

Egoism is so deep-rooted a quality of all individuality in general that, in order to rouse the activity of an individual being, egotistical ends are the only ones on which we can count on with certainty.

—Schopenhauer, *The World as Will and Representation*

6 FEBRUARY 1908
WEIMAR, GERMANY

REASONABLE , adult, mature, dependable, reliable, trustworthy. To whom do these words apply? I have never met anyone in my entire life who resembles this collection of characteristics. Surely these attributes comprise the greatest fictional character of all. Certainly *I* am not like that, though I can be reasonable and sometimes reliable—but truth to tell, only when it satisfies my real needs. It is difficult for me to believe that I am really eighty-two years old. I have the same tempestuous emotions that I had when I was a child, when I was an adolescent . . . I am still envious, still jealous . . .

Clara. There is an inextinguishable part of me that still wants her. Her alone. That part of me tells me that no one else will do. Not even my beloved, kind and loving as she is. I don't think of Clara for years and then a phrase of music, or the sight of a grey silk dress, or a pair of large brown eyes, hooded, the iris darker than the pupil, causes everything to flow back and I know that she is part of the tissue of my brain.

After being deflowered by Mr. Strooksbury (I always referred to him that way in my mind), I felt uncomfortable in my father's presence and I avoided him as much as possible. I was fifteen years old and completely self-involved so that I did not notice that he too felt some constraint. We no longer had our chats in the library; he no longer inquired about my schoolwork. He rarely glanced at me at all. He never addressed a question to me at the dinner table, and I believe my strong erotic interest in him would have ebbed had not Vanessa come to live with us for three months. Her nightly flirtations with him at the dinner table aroused all the old feelings.

Jealousy. How it consumed me! And envy. Now when I think of her I see the four of us: Clara, me, Vanessa, and in Vanessa's shadow, the figure of Nanny Grindal, who was Vanessa's maid during her stay with us.

—◈◆◈◆◈—

I remember the date, it was the fourteenth of January, 1842, when my father announced at the dinner table quite casually, without any preamble of any sort, that Vanessa would be staying with us for an indefinite length of time. From my mother's obvious lack of surprise I understood that she had known about it beforehand.

The following day painters and plasterers arrived to redecorate and refurbish the day nursery according to my father's design, making it suitable for a young lady who was to begin her first London season. Furniture was bought, wall paper chosen, curtains made and hung, old carpets picked up and new ones laid down. And then when the "pretty little nest" (my father's obnoxious term) was ready and completed, Vanessa moved in.

Her mother, my Aunt Mathilda had succumbed, Poppa told us, to a mysterious illness, rendering her incapable of chaperoning her daughter in this most crucial year of her life, Vanessa's official entree into society. Someone must oversee her. Since Guinivere was pregnant, Theodisia obviously incapable, and Brian too busy with Mathilda, my father had volunteered his services. A dry run, so to speak, since the following year he would have to do the same for me. Together with Sir Ravenscroft's son, Lord Cecil, the two gentlemen would steer "the young beauty through the treacherous shoals of London's aristocracy to the safe harbor of an advantageous marriage."

Before I begin the account of the next three months there are one or two things that I must clear out of the way.

Mr. Strooksbury. Looking back I see that I had for my era—a time in which prudery and boredom were a way of life for the average young woman—an unusually strong sexual drive. And though Mr. Strooksbury was no longer a presence in my life, my sexual feelings were.

I had not been romantically in love with him, of course—he was far too old and unattractive for that. Nevertheless, on a subconscious level I felt bound to him. He had, after all, penetrated the deeper reaches of my libidinal self. But difficult as it may be to believe, when he was removed from my life I forgot about him. It was as if he had never existed. I was aided and abetted in this conceit by my father and Mrs. Farnley, who never mentioned the incident again. I had spent five Wednesday afternoons with him, and except for the fact that my body had been fully aroused and satisfied (thank God) I blocked him out of my conscious mind. Such was my way of coping with the incident.

My sexual impulses were now directed to "socially approved" ends such as Greek and Latin accidence, piano practice, and the memorization of prodigious amounts of Horace, Ovid, and Catallus.

But without Strooksbury, I focused once more on Clara. I became obsessed with the preposterous idea of absolute intellectual intimacy with her, with the idea of yielding my whole ego into the relationship with her as one does with a lover. I allowed myself to become recklessly and completely absorbed in Clara, to send her the last reserves of my soul, to lose myself in her without reservation. The world narrowed down to her alone.

And then my father quite casually informed us at the dinner table that my cousin Vanessa would be staying with us for a while!

How many times in the past had I worried over Clara's becoming enamoured of Vanessa and abandoning me? How grateful I was that luck had been with me, and that they had met only a few times, briefly, not long enough for Clara to become ensnared by Vanessa's beauty. Still, in the back of my mind there was always the fear that a prolonged association would result in Clara's preferring her over me. Now the worst of my fears were going to be realized. Vanessa was coming to stay with us for an indefinite length of time. My father had decreed it. I would be abandoned.

Decreed is right. My father was the classic authoritarian. He believed in individual liberty only as it pertained to making money. Nothing else. He certainly did not believe in women's rights, or their claim to equality. Elijah's authority was so closely woven into the fabric of our household that it was scarcely more noticeable than the air we breathed. It was only really recognized when it was flouted or disobeyed. His authority was the bedrock of our society, the foundation of its morality, the foundation of our character.

Physically attractive, mentally stimulating, he possessed in great measure that mysterious thing called charisma. In one sense I believe that all of us, even my mother, perceived him as better than ourselves so that his authority as "Poppa" seemed only natural and proper. We had certain duties and obligations in common as members of the Forster family and one of them was to obey Poppa. We were aware to some extent that Aunt Guinivere and Uncle Solomon, though they had a similar arrangement, worked it out a bit differently. And of course Aunt Mathilda and Uncle Brian were very different indeed.

My father's ubiquitous and all-pervasive authority did not, however, prevent us—the women of the household—from forming that secret life that women have with one another, a life as secret as the one I and my brothers and cousins had during our childhood. Sometimes for a woman secrecy is a way of life, offering as it does the only possibility of her own world alongside the visible one. It is this intense and secret world that we formed among the four of us—Clara, myself, Vanessa, and Grindal—from the end of January to the end of April 1842 that I shall now speak about. A time in which our emotional temperatures rose from day to day (every gesture, every glance meant something) and the third floor, the world in which we lived, began to resemble nothing less than the stove house of the Winter Garden, wherein, by a marked increase in heat, certain exotic flowers are "forced" to flower earlier than their normal season.

I had not seen Vanessa for some time. She had spent the last two Christmas holidays with a wealthy family in Yorkshire, and since our family no longer convened at Saddler's Grove during the summer months it had been more than two years since we had been together.

We waited for her to arrive in my mother's morning room: my mother, myself, and Clara, at two o'clock on Thursday afternoon, the tenth of February; that date too is engraved upon my mind. Mrs. Farnley announced her. Seconds later Vanessa entered the room.

She was wearing the latest fashion, a periwinkle-blue woolen dress with a large expanded skirt that reached to the ground and over it was draped an immense shawl. Her golden blond hair hung down in long curls from a bonnet that framed to perfection her face, which was perfection itself. She was even more beautiful than I remembered. I suddenly felt cold, as if the brilliance of her beauty had temporarily obscured the light within me . . . as when the sun, passing between the moon and the earth, causes a total eclipse. A feeling of dark despair came over me. I glanced surreptitiously at Clara—what was she feeling?—but I could tell nothing from her face, which was as calm and closed as ever.

Vanessa was speaking, her voice a perfect accompaniment to her form. ". . . so it is in the beginning of April, Aunt Theo, that I am to be presented to the Queen. I do hope Momma will be recovered then. But what is really wrong with her? She is fatigued, Poppa tells me. What does that mean? And why should it require nurses and Dr. Lacy visiting her twice a week? If you know, dear Aunt Theo, do tell me. I am old enough to be told the truth. If there is something seriously wrong with Momma I wish to know."

My mother blushed. "I only know what I myself have been told, Vanessa. Fatigue, pure and simple. That is all. But come, let us speak about more pleasant things. I have a list of things that your Uncle Elijah has given me that I must do with you and for you. All the parties you are to attend, the balls, the teas . . . and dressmakers, we must start with them tomorrow. You need not worry about anything, Vanessa. Guinivere knows all about it. She was presented to King William when she was young. She will tell you what to wear, what you must say, how you must curtsy. . . ."

Through the open door I could see our servants carrying trunk after trunk up the stairs to Vanessa's new quarters. Grindal, who had arrived from Saddler's Grove the day before, was supervising the invasion.

As yet Vanessa had not so much as glanced at me. Or Clara. Then she addressed me: "Dear little Emma . . . how nice to see you again. When was it last? And Mrs. Lustig. Momma has told me that you are our second cousin once removed. How nice to see you again."

"Thank you, Vanessa," Clara replied without a smile or a handshake.

Annoyed by this cool response, Vanessa turned her back on Clara and said to Momma, "Auntie Theo, please come with me now, I insist. I want to show you all my new frocks, and the most delicious new bonnet I have ever owned. It's the exact color of my eyes, and with the most beautiful curly feathers in the back of the brim."

They both left without saying another word to either of us. I went over and sat down on a chair close to Clara, who was seated on the couch.

"Well, you will finally get to know her . . . Vanessa," I said.

"Yes I shall."

"She is inhumanly beautiful, isn't she?"

"Yes. I would say so . . . an inhuman beauty . . . not mortal. Quite astonishing really."

Her every word pained me. How ugly in comparison I must seem to

Clara. Would she abandon me now? Would she join forces with Vanessa? I sat there sullenly, feeling completely defeated. How unfair life was. I had only one friend, Clara. Vanessa had as many as she might want by merely appearing, crooking a finger, smiling . . .

Clara slipped her small watch out of her dress pocket.

"It is exactly three-oh-four. We have time for our music lesson before tea."

"Must we?" I felt as if I could hardly breathe, much less play Haydn.

"We needn't, but the piece is so beautiful and you play it so well, not only technically but with appropriate feeling. I am sorry the Contessa Rimini, your uncle's wife, cannot hear you play. Your proficiency would have pleased her. If you practice, Emma, diligently, you shall be a fine pianist one day."

I followed Clara into the piano room and began to play. When I had finished she praised me. "The phrasing is perfect. You have done well."

I could wait no longer. I must know what she felt about Vanessa. She had agreed with me about her beauty. But how had it affected her? Was she a new worshiper at my cousin's altar? I must know.

"What did you think of Vanessa?" I asked her.

"I think you think too much of her," she replied. She was seated next to me on the piano bench and her fingers roamed the keys.

I caught her hands and held them. "I must know how you feel. Her beauty is so dazzling. Sometimes I cannot even think when I am in her company. Did that happen to you? Did you feel drawn to worship her? Do you feel the same way?"

"No. It is true I have an *interest* in one or two goddesses, Emma— 'worship' is too strong a word—but Aphrodite was never one of them." And with that she removed her hands from mine and played the Haydn piece for me. "Do you see how in this movement the pianissimo functions? Watch my hands, Emma, see how my wrists move, how my fingers hit the keys. The clavichord. He wrote it for the clavichord. Keep that in mind when you play it. A light touch, quick, fleet, but light ever light . . ."

⚬⬦⚬

At dinner that night there was a new torment. I watched as my father and Vanessa flirted with one another. She was dressed in white moire and she wore amethysts in her ears and at her throat. She was so tightly laced her budding breasts protruded over the edge of her oval neckline. To make matters worse, she was seated on his right, formerly my place. Who had decided that, I wondered. Theodisia? Elijah? I could hardly eat a mouthful as I listened to their teasing, idiotic banter. They were so obviously delighted with one another. Two narcissists gazing into the pools of each other's eyes. I noticed for the first time that they resembled one another markedly. Though his masculine features were stronger, more prominent, of course, his face had a feline grace as hers had a certain puissant quality to it.

". . . the time, the bother you put into choosing just the right fabric, the right pattern for the wallpaper. Mrs. Farnley told me. I am truly grateful. Overwhelmed. You are my favorite uncle. But then you always have been," Vanessa said. As she smiled her body turned to him.

"And you my favorite niece," Elijah replied.

It occured to me that my mother, even though she was fond of her niece, might be somewhat annoyed at this blatant coquetry with her husband, so I looked at her. But like Clara, her face emitted nothing. There was no clue as to what she was feeling.

At the end of dinner we three, Theodisia, Clara, and I, had not been addressed one word by either of them, nor had we uttered one word. That night I went to bed devising ways and means of murdering Vanessa. I drifted off to sleep with the vision of a team of Clydesdale horses galloping over her body, their large hooves grinding her beauty into dust.

I did not think I could bear it, but what actually happened was that I did not see much of Vanessa at all during the weeks that followed, her schedule being quite different from mine. Hers was geared to the important business of being received into society so that she could make the advantageous marriage as a wealthy heiress. She made morning calls with my mother, went to the dressmakers, rode occasionally in Rotten Row from twelve to two chaperoned by Grindal and Aunt Guinivere, returned home to change, went out again at three to a concert or tea at someone's house, and would then come home once more to change for dinner. After that, she would go on to the opera, or to a ball, sometimes concluding with a cotillion at three in the morning. In the evening she was always accompanied by my father or Lord Cecil— or, on rare occasions, when my father claimed he was "fatigued," and indeed he did look tired, by my mother. As the season continued Vanessa began to sleep later, seldom awakening before noon and break-fasting in her dressing room.

So I saw little of her except at dinner, when I learned what she had done that day, for she spoke ad infinitum about her activities. For the most part only she and Poppa conversed. He seemed enchanted with her. Everything she said and did he praised, encouraged, supported, and agreed with. It was as if she were a new and beautiful young wife with whom he was smitten, with whom he had fallen in love. After dinner, on the rare occasions they stayed at home, he would listen seemingly enthralled as she played the piano or sang accompanied by Clara. If it was not a musical evening he would read aloud to her as she did her needlework, which he made a point of admiring.

Then one night at dinner, after she had lived with us for over a month, Vanessa asked my father once more about her mother's state of health. It interested me that though she asked my father frequently how her mother was, his answer was never serious or even informative. It seemed fairly obvious to all of us that her mother must really be quite ill. And that my parents knew the precise nature of the illness. But for some reason Vanessa was not to be told. Reluctantly, I had some feeling of sympathy for her, for though Vanessa might have been selfish and vain she did love her mother. I had been meaning to ask Mrs. Farnley, who I was quite sure knew the real story, but I had not got around to it as yet.

"Momma is not seriously ill, is she, Uncle Elijah?"

"No, of course not. Your father told me only yesterday that Dr. Lacy assured him that in a matter of weeks your mother will be up and about as fine as ever."

"But what is wrong with her then?"

"It is proving difficult to diagnose apparently, my dear, but it is not something for you to worry your exquisite little head about. In any case, a sick household is a dreary business, my dear. It is best that you continue to stay with us. Have you already grown tired of your favorite uncle?"

"Oh no, of course not. I am just worried about Momma. She looked so pale when I saw her last. But since you have reassured me I shall worry no longer."

Though she said that, I could see clearly that she was not reassured.

In a much colder tone my father addressed my mother. "I have received two letters today, one from Edward, the other from William. They send you their love and hope you are well. They complain that they hear nothing from you. Perhaps you should visit them."

"May I? That is, if you don't mind."

"Mrs. Lustig," my father said dryly, turning to Clara, "you have, as I know, an excellent memory for what was said by others long ago. I shall now test your memory in relation to what was said a moment ago. Tell me, did I not say to my wife that she should visit her sons. Answer yes or no."

"Yes, I heard you say so."

"Then am I not being misunderstood?"

"My father told me once that to be misunderstood was a mark of greatness, Sir," replied Clara.

"You have a decided talent for diplomacy. Theodisia, you should appoint Clara as your ambassadress."

How awful those dinners were. My father flirting with Vanessa, sniping at Theodisia, ignoring Clara and me for the most part.

One day I asked Clara if she had noticed how much attention my father paid to my cousin. I was surprised at the vehemence of her response.

"I would have to be blind or deaf not to notice! It is decidedly annoying. It is as if we three, you, your mother, and I, did not exist. Three dead women sitting at the table watching them."

I could hardly believe she answered me that way. I decided to take the opportunity to ask her again how she felt about Vanessa.

"You have asked me that before. Now I can answer you. I have no feeling about her or towards her. I admire her beauty, but she evokes no other emotion in me. I do not like her. She is both vapid and shallow. A beautiful form with little or no content. I am not intrigued."

I could not help telling her how happy that made me feel. "I was so terribly worried that you would prefer her to me."

"I know . . . and by the way, I also know what is wrong with Aunt Mathilda. Would you like to know?"

"Yes, of course."

"It must be kept secret. Particularly from Vanessa."

"I promise not to tell her."

"Your Aunt Mathilda suffered a miscarriage a month and a half ago. After which she developed a stubborn infection. For a short time it seemed as if she might actually die, but they believe she will pull through now—"

"A miscarriage?"

"Yes, she was four months pregnant—" And then Clara proceeded to tell me what she thought must have happened in fairly technical terms, each term being explained carefully to me.

Later on, as I was lying in bed that night, I thought of my Uncle Brian. Sweet, soft-spoken, but lively. Brian coupling with my Aunt Mathilda. I pictured them in bed. Would he be like Mr. Strooksbury? I didn't think so. I thought of my aunt, divested of her clothes, her large breasts spilling out of her chemise, her blond hair grazing her plump shoulders. Perhaps she was less strident then. Less talkative. I was quite sure she was not like my mother. Brian making love to Mathilda . . . implanting his seed . . . The embryo forming, the fetus and the miscarriage, and then . . . the infection. I felt pleased that I knew something Vanessa did not know, that no one would tell her. And Clara had told me she did not like Vanessa, that she found her shallow. I was overjoyed, but that feeling of happiness was not to last long.

I don't know when it was exactly that I realized the way I felt about Clara was the way Grindal felt about Vanessa. For as little as she had loved or cared for me when I was in her charge, so the reverse was true now that she was Vanessa's servant. She adored her. She was besotted, stupefied with love for Vanessa.

I began to notice how her eyes would follow Vanessa's every move, the way mine did Clara's. And how for Grindal the only voice in the world that meant anything to her ears was Vanessa's. We could be in a crowded room and Grindal's face would remain blank until Vanessa spoke, and then her whole face would come to life and she would hang on every word her darling said. She was tender, solicitous, thoughtful of her needs: Was Vanessa comfortable? Might she need another pillow for her back? Was the lamp too low, or too bright? Was her darling cold, perhaps more coal on the fire, or should she bring her a shawl?

Grindal's behaviour towards my cousin stimulated many different feelings within me. First bitterness. I had longed so much for what she freely gave my cousin when I was much younger and in her care. My mind reviewed the beatings she had given me, the times she had locked me in the closet, the same closet that was now bursting with Vanessa's gorgeous frocks. I remembered my repeated humiliations at Grindal's hands. How I had been made to sit in corners, punished for every infraction of her arbitrary rules. And how perversely I had also longed to be beaten by her at times, for then at least I would be held. I remembered the days and nights I had hungered for her to tell me that she loved me, which was even odder and more perverse, perhaps, because the fact was that I had never loved her. I had always disliked her. I had always thought of her as a stupid coarse vulgar woman—part of my defiance towards her, for I was defiant, was rooted in the fact that I felt I was innately better than she was. But human beings, being what they are, do dislike, and even hate, their "Grindals" while still longing to be loved by them. And even worse, beg to be loved by them in ways that are ruinously demeaning.

However, I noticed that, unlike Clara, who was generally cold towards me except when I had done exceptional work, my cousin Vanessa responded with a measure of warmth and affection to Grindal's uncritical adoration of her. At times she would even spontaneously hug Grindal, bestow kisses on her, call her pet names. Though naturally she could be cruel, as people are who have been granted so much power. Vanessa could wound and she did. There were times she would complain out loud about Grindal and even attempt to inveigle Clara and me into agreeing with her criticism of the servant.

"She looks like a fat goosey gander, doesn't she? Plump and ready to be cooked for dinner [during the last few years Grindal had put on

an enormous amount of weight]. Yes, on to the spit with you. You are
to be turned 'round and 'round and roasted." Or at another time: "You
look terrible today, I cannot be seen with you. It would ruin my rep-
utation. You should spend the day in the closet with a face like that.
Look at her, she looks like a halfwit!"

Grindal would cringe and say nothing in reply, her face anxious, her
whole demeanor submissive, waiting only for her mistress's tone to
change, like a dog waits for its mistress to smile, to show him that much-
needed life-preserving approval. Though at other times Grindal might
try to coax Vanessa into a better mood.

"My poor lamb is tired," she would say or comment that her "dearest
didn't feel well" and no wonder her dearest complained: "There are
just too many things my darling must do, too many people asking this
and that of my lambkin." And then she would try by playing the buffoon
to coax a smile to her beloved's face, sometimes by using towards herself
the same deprecatory names that Vanessa called her when she was
irritated. "Old goosey gander," Grindal would say, "tiresome old halfwit that she is, wants lambkins to put her tiny precious feet into her
large rough hands so that she can massage them."

I would attempt to discuss with Clara how cruel Vanessa was to
Grindal, how disgustingly abject Grindal was to Vanessa. Sometimes
she would agree, but then she would add that Grindal need not behave
in such a fawning manner towards Vanessa, need she? But since she
did she could expect those consequences. I was never satisfied unless
Clara agreed entirely with me. Like most obsessed people I could not
accept anything less than total agreement, and I would persist in trying
to change Clara's mind just as Grindal would persist in trying to change
Vanessa's mood. I, of course, had no success with Clara.

I don't know exactly when it was that I realized that Vanessa was
beginning to take an interest in Clara. I think it was near the beginning
of the second month of her visit.

⋄━◦◦◦◦━⋄

Here in Weimar, I have been re-reading Pope's ingenious masterpiece,
The Rape of the Lock. Clara was fond of Pope and his "friends" Swift
and Gay, and I was made to memorize sections of their poems. I amuse
myself as I lay awake by imagining what Dr. Freud would make of it,
beginning with its title, were he to deign to examine this enchanting
"trivia." For it seems to me that since the Doctor's advent there are
no longer "inessential" matters; all things are fraught with significance,
including women and their "frivolities." With what intensity he and his
colleague, Dr. Joseph Breuer, scrutinize and analyze every word of

Fraulein Anna.[36] Frau Emmy, Fraulein Elizabeth, Katharina, and Miss Lucy. Never in two thousand years have men paid as much attention to the utterances of women!

All these thoughts go through my mind as I lay awake at night. I sleep less and less. I fear the advent of death—"Each man's body follows the call of overpowering death."[37] I have come to the decision that I do not want to die here in Germany, in a foreign country. No, I shall return to Marlborough Gardens, if not to live there, to die there, with or without Beloved. She tells me repeatedly she does not care for England, that she cannot conceive of living there. I say nothing and make my plans accordingly.

Sleep is the nearest approach to death in living experience, says Xenephon. I believe that. Now when I sleep I am visited by messengers of death and dream about those who have died. My brothers, my mother, my aunts, in particular Vanessa . . .

—————◆◇◆—————

Vanessa stayed with us a mere three months, and yet in that short span of time our future lives were shaped. Actual hostilities among us began with a skirmish.

But before I begin describing that action perhaps I should tell you that just as I had noticed Grindal's obsessive and erotic interest in Vanessa develop, I also began to perceive Vanessa's increasing interest in Clara. At that point Vanessa inevitably made attempts to engage Clara in conversation, or if that were not possible she would speak to me.

But during our conversation her eyes would rest on Clara, and something in the way she moved her body, a particular kind of seductive movement, almost touching Clara but not quite . . . It is difficult, if not impossible, to describe these subtle distinctions of behaviour, except to say that I was not the only witness to Vanessa's tantalizing physicality. Grindal observed it too. And she took immediate action, when and if she could, by boldly placing her large substantial body between her beloved Vanessa and Clara, defying her mistress to tell her to move out of the way.

Of course, nothing of this was ever alluded to or discussed. And Clara? She seemed amused but remained aloof as always. I wonder

36. Emma is referring to Sigmund Freud's and Joseph Breuer's pioneer study, *Studies in Hysteria,* published in Germany in May 1895. The book traces the beginnings of psychoanalysis. Emma had been living in Weimar, Germany, since 1875 when she wrote this.—*R. Lowe*

37. Emma is referring to a Pindar fragment, fr. 116B.—*R. Lowe*

now if she was not aware that it was her apparent indifference to Vanessa that stimulated my cousin's interest in her. And if she knew, did she care? Was her detachment a response or a defence? And of course the interchange among the four of us was still at this stage so very gossamer, so tangential (nevertheless intense). But what could you actually discuss? Threads of feeling? Mute intentions? Stirrings of intangible suspicions? No, it was still too obscure, too ambiguous . . . everything was still action out of the corner of one's eye, fleeting, tenuous, already gone by the time you might confront it. Just this chronic sensation of simmering, an impression of gentle seething. Nothing to discuss—yet. At least not with Clara the rationalist, Clara the scientist. She would deny everything. Where is the proof, she would ask. Where is the evidence? And yet I knew, we all knew, that something was giving way, coming apart. It reminded me of the days just before I and my cousins went to war with one another.[38]

Poor Vanessa. She was not used to indifference. She was used to being stared at, gazed at as one does an object d'art, with prolonged awe and admiration. She had, after all, been created by God for that purpose, hadn't she? She was quite sure of that. It was her due. Her physical presence created a binding effect, as if a web of beauty spun out from her and we were caught inextricably in it. We all were, whether we liked it or not. But not Clara. She hardly ever looked at Vanessa, and when she did it was merely to glance over or past her. For the first time in her life Vanessa experienced rejection. And so, even though she was ensconced in the turbulence of the London season, she decided to take a decisive action. She crossed over the boundary and stepped boldly into our territory—the classroom.

The four of us lived together on the third floor. Grindal and Vanessa occupied the south side, which included the day nursery, enlarged to include a dressing room; the night nursery, where my brothers had slept; a storage room that had been transformed into a sitting room for Vanessa; and a small room Grindal occupied. We, Clara and I, were confined to our respective bedrooms in the front of the house; a commodious room between us, which was the classroom; and a small room that was set up as a laboratory where we did our experiments.

By the tacit communication women are so adept at we had arranged within the first week the space on the third floor in regard to ourselves; so that there were designated territories and, albeit imaginary, absolute boundaries, which if crossed constituted a clear transgression. We were

38. On May 26, 1837, Emma and her cousins engaged in a battle in Marlborough Gardens, which she referred to thereafter as the Marlborough Wars. See *City of Childhood.*—R. *Lowe*

not allowed in Arcadia (Clara's term for Vanessa's quarters); they were not allowed in "our" classroom. That was our "private preserve."

"What a funny little room you study in," Vanessa said, walking into the classroom one morning.

I was in there alone reading before class, which was to start in another half hour. I ignored her. I could not believe that she had actually dared to trespass. Walking over to a table, she picked up one of the books lying on it and read its title out loud: "*Interior Castle.*"[39] And running her gaze down the page, she read out loud: "I began to think of the soul as if it were a castle made of a single diamond—"

"Give me that book!" I said.

"I shall not."

I tried to snatch it from her, but holding me at arm's length she continued to read aloud.

". . . or of very clear crystal in which there are many rooms just as in Heaven there are many mansions. Good God, Emma! Have you become a 'religieuse'?" She put the book down, and I snatched it up.

"You know, Emma, you are a very strange person. Quite queer. I don't know how your parents put up with you. You're very unsatisfactory. You always have your nose in a book. Your hair always looks frightful, your dresses have smudges on them. You're by far the most unattractive creature I have ever seen in the world, I am sure."

"And you are the rudest and the most stupid. I am sure there are a dozen ridiculous things for you to do today that will profit no one, including yourself, and that will neither instruct nor amuse nor edify anyone. Because besides being rude and stupid, you are also steadfastly boring!"

"How you do carry on, Emma. You are jealous of me. Jealous of my beauty. Jealous of the attention people pay to me. Boring, am I? Well now, your father doesn't think so, does he? Oh, I have seen how you look at him when he looks at me. You cannot contain yourself, you watch our every move. I think I shall flirt with him again tonight at supper. He is easy to flirt with. He, too, has a talent for it—"

"Poppa hates you!" I said, on the edge of tears.

"He does not. He thinks I am beautiful. Looking at me pleases him. Even your mother prefers me to you. I know by the way she looks at me. And both your brothers are in love with me. Edward writes me letters, he calls me Diana of Blenheim Wood. Looking at you pleases no one!"

---

39. *The Interior Castle*—or *Las Moradas* (*The Mansions*), as the book is known in Spain—was written by St. Teresa of Avila in 1577. Like George Eliot, Clara admired St. Teresa, who in her time was as assailed and reviled as any suffragette of the nineteenth century.—*R. Lowe*

"It pleases me," Clara said, coming into the room. "I like a quiet, studious look. I prefer it. I find the modest wren far more alluring than the flamboyant peacock. But what are you doing here? This is not your purlieu."

"What business is it of yours?" Vanessa said. "I may go and come as I wish."

"You may not. This is my classroom and you have not been invited."

"How dare you speak to me that way! You may claim kinship with us but you are in fact nothing but a servant!"

"Emma," Clara said turning her back on Vanessa, "we shall begin our lesson. Take out your Heroditus and read out loud to me the translation of the passage I assigned you yesterday . . ."

"I have no more time to give either of you!" Vanessa shouted as Clara continued unperturbed, giving a quick sketch of Heroditus: " . . . an easy prosy gossip, a bit long-winded, fanciful—"

"I must dress for the ball I am going to," continued Vanessa. "To which neither of you have been invited!"

". . . even a bit foolish," Clara said, maintaining her course, "but still amusing." And then added, as if it were an afterthought, "Unlike our uninvited visitor."

Vanessa left without saying another word.

So ended our first altercation.

Some days later I came home from an early morning walk in the Gardens to find Vanessa in my room.

"What are you doing here? How dare you!"

"I am doing what I please," Vanessa said.

"And what is that?"

"I am perusing your books. I told my uncle about the religious book I found in the classroom. He asked me to search further and to bring him any odd book that I might find either in your room or in the classroom."

"You're lying. Poppa would not do that."

"If you don't believe me ask him yourself," Vanessa said.

"Why do you think your father sent you here? Obviously he doesn't want you with him."

"I was invited by your father."

"Your father doesn't care for you. He loves your sisters more than he loves you. My father loves me best. He told me so once. He told me he loves me more than my brothers and more than my mother. Your father never told you that."

"Your mother doesn't love you. My mother loves me more than anything or anyone in the world."

"Yes, *far* too much. Poppa says your momma is in love with you."

"Momma told me," Vanessa said, "that your father is immoral, that he is a womanizer!"

"My father is not!"

"Your father is not what?" asked Clara, standing in the open doorway. "Your shrill voice interrupted my studies, Vanessa. He is not what?"

"Immoral and a womanizer—Vanessa called him that," I whispered.

"Immoral and a womanizer . . . But how do you know about such things, Vanessa? Ah, how you have deceived us, Vanessa. We thought you were a *virgo intacta* but now we see you have the knowldege of a slut."

"How dare you! How dare you!" My cousin's face was beet-red with rage. "I shall tell my uncle what you have dared to say to me!"

"Do that," said Clara. "I shall tell him what you have said about him. And we shall see what pleases him the least—or the most."

I was not aware at the time that my father had slept with Clara and that she may have been suffering as much as I by the nightly spectacle of their light-hearted bandinage with one another. Ironically, for someone as obsessed as I was with Clara, I knew very little about her activities. I did not as yet know about her correspondence with her brother-in-law, Johan, or her sinister connection with Nicholas, or her short abortive affair with my father. But then on the other hand she knew nothing about Mr. Strooksbury.

For a week or two we hardly saw Vanessa. And then she came around again. This time she came bearing gifts. Her mother, she told me, had given her a brooch to give to me and she handed me a small box. "She is much better. I shall be leaving soon."

I heard Grindal's voice in the hall. "Where is my lambkin?"

"I am in my cousin's room, Nanny," Vanessa called out to her.

"Ah," said Grindal, "you are dressed far too lightly for a day like this. The first weeks of spring are treacherous, they cause catarrh and fever and all sorts of nasty things. Here, I have brought you a shawl. I knew you were being a naughty girl." She went over to her and put the shawl around Vanessa's shoulders.

Though Grindal was still quite young she looked far older than she was. In the last years, since Maria's husband, Ricci, had returned with my aunt the Contessa to Florence, Grindal had gained at least seven stone. Her once flawless skin was now blotched. I could hardly connect the present Grindal with the one I used to watch from my bed stroking her naked body in front of the mirror before she dressed for the day.

"Ah, Nanny, you are so good to me," Vanessa said.

"But how can one help being good to you, my love," Grindal said.

"I feel like dancing," Vanessa said. "Come now, Nanny Grindal, you must dance with me." She hummed a waltz and began to drag Grindal around the room. The maid was shortly out of breath and pleaded with Vanessa to let her go. "No, you must dance," said her tyrant, and Grindal tried to keep up with her even though it was obviously difficult. Finally Vanessa deposited her on a chair.

"There, you old fat goosey gander," Vanessa said.

"Yes, you are right, your Nanny is far too fat, not like my dearest one . . . light as a feather . . . graceful as a swan. How many hearts shall you break? How many hearts have you broken already?"

"I have broken yours, Nanny, haven't I?"

"Yes, you have, you naughty girl."

"Tell Emma what you call me when you are alone with me."

"I don't wish to hear it," I said. "It is disgusting. You have cast a spell on her like Oberon cast on Bottom."

"You are hateful," Vanessa said. "I came here today to try to be friendly to you but it is impossible. Do you know what the servants call your governess and you behind your backs? They call her Miss Slyboots and you her Cat's Paw! And they are right. You are nothing but a mealymouthed puppet. You would jump into a burning lake with serpents in it if she told you to."

"Well, I'd rather be a puppet. At least it's useful, not like you, a 'mindless beauty,' that's what Clara calls you."

"Mealymouthed puppet!"

"Mindless one!"

Vanessa rushed across the room and struck me. I was just about to strike back when Grindal heaved herself out of the chair, rushing towards me, and struck me hard on my cheek. Then, pulling Vanessa away, she hurried her out of the room.

Later, when I told Clara what had happened, she said, "That she-lion has a hard wallop. It's still red."

"Yes. She always did have."

"I think if you bathe it in cold water it will be all right. The skin is not broken. It will not leave a mark."

"We shall say nothing, of course."

"Of course not. Your father would not understand and your mother would understand too much," Clara said, laughing.

I was gratified, delighted by Clara's continuous scorn of Vanessa. The fact that Vanessa was powerless over Clara thrilled me. That night she spoke to me in a way she had never spoken to me before.

"Too much has been made of Vanessa's beauty, beginning with her mother. It is true, Ovid is right when he says that beauty has power, but it has not drawn *me* into her orbit. I have thought about why this is so and I have come to certain conclusions which I do not entirely understand but which I shall now share with you.

"It is because she has not suffered. You look surprised, Emma. Let me try to explain it. It is not that I am drawn to suffering or, as you realize by now, I am sure, that I have a particularly compassionate nature. On the contrary, people who suffer or who have suffered usually provoke impatience and anger in me and sometimes even disgust, and yet there is that inside me, perhaps something that has connected to my own suffering, that when I encounter it in others, whether it repels me or not, creates a bond with him or her. I would if I could break that bond, but despite my conscious wishes, whatever it is inside me makes that leap to that other suffering person, the suffering we never express to one another, the suffering we pretend does not exist. Well . . . that leap did not happen with Vanessa. But the worst of it is that even when it happens it does not always mitigate my cruelty towards that person—on the contrary, it sometimes stimulates it."

It was the closest moment we ever had together. I have thought of it often and I believe it was her way of apologizing to me for what she had done and would yet do. But in the end Clara was a cypher to me. Had she ever loved anyone, I used to wonder.

Once I asked her: "Was it philos or eros between you and your late husband?"

She did not take offence. Clara never took offence at anything that displayed precocity.

"A bit of both, thank God. He was quite handsome, sensitive . . . romantic. Not at all a business type; a disappointment to his father, who nevertheless loved him very much. My father-in-law would speak animatedly about the new turnip crop in the Caucasus and Franz would change the subject to the new performance of . . . *The Marriage of Figaro,* for instance."

It seemed a good time to pursue her personal history, so I asked her, "How did you meet him?" But she changed the subject.

"Enough personal history. Let us dissect frogs."

And we donned our chemist's aprons that she had brought for us and went to the room where she had set up a sort of laboratory to continue our experiments.

———✦◈✦———

Vanessa continued to interrupt our lessons.

"I am sure I left my gloves in here."

What an absurd lie, I thought, but a second later I would hear her say, "Ah, here they are!" and from behind a pillow she would draw the most beautiful pale silk lavender gloves. She must have placed them there! I would think.

"Continue, Emma, I am all ears," Clara said, for I had stopped translating when the door opened and my cousin rushed in.

"'And what did he say before his death?'" I was translating the first page of Plato's *Phaedo*.

"May I stay?" asked Vanessa

"No," said Clara. "Continue, Emma." And to Vanessa: "Do not interrupt us again."

Vanessa left without another word.

How strange people are. I was the one who became intrigued by Vanessa's simple request: "May I stay?" The three little words repeated in my head. And so it was I who beseeched and begged Clara to allow Vanessa to join us in the classroom. I wanted to show Vanessa how bright and clever I was, how much brighter and cleverer than she. She might be beautiful but I was intellectually brilliant. Alas, it is always our defects of character that do us in. Mine was my intellectual vanity. I told Clara that it would not disturb me, that after all she was my cousin, that she was a guest, and lastly that it might prove to be good for her!

Clara being Clara did not consent at once, but as Vanessa continued to interrupt us, Clara said to her one day, "You might as well stay since you want to. But if you do you must be silent and only listen. Today I am lecturing on Augustus, the first Roman emperor."

She spoke her usual forty-five minutes on Augustus and the Idea of Power, comparing Augustus to Louis XIV and the present Queen Victoria, pointing out to us that though they lived at different times they had one thing in common: an absolute belief that they were appointed from above to govern other people. On the whole Clara tended to look at history like Thomas Carlisle; that is, via the personality of those who were in power. As usual the lecture was fascinating. She had a mind that could conceive interesting hypotheses.

Clara was taking a chance when she lectured in front of Vanessa. She spoke about sexual things. She mentioned the word "sodomite" in relation to Louis XIV's brother, the Duc d'Orleans, and she ended the lecture by stating, "Ultimately power is not in the sex but in the institution. The Queen's consort is not King Albert, but Prince Albert. She is the Queen!"

What would Vanessa do? And why had Clara done it? Was it to challenge her or seduce her, I wondered? Why had Clara really let Vanessa stay?

Vanessa had been quiet and intent throughout the lecture. And afterwards she had said nothing, but she had looked thoughtful. I wondered what would happen.

A few days later she came back. How melodramatic we are when we are young. How fraught with meaning everything seems to us. A glance, a sigh, a cough, a whisper, a gesture . . .

"Here are some essays," Vanessa said to Clara, "that I wrote on various subjects when I was in school, Mrs. Lustig. Would you care to read them? My teachers commended me on how well they were written and how original they were in thought."

"Leave them on my desk, Vanessa."

"Are you lecturing today?" asked Vanessa.

"Yes. On the Greek negative. A dry subject to those who do not value subtleties."

"May I stay?"

"No. The topic is far too advanced for you. But come tomorrow. I shall be lecturing on Aphrodite, the Goddess of Love, and her humiliating role in the *Iliad*."

As you can imagine, Grindal did not like this development at all. And they had a spat about it in the hall. Grindal, obviously unable to contain her emotions, threw discretion to the winds despite the fact that she knew both Clara and I could hear every word she said.

"She doesn't like you. She means to do you harm!"

To whom was she referring, I wondered. To me or to Clara?

"How dare you speak to me that way?"

"I have seen the way she looks at you when you are not aware of it! Her eyes are filled with hatred—"

"I will hear no more."

"What good can they do you? Especially when neither of them likes you and they are only jealous of your beauty. And your wealth. Aye, the money that the old man, your grandfather left only to you, his darling—"

"Leave me alone. You are impossible! Anyway, I shall do as I please."

"Yes, that is the trouble."

After that Clara was colder than ever to Vanessa and forbade her to come into the classroom ever again. And so Vanessa took the action that on the surface seemed puerile but resulted in changing our lives, mine and hers. The effect on my life was immediate, while with her the effect lay like some dormant virus in her system, emerging much later in her life and in a far more devastating way.

She drew a vicious caricature of Clara and me and pinned it on the classroom door. The drawing was merciless. Anyone other than Clara would have been enraged. But not Clara. She was unique. She took it down and examined it carefully, after which she said, "It's very good. As a matter of fact, it is excellent. Your cousin Vanessa has talent. See how she has caught my lower lip and exaggerated just enough to have the proper satiric effect? I must speak to her about it. Did you know she could draw, Emma?"

Reluctantly I told her (I felt a foreboding) that ever since Vanessa could hold a pencil she had drawn. And that she had done a series of sketches of the Gardens as well as Saddler's Grove. "But she does it in fits and starts. She has no discipline. Why do you ask? Is it important?"

Was it only a week later that I found out that Clara and Vanessa had spent an afternoon together at the Mansion House[40]—I'm not sure—without asking me to accompany them? They had gone off together alone without telling anyone. Though when they came back they spoke about it in front of us as if we had known all about it. Their faces glowed with excitement as they related their impressions.

"She has an eye, a real eye," Clara said to me when we were alone the next day. "Strange isn't it that behind that facade of beauty there is real beauty? She has talent. She has shown me her drawings. They are not only beautiful, they are interesting. Sometimes I think that's all that matters. Creativity. I shall introduce her to Robert Hill. He will teach her what she needs to know in order to become an artist . . ."

As she spoke a feeling so fierce swept through me I thought it would topple me. I hung on to my school desk as Clara chatted on about painting. If I thought I was jealous at my father's table when my cousin and my father carried on together, it was nothing compared to what I felt now listening to Clara speak with such eagerness and enthusiasm about Vanessa. What talent did I have? A talent for translation! For memorizing other people's works! The pain I felt must be the kind of pain people experience who are being operated on without the drug of opium, their inner organs, formerly hidden and protected by flesh, suddenly exposed, examined, and brutalized.

I began to dream of Agura and Aurum.[41]

Separated from Clara, all of me ached and suffered. Why had she done this to me? How could she betray me in this way? And I could

40. The Mansion House in Cheapside was the official residence of the Lord Mayor during his year of office. The principal room is the Egyptian Hall, which contains many pieces of English sculpture: There is a famous statue of London trampling Envy and the river Thames and so forth.—*R. Lowe*

41. Agura and Aurum are the names of the two sisters in a fairy tale told to Emma by Grindal when she was young. See *City of Childhood*, Appendix D.—*R. Lowe*

not speak about it. Not only was I in pain but I was ashamed of what I was feeling. No one must ever know. Oh, the agony of youth; one wonders how one ever survived it!

I envisioned the worst. Clara would eventually stop speaking to me. Oh, she would continue to teach but certainly our extracurricular relationship would end. I would retreat into that state of despair that I had been in just before Clara came into my life. After Darius had been sent away.

What I dreaded did not occur. What you dread never does. Instead Grindal intervened. She confronted the situation head-on and fought aggressively for the one she loved. Who can make sense out of life? I remember that after that I began to secretly admire my former enemy, who had the courage to do what I could not. Who can foresee the future? Grindal's love became the instrument of Vanessa's destruction.

———◆◇◆◇◆———

Mrs. Farnley was the one who told me what Grindal had done. She said she was present but I don't believe her. I cannot imagine my father allowing that. I can only conclude that she made a habit of eavesdropping.

"Very upset she was, Grindal. She bearded your father in his study without as much as a by-your-leave. She told him that if he did not do something about it, Vanessa would be ruined."

"What the devil are you talking about, woman?" your father asked.

"And then she told him how Clara was encouraging Vanessa to draw and paint and how she was filling her head with the notion of being an artist. And how Clara had told her that she had extraordinary talent, and that it was of the utmost importance that she fulfill her destiny as an artist. And every time she said the word 'artist' your father would snarl. Well, you could see that the thought of his beloved niece, valuable too as far as money went—her dowry is in six figures—ending up in a garret in Paris rather than on an estate in England, married to an aristocrat, was driving him into an insane fury. So immediately after Grindal left, he ordered the carriage brought around and off he went to your Aunt Mathilda's and Uncle Brian's house and told them. And together, the three of them decided to take certain steps, but what they were exactly I don't know."

I knew that one of the steps related to Clara because she told me about it. With great bitterness she told me every word my father had said to her, a rare act of indiscretion on her part, which I wondered about at the time. "Your father asked to speak to me privately in his study. He told me that he had been told by an anonymous informant that I was seducing Vanessa into an artistic life! Then he started shouting at me, likening female artists to prostitutes! "Prostitutes without protection," he called them! He told me that the female mind was not created to be titillated by either color or form, and to remember that, after all, he had taken me into his house out of the kindness of his heart! That I was never to speak about art to Vanessa again but that in any event I would not have the opportunity since she was leaving. I might stay if I wished to do so, but if he heard that I was in any way polluting your mind, it would mean instant dismissal. Finally, though it was a fact that we were related, I was not to forget that I was a servant in his employ and consequently dependent upon him for references!"

Later that night, as if nothing had happened—the night was warm—Clara and I walked through Marlborough Gardens and stretched out on a blanket in the field in front of the Tower Farfrum next to the canal and scanned the summer heavens.

I still remember the glory of that spring sky and lying on the dew-drenched grass next to Clara as her raised thin white sepulchral hands traced out the ancient constellations for me.

Though I continued to love Clara—I could not help loving Clara—I no longer trusted her, and even though some small part of me reluctantly agreed that she had been correct to encourage Vanessa, just as Darius had been right to encourage my brother Edward's love of music, I knew that she was not my friend, nor had she ever been. But nothing about human beings is simple. "When one loves another, which of the two becomes a friend of the other? The one who loves or the one who is loved?"[42]

The following morning in class Clara said her last words about the incident. In a flat cold tone she predicted that though Vanessa would make a brilliant marriage she would ultimately destroy herself.

In the beginning of March, Vanessa left our house. Some months later she went to Cowes on the Isle of Wight for the yachting season, a guest of Lord Cecil, accompanied by her mother. It was there that she met her future husband, the younger son of the Fifth Earl of Grymston, Sir Charles Mallow, the Viscount of Kingston.

⟶◆◇◆◇◆⟵

During that last month everything that was not connected to Clara, Vanessa, and Grindal seemed to have disappeared from my conscious-

---

42. The question comes from an early Socratic dialogue, Lysis, "Or on Friendship: obstetrics." The main discussion deals with the matter of friendship. It was the first dialogue that Clara assigned to Emma to translate.—R. Lowe

ness . . . my brothers, my cousins, my mother, even my father. Like some poor opium addict whose world has narrowed down to the pipe, all that mattered to me during that month, which seemed to go on forever, was the four of us.

When it ended I awakened as if out of a dream and perceived for the first time that something had happened to my father. Though he was still remarkably handsome, he was not as robust—in fact, he looked sickly. But the coldness I felt towards him, which had begun before he spoke to me about Mr. Strooksbury, returned. I am sorry to say I felt no compassion. I was not even curious.

I believe it was about a week after Vanessa left—I'm not certain—that he had his first heart attack.

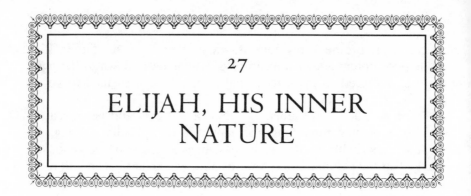

27

ELIJAH, HIS INNER NATURE

... the true being in-itself ... lies primarily in the species [hence] the generation and the nourishment of its offspring is of great importance and consequence; [hence] the excessive love of parents for their offspring

—Schopenhauer, *The World as Will and Representation*

Death is the real inspiring genius of philosophy, and for this reason Socrates defined philosophy as *thanatou melete* (practice for death).

—*Ibid.*

It was gradual, his feeling of despair.

In the beginning, when Mrs. Farnley had come to him with the horrible news about Emma and Strooksbury, he had felt an immediate rage that consumed his body and then a sudden sharp pain in his chest, as if he had been stabbed in the chest with a red-hot poker. But that went away. What did not go away were his feelings. After he had spoken to Emma—he cringed when he thought of it—after she had left, he felt a sense of grief, guilt, an overwhelming sense of shame and then fear. No one must know, no one must know, he kept repeating to himself, as if *he* had been responsible for what had happened.

At one point the desire to mutilate . . . to kill Strooksbury was so strong he thought he would have to tie himself fast with rope to a chair or his desk to keep from strangling his friend. But no one, no one must know. Emma must be protected. At least he could do that!

Elijah tried in a tremendous act of will to put it out of his mind, but it was impossible. When he was alone he would re-create the scene with Emma over and over again. From the time Emma had come into the study to the time she had left it; going over and over again what Emma had said to him that Wednesday afternoon. Not that she had said much. Only two sentences in all. "The last time I saw Mrs. Farnley she seemed to be perturbed!" and "I take it you are referring to your colleague, Mr. Strooksbury!" That was all. He had not questioned her. He could not have borne to question her.

"Seemed"! What had Emma meant by that word? He meant to understand the word in its fullest implications and subtleties . . . in its most delicate modifications. Certainly she knew that Mrs. Farnley was upset. "Perturbed," wasn't *that* an understatement! The poor woman had been distraught, hysterical; she had broken down—wept!—when she told him how she had to pull Strooksbury off Emma. "Seemed"! For God's sake, what had Emma mean by that! The word plagued him! And the other dread word: "colleague"! With its terrible nuances . . . one who joins in alliance, conspires, with its venal connections to private intrigues . . . It all stuck in his craw.

He would never never question her about it further. But perhaps it was just the fact that it was a closed issue that created what he began to think of as some kind of curious cerebral fermentation he could not control. Two dismal sentences acting like leaven on dough, kept changing into bizarre, senseless structures such as, "The last time I saw that bloody whore/liar Mrs. Farnley she was fucking Mr. Strooksbury while pretending to be upset about something *I* was doing" and "I assume you are referring to that well-known pervert, your bosom companion— Mr. Strooksbury—the one with whom you share the same whores at Malkin's brothel?"

His head would buzz ceaselessly with these insane sentences . . . and his mind went on to construct even more bizarre sentences, and the sentences boiled in his mind as if his mind were a cauldron.

With them other thoughts. The growing suspicion that Emma was being underhanded . . . untruthful. He remembered how she used to look; her face innocent, bright, shining with love for him; how when he came home after having been away she had run to him. The openness of *that* face. What had she said that night he had come from Frankfurt? *I forgive you, I shall always forgive you, no matter what you do.* Her cheeks wet with tears. But this time when he had questioned her about Strooksbury her face had not been open. He saw it before him: covert, sly, the eyes hidden, concealed . . .

He also worried about Joseph. He would think: How cruel I was towards Joseph. How smug. I've always thought of Joseph as a weakling. I have been so contemptuous . . . How truly indifferent I was to his pain and suffering. Now, Elijah thought he could understand how Joseph must have felt when Consuelo left him. But wasn't what had happened to him, Elijah, far, far worse! Only he and Mrs. Farnley knew. No one else must ever know.

During this time Elijah launched himself into a frenzy of destructive activity. One day he sold Moly's jewels, jewels that he had bought her. He demanded them from her without explanation and sold them to a man at his club for less money than they were worth. And then he had taken the money and thrown it away on three whores at Jessie Malkin's. After that he had gone to Crockford's and lost a large amount gambling. Then he had returned to Moly's and after taking her he had beaten her up because he couldn't stand the look on her face, the look of injured innocence. What right did she have to look like that?

Moly had spoken to Mrs. Farnley, and Mrs. Farnley had spoken to him, and he shamefacedly promised his housekeeper he would not do it again. So he bought the jewels back again from the man and returned them to Moly. After such bouts of madness he would be all right for a time. He would attend to his business at the bank properly, but then it would happen again. He would see Strooksbury at someone's house, or at a church committee meeting, and the same rage he felt that first day would seize him. He would want to kill the man then and there. He could not look at him. He could not stay in the same room with him. And yet he could do nothing to him. He had to protect his poor Emma.

He constantly thought of ruining Strooksbury, financially, socially, but he did not seem to have the energy to do it, and the thought that Strooksbury might take revenge in some way, in a way that might threaten Emma, prevented him from taking action. He would not allow the other thought—that if he did go after Strooksbury, Strooksbury in some way might injure him—come to consciousness. He did not allow himself to feel his fear, his cowardice. Instead he went through the daily rounds as always, but he felt crazed, as if somehow he had been "squeezed" out of society. That by Strooksbury's vicious action against his child Elijah's "place" in society had been taken away from him. For the first time in his life he felt as if he were an outsider.

The fact that he was unable to act forced him to see everything from a very different perspective, almost as if he were a child again, his vision of the world unobstructed by the associations he usually brought to his perceptions of people and the "established order." Everything now seemed to be covered with a coating of slimy hypocrisy. They were all actors, he felt, playing roles. Envy, jealousy, sloth . . . all seven deadly sins, the desire for unlimited power, masked by professional jargon, or mouthings about duty, humility, responsibility, religion . . . He now saw his "colleagues"—Redbury, Ryder, Rothschild, Strooksbury—as monsters in the way a child with clear vision might see them. He thought he now saw how money and the things that went with money—power and position—were all that mattered to these people despite what they said and for which all was sacrificed—affection, wife, children . . .

After a while he felt as if he were living on the inner edge of a crater, his fingers desperately holding on to the rim. At other times he envisioned himself in a building that was on fire and himself racing from room to room searching for Emma, but as the flames came closer realizing that there was no way out.

If only, he thought, he could unburden himself, talk to someone about what happened. What was happening to him now. Once he thought of going to confession, but he stood outside the Catholic church and he could not go in. His prejudice was even stronger. He thought of Reverend Bottome. Absurd. Impossible. He could no more speak to Reverend Bottome about what happened any more than he could speak to Solomon. Or Brian. Or Theodisia. Bottome, Elijah was quite sure, would at first pretend not to understand, and then he would offer bromides and platitudes, sending him away with the final platitude that he should trust in God; a notion Elijah had never contemplated and now, considering what had happened to him, would be impossible. Though Elijah was a churchgoer, he was not a communicant.

There was no such thing as God. But what was there? What was beneath the surface of things? Was there something? Or was it void? A nullity?

His dreams were the most upsetting. A month after the terrible event, he began dreaming of Strooksbury having sex with Emma. The first time he had waked himself and rushed from the bed and vomited on the floor of his dressing room. From that time on he could no longer look at Emma. That was in the beginning of January.

Shortly after that, Mathilda fell ill and he invited Vanessa to live with them. A decision that had proved to be a wise one as far as he was concerned. Flirting with Vanessa had distracted him temporarily at least from his bizarre and obsessive thoughts. That is, until Grindal had told him what Clara had been up to. And he was left alone with Emma again, so to speak.

He had loved one person in his life (and perhaps that had been the grievous error). Only one person—Emma! He had loved her wholly, unconditionally, and that love had been destroyed. The thing he loved with that loathsome man! The man whom he had invited into his house . . . Then one night he dreamed that he and not Mr. Strooksbury was sleeping with Emma, and the day after he had the heart attack. He remembered very little of the dream except that horrible moment when the figure rising from Emma's bed turned towards him and he saw it was himself, Elijah.

The heart attack occurred at the club. Elijah had finished eating about half an hour earlier and had gone into the card room. He had decided that he must, despite everything, make an effort to forget what had happened. To take hold of his life again.

But when he got to the card room he wondered why he was there; he had forgotten the purpose, and he sat down in the nearest chair, suddenly feeling both a tremendous fatigue and as if he were going to suffocate. The sharp pain commenced just then; he felt as if a red-hot ember from the fireplace had become lodged somehow in his chest a few inches below his cravat.

The pain, he realized, had begun some time ago in his neck and back—a spot of neuralgia, he had thought, or perhaps a bit of indigestion. His left arm then began to be in pain, and suddenly a viselike pain seized him across the chest and would not let go. His left arm was numb. Struggling upwards, he gasped and fell, as if he had been pushed, to the carpet, and lay there senseless while the urine poured out of his bladder down his legs and into his shoes.

Luckily the porter saw him fall and rushed into the dining room to fetch Sir Francis Withering, a well-known physician, who was eating his lunch. Telling the porter to fetch his bag, the doctor went to Elijah. When the bag was brought to him, Sir Francis first took out a strong solution of smelling salts and held it to Elijah's nose. Elijah came to a bit, and the doctor pried his mouth open, slowly unclenching Elijah's teeth. Then, placing his own handkerchief between Elijah's teeth— quickly, efficiently, without drama or fuss—he prepared a solution of ten grains of morphia in creosote in a tumbler. Removing the handkerchief, he administered the dose with an eyedropper.

Solomon was immediately fetched from the bank, and he took the drugged and comatose Elijah home.

For days after the heart attack Elijah drifted between sleep and wakefulness wrapped in a cocoon of opiate dreams, which he could hardly remember, except that they were strange and wonderful. Then one morning he awakened feeling better, but not aware of what had happened.

His wife's frightened face was staring at him, and he heard her say,

"He's come to! Oh, my God! He's come to!" From behind her he saw the figure of Mrs. Farnley slip forward into view. She, he noticed, did not look frightened. Theodisia began to cry, dabbing her eyes with her handkerchief while she kept repeating the idiotic phrase, "He's come to, he's come to . . ."

"Mrs. Farnley!"

"Yes, Sir."

"Please escort my wife out of the room and return by yourself."

"Yes, Sir." She led Theodisia out and returned a moment later.

"Explain to me briefly, but precisely, what has happened to me. And why am I in bed?"

Mrs. Farnley did exactly that. She told him precisely what had happened to him from the time he had fallen senseless in the card room in his club to that very morning.

"Thank you, Mrs. Farnley." Then he asked her to bring him some nourishment for he was starving.

—◆◇◆—

There were a series of doctors who attended Elijah after his heart attack. The first was Dr. Harlowe, the family doctor whose opening statement before examining him startled Elijah.

"You have your father's heart. Rheumatic. And he lived until . . . eighty-five, wasn't it? So you need not take what has happened to you to heart."

Having said that, Dr. Harlowe laughed and lifted Elijah's left wrist, pulled out his watch, and began to take his pulse. Speaking to him as if he were a schoolboy, Dr. Harlowe ordered him to throw his shoulders back so that his chest "might protrude," and with extended fingers held together in a gloved hand, he thumped Elijah's chest, first on the right, then on the left.

It annoyed Elijah to be spoken to in that manner. It further annoyed him that Theodisia was present to witness it.

After the examination Dr. Harlowe—a self-satisfied smile on his lean face—said: "A slight murmur, but no really morbid sounds, some fibrillation, however, but no evidence of syphillis, no presence of cyanosis . . ." While speaking thus he had pulled out of his big black bag, like a magician, a large glass jar filled with leeches—"The *very* best from Lord Spencer's pond"—and while cupping him and bleeding him told Elijah what he must eat from now on.

"Animal organs—kidneys, hearts, livers . . . build up your strength. Your father profited greatly from my regimen, as you will."

But Elijah did not regain his health, and he detested liver, kidney, and hearts, so when Brian, who came to visit him frequently, began to boast about the medical paragon who had brought Mathilda "back from the brink," a Dr. Roger Lacy, Elijah sacked Harlowe and became Lacy's patient.

Dr. Lacy during the course of his initial examination told Elijah that he believed tar water was the panacea for any ailment. "Capable of curing anything, Sir, from complaints of the bowel to gravel, containing as it does the vital elements of the universe. 'Twas tar water that restored your sister's health."

Lacy listened to the sounds of Elijah's thorax, but while he tapped, he held a paper cylinder to Elijah's chest and pressed his ear close to the opening. "Mediate auscultation," he explained, "the latest discovery from Paris. I am happy to tell you that you do not have liquid trapped in your pleural cavity, Sir."

Naturally, he prescribed more tar water. "You are suffering, Sir, from an insufficiency of chemical elements. Tar water will cure that."

So four times a day Elijah imbibed the sooty resin. He did this for two weeks and felt no better. Though how he felt he could hardly describe. He would start to explain and the words would elude him. He dismissed Lacy.

All this happened within a month.

Elijah had started thinking about death soon after his fortieth birthday. But he had never expected to come close to dying for another forty. As a matter of fact, he had intended to live longer than his father had, and certainly longer than either of his brothers. One of his more pleasant fantasies, which he indulged in when he was annoyed by either of them, was to envision their funerals, and himself grieving at their gravesides. And now this unexpected thing had happened to him. Something he had not planned or intended at all. And according to Mrs. Farnley had it not been for two pieces of fortuitous luck—the porter seeing him fall, and the presence of the physician Sir Francis—he, Elijah Forster, would be dead. It was difficult . . . impossible for him to really comprehend that. He did not want to die. Dimly he recalled that his sons and daughter, his brothers and sister, their spouses, and his wife had been present around the bed during the crisis. He thought he had been dreaming, but no, they had actually been there. And the strange men . . . he remembered wondering: Who are they? What are they doing here? He realized they must have been several doctors standing grave-faced around his bedside, wondering if and when he would die.

For a long time he would not admit to himself what ailed him. For despite what the various doctors had diagnosed he knew very well what *really* ailed him. It was really quite simple, wasn't it? *He was heartsick. Sick at heart. That* was what was wrong with him. Why is it that no one, not one doctor, had said that? Why hadn't they said: "We know what has happened to you. You were in a state of anger, a state of grief, a state of dread, and your heart broke." A broken heart. Was there a cure for that?

Still he did not want to die, so he went from doctor to doctor. All prescribed bed rest and light nourishment. Within three months he had lost twenty pounds and was considerably weaker.

He had never felt weak in his life. He didn't understand weakness. It enraged him to have to ask for help, for instance, when he had to use the commode. Physical weakness—he could not comprehend what that had to do with him.

After Mr. Redbury's doctor, Dr. Chester, had told Elijah that he was suffering from gallstones—"I urge you to allow me to remove them; only a matter of seconds, Sir, a mere fifty-four, stands between you and relief that you have never known before"—Elijah finally agreed (at Solomon's suggestion) to see Solomon's doctor, Dr. Blundell. Dr. Blundell advised a prolonged stay at Saddler's Grove.

⟼•≪≫•⟻

Not only was Dr. Blundell a physician, he was also a "savant." He was familiar with music, philosophy, history, and literature, besides chemistry, anatomy, physiology, pathology, and botany. Healing suggestions dropped from his lips in faultless extempore Latin or Greek, as he outlined what he called his Theory of Pore Restoration: "The theory began with Aristotle's little-known thesis *Peri Epidermis,* 'Concerning the Epidermis', which I myself have translated for the benefit of mankind . . ."

At first Elijah listened with amused disbelief, still he could not deny the man had an aura of power about him; besides, his voice was musical and in itself healing.

Dr. Blundell spoke of the skin and the pores, which he called "perforations, those minute openings of the glorious sweat glands," the key to good health. He spoke about the skin as a whole, its particular aspects and its general structure, its pigmentation, the *all-important* heating and ventilation of the pores. *And* the necessity for sweat. He instructed Mrs. Farnley to maintain a fire in the fireplace, no matter how warm the weather was. The hotter the better.

He was a charlatan, Elijah thought, but he liked him. He looked well, dressed well, smelled good. Rosy-skinned, luminous, his face not like the ashen countenaces of Lacy, Harlowe, Chester . . . and he didn't dose him, leech him, or immerse him in cold baths. So Elijah ordered a suit of clothes and undergarments and shoes to be made for him according to his new doctor's specifications. And he felt better. Following Dr. Blundell's suggestion (Dr. Blundell was an amateur botanist), Elijah became interested in plant life. He began to take short walks in the Gardens using a cane, accompanied by Norris, his coachman, when the weather permitted.

And then one night near the end of August, he decided he was well enough to attend his sister's birthday party and saw Strooksbury mingling with the guests (as if nothing had happened!), and the same hot spark of pain that he had felt that day in the club returned. "Oh, let me not die!" he pleaded to something unknown. "Let me not die! Not here. Certainly not here. In the presence of my enemy!" Oh, the excruciating pain. "Oh, God! Not that!" Dr. Blundell's ridiculous incantation, with which he closed each lecture about pores and skin, ran through his head, and he said: "Allow me to partake of the radiance of life, let me be open and willing to experience the divine flow of the universe," and miraculously—thank God!—the terrible pain subsided, but as it did he began to feel dizzy, faint. He called out to his brother Joseph, who was sitting nearby, and when Joseph came over he whispered to him that he was not feeling well and asked Joseph to take him home.

Shortly after that Dr. Blundell advised him to go to Saddler's Grove. "The peace and quiet of a country estate . . . good fresh air. So much better for the perforations. You will come back rested, restored . . . a new man."

After arranging to have the tenants move to the gate lodge, he and Theodisia went down to Saddler's Grove. While at Saddler's Grove Elijah came to realize that his entire life had changed.

That it would never be the same again.

———◆✧◆———

The minute he moved down there he knew it was a mistake. The house was cold and drafty, the housekeeper, Mrs. Capacity (his father's housekeeper), a doddering incompetent by then. Besides, it brought back unpleasant memories. And, there was Theodisia.

Two months had passed since the first major attack. During that time (which had seemed endless) he had concentrated on himself alone, concentrated on getting through it, remaining alive. He had been barely aware of others. Only he existed, and the various doctors that attended him. Now in Saddler's Grove he was alone with *her*. He had forgotten how much he disliked her. He met the difficulty by arranging to avoid her, meeting her only once a day, at the dinner table. He was relieved and somewhat amused to realize that this tacit agreement seemed to satisfy her too. It was not very different from their London life together, except for the fact that only Theodisia was present at the dinner table, and that gave her presence more weight.

However, though he was bored and uncomfortable there was, he kept reminding himself, no danger of running into *him*. So yes, it was a mistake in a way, but he decided to make the best of it. At least for now. He would have liked it better if his coachman, Norris, a bluff but kindly man, could have come down with him. But Norris himself was ill, having suffered a slight stroke. Or Grindal. But Grindal had joined his sister's household. So he was obliged to hire the Serrichers, a couple who worked at the local hospital, as his "sick-nurses," a lugubrious pair to assist Mrs. Capacity. The husband kept Elijah's room clean and fresh and attended to his physical needs, while the wife prepared the special foods Dr. Blundell had recommended that would "maintain open perforations." Mainly vegetables loaded with garlic, according to the doctor, opened the pores better than anything else.

The pair themselves looked in ill health, and had the subdued quality of the perennially poor. But they were quiet, and performed their duties methodically, and kept resolutely to themselves.

It was all terribly boring. There was little to do except read or walk in the garden . . . attend church (the rector came to visit once a week). True, his friend Redbury came down once or twice and there were the weekly business letters from Solomon to peruse—he was somewhat perturbed that Solomon had been left in charge; Joseph was no help, as usual. But truthfully, since his illness, the bank and its business seemed like a foreign land, so that though he read every word Solomon wrote him, the letters did not seem to affect him personally. He was happy enough, however, to read in one of Solomon's letters that Mr. Isaac Coverly had volunteered to act as a temporary adviser in the affairs of the bank. That whole business with Coverly—the tin mines in Peru—that seemed like a dream too. Nothing seemed real to him except the ticking of his heart. And when Solomon and Mr. Coverly came down once or twice to discuss business Elijah felt himself drift off even as they spoke excitedly about some new business deal. He made all the appropriate responses, of course, but it all seemed "much to do about nothing."

So the time passed, and despite the boredom he began to feel physically stronger. Still, he did not feel like his old self. He was stronger— but different somehow.

One day as he was sitting in the room that looked out on the small enclosed garden in front of the house, he saw a carriage drive up. Theodisia, who was sitting at the far end of the room, jumped up and exclaimed, "It must be my brother William and his wife."

"Who?" he asked.

Not looking at Elijah, she said, "My brother William and his wife, Mary."

"But I don't want them here," he said. "How dare you invite them without my permission?"

"I know you don't want them here. But *I* do."

Mrs. Serricher came in and announced them.

Elijah welcomed them in a cold voice, remarking that he had not been aware until that very moment that they had been expected. He was happy to see the young wife blush and Theodisia's brother look uncomfortable. "I do not wish to intrude—" William began.

"You are not," said Theodisia. "You are welcome here. You have always been welcome here. This is my home, too. It is one of Elijah's jokes. I told him you were coming and he was delighted."

They stayed for two nights, during which Elijah stayed in his room, refusing to dine with them.

The morning after they left Elijah told Theodisia he wanted to speak to her.

She came into the drawing room. Her face had a defiant look about it and something else that Elijah could not determine. He also noticed that she looked more attractive than usual. She was wearing a red striped silk dress with a black sash.

"Sit down," he told her. "I am very displeased, Theodisia. Without asking my permission, without informing me, you invited people to stay at the house. You are not to do that again. Do you understand? I may be indisposed but I am still in charge of such matters." She said nothing. She just sat there in front of him, sullen and rebellious. He wanted a response. He went on.

"I have been ill, Theodisia. I have been at the point of death. During all this time I have not once complained to you about my aches and pains. I have not asked you to discommode yourself in any way. I have been patient and considerate with you despite my physical incapacities. You were not given extra duties. It was Mrs. Farnley who stayed with me at night; it was Mrs. Farnley who read to me during my convalescence; it was Mrs. Farnley who administered my medical draughts . . . I think I am right in saying that throughout my ordeal you have had an easy time of it. I recall how Guinivere behaved when Solomon was ill. She would have not behaved in as thoughtless a manner as you have—"

"*They* are *not* 'people.' They are my brother and his new wife!"

"I don't care if they are Jesus Christ himself! You are not to invite anyone to this house again without asking my permission!" Her face still had a defiant look about it. He wanted to shake her. He exploded. "If you ever invite people to my house again without my permission I shall beat you—"

"I seriously doubt if you can beat me, Elijah. You can hardly stand to piss!"

"What!"

She stood up and began to leave.

"Come back here, you bitch! Don't you dare leave this room! If I cannot beat you, I shall hire someone to do it!" he shouted at her retreating back. "You may go now," he said. But she had already left the room.

After that incident he did not speak to her for a week. He had half expected her to come to him and beg him for forgiveness. Instead, whenever he caught sight of her around the house or garden, she seemed to be happy. Once he caught a glimpse of her in the hall waltzing with one of the gardener's children.

Until now he had always considered Theodisia lacking in spirit. It was one of the reasons he had disliked her. She had been so overwhelmingly grateful to marry him. That whole first year she had been so totally subservient to him. He might want submissiveness in a mistress, but he had envisioned marrying a woman with what he termed "aristocratic mettle." Someone he could have broken and tamed. Theodisia had lacked all sense of personal pride. She had disgusted him.

So though he was enraged, he was also intrigued by this "new" Theodisia. He began to watch her covertly. He took to having dinner with her again. She would not engage in conversation with him though he tried. Her replies when she made them were civil enough but monosyllabic. And that same odd expression, the one that had puzzled him the morning she had defied him, still appeared on her face whenever she looked at him. But what did it mean? She was sullen, she was defiant, but there was something else. He couldn't make it out. Could it be pride? No, it wasn't that. Contempt? Could it be that? He tried imitating the expression with his own face and sometimes he thought that yes, that was it, contempt, but then he would change his mind. It was a mixture of feelings, he decided, but what precisely? What mixture precisely? It irritated him. He couldn't let it go.

—◦≻◦◊◦≺◦—

"That color suits you, Theodisia."

"I thought so, which is why I chose it."

They were seated on two chairs on the lawn. His manservant, Zekiel, had brought them out. And a small table. They were to have tea there.

She was wearing an emerald-green voile dress, her hair, dressed simply, fell in natural curls to her bare shoulders. Her straw bonnet lay beside her. She looked at him, that mysterious expression on her face again. What in bloody hell did that mean, he wanted to ask her. What are you thinking about, or feeling, when you look at me that way?

"I never lived here when I was a boy," Elijah said. "Jorem bought it after he created the Gardens. But then you know that, don't you? No, as a boy I lived in a grim old house on Chancery Lane. My mother died here, though, in Saddler's Grove, but for years before that she lay wasted and ill in the other house. . . . Do you know, Theodisia, you look a bit like her? I never noticed until now how much you resemble her. . . ."

While he spoke he sensed that she was uninterested in what he was saying. That she was barely listening. He watched her hands as her fingers clasped and unclasped, watched as her small neat head turned restlessly from side to side.

"You seem distracted, Theodisia. I am speaking to you. I expect you to be polite and pay attention. It is the least you can do."

"I heard what you said."

"But you are not interested."

"I don't wish to quarrel with you."

"No, you don't wish to quarrel, but you are disagreeable nevertheless. Here, help me up. I no longer wish to have tea with you."

She stood up in front of him, but instead of reaching out her hand so that he could take it and help himself out of his chair, she just stood there, her hands at her sides. He did not want to, he was livid, but he was forced to ask her for her hand.

That night as he lay in bed awake it finally came to him what that look meant. She was no longer frightened of him! *That* was it. And an image that had come into his mind during the first few weeks after the attack came back into his mind, an image of a gelded bull. That was how he felt! Castrated! And she, she felt that way about him too. He could no longer perform.

Thoughts of women, of having them in all kinds of ways, thoughts that had plagued him most of his life, ever since he had been a boy, those thoughts had disappeared since the attack. His hands reached down to his penis. Limp. Useless. What did the French call it, this impotency, this impuissance . . . what was their quaint, ironic term for his condition . . . a small dress rehearsal . . . *une petite couturière* . . . yes, before the actual, complete, and whole death of the body.

He lay there trembling with rage. His mind flooded with pornographic images. His hands moved up and down his penis. It began to swell. It began to harden. When it was fully erect he got out of bed and walked out of his bedroom, down the hall to her room.

She was asleep on her stomach.

She awoke instantly, her hands curling into fists that flailed his chest, as he lifted up her nightdress with one of his arms and with the other steered his penis into her and penetrated her. She screamed at him as he moved his penis in and out of her "I hate you! I loathe you! I wish you would have died! I wish they would have brought you home dead!" He caught her hands by the wrists. He was ill, he was wasted, but he was still ten times stronger than she was.

"Scream away, Theodisia. No one will hear you. We live in a house with incompetent, doddering, idiotic servants—"

"I prayed you would die! When they brought you home I was overjoyed!"

"Were you now? Do you mean that when you sat by my sickbed with that stupid face of yours, you were thinking 'Die, die, die'? I must have heard what you were thinking, Theodisia," he said, ramming his penis in and out of her, in and out . . . "I want you to know it helped me through. Yes, every time you said 'Die' I thought, 'You first, my love, you first!' And every day I got stronger and stronger." He thrust his penis into her as if it were a bayonet. "See how strong it's made me?"

She lay limp in his arms. He lifted up her head by pulling at her hair. "Do you know what you are, Theodisia? An idiot—a dull, hopeless idiot." Suddenly she spat in his face and tried to struggle out of his grasp, but he held her fast. And then, suddenly, a feeling that he had not had for three months started up in him. Oh, Christ! It was happening, thank God! He felt his climax coming. It was coming! He was not dead! He was alive! Alive! He moved faster. In and out. Faster! Then, tearing her nightdress open, he lifted up her right breast and bit her nipple hard, and when he heard her moan in pain he came!

After it was over he rolled off her and lay there for a second next to her limp body. Then he got out of the bed and, lighting the candle that stood on the table next to the bed, he held it up to look down on her. The nipple, he noticed, was bleeding slightly. He held the candle close to her face. The look was no longer there. Good!

He put the candle back down on the table and started walking out of the room. She hurled herself out of bed and fell on him. Snarling, he turned around swiftly to push her away, but his foot got caught in her nightdress and he fell to the ground beside her. She rolled away from him, hissing and swearing. "Cripple! Weakling! Monster!"

He lay there unable to move.

She was crying now. Weeping.

"Oh, you don't know," she moaned, "you don't know the pain you've caused me! I was so much in love with you! I was only seventeen when I married you. I could not believe my luck," she sobbed, "when my father told me I was to marry Elijah Forster, Jorem Forster's son. I was so in love! I came to you in marriage and gave you my whole heart, with all its feelings, all its love for you. That day, the day I married you, was the happiest day of my life. But never once—*never once* in all those years—have you ever looked into my eyes and acknowledged that love." She began to cry again. "All the love a woman feels for a man . . . it struggled, oh, how it struggled to survive, and then finally it began to wither, wither and die. . . . Well, now I hate you. You have destroyed any love I ever felt for you. What you have done to-night . . . this brutality . . . this rape! This is your idea of love! You are a monster! I cannot wait until I stand at your bedside to watch you breathe your last. . . ."

He could get up. If he were careful. He prayed that he had enough strength to get up and leave the room without falling again. He lifted himself up by placing his hands against the wall. She did not stop him. She was rocking back and forth now and moaning words he could not understand. Without saying a word to her he left the room.

"Monster!" she screamed after him. "Cripple! I hate you. I have hated you for years! You disgust me . . . disgust me . . ."

He walked out of the house. He would not stay there another second. He would awaken Zekiel and have him drive him home to Marlborough Gardens. He would leave here. Leave her. Never return. The words kept ringing in his head, "Cripple. Weakling. Monster . . ." He got as far as the garden gate. He could go no farther. He sank to the ground. He could not take another step. He could not move.

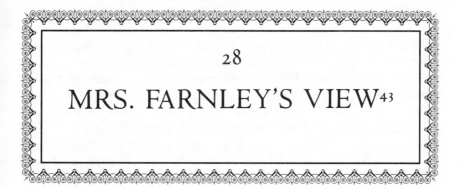

28

MRS. FARNLEY'S VIEW[43]

WHEN I first met Nicholas Renton I didn't like him. Nor did I like the idea of spying on my master. But ever since he let me know what that child-fucker Mr. Strooksbury (I like to call a spade a spade) was doing to Emma I've been on his side. And he *is* a generous man.

As for Elijah, poor man, ever since I ran to him with the horrible news he's gone from bad to worse. Crueler than ever to his wife, as if it were her fault. Irascible with the servants (though not with me), and in his cups night and day. Emma was the only thing in the world he loved and she'd been used and abused as if she were a common whore. *And* by a close associate of his. So when the master admitted to me that he had beaten Moly—actually he broke the poor girl's jaw—I thought I knew why he had behaved in such a way toward her. Still, I took advantage of it and was able to make a most satisfactory financial arrangement for her.

As I said, I could understand his pain. But at the same time I had not forgotten that when he set up Moly in her own quarters, he once invited Strooksbury to have her. And she was only fourteen then. True, we made a bit of money from him. And Moly, poor innocent that she was, did not see the wrong in it. And she did so love her pretty dresses and her cunning house. I must admit also that in a way the child was lucky. 'Twas a better fate for her to be kept by Elijah under the circumstances than to be incested by her father and her brother, weren't it? Now what would she have got for that? Not a tuppence. Only a succession of bairns and a lifetime of slavery waiting on her kin.

So Moly's set up now. And because of the "contract"—I should have

43. Constructed from a series of notes written on the back pages of Mrs. Farnley's daybook of 1840.—*R. Lowe*

been a barrister, so cleverly did I word the agreement—Moly has a pretty little cottage of her own all free and clear. She writes me through Finley that she misses Elijah. "I wonder, shall I ever see the Master again? Was it something I done that made him give me up?" Strange, isn't it, how those who are clubbed and battered and abused are always so eager to be blamed, and those who club and batter and abuse just as eager to have them do so. Eighteen she is, and still fresh-looking and with a bit of money. I have every reason to expect my niece will marry well. I for one will see to it that she chooses wisely, for as I have told her (again and again) 'tis marriage that seals a woman's fate.

When Miss Vanessa came to live with us—and what a stuck-up, vain, and silly creature she is!—I saw that Elijah rallied immediately. She was like a strong tonic to him. He was almost his old self again. Women and Elijah. He's needed women ever since he was a young boy. Sometimes I see his craving as a sickness that he cannot control. When Vanessa left he began drinking again. Many a night he'd come to my room and cry.

I wonder about the Vanessas of the world. What must they think of it? What a strange view they must have of it. Seventeen she is, and what does she know of the world except that everyone—that is, men—wants something from her and bows and scrapes to her because of this something she possesses, something that must frighten her at times, for how can she understand it. Something that shall disappear, for 'tis not like money, it shall fade in time. How long does that kind of beauty last? Ten years? And then all that hullabaloo will be over and she, poor lamb, will join the rest of us mortal women bowing and scraping to men. Once or twice I thought I saw a flicker of that knowledge in her eyes.

Women! 'Tis a wonder those four did not kill one another. Four cats are what you are, I told Grindal, the four of you caged together on the third floor. What you need is a lion tamer, I told her when she would come weeping to me about what Clara had said to her or done to her, or Emma, or her precious Vanessa. The poor fool, lovesick over Vanessa, and poor Emma lovesick (for years!) over that cold bitch Clara. And all of them fighting with one another. And over what, pray tell me. A crumb of power. And what if one of you fools, I kept asking her, did manage to sweep up a few particles of power—what is it but crumbs of power that happened to fall off the master's table, for no woman except the Queen has power. But Grindal never understood what I meant. I meant, of course, the kind of power Elijah had. *Had.* He no longer has it. Not since he finally came home from Saddler's Grove. 'Twas then I saw that things had changed between Elijah and Theodisia. And seeing it, I made my choice.

There must have been some ruckus, a real Donnybrook. And one that she won. I tried to worm it out of her but she wouldn't tell me. Oh, I would have liked to have been there to see him get his lumps. And yet I cannot say that I dislike him. In his day what a man he was! I like arrogant men. Had I been born a man I would have lived like him.

But Theodisia, now that's another matter. I was right when I judged her to be craftier than she looked, far stronger than she allowed herself to appear. But there's always a struggle in marriage, isn't there? I've seen it time and time again, and sometimes to the death between the man and wife. I saw that with the old man Jorem and that poor chick Jessica. She never stood a chance with him; she had no mettle. A woman must have that. Though sometimes it can be the other way around, can't it, like the cuckold Joseph and his Italian whore.

My Theodisia is riding high, she has taken to authority as if she were born to it. But then it is an exhilarating sensation. She sees only that she has been victorious. But I see something quite different. I do not trust Elijah. Elijah is a guileful adversary.

And there is Edward. Edward is the heir. A fact that my Theodisia has apparently forgotten or does not understand the true meaning of. Or both. She is hopelessly naive. I had a hard youth, but when I see how Theodisia behaves I am grateful for it. It has forced me to see past appearances and kept me ever alert for what might happen. I do not wish to end my days (and shall not) in an attic room in front of a cold grate with sugarless tea to drink and hard biscuits for supper. A woman in my position cannot be too careful.

Edward. Now that's a deep one. I have not said a word to Theodisia about what I have seen between Edward and Clara. The less said the better is a rule I've lived by all my life. But it's a wonder she does not see it. How can a woman be so blind? He has fallen in love—and only God knows why, since the woman is as ugly as sin—with Lustig. How I dislike that woman. He moons over her, he blushes when she enters a room. He is sixteen; she—what? twenty-three? twenty-four? though she looks older than that.

First the father, now the son! Not that Edward and Clara have been to bed together. I have my lookouts. But now that he has come down from Warrenton for the term to be with us in our time of trouble, they are always together. They play music together, they take walks together, they play games together, they laugh together. What will happen, I wonder, when Elijah becomes aware of this? Now he is involved in his struggle with Theodisia. That and his plants.

I have the feeling Elijah will die soon and Edward will be master here. If he marries Clara, impossible though it seems, but if he does . . . perhaps I should be more accommodating to the bitch. I shall have to think about this and make my plans accordingly.

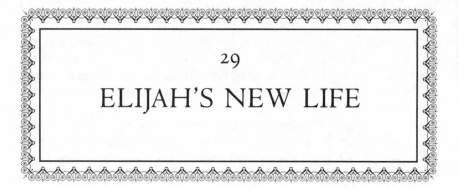

29

ELIJAH'S NEW LIFE

Death is the real inspiring genius of philosophy, *and* for this reason Socrates defined philosphy as *thanatou melete* (practice for death) . . .

—Schopenhauer, *The World as Will and Representation*

At first sight in seems extraordinary that events experienced so long ago' should continue to operate so intensely—that their recollections should not be liable to the wearing away process . . .

—Freud and Breuer, *Preliminary Communications*, Part I

MARLBOROUGH GARDENS, 1842

Did one cease to live after death? Did the psyche leave the body or did some trace of personality survive? And if it did, were the ghost and the corpse consubstantial? And was there reward and punishment after death?

Elijah's mind tended to weave in and out of these questions even while he cared for his plants, listened to *A Journey Down the Amazon* being read to him by Emma, socialized with his visitors (his brothers, his friends, Redbury, Coverly, Ryder's steward, Pierre Mboza . . .), chatted with Norris, bickered with Theodisia, listened to Clara and Edward perform piano and violin duets for him, ate, urinated, defecated, and dreamed.

The death ruminations had begun the night he had tried to run away from Theodisia and instead had slumped to the ground (with his second heart attack) in front of the garden gate at Saddler's Grove. From that point on, when he no longer could deny the fact of his bodily decrepitude, he had to face the dismal fact that his penis no longer functioned sexually but lay there limp, supine no matter what he did to it.

Oddly enough, though his impotence was a grim fact, his will to live had not diminished. On the contrary, despite his increasing loss of physical strength, his slide into a general condition of helplessness and weakness, his will had strengthened. He staved off the fear of death by ruminating on those four questions as a cow might chew her cud.

Theodisia, however, was another matter. The new Theodisia. When he had regained full consciousness the following morning he remembered in bits and pieces, as if they were sword thrusts, that long melodramatic speech she had given over him while he lay there helpless on her bedroom floor, unable to leave. He shuddered as he recalled the pent-up venom spewing out of her, the words like a river of black mud pouring out of her mouth, her face alive at last, glittering with malice and hatred of him. What was he to do? Declare her a madwoman and have her locked up? He thought it through carefully and reluctantly rejected the idea. There were too many problems attached to it. Too many possible mishaps. Besides, Theodisia was crafty—he knew that now—she would never behave that way in public.

He could, of course, send her to Saddler's Grove on some trumped-up excuse or other and stay on here in Marlborough Gardens alone. Or he could return to Saddler's Grove "for reasons of health". . . . But underlying all this conjecture was the nagging, desperate sensation that no matter what he did or arranged he could not escape from this new Theodisia. That she would continue to pursue him as the Furies had pursued Orestes. For that was how she had appeared to him that night—a Gorgon, her face black with rage, utterly repulsive, her wild long hair writhing like snakes, her nostrils snorting, "her bloodshot eyes dripping foul ooze," her bloodstained robe "unfit to bring before the statue of a God . . ."

Incomprehensibly, however, the violent episode between them had erased the pain of the recent past. What had happened between Emma and Strooksbury no longer haunted him. A force inside him now turned a blind eye to what might interfere with his enduring. Death and Theodisia were his adversaries now, not Strooksbury.

———◈✦◈———

Once he was firmly ensconced in Theodisia's morning room (he had overridden her objections by pleading abjectly, having discovered quickly enough how to manipulate through his new lack of strength) and had organized a new pattern to his life, Elijah began a new fantasy connected to the question Is there an afterlife?

He imagined himself to be a high Egyptian official during the reign of Amenhotep IV, imagining that among his duties was the building and furnishing of his tomb for a comfortable afterlife. What he should take with him was the meat and the bones of his fantasy. The essentials, of course: a feeding tube, his mother's tent bed, his father's desk, some chairs, *all* his travel books, possibly Norris or someone like him, women . . .? At that point in the fantasy he would place both his hands inside his trousers and stroke his flaccid penis . . . would the condition ever change, he wondered?

Then a burst of rage would overcome him—it was not just! He was far too young! The pain would start then, a bright hot pain a little under his sternum, and quickly he would recite Dr. Blundell's message (though he no longer saw him), and when the pain subsided he would continue the fantasy . . . perhaps he would take the Rockingham china. Now that seriously would annoy Theodisia. Perhaps the gold cutlery . . .

He began to amuse himself by speaking of any "gift" a visitor might bring him as being destined or not destined for the tomb. If he liked it he would say, much to the visitor's alarm, "What a perfectly lovely tray. Be assured it shall accompany me into my afterlife." Only Joseph had laughed when Elijah said this to him. The statement enraged Theodisia. Though her reaction puzzled him, it nevertheless gave him pleasure that he could still arouse anger in her. He filed that discovery in the back of his mind. It was a good thing to know.

Having begun to engage his visitors, despite their obvious discomfort, in this new game, he would sometimes ask them when they came to visit: "Well now, have you brought something for me to add to my tomb collection?" And then he would laugh. He liked Reverend Bottome's reply and told Joseph about it. "You are an English Anglican gentleman, Elijah, and therefore as a baptized Christian gentleman, you shall go to a Christian heaven not an Egyptian pagan afterlife."

Elijah knew very well where he would be buried when he died. He would be interred in the graveyard behind St. Swithins Church in Donnington near Saddler's Grove where Jorem; his mother, Jessica; his infant son; and his stillborn daughter were buried.

Since his sickness—though he was not really sick, was he? That is, he had no fever, no seizures . . . so then what was the correct appellation for his condition? Malaise? Disablement? Was it a valetudinous condition? A state of devitalization? What?—he had begun to think more and more about his youth.

It was truly remarkable, he thought, how much and how clearly one could remember, that is, if an effort were made to remember; how vividly things could be recalled to mind.

Elijah had been born in the parish of St. Bride near Fleet Street in Chancery Lane, No. 192. He remembered distinctly the grim, narrow, five-story house he had been brought up in—it had once been a mercer's school—and the iron bars on all the windows, which were hung with dingy yellow satin curtains. The house stood opposite the wondrous gilt-and-painted shop called Mrs. Salmon's Waxworks, inside was "The Royal Courts of England," a panorama of over a hundred wax effigies of English kings and queens. For a sixpence (put into the hand of the cripple who sat in the doorway) one could go within and see them. What pleasure he had had there.

What he chose to remember sometimes puzzled him . . . there had been a strange-looking man who seemed to live in the shadows of the dark, narrow rooms of his father's house, a thin man with splayed feet and light-colored protruding eyes that seemed to float in the gloom. Mrs. Capacity's husband, his father had told him. Elijah didn't recall at all the printers of Fleet Street or the booksellers, but he remembered vividly, as if it were before him now, the singular clock with four faces showing the age of the moon, the day of the week and month, the time of the sun rising . . . and the man whose shop the clock stood in, the man with the mountainous belly and three gold teeth. And he remembered the sound, the chronic sound of his mother's cough . . . like the flutter of bird's wings.

And St. Bartholomew's Fair . . .

Jorem had taken him and his two brothers to it and he had gotten lost. He was six years old at the time. Solomon, he remembered, had been mounted on Jorem's shoulders, and he and Joseph had been warned to hang on to Jorem's coat, otherwise they would get "lost in this seething mass of humans."

The fire eater had made him forget Jorem's warning, however. They had been to the shooting gallery, the peep show, the acrobatic performance, the arcade with its toys, and had taken two rides on the roundabouts, and he was tired and wanted to go home, but then in front of one of the booths he saw a man in black clothes suddenly take a long sword and plunge it down his throat. Elijah watched transfixed as the sword went straight down the man's throat, the hilt sticking out of the man's mouth. "A fire eater," his father told them scornfully.

Elijah watched the man remove the sword quickly—everything the man did, he did quickly—and begin to pull roll after roll of colored ribbon out of his mouth and then (this time the man moved so quickly that Elijah, for the life of him, could not make out how it had happened)—the ribbon was on fire! He had never seen anything like that in his whole life! A man swallowing ribbons of fire! It was not until the man passed his hat around that Elijah realized he had lost his father.

He remembered the beginning of the story and the end, when Jorem found him, but what was in between he remembered only vaguely. A man with a long beard was carrying him when he saw Jorem, his face white and wild-looking. Elijah cried out "Poppa!" He remembered clearly his father's face as Jorem held him tight in his arms and tears trickled down his cheeks. It was the first and last time he had ever seen his father cry.

And even stranger was the fact that this "world of childhood" was now far more real to him than that other world had ever been. The world of Forster Midland, the world of money, women, and card games, now seemed like a dream lived by another "him" in some other lifetime.

One day he thought about Dr. Pond and how much they had liked one another. Dr. Pond had read Faust with him and Wilhelm Meisters Lehrjare: "Two souls are delling in [my] breast," "The first vocation of a man is to be active." The headmaster had once jocularly suggested that one day Elijah might want to teach at Warrenton. He had been horrified at the suggestion at the time. Now he wondered what his life would have been like had he said yes. Not that Jorem would have allowed it.

Elijah hardly left his room anymore; there were not enough hours in the day to complete the tasks he had set for himself. Since Dr. Blundell first encouraged him by his enthusiasm to become interested in nature, he regularly corresponded with a Yorkshire horticulturist whose brother was living in the Amazon. He devised botanical experiments, he studied Linnaeus. . . .

He began to like the idea of living in one room. He liked Norris as a companion. He liked wheedling Theodisia. He liked asking her for things he knew she did not want to give him. He saw that she was still frightened of him, though she pretended she wasn't, and when he really wanted something, and she refused, he would force himself to stand up and use the old voice, the sarcastic, flesh-tearing voice. He was gratified to see how effective it still was. *That* was interesting. Theodisia interested him greatly now, not like Reverend Bottome, who bored him. He usually thought of furnishing his tomb when Bottome came to speak to him about the state of his soul.

Isaac Coverly came to visit him, too, and *he* was interesting. Actually he was fascinating. Coverly spoke to him about the people who lived in his shelters, about their lives. He liked Coverly, but he wondered why Coverly came to visit him as often as he did. Furthermore, he wondered if Coverly liked him. For sometimes in the middle of one of his truly intriguing stories, an expression would cross the man's face that was not at all friendly—a cold and ruthless look. What did it mean? Elijah wondered.

Redbury bored him. All his business acquaintances bored him now. He was no longer interested in trade, he told his brother Solomon. Finance bored him. He felt closer now to Joseph than he did to Solomon.

One day Joseph brought Elijah a painting that he had painted of Elijah as a boy. Elijah could hardly believe it. It was so accurate. There he stood in his sailor suit and the little pilot coat with its two rows of brass buttons, the fringed ends of the white woolen muffler showing beneath the bottom of the coat, standing in front of a tent, the expression on his face rapt . . . what could he be looking at so intently? But of course—how clever of Joseph. The patterns on the side of the tent were silhouettes of flames. The boy was looking at the fire eater. How had Joseph known how Elijah felt about the fire eater?

That was on his birthday, after the second attack. There had been a party going on in his honor in another part of the house. He had remained in his room. From time to time guests and family members would come in and extend their "heartiest felicitations." His nephew Albert had stayed with him for most of the evening, and he told Albert what he knew about Marlborough Gardens and its origins.[44] And that too was new and interesting, his friendship with Albert. His own sons, he knew, disliked him. He no longer pretended about such things. Neither Edward nor William liked him. But Albert did, which was strange. However, on reflection he thought, Why not? He had not injured Albert, as he had Edward and William. He no longer pretended about such things as well. Not that he felt guilty towards them, not that he wanted to make amends. It was just one more fact among so many other new and fascinating facts. Something to be acknowledged, recorded, examined . . . observed.

<hr />

Theodisia was furious. The fact that Elijah seemed perfectly happy in her morning room and apparently content to remain there for the rest of his life, an invalid who was enjoying himself, an invalid who was not really an invalid, who could if he wanted to stand up and walk but wouldn't out of spite, annoyed her more each day. The victory she had won at Saddler's Grove when she had vented her spleen seemed to fade just a bit more each day that he sat there. His presence was an irritation. On her insistence another doctor, a Dr. Nichols, came to examine

44. See *City of Childhood*, Research Paper No. 1.—*R. Lowe*

Elijah. After the examination he told her that he really could not understand why Mr. Forster was not making use of his legs. "Since there is nothing wrong with them. What I mean, Madam, is that there is no physical reason for your husband not being able to walk. It is purely a matter of will, Madam. He is simply not willing to walk. I guarantee you that my colleagues will agree with me on that point."

After the doctor's departure she had flown into his room screaming, insisting that he immediately vacate "her" morning room. That he remove himself and all of his vile belongings immediately! "You are nothing but a malingerer," she shrieked at him. "You malinger in order to annoy me! Dr. Nichols has told me that there is no physical reason why you cannot walk. Well, you shall walk if I must set fire to the chair itself! Norris!" The coachman blanched. "Start removing those plants—"

"No! Don't do it. They will die if they're taken out of this room."

"Immediately, Norris! Immediately!"

"Touch one plant, Norris, and I shall have you arrested for stealing and thrown into Fleet Prison!"

"He's lying, he's lying, Norris. Do you know what your master is? He is a liar. A liar! He is pretending to be ill to annoy me. He isn't ill at all. There's nothing—*nothing*—wrong with him." The Gorgon screamed, her eyes flashed. She ran to the stand on which several of his plants had been carefully placed—he would kill her!—and putting two of them in her arms raced over to Norris, who stood there frightened to death, unable to move. "Here! Here, take them right now!" And she tried to force the plants into his arms.

"Milady, p-p-please . . ." Norris stuttered, and then, looking at both of them, ran out of the room.

"Come back here, you coward!" Elijah screamed.

Turning to Elijah, a malicious look on her face, Theodisia held out both plants and as her eyes widened—she truly looked insane—she dropped them onto the floor.

Elijah screamed; he howled: "Die, bitch! Die! Die! You harpy! You rotten sack of pus! Die!"

Solomon, who was chatting with Mrs. Farnley (he had come to visit before going on home to supper), rushed into the room. "Oh my God! What is wrong? Theodisia! What is going on here?

"Theodisia!" Solomon thundered as he saw his sister-in-law move towards his brother with a raised poker in her hand. "What in God's name are you doing?"

Theodisia looked at him blankly. What was *he* doing here?

Mrs. Farnley, who had come in after Solomon, went over and took the poker out of her hand.

"Ah, I am glad you are here to see it!" said Elijah. "She is mad, Solomon. Totally deranged! I have not told you about it. It is too shameful, but now you see for yourself what I have had to put up with ever since I have fallen ill!" And then he began to cry. "My poor plants. Oh, Solomon, I cannot tell you how much they meant to me. Mrs. Farnley, pick them up, perhaps they can be saved." Then he looked at Theodisia. "You shall pay for this outrage dearly."

Theodisia now began to cry. Turning to Solomon, she said, "He threatened to do away with himself. He said he could no longer live like this, that he would rather die. Oh, Solomon, I had to stop him in some way."

"Liar! Bitch! Don't believe a word she says, Solomon. She is insane. You saw for yourself, with your own two eyes, that she was going to attack me—"

"Not another word! No, Elijah! No, Theo! Not another word!" Solomon was perplexed, but he was also absolutely sure that he could bring order out of this chaos of emotions. "Not until you have both calmed down. Not until you have been restored to reason. I see that the strain has been too much for both of you."

"*Both!*" screamed Elijah. "*I* am not strained. It is not *I* who attacked her with a poker!"

Solomon looked at Theodisia. Perhaps it was *that* time of the month— he knew from experience that women were a bit unnerved at that time, even Guinivere. If only Guinivere were here. "Come, Theodisia, calm yourself. There, there, dry your tears. . . . Mrs. Farnley will take you to Guinivere. She will take care of you. I shall stay here with Elijah."

Theodisia, her eyes cast down, allowed Mrs. Farnley to take her by the arm to where Guinivere waited in the front of the house.

Solomon, having decided that poor Theodisia had broken down because of her devotion to and love for Elijah, also decided that her behaviour was therefore understandable. Having to witness her poor husband, day after day, in this terrible condition (Solomon himself could hardly believe that this man, this weeping invalid, could be Elijah), and finally realizing that it would not change, the poor woman had broken down. And who knows, perhaps she was telling the truth, perhaps his poor brother *had* wanted to take his own life, an act that would have been horrifying. Still, seeing Elijah the way he was now, Solomon could understand it even though he could not condone it.

Though Solomon questioned Mrs. Farnley when she returned, he could not get a word out of her about her mistress except that Theodisia was perhaps too devoted to the master for her own good, which explanation, because it agreed with his thinking, Solomon accepted without question.

After discussing the incident with Guinivere, Mathilda, Joseph, and Brian, Solomon decided that it would be best for all concerned if Theodisia went back to Saddler's Grove for a while. Without Elijah. "Absence makes the heart grow fonder," Solomon said to Theodisia as he explained it to her. "And you will not be alone. Guinivere has said she will go with you. *And* our good friend Isaac Coverly has offered his services. He shall accompany both of you. So there, we all care for you. You'll see, trust me, everything will turn out all right."

Though Solomon soothed Theodisia's feelings, he was a little disturbed by Theodisia's accusation of Elijah's "malingering." He decided to speak to Dr. Nichols himself, who told him exactly the same thing he had told Theodisia. Solomon thought about it for a while and then came to the conclusion that if what the doctor said was true—and there was no reason to believe it was a misdiagnosis—that his brother could walk but did not wish to, it was none of his (Solomon's) damn business. He could see no reason for Elijah to do something that he did not want to do. It hurt no one, after all, except, perhaps, Theodisia. She seemed so insistent on having back her morning room. Somewhat petty under the circumstances, Solomon thought. When she returned he would suggest to her that she consider using the drawing room as her morning room. True, it did not have the sun, or the view of the Gardens, but really she must not be allowed to behave in such a selfish manner (perhaps it was her yeoman's background). By the time she returned, fully rested, Solomon was quite sure that she would have come around. If not that would be too bad for Theodisia, for in this case, Solomon decided, his brother's will must prevail. After all, poor Elijah had little enough in his life that he could control.

So when Theodisia returned in a month Solomon told her all of this and, just as he expected, she accepted the decision without any remonstrance.

———◆◇◆———

During the time she was away Elijah began to attempt to masturbate. Or, as he put it to himself, *praeputia ducit* ("pulls the foreskin").[45]

Holding his penis, he would whisper all the obscene Latin words he knew for the name of penis: *mentula* ("prick"), *virga* ("rod"), *coleatam cuspidem* ("the betesticled lance"), *rutabulum* ("poker"), *vomer*

45. Juvenal: Satire VI Most of Elijah's sexual vocabulary came from the Latin texts he had read, construed, and studied atWarrenton—the forbidden passages. If the study of classical texts developed a powerful memory, and orderly mind, a method to express oneself in an elegant and correct manner, it also equipped schoolboys with sexual terms, since Ovid, Catullus, and Juvenal had an avouched sexual content.—*R. Lowe*

("ploughshare"), *falcula* ("sickle"), *natrix* ("water snake"), *vas* ("tool"), *peculium* ("private property"). And then would go on to whisper the obscene word for the female pudendum, the vagina. Over and over again he would whisper *cunnus* and the compound *cunnylingus*.

He would move back the fold of skin, the *prepuce* ("before the penis"), to touch the soft, smooth, hairless, sensitive tip, the *glans* ("the acorn"), murmuring the words over and over again: *mentula, virga, coleatum cuspidem, rutabulum, vomer, falcula, natrix* . . . But the four-inch erectile tissue remained flaccid. How *could* that be? What was wrong with him? How could it be? He longed for an orgasm (to boil over); he envisioned the sperm shooting out, the penis engorged with blood, thick, erect, large! He wanted, he longed, he prayed for, an ejaculation (to throw out), but nothing happened. And the grim and desperate words of Juvenal came back into his memory to torment him: *Et quamvis tota palpetur nocte, iacebit* ("And though they toil the whole night long, limp it remains." Juvenal, Satire 10.)

———

He began to fantasize about Millie, the young woman he had been so passionately in love with when he was ten and who had been taken away mysteriously. He saw her in his mind's eye bathing him; he saw her kneeling by the tub; he saw the towels, the kettles shining nearby. She would say, "Stand up, little master." And he would, and she would begin soaping him, first his feet, lifting up first one foot and then the other. She would call them "turtledoves," her pet name for them, and then she would soap his legs, humming and smiling, and then his thighs . . . and then his "weewee," for that is what she called it. He would stop the fantasy right there, and, as if it were a painting he could enter, he would bring himself up close to that precise moment frozen in time to concentrate on the moment her red-skinned, plump-fingered hand, with the cake of soap in its palm, began soaping his "weewee" and his testicles. Yes, that was it, he would say to himself and then allow the fantasy to continue, himself as the small boy in the tub looking down and watching his penis grow miraculously, feeling the desire to have it grow and grow. . . . She would say, "Ah, the little master is feeling his manhood."

He went over that part of the remembrance, just that part, over and over again. But nothing happened. Why?

When Theodisia returned, he stopped. But one day when she came to visit him and nag him about something—he had forgotten what it was, but she could always find something to complain about—she sat down in a chair near the window. When he glanced at her, he realized with some surprise that he could see through her dress and her petticoats to her genitalia. And he saw something that did not surprise him at all. He saw that she had grown a penis. The "new" Theodisia was a hermaphrodite. He turned his head away. It would be best, he decided, if she did not know that he had discovered the truth about her. Such creatures were not to be trusted. Aristophanes had said: "[Once upon a time] there was a third sex whose name survives though the thing itself has vanished. A man-woman thing, sharing equally in male and female aspects." Hermaphrodite.

He remembered his Grand Tour, when he and his brother had gone to Florence and encountered the statue of Hermaphrodite in a famous gallery. Life-sized, recumbent; the hermaphrodite leaned slightly forward on his arms, his plump breasts exposed, the serpentine, voluptuous body twisted so that one could see both the female sex and the male one. Joseph had turned away in disgust, Elijah remembered, but he . . . he had not. It was monstrous but fascinating.

Theodisia rose, said something sharp, calculated to irritate, and left the room.

After that "revelation" he took to wearing a blanket around his waist, one that covered his lap and legs. Then one day he slid his hand down underneath the blanket and took hold of his penis. It became a habit; he would slide his hand down, open his trousers, and hold his penis. He would strike it. Stroke it and pat it. Even when people came to visit. Emma (though she came rarely), Theodisia with her new penis, Coverly, Solomon, Guinivere, Joseph . . . all of them. He would listen to them, make appropriate responses while holding his penis, and wonder what they would say if they knew.

When Norris suffered another stroke, Theodisia hired a young woman whom Elijah disliked. After she was dismissed an elderly woman, whom Elijah liked even less, took care of him for a while. Then she became sick. So when Isaac Coverly offered to help—he knew so many boys who would jump at the chance to work for such a wonderful family, to take care of such an important man—Solomon begged him to choose one and send him around.

The following week Nicholas sent a fifteen-year-old boy named William Starling, who was called Billy, to be interviewed. Neat, clean, fresh-faced, with the scent of youth about him. It was decided that Billy would sleep on a cot in the room with Elijah. After a while Billy took care of Elijah completely.

Elijah lost his enthusiasm for most of his projects after Billy's arrival. Even his plants. One day he told Billy to take them all to the Winter Garden. What is the point of doing anything, he told Joseph when he came to visit. "It's all really useless, you know. Everyone hurrying about as they do, here and there. And for what? What is the use of it anyway?" Since he had discovered Theodisia's secret he no longer cared about making Theodisia angry. And she on her part stayed away more and more from the sickroom.

One day during his breakfast (an invalid's breakfast of porridge and coddled eggs), Elijah lay down his spoon and told Billy he would have to feed him. He said he was too tired to feed himself. And Billy—good-natured Billy, forever smiling—cheerful, amiable Billy did. After Billy emptied the commode, he told Elijah it was time for his bath. And Billy left the room and came back with the bath, the towels, and the glistening kettles of hot water.

Then Billy undressed Elijah and lifted his wasted body up out of the chair and lowered him gently into the hot water of the hip bath. Looking around him at the empty kettles, steam still coming out of their spouts, at the heap of snow-white towels, Elijah let out a sigh.

Billy started soaping Elijah's torso first, then his belly, and when Billy got to his penis Elijah felt something, something he had not felt for a long time. Elijah looked down into the soapy water, watched the boy's rosy-colored hands wash his penis, his testicles, and saw his penis—his *mentula,* his *vomer,* his *rutabulum,* his *falcula*—get thicker and larger . . . he felt the blood engorging the erectile tissue. . . . He was alive! Without stopping to think he took the boy's head and lowered it towards his penis and with his thumbs opened up the boy's lips. The moment the tip slipped in he came; the semen oozed onto the boy's pink-lipped mouth and then, dripping out of its corner, fell into the soapy water of the bath.

It was over in seconds. Elijah's mind raced. What had he done? What would the boy do? The boy's face—he couldn't see it—his head was bent down. If Billy ran screaming from the room Elijah would deny it. He would deny everything. Why didn't the boy say something? Elijah coughed, and in the silkiest of tones he said, "I imagine that startled you, Billy. I've been thinking lately that I should pay you more for all you do for me." What if the boy refused to accept payment? But how could he; the boy had nothing. Nothing. "Perhaps five shillings a week more, shall we say."

The boy was saying something now but Elijah was so frightened he could not hear him. "Speak up, boy. I can't hear you."

"I said you were slippin' that old horney into my mouth. But I don't think five shillings will do it . . . Sir. For if this be done on a regular basis, Sir, I be thinkin' I deserve more, don't you?"

A regular basis! Five shillings won't do it! Elijah began to laugh uncontrollably. And he had been worried! Oh, thank God! Thank God for street boys. Thank God for Coverly's shelters and their denizens.

"Master, control yourself. They'll hear you and want to know what's going on."

And shrewd and clever and discreet too. Elijah, nodding in agreement, put his hand over his mouth. He cried with relief. Oh Christ! Christ! It works! It works! A few moments later he lifted his head—he couldn't remember feeling better—and asked Billy: "Well, what are the terms then?"

"I don't know, Sir. I shall have to think about it. But when I know I shall tell you, never fear."

Elijah put his head against the tub. Oh, he couldn't stop laughing. He couldn't stop. He must control himself. No one must know what had happened. In particular, Theodisia.

. . . from the moment love has obtained its satisfaction it de-
creases perceptibly. Everyone who has ever been in love
will . . . be astonished that what was desired with such longing
achieves nothing more than what every other sexual satisfaction
achieves. . . .

> —Schopenhauer, *The World as Will and*
> *Representation*

'The world is my representation' is, like a Euclidian axiom, a
proposition which everyone must recognize as true as soon as
one understands it, although it is not a proposition that everyone
understands as soon as one hears it.

> —*Ibid.*

As Elijah was a changed man, so too was Nicholas Renton, though
for different reasons. He had discovered during their stay with Theodisia
at Saddler's Grove, much to his dismay, that he no longer felt anything
sexual for Guinivere. It was not because she was pregnant, though she
was beginning to show. Actually, her pregnancy had given her, even
though she was over thirty, the luster of youth, temporarily at least.

In the beginning of his stay, when he had witnessed Guinivere's almost
saintly behaviour towards her sister-in-law, her daily ministrations, her
endless patience with the childish stupid woman, her warmth, her sweetness towards Theodisia, his love for Guinivere had increased. Bur-
geoned. It astonished him, in a sense it brought him to his knees, to
see the woman he loved, the mother of his future child, carry on day

after day in this unfailing, unselfish course of action. For a woman who did not in any way appreciate or reciprocate Guinivere's devotion to her. On the contrary.

Theodisia had been impossible. At least in the beginning. She had cried, fainted, screamed, cursed, accused, made dire threats. . . . She had even tried to run away two or three times! And she had occasionally imbibed too much, during which time she had flirted with him outrageously. The woman was obviously mad, he remembered thinking. Elijah was right, and he cursed himself for having put himself forward. But the prospect of being with Guinivere for a month had been too tempting.

During the first two weeks, Theodisia suffered alternately from insomnia or its opposite, drowsiness; from fear of open places or fear of closed places, from fear of society or fear of being alone. She often spent the entire night crying, when she would fall into fits of violence and try to tear up her clothing or run downstairs to the pantry and smash crockery. When she was like that she would throw food on the floor, claiming it was poisoned. She was either melancholy, depressed, or feverishly overjoyed.

She had frightened the local doctor who had been called, and he had liberally dosed her with opium. After telling them, "All indications show that her reserves of mental strength have been exhausted," he diagnosed Theodisia to be suffering from "severe uterine irritation" and refused to return though he was summoned.

Nicholas, on the other hand, eyed her as a potential murderer and kept his bedroom door locked. Under these circumstances how could anyone make love? Finally, he grew angry with Guinivere. It was unbelievable to him that Guinivere should put up with her sister-in-law's behaviour in such a totally ineffective and passive way, a kind of martyrdom.

He did not wish to admit it to himself, but the fact was that he was bored with Guinivere's unselfish, sweet-tempered devotion to Theodisia. Nicholas was tired of self-sacrifice, infinite kindness, endless devotion. . . . He was tired of duty, responsibility, fealty, trust. . . . Theodisia was impossible, that was true, but at least *she* was interesting.

Of course he had restrained himself; he had longed to beat Theodisia senseless two or three times. He had longed to take Theodisia by the throat and throttle her. And the things that had come out of her mouth! The bizarre and obscene accusations! She remembered every single thing Elijah had done to her, from the most heinous (he had once tried to choke her to death!) to the most petty (he had taken away her morning room!). And she repeated the accusations ad infinitum to Guinivere and Nicholas as if she had never said them in the first place.

Sulks and withdrawal were followed by abject pleading, on her knees no less, to both of them to be forgiven for her terrible behaviour, but that would be followed by torrents of anger that would, after she had spent herself, be followed by somewhat reasonable and calm behaviour, except that she would begin to flirt with him again. The woman was obviously mad, he remembered thinking. Still, there was something sensual . . . lascivious about her. It made him feel sexual, which made him feel uncomfortable, which in turn made him more angry at Guinivere.

Then one night Theodisia had run out of her room and out of the house onto the lawn in her nightdress, which she tore off. When she was entirely nude she danced around the trees, singing. Guinivere tried to catch her and failed. She pleaded and begged her sister-in-law to come to her senses, to no avail, so she decided (reluctantly) to ask Nicholas for help. She had awakened him (it was two A.M.) and, after reminding him that he should not judge poor Theodisia, she explained the circumstances. "Be gentle with her, Nicholas. Remember: 'Judge and ye shall be judged.' "

They went downstairs. The moon was full and he could see Theodisia clearly, waltzing nude on the lawn. He carried a robe over his arm, Theodisia's robe, which Guinivere had given him. Standing on the edge of the lawn he called out to her, "Theodisia!" When she heard his voice she stopped dancing momentarily and then, looking straight at him, stuck out her tongue. Then she turned around and began dancing again.

He watched her. There was, he could not deny it, a wanton sensuality about her. She glided in and out of the trees . . . sinuous . . . serpentine . . . her body white and golden in the moonlight, her feet suprisingly elegant, narrow, her graceful body gamboling on the silvered grass. Every so often she would turn towards him and smile at him in a secretive, knowing way. Once she cupped her naked breasts in her hands and—in an ancient gesture—proffered her breasts to him.

Finally, Guinivere's voice brought him back to his senses, reminding him of his purpose for being there, which obviously he had momentarily quite forgotten.

He called her name again. "Theodisia," he called, "come to me." And she did. She listened to him, allowed him to cover her with the robe, and then, docile as a young schoolgirl, she went with him up to her room, telling him she would have no one else but him. Asking him in a gentle and subdued way to stay by her bedside until she fell asleep. Elijah's wife! he had thought to himself. Elijah's wife! He stayed with her until dawn.

Finally, how or why he didn't know, in the days that followed she seemed to calm down.

Near the end of the month Solomon had come to Saddler's Grove and begged Theodisia to allow Elijah the use of her morning room. And to everyone's amazement and relief she had yielded gracefully. "She is her old self," said Solomon. A few days later they all returned to London.

One of the very first things Nicholas did on his return to London was to order Toby to arrange for the disposal of the dollhouses.

"Send them to a workhouse, an orphanage, a prison perhaps, or a Magdalen[46] . . . but get them *out* of my room!"

Nicholas did not know why he no longer wanted the dollhouses, but since he was principally a man of action he did not question his decision. The man who had conceived the dollhouses, who had gone to such trouble to make sure everything had been executed to scale, no longer existed, was no longer in charge.

The next thing he did was tell Mrs. Kitto that she could have Guinivere's suite of rooms to use as she wished. Nicholas did not remember the back of Kitto's store as large, but she was always complaining, wasn't she, about the "small and sorry space I have to live in now," as compared to what Mrs. Farnley and Mrs. Bridgewater and Mrs. Page (Mathilda's housekeeper) enjoyed. The four women had become friendly with one other and occasionally met over a cup of tea.

Nicholas still believed he loved Guinivere. She was, after all, going to be the mother of his child. He had already made plans so that he would not be separated from her or the babe. He had arranged to become indispensible to Solomon as well as Guinivere. Recently he had lent Solomon the necessary money to tide him through a small bank crisis, charging him a minimum interest rate. The Forsters' affairs had become his affairs. He was now connected to them by ties of blood. But soon after he returned from Saddler's Grove, Nicholas confessed to himself that, though he still loved her, he no longer wanted to have sex with Guinivere. The very things that had made her so desirable— her gentleness, her purity, her sweetness—now bored him and made him feel resentful. He began to ask himself the age-old masculine question: Why is it that a woman never senses when an affair is over? The Grand Passion of his life was now just "an affair."

It fell on Toby's shoulders to tell Guinivere when she came to see Nicholas—an ill-concealed desperation in her face—that Nicholas was

---

46. Magdalen was the name of the homes for prostitutes who were suffering from venereal diseases in the nineteenth century.—*R. Lowe*

not at home, or though at home was too busy or "not feeling well." It was Toby who was forced to see the confused pain in the woman's eyes, the disbelief . . . the horror.

Toby spoke to Nicholas about it.

"You cannot do this to her. You have a responsibility to her. She is going to have your child. And she is not the kind of woman to fight you on this, Nicholas. Unfortunately, she will accept your terms but she will waste away. She will kill herself quietly without fuss. And Nicholas, if she does, I shall not forgive you. I shall not. It will be your fault. It is your indifference that will kill her."

Nicholas sighed. "What do you want me to do? Do you remember what you said to me, not so long ago, when you found out that I was in love with Guinivere? You said that she was dull and passive. What could I see in her, you asked. And you intimated that perhaps her so-called goodness might really be a lack of imagination on her part, perhaps even a lack of intelligence. . . . Well, what if I told you now that I think you were right. No, wait Toby, hear me out. I love her, I do, I shall always love her, but she is—how can I say it without making you angry—she is boring to me now. Her pale golden hair bores me, her sweet pure mouth, her eyes that I thought I would never tire of looking at, now bore me. *It* is bored." He made a gesture towards his genitalia. "My intellect, my reason, may still love and admire her but"— he made the same gesture again—"*it* no longer does."

"Well, all I can say is, thank God I am too small, too ugly, and too poor to be the target of such a capricious instrument of fate. But that's neither here nor there. What about Guinivere? You must do something. What are you going to do?"

"You are right, of course. I must do something—I will not sleep with her again—"

"Oh no, of course not, but you *will* sleep with the other one—"

"Who are you talking about. What other one?"

"You know exactly who I mean. You may deceive yourself and others, but you do not deceive me. Why do you go so often to Elijah Forster's house? It is not only to visit your enemy and gloat over him. It is to see his wife. Come, tell me, I want to hear it from your own lips, the name of the other woman who interests you."

"You are too shrewd for your own good. But I shall say no more about any of this. I have work to do. And so do you." Dismissed, she left the room.

"The other one"—he liked Toby's appelation. But he did not "gloat" over his enemy. Toby was wrong about that. On the contrary, it had enraged him that Elijah had fallen ill on his own and not by Nicholas's will, not by one of Nicholas's prearranged "accidents." Elijah's illness had been an unexpected collapse. It had upset Nicholas's plans of slow ruin and humiliation for Elijah. It annoyed him that fate had given Elijah the coup de grace and not he, Nicholas Renton. Still, after coming to terms with that, he did go there frequently to view the man who was in the place in society that he, Nicholas Renton, should have been as Jorem's son: the head of Midland Forster, admired by all, the owner of the Gardens, married and producing legitimate Forster children.

In the deepest part of Nicholas's mind he had constructed the following autobiography: Once upon a time a man named Jorem Forster, a banker, the creator of Marlborough Gardens, had a child named Nicholas, whom he loved dearly, by an unknown woman, who, for some mysterious and appalling reason, had been sent to Newgate with their precious child, Nicholas. Jorem had desperately sought the child, and when he finally found him, Jorem had immediately had his lawyer, Jasper Hemsley, draw up the proper papers, and he, Nicholas, was released from Newgate.

That the story did not hold, that certain facts contradicted one another, that it did not connect or really actually prove anything, did not deter him from believing it.

The fact that he loved Jorem and bore no resentment towards him and hated Elijah and bore all resentment towards him also did not bother Nicholas. He acted out of both modes of thought as if both were logical. Still, because there were from time to time stabs of doubt— for there was another part of his mind that reviewed the evidence and found it insufficient—he retained the young lawyer Stanthorpe, the one who had found him at David Kitto's shop, to search out the "hard facts" that would connect him legally to the Forsters. For though the deepest part of his mind *knew* that he was Jorem's son, he wished to silence once and for all the other part, the skeptical part, of his brain with its recurrent nagging doubts.

He began to think more and more about Elijah's wife, Theodisia— "the other one," as Toby called her.

Not only did he find himself attracted to her sexually, but the fact that she was Elijah's wife made her almost irresistible. And there was something else too. Unlike Guinivere, who despite her sexual betrayal of Solomon still loved her husband, Theodisia hated Elijah. And, Elijah was dying. Each time he pondered these facts he began to think of ways to hasten Elijah's death, for the idea that with Elijah dead he, Nicholas Renton, could become Theodisia's husband had begun to take root in his mind. Why not? Elijah was ill. Theodisia was attracted to him. What it would do to Guinivere barely penetrated his consciousness. Somewhere deep inside him he understood that if he presented the decision to Guinivere as a necessary sacrifice on her part she would do as she always did, muffle her rage and not betray him. He was quite sure he could handle her.

The thought of being Theodisia's husband intoxicated him. Something had to be done. Elijah could go on for years the way he was. As a matter of fact, since the boy Billy was taking care of him (Nicholas, of course, knew *what* the boy was providing for him), Elijah was in better physical condition. Elijah's strength was returning. That was not good. So some weeks later, in the latter part of August, Nicholas decided to take an action and change that.

When Elijah had first fallen ill Nicholas had consulted the only doctor in London he trusted. A man who no longer practiced medicine officially, a man whose use of alcohol had landed him in one of Nicholas's shelters. Dr. Francis Underhill had first studied with Corvisart, the man who had tapped Napoleon's imperial thorax with his fingertips, and Underhill had also studied with the great Hyacinthe Laennic, the doctor who had written the treatise on the acoustics of the heart called "*De l'auscultation Mediate*" in Paris.

Nicholas used Underhill, in an unofficial capacity, as a medical consultant for himself. He used the man's skilled services as well, for other more mundane tasks such as removing an occasional bullet or attending wounds that one of his troops might have incurred in the performance of his duties. So, when Elijah had been taken ill Nicholas had immediately gone to Underhill with the information that Solomon had given him. And almost before the family knew, Nicholas knew that what Elijah had suffered when he had collapsed at his club was called "coronary failure."

"What that means, Sir," Underhill told Nicholas, "is that Forster's life's blood stopped feeding his heart . . . momentarily. And had the heart not resumed its feeding Forster would have died. It was the doctor's presence together with the magical drug opium that saved him . . . temporarily."

Now, having made the decision that it was time to act, Nicholas went to visit Underhill again.

Francis Underhill lived in a house that Nicholas had bought for him near the East India docks. He lived there alone with only one servant, an old woman who might have been his wife. Though Underhill worked for Nicholas, he was not in the least enthralled or as impressed by him as Kevin was, for instance, or Guinivere. He was somewhat grateful for Nicholas's financial assistance, which made it possible for him to perform his experiments, but he assessed Nicholas as just one more ignorant miscreant in a world filled with them.

The doctor, seated in a vast armchair, his feet resting on the bronze ball of a fire dog—the house was perpetually cold and damp and a fire always crackled in the large hearth—opened up the conversation with the dry observation that Nicholas did not look well.

"Perhaps you have a stone in your liver, or a growth in your stomach. I'd see a doctor if I were you."

Nicholas was used to Underhill's form of macabre humor, so he ignored it and came straight to the point.

"Is it possible for a human agency to cause a coronary attack in a human being?"

"Ah, I take it you wish to know whether or not it is possible that the particular heart of a gentleman named Elijah Forster, the 'human being' you came to consult me about some months ago, can be destroyed, murdered really, by some outside agency like yourself, for instance." Dr. Underhill had a penchant for coming straight to the point, which is why Nicholas employed him.

"It is."

The room in which they sat held many tables strewn with all kinds of vials and porcelain pots and jars, among which lay a profusion of different instruments, files, scissors, and pincers, as well as various portfolios of anatomical prints. On the wall behind Nicholas floor-to-ceiling bookcases were crammed with Latin and Greek medical texts in crushed morocco. Works by Galen, Aristotle, Herophilus, Diolcles, Hippocrates, Thessalus, Rhasus, the Canon of Avicenna . . .

"An interesting question . . ." Underhill leaned back in his chair and put his long slender fingers together as if he were about to pray. "I believe it is possible, Sir, though there are many colleagues of mine who would disagree. It is in my opinion almost a certainty. But if that is your purpose in visiting me tonight—to find out how to do this, exterminate Elijah—I must first give you a short lecture on the heart itself. Once you can 'envision' the attack you can produce it."

"I am all ears."

Underhill laughed. "Good. Now relax, Nicholas. Sit back, sip your brandy . . . it will do your heart good." Underhill laughed again and began his oration on the heart.

"The heart is a four-chambered muscle, roughly cone-shaped, approximately the size of my fist." He made one and held it up. "It weighs about three hundred grams, less in a female. A muscular pump, really, and although the design is relatively simple from the standpoint of mechanical structure, it is exquisitely sensitive and complex from a functional standpoint. Its action is propulsive. With every heartbeat the blood—your blood, Nicholas—douses down through the caverns of this four-chambered muscle.

"Blood, Sir, is the sovereign principle of life. Blood is the first thing to live and the last to die. Blood is the cause of a short life, a long life, the cause of genius, the cause of cretinism, the cause of weakness, the cause of strength. It is Life itself! And it *must* flow, Nicholas. That is its function. If . . . and when . . . it stops flowing, death succeeds.

"The heart lives on blood. It is fed blood by its very own set of arteries, called the coronaries, Latin for 'wreaths', that rise out of the root of the aorta and are entwined like a vine around it.

"The heart is greedy, Sir, greedy and impatient. It insists on being fed blood, more blood than any other organ in the body and *before* any other organ in the body. Now—listen closely Nicholas—*if* the flow of blood in the coronary is impeded in any way there will occur that which happened to your 'friend' Elijah at his London club—a coronary attack. Mild or severe, depending upon the severity of the stoppage.

"One last thing to know—two words—'diastole' and 'systole.' Diastole is the relaxation stage of each heartbeat between contractions, when the heart fills with blood. Systole is the contraction of the heart and arteries that drives the blood outward. The heart thrives on high tension. That is its heartbeat, its cadence, its music. Now, *if* a man—let us say you, for instance—impedes, meddles, in some way with those contractions, prevents the heart from receiving its *vital* flow of blood, why then—"

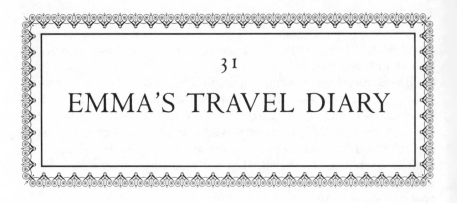

31

EMMA'S TRAVEL DIARY

PARIS, SPRING 1853

THE manager has just told me that he has been informed by a representative from the coaching company that the passes are finally open and declared safe to travel through, and that I should make my arrangements immediately if I wish to travel to Italy. It will take, he said, three weeks to get to the border and another fortnight to arrive in Florence. I wonder whether it will be quite as beautiful as I imagine it from Darius's description of it.

Yesterday the Polish count left for his estate, amid a great flurry of attention from the staff. During my solitary dinner I thought of Elijah. Like the count, he too had lived in a sea of admiration. Equally as handsome. And like the count indubitably masculine. When I was young I thought he was immortal . . . .

⸻ ⬧◇⬧ ⸻

When my father and mother returned from Saddler's Grove my father installed himself in her morning room with his plants, to which he had taken such a fancy. It was his bedroom, his dressing room, his dining room, his study, his hothouse. A fire burned continually in the hearth. The room smelled of burning wood, medicines, food, and faintly of excrement and urine. There were two commodes: one stood by his bed, a tent bed that he had had moved down from the attic, a bed he claimed his mother had died in; the other was next to a large upholstered chair that he sat in for most of the day.

I did not wish to see him but of course I had to. My mother decided that I should read to him. And so I did.

The first sight of him hunched in that chair that he was obviously going to spend the rest of his life in, and the extent of his physical debilitation, dismayed me . . . frightened me.

He had left for Saddler's Grove a convalescent; he returned from Saddler's Grove a permanent invalid, his superb heroic physique—I thought of him in those terms as an "anax,"[47] a conquering hero—shattered. The first horrifying thought that went through my mind when I saw him sitting there, pathetic and ignoble, was that this was what Thersites[48] must have looked like! Debased . . . "the ugliest man who came to Illion." Elijah's hair was thinner, no longer burnished gold; his eyes were sunk into his head; his legs, propped up on a footstool, seemed lame. Useless. Theodisia, who had followed me into the room, pretended not to notice how his appearance had shocked me. She led me to the chair beside his, placed a book into my hand, and brusquely told me that I was to commence reading to him from a book entitled *The Account of a Voyage 'Round the World in 1769–1771*, by Lieutenant James Cook.

"Your father," she said in a smug tone, "has become interested in far-off places."

I would like to relate that I felt compassion for him, some measure of tenderness, but I did not. After the initial shock I felt mostly indifference. I was sixteen then. Soon I too, like Vanessa, would enter society. The world out there fascinated me. I, too, would marry, have children, run my own household. But I had ideas about that. My life would not be like Theodisia's. I would have some measure of authority and control of my household. I would be careful to choose a man who was not the autocrat my father was. Elijah, and all the feelings connected to Elijah, was part of my childhood. I was no longer a child. I was a young woman. My anger towards him vis-à-vis Darius's letters and the Strooksbury incident had not completely abated but it was not important any longer. The present was mine. I felt my own power. I felt potent, alive, vibrant. I viewed him with displeasure. I looked at him through the supreme arrogance of youth. He was superannuated, desiccated, no longer sexually attractive to me. I would not have wanted him to ask me for physical affection; I would have shuddered had I been asked to give it. Not that he did. It did not concern me to wonder what had happened to him. His new state of physical weakness repelled me. I realized, of course, that he had changed not only physically by psychologically. He had an amused expression on his face. Though what could have amused him I don't know.

I spoke about some of these observations and feelings with Clara, who would laugh knowingly and subtly egg me on to criticize him and pick at him further, which made me realize (what a shock) that she did

---

47. Agamemnon was an "anax," as were Menelaus, Nestor, Achilles, etc. *Anax* is the Homeric Greek word for king, lord, protector.—*R. Lowe*
48. Thersites was the name of the lower-class rebel in Homer's *Iliad*, Book II.—*R. Lowe*

not like him at all. At the time I attributed her attitude towards him to his verbal abuse of her after Grindal had come to him about Vanessa. Still, even then I thought Clara's hostility towards my father was a bit excessive. I did not know, of course, anything at the time about what had happened between them.

My measure of independence from him also included a measure of independence from Clara. I no longer obsessed about her. I no longer watched her as I used to. Though I still cared for her approval, it was no longer a matter of life and death. I now helped her with her articles not as her charge but as her assistant. And to my intense satisfaction she occasionally listened with respect to my ideas on whatever subject was being discussed and at times elicited my opinion.

Then one day out of the blue she began to speak to me about her brother-in-law, Johan Lustig. Johan, she told me, was a university student, the University of Freiburg, a member of the student association (Burschenschaften), a follower of Hegel, one of the leaders of his gymnastic club, a duellist(!), a member of the Young Germany movement, and a follower of Welcker.[49]

"He is handsome, even more handsome than your father. Tall, blond, broad-shouldered, blue-eyed . . . a romantic . . . oh, he is wildly romantic, interested in everything from poetry to revolution. Equally at home, Emma, in a salon or a debate. You must remember that Germany is not England, Emma. In Germany every student who is worth his salt is a revolutionist of sorts."

"But troubled and troublesome," she confided in me, "to his family, who are bankers like your father and uncles, and are, as a matter of fact, business associates of your family. Troublesome to Mr. Lustig in particular because Johan, like Franz, my beloved husband, shows no interest in banking."

From then on she read portions of his letters to her aloud to me. Here was a whole new world, another language, another country. The way she spoke to me about him excited me. He was courageous, brilliant, romantic, handsome, daring, defiant . . .

One day she suggested to me that I write him, saying that she had told him about me and that he had evinced an interest in "your English pupil. Surely no one can be as delightful as you have described her to me. Perhaps she may feel inclined one day to write me a few words. . . ."

I did not need to be coaxed. I had already had a dream about meeting him, looking into his azure-blue eyes and falling in love. And so Johan

---

49. Karl Theodor Welcker (1790–1868), a professor at the University of Freiburg, was part of a political and social movement that was liberal and nationalistic.—*H. Van Buren*

and I began a correspondence in English. His letters to me, charming, informative, and calculatedly seductive, were enclosed in the letters Clara received from him.

An enormous sexual excitement began to build up within me, so that I began to masturbate again. This time my sexual fantasy had Johan Lustig at the center of it. Though Clara and Darius had both described human copulation to me, and I had had intercourse with Mr. Strooksbury, I was still rather vague about the act itself. In my fantasy about Johan making love to me I merely reenacted what Mr. Strooksbury had done to me. Except for one fact: when Johan, fully dressed of course, unbuttoned his trousers I saw in the darkness of my room a huge golden lustrous penis emerge, and the sight of that alone made me come. I resolved to learn German, and Clara began tutoring me.

My obsessive passionate nature gradually became as involved in Johan as it had once been in Clara . . . in Darius . . . in my father.

At the same time I could not help but observe how everything had changed in the household. It was quite obvious to me now that the reins of authority had shifted and that my mother and Mrs. Farnley now reigned jointly. All decisions, all orders, emanated from their duel queenship.

And the stream of visitors! Mr. Isaac Coverly, a man I did not really know, but did not like for some reason, came at least three times a week. And Uncle Brian, Solomon and Joseph and Aunt Guinivere, and Aunt Mathilda, now fully recovered and as bossy as ever. And from time to time a strange young black man, tall, imperious, named Pierre Mboza, Miles Ryder's steward, would come to deliver a message. What in the world, I used to wonder, could they, my father and the black gentleman, have to say to one another?

I don't know when I began to notice that Edward, who was now at home, having come down from Warrenton because the head of the family was ill and he was the heir, was interested in Clara. I would catch them talking to one another, their heads close together, chattering away, laughing and playing word games with one another. My mother did not seem to notice, or if she did notice she didn't seem to care. I wondered about it idly, but my head was filled with thoughts of Johan and the possibility that he would come to England. In one letter Johan had written to me he told me that his father had laid down the law: he must study banking or else! His father had written my Uncle Solomon to see whether or not he might not allow Johan to apprentice in his bank since Johan spoke perfect English.

Clara told me that Solomon had written Mr. Lustig telling him that he would be more than delighted, that he would be grateful for Johan's assistance, and that, under the circumstances, he felt it would be beneficial to himself as well as Johan if Johan would live with them while he was in England. "And so," Clara told me, "it has been decided that Johan is to come to England soon."

He was coming to England! It was all I could think about, for though I had not seen him yet in the flesh I was already in love. I awaited his arrival in a state of delirious excitement.

I began to read Hoffman's strange novel *Die Elisiere des Teufels* (*The Devils's Elixers*) in German. His world of demons, a world forever struggling with everyday reality, a world changing incessantly, a world that was not clear or serene but tempestuous and turbulent, an irrational world, seemed to echo my own adolescent state. Marlborough Gardens took on the atmosphere of a dream or a fairy tale.

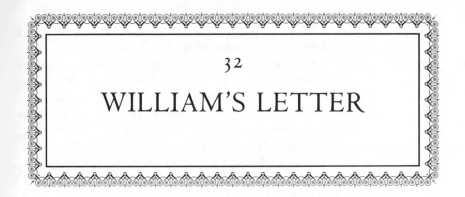

32

WILLIAM'S LETTER

Of the three children William was the sweetest, the most love-
able. But when he went away to Warrenton that all changed.

—Mrs. Farnley's Daybook, 1876

I am sincerely happy I outlived William. There is some justice
in the world after all. Had he outlived me he would have burned
all the Forster archives. He had no family feeling . . . none at
all.

—Emma Forster's *Weimar Journal*

18 DECEMBER 1880, MELBOURNE

Dear Albert,
The answer is NO!
    I am not at all interested in contributing any money for a
special wing to be adjoined to the Winter Garden that would
re-create my father's rare collection of tropical plants. I care
as little or as much for the memory of them as he cared about
me when I lived with him and was in his so-called paternal care.
    As you know, I have children of my own now, three sons
and a daughter. I love them all and I sincerely believe they
love me. I "care" for them. And though I now understand
more fully why Elijah preferred my sister, Emma—I too am
more attracted to my daughter, Sarah—nevertheless I *love*
my sons.

I find it difficult to discuss this with you, Albert, because of Solomon. Solomon was so different from my father. It seems curious to me that you who were so close to our family can be so completely unaware of the difference. To put it bluntly—and the older I get the more blunt I become—your father was a good man. My father, Elijah was not. Your parents had a mutual affection and respect for one another. They were kind to one another and their children. Nothing like that existed between my parents. My parents hated one another and humiliated one another repeatedly; their marriage was in a fact one long painful struggle. Malevolent really. Violent at times. It brought devastation to all of us. I would not have written you this except that ever since we have begun our correspondence you have, unerringly, time and again, put your finger on those incidents in the past that have caused me the most pain.

Those tropical plants, his collection, that you are so concerned about mean something very different to me than they mean to you.

If you remember, my father's second heart attack was followed by a prolonged invalidism in which he could no longer make use of his legs. Mysterious, because the paralysis, according to one of his doctors, had no physical signs, no evidence of physical pathology.

Anyway, by the time I saw him he had already ensconced himself in Theodisia's morning room, the sunniest room in the house.

I remember for the first time in my life I was looking forward eagerly to seeing him. I had had great success at school. I had won prizes, as you know. I had made friends of my own. Edward had left Warrenton to be at home, you were already in Oxford. I was developing a life of my own and I was anticipating my own exclusive relationship (at last) with my father, not as my mother's child but as Elijah's son.

When I walked into the morning room that day I could not believe what I saw. The man I knew as my father had disappeared. Instead in his place, sitting on a chaise, propped up by numerous pillows like some tawdry courtesan, his wasted legs wrapped in several blankets, was a gaunt and shrunken stranger. I could not believe it was the same man. He had collapsed. All the arrogance, the cruelty, the glittering force of his nature had disappeared.

But it was not only Elijah who had changed. My mother,

too, had changed. I saw immediately that the monstrous struggle that had been going on between them all these years had taken yet another sinister turn.

I remember clearly the first time I heard her say no to him. It was in reference, by the way, to his tropical plants. And that was difficult to comprehend too. My father, the imperious banker, the womanizer, the reckless gambler, now an amateur botanist! Who would have believed that possible? He wanted to go out; as a matter of fact, he wanted to go to the Winter Garden to check on some new tropical plant of his. It was raining that day, but it was a very light rain, hardly any precipitation at all. And the weather was warm. Our coachman, Norris, could have wheeled him to the Winter Garden and easily shielded him from the few scattered raindrops with an umbrella. Clearly my father was anxious to go.

"No," she said. "No, Elijah, you may not go out this afternoon. It is raining. If you catch cold it is we who will have to take care of you."

"I shall take care to bundle up, Theo," he said.

"No."

I could see her barely concealed delight when she said no to him. As a matter of fact, she smiled each time she said it. And then I noticed how much better she looked. How much more robust than he. She had gained some weight, but her clothes, all new, seemed to fit her better. And she had changed the way she wore her hair. However, to me there was something vaguely repulsive about this new, what can I call it—energy? life force?—she seemed to possess.

It was not that I was entirely unsympathetic to her. It had been painful to watch him humiliate her again and again. You never witnessed that. Or rarely, for yes, I do remember he used to humiliate her now and then publicly. But at home it was chronic. My school holidays were ruined by his constant snipes at her. Though I was also angry with her. Why didn't she once do something about it! Still, this new development between them was not to my liking either. It was as painful for me to witness this behaviour as it was the other.

Now she turned and smiled at me, jerking her small chin upwards as if to say: "See what I can do now. He is weak now. Each day he gets weaker. Each day more obedient."

Since I could not stand watching them behave that way, I made up some silly excuse and walked out of the room. Later that day she cornered me.

"Why did you walk out of the room?" my mother asked

me. "He was very upset. He told me so. And your excuse was ridiculous, an appointment with one of the twins to go boating! In the rain! The doctor said he was not to be upset. Apparently you don't realize how sick your father really is—"

The nerve of that woman! I wanted to shake her.

"I am sorry," I said. "I shall apologize to him."

"And what about me? You must apologize to me too. After all, I was in the room, too."

"Please accept my apologies, Momma. If I was rude to you, I am truly sorry for it, Mother."

"He would like it, he told me, if you would read to him. Your father has become interested in far-off places like Africa and the Amazon. He collects travel books now. It is his new diversion."

"Is that all, Mother? If it is, I shall go straight to him."

"No. I wish you to accompany me to Lady Devanter-Winter's home this evening. She is being honored for her work at the London League."

"You will have to excuse me, Mother. I am not feeling well. Ask Edward."

"I want you to escort me, not Edward."

I looked at her and presumably what she saw in my face forbade her to pursue the matter further. I started up the stairs to my room. When I was at the landing I heard her follow me. "William, William," she cried out, "please do not do this to me . . ." But I paid no attention to her and she gave up.

I believe it was then that I began to hate him. And to hate her. Seeing him in that condition, totally divested of all the vital forces of his nature, the father I had feared all my life, his hubristic arrogance, his singular glittering wit that had been so malicious, so devastating, that had made him the formidable but fascinating parent, gone, vanished completely—I don't expect you to understand what I am going to say now, for I still don't—made me feel as if I had been cheated. Betrayed. His cruelty, his arrogance, his coldness had heretofore given him an aura of strength and power. And now nothing was left of that hard surface, that metallic glitter, that had drawn me towards him, despite myself, despite the fact that I knew he was morally wrong in his treatment of Momma. Once there had been a sense of magic to him. Once I had wanted to be part of that magic. Now it was gone. I don't know what Edward felt. As usual we did not speak to one another about it.

As for Emma. That was another enigma. Emma, who I know had adored him, worshipped him, now rarely saw him or spoke to him at all. I could have imagined her playing nurse and doctor, never leaving his side, provoking one of those long, drawn-out, cunning, and devious battles between her and Mother—their voices poisonously sweet—as to who would control the sickroom.

Puzzled, one day I ask her point-blank, "Why do you avoid the sickroom, Emma?"

"I cannot bear to see him in that condition."

"Is that why you have allowed Momma to take control?"

"I think she does as well as can be expected."

Her defence of Momma angered me.

"So then you are on her side in this matter."

"I don't know what you are talking about, William."

Her denial angered me even more.

"Oh, come now, Emma. Surely you see that she is slowly crucifying him. Have the two of you decided to band together and do the gentleman in? Women closing their ranks against the man, so to speak? I should have thought *you* would have controlled the sickroom. I thought your life's ambition was to 'take care' of Father and 'do' Mother in."

"You are being absurd, William. I shall no longer listen to you." She began to walk away. My anger exploded. I ran after her and caught her and held her arm. I wanted to hurt her.

"What has happened here?' I demanded. "Why is everything changed? Yes, Poppa is ill, but what has happened besides that? If you do not tell me I shall hurt you."

"Let me go!"

"No!"

"Let me go. There is nothing to tell other than what I have already told you."

I let her go.

As I said, though I had little sympathy for Elijah, it was just as hard to see him being mistreated in his now degenerative physical state by his former victim, my mother. It was as if his arrogance, Elijah's lifeblood, had somehow been sucked out of him and transferred to Theodisia's bloodstream. A melodramatic image, I admit, but that is the way I experienced it.

One of her favorite ways to plague him was by denying him the right to buy a new exotic specie of tropical plant, one that he had set his heart on.

It seems, by the way, that my father was not the only English gentleman who was interested in the Amazon and its botanical specimens. There was a whole coterie of men (and women) who shared his botanical passion. A Yorkshire horticulturist received from his brother, a botanist in the Amazon, a regular shipment of rare plants that grew in the tropical forests of Brazil. Once a month Mr. J. D. Mallory (the horticulturist's name) would send a letter to his subscribers telling them what was available, and the price.

Even after all these years I remember the name of one of the plants my father so passionately desired. It is strange what you remember and what you don't. *Rapatea paludose.* A swamp plant. Quite ugly, it seemed to me. Mr. Mallory had included a colored drawing of it. Elijah asked Theodisia to buy it for him.

To this day I do not understand what financial arrangements they had between them at the time. Apparently, he had given up some measure of his financial control.

No, he could not have it, she told him. "No, it is far too expensive. I have been going over the accounts with Mrs. Farnley. Perhaps you do not realize how extravagant you are. Why only last month you spent thirty-three pounds on those outlandish specimens, three of which have already died."

When my father began to beg I left the room. This time without an excuse. That night at dinner Mother commented on my rude behaviour. But I would not apologize this time.

"I demand an apology," she said.

"Demand away," I replied

"How dare you speak to me that way!"

I could no longer contain myself. Thirty-three pounds! A man who had well over a million pounds! Her cruelty! Her petty tyranny!

"You disgust me, Mother. You and Father. I shall return to school. Please ask Mrs. Farnley to have my bags packed."

I left the table and this time she did not follow.

As you know, I did not return until the funeral.

For a time I wanted to forgive him, to love him; to forgive her, and love her, regardless of what they had done to each other and to each of us. I tried to forgive them, but I found it made me sick, and so I had to take back my forgiveness and replace it with anger. I forgave neither of them and felt better for it.

But I must not complain. Of the three of us, Edward, Emma, and me, I have been the luckiest. After almost destroying myself, I married a woman who turned out to understand me and whom I could love. Australia has been good to me and for me. And so has my wife, Agatha.

Incidentally, my wife told me shortly after we were married that she understood there had been an agreement between our fathers that Emma would marry one of her brothers. But all adamantly refused, though they did admit her dowry was tempting. She was too odd even then. Entre nous, Albert, I feel I must warn you about Emma. She is truly lethal. Pure poison. *Never* believe what she says about me! She is *not* to be trusted.

Families! Domestic arenas for extended conflicts. Family speech! An exercise in evasiveness, everyone speaking in code . . . .

Now that I have said all this perhaps I shall send you some money after all. The past is the past is the past. I am sure if I think hard and long enough I shall remember the pleasant moments.

I will never come to England again. I doubt if you will ever come to Australia. Strange that we who played as children day after day with one another in Marlborough Gardens (those are pleasant memories indeed) now live on opposite sides of the earth. But you met my boys, of course, when they were at Warrenton. They adored you and your father, Solomon.

Before I close I must tell you what Edward disclosed in his last letter to me. (I never hear from Emma, by the way. She lives in Germany now, doesn't she?) Do you remember when we were at Warrenton and Edward would disappear on Monday afternoons and we would speculate endlessly about where he went? Had he gone to the dogs (ha ha) or to the bars, or brothels or betting parlours, or, as one of the twins conjectured, to some private place where he could indulge in onanism to his heart's content without interruption? Well, it was none of those things, Albert. We were all wrong. Edward went to see a Dr. Fritz Hergzborg, a violin teacher, to learn to play the violin. Do you remember how Darius was going to teach him to play and Poppa would not allow it? I always did wonder how Edward suddenly knew

how to play the violin. One day he came home from Warrenton and joined Clara Lustig in a piano-and-violin duet.
But then Edward was very good at keeping secrets. We all
were.

My best wishes to you, your wife, your children, and your
grandchildren.

Agatha is thinking of going home and staying for a while.
Her father, who has been so kind and wonderful to us, is ill.
She wants to see him before he dies. I shall write and give
the exact dates of my wife's arrival if she decides to come.
Perhaps you will be kind enough to meet her at the boat.

With sincere affection,
William

33

CLARA

The year Elijah died was the year Johan came to Marlborough
Gardens. That was the year Clara disappeared.

> —Emma Forster, *The Metaphysics of
> Sex*

I was devastated when Clara did not return. I blamed Mother
for her disappearance and soon after the event I planned my
revenge.

> —Edward Forster's *Journal of Moral
> Inventory,* written for Reverend
> Garth Blackstone

O<small>N</small> a visit to the only friend she had in London—Sophie Hussaye—
Clara sat impatiently listening to Sophie describe the new novel she
had written. Clara had come to tell her friend something that had put
her into a state of despair, but she had not as yet had the courage to
speak about it.

"... *and* it is going to be published in three small 'post octavo'
volumes," Sophie said to Clara, who was smoking one of Sophie's
cigarettes and drinking wine. "Six hundred copies, and they have
bought the copyright for four years! For sixty pounds!" The two women
were seated in Sophie's sitting room on her couch next to one another.

Sophie Hussaye was older than Clara by twenty years. French, Sophie
had emigrated to England from Paris about five years earlier. She belonged to the bohemian fringes of the London literary set that included
George Lewes and John Chapman.

Clara had met her in the London offices of *Blackwoods',* where Clara had sought to interest the periodical in publishing a monthly column of foreign news (and had failed). They had struck up an immediate acquaintance, or rather Sophie had. But Clara, entertained by Sophie's unconventional speech and rakish manners, allowed herself to be pursued.

It was difficult for Clara to communicate with another female honestly. All her life she had moved in society, despising its values, rejecting its purposes, but was unwilling to express her rebellion openly. Though she had contempt for Sophie's intellectual ability, she admired her for fighting unreservedly for what she believed in. Sophie believed in women's rights and belonged to organizations that fought to give women the vote. Clara was too wary of being caught and hence compromised in some way.

"Oh, I have done very well for myself," said Sophie, nodding, taking short quick puffs on her cigarette. "Soon I shall be rich enough to take a lover." She was plump with obviously dyed red hair, wrinkled, had a small mustache like so many other French women, but she possessed a sexual life that was indefatigable. Since Clara had known her, Sophie had had three lovers.

After years of writing romantic slush, using the pseudonym Oliver Henshaw, for the Sunday papers such as the *Dispatch,* and *Lloyd's Weekly,* and even once or twice (she confessed) "writing one of those books that 'are disemboweled out of the filthy cellars of Holywell Street,'" Sophie had written a novel that *Blackwood's* had bought. The story concerned a wealthy heiress from Bruges who married her deceased sister's husband, and it was entitled *A Legacy of Ruin.*

Sophie was the only person in London with whom Clara felt at ease. She had told Sophie about her brief and painful sexual fiasco with Elijah, and even a little about Emma, William, and Theodisia. Lately she had begun to confide in her about Edward. But she told her nothing about Nicholas Renton or Johan.

After Elijah's second heart attack, Theodisia had told Clara that she was no longer expected to dine with the family. Clara expressed the change in the household to Sophie thus: "Apparently the long reign of the phallus has ended in the Forster household, and the reign of the cunnus has begun." She would not have dared to express herself to anyone else this way. As she had expected, Sophie howled with laughter.

Theodisia had given her a choice: "You may dine alone or with the servants." She had chosen to dine alone, of course, but she was lonely. Emma, ever since Elijah's return from Saddler's Grove, had begun to gravitate towards her mother, a phenomenon that had puzzled Clara, but intent on her own course of action, she had not bothered to investigate.

So intensely lonely (a fact she concealed from Sophie) that she had taken advantage of Sophie's interest in her, she now, as often as she could, spent her evenings with her friend. Naturally she considered herself far brighter than Sophie, and better educated, but admired her, albeit reluctantly.

For Sophie had come to London alone and without money, without friends, without connections of any kind, and yet she had triumphed. She had worked, struggled, and—triumphed. Clara sensed a courage in Sophie that she herself did not possess. Whenever she contemplated being on her own like Sophie the faces of those wretched people, the people who had swarmed like lice around the carriage that had taken her through the back streets of Marlborough Gardens to Nicholas's house, floated into her consciousness and drained her of any courage that she might have possessed. Were she to let go of what she had she might become one of them. Swept away into a meaningless oblivion. She was a coward. Sophie was not.

Throughout Elijah's illness as she perceived the gradual emergence of Theodisia as the new domestic force to be reckoned with, Clara had become more anxious. What would become of her? Would she be dismissed? She had written Johan about it, urging him to come, there would never be a better time, the household and its occupants were more vulnerable than ever (what did it matter that it wasn't true; it was true about her, she needed him; he must come), Emma was the prize that he could win, shaken and confused as she was now, a dowry of twenty thousand pounds! "Come, Johan, come bearing gifts, come and claim your booty. Do not procrastinate, give up your baroness, procure your trophy. Now is the time! The golden opportunity," she wrote him.

Occasionally she wondered why Theodisia had not contrived to dismiss her on some pretext or another. But perhaps she enjoyed humiliating Clara. For she did so at every opportunity. Clara had been successfully isolated. She was expected to eat alone, sit by the fire alone, walk in the Gardens alone . . . she was totally ignored by the servants now, and her requests (if she had any) went unacknowledged. Except for Emma—though that had subtly changed too—no one in the household spoke to her. Had it not been for Edward she would have seriously considered leaving or committing suicide. The sight of Nicholas as Isaac Coverly, so entrenched in the family, the godfather of Guinivere's baby daughter—Solomon had asked him; and why not, after all, he had sired it, hadn't he?—galled her. But then Edward had come home from school and had arranged to remain there indefinitely until his father's condition stabilized, and his sudden and eager desire for her companionship had sustained her and given her the hope that her life was not over, that it might actually be beginning again. It was the topic of most of the conversations she had with Sophie nowadays.

"I encouraged him discreetly. I was afraid it would be noticed. But

I was mistaken—Theodisia hardly ever notices him. Only William, whom she loves, and Elijah, whom she hates, concern her. Edward means nothing to her. Her eye glances off him as if he were a piece of furniture. He is almost sixteen. I am almost twenty-five. A nine-year difference. He is solemn, vulnerable in a way that neither William nor Elijah is—"

"Mais je comprends tout!" said Sophie. "The boy has fallen in love with you. Ah, first love! Is that not the most passionate feeling we shall ever experience? Never before and never after is the feeling so exquisite, so painful, but we do not know it at the time. . . . So confess you are thinking that now that the master is ill, that he might even be dying, that the young boy so enamoured of you shall inherit . . . and what might that not mean for you?"

"Really, Sophie! There have only been a few conversations between us, a few duets . . . à propos, he is a fine musician—and you already have him hopelessly in love with me. Believe me, the English temperament is not similar to the Gallic. Soon you will predict marriage."

"But I do, I *do,* cherie. No, do not say no, do not shake your head. There is only one small fly in the ointment. If only you had not slept with the father!" Clara gasped. "But how could you foresee that Elijah would fall ill and Edward would become the master way before it was expected to happen? Ah, yes, Clara, I comprehend everything. It is a difficult role you must play now; you must keep him on the proverbial string so that he will not go off 'half cocked,' as the English say, and tell Poppa that he has fallen in love with his sister's governess and desires to marry her. No, that *must* not happen. That would be a disaster! You see your chance, Clara, and for once in your life you have one. Forgive me for that but it is true, n'est ce pas? Ah, how wonderful it would be to be mistress of that house, to have one's dream of revenge fufilled. *What* a beautiful novel that would be."

Sophie had said all of what Clara could not say out loud. However, Clara pretended not to agree. She would admit nothing.

That conversation had taken place a few months earlier. Since then the boy had become more amorous. She thought of him as "the boy" even though in the last year Edward had grown considerably, and was now as tall as his father and his two uncles. But because he had grown so fast and so suddenly he did not have that manly heft and he looked, in a way, more boyish than ever.

"I have fallen in love with you. I want you to be my wife," Edward had told her the day before.

"Edward, I have forbidden you to speak to me in this manner."

"Why? Why can I not speak to you this way? Why can I not tell you what is in my heart? Do you know how lonely I have been most of my life? And now to have found someone who understands me. Because you do. You have said things to me about myself that no one has ever said. Darius was right, my father knows nothing about love or beauty. But it is people like you and Darius who know. I wish to spend the rest of my life with you—"

"I am overwhelmed. You are too impetuous, Edward. We must be careful."

"Why? I am the heir and he will die soon. Every day he gets weaker. His spirits are good . . . he seems actually happy, but he is dying. I know it. I feel it. More and more every day. He will not see another season."

"You must not speak that way about your father—"

"Why not? You know how cruel and vicious he has been in his life-time. You have seen how he has behaved towards us. Now he must pay the piper. I will not mourn him. Nor will William, nor will Mother."

"Well, if you are so sure that his death is imminent, why not wait a little longer?"

"I want him to know before he dies that I have chosen to marry you and not the heiress that he had in mind. Let him know before he dies how I have defied him."

"And if I ask you as a favour to me—because, as you say, you love me, Edward—to wait until I feel more prepared, will you do that for me?"

That conversation with Edward had sent her hurrying to her friend for advice tonight. What was she to do? Elijah would with the greatest delight and cruelty tell the boy that he had slept with Clara, though his words would be cruder than that. But that would be just the beginning. Elijah would describe to the boy exactly what had happened. How often and where and what it had been like for him. Elijah was a cruel man. His pride and rivalry with his son would make him even more vicious than usual.

Sophie listened, her clever little head already calculating how to out-wit the two men.

"Now, if this were one of my novels, Clara, I would have you poison the master to be on the safe side. Has the thought crossed your mind?"

"I have already bought the poison."

"Clara!"

"No, I haven't, but of course the thought has crossed my mind. If he only would die. Everyone in the household feels that way, I think. Theodisia wants him to die. But she is so stupid she does not realize that when he dies she shall have a new master, and someone whom she has never gone out of her way to please, her oldest son. Mrs. Farnley wants it to end, I think, in order to start the new "order," to serve her new young master, Edward. Now there, Sophie, is a clever woman. Farnley has always and now even more so been respectful and attentive to Edward's needs. The only person that I can think of who may not want Elijah to die is his brother Joseph. Even Solomon I suspect wants him to die now. He is useless to everyone, more of a hindrance than anything else. Everyone wants to get on with his or her life. It's as if the fact that he is alive is in some way preventing us from living."

They had another glass of wine. Lately Clara had begun to enjoy the effects of drinking. For the most part she had abstained from liquor, but now she liked the muddled feeling too much wine gave her. It stilled some of the dire thoughts that filled her head.

"I shall tell you something now," said Sophie, "something that you yourself would have told me. You are such a clever person, Clara. Far more intelligent than I am. I have read your articles and your notes on Goethe. I have been impressed by them. It is too bad you do not have a special man or woman in your corner to further your interests, but alas you do not. Now listen to me—you will lie, that is what you will do. You will tell Edward that you did not wish to tell him exactly what you are going to tell him, the lie that you yourself, Mademoiselle Mendacity, would have thought of yourself, except for the fact, *ma pauvre,* that you are too frightened now to think properly.

"Edward knows that his father—how could he help but know—is a lecherous man. . . . Tell the boy that his father, Elijah, tried to rape you when you were asleep, defenceless, and when you awakened and resisted him and threatened to call out for help he left, but from that time on Elijah has been your enemy. *C'est tout.* That's it. The boy will believe you. He is in love! And for the first time! Then you will ask him to make a lover's vow. His first lover's vow! Ah, how romantic— he will do it. He will promise you to say nothing to his father until you are ready."

The hour was late when Clara said good-bye to Sophie, sincerely thanking her for her advice. On the way home she thought about what Sophie had said. She was right, of course. Clara would have thought of it herself had she been her usual cool, detached self. But she had so many feelings and they were so varied. How did she really feel about Edward? She didn't really know. And Elijah . . .

What a bitter disappointment that had been. And how horrible to see him now, even though she hated him, faded like that, that bright star of a man, for she still remembered vividly the way he had looked the first time she had seen him, the essence of virility. Nothing was left of that, that special force that exuded from certain men that made you want to fornicate with them. Johan was coming, though. It was all arranged. That had been a bit of luck too. She had almost given up and then Solomon had told the family that he had decided to accept Mr. Lustig's offer to use his youngest son at the bank. The arrangement would satisfy both families, Solomon said, because Johan had been wanting to come to London, it seemed, for some time.

Clara knew the Lustigs did not like her. They had tolerated her, but when Franz, their favorite son, had died, they made it clear that they would be relieved if she left their home. His death had undone her. She still felt the loss. Parents. How stupid parents were. The two of them, Elijah and Theodisia, had denied Edward their love without even thinking about it or wondering what might happen to him because of it. So that now she, with the smallest effort on her part, had won his all-too-vulnerable heart.

She and Edward, man and wife; Johan and Emma, man and wife. That was the plan. And it could actually come about, if only Edward and Emma did what they were supposed to do. If she could control them. Emma could be controlled, Clara was positive about that, but Edward was another matter. He was in love with her, but there was a force within him . . . he was not dependent on her in the way Emma was or had been. He wanted her approval, yes, but he anticipated that he would have it, which is something Emma never had anticipated. *That* was the difference. That was what made it so difficult to control him, she finally realized as the carriage drew up to the house.

She let herself out of the cab and hurried up the steps with the key in her hand. It was ten o'clock. She had told Edward she was visiting her sister, who was ill. She opened the door and was about to go in when she heard the morning room door open on her left. Edward was coming out of the room. He looked pale, as if he might faint. His face told her everything! He *knew*. Elijah had told him. And then he saw her standing at the open door and his hands went up to cover his face. "Oh, my God! Clara! Clara!" he screamed, "Help me, help me. . . ." And he came towards her. "Clara . . ."

She turned and fled.

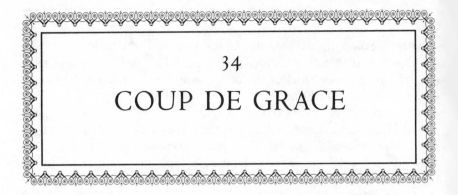

34

COUP DE GRACE

Pallida mors aequo pulsat pede pauperum tabernas Regumque turris ["pale Death, with impartial step, knocks at the cottages of the poor and the palaces of kings."]

—Horace

Mrs. Farnley let Nicholas into the house. It was some time after the dinner hour. Saying he would keep his hat and cane, Nicholas cautioned her not to tell anyone else that he was present, and as a matter of fact to forget altogether about his visit to Elijah, and that no matter what happened, what outcries she might hear, she was not to come even though she was summoned. Having said this he went straight into the morning room without knocking.

"I wish to speak to you, Elijah," Nicholas said, "about something highly confidential. It would be best if we were alone together."

Billy was seated next to Elijah's chair polishing his boots. The fingers of Elijah's right hand were stroking Billy's thick hair. The boy looked startled.

"You had better dismiss the boy. The matter is of some urgency," Nicholas said, staring at Elijah. God, he detested him. Hated him. Felt repelled by him. Elijah looked . . . what? Gelded. The word came to him with a sort of shock. The lack of physical exercise had put weight on Elijah. . . . It had broadened his hips, it had made his chest seem fuller . . . and the way he was sitting . . . his legs crossed at the ankle . . .

Somewhat perplexed, Elijah smiled at the boy. "Well, Billy, leave us. Go and ask Mrs. Farnley if there is something you can do for her."

And his voice, thought Nicholas, lighter, softer, higher . . .

"Well," said Elijah when the boy left the room, "what is so pressing that you feel compelled to visit me at this hour? I am curious. I am waiting. What can it be, Isaac?"

"Yes," Nicholas agreed, "I shall come straight to the point. Firstly, *that* is *not* my name." Elijah looked at him blankly, his face void of expression. "Isaac Coverly is not my name. *My* name is *Nicholas Renton.*" Nicholas was watching Elijah closely. Now *that* bit of information had been a shock, hadn't it? Elijah's countenance had paled. Nicholas repeated the sentence: "My name is Nicholas Renton."

"What in God's name are you talking about! What do you mean, you are Nicholas Renton! And why are you telling *me* this! Have you taken leave of your senses?"

"I thought it was time to tell you the truth."

"The truth, you say! Well, then, tell me who was the man at Jessie Malkin's?" Elijah asked.

Elijah looked puzzled, but not only puzzled, noted Nicholas. He looked frightened. His eyes gave him away. Fear flickered in their centers.

"One of my minions. A former clergyman, a drunkard by the name of Samuel Stokes."

The fear in Elijah's eyes grew. "Why are you telling me all this?"

"Why not?" said Nicholas. "By the time I leave this room you will be dead."

Nicholas had wanted to draw out the cat-and-mouse game with Elijah a little longer, but the sudden desire to kill Elijah, to administer the finishing stroke quickly, had overcome his desire to play it out slowly.

"What! Have you gone mad! Has everyone gone mad! First Theodisia, then you! Get out of my room! Get out! Immediately! Or I shall ring for Mrs. Farnley—"

"She will not come. I have given her orders not to."

"*You* have!"

"Yes. She is as much my servant as yours. I pay her as much if not more than you do." As he said this Nicholas noted with growing excitement that Elijah was deathly pale now. "You see, Elijah, I know everything that goes on in this house. *Everything.* I know, for instance, about Moly, Clara . . . I know exactly what Billy Starling does for you." Elijah was licking his lips now as if he were thirsty. "Billy works for me, too . . ." He watched as Elijah's forehead broke out in sweat when Billy's name was mentioned. Diastole . . . Systole . . . Elijah seemed to be having difficulty breathing.

"Leave me," gasped Elijah. "Leave me, whoever you are!"

"No. That is precisely what I shall *not* do. I shall not leave until I have told you everything I have come to tell you."

"Oh, there is more!"

"Yes, more." Diastole . . . Systole . . . Now to discharge the next shock. "I am Guinivere's lover. I am the father of Guinivere's child—"

Elijah began to shout. "Help! Help! Help! Someone help me!"

Nicholas ran to him and covered Elijah's mouth with one hand; with the other he held Elijah's hands fast. Elijah struggled, but not that much, Nicholas realized with surprise. Elijah was quite weak. Then Nicholas bent his head down to Elijah's ear and in a cold and vicious voice he said, "When you are dead, Elijah, I shall marry Theodisia. *I* shall be her husband."

A terrible pain began in Elijah's chest . . . a prolonged squeezing, as if some outside force had picked him up and was forcing his chest to press together . . . intolerable, insufferable! A feeling of nausea and dread came over him . . . *pallida mors.* . . . Then Nicholas poured the final draught of poison into Elijah's ear: "I know about Emma. I know about Lionel Strooksbury and what Lionel did to Emma—"

Elijah moaned. The incredible pain stretched to Elijah's shoulder, his arms . . . his jaw . . . Oh, he could not breathe! He could not breathe! Damn Isaac! Damn Nicholas! Whatever his enemy's name was. Oh, God! He was losing consciousness. He mustn't, but—Oh, God!—he was. He made one last effort, a desperate instinct for survival rising in him; he lifted his arms, he stood up in his chair. Oh, God, how weak he was; he could not believe it. He reached out to strangle his tormentor, his assassin, and fell to the ground in front of his chair senseless.

Nicholas looked down at Elijah, lying there close to his feet. His face looked cold but also curious. Nicholas took out his watch and noted the time. Eight thirty-two. He placed it among the curios on the small table standing next to him. A moment later he picked up the book that had fallen out of Elijah's lap when he rose so precipitously. *Adventures in the Amazon.* He sat down in Elijah's chair and, turning the pages, began reading the book aloud " 'At first sight the Amazon is a paradise—in reality it is an Inferno, scarcely habitable by man . . .' "

The minutes ticked by. Half an hour passed. He put the book down and went over to Elijah. The body was still warm. He turned him over.

Elijah's heart had stopped beating, his moist skin looked blue. Nicholas felt his pulse. There was none. He lifted an eyelid; the pupil was dilated. It was all as Underhill had said it would be. "Once the blood flow to the heart has ceased, it will take half an hour for the heart muscle to die." Exactly.

Nicholas looked down at the dead body of his enemy and said: "*I am Jorem's son.*" Then he picked up his hat, cane, and gloves and let himself out of the room.

———◆❉◇❂◆———

Edward, who had just returned from a walk, found his father. It was around midnight and just at the time Clara let herself into the house. He looked to her for help. But she seemed terrified and ran off.

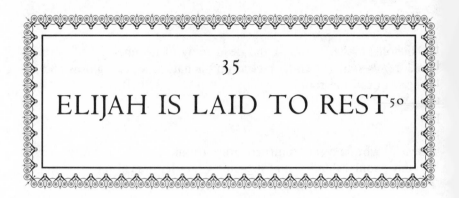

35
ELIJAH IS LAID TO REST[50]

> If a continued existence after death could be proved to be incompatible with the existence of gods, (men) would soon sacrifice these gods to their own immortality, and embrace atheism.
>
> —Schopenhauer, *The World as Will and Representation*

AFTER Elijah's death certificate was signed by Dr. Harlowe, the Forsters let the body lay in the morning room in the same position as it was found, face-up in front of his chair, his arms outstretched, for three days, by way of Elijah's written instructions. Elijah, like so many Victorian gentlemen, feared being accidentally buried alive. When he did not rise on the third day, Solomon had him removed to the library and then sent for Mr. Adderly, the embalmer and undertaker, who had prepared Jorem and Sidney several years earlier.

Mr. Adderly, of Adderly and Company Ltd., whose sign above his door on Holborn Road read "Funerals Completely Furnished, Speed, Cleanliness and Efficiency," came to the house the following day with his assistant, a plump young lad with a round head, named Rowly.

A small-boned, cheerful-looking man, Adderly arrived on the morning of the twenty-third of August, 1842, to begin his work—as he said, "Before grave post-mortem de'ydration commences. *Deo gratias.*" Adderly knew just enough Latin to appease his customers, though he did not always use the appropriate phrase.

Mrs. Farnley ushered him into the library and he immediately began

---

50. This is Emma Forster's unedited chapter from *The Metaphysics of Sex.*—R. Lowe

to set out the tools of his work; a coffin board on which to lay Elijah's body, a sheet to lay under the body, a special soap with which to wash the body, needle and thread to sew Elijah's jaw in place, a sharp knife, a suction apparatus, ligatures, a rubber drainage tube, a catheter, scalpels, scissors, forceps, several types of needles, a decorator (a tapered piece of steel with a groove along one side), a separator made of bone, tubes, containers, a hand pump, and a large vat.

Elijah's body had been carried by Solomon, Joseph, and Dr. Blundell into the library, the place where Elijah's brother had decided it was to be viewed. "His favorite room," Solomon told Dr. Blundell, "before illness overtook him." The large kidney-shaped desk had been removed to make room for the body.

The embalmer and his boy began to undress Elijah. Mr. Adderly instructed Rowly, who was learning the trade. "Rigor mortis has passed away and, as you might expect—Rowly, please take note—the corpse is now in what they call a state of 'secondary flaccidity.' " It was Mr. Adderly's habit to maintain a running commentary of all he did so that his apprentice, Rowly, an overweight lad of fourteen who lived with him and his wife, might profit from his technical expertise. The embalmer had longed for a son, but as he said quite often, "*Ex nihilo nihil fit.*" Rowly was a good lad, honest, and wanted to please, though as Mrs. Adderly kept saying, he was "a bit thick."

"Pale and blotched 'ee is," Mr. Adderly said as they undressed Elijah, " 'Twill be pink dye we'll be usin', Rowly . . . we'll 'ave to add some pink dye to the embalming fluid, Rowly. 'Tis a good thing I brought the stuff with me. Be prepared, Rowly. *Always* be prepared."

The man and the boy removed Elijah's shoes and socks and added them to the neat pile of clothes on the chair next to the corpse. Then gently but firmly they pulled Elijah's outstretched arms down to his sides.

"Now that's a funny way to die, don't you think, Mr. Adderly, wid your arms outstretched?"

"No, Rowly, I don't think about such things. I just does me work. And there's lots of work to do. 'Ere now, 'and me my gloves."

Mr. Adderly lifted up Elijah's eyelids. "Note, Rowly, cornea cloudy, lips reddish black . . . the gentleman must 'ave fallen wi' his face downwards . . . the face is purple, Rowly. But we'll take care of that, won't we, when we remove the blood?" Mr. Adderly was proud of his skill and technique. The "hypostatic" blood would be removed and the discoloration cleared. It was too early in the game, Adderly thought, to teach Rowly the technical terms. Rowly was a good boy, but his wife was right he was "a bit thick." If only he could find a bright ambitious boy . . . .

Now where were the gentleman's clothes that he was to be buried in, Adderly wondered. Not that he would need them right away. There was a lot of work to be done before that. He looked at the corpse of Elijah. Such a handsome man, one of the handsomest he had ever seen . . . and so young . . . half the age his father had been.

There was a knock on the door and a boy came in with Elijah's burial clothes: a frock coat, a clean starched shirt, underclothes, a highly polished pair of boots, a cravat, a gray suit, and a yellow vest.

"Ah," said Mr. Adderly, "the burial clothes. Very good. I was wonderin' . . . lay them over there on that chair, lad."

Billy put the clothes on the chair, taking a long hard look at the body as he passed. Mr. Adderly noticed.

"What's you name, boy?" he asked.

"Billy. Billy Starling. Sir."

"Billy Starling. And the sight of a dead body don't frighten you, do it, Billy?"

"It do not. Sir."

"Hmmm . . . well then, p'raps you can stay and 'elp. Rowly can use a bit of help, can't you?"

"Yes." The apprentice smiled. "I can always use a bit of 'elp, Sir. I can that."

"Well then." Mr. Adderly smiled. "Let's get to work, lads." He picked up his scalpel and said to Rowly, "While I'm doin' this 'ere, Rowly, you can show Billy 'ow to sew 'is jaw in place." Having said that, Adderly made the proper incisions speedily and efficiently, while giving a sort of anecdotal lecture, as it were.

When the job was finally done, the blood removed, the embalming fluid injected, Mr. Adderly massaged Elijah's naked body with some cream. "T'will inhibit the growth of mould. 'Ee's to lie 'ere, I understand, for three or four days and then be taken down to Saddler's Grove, to be buried there in the graveyard behind St. Swithins, the old church where 'is father, Jorem, was buried six years ago. I embalmed the old gentleman too. I niver thought I'd be asked back so soon."

Adderly removed his gloves and began to wrap his instruments in a fresh cloth that he had brought with him. Then he turned to Billy and said, "Well, Billy, you done a good job. You seem to 'ave a real interest in the dead. 'Ow would you like to join the firm of Adderly and Company, Ltd.? You'll be treated as part of our family. You'll sleep with Rowly . . . share his bed. And sup with me and me better 'alf and me four bloomin' girls. What say you?"

"Thankee, Sir, an' I says yes."

Mrs. Farnley and Solomon arranged the funeral, but not until after Mathilda and Solomon fought over the kind of coffin to be used, the wording of the funeral announcement, and the decorations of the mortuary chapel in Saddler's Grove. Mathilda's feelings were so hurt, she complained to Guinivere, that she was actually considering not attending her own brother's funeral!

Between them, Mrs. Farnley and Solomon decided on an oak-paneled coffin with silver-plated handles and a padded silk interior, and for its pall a black velvet cloth with an edge of white silk spread over the coffin. There would be six horses for the hearse—Mr. Adderly had tried to persuade them to convey the corpse by train since a line had just been opened near Saddler's Grove "and the cost is only six pence per mile"— but they decided against that.

Solomon would be the chief honorary pall bearer. He would wear a cocked hat with black plumes, while the other honorary pall bearers (Joseph, Brian, Mr. Coverly, Mr. Redbury, and Mr. Strooksbury) would only wear black crepe hatbands. All, of course, would wear black ties, black gloves, white silk scarves, carry rolled-up umbrellas, and have a white rose from the rose garden of Marlborough Gardens in their button hole.

The body, placed on its back in simulation of natural sleep, was to be viewed in the library of Elijah's house for a week beginning on the twenty-sixth of August. Mourners were to be met at the door by Mrs. Farnley herself. Spiced wine and currant bread which the guests could partake of before or after viewing the body, were to be served in the hall. Theodisia was to be seated at the head of the coffin, with Daisy by her side in case she should feel faint or need anything.

The body would be taken to Saddler's Grove in a hearse drawn by six horses and followed by fourteen mourning coaches. They would be met by Reverend Knolly of St. Swithins in Donnington, who would receive the body at the entrance of the churchyard.

After the funeral, Mrs. Farnley, Mrs. Capacity and her daughter, and Mrs. Serricher were to arrange a dinner at Saddler's Grove for the family and the funeral guests.

Every detail was gone over three or four times until Mrs. Farnley and Solomon agreed with one another, until the solemn ritual had been carefully ironed out so that all could work smoothly. There should be no snags, no unexpected revelations.

In the meantime, Mrs. Adderly had sent over the crepe to be sewn on to the men's and boys' hats, and women's bonnets with their black brims and black bows, as well as black ribbon for their underwear. Of course the women would wear black dresses and mantlets, black lace handkerchiefs, black shoes and gloves.

Theodisia's widow weeds, "it was decided," would consist of a huge skirted black bombazine dress, enormously heavy and itchy, and a black veil that fell almost to her knees. Hair had been cut from Elijah's head and lockets had been purchased and given to Theodisia so that she and each of her children could wear a lock of Elijah's hair around their neck.

When everything had been arranged, each detail attended to all the practical details thought of, Mrs. Farnley and Solomon announced that the funeral rituals could begin.

36

JOHAN

I fell in love. Impetuously without a single reservation, with no regard at all for the consequences. I fell in love; drowned in love; almost died in love. And I am glad of it.

—Emma Forster's *Memory Journal*,
Volume 1, 1884

P ERHAPS the stories of one's youth are best read at the beginning of each spring in meadows thick with hyacinth, beneath April trees at the edge of a grove, where from deep within, invisible among the trees, the nightingales sing of beauty, passion, and immortality.

My father died in 1842, but I did not mourn him until almost a quarter of a century later. At the time he died I had little or no feeling for him. Had he died when I was twelve years old I have no doubt that I would have succumbed totally to grief and followed him into the grave shortly thereafter. But at the time of his death, I, his only daughter, felt nothing. Of course I had no way of knowing that my feeling for him, my intense love for him, would return to me many years later like the eruption of an underground geyser.

At the time of his death I was interested in one thing only: the imminent arrival of Johan Lustig from Frankfurt, Germany. That and only that was the focus of my attention. He was supposed to arrive on the second of September. I knew he was coming. He had written telling Clara and myself that he was. My whole body and soul awaited him. And that was true even though my father had died. Even though Clara had disappeared.

As the days passed and Clara did not return, I admit I was disturbed, though not for her sake, I am ashamed to say. My concern was what would I say to Johan when he asked: "Where is Clara?" But somehow I suspected that she had written to him and told him where she was. Besides, I reasoned, perhaps she would return before he arrived. But what difference did it make? The only thing that really counted was that Johan was coming.

I had plied Clara with endless questions about Johan. "What does he look like? Describe him feature by feature," I asked her. "What kind of person is he?" "Has he ever been in love, Clara?" "What did he do when he was at school?" "What does he do when he is at home?" And so on. And Clara patiently answered each of my questions. I had not met him, but I was already in love with him through his letters.

Despite my incredible self-centeredness I did notice that Edward had been crying; his eyes were continually red and swollen. I was quite sure that it was not because of Elijah's death but because of the sudden and mysterious disappearance of Clara. He had been in love with Clara. She had vanished without a letter, a note, or a message of any kind. Naturally the family thought Edward's grief was connected to Father's death. Not that I spoke to him about it. We had grown apart while he was away at school. Nor was I close to my brother William who had come home from Warrenton calm though a little dazed. The friendship we had once had was no longer.

All during that week while my father lay in his coffin in the library being viewed by the "hordes" coming to pay their last respects to him, I thought of nothing but a certain letter that lay unopened on Clara's desk in her room.

A messenger had brought it to the house the evening Clara disappeared. Mrs. Farnley had put it on her desk, where she always placed Clara's mail. I knew it was from Johan. I recognized his handwriting, and besides, his address was written on the back of the envelope. The day after my father's death, I went upstairs to Clara's room and slipped the letter into one of the desk drawers so that neither Mrs. Farnley or one of the maids would make off with it—or worse, give it to Theodisia or one of my uncles to hold in "safekeeping."

When Clara had still not returned by the third day, I took it out of the drawer to open it, telling myself before I did that if Clara returned and asked for her mail I would tell her she had not received any or that I, myself, had not seen any. Reasoning thus I took the letter to my room, opened it, and read it.

If I was in love before I read the letter, after I'd read the letter I was feverishly in love.

It was dated 2 August 1842.

Meine Liebe Clara,

I cannot wait to come to England. At last, I shall actually be in London with you, and all the people you have written about to me these past five years. I shall meet each one of them at last: Theodisia, Elijah, the brothers Joseph and Solomon, their wives and children. . . . Oh, how my heart longs to see you . . . but best of all I shall finally meet Emma.

Because of all you have told me about her, I feel I know her intimately; what she thinks of, feels, her entire heart and soul. You will see, she will fall in love with me. Yes, and we shall be married, Emma and I, just as we've planned for so many years. Bright, innocent, intelligent, loving Emma . . . I cannot wait to meet her!

The future is ours, Clara! Let us make the most of it!

auf Wiedersehen,
Johan

"Who ever lov'd, that lov'd not at first sight?"
—Shakespeare,
As You Like It

Johan came late. By the time he arrived I had given up hope that he would ever come. He was expected at four with my Uncle Solomon, who had told us the day before that Johan had brought gifts for us, which they would bring with them.

The doorbell rang at three minutes after five. What could have delayed them? Mrs. Farnley, who had just come in to ask whether or not she should begin serving tea, left to answer the bell. It must be them, I thought: Johan and Solomon. It *must* be.

I sat almost unable to breathe, next to my mother, enveloped in her black weeds, on the couch in the freshly cleaned morning room. Everything in it had been washed and scoured, the bed and the commodes had been removed—I never saw the chair Elijah lived, sat, and died in again . . . what did they do with it?—all my mother's pretty furniture was returned. It was her morning room again.

William—increasingly sullen—sat in a chair next to the door. Ever since he had returned home he had pointedly shunned all of us. Edward, in his new role of lord of 43 Marlborough Gardens, was standing by the mantel, his elbow resting on it, speaking to Momma. Since Elijah's death not only had Edward taken control of the household but he seemed to have taken more and more control of Theodisia.

It was but a week since Father had died. A week since Clara had disappeared, but one could not deduce either calamity from Edward's countenance or manner. Indeed, the opposite was true; it was as if (for him at least) a celebration was in the offing. His inheritance had finally come due. And yet I knew he had been crying, for I had heard him. Had it been for Clara? Or Elijah? Or both . . .?

"It is inappropriate," he informed Mother, "of Uncle Solomon to bring a comparative stranger, this Johan Lustig, to our house. At this time—with gifts no less!—while his own brother is lying dead in the other room. What can he be thinking of? To come to us to pay a social call with a new acquaintance, a new employee, really! And unconscionably late besides!"

The door opened. Johan came in last . . . behind Mrs. Farnley, behind my uncle, carrying a large portmanteau that he put down beside him. My uncle must have introduced him to us, of course, and we to him, but I remember none of it. I only remember seeing Johan: Johan standing there in his dark green wool suit, far far more handsome than I had ever imagined him to be.

I shall not belabor the agony and ecstasy of first love, its insane hopes and expectations, except to say that I fell in love immediately . . . as one slips into a body of water and drowns.

Startlingly blond, his golden hair and mustache looked as if they were streaked with sunlight . . . narrow, long blue eyes with thick, straight dark lashes . . . he smiled, showing his perfect teeth.

So this was Johan Lustig, Clara's brother-in-law. The words of his last letter glowed through my brain: "I cannot wait to meet her." A sharp desire to be loved by him went through my body with such force it pained me.

I was alone in the room with him. Everyone else had faded from view. I saw only him. Heard only him. This was the man I would marry . . . with whom I would have children. I lowered my eyes, feeling somewhat dizzy.

As if his voice came from another room, I heard my uncle say something about gifts.

". . . alas, a gift for Elijah too. Of course, when Johan started his journey from Frankfurt a month ago my poor brother was still alive . . . indeed, Elijah seemed to be recovering his strength. . . ." Solomon sighed. "There are things I do not understand. Ah, well, Johan first wants to pay his respects to my dearly beloved brother before he gives you the gifts he brought for you from Germany. Come, Johan."

The two men walked out of the room leaving the portmanteau behind. We sat in silence. I looked up at Edward, who now stood with his arms folded together, disapproving of Solomon, of Johan, of William, who began humming and drumming his fingers on the arm of his chair. I

glanced at my mother. She was staring into space, her face a total blank.
How grubby, I thought, how shabby they all looked next to Johan.
Petty and malicious. They had just met a superior being, far superior
to any of them. For a moment I was incensed. They seemed so singularly
unaware of what had just happened. What was wrong with them, I
wondered, that they did not notice, that they were deaf, dumb, and
blind to his radiance?

A quarter of an hour later the door opened again and Johan and
Solomon returned. The room and everything in it seemed suddenly
brighter because of his presence.

"Tell them what you said," my uncle said to Johan as he came into
the room. " '*er scheint zu schlafen*'—'He seems to be asleep.' Johan
said. And it is true, he does. Ah, if he could only awaken . . ."

"But he has, hasn't he?" said William in that obnoxious, clever
schoolboy tone of his. "Awakened in another time, another place.
Eternity and Heaven. At least that is what our dear Reverend Bottome
has led us to believe these past few days . . . ad infinitum, may I add."

"William!" said Edward.

"Yes, Edward."

"Assist Momma. She has dropped her prayer book."

"Of course, Edward," said William. Rising from his chair, he went
over and picked up the book Momma had just let fall out of her hands—
a prayer book she had begun to carry with her ever since Elijah died—
and replaced it in her lap without ever once looking at her.

"Do go ahead, Johan," my uncle said, blissfully unaware, as always,
of the varying tensions in the room. "Open the portmanteau. I myself
have seen all your presents already. Thoughtful . . . exquisite. And we
have received ours. Also exquisite . . . thoughtful. 'Beware,' I said to
him that first night he came. 'Beware the Greeks bearing gifts.' " And
Solomon laughed as if he had said something daring and original.

"But, Solomon, do you really think—" queried Theodisia tentatively.
I looked at William—Momma was already responding on cue to Edward's directions—but he deliberately looked away.

"Do I really think what, my dear Theodisia? I know we are all in a
state of grief over Elijah's death, but Johan has come all the way from
Frankfort am Main, bringing gifts with him. And so we are bound—
bound, Theodisia, by the sake of *virtue*—to accept gladly and graciously
this good fortune."

William, unable to contain himself, rose to leave the room.

"William!"

"Yes, Edward?"

"Remain seated."

"Johan," my uncle said.

"Bitte."

"Dispense the gifts."

"Wirklich? Ach so. . . . You will forgive . . . I feel like an intruder . . . *seltsam*—"

"Nonsense, Johan. As I said—rather as Aristotle said—the aim of life is pleasure. Come now, no more delay."

"Natürlich," said Johan. He smiled; his eyes seemed to understand all the working of our hearts and minds, seemed to sympathize with all our difficulties. He bent down next to his portmanteau and lifted out his first gift, a walking stick. "It was to be for the master of the house," he said as he walked over to Edward, who looked stern and frightened simultaneously. "And you are that now of course, *nicht wahr?* Perhaps a bit too rich for an Englishman, but my father insisted. It has been in our family for years. It was given to our family by the Margrave Louis of Baden in the last century." His melodious voice had just enough of an accent to make it irresistible.

The walking stick was wooden, its handle a silver sculpted statue of the goddess Aphrodite, made in such a manner that as the owner's fingers grasped the stick they would of necessity grip the coral nipples of her silver breasts. Edward blushed and made no move to take the gift.

"It is too rich, perhaps, too fantastical?" Johan asked.

"No. I am delighted." Edward took the stick finally by its middle and held it that way by his side. Edward was always polite even when confounded. Later, I would find the stick resting in his bureau on the bottom drawer, never to be used.

All the gifts were lavish. Too lavish. Spectacular like Johan himself. For William a gold-plated watch. For my mother a slim volume bound in red morocco, *Goethe's Poems.* He bowed in front of her. "From my mother to you . . ." His profile was beautiful—I was content to merely stare at him—his straight nose, resolute chin, and fair complexion. His silken mustache floated like a golden wave above his beautiful lips. His physical closeness sent my heart leaping. I knew that I was blushing, but there was little I could do about it. I drank in his delicious odor; a mixture of cologne and tobacco.

The he stood in front of me and bowed.

"And now for Emma," he said.

He reached into his vest pocket and drew out of it a small square box covered in red velvet. Bending towards me, he opened it. Resting in the center on its bed of red velvet lay a golden heart. A small diamond in its center twinkled. I loved him. I looked straight into his eyes—grave yet gay—which were scrutinizing me. There was no doubt in my mind. None. He loved me too.

I saw him once more before the funeral.

burned with the fever of love. What I had felt for Clara now seemed pale in comparison. I also knew without Johan's telling me that he knew where Clara was, though neither of us mentioned her.

The following evening I saw him again at Uncle Solomon's house. The whole family was there. Vanessa too. He had been placed next to her. Who had done that unforgivable thing? How beautiful he looked in his evening clothes. He smiled across the table at me. He loves me; I love him. The words repeated in my head.

Throughout dinner I kept looking at him, and he returned my glances, as if to assure me that the presence of the beautiful young woman on his right, my cousin Vanessa, meant nothing to him . . . as if he knew what I might be fearing. Once as my gaze ran to his, it rested momentarily on William, who was in the midst of an animated conversation with Albert. William returned my glance as if to say: "For God's sake; be more cautious." For a moment I felt it as a check on my joy, but then my happiness soared again and I thought, I shall never be happier.

The next day we went to Saddler's Grove to bury Elijah.

The procession to the graveyard was led by two beadles, each of whom carried a long staff at the end of which was a knob of silver. And after Reverend Knolly came the great oak coffin with its silver handles that held the body of my dead father, Elijah, carried by six pallbearers whom we followed: Theodisia, Edward and William and I. Next came Joseph, Solomon and Guinivere and their children; after them Mathilda and Brian and their children. Finally our guests, two by two, made up the rest of the procession.

At the open grave I stood next to my mother and my brothers listening to the Miserere. "Lord have mercy upon us, Christ have mercy upon us, Lord have mercy upon us."

Standing between Solomon and Guinivere, Johan was taller than Solomon, slim, erect, powerful, the ends of his golden hair curled into the folds of his crisp white scarf. I gazed with a fierce passion at every detail of his face, the curve of his eyebrows, the contour of his nose, the firmness of his mouth, the directness of his glance, in particular his eyes, penetrating, alert, and intelligent.

My mother wept uncontrollably. Next to her Mr. Coverly hovered. Behind him was my seducer, Mr. Strooksbury. But I felt detached from all of them and instead invisibly connected and joined to the stranger in our midst, the incredibly handsome young man from Frankfurt.

I barely heard the words: ". . . the grace of our Lord, Jesus Christ, and the love of God, and the fellowship of the Holy Ghost be with us for ever more, Amen."

I watched as the coffin was lowered into the ground and a clod of earth was thrown on it. For a moment reality intervened. I stared into the open grave filled with its new occupant. My father whom I loved was being buried. Dead at the age of forty-two. I felt a momentary anguish; I thought, I shall never see him again! But as I lifted my tear-laden eyes they met Johan's eyes across the open grave and the same passion that I felt before returned. He smiled at me. I smiled back at him.

After the graveside service, as William and I began to walk towards the carriages standing outside the graveyard, I heard a voice that jolted me.

"You needn't bother, Mr. Coverly. *I* shall accompany my mother to her carriage."

It was Edward's voice but changed somehow. I looked up, He was standing there, my brother Edward, tall, arresting, handsome, grave—authoritative. The heir. I realized that Edward's voice sounded so much like Elijah's that for a panic-stricken moment I thought Elijah had risen from the dead. But it was only Edward, his arm curled protectively around our mother's shoulders as he helped her up the coach steps.

I stepped into the carriage and sat down next to Theodisia. Turning my head to look out, I hoped to catch one last glimpse of him. And there, outside the window looking in at me, stood the young man I loved. Once more our eyes connected.

I was just sixteen. At that moment it did not matter that my father was dead. *I* was alive and in love with that beautiful man who was standing outside the carriage looking at me with love in his eyes.

⊹⊱◈⊰⊹

The following day I woke up in a decidedly different frame of mind. The past . . . its tragedies seemed to have a solid grip on me. I found myself thinking of Darius's attempted suicide . . . so young . . . and Sidney's death . . . so young. My own father! Dead! So young! All the sudden elation and feverish excitement that I had been experiencing since Johan's arrival had mysteriously disappeared. That feeling of profound well-being, the understanding that the world was a marvelous and wonderful place to be in, to live in, and that such simple things as the scent of a flower, the curve of a cloud, sunrise, sunset, were but an infinitesimal part of the myriad glories that the world offered; that promise of infinite joy had somehow vanished. And the real truth was that I was alone now. My father had died, Clara had disappeared, Darius was no longer available.

A restlessness overtook me. Suddenly, I wanted to run away. I could no longer stay in our house another moment. And then the strange idea came to me that I must visit Sidney's grave. I must in some way pay my respects to him. I had not done that. I had been petty and mean about his death. I had not liked him. Now I felt compelled to go to his grave. I sensed that somehow going there, being there, would be an atonement for my uncaring. And it would be in keeping with what I felt now, so urgently.

Grabbing the black cloak I had worn to the funeral, I left the house and made my way quickly through the South Gate down the path that led to the enclosed rose garden where Sidney was buried. How emotional the young are! How romantic! How intrigued they are with both life *and* death.

My hand was on the gate to the rose garden to push it open—I had already unlatched it when I heard his voice.

"Fraülein Forster . . ."

Johan! A bolt of pleasure went through me. A thousand thoughts filled my mind. But the predominant one was the dread that I did not look my best. I had rushed out of the house not caring how I looked. If only it weren't such a clear day, a cloudless sky flooded with brilliant sunshine. If only it were cloudy, dark, so that the nevus wasn't so visible. I turned around.

He removed his hat, he bowed. He was about to take one of my gloved hands in his and kiss it when I drew away from him sharply.

Unflustered, he smiled and said, "I am fortunate to have met you alone, am I not? Come, Fraülein Emma, we will walk together and you will show me Marlborough Gardens . . . the temple, the statue of Nemesis, the sunken garden, the Tower . . . Calypso's Cave . . . you see, I know all about the Gardens. That is, of course, if you wish to. But you do, don't you? You will do this for me? I am eager to see and experience everything."

I looked into his face. He was life. He was joy. He was happiness. He extended his arm.

We walked that morning down paths already covered with nut-brown leaves. Fall was early that year, I remember; there were splashes of color, the red foliage of maple, the gold of oak—in a predominantly bronze and ochre universe.

I exploded with information. I felt as if my heart was winged and about to fly out of my body. I told him all I knew about the Gardens. Its history, our life in the Gardens when we were young, the coming of Darius, the battle . . . everything.

When we came to the lake where the black swans lived, I told him about the black swan named Maartel, and the story, called "The Creature of Hope" my grandfather had told us when we were young. I even told him about how when I first saw Clara I had thought of her as that—the Creature of Hope. But that was the only time we spoke of Clara.

He said little, but it seemed to me he listened to everything I said with the utmost attention. It seemed to me that morning as if I were beautiful and that pleasure and the consummation of every flame of passion, chaste or sensual, could be fulfilled. When we parted he again removed his hat and this time even before he reached for my hand I gave it to him.

"Tomorrow, you will take a walk again, Fraülein Emma?"

"Yes."

"Around eight o'clock, shall we say? I love the early morning. I trust you do."

"Yes. That would be fine."

"Then I say *auf Wiedersehen,* Fräulein Emma. It was a pleasure to meet you. I look forward to tomorrow."

Alone in my room I took out Johan's letter—I had hidden it between the pages of my Greek grammar—and read it again. "But best of all I shall finally meet Emma . . . I feel I know her intimately; what she thinks of, feels, her entire heart and soul. . . ." As I read those words all the loneliness that I had felt seemed to melt away, and something pure and shining began to take its place, began to fill my heart. His words touched the deepest part of my self. I pressed the letter to my breast. I felt the power of love. I felt transformed. Transfigured . . . my ideal had become reality, truth and fact were one.

"Oh, yes," I whispered to myself, swimming in a tide of exultation. "Yes, yes, it will be as you have written, Johan. . . . The future will be ours! And we *shall* make the most of it!"

SHADOW OF THE RED MOON

Walter Dean Myers

illustrations by
Christopher Myers

SCHOLASTIC
HARDCOVER

SCHOLASTIC INC.

NEW YORK

High School Library
Mooseheart Illinois
60539

Copyright © 1995 by Walter Dean Myers

All rights reserved. Published by Scholastic Inc.

SCHOLASTIC HARDCOVER is a registered trademark
of Scholastic Inc.

No part of this publication may be reproduced, or stored in a retrieval
system, or transmitted in any form or by any means, electronic,
mechanical, photocopying, recording, or otherwise, without written
permission of the publisher. For information regarding permission,
write to Scholastic Inc., 555 Broadway, New York, NY 10012.

Library of Congress Cataloging-in-Publication Data
Myers, Walter Dean, 1937–
Shadow of the red moon / Walter Dean Myers.
p.   cm.
Summary: As the Fens attack his home in Crystal City, fifteen-year-old
Jon is sent into the Wilderness with other young Okalians to search for
the Ancient Land, but what he finds is something very
different.
ISBN 0-590-45895-7
[1. Fantasy.]   I. Title.
PZ7.M992Sh   1995
[Fic]—dc20   94-42298
CIP
AC

12 11 10 9 8 7 6 5 4 3 2 1   5 6 7 8 9/9 0/0

Printed in the U.S.A.   37
First printing, November 1995

PROLOGUE

This is the story of a people. They call themselves Okalians, which means "The People Who Dream Greatly." The Okalians trace their history back to a time when stories were not written, but passed from generation to generation by word of mouth. Eventually they came to write their story in the Book of Orenllag. The Book became the legend of their triumph, their rise to greatness. It was the truth as they knew it to be, and the truth by which they would try to live.

They had settled in the southern part of the land, where the sea formed a protective border and the foods were plentiful. Here they lived in peace and security for tens upon tens of generations. Then came the calamity, which, according to their own legend, was one of the trials that proved their greatness.

There had been first a great disturbance in the sky. The rains poured heavily for six days and lightning ripped across the horizon like the brilliant fingers of an angry god. Some said they saw the meteor when it first appeared, others saw it only after it had broken into a thousand smaller meteors burning in the night air before crashing heavily to the ground, lifting a great black cloud that rose many times higher than the mountains. The entire sky darkened with the thick, choking dust and all the world was plunged into a numbing cold. All living creatures suffered. It was then that the Okalians were forced to leave their homes and journey across the Wilderness looking for a place free from the settling dust, where they could begin to build and to renew their lives.

When they found this higher ground, this place of new beginning, they built a city whose walls were made of solid crystal. The crystals held what little sunlight filtered through the dust and made life bearable. Even though this Crystal City, as they called it, was a wondrous invention, life for the Okalians had still been hard. But they had survived, and in their surviving had become stronger and more convinced of their greatness.

The dust eventually grew less dense and the world began to warm. They saw that a New Moon had appeared in the distance. Unlike the Red Moon they had always known, the New Moon seemed cold and menacing. Some saw it as a good sign and thought it was the omen of a new prosperity, a new tranquility. But with the warming of the world came the great plague.

The Okalians, behind the protective walls of Crystal City, were not affected by the plague, but were witness to its terrible effect. Whoever was exposed to the plague, with few exceptions, was struck down between the sixteenth and seventeenth year, creating in the Wilderness a world composed almost completely of children. When this was discovered, the Elders in the Crystal City decided to lock their gates and keep out the plague, and all strangers who might bring it into the city were turned away.

Of all the people who once lived in the Wilderness, the Na'ans, the Kargs, and the Fens, the people most affected by the plague were the Fens. Many of the Fen children immediately died of starvation or were killed by roaming bands of wild animals. Only the strongest survived, those almost as wild as the animals that attacked them. The Fen children formed their own society and began to dominate the hard world about them. In the process they wrote no book, but did create their own version of truth and seek their own place in the world. Not finding such a place in the Wilderness, they finally turned their eyes to the Crystal City, the one place that had been closed off to them, that had shut them out.

on was so scared. So scared. They had told him that it was the Okalian children who would save their world, but they didn't tell him anything about how scared he would be. The Fen children had been surrounding Crystal City for months, hurling rocks and stones and sharpened flints, trying to tear their way inside the gleaming walls. Months before, in the middle of the night, they had sent out nearly a hundred Okalian children, who attempted to steal through the Fen camps. But the signal fires they were supposed to light were never seen and no one in Crystal City knew how many, if any, had survived. Now the Fens had made cracks in the walls, and it was only a matter of time before they broke through.

"You are the hope of our people," his father had said. "You last children."

There were only twenty-four Okalian children left in the city. Everyone sixteen and over stayed back to hold off the Fens. The youngest children, those under six, were kept with their families. The others were going out of the tunnels, one by one. It was hoped that the older children and the adults could hold off the Fens long enough for the twenty-four of them to make their way through the ventilating tunnels and into the Wilderness. From there they would have to find a way back to the Ancient Land, to make a new start for the Okalians.

The tunnel was inky dark. Jon couldn't see his hands in front of his face as he edged along the damp wall. There was a slight breeze, cool wind in his face, as he neared the opening that led to the grounds outside the tunnel. In the distance he could hear noises. He imagined what they would be. Sounds of battle? Sounds of people crying out in agony? Don't think, he told himself. Just get to the entrance to the tunnel.

He sucked in as much cool air as he could as he reached the grating that covered the tunnel.

He pushed on the grating. At first it didn't move, and he panicked. He didn't want to be trapped in the tunnel, to have the Fens find him there. He clenched his teeth and pushed with all of his strength. One side of the grating gave way and then the other. He pushed it aside and climbed out. He was on his hands and knees. The ground was wet and icy cold. He crawled forward, lifting his head, squinting his eyes.

He remembered that there were two hundred and sixty paces between the walls of Crystal City and the first stand of trees. Pushing himself to his feet, he tried to remember in what direction the trees were.

For a moment an image of his mother came to him. It was the look on her face as she watched him go through the door for the last time. The noises of the fighters had been getting louder and louder. He had been so scared. There was such a terrible look in her eyes, such a desperate, terrible look. They were losing each other and they both knew it.

"It is only our children who can save us," his father had said. "They are the ones who must carry our dreams."

Jon wiped quickly at the tears in his eyes and started forward. Just as he spotted the trees a torch flared to his left. The Fens were starting fires near the tunnels. Jon dove to the ground. A sharp pain ripped through his knees and he clenched his fists tightly to keep from crying out. From somewhere in the darkness there were screams and shouting. The Fens had found the tunnels and were attacking them.

The noises, the cries, seemed to come from everywhere. Jon looked back toward the tunnel. He saw, or he thought he saw, shadows moving behind him. He forced himself to crawl forward for a while, then to stand and run as fast as he could toward the darkness of the trees. Behind him an alarm clanged noisily, drowning out all other sounds. The outer walls had been penetrated. The Fens were in Crystal City!

He reached the first line of trees and went on, stumbling through the darkness, his breath coming in short, rasping gasps, his knees aching, the low tree limbs tearing his face in the darkness. His heart pounded wildly and small whimpering sounds came from his throat.

He kept running away from Crystal City. He ran until he couldn't run anymore, until his body screamed with pain and his legs, heavy with fatigue, just stopped moving. Ahead of him he saw the outline of a gnarled tree, its petrified branches splintered and twisted as they had been for a hundred years. He pulled himself into it, climbed as high as he could, and clung desperately to the thick trunk. He looked back toward Crystal City and saw it surrounded by the flickering lights of a hundred torches bobbing in the night.

He clung to the tree limb with all his might. He thought about his mother again. He had been glad to leave when he heard the sounds of the battle. For all of her heartbreak and his father's talk about being proud of being an Okalian, nothing had mattered to him but how scared he had been, how he had wanted to escape.

He was afraid to stay in the tree, and afraid to let it go. Scenes flashed through his mind. The children sitting together when they were told who was to try to break out, and who was to remain behind.

"Plagues end," the Elder had said. "We don't know if this plague has ended. If it has not ended, then it won't do us any good to have the adults or older children leave the city. You are the ones who are left, and you can save that precious ideal of what it means to be an Okalian."

He hadn't said anything about the Fen children who lived in the Wilderness, who were attacking them.

Jon told himself that he would reach the Ancient Land. That somehow all of the Okalian children would make it there and be safe again. Maybe, he told himself, the Fens would spare the others in Crystal City once they had broken through the walls. He searched himself for hope, for some small comfort he could believe in, but the only thing he could find was his cold cheek against the tree and the awful sense of being more alone than he had ever been. After a long time he fell asleep.

He woke with a start. The sky was barely light, the day a gray, silent veil around him. He looked toward Crystal City. It was farther away than he had thought it would be, but he could still see it through the mist. Fires from the attack still burned. Where the gold and crystal spires had once gleamed, there were curled wisps of black smoke. Even as he watched, another tower crumbled, seeming first to bow, then to lean heavily to one side before finally falling.

"Move." He spoke the word aloud to himself. He had to keep moving.

Each of the children had been given directions to reach the land where the Okalians had first found their greatness. There had been disputes among the elders as to how far away it was, and what dangers lay ahead of them, but with the Fens breaking through their defenses, it was their only hope.

There were no signs of Fens near him. Had they all rushed to the Crystal City? What were they doing there? Don't think, just keep moving.

Jon searched the skies until he found the twin Shan stars. He remembered his mother holding him on her knee when he was a child

10

and pointing them out to him. She made a little rhyme about them, how if he were good they would point to his true love.

"All in due time, of course," she had said, smiling. "All in due time."

He lined up the Shan stars with his hand, pointed to the direction they indicated, and started walking.

He told himself that he wouldn't look back at Crystal City, but he did. Turning, he shielded his eyes with his hand and searched the horizon. A misty fog had already partly concealed the city of his birth. He thought he saw lights still on, but wasn't sure. He had always been taught to celebrate the wonders of the city, and the wonders of being an Okalian who lived there. Now there was a sadness about the distant shapes that seemed less than solid, almost less than real.

They hadn't been given maps, but they had all memorized the Book of Orenllag and the story of how the Okalians had left the Ancient Land after the meteor and the great dust clouds. The book had been started at Orenllag, and had been finished in Crystal City. Jon thought he might add to it when they reached the Ancient Land.

The land was rough, mountainous. He knew he should come to a river soon. There was a ridge ahead of him and he headed for it, going to his knees as he reached it.

He made his way slowly along the rising earth, feeling his feet slip as the crusted ash gave way beneath him. At the top of the ridge he flattened himself before looking over. Below him was a narrow gorge, only half filled with dark water, and a small wooden bridge that crossed it. For a brief moment he felt a sense of joy, glad to find something he had heard about, but had never seen. But the joy quickly changed to horror. For there, sitting to one side of the bridge, was a Fen.

Before the plague, the Fens, according to Okalian history books, had been a hardy people who devoted most of their time to simple survival. Some, his father had said, seemed capable of more advanced living and even some ingenuity, but it was not the rule.

"But . . . ?" Jon had glanced toward where his mother was mending a shirt.

"Your mother has some Fen blood in her," his father had said. "There was a time when we traded with them."

Jon looked down at the Fen guarding the bridge. It was a boy who looked nothing like his mother. His mother was small, and thin, but graceful in every movement. The Fen below

was short and squat. His hair was red, much lighter than Jon's. Most of the Fens had red hair.

Jon was thinking of turning back, looking for another way to cross the river, when something moved in the tall grass to his left. He looked closely and saw two figures. They were dressed as he was, in tunics and pants instead of the animal skins the Fens wore. They were Okalians.

on caught his breath sharply. It was wonderful to see Okalians. Wonderful. He wanted to stand up and shout to them, to scream out that he was there, too. But just a glance at the Fen near the bridge and he knew he didn't dare give away his position.

From where he was, Jon couldn't tell if the Okalians were boys or girls. He looked for a way to signal them, a small stone, something. He looked back to the bridge, and saw that another Fen had neared it. Jon watched the Fen as he moved slowly, carrying what looked like a bundle of sticks. The Fens had short, stocky legs and seemed to rock from side to side as they walked.

He looked back to where the Okalians had been and at first didn't see them. He felt a moment of panic, a moment in which his stomach seemed to clench and his breath stop. Then he

15

saw them again. They had moved a little closer to the bridge and were huddled together behind a wide, gnarled tree. Jon put his hands flat against the ground and started inching his way down the side of the hill.

By the side of the bridge the two Fens were putting branches into a pile.

He looked back toward the Okalians and saw that they were looking right at him. He lifted his hand and waved nervously, keeping a watchful eye out for the Fens.

The girl looked a year, perhaps two years, older then the boy. She nodded and pointed toward the Fens. Her hair was long and black and she had it tied around her head so that from the distance it had been hard for Jon to see that she was a girl. But up close she was very pretty, with large dark eyes that held him in her gaze. The boy with her looked as if he might be her brother.

"My name is Jon." He whispered when he had reached them. "Are you all right?"

"Yes," the girl said.

The boy didn't answer and Jon saw that his face had been badly scratched. A rag had been tied around his waist and Jon thought that the dark stain on it might have been blood.

"We have to try to make it across the bridge," Jon said. "All the routes go that way."

16

The girl nodded. The boy was on his knees, looking at the Fens. His chest went up and down quickly and Jon could hear him suck in the cold air.

"Can you go first?" the girl asked.

"Y-yes," Jon answered.

He looked down at the Fens and then at the bridge. If they wandered just a little farther away, he thought he could get across the bridge without being caught. He looked back at the girl. She was holding the boy's shoulders, making him look into her eyes. Jon knew the boy was scared. So was he.

He watched the two Fens who guarded the bridge. They had their fire going now, and pushed branches onto it. They had already cleared the area around them and now were moving farther and farther away to gather wood. Jon waited until they were both a distance from the bridge with their backs turned.

He ran as fast as he could, pumping his legs furiously.

Halfway across the long bridge Jon's leg began to cramp up, but he didn't stop until he had reached the far side. He turned around and saw the other two Okalians running across the bridge with the Fens close behind them.

"Come on! Faster!" Jon called to them. He started backing away as they came closer.

The two Okalians ran as fast as they could. The Fens, who had been gaining on them, began to fall back.

When the boy and girl had crossed the bridge, Jon started to run again. He looked over his shoulder and saw that the Fens had stopped once they had crossed the bridge. The three Okalians kept running, the boy and girl close behind Jon, until they had gone past a rock-strewn field and collapsed in a patch of coarse grass. The Fens were nowhere in sight.

Jon sat up, trying to catch his breath. "We can rest here for a minute or two," he called to the girl. His chest was pounding. "Then we'd better move on."

"Go away!" the boy spit the words out angrily. "Go away!"

Jon looked at the boy for a moment, then at the girl as she sat on the ground, her back against a rock.

The girl seemed all right, but the boy was scratched, and maybe wounded. Still, Jon was glad to see both of them.

The coarse grass cut his hands and he had to shift position to get comfortable. The field was nearly flat. They would have to find a place with more shelter, Jon knew. He didn't know where they were, or how far it was from one landmark to the next. He only knew that somewhere in the vast area they called the Wilderness, he would have to find them. When the Okalians had made the long journey from the Ancient Land to the place on which they had built Crystal City, they had crossed all of these places, and had written them down in the Book of Orenllag.

First there would be the Plain of Souls and, somewhere to the west, the Swarm Mountains. There, if anywhere, the water would be pure. There would also be the chance of finding fruit trees. But the first thing they needed to do was to get out of the field they were in.

"I think we should move on," Jon said. "In case the Fens are following us."

The boy looked away. Jon turned and started slowly across the field. It took a few minutes for the girl to catch up with him. The boy was trailing them.

"Is he all right?" Jon asked the girl.

"Yes," she said. Her voice was flat, labored. Up close she looked to be about fourteen, the boy twelve, no older.

"Have you seen other Okalians?" Jon asked them.

"We were in the first group that left," she said. "We were attacked as soon as we left and we split up. Kyra and I stayed together. I haven't seen any of the others since then."

"Have you seen other Fens?"

"Fens, yes," she said. "And dogs."

"Dogs?"

"I think they were dogs," she said. Her voice was husky, and she spoke slowly. "They were strange, though."

"Did I tell you my name was Jon?"

"I'm Lin, my brother is Kyra," she said. "He's had a hard time."

She didn't go on.

They walked across the field, looking back frequently to see if they were being followed. Jon knew that there would be Fens all along their route, and that they would have to be watchful. He wondered what Lin meant when she said her brother had had a hard time.

The Plain of Souls was a long stretch of rolling hills and ravines. There were trees dotted across the landscape, but little greenery. The whole area had once been covered by a thick, gray layer of dust. Now there was some green, some few signs of new life.

The sky above them was a patchwork of reds and golds. In the distance it was darker, almost brown. Jon remembered seeing the sky from Crystal City. It was beautiful when it was safe.

"I don't think they've followed us," Jon said,

stopping near a small plant. "But I think we might be better off if we travel together."

"Why?" Lin asked.

"We can take turns resting and being on guard," Jon said. "And . . . I really don't want to be out here alone."

"Neither do I." Lin stopped a distance from him.

"You look like a Fen." Kyra's face was puffy.

"No, he doesn't." The girl spoke quickly. "It's just that you don't see many Okalians with red hair."

"My mother was part Fen," Jon said. "Tell me about the dogs."

"There were two of them, and they walked side by side," Lin said. "They were so close I thought it was one animal with a lot of legs."

"Everything is scary out here," Jon said.

"I'm not scared!" Kyra's voice was defiant.

Lin put her hand over her brother's. "What route were you given?"

"To follow the twin Shan stars," Jon answered. "East of the Plain of Souls, across Gunda's Hope, then to the Swarm Mountains, Orenllag, and then the Ancient Land."

"We went out before the Fens had actually started the attack. We headed west of the Plain," Lin said. "But we ran into the Fens

High School Library
Mooseheart Illinois
60539

21

about four days out. There were five of us. I don't know what became of the others."

As she talked, Jon tried to remember whether he had seen her in Crystal City. He thought he might have spoken to her once when he discovered her playing a lute in one of the city's three gardens. She had been younger then, and the times more peaceful.

"You can travel with me," Jon said.

"We don't want to travel with you," Kyra said. "You're part Fen!"

Jon turned to face Kyra. He was almost as tall as Jon, but his face was rounder, his eyes set deeply beneath a high forehead.

"Whatever you want," Jon said. He wasn't going to defend his mother's having been part Fen, not out here in the Wilderness.

"I want to travel with you," Lin said. A swirl of dust rose up from the ground in front of them and spun skyward for a brief instant before seeming to fold in on itself and settle again to the earth. "We only have each other."

"Good." Jon touched Lin's shoulder lightly.

He started to walk again, and saw from the corner of his eye that both Lin and Kyra were following. He was glad.

They walked for hours, until Jon's knees ached with the effort. There were few places to walk in Crystal City; it was less than seven kilometers wide and most of it was taken up either with living spaces, centers where they grew the food they ate, the gardens, or the Societal Planning Centers. It was in the Planning Centers that they exercised three times a week. Okalians over fifteen, before the Fen attacks began, could go out of the City to hunt for new foods, or the occasional piece of fruit. Both men and women over eighteen went out once a week on safety patrols. It was on one of these patrols that they had first learned that the Fens were planning to attack them.

Jon slowed down when he thought they should rest. Lin and Kyra at first slowed down, then Kyra moved ahead.

"I thought we could stop here," Jon said, stopping in a field of coarse grass. "There's enough shelter and we can take turns sleeping."

"All right," Lin said.

She went a short distance from him and sat on the ground. Kyra turned back to her, but, instead of sitting, walked back and forth nervously.

Jon took his boots off and realized that the side of his ankle was sore. His feet and legs ached. He looked over at Lin. She saw him looking and turned away.

The night was relatively clear and he searched the sky for the twin stars. He found them and drew an arrow on the ground pointing in the direction indicated by lining up the two stars. Far to the south, like a red eye burning over the brooding hills, was the Red Moon that hung over the Ancient Land.

"I think I've seen you at Crystal City," he called to Lin. "You were playing a lute. I said something to you."

"I don't remember you," Lin said. "But I know who your mother is. She's a small woman, almost fragile."

"Yes." Jon closed his eyes. An image of his mother, he had never thought of her as fragile, came to him. The fear he felt when he heard the sounds of the fighting, when he saw the changed looks on the faces of the adults, had entered him, had filled his chest like a vulture consuming him. Maybe it was just the way his body reacted, heart pounding, arms and legs trembling, mouth dry, that made him think so much of himself, to fear so much for himself. Now, in a moment of relative calm, he thought of his mother, and every feeling that had gathered in his chest rose into his throat and filled his eyes with tears. He rolled onto his stomach and put his face on the ground.

He woke with a start, opening his eyes to a sky shimmering with the first rays of sunlight. He didn't see or hear anything wrong, but he knew something had awakened him. Then there was a noise from somewhere ahead of him in the deep grass.

"Lin?" He looked around for Lin and her brother. He didn't see them.

The noise ahead of him sounded like something thrashing about through the grass. He imagined Fens. Pushing himself up slowly, he edged toward the sound. Then it stopped. Jon listened. He heard something that could have been heavy breathing.

In the middle of the clearing, standing in a shaft of morning light filtering softly through the low treetops, was a black unicorn. It was caught in a trap of thick vines, which bound its legs.

The unicorn's eyes rolled wildly as it twisted and turned trying to free itself. Its coat was shiny, and sweat foamed like pearl droplets on its powerful neck. The sun glinted off its black body as it reared back and twisted in a vain effort to free itself. Then it fell to one side and pawed at the vines with its feet. For a while it was still, and then it began to struggle again.

"What are we going to do?"

Lin's voice startled Jon and he jumped. She smiled at him and he smiled back.

"I don't know," he said. "Do you have any ideas?"

"When he moves, the vines tighten," she said.

"He needs help. We could free him if he lets us get close enough."

"Could be," Jon said. He looked around for a loose branch and found one. He picked it up and it broke in his hand. He looked over to where Lin, and now Kyra, watched.

Jon took a step toward the unicorn. The frightened animal twisted and tried to pull away from him.

"It's going to hurt itself," Lin said.

"Somebody set this trap," Jon said. "If we're going to free it, we'd better do it quickly!"

He went toward the unicorn again and it tried to wrench away from him.

"Remember the unicorns back in Crystal City?" Lin said. "If you approach them gently, they don't run away."

"If this one is from Crystal City it's probably been through as much as we have," Jon said. "It's terrified, and we can't spend too much time here."

Jon looked for another branch, picked up several before he found one that didn't break, and poked it toward where the vine had been tied to a tree. The unicorn lunged at the branch, only to be pulled up sharply by the vines. It fell again. Lin ran to the tree and tried pulling at the vine.

"Kyra, help us!" Lin called to her brother. Jon

looked over at the boy, who shook his head and backed away.

Jon pushed the branch toward the unicorn to distract him as Lin struggled with the vine.

"Kyra!" Lin called to her brother again and this time he went flying toward her. He threw his weight against the vine, pulling with everything he had. One vine came loose but there was another one to deal with, too. Jon took a deep breath, and went quickly to the unicorn. He put his arms around the unicorn's neck and held on as tightly as he could.

The unicorn shook violently in his grasp, knocking Jon away. The animal lunged at Jon once and then turned toward Lin and Kyra.

"He's free!" Lin cried as she scrambled away.

The unicorn snorted, twisted, and leaped nearly straight into the air. Then, realizing it was free, it lowered its great head and raced off with long, powerful strides.

Jon, struggling to catch his breath, watched as the unicorn moved easily along the far edge of the field.

"It's so beautiful," Lin said. "But we'd better get out of here. If there are any Fens around, they had to have heard us."

They started out again, talking about the unicorn. Okalians didn't eat flesh, and the unicorns were the only animals in Crystal City.

They were largely kept in one of the gardens, but it wasn't unusual to see them wandering about the city.

They walked faster than they had the day before, and after a while Lin and Kyra dropped behind and walked together. They walked for hours, until they reached what looked like a sunken field. Its dusty surface was flecked with shiny chips of hard stone. They decided to go around it.

Along the edges of the field, barren trees pointed at odd angles toward the east. At the base of the trees was a green shrub.

"Berries," Lin said.

"They might be poisonous," Jon answered.

"No, look."

A tiny bird, black except for yellow markings on its wings, hopped near the shrub. It went from branch to branch pecking at the berries.

Lin watched the bird and then went to gather some of the berries herself. She brought the first handful to Kyra, who sat apart from them. She brought some to Jon.

"You said you ran into Fens?"

"When we saw them we panicked." Lin spoke softly. "Everything I had been taught just went out of my mind. We were all screaming . . . I was screaming. It was just horrible."

"Were many . . . injured?"

"I don't know. I can only remember it in bits and pieces," Lin said. "Does that make sense?"

"I think so," Jon answered.

"I remember us running. Screaming. Kyra fell and they grabbed him and were dragging him somewhere. That's how he was scratched up. He was kicking and swinging at them and I was yelling and trying to knock them off. Somehow we got free. He was like a wild person. He's been different ever since."

"He's young," Jon said.

"He's older now," Lin said. She had the juice of the berries on her face. "After the fighting was over, when Kyra and I had managed to get away, I didn't feel very much like I thought I should feel."

"Like an Okalian?" Jon asked.

Lin nodded.

Jon thought of saying that he didn't know if he felt the way an Okalian would feel, either. He didn't feel particularly brave, or noble, or strong.

"When we reach the Ancient Land it'll be different," Jon said. "We'll be real Okalians again."

"Yes. I believe that," Lin said. "I believe that with all my heart."

"It's following us!" Kyra called out suddenly.

Jon turned quickly to where Kyra knelt.

"I see it!" Lin said. "It's the unicorn we freed."

The unicorn stood off from them, motionless. Jon shielded his eyes from the bright haze and looked at it. It moved slowly ahead a few steps, stopped, and then retreated.

"Let's walk a bit," Lin said.

They started to walk and the unicorn started also.

"It's got to be one of the unicorns from Crystal City," Jon said. "And it's out here the same way we are, trying to find something safe in the Wilderness."

"It's beautiful." Lin shielded her eyes with her hand. "And so black it looks like a shadow against the sky," she said.

"I think it's good luck," Jon said.

"Fens believe in luck," Lin said. "We were taught that in school."

Jon took a deep breath and put his head down as he walked. Was that the reason that he did not feel like an Okalian? Because he was part Fen?

"It's still following us!" Kyra called out. He ran ahead of them, delighted to see the unicorn.

Lin caught up with Jon. "Jon, I think I believe in luck, too," she said. "I think we'll need a lot of it."

The wind, which earlier had come from the west, now came from the south into their faces as they walked. It was a strong wind, more humid than the one from the west, and heavier with dust. They talked less and rested more often.

"There's more new growth," Lin said to Jon as they came to a wide valley. "Look, there and there."

There was more green than he had been told to expect. Low shrubs dotted the floor of the valley and a few of the trees had leaves, but most were covered with a dull green growth around their trunks.

"You're in a good mood today," Jon said.

"She's always in a good mood," Kyra said. "She's the best sister in the world."

"And Kyra is the best brother," Lin said, putting her arm around him. "We both feel a little better about our chances. We haven't seen any Fens since the bridge. Maybe they're all up at Crystal City."

"And our parents are beating them," Kyra said. "The Fens are going to be sorry that they attacked us."

"I think so," Jon said.

"It's simple. What we have to do," Lin went on, "is just to stay strong. It should take us twenty-four days at the most to reach the Ancient Land. We're all strong enough to do it. I know we are."

"We can get across this valley in no time," Kyra added.

"No, this is the Plain of Souls," Jon said. "Once we're in the middle of the Plain we can be seen from every side. That's what happened to the Okalians when they were on their way to start Crystal City. We'll be better off going east. Over there."

Jon pointed toward the rim of the valley.

"Going around will be harder," Lin said. "Maybe even a lot harder."

"Can you make it?" Jon asked.

"I have to make it," she answered.

Lin started walking and Kyra started after her. Jon let them get a short distance away from him before he started after them.

Lin was walking fast, faster than Jon thought she should. He had a funny feeling about how she looked. He thought about what she had said, about it being simple to reach the Ancient Land. His father had spoken like that, too. He had given Jon long lists of rules and things to look out for. Many of the things his father warned him about he already knew from school. Don't eat strange plants or fruits, don't let the dust that covered nearly everything stay on your skin for very long, and never underestimate the periods of cold. It was his mother who told him that there were more important things to think about. Like the way the sun felt on his skin, or the lingering taste of fresh fruit in his mouth.

He thought of a tune his mother often played on the orange lacquered lute she liked so much. He thought of her sitting in the soft glow of candlelight in the evenings, her fingers dancing across the strings of the instrument, a faraway look in her eyes.

"The lute is a happy instrument," she used to say. "Meant to be played by happy people. Or people who want to be happy."

Both of his parents had come to him the night before he left, when they first realized that Crystal City would fall to the Fens. His father had told him he depended on him to be strong. His mother had found a reason to stay behind, as she always did, and had told him to think not only of what he would be leaving, but of the love he would take with him as well.

Jon caught up with Lin.

"Kyra's walking really fast," he said. Kyra was up ahead, walking in long, loping strides, both arms stretched out to his sides.

"I think he needs to use up a lot of energy," Lin answered.

"He seems to be getting on all right," Jon said.

"Sometimes at night he cries," Lin said. "He doesn't want you to know it."

"It's all right to feel bad, even to cry."

"Your mother really doesn't look like the other Fens," Lin said, changing the subject.

Jon looked at her, and then away. "No, not really," he said. "She's taller, much taller. She's only part Fen. At any rate my father says that most Fens look the way they do because they have bad diets. If they ate better they would be like us . . . like the Okalians."

"Do you really believe that?" Lin asked.

"I don't know."

"Do you look like her?"

"Same hair, same eyes," Jon said. "Sometimes, when my father wasn't around, she would make me stand in front of the mirror with her and we would stand there looking at each other. She used to say 'Our souls come together in our eyes.'"

"I try not to think about my parents," Lin said. "Or about Crystal City."

"The thoughts keep coming, though," Jon continued. "They keep coming and it just hurts . . ."

"It just gets to the point where I feel the pain is part of me," Lin said. "The part that hurts so much. I can't talk about it, even with Kyra, without crying."

"It's the not knowing . . ." Jon started to say more, but Lin lifted her hand for him to stop, and he did.

They walked on without talking for a long while. There were things Jon thought about saying. He wondered what Lin's parents were like and what they had told Lin and Kyra. He also wondered what Lin really thought about the Okalians who were caught by the Fens.

Quickly he shut the thoughts away. He made himself think about his route and about the Book of Orenllag. The Okalians had made it from the Ancient Land as a people, across the difficult lands, through Gunda's Hope and the Plain of Souls, to reach a new beginning. He told himself that he and the other Okalian children would make a new beginning as well.

Kyra stopped first and sprawled on his belly. In the distance the unicorn loped easily. The boy was watching him.

"Kyra," Jon called. "Let's give him a name."

"I've got a name," Kyra called back.

"Not you," Lin said, "the unicorn."

"Let's call him Shadow!" Kyra said as Lin and Jon neared him.

"Then it'll be Shadow," Jon said. "Shall we touch hands or something?"

"Is that what Fens do?" Kyra asked.

"Jon is not a Fen," Lin said quietly. "He is an Okalian."

"We can touch hands if you want," Kyra said.

They stood, touched hands with Lin's on the top on her brother's and Jon's on the bottom. Jon lifted their hands slowly. "We have named him Shadow!" he said.

They found comfortable positions and rested. Jon closed his eyes and rolled his shoulders forward. It felt good.

"Shadow's leaving," Kyra called.

They sat up. The unicorn they had just named was off to their right. They watched as the dark shape moved easily across the field, silhouetted against the flat gray-white sky. Shadow was a perfect name for him.

"Kyra! Over there! Can you see them?" There was panic in Lin's voice.

"What is it?" Jon asked.

"There!" She pointed straight ahead. "That's why Shadow is leaving. It's the dogs!"

Jon didn't see anything that looked like dogs in the direction Lin was looking, only a vague gray mass that seemed to move of its own accord. Looking closer, he saw that the mass was really a pack of living creatures, one jammed against the other, pushing and jostling one another as they made their way toward them.

"Into the trees," Jon said.

They moved quickly and without speaking. They found a tree they thought they could climb and stood near it. Then they turned back to the dogs.

The beasts seemed to be wandering aimlessly, their heads close to the ground. Their howls were like the whistling of a distant wind, cold and eerie.

"They're the same kind I saw before," Lin said. "We didn't learn anything about them from the Council. Did you?"

"No," Jon answered. "What were they doing before?"

"The same as now," she said. "Just moving together like that."

The dogs on the outside of the pack kept going in toward the center, pushing their way into the middle of the others, forcing other dogs to the outside. They went along at a slow pace.

"Look, they've stopped," Lin said.

They had. They were yelping now, and most of them sat or lay down. Two of them circled the pack. They went around and around. The pitch of the yelping got higher. Then, suddenly, they started again.

"Into the tree! Quickly!" Jon said.

Jon started to give Lin a hand up. The tree was rock hard.

"It's dead!" Lin called out. "The limbs might break off!"

The dogs were getting nearer, picking up speed. "We don't have a choice!" he said.

He pushed Lin up as far as he could until she reached the bottom branch. She pulled herself up slowly. She went up into the tree until she reached a thicker branch and stopped there. Kyra was up next, stepping roughly on Jon's shoulder. The yelping of the dogs increased.

"Jon, hurry!" Lin's voice was filled with urgency.

Jon had to wait until Kyra had cleared the bottom branches. The dogs were coming faster, yelping and growling. He watched as Kyra got into the higher branches.

"Kyra, be careful!" Lin called down. "Stay near the trunk!"

"I'm being careful," Kyra said. He was watching the dogs as he climbed.

"Hurry! Hurry!" Lin's voice pleaded, and Jon

pulled himself up just as the dogs reached them.

The lowest branch seemed weak, but it had taken all of Jon's strength to reach it. The dogs raced past the tree, and on to a small mound beyond it.

Bigger than they seemed from a distance, most were gray and only a few black.

"They're stopping," Kyra said. His voice was calm, calmer than it should have been.

The dogs were settling on the hill. Two dogs broke loose from the pack and began to circle it, their noses close to the ground. The yelping of the dogs circling the pack changed, as if they were signaling the others. The pack shifted slowly, took up the yelping, and headed back toward the trees.

This time they came slowly, jostling and pushing against each other, until they came to the tree where Jon, Lin, and Kyra waited. One dog moved heavily into the trunk. He sniffed at its base and then put his paws on the trunk and began to yelp. Jon carefully moved to the next branch. The dog was close enough for Jon to see why they moved in a pack, and so strangely. He looked down at the snarling mouth and the white, sightless eyes, and trembled.

aack!" Kyra made a noise and started spitting at the dogs.

"Shut up!" Jon yelled at him.

The dogs kept up their snarling and yelping for a while and then moved a short distance away, piling onto one another. At first the pile was loose, but it got tighter and tighter as the dogs settled in.

"Hang on!" Jon called out. "We have to stay strong."

"You're scared!" Kyra called out.

"Yes, I'm scared."

"I'm not!" he called back.

At the sound of their voices, the dogs rose and began yelping and growling. They headed for the tree, some stopping a few meters away and baring their teeth.

Jon looked up at Kyra. He was clinging with both arms to the tree. He was scared. Not as scared as Jon was, perhaps, but still scared.

One dog came up to the tree and barked. He lifted his head, baring a row of vicious-looking teeth. He went around the tree several times, and then went back over to the pile of dogs and pushed his way into them.

They kept as quiet as possible. Jon was scared, but he was angry and frustrated, too. He had left Crystal City with the other children, running from the invasion of the Fens. Now he was cold, and terrified of the dogs. Was this to be his life, running from everything? Struggling just to survive?

"Shadow!" Lin broke the silence.

A dog, hearing Lin's voice, yelped and ran around the base of the tree. He was answered by other dogs.

Jon saw Shadow. The unicorn stood on a small crest near the edge of the valley. Jon knew that even with his great strength he would be no match for the dogs. There were too many of them.

It began to snow. It swirled about the tree as the wind picked up.

Both Lin and Kyra stretched out their bodies on branches above him while Jon sat with his legs over a smaller branch, his arms around the trunk of the tree. The snow went down the back of his neck and he began to shiver. His fingers ached from the cold and from time to time his foot would go to sleep. Below him, huddled against the swirling snow, were the dogs. In the distance, the movement of shadows and lights were nightmare dancers that called to him, their voices through the dead branches inviting him to release his grip from the tree.

Jon fought the sleep that tugged at him. Each breath became painful as the cold air froze the moisture inside his nostrils.

He could see Kyra plainly; one of the boy's feet dangled from a branch just above him. He was turning his face, trying to avoid the stinging snow. Jon looked for Lin but wasn't sure the dark spot above him was she. He looked down to the ground, but he didn't see her there, either.

"Lin!" He called to her.

"I'm still here!" The answer came from high above him. Lin had climbed farther into the tree.

"Is Kyra awake?"

"Yes!" the boy answered. "There are Fens coming!"

Everything on Jon's body hurt. He looked down at the dogs. They were moving again, going about in quick circles, searching for a scent. Then Jon smelled what the dogs had — the strong odor of smoke.

"Where are the Fens?" Jon called out. "Are they headed this way?"

"They're on the far side of the valley," Lin said. "I don't know if they're really Fens, and I can't tell if they're coming this way. They're carrying torches."

Jon strained to see through the snow, but couldn't. Below him the dogs circled about the tree and yelped. Some howled. The circle grew wider. One dog started off, then two others followed it. They caught up with it and the yelping began again as they huddled away from the others. The others followed, bumping and jostling each other until they were all assembled. They started off in a quick pace away from the odor of the smoke. They moved fast and were soon nearly invisible in the falling snow.

"The torches are headed in this direction," Lin said.

When it was clear that the dogs were gone, Jon slid down to the ground. Kyra came down and then Lin. Halfway down the trunk of the tree she pushed away from it and jumped. She landed on her feet but her legs gave way and she fell to the ground.

Lin winced. Her hair fell across her face and she pushed it away in anger.

"Why do we have to be out here?" she cried. "Why?"

Kyra knelt by her side as she gritted her teeth.

"We have to go on," Jon said.

Lin looked up at him, her eyes filled with tears, and tightened the corners of her mouth. She pulled herself to her feet, wincing as she did.

Jon could see the faint lights from the torches. They weren't that near.

"Those Fens will tear up the dogs," Kyra said, seeing Jon look toward them.

"I don't know," Jon answered. "If the dogs aren't afraid of the fire, it will be children with sticks against wild dogs. I don't know —"

"They're not children!" Lin's voice was filled with anger. "They're not children! *We* are children. They are Fens!"

"Most of them are younger than I am," Jon said. "Some people on the Council think the plague might be over, but they still don't live that long."

"I don't care how long they live!" Lin said. "It's because of them that we're out here. We're children and children shouldn't be out in the cold and running from dogs and climbing into trees and . . . and being away from our parents.

They aren't children. Children don't attack Okalians!"

"We have to go on," Jon said quietly.

He walked ahead of them, letting his feet drag so that he broke a path through the fallen snow.

He was cold. He had almost forgotten that he was cold, or how cold he was. As he walked he thought about what Lin had said, that the Fens weren't children. He wondered what the Fens thought of them.

t was during the time of Gunda that the Okalians were forced to leave the Ancient Land," Jon said, as much to hear the sound of his own voice as anything else. "The dust was thicker over the Ancient Land so that they couldn't even see the moon. It was just a dark shape in the sky."

"I know that," Lin said. "You don't have to give me history lessons."

"Did you know that it was on the Plain of Souls that more Okalians had their dreaming stopped than at any other place on the journey?" Jon went on.

"Yes, I've read the Book of Orenllag," Lin answered sharply. "The same as you. But it didn't tell us about the Fens."

"The Elders who wrote the Book of Orenllag didn't know the Fens would ever attack us," Jon said.

"Attack us?" Lin glared at Jon. "The Fens *kill*

people. In Crystal City the Okalians dream until they have grown old and their dreaming stops, or some . . . some terrible chance has fallen on us. But the Fens *kill*! They kill animals to eat. They kill Okalians. That's what makes them different from us. They kill!"

"I know that," Jon said. He turned sharply on his heel and walked away from Lin. He could feel the hurt and anger rising in his chest, his face burning. He was part Fen. Perhaps it was not a large part, but still it was true.

He walked as fast as he could, hoping that Lin and Kyra wouldn't keep up with him. He knew his route. He would follow the twin Shan stars, stay east of the Plain of Souls, cross Gunda's Hope, and go past the Swarm Mountains on to Orenllag. From there he would be able to see the Ancient Land. He didn't need to be with anyone. He could be with himself.

Off to his right there was a noise. It sounded far away. Jon couldn't think of what the sound was; he almost didn't care. He thought of his mother, half Okalian, half Fen. He had never met his Fen grandmother. It didn't matter. Nothing mattered except that he was strong, and that he would find the Ancient Land.

"Jon, I'm sorry." Lin was breathless as she caught up to him. "I forgot that you were part Fen."

"It doesn't matter," he answered.

"It matters," Lin said. "I don't want to hurt you. I want us to be together."

Jon stopped. He looked at Lin to see if she was sincere. She looked at him, pleading with her eyes for him to put aside his anger.

"So it matters," Jon said. "I know what the Fens have done, and I hate it as much as you do. But we are Okalians, you and I, and I know that you took the same vow as I did, to find the Ancient Land and —"

"— and a new beginning," Lin finished the oath they had all taken.

Jon began walking again, this time more slowly, with Lin at his side.

They pushed on for hours, half looking for a place to stop and rest, half afraid to stop. When they finally did stop it was near a small frozen stream that ran between the Plain of Souls and a rocky ridge. There were small animals on the ridge with lizard tails and horned backs. They darted along the ridge, stopping abruptly to some unseen signal, only to mysteriously resume their frantic flights along the hard earth to disappear in the darkness or beneath the snow.

"We can take turns sleeping," Jon said.

"I know that," Lin said. "We're equals here, you're not our leader."

"I didn't say I was," Jon said. "It's just that the thought of sleeping sounds so good to me. Closing my eyes even for a moment is like something so good I want to eat it."

"Then close your eyes," Lin said. "You sleep first, and then we'll wake you and we'll sleep."

Jon lay on his stomach and closed his eyes. He called sleep, welcomed it, tried to suck it into his lungs, into his belly. But sleep didn't come. Instead came the thoughts that he had been pushing aside for so long. What had happened at the city? He imagined what he had not wanted to imagine, the Fens breaking through the outer walls, running through the halls of Crystal City, stopping the dreaming . . . killing the Okalians.

He thought of Veton, his father. His father would be brave and resourceful, not like him, scared. He squeezed his eyes tightly shut and tried desperately to block out the images that tumbled into his mind. They were images of his mother. Of her standing in the halls, her gentle hands before her, the hands that had caressed her lute, and her son. He imagined her looking at them, wondering what she should do with them as the Fen children came toward her . . .

When Kyra woke him, he saw he was lying on the ground near Lin's feet. He raised himself to his elbow.

"What's wrong?"

"Nothing is wrong. The unicorn is back," Kyra said. There were dark marks on his face — stripes on his forehead and smudged diagonals under his eyes.

"What's that on your face?" Jon asked.

"Nothing," Kyra answered.

Jon had seen markings on the faces of the Fens. Kyra didn't look like a Fen, but he didn't look like himself, either.

They were on a small hill and Shadow was standing at the bottom of it. Jon wondered if the unicorn thought they would lead him back to Crystal City.

"Their gentleness and elegance," his father had said, "symbolizes our way of life better than any other creature or thing."

When Lin was fully awake, Jon told her to look at her brother.

"Why?" she asked.

"Just look at him," Jon said.

Jon watched as Lin went to her brother. She at first frowned and looked away, and then took Kyra's face in her hands. She touched his face and tried to wipe the markings off, but he wouldn't let her. Lin moved away from him, but she was clearly shaken. Kyra walked ahead of them, sometimes moving straight ahead, sometimes hurrying to a tree or bush where he would stand for a moment, as if he were stalking something, before moving on.

"Is he okay?"

"He's fine," Lin said.

"Why did he mark his face up?"

"I don't know," Lin said, her words spoken so softly Jon could hardly hear her. "He'll be all right."

There had been a time when Jon thought that the Okalians understood most things. Now, even as an Okalian, he saw that there were things he didn't understand. Kyra was one of those things.

Jon wasn't at all sure that Kyra would be all right, or even strong enough to make the journey to the Ancient Land, but he didn't say that to Lin.

Most of the Plain of Souls had been barren and sandy. There were patches of short, matted grass and occasionally a shrub with tiny white flowers. As they went farther south, the grass was thicker and there were trees with thick, twisted branches.

Jon saw a bug crawling in the undergrowth. It was bright red with yellow spots and had red and yellow spikes on its body. Jon had never seen one like it before. For Jon it was as if there were a whole new order of life, things that had come into being only after he had left Crystal City.

"Jon, over there!" Lin whispered hoarsely.

Jon looked quickly toward where Lin was pointing. Squinting, he saw a crudely built fence that closed off a circular area. In front of the fence a kneeling figure was digging with a stick.

Jon motioned for them to get down. Behind them Shadow pawed anxiously at the ground.

Lin crawled to Jon. "What is it?" she asked. "Some kind of fort?"

"I don't know," Jon answered. "I think we'd better stay clear of it."

"It's a boy," Lin said. "He's standing!"

Jon looked and saw a tall, thin young man. He was looking intently at something cradled in his hands. He started away, then went back to where he had been digging. He knelt and started digging again with the stick.

"I think he's an Okalian," Jon said.

They watched him a while longer and Jon realized that he was glad just to find another Okalian.

"Are you sure?" Lin asked.

"No."

Just then the figure straightened up again and

looked out toward them. He dropped what he had been digging and shielded his eyes as he looked around. Behind him Jon saw a thin wisp of smoke rise slowly and then flatten out in the heavy air.

"He's an Okalian," Lin said, standing. She waved to him, and he waved both arms over his head.

Jon glanced over toward Kyra. The boy was kneeling, his hands clutched in front of him. He was afraid. Jon couldn't blame him; Kyra had been captured once. Jon turned his attention back to the fence.

Jon stood and they started toward the fence. As they drew near it was clear that the figure was an Okalian. He wore a metal band around the upper part of his right arm, as some older Okalians did.

"Hello, friends!" His voice was cheery enough.

"Hello!" Lin responded.

"Come in, come in," he said, motioning toward an opening in the fence. "I thought you looked like Okalians."

"How long have you been here?" Jon asked, stopping in front of the crudely made door.

"Awhile," he said. "But come on in. You can't be too careful, you know."

Jon felt uncomfortable going into the opening. The boy's clothing was dirty and torn, and he seemed strange. Near the door he stood to one side, nervously rubbing his thin arms.

"Two? Three of you! That's good. Are there more?"

"Us, and Shadow," Jon said, looking around for the unicorn. He saw him and walked toward him, only to see the animal move quickly away.

"He'll come later," Jon said. "He follows us."

"A unicorn? Wonderful. It's been a long time since I've seen a unicorn."

"My name is Jon."

"And I am Ceb," he said. "We call this place the Compound, for want of a better name."

"What route are you following?" Lin asked.

"This is my home," Ceb said. "You're welcome to be here. What are your names?"

"I am Lin." She stepped forward. "This is my brother Kyra. How long have you been here?"

"We were wandering along the edge of the Plain," Ceb went on, "like you. Then we came upon this place. It must have been built ages ago."

"There are others here?" Jon asked.

"You'll meet them," Ceb said. "Do you want water?"

"Yes," Jon heard himself say quickly.

Ceb smiled. "We have fresh water," he said. "Come."

They had moved away from the opening in the fence and Jon saw that Shadow had come into the Compound. It made him feel somehow more secure.

From the inside the fence looked stronger than it did from the outside. There was a heavy bolt that could be placed across the gate that would keep out animals, but the fence was too low to keep out Fens.

Inside the Compound was a large structure surrounded by smaller ones. The smaller ones were little more than huts made of stone and mud. Jon saw faces in the doorways, sometimes just parts of faces, eyes peering from the shadows. The large structure, the one that Ceb led them into, was made of branches woven together and sealed with a dark material.

Jon saw Lin looking around in the dim light with the same wonder he had.

"You said you've been here for a while," Lin told Ceb. "Why do you stay?"

"We stay because we are happy here," Ceb said. He smiled in a strange, almost pained, manner. "We weren't in the city when the Fens attacked."

Shadow whinnied and stamped his foot.

"For a while we wandered around like I imagine you're doing," Ceb went on. "Being afraid of everything, and for every moment of our lives. Then we found this place and stopped to rest."

"You're going to stay here?" Lin asked.

"Until it's time to leave," Ceb answered quickly. "Are you a family?"

"Yes," Lin answered before Jon had even thought about what Ceb meant.

"Then I'll try to find you a place together," Ceb said. He smiled broadly before leaving.

"What is this place about?" Lin wondered aloud when Ceb had disappeared through the low door.

"I think we're being watched," Jon said. "Did you see them?"

Lin nodded.

"We'll have to be careful," Jon said.

Presently Ceb came back. There were two Okalian girls with him and a boy no older than Kyra. The girls seemed to be nearly as old as Ceb. They carried gourds of water.

"What do you think?" Lin whispered in Jon's ear.

"I don't know," he answered under his breath.

"This is Atalia and her sister Pan," Ceb introduced the two girls. "And this is Atun. They've agreed to share their space with you. We don't have that much room here, so we do the best we can."

Ceb nodded and left them with the girls and boy.

Lin drank hungrily from one of the gourds. The water ran down her face and onto her tunic. Kyra drank next, and then Jon.

"Come with us," the darker girl said.

"How many of you are here?" Lin asked, as they followed them.

"Twelve of us," Atalia said, glancing back at Jon.

The inside of the tiny hut looked like a cave. It was clean and neat, though, and away from danger. The soup they were given was warm and delicious, and Jon felt himself relax. The girls began to talk, to ask how things had gone at Crystal City.

"Not well," Lin answered. "We don't know the final outcome . . . but it didn't look good."

"Let's not talk about it," Pan said.

"How old is Ceb?" Jon asked.

"Eighteen," Pan said. "He knows a lot."

Jon felt that the Compound was wrong and the Okalians who lived there, who did not want to make the journey to the Ancient Land, were somehow wrong, too.

They drank more of the cool water, and then

were given places to rest. Jon wanted to think about the Compound, to figure it out, but in minutes he was asleep.

When he finally woke it was to the sound of girls' voices.

"Look who's with us again!"

Jon looked up and saw Atalia. She was wrapped in a white cloth and her hair was loosened about her shoulders.

"Have I slept long?" he asked.

"Forever," Lin said from the other side of the small hut.

"How are you doing?" he asked.

"Well enough to start traveling soon," she said. There was a seriousness in her eyes as she looked at him. The corners of her mouth moved slightly, as if there was something more she wanted to say, that simply wouldn't come.

"There's no hurry," Atalia said. She spoke quickly. "We're glad to have you here."

"Don't you want to get to the Ancient Land?" Jon asked her.

"Maybe." Atalia giggled. "And maybe not."

In the dim light Atalia's teeth looked dark.

"How do you spend your time here?"

"Sometimes we tell stories." Atalia was preparing food. "We have the Book of Orenllag. Sometimes we read to one another, or just rest."

"We visit each other a lot," Pan said. "Come on, I'll show you around."

She took Jon's hand and pulled him up. He looked around. He didn't see Kyra.

With Pan holding his hand, he left the small hut and went out into the courtyard. It was nearly dark and he closed his eyes to get used to it. When he opened them again, his whole body tensed and he stepped back quickly, bumping into Pan and nearly falling.

"Don't be afraid!" Pan said quickly. "They won't harm you."

"What are they doing here?" He stared straight ahead at three Fens. They stood together in the center of the inner court of the Compound.

"We live in peace here," Pan said. "We've learned to do that."

"You learned that from Ceb?"

She didn't answer.

The Fens, with their peculiar, waddling gait, started toward them. Pan, who was slightly taller than the Fens, stepped forward and touched her fingertips together in front of her face. The Fens did the same thing. Then they smiled, or at least Jon imagined that what they were doing was smiling. Their eyes narrowed to slits and their lips moved away from their red-stained teeth.

62

"It means that all of our thoughts are of peace," Pan said.

"I think I'll check on Lin," Jon said.

When he got back to the hut he had slept in, Lin was waiting for him. She searched his face, trying to read his reaction. Kyra was there, too, sitting in the shadows. His arms were folded in front of him as he rocked back and forth. Jon wondered what was going on in the boy's mind. He knew that both Kyra and Lin had seen the Fens who lived in the Compound.

"Okalians have the mind to understand things," Atalia said, without asking if he had seen the Fens. "When you understand the ways of peace everything will be all right."

"We've taken an oath . . . ." Jon heard his voice tremble. "We've taken an oath to reach the Ancient Land."

"Of course," Atalia said, smiling. "Have some soup. Rest. There is so much in your head now. Later things will be easier."

Atalia ladled out the soup. She gave some to Lin, and then to Jon. She offered it to Kyra. He didn't look at her, just kept rocking to and fro. She put it in front of him.

He didn't touch it.

Jon tasted the soup. It was warm, and filling. He looked over at Lin. She was watching her brother.

"There were nearly white clouds in the sky last week." Pan spoke to Atalia. "Did Ceb tell you?"

"Yes, it means there might be clear rain soon," Atalia said.

"When I was young I used to imagine myself riding on a white cloud and going to a secret place that only I would know about." Pan went on as if Jon and Lin and Kyra weren't there, as if they hadn't seen the Fens and weren't filled with wonder and fear that these creatures would attack them.

"Ridiculous," Atalia answered. "Because I know all the secret places that have ever been."

They laughed. They talked more, almost without stopping. They would go from one thing to the next almost without reason. They talked of Ceb a great deal, and it was clear that he was their leader.

Atun, the boy, wandered in and out of the hut, usually without speaking. Sometimes Jon would catch the young boy looking at him, only to see him look quickly away when their eyes met.

"Atun must tell a story," Pan said, noticing that Jon was looking at the boy. "He tells wonderful stories."

"I-I can't," Atun stammered.

Pan first, and then Atalia, went to him, and

they put their arms around him and their faces against his chest. Huddled that way, they even looked like Fens.

"Then you must have some sorpos," Pan said to Atun. She spoke to him, but she looked at Jon.

"All right," the boy said.

She went to a corner and reached into a basket, and took out a piece of reddish fruit. Atun took a bite from it while it was still in her hands. Then she gave it to Atalia.

Jon watched as Atalia bit greedily into the fruit. There was no control in the way the Okalian girl stuffed the fruit into her mouth. It was a hunger, a hunger that Jon had never seen before.

The sorpos was half as large as Pan's face, with a bright red and yellow peel. Inside it was dark red and shiny with juice. Atun greedily took more of it from Pan. The moment he had taken as much of it as he wanted, he turned and walked away. Without saying a word, he leaned against the wall and slid down until he was seated. His face was in shadow while a triangle of light fell across his thin legs. Atalia took several bites of the sorpos, ran the back of her hand across her mouth, and went to another corner and took a small ball from a nearby table. She sat cross-legged on the floor and began to play with the ball slowly, rolling it from one hand to the other.

Pan was standing in the middle of the room as the rest of the group watched. Her head was down and she was eating the sorpos. Then she lifted her head slowly and held out what was left of the fruit.

"Do you want sorpos?" she asked. She was smiling.

Lin turned away and went to the mat she had slept upon the night before. Pan, still smiling, offered it to Kyra.

"It doesn't bite, you know," she said.

Kyra took a small bite of the sorpos. He turned the fruit so he would not have to bite where Atun had. Pan went to Jon next and offered him some.

"What is it?"

"It gives you a nice feeling," she said. "I think it's one of those things between fruit and flesh."

"You know I don't eat flesh," Jon said, turning his head to avoid the sorpos.

"Of course not," she exhaled impatiently as if Jon had said something stupid. "I just mean it feels that way. I'm Okalian, after all."

Pan moved it near his mouth and then, stepping nearer, rubbed it gently across his lips. Jon moved his head back and pressed his lips together.

"It feels prickly," Pan said with a low giggle, and Jon bit into it.

"It does taste like fruit, but different," Jon said as he rubbed his mouth.

Kyra said he wanted more, but Pan wouldn't allow it. "Later, perhaps," she said.

She finished the rest of it herself while Kyra went over to where Lin was lying on a mat near the wall. Lin looked tired. Her breathing was shallow and her shoulders drooped. Kyra sat next to her and she put her head in his lap, but it was he who went to sleep first, with Lin following shortly. Soon Atalia and Atun were also asleep.

"What did you do in the Crystal City?" Jon asked Pan, who was still awake.

"I was going to be a teacher," she said. "I would have liked that, I think. Sometimes I try to teach Atun, but he doesn't want to listen. What were you going to do when you grew up?"

"I don't know," Jon answered. "My father thought I could be a scientist. My mother said maybe by the time I grew up we would have musicians again."

"You like music?"

"Yes, a lot," Jon answered. He felt as if he were going to sleep. He wasn't tired, but he knew something was happening. The small spot of sunlight on the floor before them had spread slowly. Jon felt it sucking him into its warmth, making him drowsy. Pan's voice continued. She was talking about water, how wonderful it was, and how she had felt once when she had waded in a stream in the Crystal City.

"It was as if I were flowing with the water," she said, "as if I were lighter than the air about me. I felt like one of those small things that spin webs and hang from trees, except that I wouldn't change into anything, just blow forever in the wind."

"That was good," Jon said, as he tried to stay awake.

"When I came here I was depressed," she said. "I thought I would never see real water again. Not the kind you can bathe in or swim in."

"There's none here," Jon said.

"No, but it doesn't matter," she said.

She came and sat next to Jon. Her eyes looked as if she might be crying, but when he leaned toward her and looked closer he could see that she wasn't. She leaned toward him, imitating what he was doing, and laughed. Her laugh was deep and pleasant.

"Where do you get the sorpos?" he asked.

"The Fens collect it. They leave at night and bring it back. They know where to get everything. They have sorpos and herbs that heal sickness. They're our ages, even younger, but they act older. You know what I mean?"

Jon's eyes had closed and he was not sure if he was awake or asleep. He had just suddenly slowed down. When he forced open his eyes, the top of Pan's head was in front of him and he saw that she was leaning toward him. He touched her hair. It was soft. He slept.

It was not exactly a dream, and not exactly wakefulness. He was somehow aware of the familiar things of his home back in Crystal City, the warmth, the comfort of knowing he could open his eyes and see his mother there as she had been so many times, sitting at the great carved table with her spinning. Perhaps it was half memory and half dream.

When he had awakened from his semi-dream he saw that Pan was sitting at the entrance of the sleeping place, talking with Atalia. She had a way of looking at Jon, a way that he liked, sliding her eyes toward him without moving her head.

"Peace to you!" Pan touched her breast over her heart and then held her open palm toward him.

"Peace to you!" Atalia said. She made the same gesture Pan had.

"Peace to you, too," Jon said, touching his chest quickly and holding his hand up.

"When someone offers you a greeting of peace you must return it," Pan said. "Peace is the secret of what we are about here."

"We're not Okalians, or Fens, but brothers

and sisters in peace," Atalia said. "There's fresh fruit here, and water outside in the center."

The already dim space darkened as a Fen stood for a moment in the doorway. Then she came in and Atalia and Pan started talking to her. It wasn't as if they were talking to a friend. It was as if they were talking to an honored guest, some person of esteem, a Council elder.

Jon stared at the Fen, straining to recognize something familiar, something of his mother. He remembered how his father would wonder aloud why she insisted upon claiming the strain of Fen blood that she had. Jon used to think that it was a charming thing, a sweet and gentle accent that made her just a little different, a little more special. This Fen girl seemed neither charming nor gentle. She was wearing an Okalian tunic over her shoulders, and her bare arms looked strong. She looked at Jon intently, almost defying him to return her gaze.

Jon took a deep breath, got up, and went out of the sleeping space. He felt good walking about the courtyard of the Compound. Mostly it was because of the warmth. The howling wind and the gelid air were beyond the fence of the Compound. Even if it got colder, he felt they could survive in the Compound.

There were more Fens. Jon tried to avoid their eyes as he looked about the Compound.

"Gebus!" Two of them spoke the word clearly as they stopped in front of him.

Jon stopped and looked down at the ground.

"Gebus!" One of them touched his chest and held an open hand toward Jon.

"Gebus," Jon said softly.

"They use the same word for peace, birth, and friendship." Ceb came up and laid a hand on Jon's shoulder. "They're being friendly."

There was a water bag in the middle of the Compound from which everyone drank. Jon poured some water into a gourd that was tied to the side of the bag. It was incredibly cold and good. Another Fen, his teeth almost glowing red from the sorpos, his eyes distant, came to the water bag and drank a little and poured the rest over his head. Then he walked away. Jon drank more, letting the cold water pour down his throat until it ached. It ran down the sides of his face and onto his neck and chest until he shivered with the delight of it.

"Lin is sick."

Jon turned to see Kyra standing next to him. "She's tired," he said.

"She'll be all right," Kyra answered, looking at Jon as if he expected he would answer some question he had not asked. "Pan said so."

Jon went back to the sleeping space and Ceb

was there. He was sitting with Pan and Atalia. There was a Fen sitting with them as well.

"Are there any medicines here?" he asked Ceb.

The Fen spoke to Jon. He thought he recognized some words in the language of the Okalians, but he wasn't sure.

He looked at Ceb.

"He understood you," Ceb said. "But the Fen people who live here don't always have the healing herbs. If they have them, they wear them in pouches about their necks."

"Do they really work?"

"For most things," Ceb said. "But the sorpos will help her as well. She hasn't taken any of it."

He put the sorpos down in front of Jon. "It will help her," he said.

Jon picked up the sorpos and took it to Lin. He touched her shoulder and she turned to him and tried to smile. He offered her the sorpos.

"I don't know if I want it," she said.

"They think it might help with your illness."

Jon started to move away but she caught his arm. She pulled herself up to one elbow and bit into the sorpos. Then she turned away again.

Jon told himself that the sorpos would help Lin. He was tired, and a feeling of sadness made it even worse. He lifted the sorpos to his lips. When he reached the mat he had slept on earlier, he stretched out on it.

For a long time he lay with his eyes closed, halfway between sleep and wakefulness. There was the sense that he wasn't really there. He lifted his hand to see if he could feel his face. He did, but it was an uneasy feeling. He felt suddenly afraid.

Opening his eyes, he pushed himself up from the floor and the world spun around violently. There was a lamp with a bright yellow flame on a hook on the wall. He lifted it and looked about as the reeling slowed. He could see the bodies of Pan and Atalia, Atun, and Ceb lying about the floor. They were all asleep. Jon crawled over to Lin and touched her head. It was cool and damp.

There was a noise from Ceb as he shifted position unconsciously. Jon looked and saw that Ceb had rolled onto his back. His eyes were only half closed and his mouth was wide open. A small insect settled on his face, walking near the red-stained mouth.

Jon crawled out of the sleeping space and into the darkness of the Compound.

The Fens were in the Compound. They had formed a line and were carrying something over their heads. He wanted to know what they were doing and hoped his legs were steady enough to follow them. Jon licked his dry lips and swallowed hard as he made his way along the wall to where Shadow had been earlier.

When Jon found Shadow trembling, he took off his tunic and put it over the unicorn's neck.

"It's all right, Shadow," he said. "It's all right."

He looked to see if Shadow had been injured but saw nothing. Jon put his arm around the animal's neck and turned his attention again to see what the Fens were doing.

It wasn't clear. He knew they were carrying something, something they had on a kind of platform above their heads. Two Fens with torches walked before it and two followed. They went across the center of the Compound to the entrance. One of them opened it and they carried the platform out. Moments later they returned. The entrance to the Compound was again closed and the heavy bolt that secured it put in place.

ne by one, the torches went out until there was only one lit. This was held by a Fen who went to the gate and put his ear to it. Then he walked away. Jon watched in the darkness. The sorpos had left him feeling unsure of himself. He thought about going back to the sleeping space and looking for more of the red and yellow fruit, then decided not to.

Jon was about to go back to the hut when he saw the Fen with the torch go back to the gate and put his ear to it again. After a short while he waddled away.

As quietly as he could, Jon started making his way toward the gate. Reaching it quickly, he put his ear against it as the Fen had. He heard nothing.

The Fens had gone just outside the gate. Whatever it was they had carried, they had left there. Jon's hand went to the large bolt and pulled it back.

As the gate to the Compound closed behind him, he realized how scared he was. He didn't want to be out of the Compound, but he had to know what the Fens were doing. He stood near the gate for a while. It seemed to have grown colder. The New Moon shone on the gently falling snow. He listened but didn't hear anything. Now and again, between the slow, almost hypnotic patterns of the falling snow, he could see the twin Shan stars in the east.

He looked around, found the Fen footprints in the snow, and followed them with his eyes. They didn't go far, no more than twenty meters. There was something there, something still. He pushed one foot in front of him and then the other. He was afraid to look ahead and afraid not to. Finally, he reached a point near the still object and took a closer look at it.

There, face down, the piling snow already partially covering the shaggy skins over its body, was a Fen whose dreaming had stopped. He was still on the small platform on which the others had carried him out of the Compound. He had somehow stopped dreaming, and they had taken his body and put it away from them outside the fence.

Jon turned him over and looked closely. The Fen seemed older than the others, but not much. He looked at his mouth, now gaping open as if he were in a state of surprise, and saw the red stains of the sorpos.

He was about to start back toward the Compound when he heard a strange noise. At first he turned to the Fen, thinking it had come from him. The body didn't appear to have moved. Jon listened for a while, watching the Fen's mouth to see if he saw signs of breath.

The sound again. It was low, menacing. Then there was a yelp. The dogs!

Jon looked about frantically. He didn't see them but knew they were out there, among the shadows. It was what the Fen had been listening for.

Backing toward the gate, Jon saw a shadow move across the snow in front of him, then another. There was another yelp, and then a low growl. Now he saw the pack, jostling one another, pushing together as they scented their prey.

He touched the fence of the Compound and felt for the gate, opening it just as the pack surrounded the still figure on the platform.

The bolt was clumsy, and with his stiff fingers he had trouble moving it, but finally he managed it. Putting his ear to the door he heard the whining, growling dogs as they devoured their prey.

79

Ceb was spread-legged in the sleeping space. With his mouth open he looked like the Fen outside the Compound. His chest moved, though, and Jon knew he was still dreaming. He looked at the others. Pan and Atalia were sleeping next to the Fen girl they had been speaking to earlier. Kyra was by himself in a corner and Lin was next to the far wall. Jon went to her side and touched her face lightly with his fingertips.

Her eyes opened quickly and she looked at him. For a moment she didn't seem to recognize him, and then she smiled.

"Is it day?" she asked.

"Not yet," Jon answered. "How are you feeling?"

"Good," she answered. "It's warm here. Is Kyra asleep?"

"By himself in a corner," Jon said.

"Are you all right?"

"Yes," he said. He didn't want to worry her. "I was outside the Compound for a while. I saw the Fens taking something outside and leaving it. I wondered what it was and I went to look."

"What was it?" she asked.

"The body of a Fen," he said. "His dreaming had stopped. They took the body out and left it for the dogs."

"I don't think the dogs would be in this area," she said.

"Perhaps not," he said. He didn't tell her that he had *seen* the dogs, or that a Fen had listened for them at the Compound gate. He didn't know what to make of it and decided to ask Ceb about it later.

"Was it cold out?" Lin asked.

"No, I thought it would be colder," he said.

There was no answer. Jon raised himself to one elbow and looked at Lin. She was asleep.

He closed his eyes. It would be a long time yet until it was daylight, and he wanted to sleep.

Jon's thoughts faded into sleep and he began to dream a frightful dream of the dogs chasing him, rushing past him in their blindness, making him think he had escaped them, only to come again, always to come again. He opened his eyes and faced the darkness. It was better than the dreaming. He thought of the Fen on the platform. But there was something wrong, something that was all around him, and yet he couldn't see it. He forced his mind back to the Fen on the platform and tried to relive what he had seen.

Nothing. He closed his eyes again. In the darkness Lin's hand in his own was soft and comforting. He felt peaceful. Even Shadow was not ill-at-ease here. Shadow!

Quickly, he sat up. He had felt that there was something wrong. Now he knew what it was.

on reached for Lin and shook her gently.

"What is it?" she murmured sleepily.

"It's Jon," he said. "We have to leave!"

"Leave?" She moved against him as she adjusted her position. "Where? Why?"

"You asked me if it was cold outside and I said that it wasn't," he said. "But it had to be. It was snowing. And when I came back into the Compound my fingers were stiff, it had to be from the cold."

"I don't know what you're talking about," Lin said.

"There was snow on the ground outside," Jon said. "And Shadow seems cold."

"I'm not cold," Lin said. She took his hand. "Jon, are you all right?"

"You were cold before you took the sorpos!" he said. "Everyone here takes sorpos, it just makes them feel warm. No one gave Shadow sorpos, which is why he was cold. We've got to get out of here and head for the Ancient Land again. Are you well enough to leave now?"

She didn't answer but began stirring about, collecting her things. Jon went over to Ceb and started shaking him. Ceb pushed Jon's hand away twice before he woke.

"Ceb! Come outside with me!"

Ceb scratched the back of his neck and shook his head. Jon pulled him to his feet.

"What's wrong?"

"Come outside," Jon said in a loud voice.

He half led, half pulled Ceb to the middle of the Compound. Then he looked around and finally found the small gourd they used to drink water. He gave some water to Ceb, who drank it slowly. There was a small amount of water left in the gourd and Jon hoped it would begin to freeze to prove his point to Ceb.

"Ceb, you have to listen to me," he said. "This place is cold and getting colder. When the really cold weather hits, the Compound fence won't help you. It's the sorpos. The sorpos makes you think it's warm here."

"We can't leave here," Ceb said, shaking his head. "You have to stay here or the dogs are going to get you. I know what I'm talking about."

"Dogs? Then you know about the dogs?" Jon

asked. "And you mean you *know* it's cold in here? You know this and still you stay?"

"What are you looking for?" Ceb turned and started away. "We have a place here. . . ."

Jon followed Ceb, grabbed his arm, and spun him around. "Ceb, you're an Okalian!"

"Jon, you're making too much of this," Ceb said. "We've got plenty of time to . . . do whatever we have to do. Plenty of time."

Jon watched Ceb walk away. He stumbled after him in time to see him stretch out on the floor of the sleeping space. Pan and Atalia were sitting up. The lamp was on the floor between them. Pan touched her chest and lifted her hand to Jon. The sorpos was in it.

"They know it's getting colder," Lin said. "They know everything."

Jon turned away and picked up his tunic. A moment later he heard Kyra's voice and he knew Lin had awakened him. Jon went back outside to where Shadow waited.

A small figure waddled across the square, stopped at the water, and then waddled back to where it had come from.

"We're ready," Lin said.

Jon looked at Kyra's eyes and saw that they were wide, as if he were frightened.

"It'll be all right," Jon said to him.

It was growing somewhat lighter. From where they were, Jon could already make out the entrances of sleeping huts along the other side of the Compound. When they got to the entrance they found it guarded by a sleeping Fen.

Jon touched the heavy bolt across the door and then, with a heave, pushed it back. The Fen awoke with a start, wiped at his face, and grumbled as he reached for a torch that smoldered dimly. He blew on it until it flared up suddenly and held it above his head so that he could see the three of them. The Fen looked at Jon, and then Lin and Kyra.

Jon reached for the gate and the Fen put the torch close to him to examine his face. He said something, it might have been "Open gate," and Jon was surprised that he spoke Okalian. Ignoring the bright questioning eyes, Jon pushed the bolt. The Fen stepped toward Jon, puffing himself up and twisting his shoulders so that they slanted to one side, letting the torch go low so that it lit up his face from below.

In the time it took to lower the torch, Kyra had stepped toward him, pushing him back. Jon thought there would be a battle, right then and there.

There were footsteps behind them and the

Fen looked over Kyra's shoulder, holding up the torch again. It was Atun. He had a small bag under his arm.

"I'm going with you," he said.

The Fen turned toward Jon and looked at all of them again. Then he stepped aside.

They hadn't realized how still the air was within the Compound until they had stepped out of it. A cool breeze rushed across Jon's skin, and he felt clean and good.

"We'll have to be on the lookout for the dogs," he said.

They walked a short distance under the stars without knowing which way they were going and without speaking. Jon headed for high ground, hoping to see a direction they could take.

"It's getting colder," Kyra said.

"I know," Lin answered. She put her arm around his waist. It would be getting colder fast.

The cold would be their enemy, waiting for them to slow down, to falter. Jon thought about the dogs, yelping and whining and growling after them, unseeing, unknowing, uncaring, hungry.

The uphill climb was hard. Jon tired quickly and could hear Lin sucking the air between her teeth even though they were going slowly.

They hadn't been in the Compound long, but they all seemed weaker than before.

"Wait here," Jon said. "I'll go to the top and look over."

"We can all go up," Kyra said.

He started up and Shadow went with him. It was easier for Shadow. Jon went slowly, reaching for small branches to grab and pull himself along the steep incline. The sky was a dark bowl above him, filled with distant stars that threatened at any moment to come tumbling down and fall in a glorious heap about them. For a wild moment he felt he could leap up and reach them.

Shadow reached the top first and whinnied softly. He reared up, pawing the air. Jon got there a moment later with Kyra, and Lin and Atun followed. Atun sat down near a large rock and covered his head with his arms.

Jon knelt down beside him. "I'm glad you came."

"Is it true," Atun asked, without lifting his head, "that there is no Ancient Land?"

"Don't be silly." Jon shivered with the chill of the words that came from Atun and wondered how he could have held the weight of them as he labored up the mountainside. "Anyway, Ceb doesn't know as much as he pretends."

"He's my brother."

"Oh." Jon changed position. "Anyway, I'm glad you came, Atun."

Atun didn't answer, and Jon let him be and went to look around.

The other side of the crest dropped sharply, too sharply for them to try. But just beyond it was a high mesa that he knew must be Gunda's Hope. That was the place the Okalians thought would be the most challenging part of the journey from the Ancient Land to the new beginning that was Crystal City. They had looked at the mesa as a place of despair, but Gunda had called the Elders to a meeting, had joined hands with them, and then, lifting their hands together, had named the mesa Hope. And from that time on they had called it Gunda's Hope.

Behind them, to the north, Jon could see the Plain of Souls clearly. Off to the right he could see the twinkle of campfires, or perhaps they were just torches. It was hard to tell. Jon lined one of the fires up with his thumb for a long while to see if they were moving. They weren't. He wondered if they were Fens, or Okalians who had made it that far.

"Are they Okalians?" Lin's voice broke the silence, reading his thoughts.

Her face startled Jon as he turned toward her. She was paler than the moon, as if all of her life forces were being drained away slowly. She had grown thinner, so that her eyes looked much deeper in her head. Jon pushed away the hair from her face.

"I can't tell," he said.

"Why are the Okalians staying back there?" Lin asked. "What's wrong with them?"

"Atun said that Ceb doesn't believe there's an Ancient Land," Jon said. "If he doesn't have that hope, maybe he doesn't have a reason to go on."

"And what do you believe now?"

"That it's time for us to move on toward whatever it is we find," he said.

Lin grew weaker as they went along. Atun was just sad, and began to cry and to complain that they were going too fast. Jon lost his patience with him.

"Why don't you try being quiet!" he said.

"He's used to the sorpos," Lin said.

Atun stumbled along with his head down, staying as close to Kyra as he could.

In the daylight they could see Gunda's Hope clearly. They found a dark green swath that led up to the mesa flat and decided to follow it. They had pushed on for only a short time before Lin fell, sick and exhausted.

Jon picked Lin up and began to carry her,

but he knew he wasn't strong enough to go very far.

"Do you want me to carry her?" Kyra asked. He pushed the words out slowly, knowing he wouldn't be strong enough to carry his sister.

"No, maybe we can do something else," Jon said. He laid Lin carefully on the ground. "Do you have any food?"

Kyra looked first in the pouch he carried and pulled out a small piece of fruit. "Part of it is spoiled," he said.

"That may be all right," Jon said.

He took the fruit and looked around until he saw Shadow. He saw the animal and sensed the unicorn was aware of him. Without rising from his kneeling position, he held out his hand with the fruit in it.

"You think he'll carry her?" Atun asked.

"I don't know," Jon answered.

Shadow took a few tentative steps toward them, then stopped. Jon held the fruit higher. When the unicorn reached Jon, he took the fruit from his hand.

Standing, Jon put one hand carefully on the animal's neck.

"Please, Shadow," Jon whispered. "Please take her."

He knelt and lifted Lin's thin form in his arms. He placed her across Shadow's broad back and watched as the girl put both arms around the unicorn's neck.

They traveled all day. Jon pushed one foot in front of the other until his legs ached and he was so tired he had to think about each step. Push a foot forward. Then the next. Then the next. They saw the dogs once. First they heard their yelping and then they saw them far off to the left. The gray huddle was moving away from them. They watched for a while and then moved on, too tired to make much of it.

Atun trailed them and Jon thought it might have been a mistake to bring him along. But what if they had left the boy behind? He was still an Okalian while the others were, somehow, no longer Okalians. They had given themselves up to the sorpos. It warmed them and told them that their home was warm, and that life was good, and that there was no purpose except the peace the sorpos brought them.

Kyra was always ahead of Jon, next to Shadow and his sister. He had put the marks on his face again. Sometimes, as he walked, Jon saw him swing his head from side to side.

There are nightmares in his head, Jon thought. They whispered to him and he answered with a hunching of his shoulders, a twisting of his body. Kyra was changing, and the other Okalians in the Compound had

Jon remembered the Fens passing them, heading in the direction of Bemen's Plateau. Back at Crystal City he would have gone to one of the Elders who had been trained in medicine, but out here the only thing he could think of was to find a Fen camp and look for their healing herbs.

"It won't work," Atun said. "They won't give them to you."

"I'm not going to ask them," Jon said. "I'm . . . just going to take the herbs if I can find them."

"That's wrong," Atun said.

"If you think it's wrong then you should stay here," Jon said.

Atun scowled. "I'll go."

They walked on until Jon saw the flickering of Fen campfires in the distance. He pointed them out to Atun and they headed toward them. The fires looked very far away at first, until Jon realized that he and Atun were walking through a small valley. Once out of the valley they could look down on the fires, which were along a hillside.

"It won't take us long to get there," Jon said. "Let's go, but keep a lookout for Fens."

"Will you attack them?"

"I'll defend myself if I have to," Jon said.

"What does that mean?"

"Whatever it has to mean," Jon said. "Lin is very sick."

"It's okay if you tell me what to do," Atun continued. "I'm just a child."

"How old are you?"

"Nine."

"You'll be all right," Jon said. "Don't worry."

Jon didn't want to tell Atun what to do. He didn't want to be responsible for him. But he knew what Atun wanted. He wanted to be a child again, as he had been back at Crystal City. In the Wilderness it was hard to be a child.

"I didn't see any Fen children," Jon said as he started again toward the fires.

"There were Fen children at the Compound," Atun said. "Their parents weren't really old, though."

"I think they were as old as Ceb," Jon said. "I didn't think they would even be that old."

As they neared the Fen camp they could hear

the sounds of the Fen flutes in the wind, and once in a while they could see one of the Fens silhouetted against a fire. There was a strong smell in the air, and Jon thought that it was something the Fens were burning to keep the dogs away.

Jon didn't know if the Fens had posted guards. He hoped that they would be like himself, afraid of what they could not see, lighting their fires so the darkness would not seem so near, so menacing.

"Be quiet."

Off to their left a branch, caught by the wind, whisked across the ground. It wasn't a dog. They waited for a long moment and then continued.

"We never played games at the Compound," Atun said in a whisper.

"Did you play games at Crystal City?"

"Yes, a lot of games," Atun answered.

"I used to like to play games," Jon said. "My mother wanted to play all the time."

"I think about my mother sometimes," Atun said. "She's really pretty. Like Atalia."

"Shh!" Jon said. "You want to let every Fen in the world know we're here?"

He didn't want to think about Atun's mother, or his own. He didn't want to think about games they used to play back in Crystal City, or anything else. He just wanted to find a Fen with the herbs they used for healing. He didn't know how he would get them from the Fen, only that he had to get them.

When they reached the edge of the Fen camp, Jon told Atun to stay behind.

"I'm going to try to sneak into their camp and look for the herbs," Jon said. "Stay here. If you think that something went wrong . . . go back and tell the others."

"Suppose you can't find herbs?"

"I'll find them," Jon said. "Don't worry about it."

Jon moved along the edge of the camp. He could actually see the Fens now, huddled together, sometimes with their arms around one another. He looked around until he saw one lying alone.

The lone Fen slept on his back with both arms stretched out. Next to him there was a dark form that Jon thought might have been another Fen. From where he crouched, Jon could see two pouches tied to a cord lying on the Fen's heaving chest. He glanced over at Atun, saw that the boy was watching him, and then began slowly crawling toward the Fen.

Asleep, the Fen looked more like a child than any of them did awake. Jon watched as the Fen's chest rose and fell. He looked to see if the

Fen had a weapon and saw that there was a bit of cloth around one wrist. He was sure now that the Fen was a girl. The dark form was a large skin, or maybe several joined together.

The Fen's mouth was open and Jon could see that her teeth were dark. Sorpos. He moved close to the sleeping Fen, trying not to make a noise. Carefully he opened one of the pouches. It contained bits of sorpos. The other one was half filled with a green powder. He was about to untie the pouch with the herbs when he heard the sound of high voices behind him.

Two Fens were coming toward him. Jon ducked his head close to the Fen. Quickly he pulled the skin over his shoulders and tucked his legs near his chest. In the darkness under the stinking skin Jon tried to be still, tried to keep himself from shaking with fear. He could feel his heart beating in his temples as the voices came near him.

The Fen voices were over him now. A cold trickle of sweat ran down the side of his face and onto his neck. He felt something step over him and then heard a grunting sound inches from his ear. Then nothing.

For a long time he lay still, not daring to move. He clenched his teeth and fists hard, and opened them again slowly.

The thought came to him that the Fens might have stopped near him, and were just waiting for him to come out from under the skin. Or maybe they had left. Slowly he pulled the smelly skin away from his face. He turned his head to see if anything was behind him. Nothing. In the distance a thin line of dark clouds rolled quickly past the pale moon. The fire near the center of the camp had died down.

Jon sat up and looked at the Fen lying next to him. One of the pouches was gone. Jon quickly took the other from the string and moved away. He looked inside. It was the herbs. The other Fens had taken the sorpos.

He crawled away and almost stepped on another sleeping Fen. He carefully took both of his pouches and then started making his way back to where he had left Shadow and Atun.

"EEE! EEEE! EEEEE!"

The sound sent chills through his body. He looked up and saw a Fen standing over him. The Fen held a stick — it could have been a spear — high over his head. Jon pushed himself forward as fast as he could, grabbing at the Fen's legs. He felt the Fen grab at the back of his neck as they went sprawling into the dirt.

The Fen grabbed his leg and Jon kicked out with his free leg. He kicked him again and again and the Fen rolled away. Jon got to his feet quickly and for a moment he couldn't see the Fen.

"Jon! Jon!" It was Atun.

"EEEEEE! EEEEEEE!" The Fen had moved away and was jumping up and down, trying to wake the other Fens.

Jon began to run; he saw Atun and they ran together. He looked over his shoulder and saw that there were torches being lit behind him at the Fen camp, but none were moving in his direction.

Jon was exhausted. It was even difficult to take one breath after another. "Let's go," he said.

"I saw you fighting that Fen," Atun was saying. "You're very strong. You should be our leader. You can tell us all what to do."

Atun lifted Jon's arm and put it around his own shoulders.

"You all right?" Jon asked.

"Sure," Atun said. "I didn't know you could fight like that. You knocked that Fen down like it was nothing, right?"

Jon didn't answer. He was close to crying. Tears came so quickly now, so easily. He remembered his father once had said he was very brave, that he had outgrown tears. He had fallen and hurt his elbow. He had wanted to cry but knew that his father didn't like to see him give in to pain, so he had held back the tears. His father had put his arm around Jon's shoulders, the same way his arm was now around Atun's shoulders, and told him how brave he was. Later, alone in his bed, he had cried.

Atun kept talking about how brave he had been, and how he had knocked down the Fen. It was the first time he had ever tried to hurt anything in his life. He hadn't been brave, he had been desperate, and so filled with fear that he had struck out at the Fen with all his strength. The Fen had been startled to find him there and couldn't have seen him very well in the darkness. Jon knew if the Fen had seen his face he would have seen the panic in his eyes, the horror in his face.

He hadn't seen the Fen very well, either. All he had seen in the hurried flicker of shadows was something he feared.

"Kyra was afraid you weren't coming back," Lin said. She seemed so weak. Her shoulders formed a fragile bow that held her body barely safe from the wind. "I told him you would be back."

Jon offered her the pouch.

"I don't know what it will do," he said. "I've only heard . . ."

"Thank you, Jon." Lin smiled and touched her cheek to his hand. Her face was warm but her hands were cold.

Jon thought the herbs would help Lin, but he also thought she needed rest. Not just to be still, or to sleep, but to have the peace of knowing everything would be all right in the next day, the next hour, the next breath. That would be real rest.

"Jon fought with one of the Fens," Atun said before Jon could stop him. "He stopped his dreaming."

Lin turned to Jon quickly, searching his face. "You did what?"

"I didn't stop his dreaming," he answered, angrily. "Look, we'd better get going. In case they're following us."

"Are you all right?" Lin asked.

Kyra came close.

"Yes, I just . . . we were both surprised to see each other. I don't think that . . . it was very quick. I don't think I hurt him."

"You can stop a Fen's dreaming?" Kyra asked. There was something childlike in his voice.

"I wouldn't want to," Jon said. "Now, let's get moving."

The wind wasn't as strong, but it was colder. They walked with Lin hunched on Shadow's back, Kyra walking ahead, and Atun following him single file. Jon brought up the rear, his shoulders aching from tensing them against the bitter chill.

They walked through the night and into the next day, stopping for only a few minutes now and again when either Kyra or Atun was too tired to go on. There were times when Jon was too tired to go on, times when the frozen ground would send shards of pain through his feet and his fingers would curl with the cold and he had to push one hand against the other to straighten them out.

Atun came up beside Jon and touched his shoulder. Jon looked at him and saw him point toward a small hill to the left. It would be shelter against the wind. Jon nodded, and led Shadow toward it.

The ground was too hard to leave footprints and Jon doubted if any Fens were around. There was a dark area off to one side and Jon thought it might be a cave.

"Kyra, help Lin off Shadow," Jon said. "I want to look around."

Kyra nodded grimly.

Cautiously, Jon went to the dark area he had seen. It was a cave. He found a rock and threw it in, then another. There was no response.

Lin didn't want to move from where she was lying on the ground. Jon thought if she fell asleep there it would be bad. He told them about the cave and they struggled into it.

They settled Lin just inside the mouth of the cave, and Atun and Jon went out again to look for dry sticks. They found some that were dry and others that were damp but took them all the same. The idea of a fire appealed to Jon.

Jon hoped he could remember how to start a fire with stones. With Atun sheltering him from the wind, he banged the rocks together over a small pile of dry leaves. It took him long minutes to get it started, but finally they had a small blaze. Jon put in one end of a stick until it caught, then stamped out the rest of the fire.

They got back to the cave and decided to try to find their way farther in before lighting a larger fire, so that the smoke wouldn't give them away. They made their way in the darkness with Atun in the lead and Kyra and Lin following. For some reason Shadow wouldn't go into the cave. Jon thought he might come in later.

They moved as far back into the cave as they dared, not really wanting to get too far from the opening.

The cave was warm. Atun and Jon put the dry sticks and some leaves they had gathered in a pile and lit them.

"I feel a small breeze," Atun said. "Maybe there's another opening somewhere."

Jon lit one of the sticks and held it up. The cave was huge, much larger than he thought it would be. It seemed to go down forever. He looked up at the path they had used to climb down into the cave. It was narrow and twisted along the nearly yellow walls of the cave.

The smoke from the fire went to the right and collected in a small pocket. It was possible that it would get smoky in the cave, but that was all right. For the moment, they were out of the cold.

"Shadow didn't come in?" Atun asked.

"No, but it's okay," Jon said. "We'll just rest here a while, maybe get some sleep, and then we'll move on. We'll find him again."

In the glow of the small fire, Jon could see Lin's face. She was pretty. He thought about what they would do when they reached the Ancient Land. He had asked his father what they would do, and his father had said that he would have to find a mate. He wondered if Lin thought that he would be a good mate.

"Jon." It was Lin's voice. "Where do you think we are?"

"Gunda's Hope," he answered. "I'm sure of it. When we get past here it'll be a short journey to the Swarm Mountains."

"Then up rose Puc!" Kyra said, quoting from the Book of Orenllag.

"Then up rose Puc!" Jon repeated, closing his eyes.

He fell asleep quickly.

In a dream the Fen he had fought was lying on the ground and, for some reason, Jon sat nearby watching him. The Fen lay motionless as Jon watched. After a long time he stirred, lifting a huge arm to shield his eyes from the sun. The Fen looked around, dazed, and began to grope around the ground for his weapon. Still, in the dream, Jon was motionless. Even when the Fen had wrapped his fingers around the spear and was getting to his feet, Jon was unable to move. But now he saw his face. It was the same one he had fought. The Fen screamed at him, the sound hurting his ears. Jon screamed back. It was the same sound.

"Jon! Jon!"

Jon felt his shoulder being shaken and he felt something pushing against his legs. He opened his eyes and saw that it was dark except for the small pile of glowing ashes in front of him. For a moment he didn't know where he was. Then he remembered the cave.

"What is it?" he asked.

"Lin thinks we should move on." It was

Atun's voice. "She thinks there are dogs in the back of the cave."

"See if you can build up the fire," Jon said.

"I'm scared! I'm scared!" Atun's voice was high and wavery.

The sound of a dog yelping was no more than a few meters away.

The fire flared up as Atun stirred it. Jon could see Lin clearly now, the flames lighting her face from below, giving her an eerie look. He looked around. There was only one dog near them.

"The others are over there," Lin's voice cracked as she spoke. "He's looking for us."

Jon looked and saw the sightless, glowing eyes of the other dogs, and the moving mass that was their bodies. He took a stick and lit the end of it and pushed it toward the dog that was near them. The dog moved away from the smell of the smoking stick, howling.

"The others are beginning to move this way!" Kyra called.

Jon took the stick and pushed it closer to the dog. The animal growled and lifted its head. It bared its teeth and bit at the air. Then it lowered its head and pushed forward, trying to contact whatever was near it. Jon pushed the flame against the dog and watched it recoil. The dog moved away, crouching so its belly was touching the ground.

Jon looked up and saw the other dogs still moving toward them, pushing into each other, lifting their heads to find the odor of the intruders. He pushed the stick as hard as he could into the dog's side. The dog turned and attacked the stick and Jon held it against the dog's side as hard as he could. The dog rolled over and started yelping in pain. Its fur was on fire.

The other dogs, signaled by the change in tone of the yelps, stopped, and began howling in a high pitch that Jon had never heard before.

The dog that was burning ran in a small circle, twisting back onto himself trying to bite whatever was causing him the pain. Finally he got back to the pack.

The howling stopped, and the yelps began again, and the growling that signaled they were about to attack. Jon held the flame high and watched as the dogs attacked the one that he had set afire. In moments it was over. They had killed it.

They bunched together and edged toward the mouth of the cave. Behind them the dogs fought their way through the huge pile to tear at the injured animal. Jon pushed Lin ahead of him.

"I can't see where I'm going!" Lin said.

"Just stay close to the wall."

It seemed to take forever until Lin said that she thought they had reached the mouth of the cave.

"Be sure!" Jon said.

The echo of the words had barely died when an icy gust of wind hit them.

They scrambled outside, Kyra falling and rolling part of the way down the hill. The wind drove Jon backward, taking his breath. He took Lin's hand. She leaned forward and gritted her teeth as the wind whipped her hair into her face. At the bottom of the hill they looked for Shadow.

110

It was Lin who saw the unicorn silhouetted against the distant moon.

They started again, trying to push ahead faster as the wind picked up. Bits of debris tore into Jon's face and he found himself leaning far forward just to stay on his feet. Behind them they heard yelping. The dogs were out of the cave.

They were in a dust squall and Jon could taste the dust in his mouth. He had seen the squalls when he was in Crystal City, darkening the skies and covering everything in their path. Sometimes, when the wind shifted, the thick clouds of dust seemed to leap into the air like some great monster. From within the walls of the city it had been a wondrous sight, but he was not in the city and the sand and dirt cut into his skin and choked his breathing. Jon turned and saw the dogs headed back toward the cave.

They went on until they came to a small stand of trees. They all sank to the ground near them. Jon thought about the dogs, imagining the beasts huddled against the dust storm even as the Okalians were. He closed his eyes, shielded his face the best he could, and let the wind do what it would. It was not just his body that was tired, it was his soul.

It took forever for the dust storm to stop, or

111

at least it seemed forever. Jon lay gasping on his side. He looked over to where Lin crouched. He tried crawling to her but his hands, cut and bruised from climbing down the rock, were too sore to move along the ground.

"Lin!"

She didn't answer, just raised a thin hand.

When the dust settled they all looked terrible. Kyra looked the worst as he stood panting against a dead tree, the whites of his eyes peering from the black grime on his face. Lin was trying to get some sticks from her hair. Jon went to see Atun and found him clinging to a small tree. He looked unconscious. Jon knelt to examine him. Gently he moved the boy's arm from his face. His eyes were barely open. There was moisture on his face as well as dirt. A small cut on his brow formed a perfect crescent over his left eye. Jon looked at his mouth. At first he thought it was bleeding. He pushed the red lips back. Sorpos!

There was a pouch next to him and Jon didn't have to open it to know what it contained.

When everyone had recovered, Jon realized they weren't as bad off as he had thought they would be. They had accomplished a small victory over both the dogs and the dust. Lin managed a smile, and even Kyra, once he had cleaned himself up and had started grumbling about the dogs, seemed in fair spirits.

"We'll have to carry wood for torches," Lin said. "It works against the dogs."

"And hope they all avoid the smell of smoke," Jon said.

"You can fight them," Kyra said to Jon. His eyes were narrowed into slits and Jon thought he had put even more marks on his face. "You can stop their dreaming — the Fens and the dogs."

"I didn't stop the dreaming of the Fen —" Jon said. He felt his face flush. "I did *not* kill the Fen."

"Maybe the other Fens killed him when they saw that you had beat him," Kyra said. "Like the dogs. The other dogs killed the one you beat."

Jon turned to answer Kyra, but he saw the boy wasn't talking to him anymore. He was having a conversation with himself, rocking to and fro, nodding as he agreed with his own vision of what had happened. Jon looked at Lin, and she went to Kyra and put her arms around him.

They started walking again. Atun kept off to himself, and Jon felt that was good because he didn't want to speak with him. As they walked, they rechecked their course.

114

They decided to rest when Atun spotted a small stream. They weren't sure if it was clean, so they used its waters to wash themselves as best they could and chewed on plants along the edge of the stream for moisture.

They decided that Lin and Kyra would sleep while Atun and Jon kept watch. Jon had thought that Kyra would not sleep, that he would pace as usual, but he did sleep, breathing heavily and tossing about as he did. Jon sat next to Atun and asked him how he was doing. He didn't answer.

"I know what you have in the pouch," Jon said.

"I don't care," Atun answered. "I'm going back to the Compound anyway."

"You'd be lost if you went back," Jon said. "Especially with that stuff."

"Ceb was right," Atun said. "We should just find a safe place to be."

"The Book of Orenllag says that there is an Ancient Land," Jon said. "Do you believe Ceb or the book?"

"I don't know what to believe anymore!"

"Atun, if you're going to stay with us you have to do without the sorpos," Jon said. He searched for something more to say to Atun, something comforting, but nothing came.

Atun fell asleep and Jon let him. Somewhere

between worrying about Atun and wondering if they were still going in the right direction, he fell asleep himself. When he woke, he found Lin sitting over him. She had pulled his head into her lap and was smoothing his hair with her hands.

"It's only me," Lin said. "I thought you would want to know that Shadow is back."

Jon lifted his head and saw Shadow. His legs were covered with dust and dirt.

"He just got here a few minutes ago," Lin said. "I tried to get near him, but he shied away. He's getting wilder."

"How long have I been asleep?"

"Not long," she said.

"Are you all right?"

Lin put her arm around Jon's shoulder and put her cheek against his. "No," she said. "I'm out here in the Wilderness, and I'm tired and cold and hungry. But maybe it's not as bad as it could be."

"Sounds pretty bad."

"I have you," Lin answered. "It could be worse."

It was warmer.

There's something coming!" It was Kyra's voice.

Jon felt Lin move away and he sat up at once.

There, clearly silhouetted against the horizon, a hooded figure rode toward them. The figure was on a large, humpbacked ox.

"What are we going to do?" Lin called to Jon. She was leaning forward, straining to see what was coming.

"Wait for it, whatever it is," he said. It was moving toward them very quickly.

Shadow pranced about and reared up.

Jon looked beyond the figure and saw nothing. Whatever it was, there was only one of it. It slowed as it came nearer and Jon could see that it was large. There was a hood the color of dried blood and a cape to match. Beneath the hood and cape were other colors and cloths. Jon couldn't tell where the cloths stopped and the person, if it was indeed a person, began.

It stopped. For a while it didn't move, and then it came slowly into the clearing in front of them. An arm went up and the hood was pulled away. There was a face that could have been Okalian if it had been less tortured, if the eyes had been less piercing.

"Who are you?" Jon called out.

"Who are you?" the figure repeated in a low, strange voice.

"I am Jon, of the Okalians," Jon answered.

"I am Jon, of the Okalians," the visitor said, and laughed.

Silence. Birds flew to the ground and pecked at fruit that Lin had dropped.

"What do you want?" Jon said.

"What do you want?" was the reply.

Silence.

"We are looking for the Ancient Land of our people," Jon said. "The land of the Okalians."

The figure breathed deeply, and exhaled slowly.

"I am the Soo, the Fire Bearer." The figure produced from beneath his robes a brass ball from which came wisps of smoke. "Perhaps you have need of fire? The price is good."

"We have nothing with which to pay."

"Pity! Pity!" he said. "But perhaps you will allow me to have my meal with you?"

Before Jon could answer, the stranger leaped nimbly from the ox and, taking sticks that he had bound to the side of the animal, began building a fire. First he made a pyramid of small sticks, then he placed larger ones over it. He took the brass ball and swung it around the pile several times before stopping it. Then he took the top off the ball and placed a small stick in it. The stick began to burn and he placed it quickly beneath the pile.

"Sit," he said. His voice was friendly.

He took off his cape and some of the things he wore beneath it. Some were cloth and some were the skins of animals.

"I'm glad that you aren't Fens," he said. "They are not trusting. Okalians are always trusting."

"Do you know many Okalians?" Lin asked at once.

"A few," the Soo said. "A few pass this way now and again."

"Do you know where they go?" Jon asked.

"Where do they go? Where do they go? It's a very good question," he said.

The fire crackled and flickered, sending its warmth to all of them. It seemed like a friend that he had brought along.

"Who are you?" Lin asked. "What are you?"

"What am I?" he asked. He pulled at his shaggy beard. "I am the Soo, the Fire Bearer. It is what I do and who I am. Here there is cold that creeps and kills. It is fire that holds it off."

He swung the brass ball about, leaving a wispy trail of smoke in the air.

"Here there are dogs that follow the scent of warm blood," he continued. "It is the fire that drives them off."

The Soo sat facing the fire, his pale and scaly legs crossed, staring into the blaze.

"Are you hungry?" the Soo asked, pulling out a pouch from his garments and unwrapping it. In the pouch there were leaves with pieces of a purplish stem still attached. No one admitted to being hungry.

"You say you have seen others like us," Lin spoke slowly, deliberately. "Do you know of the Ancient Land of the Okalians?"

"The Okalians?" The Soo pulled out a wide metal blade with which he scraped his legs. "They pass from time to time, going where they go. Weren't they the ones that fled when the Beasts attacked the Swarm?"

"You don't know anything." Atun walked away from the fire.

"It was the Okalians who rose from the Swarm," Jon said.

121

"One time," the Soo went on as if there had been no interruptions, "in a land far, far from here, there was a strange but happy tribe. They had learned many useful things. Nice things. Nice things. They invented a way to bring the heat of fire to cold places. They invented a way to take water to the places where there is no water. Then they had the nicest idea of all. They invented themselves. You should have seen how they enjoyed that invention."

"You can't invent yourself," Jon said.

"No? That's not true?" the Soo looked up at Jon. One eye nearly closed beneath the shaggy white hair. "As I grow old I have trouble knowing what is true. They did not invent themselves?"

"Of course not," Lin said.

"But none of this was important to this tribe. Nice, but not important. In seasons past there were many ways to do things and none was more important than the other. Then, one day, as many seasons past as there are stars in the sky . . ."

"How do you know this?" Kyra said.

Jon looked at Kyra and he looked down at the ground before him. "Let the Soo speak," Jon said.

"Ahh, let the Soo speak," the Soo said.

"Tell us more about this tribe," Jon said,

when the Soo seemed more absorbed in his scratching than anything else.

"One day," the Soo went on, "some of the tribe were alone, waiting for the others to return to their camp. The ones who waited were on a high hill, higher than the nests of the great birds. It was a place in which they thought they would be safe from other animals who might eat them. Did I tell you they did not like being eaten?"

"I had guessed it," Lin said. She smiled.

"Possible," the Soo said. "At any rate, there were nine of these creatures on the hill. Those who had left the camp were many times that number. Maybe even more. After a great while those on the hill saw, off in the distance, those returning from the hunt for grains, which was what they ate — that and a little fruit for the bowels."

Jon looked at Atun. He was bringing his hands to his mouth in a way so no one could see what he was doing. Jon knew it was the sorpos again. Lin had her arm about Kyra and Jon moved closer to them, away from Atun.

"One of them saw off in the distance, opposite of where they were, a frightening sight," the Soo went on. "It was the Beasts. Big things with curved teeth that ate everything."

"You mean the dogs?" Lin asked.

"Bigger than the dogs. Many times bigger than the dogs. It was the Beasts that drove the dogs into the caves where they lost their sight. No, the Beasts were nightmares with five legs and twenty teeth, maybe forty teeth. Who knows?"

"Five legs?"

"Maybe seven, maybe three. But they attacked this great swarm of a tribe that wanted only to live with quiet hearts. They attacked, and all the tribe stayed together bravely to fight them off except for one small group that ran off."

"What are you talking about?" Jon asked. "Are you talking about the Swarm? Have you read the Book of Orenllag?"

"I don't think the Soo reads," Lin said.

"I bear fire, not words," the Soo said. "But words are good, a comfort that can be shared. Not as great a comfort as fire, but a comfort."

"You speak of a land far away." Lin pushed herself forward on her knees. "Do you know where this land is?"

"Are there other tribes still around?" Jon asked.

"There is the Soo." The Soo touched his chest. "The Soo is of the Kargs. There are so few of us. It is sad. There are tales of the Na'ans, but I have never met any of them."

"They are written of in the Book of Oren-llag," Jon said. "They are a tribe."

"Then there are the Fens," the Soo said. "The Fens are not a trusting tribe."

"Where is this place that the Beasts attacked the tribe you speak of?" Jon asked.

"I have heard it was that way," the Soo said, pointing in the direction of the Crystal City.

Jon turned away. "I don't think so," he said.

"Do you always travel alone?" Lin asked.

"Alone? Yes, alone. The fire doesn't speak to me. I listen, but it doesn't speak." The Soo held up the brass ball. "Would you like the fire? Would you like to be a fire bearer? I will give it to you in exchange for one of the boys. Which-ever one talks the most. I'll teach him to be a fire bearer."

"We're Okalians," Lin said. "We don't give each other away."

"Pity, it's such a good trade," the Soo said, grinning. He scratched again at the silvery scales on his legs. "Nothing can live in the Wilderness long without fire. You can't. I am the Soo, and I can't."

"We'll take the fire from you!" Kyra said.

Jon looked at Kyra. His teeth were clenched and his face tightened so that Jon could hardly recognize him. The boy hurled himself across the space between him and the Soo and sent the old man tumbling backward.

"Kyra!" Lin screamed at her brother.

Kyra and the Soo tumbled over in a mass of rags and bare legs. Jon saw the blade that the Soo had been using to scrape his legs and picked it up quickly.

The Soo pushed Kyra aside and sprang quickly to his feet. He saw Jon standing with the blade and his dark eyes rolled about from one of them to the other. The brass ball of fire was on the ground between them.

"Jon stopped a Fen's dreaming," Kyra shouted from where he lay. "He'll stop yours!"

The Soo looked at Jon and pointed a bony, yellow-nailed finger. "You?"

Jon knew it wasn't true, but he nodded anyway.

"You want to take the fire from me." The Soo spoke quietly, almost sadly.

"You said we can't live without it," Lin said.

"And you are Okalians?"

"We are Okalians," Jon said.

The Soo took a step toward the brass ball, but Kyra beat him to it and kicked it toward Jon. The Soo looked at Jon, looked into his eyes, and down to the blade he held in his hand.

"He's afraid of us!" Kyra said.

"There's no need to be afraid of us," Jon said. "We don't need his fire. We are Okalians. We can make our own fire."

He threw the blade to the ground at the Soo's feet. The Soo bent quickly and picked up the blade and the brass ball that contained the fire. His lips were thin and pink, and when he pursed them to blow on the fire he looked like some wild animal that had managed to stand erect and to wrap itself in the tattered disguise of a higher creature.

The smoke came from the ball in a small blue cloud, then narrowed to a wisp, which pleased the Soo. He wrapped his face again.

"Yes, you are truly Okalians, wandering along the edges of your darkness," he said, his voice raspy and low. "Is this the darkness you dream in?"

"We are Okalians," Kyra said. "The people who dream greatly."

"The people who dream greatly," the Soo repeated.

"He's afraid of us," Kyra said again.

"It's time for us to leave now," Jon said, stepping in front of Kyra.

"Which way?" Lin asked. "The Soo pointed back to Crystal City."

"The way we know," Jon said. "Come on."

He put his arm around Kyra and started off. Lin walked behind them and Atun followed.

Jon turned to see what the Soo was doing. He saw that he had settled again in front of his fire, rocking to and fro. From a short distance away he looked like an incredibly old man in front of a fire, and from a farther distance like merely a pile of rags, and from still farther like a fire whose smoke had failed to rise and had settled next to its own flame for warmth.

As they walked, Jon thought about the Book of Orenllag. He told himself that what was written there was true, it was the Okalians who had risen from the Swarm and become a great people. They had not run away, but had been led by the great Puc, and had risen. Had truly risen.

They had reached the far end of Gunda's Hope, the vast mesa over which the Okalians had struggled on their way northward to the area in which they would build Crystal City, so long ago. They had climbed down the mesa, holding on to the small trees that dotted the far side. It was evening when they reached the ground below and the Red Moon of the Okalians hung in all its fullness and beauty in the distance. The Red Moon heartened them, even as the sprinkling of trees on the mesa side had. It was warmer on this side of Gunda's Hope, and more trees and plants were growing. Jon felt it was a good sign. But from the edge of the mesa they had also seen how far they had to go. The Swarm Mountains, dark and forbidding, were at least a day ahead; to their left and even more distant there was a tiny patch of blue green that Jon saw and hoped in his heart was the lake of Orenllag.

They decided to sleep. They found tall grass and found places in it. Jon was the last to lie down, looking around first to see if there were any signs of danger. He didn't see any and allowed himself to stretch out completely on the ground, looking up at the darkening skies. He fell asleep thinking about the Soo. He told himself over and over that he didn't care what the Soo had said. The old man had challenged the Book of Orenllag, had given his own version of how the Okalians had faced the Beasts and how the Okalians had fled to save themselves. It wasn't true, Jon told himself. The Soo didn't know how Okalians had always risen, had always learned to dream greatly. It was the reason they had built Crystal City, to keep creatures like the Soo out. The Soo and the Fens.

Lin moved from where she was lying and came near enough to Jon to take his hand.

"How are you doing?" he asked.

"I'm tired, as usual," she answered, then lifted his hand to her mouth and kissed it gently.

Jon couldn't sleep as long as Lin held his hand. It was only when she had fallen asleep and had released his hand that he finally drifted off.

He woke up with a start and looked about

him. The air was damp, still. Lin was asleep not far from him, her body angled oddly, her fingers spread against the ground as if she felt for its warmth. Jon watched her for a while, seeing her stretch in her sleep, thinking she was beautiful. Kyra was near her feet. He moved about uneasily in his sleep, jerking his head from side to side. He reached out with his hand until he touched Lin's bare leg just below the knee. Then, holding it, he became calm again.

Jon sat up slowly. What was it that he was sensing? He looked around, squinting into the semidarkness, until he saw a movement in the shadows. For a moment he froze and then, slowly, he began to recognize the shape and knew what was happening. It was Atun, preparing to leave.

Jon couldn't see his features, but he saw when Atun stood and looked about. Jon let him go a short distance and then went after him, catching him just beyond the little camp they had made.

"Why?" Jon asked.

"Ceb needs me."

"He doesn't need you or anybody else."

"He does," Atun protested. "You don't know."

"He has the sorpos," Jon said. "What does he need you for?"

Atun turned away and started on.

"I think you're going back for the sorpos."

Atun whirled toward Jon, his face twisted and angry, his thin shoulders hunched forward. "You don't know anything!" he hissed. "You don't know anything!"

His teeth were dark at the edges. Jon knew he had been at the sorpos again. "You won't make it back," Jon said. "The Fens will catch you before you get past Gunda's Hope."

"I'll make it back," he said quietly.

"Atun." Jon spoke gently to him as he backed away. "There's no real life in the Compound. They're living in a made-up world. You have to know that."

"Maybe that's better," Atun said. "I don't know."

He half walked, half stumbled off, looking frail and small in the great Wilderness.

When Lin and Kyra woke, Jon told them that Atun had left. Lin cupped her elbows in her hands. She began to cry, loud sobbing that shook her whole body. Jon put his arms around her and held her until she had recovered. She pushed away from him and stood. Her mouth tightened and she rubbed her face briskly with the palms of her hands.

"We had better start again," she said.

Kyra looked off in the direction that Atun

had gone. He rubbed his own face, as his sister had, smearing the markings.

Jon knew that they weren't so concerned with Atun's leaving, or even with the fact that he might not make it back to the Compound — they all had doubts that any of them would make it to safety.

They hadn't seen Shadow for a while. Jon pictured him running freely through the Wilderness, finding his strength in freedom, his joy in the wind racing past his head.

Beneath their feet was a tangled mass of dead material that forced them to lift their legs higher than they would normally. But there were also green buds that pushed up as well, living material rising from the dead. Jon tried to remember the passages from the Book of Orenllag that would tell them where they were. They would soon reach the Swarm Mountains, and if they climbed one of them they might even be able to see the Ancient Land.

Lin walked closer to Jon. When they had started, she had always stayed closer to Kyra.

"Those low clouds over the mountains are really dark," Jon said. "You think it might rain?"

"I don't feel like talking," Lin said.

"Is something wrong?"

"It's just too hard," she said. "It's all too hard. Just be quiet and keep going."

134

Jon glanced at her out of the corner of his eyes. She was strained; they were all strained. He walked faster, knowing that she would have to work harder to catch up, not knowing why he would want to make her work harder. After a while he slowed and looked at her, and she returned his look with defiance.

Later, when he stopped and said it was time to rest, it was Lin who ignored him and walked on. He had already sat down and had to get up to follow her.

Kyra, always behind them, had begun to mumble to himself.

The next day was a nightmare of pain and confusion. Jon couldn't tell if they walked more, or if they spent most of their time lying on the ground. When the sun had almost gone down, outlining the mountaintops with golden halos, they found a berry bush. It lifted their spirits, and they sat around the bush and ate as much as they could.

"You have berry juice all over your face," Kyra said to Lin.

Lin responded by rubbing the berries into her face and licking off the juice with a smile.

"There's nothing like food to make you feel good," Jon said.

"Makes me feel good," Lin said.

"Me, too," Kyra said. "I didn't eat much back

135

in Crystal City but now I think about food a lot."

"I think we all do," Jon said. "We have to make peace with food, and with the weather, and with each other."

Lin held out a handful of berries to Jon. "But when you have food it is easier to make the peace," she said.

That night they all slept soundly.

It was late in the morning when Jon awoke. Lin had gathered some more berries for them to carry, and Kyra had painted his face again, this time using the juice from the berries to make the markings darker. Lin seemed in a good mood.

They were talking about a dance Lin had learned in Crystal City when they heard sounds drifting toward them from the distance. The hills nearby were not really the start of the Swarm Mountains, but they were high enough to see for some distance.

"Wait here," Jon said.

He ran up the hill as fast as he could and found a small ledge. He looked down to where Kyra and Lin were watching him. Lin gestured with her palms up, wondering what the noise was.

Jon was about to call down that he didn't see

anything, and then he looked toward his right, at the flat, marshy grounds that he knew the Okalians had avoided on their way to Crystal City. A band of Fens marched along in twos, carrying a platform. There was something on the platform but they were too far away and Jon couldn't make out what it was. He beckoned for Lin and Kyra to come up to the ledge.

"What is it?" Lin asked when she had reached him.

"There." Jon pointed toward the Fens. "There are about sixteen of them."

"They have spears," Kyra said.

"Jon, it's Atun!" Lin said. "He's on the platform."

Jon looked again. Sure enough, the figure sitting on the platform, two ropes around his neck, was Atun.

They watched silently. Jon felt sick to his stomach. Lin had put her head down and folded her hands in her lap.

"We'd better get going," Jon said. "They're not coming toward us. We'll be all right."

"We have to do something," Lin said.

"There are too many of them, and they have spears," Jon answered.

Lin stood, nodded, and started down the hill.

"Look!" Kyra called out.

Jon had started down the hill after Lin, then stopped and went back. He hoped he would not have to see the Fens stop Atun's dreaming.

From the ledge he saw that the Fens had stopped.

"Look behind them," Kyra said.

There was a lone figure riding toward the Fens.

Lin had reached them and pushed her way between Jon and her brother.

"It's the Soo," Jon said.

They watched the Soo move quickly toward the stationary Fens. The Fens put the platform down and formed a circle, their spears pointing outward. The Soo slowed as he reached the Fens, and then stopped within a spear's throw of the platform.

Two Fens moved toward him menacingly. The Soo reached into the rags he wore and pulled out the brass ball. He lowered it carefully to the ground and pointed to the platform.

"He's trying to trade the fire for Atun," Lin said.

None of the Fens moved. The Soo didn't move. Away from them, graceful black birds, their wings spread wide, etched slow circles against the sky.

"What are they doing?" Lin asked.

"I don't know," Jon answered.

"Maybe they're waiting for more Fens to come," Lin said.

What seemed to Jon an eternity passed before one of the Fens near the Soo pulled his spear back as if to throw it. Still the Soo did not move. The Fen lowered his spear and went near the smoking brass ball. He picked it up and moved quickly away from the Soo and joined the others. Then the Fens began to move on, some looking back at the Soo and the platform they had left behind.

"He's untying Atun," Lin said.

They watched as the Soo lifted the Okalian boy onto the back of his ox and started slowly away. As the ox picked up speed, he left a cloud of dust. When the dust had settled, the ox, the Soo, and Atun were nowhere in sight.

"We can stop the Soo!" Kyra said. "We can catch him and stop him!"

"I think Atun will be all right with him," Jon said. "We don't have to catch him."

"Kyra, he doesn't want to be with us," Lin added. "We can't force him to be with us. He wants to make his own way, and maybe he can with . . ."

Kyra's face twisted and his lips were moving; he was talking to himself again. He wasn't lis-

139

tening to his sister. For a while Jon thought he might go after the Soo alone. It was Lin who got them started again.

They were headed toward some woods. This was a good sign. Jon could see the trees, taller than any they had seen before, with green leaves around the tops of their trunks. The branches were mostly bare, but the little vegetation on the trees signaled a warmer climate. Jon felt good. They changed their course to head toward the woods, knowing it might be a wrong direction, but understanding that there was hope in any sign of warmth.

When they stopped, Lin placed a cloth on the ground, took out the berries she had gathered from the night before, and laid them out.

"What have we become?" she asked.

"Become?" Jon asked.

"We are the people who dream greatly," she said. "We, the Okalians. But it was the Soo who saved Atun."

"There will be a time to dream greatly," Jon answered. "Maybe now is just a time to survive."

The Swarm Mountains had been one of Jon's goals, and they had reached them. Lin was stronger inside than she had been when he had first met her and Kyra at the bridge, but she had grown tired.

"There's supposed to be a pass through the mountains," Jon said. "I'll go ahead and see if I can find it."

"Just be careful," Lin said.

When Lin and Kyra had settled in a stand of low trees, Jon started up the first mountain. It was steeper than he thought and he had a hard time going up.

A quarter of the way up the mountain there were signs some Fens had been there. A broken spear lay on the ground near the ashes from a fire. A gourd, its top chipped, was on a flat rock. There was a bag, half hidden in a small bush, and Jon snatched it quickly.

Jon looked, almost against his will, to see if

there was anything in the bag he held in his hand. It contained healing herbs. He was relieved that it wasn't sorpos, that he wasn't faced with the temptation.

On the far side of the hill, Jon could see the terrain they would have to deal with. The green, purple-streaked sky stretched endlessly before him. In the distance, just above the horizon, was a band of yellow that grew into a golden haze before gradually fading into green again. For a moment he thought he had heard Shadow whinnying in the distance. Then nothing. He put his back against a rock.

Off to the south, where he thought the Ancient Land lay, was nothing but haze. He strained his eyes, but he couldn't see anything clearly.

Looking downward from the hill, he could see, against the dark background of the land, wisps of smoke that curled skyward. He counted them and saw there were five of them scattered throughout the area. There were figures moving about one of the dried lake beds. Fens.

Jon went down to where Lin and Kyra waited.

He told Lin what he had seen from the top of the hill. She shook her head and clenched her mouth the way Jon had seen her do more and more often.

"We can't go around the mountains, because the Fens have huts near them. We'll have to find the pass through them. I think I should go back and look some more. It'll be better if I look when it's getting dark. The Fens stay close to their camps at night. I'll stay overnight and look again at dawn if I don't find it tonight. Will you be all right here?"

"I'll need time to quiet Kyra, he's very agitated. I don't think he slept well."

"He hardly sleeps at all," Jon said. "It's not good."

"He'll be all right," Lin said. She went to her brother and sat next to him. Jon had the feeling that Kyra would not be all right, not for a long time.

They didn't speak again until it was time for Jon to go and look for a path through the hills.

"Jon . . . be careful," Lin said.

"When I was small," he said, tying vines about his pants legs so they wouldn't catch on the bushes, "whenever I did anything risky, my mother would blow in one of my ears and warn me to hurry back quickly so she could blow in the other or I would grow up lopsided."

"That's silly," Lin said.

"I know," Jon said.

He finished tying his pants. Lin came to him, kneeling by his side. Jon started to look at her

143

but she stopped him, holding his head in her hands. She drew near and blew gently into his ear.

Jon began climbing. It was not as hard as he had thought it would be — there were a few places that were quite steep, but most of it was just plodding along. He held his breath too much, so that the very act of breathing was difficult. He knew he had to do two things: The first was to get to the top and look for a path through the hills, and the second was to find a place to hide himself so he wouldn't be seen when the day came again.

A fog of dust drifted about the base of the mountain but soon cleared up as he climbed. There were comforting, if dim, glimpses of the Red Moon through the dust and clouds. Jon wanted to stay away from the trees. He thought that the Fens would be huddled near them.

Jon heard a noise and stopped near a large rock. He listened carefully. At first he didn't hear anything, and then, from far away, came a sound that was between a cry and a moan. It sent a chill through him.

It began to rain, lightly at first and then harder. He was glad for the rain. The Fens wouldn't want to get wet and it would be harder for them to see him.

He heard the sound again, recognizing it this

time as a flute, the breathy notes rising and falling in the darkness. This time it went up even higher, and then higher still before flattening to the same plaintive note. He imagined the sounds were from the valley below, echoing along the sides of the mountain through the dank mist.

There was another sound, even more distant. It was vaguely familiar, and Jon strained to hear more of it. The sense of it eluded him, but it was still disturbing.

The sounds that he had heard first, the three notes and then the change in pitch, came again. This time it sounded closer, but he was sure he hadn't been seen and decided to continue climbing. He moved slowly, carefully, in the semi-darkness, looking for a place from which he could see most of the mountains and not be seen himself. There was what looked like a ledge above him and just to the left, and he headed for it. The ground beneath the ledge was soft and he took his time planting his feet before pushing himself up. Climbing onto the ledge, he saw it was narrower than he had thought, but from its edge he had a clear view of the mountains. He crawled to the edge to look over.

He could see only one fire in the valley below. Shadows in front of it could have been

Fens, but Jon wasn't sure. But from the darkness the sounds of Fen flutes drifted toward him, melancholy birdsongs stitching the seams of night.

Jon listened to the flutes, fascinated by the strangeness of the melodies, until, quite suddenly, they all began to play together in a haunting and beautiful chorus, then stopped.

Jon was still. Had the Fens heard some noise he had made? A trickle of sweat ran down Jon's neck into his shirt. What were they doing? Then the sudden, unexpected thought: Who were they besides the nameless creatures he had just called Fen?

Minutes went by, then hours. Jon shivered with the cold. His legs ached as the sky began to lighten. He shifted his body and sat up, straightening his legs.

There was the distant sound he had heard before. Not the flute, but the other sound that had seemed so familiar. Now he knew what it was. It was a noise he had heard Shadow make. Had Shadow returned? Jon felt instantly better.

Then there were still other sounds as the world seemed to be waking. The new sounds were clearly the high voices of the Fens. Jon stood slowly and looked over the edge again. He could barely make out a small group of Fens stirring about below. They had started another fire and Jon remembered the Soo, wondering if these were the Fens who had traded the fire for Atun. He was about to look away from the Fens, for a passage through the mountains, when he saw the unicorns. There, held in a roughly constructed pen, were at least twelve of the horned animals.

The fence itself formed a circle and the Fens were on the outside of it. They had pushed sharp sticks through the rough structure so that the unicorns could not get close to the sides without injuring themselves.

Off to one side Jon saw another sight, one that sickened him. It was a huge fire. In it were the remains of a carcass. The Fens were using the unicorns for food.

Jon crouched low and tried to think of what to do next. There weren't that many Fens in the narrow canyon, and he thought that with Lin and Kyra they could possibly avoid being seen if they stayed high in the hills. Jon thought it might be better to try crossing at night, so that Lin and Kyra would not see the trapped uni-corns.

The sky grew dark as a small dust cloud passed before the sun. Below him there was a commotion, but he couldn't see what was going on. The unicorns in the pen began to bleat and cry and Jon could see that they were moving, raising even more of the choking dust. As the sky lightened he could see that the Fens had moved the unicorns away from one side of the pen and now were opening it. They were pushing in yet another of the frightened beasts. His heart stood still. Where the other unicorns were tan-colored, this one was pure black. It was Shadow.

Think. He had to think.

Jon looked for markers, something that would show him a safe path through the Fen camp. He saw a smooth boulder, nearly flat on one side, in an area where there were no Fen huts between it and where Lin and Kyra were waiting.

There was no time to waste. There were things to do. Jon had to find a way to get through the hills, and he had to find a way to save Shadow. There were no choices. He just had to do both.

oing down the hill was harder than Jon imagined it would be. In the darkness he banged his knees more than he did on the way up, scraping them time and again on the jagged rocks. His hands were raw and his whole body was aching by the time he reached the bottom of the hill. It didn't matter that much to him. He could put up with the pain.

All the time Jon had been coming down from the mountain he had been thinking of the Fens. It was hard to hold them in his mind. Were the wild creatures who had attacked Crystal City the same people who lived in the Compound, or who played their flutes in the mountains? He tried to picture them in Crystal City. It was difficult to imagine, but Jon knew they would have survived somehow, even in Crystal City.

It took him a long time to find the place where he had left Lin and Kyra.

"Lin!"

There was no response.

"Lin!"

There was a movement behind Jon and he spun around, arms across his chest, ready. The low branches of a bush moved slowly aside and he saw Lin looking up at him. When she saw it was Jon, she got up quickly and came to him.

"What did you find out?" Lin looked up at him. Her voice was flat, as if something was wrong.

"I think we can cross the mountaintops," Jon said. "It won't be easy but it might be the best way. There's a Fen camp just over this mountain. We can go around this one and take on the next mountain. Our people came from these mountains once. We'll do all right in them."

"Good." Lin put her hand against his chest.

"Is everything all right?" he asked.

"There were Fens near here while you were away," she said. "Once early and once late. They didn't seem to be looking for anything, they just wandered by. I didn't know if they had captured you or not."

Jon touched Lin's cheek lightly. "It feels good to know someone is caring," he said. "Are you . . . ?"

"I'm ready," Lin responded.

150

"There's more," he said. "The Fens have a pen near their camp. They use it to keep the unicorns they catch. They eat them."

"*Shadow?*" Lin's eyes widened.

Jon nodded. "I saw them drive him into the pen."

"What is wrong with these creatures? Why do they have to destroy and eat what we love?" Lin exhaled sharply and clenched her hands together. "How can they be so . . . so hateful?"

"I don't know. The Elders used to discuss exactly what the Fens ate," Jon said. "They knew that very little has been growing in the Wilderness for a long time."

"Okalians don't kill to eat," Lin said. "It's the one sure thing that separates us from the Fens. We don't kill."

Lin turned away and went back to the bushes. She didn't look young anymore. The roundness in her cheek had straightened to a hard angle and her eyes, once clear and bright, had deepened.

Kyra was sitting on the ground. Jon saw that he had smeared his face with mud and had drawn dark triangles, probably with berry juice, on either cheek and on his forehead. Kyra's appearance made Jon nervous, but he forced himself to sit near the boy.

He examined the cuts on his legs. One leg had bled slightly and the dried blood made the cloth of his pants leg stick to his flesh. He pulled it away.

"What did the Ancient Land look like?" Lin asked, when Kyra stood and started walking away.

"Misty in the distance," Jon said. "Where's he going?"

"He's been anxious," Lin answered quickly. "You did see the Ancient Land, didn't you?"

"When the light hit it in just the right way it seemed to be glowing," he lied.

"Good," she said. "Good."

"Kyra doesn't look too good."

"I don't know," she said. "He was really upset when the Fens came near. I had to keep my arms around him. He wanted to go after them."

"Go after them?"

"He found a spear tip." Lin talked to her hands. "Sometimes he holds it in his hands, turning it over and over again. Sometimes he makes marks on the ground."

"Did you say anything to him?"

"I told him that I love him," she said. "But I don't know if he understands that anymore."

"Maybe he'll do better if we're on the move. We should start climbing as soon as we can,"

152

Jon said. "I don't want to stay on flat land if the Fens are walking around here."

"How long will it take to get to the Ancient Land?" Lin turned to him, then made a funny movement with her hand as if she had been about to say something else and had changed her mind.

"What is it?"

"I'm afraid for Kyra . . ."

"He'll be all right," Jon said. "We'll stick with him."

When it grew dark, they started. Climbing the hill with Lin and Kyra was harder than Jon thought it would be. Not that Lin couldn't climb, but Kyra was bad at it.

The spear tip worried Jon, but he realized that he was glad that Kyra had the weapon. Like it or not, it was something they might need.

As they climbed, Kyra quickly fell behind. Jon went back for him.

"Are you okay?" Jon tried to keep his voice down.

"I'm all right," Kyra said, his voice hoarse.

"I'll give you a hand."

"I don't need a hand."

"Stay close with us," Jon said. "You know we need you to be with us, to help us."

"I can't help you," Kyra said, his face inches from Jon's. "I'm too scared."

"It's okay to be scared," Jon said. "We're all scared."

"Not like me," Kyra answered, his voice barely above a whisper. "Not like me."

They climbed slowly once more, until Jon began to hear the cries of the unicorns. He signaled Lin to stop and rest awhile. He put his back to the mountain and leaned against it. Below him Kyra was still slowly climbing toward them. Lin leaned over him to see the side of the mountain, her body thin and warm against his.

"I see them," she said.

Jon nodded. "The Ancient Land is over there." He pointed to where he thought it would be. "We'll rest for a while and then go on. The sound travels well here, so we'd better be quiet."

The melancholy braying of the unicorns, frightened and despairing, reached them. Jon looked at Lin. There was anger in her face. Kyra felt fear, Lin anger — what did he feel? Confusion? Perhaps the pain of not knowing what to be angry about, or what to fear?

There were scratching noises on the ledge above them. It was the same ledge that Jon had been on the night before.

Jon looked at Lin. Her teeth clenched, she had flattened herself against the mountain. Jon glanced down the mountain. It would be risky, but it would be better than being caught by the Fens on the mountain. The scratching sounds stopped. Jon placed his foot on a rock projection and lifted his head enough to see the ledge.

There, barely a body's length away, a Fen facing away from Jon was trying to start a fire.

Kyra had reached them and Jon signaled the presence of the Fen. Jon put his head down and tried to figure out what to do.

in had said that some Fens had wandered past them the day before. They couldn't take a chance of going back down the way they had come up. Jon eased himself to a position from which he could see the ledge again. The Fen had moved away from them, closer to the mountain that sheltered the small fire he had built. It was too dark to see clearly, but Jon could tell the Fen had something in his hands. Jon imagined those hands. Fat stubby fingers, dirt lining the rounded nails, the thumb set off too far toward the wrist.

There were the three notes again, the sad, mourning cry of the Fen flute. Three low notes, and one high one. Three high notes, ever so slightly different from those he had heard from the other Fen, and then a note both soft and sweetly timbred, like the throaty humming of a mother's lullaby to her child.

For a while Jon stood, his forehead down on the rock ledge, listening to the Fen's tune. He had heard it before, from his mother.

There was no way that they could start back down the hill without making some noise and having the Fen discover them. Even if they did start down, they might run into more Fens below. But they had to do something.

The Fen was still facing away from him. Pushing himself up with his hands, Jon crept onto the ledge. The Fen was young, perhaps no more than ten or eleven. The eerie flute sound drifted into the coolness of a breeze and floated off.

Kyra had moved to the ledge with him. Jon hesitated for a moment. He wanted to call out to him, to tell him not to push the Fen from the ledge. If he did, the other Fens would hear the alarm. They would have to pull the Fen back onto the ledge and keep him quiet.

Jon was crouching, but Kyra was upright as he flung himself across the ledge. There was a noise that sounded almost like a loud slap. The sound of the flute stopped abruptly. Jon got to them quickly and pulled the Fen back from the edge, clamping his hand over his mouth.

"Look to see if there are others coming!" Jon whispered, surprised at the desperation in his voice.

He looked up into Kyra's face. It was so twisted Jon hardly recognized him.

"Are you hurt?" Jon asked Kyra.

Lin scrambled onto the shelf. She took her brother's arm and looked into his face.

"I'm all right," Kyra said. He turned away and went to the edge to look over.

Jon looked down at the Fen. He wasn't resisting him. Jon looked at his eyes and they closed slowly. He took a deep breath and tightened his grip on the Fen. He knew the Fens were strong; they were slow but they were strong.

"They're not coming," Kyra said. "Is he stopped?"

"Stopped?" Jon looked down at the Fen, felt his body relax against his own. The arms were soft in his grip. He moved away and saw the blood on the Fen's bare chest. Kyra had used the spear tip.

The Fen's chest moved slowly. He was still alive.

"No! Noooo!" Lin tore at the Fen's clothing, searching for the wound.

"We have to stop him," Kyra said, moving toward them. The blade in his hand caught the reflection of the moon.

"No!" Jon pushed Kyra away.

"He'll get the others after us," Kyra said. "We have to stop his dreaming."

Jon felt his head pounding. Kyra's face was close to his. They looked into each other's eyes and what Jon saw in the young boy's terrified him. The sounds of the unicorns rose from the canyon below them as the first signs of the new day appeared in the sky.

"We'll leave him here," Jon said. "Maybe . . . maybe they can save him."

"We've killed him," Lin said. "Haven't we? Haven't we killed him?"

Jon searched for something to say. A wave of sickness swept over him.

There was a whinnying from below, somehow more disturbing than the others. Jon told himself it was Shadow.

"You two go on," he said. "I have to see if I can free Shadow. Just stay close to the hills and out of sight of their camps. Go in a line with the twin Shan stars. I'll catch up with you. Go on!"

Kyra stood and looked at him. Jon rubbed his arm as Kyra stood over him, the spear tip in his hand, deciding what he would do. He walked over to the edge and looked down.

"Maybe we can stop all of them from dreaming," Kyra said quietly.

"Kyra!" Lin reached out for him and he pulled away.

Jon looked into the Fen's eyes. He was

younger than he had thought. He put his hand over the Fen's face and saw the terror mount in his eyes. He pulled the eyelids down. Under his left hand he could feel the Fen's heart beating, but the youngster kept his eyes shut as Jon had hoped he would.

"He's stopped," Jon said.

Kyra looked at Jon and at the Fen upon the ground. The Fen's flute lay next to him, and Jon picked it up. He stood, stepped as casually as he could over the outstretched Fen, and started down the hill toward the Fen camp.

The rain, which had been steady but light, came down heavily as Jon reached the Fen camp. There was a row of huts off to one side. He looked toward the pen and tried to locate Shadow, but couldn't.

There was a group of Fens gathered around a smoldering fire just beyond the pen.

Jon stopped and knelt on one knee. He turned and saw Kyra not far behind him. And beyond Kyra was Lin. Jon looked to see if Kyra held the spear tip in his hand still, but he couldn't see it.

One of the Fens saw him and leaned forward, shielding his eyes from the rain, trying to see who he was.

"Everybody down!" Jon managed a loud whisper.

He told the others to stay put and, half standing, half crouching, started walking toward the pen again. Some of the Fens glanced in his direction, but it was still too dark for them to tell for sure who he was. They huddled briefly, and then one of them started toward him.

Jon lifted the Fen's flute to his lips and began to blow into it. The notes were not as sweet as he had heard the Fens play, or as clear, but the Fen stopped, ran his hand over his face, and turned away.

Jon looked at the pen. There was one side where they took the animals out. He walked to it slowly, moving from side to side as the Fens did. He could see Shadow standing just inside the pen. Jon wondered if the unicorn's heart was racing as wildly as his own.

The walls of the pen seemed less crudely made when seen close up, but the spaces between the branches were greater than he had imagined. Walking along one side of the pen, he ran his fingers along its rough surface. Branches torn from the trees, their edges jagged and twisted, were bound together by thick vines.

There was a chittering sound behind him. Jon stopped and turned slowly. It was the same Fen who had wondered about him before. Now he moved quickly toward Jon, pointing, his voice getting higher and higher. Kyra was near him. Jon moved toward him and the Fen stopped just as Kyra reached him.

Jon turned away as fast as he could. He moved to the pen, looking for the gate. He found it just as he felt a blow to his head that sent him to his knees.

Jon pitched forward and rolled to one side as a huge stick pounded the ground near him. A Fen lifted the stick again as Jon rolled toward the pen. The stick landed heavily across his side, and he gasped for air.

The pain was unbelievable, worse than any Jon had ever known. He lifted his arms as the stick came down again.

Jon blocked the stick with his arms, but not before it had gone hard into his face, and the taste of his own blood filled his mouth. He grabbed the stick and the Fen pulled back, jerking it from his hands.

Another stick, meant this time for Jon's head, cracked against his shoulder. He lashed out at the Fen and missed him. There was another one and another, all with sticks, all screaming their anger. Lin was fighting them off as best she could but the blows rained on them until Jon was filled with pain. Somehow he scrambled to his feet just as he saw Lin fall. He kicked at the Fen nearest her, driving him back.

Jon grabbed a stick that was on the ground and swung it over his head. He could feel other sticks hit his legs and body as he swung as hard as he could. Jon hit one of the Fens across the shoulders and he backed off. Jon started backing away and felt the pen behind him.

Lin grabbed a Fen by the legs as she tried to get up and two of them went after her, swinging their arms awkwardly like ashen clubs. The pen was behind Jon and he looked up to see the vines that held the gate shut. With all his strength he pushed at the vine until, with one last effort, it was free. The gate was open.

Jon began crawling, trying to get away from the terrible beating, the nightmare screaming that filled his ears with as much confusion as his body had pain. He struggled to his feet and, eyes closed, stumbled forward. He tried to open his eyes to look for Lin and Kyra. The air was filling with a choking dust. He began to cough. For an instant the dust parted and he saw Kyra across the open space. There were Fens all around him and he stood with the blade held high, not striking with it as Jon had seen him do before, but holding it defiantly above his head. There was both madness and triumph in his eyes.

Then there was a great noise, like thunder, all about them. The ground beneath them trembled, and they were engulfed in a dizzying swell of sound and vibrations.

Around them, in a great circle, the galloping unicorns raced with a fury, knocking everything from their path. The Fens were fleeing in panic, some of them being knocked senseless to the ground. Jon could see, through the swirling dust, Shadow galloping in the front of the herd.

"Jon!" Lin, her face smeared with dirt and blood, was near him.

She reached toward him and Jon took her hand. As they watched, the circle of unicorns grew wider, forming a shield around them.

"Kyra?" Jon asked. "Where's Kyra?"

"There." Lin pointed a short distance away. Kyra was on his knees, shaking his head. There were three Fens within arm's length of him, but none of them moved.

As the circle of unicorns widened, the Fens fled through an opening in the canyon. Some were injured and were half carried, half dragged, by the others. Lin and Jon watched for a while until they saw one of the Fens on the ground, who had been still before, begin to move.

"Let's go," Jon said. "We can get out of the canyon this way."

"Are you all right?" Lin asked.

He nodded.

Then, as the sun beamed down into the

canyon, Shadow whirled to a stop. He reared up on his back legs and turned. Jon tried to feel what the great beast felt, the joy he would feel at being free again, but he couldn't. He watched him as he led the unicorns out of the canyon. These were Shadow's hills, his own ancient land, the unicorns his race. Jon watched him for a while before losing sight of him in the dust and flying hooves of the unicorns that followed.

"Cheee! Cheeee!"

Jon's heart sank. It was the cry of the Fens. He looked to see where the sound had come from and saw two Fens, one with what looked like a spear, standing at the narrow end of the canyon.

"Kyra!" Lin called to her brother. "This way!"

Kyra struggled to his feet and started backing toward his sister. The three of them started slowly toward the other end of the canyon. The two Fens didn't follow but continued their cries. One of the Fens on the ground, the one Jon had seen moving, started to get up. As he moved, the two standing in the distance began to jump excitedly.

"Cheee! Cheeee!"

Jon looked behind them. He didn't see any other Fens. Soon they would be away from this place.

Kyra looked worse than Jon. His clothing was torn and stained with blood.

"Are you hurt?" Jon asked.

Kyra didn't answer. Jon looked to where he was staring and saw the two Fens near the mouth of the canyon. The three of them watched the Fens as they in turn watched the ones struggling now to get up. The Fens were moving away from them, heading toward the mountain.

"They're afraid of us now," Jon said.

"Let's get out of here before they stop being afraid." Lin spoke between gasps. "Let's go."

As they headed toward the entrance to the canyon, Jon began to feel the pain he hadn't felt in the excitement of the battle. Every part of him hurt. The side of his head, just beyond his ear, throbbed with pain, and he tried to touch it but his arm hurt almost as much and he pulled it to his chest. Lin was at his side, tears streaming down her face, her left arm uncontrollably trembling. They needed to find a safe place to rest.

As he turned he saw Kyra, his face contorted, raise a spear tip high above his head.

"Kyra, it's okay, we're safe now," Jon said. "They won't come any closer."

"It's all right." Lin touched her brother's

shoulder. Her voice was low and soothing. "We can just go now."

"Do you want water?" Jon asked.

"Cheeeeeee!" Kyra screamed and started running across the canyon.

"Ky-raaa!" Lin screamed her brother's name. "Ky-raaa!"

The Fens were already nearly out of the canyon, and when they heard Kyra's scream they ran all the faster. Jon started after Kyra but his bruised legs were no match for Kyra's fury. In moments the boy had disappeared through the narrow opening into which the Fens had gone.

Lin ran after him and Jon after her. The canyon was covered on that side by the thickening grasses of the wood that bordered the Swarm Mountains. Kyra was out of sight by the time Jon and Lin reached the wood. There was no way to tell where he had gone.

Lin screamed, her mouth wide open, her face an anguished mask. She screamed and screamed until finally she fell to her knees and sobbed into her hands. Jon knelt by her side and held her as tightly as he could.

He looked over her shaking form toward the wood. Now and again he thought he saw something moving, but he was never sure it was more than the wind blowing aimlessly through the tall grass.

Jon waited for Lin to recover, giving her time with her grief before pulling her to her feet. She looked up at him with such despair in her eyes that he had to turn away.

"Lin . . ." Jon searched for words.

She didn't speak, but sucked in as much air as she could and started walking forward. Jon watched her for a while and then followed. When she reached a leather water bag that the Fens had dropped, she picked it up. There was another one a bit farther. Jon picked it up and slung it across his shoulder, wincing when it hit a sore spot.

They passed a wounded Fen near one of the huts. Jon stopped and saw the gash in his neck. Next to him lay the speartip that Kyra had used. The Fen's eyes were full of fear as he moved his hand toward the wound. Jon dropped the water bag and went on.

in sobbed as she walked. Her body heaved with each step she took. Jon, walking next to her, saw the skin pulled tight on her face, her teeth bared, trying to hold in her sorrow.

Jon walked behind her until they reached the bottom of a small hill. They had only to climb over its base to be out of the canyon. They climbed together, helping each other as they could. Jon knew there was a danger that Lin would be pulled into the darkness left by Kyra. The danger for Jon was that he would lose her.

It was a small hill and they didn't have much trouble. When they reached the far side, the deep brown dirt gave way to a lighter brown sand and gray and black rocks. Jon stopped at the edge of it and waited until Lin had looked into the distance, to where he had said he had seen a sign of the Ancient Land.

"You knew about Kyra, didn't you?" she said.

"About Kyra?"

"That he was changed, that he wasn't one of us anymore?"

"I don't know that he wasn't one of us," Jon said. "He put the markings on his face, and the mud, but we all learned to survive out here. We took the Fens' healing herbs when we needed them, we fought them when we thought we had to fight. Maybe Kyra just did what we were all doing, he just couldn't pretend he was doing something else."

"I love him so," she said.

"I know," he answered.

"He didn't believe there was an Ancient Land," she said. "He kept telling me that you were lying."

"What's a lie?" Jon shrugged. "I hoped. I still do hope. Hoping isn't lying."

"I think my brother was wrong," Lin said. "I know we'll find it."

There had to be, Jon thought. There had to be some Ancient Land, some special place they could go to and know they belonged, know at last who they were. None of the logic his father had taught him made the idea of the Ancient Land really true for him. There were just images he had strung together with feelings as elusive as sunlight on water. Feelings about needing to be Okalian, and of knowing clearly what that meant. He had been given the memories of a people, and had made them his own, and had loved them dearly.

From a distance the lake looked like a huge mirror reflecting the slanting sun. As they neared it, both of them realized that here was the place they had heard about all their lives.

"Jon, it's Orenllag!"

They walked faster, almost running at times. When they got to the lake they found an area of deep mud all around it. Lin ran through the mud to the lake. Jon followed her through the mud and into the cold water.

Orenllag. This was where his people had come when they left the creatures that wandered through the mountains and had become truly Okalians. There was an Orenllag.

Lin splashed water on him and he splashed her back. It was silly, and wonderful, and joyous. He was playing like a child and enjoying it.

"Maybe we can wait here for a while," Lin said. "For a few days."

"For Kyra?"

"He might be looking for us," she said, softly.

"Let's rest awhile," Jon said. He took Lin's hand and led her out of the lake.

They sat on the edge of the lake in a place where the earth beneath them was firm and tufted with brilliantly green grass. They rested.

What they would have to do, Jon knew, was to stay at Orenllag until Lin was ready to leave Kyra behind.

"Do you think the Fens think of us as monsters?" Lin asked.

Jon shrugged. "I suppose so," he said.

"Kyra's not a monster," Lin said. "Whatever you think of him — and I saw the look on your face when he ran off — he's not a monster, even if he did mark himself like a Fen."

"I don't think he is," Jon said. "But I don't know if the Fens are monsters, either."

"They killed Okalians."

"We killed Fens."

"They eat flesh," Lin said. "They live out here in the Wilderness like beasts."

"Like us, now," Jon said.

"I'm not a monster," Lin said.

"Neither am I." Jon crossed to Lin, lifted her hand, and kissed it gently.

"You are a sweet person," Lin said. "Thinking about building a life with you is not so bad."

"I think, if we're going to build a life out here, it can't be another Crystal City," Jon said.

"It'll be what we can make it," Lin answered. "If we can make it at all. We don't know that we won't have to build another Crystal City to protect us from whatever it was that killed their adults. I want to grow up, Jon. I want to grow up."

"So do I, Lin," Jon said. "We left some Fens in the camp back there. They're in pain. Maybe we can help. Maybe we can't, but if we're going to build something that's not just crystal, if we're really going to build a life, we have to start with something fresh, something good. We have to start with who we are."

"No! We're all . . ." The words filled her throat and she had to force them out. "No! Don't go back. We're all that we have. You're all that I have. If you go back they'll just fight you again.

"Jon, they're not like us." Lin got to her knees, wincing as she did so. "Or maybe they are. Maybe out here we're all the same. But all they know now is that we fought them and they'll fight you."

"Then it's time for them to learn something else," Jon said. "Lin, I'll try to get back as soon as I can, but I have to go and see what we left behind back there."

"I won't go with you," she answered, getting quickly to her feet. "I'm going on to the Ancient Land. I'm going without you."

She looked at him, then turned and began to walk.

Jon didn't know what to expect of her, or of

himself anymore. He turned quickly so he wouldn't see her walk away.

He walked slowly, not at all sure whether what he was doing was right, or if there was such a thing as right anymore. Then, not being able to resist, he turned. He could see her still, her slight figure growing ever smaller in the distance.

When he reached the pass that went into the canyon he walked slowly, cautiously. He climbed the hill and looked down into the canyon. The first thing he saw was the body of a Fen, its dreaming stopped, where it had been before, and, near a small hut, two more Fens.

One, Jon was sure, was the one who had come down from the hills, who had been playing his flute before Kyra — no, before he and Kyra — had attacked him. He was lying on the ground, and the other Fen was kneeling next to him. It looked like a female, and she was putting something on the dark spots on his shoulder. Jon imagined it must be their healing herbs.

When the kneeling Fen saw him, she was startled. She was small, smaller than the Fen lying down. She began to tremble and to pull at her hair.

Jon reached down and took the herbs from

her and finished pouring them on the wound. He touched the Fen's face and he didn't move. He watched his chest; it still moved. The girl's eyes followed each move Jon made.

The Fen was too sick to move. Jon hoped he wouldn't die. He sat down next to the still form. Jon took the Fen's hand in his, and the wounded Fen boy opened his eyes. Using the little strength he had left, he pulled his hand quickly away from Jon. There was fear in his eyes. Jon knew it was true. They had, each in their own way, made monsters of each other.

The rain had eased and there was a shimmering glow around the circle of the Red Moon. It was plainly red on one side, and darker, almost black, on the other. Beneath its hugeness Jon felt small.

They sat in silence for a long time, the girl not moving and Jon moving only as the ache in his knee forced him to change position.

The girl made a soft noise. When Jon looked at her, she touched herself and then pointed behind him. Jon turned and saw a figure coming down the small hill that he had come down. It was Lin.

Jon had never been so happy to see anyone. He smiled and put his hands over his face to keep it in. He looked at the Fen girl and she looked at him, and she, too, smiled. It was a wide smile and her small, uneven teeth gleamed even in the dimness of the canyon.

Jon stood to greet Lin.

"Are you staying with them?" she asked. "I have to know."

"No," he said. "I came back to help. She was here. I'll stay here until it's all right to leave him."

"More of them will come here," she said. "What will you do with them?"

"If they come back before he's well, maybe I can reason with them."

"That's something other than your mind speaking," she said. "Too much has happened here. Just look around you."

Jon did look around, at the body of the dead Fen, at the pen that had held the unicorns.

"Lin, I don't want to go somewhere and build another Crystal City," Jon said.

"If I helped you, we could bring him with us," she answered.

The wounded Fen moved and the Fen girl put her hand on his forehead.

"To where?"

"To a place we'll find," she said. "Or a place we'll build. It could be for all of us, and for Kyra, too, if he makes it. When he makes it."

"For Kyra, too," Jon answered. "When he makes it."

He turned to the Fen girl and put both hands to his chest. "Jon," he said. "Jon."

The girl put her hands to her chest. "Gebus."

Jon looked up at Lin. "I think it'll work," he said.

Lin knelt by the Fen and looked at the wound. Then she went from hut to hut until she found what she was looking for. She took water from the bag she still had and poured it on the leaves she had found. Then she put the healing herbs on the moist leaves and placed them on the wounds.

She moved the covering from the wounded Fen's arm and he tried to pull back. She took his arm again, more firmly, and put it around her neck. Then she struggled to stand.

Jon took the other side and slowly, carrying the wounded Fen between them, they began to make their way out of the canyon.

Lin and Jon walked ahead, struggling with the wounded Fen. Jon thought if ever he stopped he would never go again. The Fen girl trailed a bit behind, stopping when they stopped, never coming closer.

When they reached Orenllag they stopped to rest. Fatigue came down upon them like a heavy blanket, pulling them toward sleep. Jon wanted to close his eyes and let whatever would happen come to be. There had been a time when he would have had to tell himself not to cry, but now he had no tears for such small things. According to the legend, the Ancient Land was just a day's journey beyond the lake. He wanted to see for himself, to know what it was they would find.

Lin was on her knees, her head bent nearly to the ground. The Fen girl had come close to sit by the feet of the wounded Fen.

Jon wrenched himself to his feet. And pushed the hurt from his mind. He went to Lin and pulled her up.

"Lin, it's time to start again. We have to keep going."

The Fen girl was the first to hear the sound of the hoofbeats. Lin turned next, and then Jon, to see Shadow loping easily across the grassy ridge they had covered with so much difficulty. Jon watched him and felt light again.

Shadow was thinner than he had been before, and there was still a piece of vine around his neck. He circled them once, twice, and then stopped. Lin reached into her bag and found a few berries, which she took to him. She pulled the vine from around his neck and threw it down.

Jon watched as Lin held on to Shadow, her face against his neck, her bare arms clinging to him. There was a strange scent in the air. It came and went in snatches, as had the sound of the flute before. It smelled like the sea. Jon looked in the direction they were headed, but saw nothing.

"Do you think he will carry the Fen?" Lin asked.

"If he doesn't, I will," Jon said.

They lifted the Fen again, and took him to Shadow. Shadow didn't move as they lifted him onto the unicorn's back.

As he walked, Jon thought of what would be. How in years to come those who came after them might read about the fall of Crystal City, and about the pain they shared and the long trek toward the Ancient Land. They would read about how they, Fens and Okalians, had together built a city and made it into a wonderful place. And if they failed, if there was nothing to read about, no great city rising on the horizon, no way of being to hold in awe against the starry heavens, then the Red Moon alone would bear witness that one day, four sick and weary souls had come together and called themselves a people.

The End

ABOUT THE AUTHOR

Walter Dean Myers is an award-winning writer of fiction, nonfiction, and poetry for young people. His many books include *Somewhere in the Darkness*, a Newbery Honor Book, a *Boston Globe/Horn Book* Honor Book, and a Coretta Scott King Honor Book; *Malcolm X: By Any Means Necessary*, a Coretta Scott King Honor Book and an ALA Notable Book; and most recently, *The Glory Field*, an ALA Best Book for Young Adults.

Mr. Myers wrote four Coretta Scott King Award-winning books, including *Fallen Angels*, and he also wrote the Newbery Honor Book *Scorpions*. Mr. Myers is the recipient of the 1994 *SLJ/*YALSA Margaret A. Edwards Award for Outstanding Literature for Young Adults and the 1994 ALAN Award.

Walter Dean Myers lives in Jersey City, New Jersey, with his family.

ABOUT THE ILLUSTRATOR

Christopher Myers, a graduate of Brown University, is working in New York on a series of images of minstrels. *Shadow of the Red Moon* is his first collaboration with his father.